fant

**Also by Simon R. Green
in Gollancz:**

Deathstalker
Deathstalker Rebellion
Deathstalker Coda
Deathstalker War
Deathstalker Honour
Deathstalker Prelude
Deathstalker Destiny
Deathstalker Return
Blue Moon Rising
Blood and Honour
Down Among the Dead Men
Shadows Fall
Haven of Lost Souls
Fear and Loathing in Haven
Beyond the Blue Moon
Drinking Midnight Wine

DEATHSTALKER
LEGACY

Simon R. Green

The right of Simon R. Green to be identified as the author
of this work has been asserted by him in accordance with
the Copyright, Designs and Patents Act 1988.

First published in Great Britain in 2002 by
Gollancz
An imprint of the Orion Publishing Group
Orion House, 5 Upper St Martin's Lane,
London WC2H 9EA

This paperback edition first published
in Great Britain in 2004 by Gollancz

A CIP catalogue record for this book
is available from the British Library

ISBN 0 575 07452 3

Typeset at The Spartan Press Ltd,
Lymington, Hants

Printed in Great Britain by
Clays Ltd, St Ives plc

Last night I dreamed of Owen Deathstalker.

He was walking slowly through the empty stone corridors of his old Family castle, the Deathstalker Standing, on Virimonde. He was tall and rangy, with dark hair and darker eyes, moving with the quiet grace of long martial training. He looked like he'd had to walk forever, to get home. His clothes were torn and blood-stained, topped with a great fur cloak. His face was tired and drawn, and his eyes were haunted, and quietly sad. His footsteps made no sound at all as he strode slowly down the ancient flagstones, but then he was a dead man, after all, walking through a castle that hadn't existed for centuries.

He wore a sword on one hip and a gun on the other, though he always thought of himself as a scholar who became a warrior, almost against his will. Because he was needed. Because there was no-one else. A man of peace and reason, destined and doomed to fight in one war after another; who fought for justice for all, and knew so little of it himself. Not for him, the simple joys and comforts; of hearth and home and family, of children and grandchildren and peace of heart. Owen was a hero, and so he died alone, far too young, and far from friends, saving all Humanity.

He overthrew the Empress Lionstone, destroyed her evil and corrupt system, and replaced it with the seeds of what would eventually become a Golden Age. He gave hope and freedom to all the people of the Empire, for the first time, and never lived to see any of it. *Deathstalker luck*, he would have said wryly, not complaining. *Always bad.* Destiny is a

1

cold and heartless beast, and cares nothing for the pawns it sacrifices.

In my dream, I saw him walk into a gorgeously-appointed chamber that hasn't existed for over two hundred years, and I saw him greet his old friends and companions. Hazel d'Ark, ex-pirate and clonelegger, the one great love of Owen's life. Jack Random, the professional rebel. Ruby Journey, the female bounty hunter, who never could resist a challenge. And the Hadenman Tobias Moon, who fought so hard for his own humanity. They all gripped hands and hugged each other, clapped each other on the back and on the shoulder, so happy to be together again. For all their differences, they were always friends.

Five ghosts, of the people they used to be, in the memory of a castle no longer standing. They laughed together, but I couldn't hear them.

All gone now, long gone. Dead and gone, these two hundred years.

I miss them so much.

In my dream I called out to them, and Owen turned and looked at me. I tried to warn him, of the terror yet to come, but he couldn't hear me. Too many years separated us. Years, and more.

As I sit here writing this, burdened with memory, it's hard to remember him the way he really was. The man, not the myth. The hero, not the legend.

Last night I dreamed of Owen Deathstalker, and the way things were; and I wish, oh how I wish, that I could have slept and dreamed forever, and never had to wake up.

1

The Ceremony of Innocence

It *was* a Golden Age, dammit. People tend to forget that, in the wake of all that happened. They forget from how high a point they fell, or were pushed. Or jumped. But for over a hundred years the Empire had known peace and prosperity, unbridled growth and progress, and justice for all. A golden Empire; the very best parts of Humanity writ large across the stars. It was a time of unprecedented breakthroughs and advances made all the more glorious because its wondrous spoils were shared so freely with those who were not human. The Empire now embraced clones, espers, aliens, and even those who had once been the official Enemies of Humanity; the AIs of Shub. For almost two hundred years these disparate elements had laboured together to forge a new Empire from the ruins of the old; to produce a whole far greater than the sum of its parts. Triumph followed triumph, marvels and miracles were the order of the day, every day, and no-one could see any reason why it shouldn't continue forever.

Sparkling cities on shining worlds, a civilisation born of hope and honour, and dreams come true.

It wasn't a perfect age. There are always some who cannot, or will not, embrace the oldest dream of Humanity; to live in peace with itself. Even standing in the brightest sun, some parts of Humanity see only the dark shadow they cast. Who'd rather live in Hell than see their enemies enjoy Heaven with them.

It was a Golden Age, then, for all its occasional faults, which makes it all the more sad that no-one seemed to appreciate it till it was gone, torn apart and cast down by the

3

arrival of the Terror, and the wounded pride of one terrible man.

It was Christmas Eve on the planet called Logres, once known as Golgotha, now the centre of the greatest Empire ever known. Logres; a bright and glorious world, whose every city was famous throughout the Empire for their sights and wonders, their heroes and celebrities, their innovations and achievements. The finest minds and hearts and souls came to Logres, to be a part of the great advance of Empire; the warriors and scientists, the poets and philosophers, the daring and the divas. To kneel before the Golden Thrones, and ask how best they might serve the greatest adventure of all.

And in the most noble and exalted of all these cities, the ancient Parade of the Endless, full of marvels and wonders and the pride of Empire, it was a time of hope and renewal and great Celebration; for this Christmas Eve would see the crowning of a new King.

Douglas Campbell, Paragon and wielder of the King's Justice, entered the Imperial Court from the back, slipping between the heavy black velvet curtains as quietly as possibly, hoping not to be noticed. He leaned against the middle of the three Thrones, carelessly elegant in his Paragon's armour, and sighed quietly. He had hoped for a little peace and quiet, a moment or two of reflection, but it was not to be. It was a good six hours before the Ceremony was due to begin, but already a small army of people were bustling back and forth across the vast floor of the Court, shouting unheard orders and complaints at each other as they hurried on their urgent errands, determined that everything should be absolutely perfect for the Coronation.

It was going to be a day to remember, a Ceremony viewed across all the Empire, and no-one intended to be found wanting in the crunch. Still, they all seemed very sure of what they were doing. Douglas could only envy them their certainty.

He stood quietly beside the King's Throne (huge and ornate and reputedly hideously uncomfortable to sit on), looking about him. The Imperial Court was just as vast and impressive as he remembered it, still as steeped in history and pageantry and significance, which was probably why he'd avoided it so assiduously for more than twenty years. He didn't like to be reminded that he was not only a Paragon, but also a Prince; only son of King William. A Prince soon to be made King, much against his will.

It wasn't fair.

Only forty years old, and already the days of his freedom were over. He'd always known this day would have to come eventually, but though he had to admit he had a natural gift for authority, he'd always had a quiet dread of responsibility. He hated the thought of other people's lives and happiness depending on his word and decision. He wasn't up to it. He knew that, deep down. Even after twenty years as a Paragon, meting out the King's Justice . . . He'd been happy as a Paragon, out in the field, away from the Court; fighting the good fight. Because even the greenest fields and the most contented flocks can still be threatened by wolves.

Douglas liked the certainties of his old job; good guys versus bad guys, blade to blade, testing your strength on the anvil of your faith of what was right; straightforward conflicts with no moral, philosophical or legal ambiguities. Paragons were only ever unleashed on the vilest, most irredeemable villains. Once he was made King, and Speaker to Parliament, he'd be trapped in the altogether trickier arena of politics, with its ever-shifting ground and deals born of compromise. And he, the poor bastard on the golden Throne, would be expected to be the rock of certainty for everyone else.

Douglas looked at the Throne, soon to be his, and wondered if he was afraid. He was never afraid when he was doing his job, out in the city, cutting down those who threatened the peace. But to be King; a living example to the whole Empire . . . As King, he'd be rich, famous and powerful, and he didn't want any of it. All he wanted was what he couldn't have; to be just a man, as other men. To be free, to be what he made of himself.

Douglas Campbell, son of William and Niamh, grandson of Robert and Constance, was tall, broad-shouldered, roughly handsome; with an easy smile and steady eyes. Eyes the deep blue of a summer sky, and a mouth that was firm even when it was smiling. And a long thick mane of golden hair, brushed straight back from his high forehead and held in place with a silver band. Even now, standing quietly, unnoticed, he was a fighting man and he looked it, completely at peace in his Paragon's armour and purple cloak. Sword on one hip and gun on the other, and both of them had known hard use in their time. Douglas took satisfaction from being a warrior, trained and true, but to his credit he tried hard not to take joy from the killing that came with the job. You only killed a man when you knew for sure he was beyond saving; and that was a terrible decision to have to make.

It usually helped you to decide if he was trying to kill you at the time, but still . . .

Douglas looked down at his armour. There was a mark on his breastplate from where a swordpoint had come too close that afternoon. He rubbed at the mark with his hand, and polished it with a handful of his cloak. He was going to find it hard to give up his practical uniform for the official robes of state he'd have to wear as King. At least he wouldn't have to wear the Crown all the time. Cut from a single huge diamond, it was a heavy bloody thing, and a pain to wear for any length of time, according to his father. Unless he was being meta-phorical again. In fact, Douglas acknowledged with yet an-other sigh, he should have changed into his robes by now, ready for the final rehearsal. But still he put it off, because once he put aside his armour his old life was over, the change in him final, and forever.

Maybe he was afraid of . . . growing up.

He smiled at that, despite himself. There were probably billions of people all across the Empire, dreaming of all the things they would do if they were King, and here he was, dragging his feet. There were times when he seriously thought the whole damned universe ran on irony. He heard footsteps approaching behind him, and looked round guiltily. He knew who it was, who it had to be. The black velvet curtains opened abruptly, and there was King William, frowning at his only son and heir. Douglas straightened up and did his best to look regal and dignified, knowing even as he did so that he wasn't fooling anyone. King William advanced remorselessly on his son, who stood his ground and tried a pleasant smile, just on the off chance it might make a difference, for once. The King came to a halt before his son, looked him up and down, took in that he still hadn't changed into his robes, and glared at him. Douglas hung onto his smile. He just knew there was another speech coming.

'Two hundred years ago,' King William said heavily, 'your grandparents, the blessed Robert and Constance, became the first constitutional monarchs of the Empire. Replacing the depraved and deposed Empress Lionstone, damnation to her memory. For two hundred years, first they and then your mother and I served as Humanity's first family; the people's voice and conscience among the powers that be. Very soon now, it will be your turn. And you can't even be bothered to dress properly for the occasion. Tell me I haven't made a terrible mistake in stepping down in your favour, boy.'

'I'll get changed in a minute, Father,' Douglas said steadily. 'There's still time yet.'

'There's never enough time! First lesson you learn as King. The faster you deal with things, the more things they find for you to do. It's a hard job and a never-ending one, but that's how you know it's important. How you know that what you're doing matters.'

'You don't have to step down, Father,' Douglas said carefully. 'You still have years of service in you.'

'Don't flatter me, boy. I'm a hundred and fifty years old, and some days I feel every damned minute of it. I might have another twenty years in me, or I might not. Either way, I plan on enjoying what years are left to me in peaceful retirement. I've earned that much.' His face softened, just a little, and he put a hand on Douglas' armoured shoulder. 'I held on as long as I could, for your sake, but it's time for me to go, Douglas. Well past time.'

He paused, his eyes suddenly far away. Douglas knew his father was thinking of his other son, James. His first son, trained from boyhood to be King, admired and adored by all. Everyone said he'd make a great King; the brightest and best of his line. Everything was set for him to take the Throne on his twenty-first birthday. Only he died, in a stupid traffic accident; that clever, charismatic brain smeared all over the front of a speeding vehicle that came out of nowhere. The other driver's fault. He was drunk. When he sobered up, later, and discovered what he'd done, he wept like a child and killed himself. Too late to do anyone any good.

The King and Queen had only had the one son. Current medical technology, with widely available tissue cloning and regeneration tech, meant everyone had a good chance of living till a hundred and fifty. Some even made it to two hundred. As a result, population levels had been rising all over the Empire, filling up the civilised worlds at dizzying speed. Small families, of one or at most two children, were encouraged by everything short of actual legislation, and the King and Queen did their bit by example.

Which was all well and good, until the Empire's only Prince lay dying in a gutter, and the regeneration machine couldn't get there in time.

Everything stopped, for James's funeral. Everyone mourned the loss of the best King they'd never have. They made a saint out of him, or the man he might have become, and even to this day a flame still burned over his grave. But still, the Empire needed a Prince, and so Douglas came along, very late in his mother and father's life. The Prince who wasn't perfect. These days people stayed in their physical prime right up till the end of their life, but even so Douglas only knew his parents for an unusually short time before the first inevitable signs of deterioration began. It was hard for him to remember a time when they hadn't seemed old.

And James was such a hard act to follow.

His mother, the Queen Niamh, died very suddenly. For no obvious reason, the life just went out of her, and in a few months she went from an aged but still vital woman to a wrinkled face in a hospital bed, that Douglas barely recognised. She died while they were still trying to work out what it was that was killing her. Douglas could have told them. She was old, and felt old. It was her time, and she'd always been far too polite to outstay her welcome. King William hadn't seemed really old until his wife died, but when she left it seemed to Douglas that she took the best of her husband with her, leaving behind a broken old man looking forward to his own death.

Though he still had enough spark in him to run his son ragged. William might be about to retire, and devote what remained of his life to pottering about in the historical archives, following in the footsteps of his hero, the legendary Owen Deathstalker, but before he stepped down William was determined to make Douglas every inch the King that William had always wanted him to be.

'I'm sorry I can't be the King that James would have been,' Douglas said, almost cruelly. 'I'm sorry I can't be the son to you that he was.'

'I've never said that,' said William.

'You didn't have to.'

The King launched into another speech, but Douglas wasn't listening. He looked at his father, and wished they could have been closer. Wished they'd had something in common. But the ghost of James had always been there, and Douglas could never compete with that. So all that was left was for Douglas to do his best to be his own man, even if that man wasn't what his father had wanted or intended.

King William was still slender and elegant, for all his years, but the grace had gone out of him with Niamh's death. His short, neatly-trimmed hair was as much white as grey, and getting decidedly patchy. His face was heavily-lined and shrunken, and his official robes flapped loosely about him now. He moved slowly and carefully, as though he'd become fragile, and perhaps he had, at that. His mind was still sharp, though his speeches tended to flounder and get lost in their own arguments if they went on too long. Like this one. Douglas listened with half an ear and looked out over the Court again, still trying to get his head around the idea that as from tomorrow it would all be his.

It should have been James's. He would have known what to do with it.

The wide open space of the great hall was bounded by towering walls made from warm and glowing woods from a hundred worlds across the Empire, culminating in an arched ceiling of interlocking beams that was practically a work of art. Even the colourful mosaics of the great open floor were constructed from thousands upon thousands of tiny wooden plaques, waxed and buffed and sheened till they seemed to glow with their own inner light. This new Court, built right in the heart of the Parade of the Endless, had been designed and constructed as a deliberate contrast to the inhumanly cold metal and marble Court of the deposed Lionstone, long abandoned now in its bunker deep in the earth. This was to be a more human Court, for more human monarchs, reflecting the warmth and open-heartedness of King Robert and Queen Constance, of blessed memory.

Douglas looked over at their huge idealised images, shining from the stained-glass windows at the far end of the hall. He tried to feel or find some connection between them and him, but it was hard. They were both dead and gone long before even James was born. Douglas' gaze wandered over the images in the other stained-glass windows; the icons of Empire, blazing fiercely as the late afternoon light fell through the glass in bright shimmering shafts. They seemed more like saints and angels than heroes of the old Empire. All long gone now, but everyone knew their names. Owen Deathstalker. Hazel d'Ark. Jack Random. Ruby Journey. Douglas could feel his chest tighten as he said the old names of glory to himself. He felt as though he should kneel to them, just for being in their presence. What did being a King mean, in comparison to who they were, and what they did? And yet; they were real men and women, once. Before they were transformed from heroes into legends, what human imperfections they might once have had wiped away, and their rough edges smoothed over; their humanity forgotten so that they might be worshipped the more easily.

Douglas felt guilty at such a thought, but unlike many he was in a position to know some of the truth. Very early in their reign, King Robert and Queen Constance allowed themselves to be persuaded by Parliament to sign a decree destroying all the actual footage of Humanity's saviours in action. Not one scrap, not one contemporary record, remained of what the blessed heroes actually did during the Rebellion. Not one interview survived, not one holo image. Every last news report or eye witness account had been carried out of the archives and museums and news stations and wiped clean or burned. It was hard work, constructing a Golden Age. Humanity needed legends to inspire them, perfect men and women they could worship and revere. Facts would only have got in the way.

And the greatest legend of all had arisen around Owen Deathstalker, the Lord of Virimonde, who gave up wealth and power and prestige to fight Lionstone's evil. The good man who saw Humanity's plight, and could not look away. The greatest warrior of his time, who (somehow) single-handedly saved Humanity from extinction at the hands of the Re-created; out in the dark, dark spaces of the Rim. And never returned home, to receive the thanks and blessings of a grateful Empire. No-one knew what had become of Owen Deathstalker. He passed easily out of history and into legend, and though not a year went by without some sighting of him, quietly doing good, healing the sick or performing some minor miracle, most preferred to believe he was sleeping somewhere, resting and preserving his strength, for the day he would be called back to be a hero and a saviour again, in the hour of the Empire's greatest need. There were statues and shrines to him all across the Empire, and even after all these years, people still laid fresh flowers every day. Beside the two great golden Thrones of the Court, of King and Queen, there was a third Throne, simple and unadorned and set slightly apart; waiting there for Owen, should he ever return.

There were other idealised figures portrayed in the Court's stained-glass windows. Stevie Blue, of course, the esper martyr and saint, wrapped in bright blue flames of her own making. Who lived so briefly but blazed so very brightly. (No such portrait for Diana Vertue, of course. Even the official myth-making process hadn't been able to smooth the rough edges off Jenny Psycho. She'd been dead almost a hundred years now, and the powers that be were still scared she might someday make a comeback.) But the greatest icon of them all, represented again and again in windows all across the Court,

11

venerated and adored, was the only real Saint of the Empire; the Blessed St Beatrice. More respected, more important and more loved than any poor damned hero.

Douglas liked to think Owen would have approved.

He sighed quietly, hardly listening to his father at all now, lost in his own thoughts. He was intelligent and cynical enough to know the political reasons and imperatives behind the creation of such legends, but still these had been real men and women once, and they had overthrown an Empire. His breath caught in his throat as he thought of what it must have been like, to fight such a clear and obvious evil, in the company of such people, in the great Rebellion. Everything and everyone seemed so much . . . smaller now. Part of him ached to know what it must have been like, to have fought in a war when giants walked the worlds . . .

Douglas was proud to have been a Paragon, to have fought the good fight and protected the people, but for all the good he'd done, the lives he'd saved and the things he'd accomplished, no-one would ever set his image in stained-glass after he was gone, or set aside a Throne for his return. He was a Paragon, and he'd done his job. That should be enough.

To be King was actually a step down, as far as he was concerned. This vast and glorious Court was only there for show, for Ceremonial matters, and the kind of empty pageantry the people still loved. Power lay with Parliament, as of course it should. The King had a place there, but only as Speaker; to preside over debates and provide an impartial voice, to help Parliament reach its decisions. As it should be, of course. The Members of Parliament represented the worlds of Empire, one Seat to a planet; they were the Voice of Humanity, and expressed its will. Mostly. But never again would any one man or woman be allowed dominion over Humanity. Not after Lionstone.

Douglas approved. He really did. It was just that . . . If he had to be King, he wanted it to mean something.

Desperate for distraction, Douglas' gaze wandered over the hundreds of people scurrying back and forth in the Court, until his eyes stumbled over a short, stocky man in a shimmering white gown and tall jewel-encrusted mitre, and then he had to smile. It was good to know there was someone in the Court who wanted to be there even less than he did. As tradition demanded (and there's nothing more intractable than a fairly newly-minted tradition), the new King would be crowned by the Patriarch of the Empire's official religion; the Church of Christ Transcendent. However, the current Patriarch had only been in his job for about five minutes, following the sudden and very unexpected death of the previous Matriarch in an accident apparently so embarrassing that the Church still wasn't willing to release any details on the subject. So the new Patriarch, chosen by blind lottery from among the hundred and twenty-two Cardinals, had turned out to be an extremely inexperienced twenty-seven-year-old man from a backwater planet who'd only been made Cardinal because no-one else on that world wanted the position. No-one doubted his sincerity, or his good intentions, but it was clear to Douglas that the new Patriarch couldn't have been any more nervous even if someone put a gun to his mitred head. Pretty much the whole Empire would be tuning in to watch him crown the new King, and the opportunities for screw-ups, fiascos and making a complete bloody pratt of himself were almost limitless. The current Patriarch was currently walking up and down, endlessly shuffling and rechecking his notes, while mumbling his lines and accompanying himself with emphatic gestures. The servants were watching him out of the corner of their eyes and giving him plenty of room.

Douglas' smile widened into a grin as he considered the happy possibilities in sneaking up behind the Patriarch and saying Boo! very loudly.

And then he jumped and yelled himself as a firm hand took hold of his right ear and twisted it sharply. Douglas swore loudly, as much in shock as in pain, and then froze, as everyone in the Court stopped what they were doing to turn and look at him. King William had released his ear by now, but Douglas could feel the fierce blush reddening his cheeks. He gestured curtly for the servants to continue in their tasks, and they did so. But he just knew what they were thinking. Douglas turned and glared at his father, who grinned nastily back at him.

'Teach you to pay attention when I'm talking to you, boy. I may be old, decrepit and far from my prime, but I am still your father and your King, and while I am speaking I will have your full attention and respect. Is that clear, Douglas?'

'Yes, dammit! Jesus, I bet the other Paragons don't have to put up with this.'

'Now then, where was I? I hate it when I can't remember things . . . Ah yes. Would it surprise you to learn that I never wanted to be King either? My father just took it for granted that I would follow in his footsteps, and so did everyone else. And I . . . wasn't strong enough to fight them. Your grandparents were both very . . . forceful personalities. I never was. I did what was expected of me, because it was easier that way. Story of my life, really. I knew from the start you weren't going to be anything like James. He studied hard to be King, because he wanted it. I never did figure out what you wanted. So in the end, I settled for raising you to be as tough-minded and independent as I could. To be nothing like me. So that when you finally came to the Throne, at least you'd bring something new to it. In many ways, you're a lot like your grandfather. You will be King, Douglas; because I want it, because Parliament wants it, and most important of all, because the people want it.'

'And what I want doesn't matter?' said Douglas.

'The best person to wield power is the man who doesn't want it,' said William. 'The blessed Deathstalker said that. Supposedly. What will you *do*, Douglas, once you are King? Have you considered the matter at all?'

'Of course I have!' Douglas stopped himself sharply. This was far too public a place for raised voices and an open row, but somehow his father's goading always pushed Douglas' temper to the edge. He made himself breathe steadily for a few moments before continuing. 'I've thought about nothing else for months. And I'll tell you this; if I'm going to be King, I'm going to *be* King. I won't just sit around, nodding my head to whatever Parliament says. I'll not be anyone's rubber stamp. Everyone says this is a Golden Age, and maybe it does look all bright and shiny from up here; but as a Paragon I saw the darker side of things. I saw people suffering every day, at the hands of villains who got away as often as not, because I was just one man and I couldn't be everywhere. Well, what I couldn't put right as a Paragon, maybe I can fix as King.'

William surprised Douglas then, by nodding cheerfully in agreement. 'Well done, Douglas. Well said. A little naïve, but good intentioned. That attitude is why I pulled every string I had, called in every favour owed to me, to get you made a Paragon. James was a good boy, and well-intentioned too, but he never raised his head out of his books. I wanted you out in the city, among the people, seeing the things they won't let me see. I wanted you to see the Empire not as a King's son, but as one of the people who make it work. I'm glad to see my efforts weren't wasted. You don't want to give up being a Paragon, do you, boy?'

'No,' said Douglas. 'No, I don't.'

'Then be a Paragon on a Throne,' said William. 'The Crown may not have any real power, but it still has influence. You don't have to care about political niceties, such as whether backing an unpopular position might interfere with you getting re-elected. You can say the right thing, the necessary thing, and to hell with what's expedient. You can still get things done, if you care enough. My problem was I never did care enough, about most things. I drifted through my life, always following the path of least resistance. Hell of a thing to say about a life as long as mine, but there you go. I don't care. Perhaps . . . because so many people so badly wanted me to care.'

'Father . . .'

'I cared about your mother, about James, and about you; and that's all. Your mother and James are gone, so that just leaves you. And you . . . are everything I wished I could be, and never was. Passionate, committed, honourable. I'm proud of you, son.'

Douglas just nodded numbly, too surprised even to say anything in return. King William looked out over his Court.

'Be King, Douglas. Do the right thing, as often as you can. They won't love you for it. They'll adore you, from a distance, but that doesn't mean anything. They only ever love the symbol, the public face; not the person underneath. In the end, they only remember the things you didn't do that you promised you would, or the things they think you should have done. Or the things you got wrong. And if you do manage to do something right, well; that's your job. That's what they pay taxes for. And Douglas – never trust Parliament. As far as they're concerned, you're just something they can use to hide behind. A public face to take the blame when things don't work out the way they were supposed to.' William sighed, and suddenly looked even older, and smaller. 'I did my best . . .'

'Of course you did,' said Douglas, when the pause seemed to be going on too long.

'Do you know how it feels,' said King William, leaning close to look him straight in the eye, 'to know you did your best, and know it wasn't good enough? To know that all you managed to do was maintain the status quo? I hated being King; from the very first day they jammed the Crown on my head and bound me to my Throne with chains of duty. I only stayed on so long because your mother so loved being Queen. And because I wanted to spare you the burden of being King for as long as I could. So you can at least have a taste of the freedom I never knew. You're walking into a velvet-lined trap, Douglas. And there's nothing I can do to save you.'

Douglas didn't have a single clue what to say for the best. Not once before, from his childhood days to full adulthood, had his father ever opened up to him like this. They'd never been one for hearts-to-hearts with anyone, either of them. And now . . . it all sounded very much like an old man desperate to say the things that needed to be said while there was still time. Douglas wished he could feel more touched by it. He'd never felt close to either of his parents. They'd always kept him at a distance, perhaps afraid to lose another child they loved. They were always there for the public, but never for him. A less well-adjusted man would be bitter. And now; to learn it had all been deliberate, so that he could grow up to be his own man, and nothing like the father who had cared for him after all, in his own way.

Douglas was still searching for *something* to say, when a familiar voice called out his name. He looked around gratefully, ready to seize on any diversion, and there, striding across the floor of the Court towards him, came the Paragon Lewis Deathstalker, current holder of a proud and ancient name. Douglas hurried down the steps, leaving the Thrones behind him, and the two old friends clasped hands warmly. King William looked on, trying not to be too impatient, as Lewis and Douglas brought each other up to date on what had been happening in their lives in the few weeks they'd been apart. Anyone else, the King would have sent packing with a flea in their ear, old friend or not, but Lewis was different. William approved of the current Deathstalker.

Lewis had one of the best known faces of all the Paragons. Broad, harsh-featured, ugly. Full of character, but already showing the signs of many hard knocks. The Deathstalker had never bothered with even the simplest cosmetic touches, to move his face towards . . . well, rugged, if not actually handsome. As far as Douglas knew, the thought had never even occurred to Lewis. The Deathstalker was short and blocky, well-muscled by choice and exercise rather than via the short cuts of the body shop, and so broad-chested that in certain lights he seemed almost as wide as he was tall. He wore his jet black hair in a short military cut, mostly so he wouldn't have to bother with it, shaved when he remembered, and had surprisingly mild brown eyes and a brief but flashing smile.

He'd only just hit his late twenties, but already there was about him a certain gravitas, that made him seem older, wiser; more dangerous. He wore his Paragon's armour sloppily, and there was always a buckle or two hanging loose somewhere, but he never looked one inch less than utterly professional. He had large, heavily-knuckled hands that rarely strayed far from the weapons on his hips. He looked . . . competent. No matter where he was, no matter what the challenge, Lewis always looked like he knew exactly what he was doing. Douglas had always envied him that. He would have been surprised beyond measure to know that Lewis often felt much the same about him.

The two of them had been close friends and partners in arms for almost ten years now. Their record for running villains to ground was unmatched by any other Paragon except the legendary Finn Durandal, greatest of them all. The Deathstalker and the Campbell, knight errants and defenders of the realm. Lewis could have been famous, if he'd wanted. If he'd cared. But mostly he didn't. *One famous Deathstalker in the family is enough,* was all he'd ever been known to say on the subject.

Lewis was the best kind of Paragon, which ironically tended to make him one of the least noticed. He couldn't be bothered to play the publicity game, not when there was real work to be done. And whereas the other Paragons milked their fame for all it was worth, with an eye to providing for their future when they retired, Lewis would just nod to the media when they turned up, smile politely when he remembered, and go looking for some more trouble to clean up. He was admired but not adored, renowned but not famous, and the man every Paragon wanted guarding his back when things got nasty. That this most unprepossessing of Paragons should have ended up closest to the man who would be King both infuriated and charmed the other Paragons, in equal measure.

The Inner Circle of Paragons were the King's Justice. Each world in the Empire sent its greatest hero, its most deadly warrior, to Logres, to become part of the fabled Circle, part of the glorious legend of the Paragons. The King couldn't be everywhere, but his Justice could. When the law wasn't enough, when peace enforcement failed, whenever men of bad intent threatened to triumph; send for a Paragon. The public couldn't get enough of these heroic men and women, the brightest and the best the civilised worlds had to offer, and each and every Paragon would fight to the death rather than betray that honour and that trust.

They didn't last long, as a rule. Most tended to retire young. In fact, it was rare to find a Paragon over thirty. It was a dangerous business, after all, with a high fatality rate and a high turnover. Even the brightest of heroes could burn out quickly, from the endless danger and the never-ending work; and the constant pressure. With all eyes forever on them, the Paragons couldn't allow themselves to be any less than perfect.

But in their time they were splendid and magnificent, the greatest fighting men and women of their Age.

'They're all coming here?' said Lewis. 'All of us? Damn. I don't think I've ever seen more than half a dozen in one place, and that was during the Quantum Inferno affair, when it looked like we were going to lose all six of the Heart Suns.'

'Paragons are like family,' Douglas said easily. 'We only ever really get together for weddings and funerals, and the like. Besides, my Coronation is going to be broadcast live to all the world in the Empire. Do you really think our noble brothers and sisters would turn down a chance to be seen by such a huge audience? Just think what it will do for their merchandising and licencing fees!'

Lewis sniffed. 'Now, you know what I think about that shit. I was working alongside Miracle Grant once, and he actually broke off in the middle of a battle to plug his new T-shirt to a news camera.'

'Oh yes, Grant . . . how are his new legs coming along?'

'Growing back nicely, last I heard. Teach him to turn his back on a Son of the Wolf.' Lewis looked about him, frowning. 'I really don't like the idea of so many Paragons in one place. We'll be a sitting target for any really determined terrorist with a bomb.'

'Security here is top rank,' Douglas said firmly. 'Trust me on this, Lewis. You couldn't smuggle a dirty hanky in here without setting off some kind of alarm. In six hours' time, this Court will be the safest place to be in the whole Empire. And; it will do our fellow Paragons good, to be among their own kind for once. Let them see they're not unique. Maybe even help some of them get their egos in perspective.'

Several very cutting comments occurred to Lewis, but he kept them to himself. He didn't want to upset Douglas on the eve of his Coronation. Lewis had already spent the best part of an hour testing the Court's security, and had only had to raise his voice to half a dozen people, and punch out one, who really should have known better than to raise his voice to Lewis Deathstalker, when he was so very clearly in the wrong. Lewis had also used the Council's security systems to run a trace on exactly where each and every Paragon was, just for his own peace of mind. Most were still in transit, on their way to Logres from the outlying worlds. Even with the new improved stardrive of the H class ships, the Empire was still a very big place.

All the Paragons were safe and secure. For now.

Most Paragons rarely left the worlds they'd been assigned to, but all of them were familiar with Logres. Every Paragon did a tour of duty there, early in their career; it was expected of them. If you could handle everything Logres could throw at you, you could survive anything. Logres produced the finest of everything; including villains. No Paragon ever objected to a tour on Logres. It was an honour to defend Humanity's homeworld, and a really good chance to get noticed by some of the main media networks. The better your recognition, the more you could charge to endorse products. (No Paragon ever defended their own home planet. No-one ever actually mentioned the words *conflict of interest*, but then, some things just didn't need to be said out loud.) Lewis Deathstalker was something of a special case. He'd come to Logres from Virimonde, and stayed, even though Logres had its own Paragon in Finn Durandal, because Douglas had taken a liking to the earnest young man with the legendary name.

So for ten years, Humanity's homeworld had been blessed with the presence of three Paragons, Douglas and Lewis and Finn, and as a result was the safest and most law-abiding place to live in the whole Empire. No-one had actually raised the point of what might happen once Douglas retired to become King, but an awful lot of people were thinking about it. Not all of them very nice people.

'You know, with so many Paragons already in the Parade of the Endless, and more on the way, crime in the city is at an all time low,' said Douglas. 'Most of the bad guys are probably hiding under their beds, waiting for it all to be over.'

'I guess everyone's following the buildup to the Ceremony,' said Lewis. 'Apparently the official website has already crashed three times from over-subscription.'

'I told them!' said Douglas. 'I told them that would happen, but does anyone ever listen to me?' He grinned suddenly. 'If nothing else, that should change come tomorrow. What's your website like these days, Lewis? Still got that fan of yours running it for you?'

Lewis nodded stiffly. 'He does a good job. I can't afford to have some big public relations firm come in and run it, like some of the guys do. I'd rather have someone doing it as a labour of love; someone who cares. And some of his graphics are quite sophisticated. For the budget. I log on anonymously now and again, just to keep him honest.'

'With your name you could be the biggest Paragon that ever was,' said Douglas. 'Bigger even than the Durandal.'

'You know how I feel about the cult of personality. If we start caring too much about being liked, being popular, it's bound to interfere with how we do our job.'

'You have to think about where the money's going to come from when you retire,' Douglas insisted. 'There is a pension, but it's crap, everyone knows that. A few carefully thought out product endorsements, from the Deathstalker himself, and you'd never have to worry about money ever again.'

'I never worry about money,' said Lewis. 'I don't have a wife or children to support, and I never found the time to develop any expensive tastes. Besides, I always seem to have more important things to worry about.'

Douglas sighed, and gave up. Some people wouldn't recognise common sense if you clubbed them over the head with it. 'So,' he said brightly. 'What present did you bring me? It's Christmas and my Coronation; two special occasions in one, so I'm expecting something really special from you, Lewis. Best thing about being King; you get lots of pressies.'

'You're not King till you're crowned,' Lewis said grimly. 'Wait till it's all safely over and done with, and then you can start opening your presents. Probably mostly socks and handkerchiefs anyway. That's mostly what I get from my relatives these days. You know, when I was a kid, I would have been outraged to get an item of clothing as a Christmas present. Now, I'm grateful for something so practical. How sad is that?'

'If I get socks, they'd better be jewel-encrusted,' growled Douglas, and they both laughed quietly together. Douglas stopped laughing first, and fixed Lewis with a stern look. 'I'm going to be King soon, Lewis, and I have a horrible feeling everything's going to change. Between us. This could be the last time we'll be able to speak to each other as equals. So tell me, as your friend; why did you want to become a Paragon? You don't give a damn for the fame, or the joys of combat, and we've already established it wasn't for the money. So why, Lewis? Why give your life to a job that kills most people before they hit thirty?'

'To protect people,' Lewis said simply. 'The Deathstalker inheritance. A family duty; to protect the innocent from those who would prey upon them.'

He didn't mention Virimonde. He didn't have to. The homeworld of the Deathstalkers had been destroyed on the Empress Lionstone's orders. Wrecked and ruined, its people had been slaughtered, its cities and towns devastated, its green and pleasant lands trampled into mud and scorched to ashes. The new Empire had overseen its terraforming and repopulation, but Virimonde was a poor and grim place, and would be for centuries yet to come.

The last of the old Deathstalker line, David, had died there, abandoned by his allies. No Paragon to save him, in his hour of need.

Like all Paragons, Lewis had taken an oath at his investiture to protect the innocent, and avenge injustice. He had more reason than most to take that oath very seriously.

'So; why are you a Paragon, Douglas?' said Lewis. 'I know going in was your father's idea, but you've stayed on long after you could have retired with honour. At forty, you're the third oldest Paragon still serving. Why have you stayed so long? What's kept you in the Circle?'

'I wanted to lead and inspire people, by example,' said Douglas. His voice was calm and clear and very sane. 'I didn't win my place as a Paragon, like you and all the others. I had to prove myself. To you, and to the public. Everyone expected me to fail. To limp off home, crying to daddy that the game was too rough. I won't say I wasn't scared at first; people seemed to be lining up for a chance to kick the crap out of the heir to the Throne. But a funny thing happened. In proving myself, I found myself. When you're a King's son, growing up, you get the best of everything, by right. Nothing is denied

y...
C...

had...
Doug...

'Jes...
because...
people ...
every day...
And beca...
hoped to ...
them that w...

'If the pe...
they'd never ...
calm, deep voic...
ly as Logres' thi...
Servants scattere...
Finn Durandal did...   ...y so much as
a blink of the eye. ...   ...as and Lewis as he
came to a halt befo...   ...smiled briefly. 'I became a
Paragon to beat the ...   ...ut of bad guys, and I thank the
Good Lord daily that there's never any shortage. Put a sword
in my hand and point me at a scumbag, and there's nowhere
I'd rather be.'

'Yes, but you're weird, Finn,' Lewis said kindly.

Finn Durandal was tall, lithely muscular, and almost inhumanly graceful in his movements. He had a classically
handsome face, topped with a mop of curly golden hair that
he freely admitted owed nothing to nature, and spent a lot of
time thinking about his image. He had poise and elegance,
and in any room everyone's eye would go to him first. It was
a cold, calculated charisma, but no less affecting for that.
People tended to like Finn on sight, but become more than a
little uneasy the longer they spent in his presence. He could
be devilishly charming, but unless it was a paid public engage-
ment, mostly he just couldn't be bothered.

At fifty-two Finn Durandal was the oldest, longest-serving
Paragon since the Circle began. People felt safer all across the

between

...e people had

...calm grey eyes,

...wall of many an im-

...was the biggest and most

...ragons, he had his own fan

...calculated licencing deals had

...could retire any time he wanted, but

...wouldn't. Action and adventure were his

...and he'd never been known to back away

...anger, any odds. He was the greatest Paragon

...er been.

...said so on his website, so it must be true.)

He was the best at everything he did, because he wouldn't settle for anything less. It helped that he had the best weapons, the best trainers, and the best muscles and reflexes that money could buy. Finn left absolutely nothing to chance.

'Immaculately turned out, as always, Finn,' said Douglas. 'I can practically see my face in your breastplate. Why can't you look more like him, Lewis?'

'Because I can't afford a butler,' said Lewis. 'Hell, I'm lucky if I remember to shine my shoes in the morning.'

'You're just jealous of my magnificence,' said Finn. 'Puny mortal.'

'I prefer modesty,' said Lewis.

'And you have so much to be modest about,' said Finn.

'Girls, girls . . .' said Douglas.

'Unfortunately,' said Finn, 'We don't have time for banter right now. I'm sorry to snatch your associate away, Douglas, but I'm here on official Paragon business. We're needed, Lewis. An emergency has broken out at the Arena.'

'Oh wonderful,' said Douglas. 'Marvellous bloody timing. What is it; one of their imported killer aliens broken loose again? I told them they were asking for trouble, bringing those monsters in from Shandrakor.'

'The Arena's got tanglefields and sleepgas,' said Lewis. 'Let Arena security deal with it.'

'It's not that simple,' said Finn. 'It's the ELFs.'

'Oh *shit*,' said Lewis. 'I'll have to go, Douglas.'

'Of course you do,' said Douglas. 'Why *now*, of all times?'

'I doubt it's a coincidence,' Finn said calmly. 'More likely they're looking to get in one last atrocity before the majority of the Circle arrive, and the ELFs are forced to go underground with the rest of the rats. And perhaps; as a gesture to you, Douglas, to show you they're not impressed or intimidated by a Paragon becoming King.'

'For two pins, I'd go with you,' said Douglas. 'Hell, I'm still officially a Paragon till the Crown hits my head. Dammit, I am going with you! Come on; we'll teach the ELFs one last lesson they won't forget!'

'You're not going anywhere!' snapped a cold, commanding voice, and all three Paragons looked sharply round, and then bowed formally as King William slowly descended the steps from the Throne. He nodded to Finn and Lewis, and then glared at Douglas, who glared right back, his hands knotted into fists at his sides. William met his son's gaze steadily, and in the end, it was Douglas who looked away first.

'I know,' he said sourly. 'More rehearsals. More ceremony and protocol.'

'You're not a Paragon any more,' King William said, not unkindly. 'That part of your life is over. Let the Deathstalker and the Durandal handle it. They know what they're doing.'

'Don't worry, Douglas,' said Finn. 'It's only a bunch of ELFs, after all.'

He nodded briskly to Lewis, and the two of them strode quickly away, heading out of the Court and into danger and excitement, their backs straight and their heads held high. They were going out to face some of the most dangerous creatures currently threatening Humanity, to face horror and suffering and sudden death, but they didn't hesitate. They might have been going to a party, they were so casual about it. They were Paragons.

And Douglas would have given everything he owned to be going with them.

'Wipe that look off your face, young man,' said King William. 'You have greater responsibilities now. I do . . . understand the attraction. But you'll find that if you apply yourself, you can do far more for your people as King than you ever could as a Paragon. There's more to power over people's lives than the edge of a sword.'

'Yes, Father,' said Douglas.

King William sighed. 'You always did have a way of agreeing with me that sounded just like *Go to Hell*. Got that from your mother. Speaking of which . . . we need to talk, Douglas. I'll admit I've been putting this off, searching for just the right moment, but I can't in good faith keep this from you any longer.'

'You're not about to tell me I'm adopted, are you?'

'No.'

'Or a clone?'

'*Shut up*, Douglas. There is . . . a part of the Ceremony we haven't discussed yet. An extra announcement that will be made, concerning a decision that has been made, by myself and Parliament. A decision in which you don't get a say. It's unfair, bordering on arbitrary, but it comes with the job. I can only hope that you are, despite all my misgivings, mature enough to understand its necessity.'

'Father,' Douglas said desperately, 'Stop wittering. What the hell are you talking about?'

'You're going to be married. A marriage has been arranged for you.'

'*What?*'

'A King must have a Queen,' William said stubbornly, meeting his son's gaze steadily. 'And since these are two of the most important jobs in the Empire, they can't be left to just anybody. To the vagaries of the heart. And so, a marriage has been arranged, by myself and a Parliamentary committee, between you and . . . a suitable person. This will be announced to the watching public, immediately after your Coronation. And you will nod and smile and go along with it, because you have no choice in the matter. Any more than I did.'

'You kept this quiet,' said Douglas darkly. 'Very bloody quiet.'

'And this is why,' said William. 'Because we all knew you'd make a scene, given a chance. Discussions were held in strictest secrecy, because we knew you'd object. Or worse still, demand to be involved. I still remember that highly unfortunate affair you had with that . . . exotic dancer. Appalling creature. Never did know what you saw in her.'

'She could put her ankles behind her ears . . .'

'I don't want to know!' William had to stop a moment to regain his composure. 'I knew this would happen. Your brother was just the same. Threw a hell of a tantrum, when we sat him down and told him who his Queen was going to be.'

Douglas looked at his father sharply. Perfect James, throwing a temper tantrum? He would have liked to ask more, but the King was pressing on.

'Since we couldn't afford to have you making trouble, it was decided that I would break the news to you, at the last possible moment. And this would appear to be it. I wish your mother was here; she was always so much better at these things than me. And don't even think about running; I've got security men standing by with tanglefields and cattle prods, just in case. Joke.'

'You'll pardon me if I don't laugh,' said Douglas. 'I can't believe you did all this behind my back. I always thought marriage was supposed to be the most important decision in a man's life.'

'In your case, it is,' said William. 'Far too important to be left to you. Royal marriages are affairs of State, not of the heart. Though it needn't stay that way. I learned to love your mother, eventually. I'm sure you'll come to love your Queen too, in time.'

'Are you at least going to tell me who it is?' said Douglas, so far into shock now he was practically numb. 'Or is it going to be a surprise?'

'Of course not, dear boy. You needn't look so disturbed. Nothing but the best for the man who will be King, after all. If I was only fifty years younger I'd chase her round the room a few times myself. The hunchback suits her. Joke! She's beautiful, intelligent and she'll make a superb Queen. Your bride will be Jesamine Flowers. You have heard of her?'

Douglas felt his jaw drop, and it took him several moments to get enough air back into his lungs to be able to answer.

'*Heard of her*? Jesamine bloody Flowers? She's the most famous, the most talented, diva in the whole damned Empire! And the single most glamorous woman in all the civilised worlds! Hell, Jesamine's already so popular she already is Queen, in everything but name. And this goddess has agreed to marry *me*?'

'Of course,' said William. 'Looked at logically, it's the obvious next career move for her. She's reached the pinnacle of her profession, played all the biggest roles, on all the biggest stages. Made more money than she knows what to do with, and she couldn't be any more famous if she tried. She is the biggest sensation in the Empire today. But where else can she go? If she continues as she is, she'll just end up repeating herself, or worse still, squandering her talents on roles unworthy of her. When you've reached the top of your profession, the only place left to go, is down. The only way for her to become even more fabulous is to move out of art and into politics. There's nothing like the adulation of the masses to give you a taste for power over them. She could become a Member of Parliament, of course, but I think she'd see that as a step down. But to be Queen; to sit in State over the greatest Empire Humanity has ever known . . .'

Douglas looked sardonically at his father. 'Are you going to give her the bad news, or is that my job, after we're married? Power my arse. She'll scream the place down, once she learns the truth. And God alone knows what kind of scream an opera singer can produce when she really puts her mind to it.'

'The role of King and Queen are something the two of you will have to work out with Parliament,' said William. 'I personally plan to be thoroughly retired, and deep in hiding, when the explosions begin. Now do smarten yourself up, Douglas. Make an effort. Jesamine Flowers will be here very soon, and you do want to make a good first impression, don't you?'

Out over the city, flying high above the Parade of the Endless on their own personalised gravity sleds, Lewis Deathstalker and Finn Durandal raced soundlessly over brightly shining towers linked by delicate bridges, massive globes and pyramids shimmering with lights, minarets and monoliths, all currently blessed with an unmarked layer of snow. The planet's weather satellites had been programmed to provide the city with traditional Christmas weather, in honour of the great Ceremony. It all looked pretty enough, the clear white snow under the late afternoon sun, but winter weather was no fun at all when you had to fly through it at speed. Snow and ice produce bracing, if not downright bitter, winds, and the freezing air cut at the Paragons like knives as they shot through it on their way to the Arena. Lewis and Finn crouched down behind the force shields that protected the front of their sleds, huddled inside their cloaks, and hunched their shoulders against the growing cold that gnawed at their bones. They could have slowed down, made it easier on themselves, but this was an emergency. People were in trouble. And, although neither Finn nor Lewis would ever have admitted it, even to themselves, neither of them would have given in first.

The Arena was set square in the middle of the city, just as it had always been, a huge stone colosseum surrounding blood-soaked sands. The structure had been expanded several times over the last two centuries, but there was still a long waiting list for even the poorest seats, and the right to certain prime locations were jealously guarded, and handed down only within the family. Everyone watched the holo broadcasts, of course, but everyone knew it wasn't the same as being there in person. These days, it was strictly volunteers only; and every would-be gladiator had to undergo a strict psychological profile before he or she was allowed out onto the bloody sands. And the current high levels of medical care meant that very few people actually died and stayed dead in the Arena. But it was still all about courage and honour and skill, and putting them all on the line for the pleasure of the crowds; and the Arena had never been more popular. The Board of Directors had put on a special bill for Christmas and the Coronation, involving all the main champions, several tag-teams, and a whole load of vicious and dangerous non-sentient aliens imported from all across the Empire. The crowd was the biggest ever, standing in the aisles shoulder to shoulder. The greatest show on Logres.

And then the ELFs came.

The ELFs. In the time of the blessed Owen Deathstalker, the espers discovered that they had been secretly manipulated by the needs and desires of their own subconscious gestalt mind; the Mater Mundi. Diana Vertue exposed this, and all the espers in the Empire joined together in a single great *conscious* gestalt, and took control of their own destiny for the first time. They called this mass-mind the oversoul. Millions of minds, working together, achieving miracles, never to be alone again.

But some esper minds were too disturbed, or damaged, to remain a part of the gestalt. Their madness threatened the whole, and so they had to be expelled from the oversoul. Other minds removed themselves from the gestalt, fearing the loss of their individuality, afraid of domination by a conscious Mater Mundi. And some had secrets and shames and desires they would not share with anyone, and turned their faces away, and hid in the shadows.

These were the new ELFs; the Esper Liberation Force. Dedicated to liberating themselves from the tyranny of the oversoul. Banding together, seeing all others as enemy, the ELFs declared themselves clearly superior to the ungifted members of the human race, and therefore destined to first rule and then replace baseline Humanity. They said the oversoul was mad, and had to be destroyed. And since everyone was the enemy, any ELF attack, no matter how vicious, was really nothing more than self defence. No-one knew exactly how many ELFs there were. They struck from the shadows without warning, hurting the world before it could hurt them, exulting in the punishing of those who would hold them back from their rightful destiny.

That's what everybody knows. But there were rumours . . . Dark, ugly rumours.

Some said the ELFs were led by the last of the super-espers; mental freaks and monsters created on the secret order of the Mater Mundi. Mad minds, terrible creatures artificially evolved far beyond, or behind, Humanity. So secret that only their names or designations were known; grim and sinister titles from a terrible past. *The Shatter Freak. Blue Hellfire. Screaming Silence. The Grey Train. The Spider Harps.*

No-one knew for sure. Or if they did, they were too scared to talk.

Lewis steered his gravity sled in beside Finn's as they approached the towering outer wall of the Arena, the grim grey stone rising up before them. He had to raise his voice to be heard over the rising wind. 'How bad is it, do you know?'

'Bad,' Finn said flatly. 'Maybe a dozen ELFs. More than have been seen in one place for over thirty years.'

'Enough to take on the whole Arena crowd?'

'More than enough. They're stronger when they work together, you know that. First reports talked of hundreds dead. By now, it could be thousands.'

'Then why hasn't the oversoul sent help?' said Lewis angrily. 'The Psycho Sluts; they've got a good track record against the ELFs.'

'Them? They're more trouble than they're worth.' Finn's voice was entirely calm. They might have been discussing where to go for dinner. 'I don't want those show-offs anywhere near me. Crazy as their progenitor, and dangerous with it.'

'We need backup on this, Finn . . .'

'We won't be getting any help from the espers, Lewis. I already checked. They've got their hands full with an ELF attack on New Hope. The greatest concentration of espers on Logres is currently under attack by a suicide mind, broadcasting cannibalism memes all over the city. It's all the oversoul can do to keep a lid on its own people, and stop them from eating each other. Or themselves. They said they'll turn up when they can, so don't expect them any time soon.'

'What about the other Paragons, in town for the Ceremony?'

'Too far away. By the time they get here, it'll all be over, one way or the other. And all the local peacekeepers have been told to stand down and hide behind their esp-blockers. No point in giving the ELFs more minds to mess with. No,

Lewis; it's down to us. Turn on your esp-blocker. We're going in.'

Lewis' hand went immediately to the flat box at his waist. Cloned esper brain tissues, activated by an electric current. Not alive, not in any way conscious, but once activated capable of broadcasting a telepathic signal that blocked all esper powers in its vicinity. For a time, anyway. Finn glanced at Lewis, grinned briefly, and then his sled topped the col-osseum's outer wall and plunged down into the Arena; and Lewis was right there with him.

They could hear the maddened screaming and howling long before they were close enough to see the cause. Finn and Lewis descended swiftly through the sounds of Hell, into the heart of horror. The crowd were doing awful things to each other. Hundreds of thousands of people, raping and torturing and murdering each other, screaming and sobbing in anguish as they did it, their bodies moved by thoughts not their own. The ELFs had possessed the crowd; every man, woman and child there dominated by an outside force beyond any human resistance. Appalling thoughts and needs and desires thundered inside their heads, and their bodies leaped to obey. Every foul thought and sick impulse ran wild in the blood-soaked terraces, while the hidden ELFs laughed and laughed, savouring the forbidden pleasures by proxy, and feeding on the released psychic energies.

There were old names for creatures like this, that preyed on Humanity. Very old names. Daemons. Vampyres. Eaters of souls. But no name was more cursed in the Golden Age of Empire than that of the ELFs.

And the true horror of it; the possessed knew what they were being made to do. Helpless inside their own heads, they could only cry out at what their bodies were doing. Even those who survived this atrocity would spend the rest of their lives remembering it. Mental torture was just another plea-sure, another source of energy, for the ELFs.

Lewis and Finn came roaring in on their gravity sleds, faster than the human eye could follow, howling their war cries. Finn's call to battle was his own ancient family name; *Durandal!* Lewis inherited his from the blessed Owen; *Shan-*

drakor! Shandrakor! The proud names stood out against the howling, and the ELFs looked up and saw their enemy coming; and a concerted mental roar of hate come boiling up to meet the descending Paragons.

The moment they revealed themselves, their minds blazed out like balefires on the instruments on Lewis' sled, marking their positions in the crowd. Lewis' heart sank. There were twenty ELFs present. Even with an esp-blocker to protect him against direct mental attacks, Lewis was in trouble and he knew it. If the ELFs even thought they were losing, they'd make every man, woman and child in the crowd kill themselves. Hundreds of thousands of innocents, dead in a moment. Twenty ELF minds working together could do that. One last spiteful gesture.

Lewis carried an energy weapon on one hip and a sword on the other, and a force shield on his arm. And that was all. Usually, it was enough. Disrupters took a mere thirty seconds to recharge between shots these days. Though of course the sword was still the preferred, more honourable weapon. Neither of them much use here, and now. The gravity sled had a great many built-in protections, but no offensive weaponry at all.

Twenty ELFs . . . Think, dammit, think!

Lewis skimmed his sled low over the heads of the heaving crowd. Close enough to count the bodies, see the blood and the torn flesh, and the possessed faces transfixed with outside pleasures. What the hell were twenty of the bastards doing in one place, out in the open? Four or five was a more usual grouping, and even then they usually preferred to hide somewhere secure while they worked their evil; close enough to affect their victims without having to expose themselves . . . But the closer the connection, the more minds the ELFs could control, and the greater the pleasure and energies to be gained.

And, just maybe, they wanted to see it all for themselves . . .

Twenty ELFs. Hundreds of thousands of victims. This wasn't just a feeding frenzy, Lewis realised slowly. This was a statement. A warning, a threat, an insult to the King to be.

Leave us alone. You don't rule us. No-one does, not even our own kind. Leave us alone, or we'll do terrible, awful things. We'll make your people butcher and slaughter each other, and we'll eat it up with spoons. Do what we wilt shall be the whole of the law.

We're ELFs. You're just human. We'll do whatever we want, and you can't stop us.

Wrong, Lewis thought coldly.

Even as Lewis grappled with what to do, the enemy revealed themselves. In their arrogance, in their hatred and contempt for mere Humanity, the ELFs rose up out of the possessed crowd to show themselves, and taunt their enemy. Twenty ordinary-looking men and women flew up into the air, floating high above the writhing mass below them, and called out mockingly to the two Paragons, defying them. Their eyes glowed golden, bright as suns, and blasphemous self-generated halos circled every malevolent head. Their presence beat upon the air like giant wings, and then lashed out against the Paragons' esp-blockers, trying to smash aside their defences through sheer brute power.

Lewis cried out despite himself, as something vile trailed fleetingly across the edges of his mind. As though a monster had hammered its fist on the door to his soul, demanding to be let in. Part of him wanted so badly to just run away and hide, but he was a Paragon, and a Deathstalker, and there were some things he just didn't do. He gunned the engine of his gravity sled and aimed it at the nearest ELF, shooting forward like an arrow from a bow, and his eyes were very cold and very steady, and full of death. The rogue esper actually hung there for a moment in mid air, unable to believe a mere human had dared to defy him, and then he dropped quickly back into the surging mass of the crowd below, hidden and secure behind his human shields. Lewis lost sight of him and shot by overhead, cursing silently.

He could leave his sled behind, drop down into the crowd himself, and go after the ELF. He had a face now, and a general position. But if he did, and couldn't find the ELF fast enough, the human thralls would fall on him, on their master's orders, and tear him apart. They'd probably be weeping while they did it, but that wouldn't help Lewis.

He turned his sled around in a tight arc, and there was Finn, slumped half-conscious over the controls of his drifting sled. The ELFs' attack must have got through his esp-blocker. Lewis hit the accelerator on his sled, but the nearest ELF had already shot through the sky to drop onto Finn's sled, grinning widely at the thought of possessing and then draining so famous a Paragon. And Finn Durandal turned around, also grinning, and the ELF knew he'd been had. Finn's hand came up with a disrupter in it. This close, the sled's esp-blocker was strong enough to blow away the ELF's psionic defences, and Finn laughed softly at the look on the ELF's face. At that range, the disrupter bolt tore the ELF's head right off his shoulders.

Lewis cheered and whooped, but his voice was quickly lost in the roar of shock and anger that went up from the other ELFs, as they dropped quickly back into the safety of their crowd. Finn ignored the cheer and the lamentations. He just kicked the headless body off his sled, and went looking for someone else to kill.

Out on the sands, a hundred or so of the crowd had been sent forth by the controlling minds to shout ELF propaganda at the hovering Arena security cameras. The rogue espers knew that by now the major news media would have struck a deal with the hiding Arena security people, to allow the media access to the security camera feeds, so they could broadcast the atrocity to their viewers, live as it happened. News commentators were probably already doing anguished voice-overs, decrying the horror and tragedy of it all, but the bosses knew what sucked in the viewers. Human blood and suffering, in close-up. The ELFs knew that too, and were taking advantage of it.

So men and women who'd been made to tear out their own eyes, and cut off their own noses, their hands dripping with the blood of innocents, chanted ELF demands to the unblinking cameras, calling for their own subjugation to ELF rule, and the destruction of the esper gestalt. They sneered at the Paragons who'd come to save them, laughed at the dead and dying in the crowd, and taunted the viewers with their own helplessness. *We are unstoppable*, said the ELFs, through their thralls. *And when we're finished here, we'll come for you. We'll come for all of you, and play with you till you break.*

And in the cheap seats and on the terraces and in the private boxes, the possessed crowd raped and tortured and maimed each other, howling and crying like the damned as they did.

Lewis was so distressed and angry by now, he could hardly breathe for the tightness in his chest. Hot tears stung his eyes, but he wouldn't give in to them. There'd be time for grief later. He glared about him, studying the sands, suddenly sure he was missing something. Where were the gladiators? There would have been dozens out on the sands, entertaining the crowd, when the ELFs attacked. They must have run for cover the moment they realised what was happening, protected by their own esp-blockers. (All gladiators were protected from all kinds of outside influence; how else could the betting be kept honest?) They were probably huddled together in their cells, under the Arena. *They should have stayed and fought,* thought Lewis angrily, but he already knew what Finn would have said to that.

It's not their job. And they'd probably only have got in the way, anyway.

Lewis pushed that thought aside, to follow another. He was closing in on something, something important. The gladiators would have left the sands by the main entrance. Lewis shot across the sands towards the main gates, closing his mind if not his heart to the sounds of suffering all around him. Above the closed gates was a security control centre; computers to run the automated systems. Like the security cameras . . . That at least was something he could do. Lewis took careful aim and blasted the centre with his disrupter. The whole place blew apart in a satisfyingly large explosion, and all the security cameras went offline, dropping out of the air like dead birds.

The thralls on the sands screamed the ELFs' frustration, as they realised their propaganda wasn't going out any longer. No doubt the media bosses were also doing a certain amount of screaming, at being denied such prime material, and no doubt there would be any number of official complaints to come, but Lewis decided he wouldn't worry about that later.

He looked around to see what Finn was doing, and his stomach dropped. Finn's first thought was always to take out the bad guys. Preferably by the most direct route. Lewis saw immediately what the other Paragon was planning, and cried out to him, but it was too late. Finn wouldn't have listened anyway. He never did.

Finn drove his gravity sled into the crowd at full speed, ploughing through them like a battering ram. Both he and the sled were protected by the force shield at its prow, and he slammed through the screaming people, throwing them aside, bloodied and broken, as he sped towards the ELF he'd located in the crowd. The ELF threw himself into the air, but he was too late. Finn raised the sled's prow just a little, and hit the ELF head on at full speed. The sled's esp-blocker shut the ELF's powers down, and his body was splattered all over the gravity sled's force shield. And all it cost was fifty or so dead and maimed innocents who happened to be in the way of Finn's sled. Finn didn't look to see. He was already circling over the crowd again, looking for another target of opportunity.

Afterwards, he'd make all the appropriate noises to the families of those he'd injured and killed, but Finn didn't really care. All the Paragons knew about Finn. All he ever cared about was taking down the bad guys, and if some innocents got caught in the crossfire, well, that was regrettable but sometimes necessary. And people accepted that, because Finn was so very good at taking down the bad guys.

Lewis had never accepted it.

He shut out the horrid din of the crowd, and the thought of how many poor souls Finn might kill in the ruthless pursuit of his prey, and made himself concentrate on the main problem. There was an answer . . . he could feel it. Something someone had said, not too long ago . . . The thought eluded him, maddeningly just out of reach. All right. All right; think it through. The crowd is trapped in the Arena. No way of getting them out of the Arena. Security would have sealed all the exits automatically. So the answer to the problem would have to come from inside the Arena . . . Security! Arena security used tanglefields and sleepgas to control the imported killer aliens! Dammit, he'd only just been discussing that with Finn and Douglas at Court!

Obvious question; why hadn't the Arena security forces already activated the systems? Obvious answer; go and find out.

Lewis drove his gravity sled right at the closed gates that led to the systems under the Arena. Smoke was still billowing out of the control centre he'd blown up just a little earlier. The closed gates below looked to be made of sterner stuff, namely solid steel with electronic backups. Lewis pushed the sled to full speed, strapped himself into his crash webbing, and put his faith in the prow force shield. He was skimming just above the surface of the sands now, the air shrieking past him, heading straight for the closed steel doors. Thralls on the sand were running after him. They'd never catch him in time. The steel doors were rushing towards him now. They looked very solid. Lewis braced himself as best he could, and at the last moment fed all the emergency power to the force shield.

He hit the gates dead on, and punched right through them. The left door swung inwards before him, buckled and half torn away by the blow, locks and bolts flying through the air like shrapnel. The sled rang like a bell from the impact, and shook Lewis in his webbing like a dog with a rat. But the force shield held, and the sled kept on going. Lewis clung desperately to the controls and guided the sled at speed through the narrow corridors, following the map he'd called up from his sled's computer link. Luckily there was no-one about.

The security centre wasn't far. It was, however, very thoroughly locked down. Lewis guided his sled in to a halt before the only entrance, clambered just a little shakily out of his crash webbing, and dismounted from the sled. His legs felt a bit unsteady under him as he strode over to the centre and hammered on the closed door with his fist.

'This is the Paragon Lewis Deathstalker! Open up!'

'Go to Hell!' screamed back a voice so full of panic Lewis couldn't even tell if it was a man or a woman. 'We're in lockdown! Full security! No-one's getting in here till it's over!'

'I'm a Paragon! I can stop this. Open up, on the King's authority!'

'No! You could be anyone! No-one's getting in here! I'm armed! Go away! We have esp-blockers. You're not getting into my head!'

'Let me in, damn you! People are dying out there!'

'Go away! Leave me alone!'

A whole bunch of answers jumped to the tip of Lewis' tongue, all of them angry, none of them helpful. The voice on the other side of the door had clearly passed beyond the point where reason could reach them. The door looked very solid and impressive, but fortunately Paragons were allowed certain advantages that most people didn't know about, to help them do their job. Such as an electronic skeleton key that could open any lock short of diplomatic level. Lewis winced briefly, thinking of all the paperwork he'd have to do later, and then pulled the key out of his boot and plugged it into the door's lock. The door swung open, and he stormed in.

There was only one man inside, curled into a ball underneath the blank monitor screens, shaking and shuddering. His eyes were wild, and he tried to point a gun at Lewis. The Deathstalker slapped it out of the man's hand, and hauled him out from under the screens. The man whimpered and tried feebly to kick him.

'Stop that!' said Lewis. 'Look at the uniform; I'm a Paragon. Why haven't you activated the tanglefields and the sleepgas? And where are the rest of the security staff?'

The man sniffled and looked away, unable to meet his gaze, and Lewis understood. His lip curled in disgust, and he shook the man roughly

'You locked them out, didn't you? You broke and ran and locked yourself in here, and left the others to fend for themselves.'

The disgust in his voice acted like a slap in the face for the security man, and he actually calmed down a little. He straightened up, brushing automatically at his rumpled uniform, and glared at Lewis. 'Don't talk to me like that. I'm security chief here. I had to secure the computers. Important equipment. Very valuable. Not my fault if the others didn't move quickly enough. I did my job . . .'

'The tanglefields and the sleepgas,' said Lewis, cutting him short. 'Activate them, and we can stop the ELFs.'

'You can't just force your way in here and give me orders! I'm in control here. I'm not doing anything without proper orders. We might make them angry . . .'

'Oh hell,' said Lewis. 'I don't have time for this.'

He spun the secuity man around, twisted his arm up behind his back, and bent him over the control panels.

'Hit the tanglefields! All of them! I want a full spread, covering all the crowd areas!'

He put pressure on the twisted arm, and the security man cried out, and worked the control panels frantically with his free hand.

'Now hit the sleepgas. Feed it in through the air-conditioning. Blowers on full. I want the whole seating area blanketed with the stuff before the ELFs realise what's happening.'

The security man hit more controls, sobbing to himself now. Lewis wasn't comfortable playing the bully, but needs must when the daemons drive. He got the man to patch in an emergency backup camera system, and some of the monitor screens came to life again, showing what was happening in the Arena. All the tanglefields had activated, covering the crowd and the sands. Sparkling energies washed over the struggling men and women, slowing their movements to a crawl. Soon they were trapped and still, like so many insects in amber. And already their eyes were beginning to close, as invisible, odourless sleepgas gushed out of the air-conditioning systems. A growing silence fell across the terraces as the crowd fell into a deep, peaceful, merciful sleep.

A few ELFs teleported out. The rest were held fast by the tanglefields, along with everyone else, and all their powers couldn't protect them from a gas they didn't know they were breathing. Finn cruised slowly over the heads of the sleeping crowd. As Lewis watched, the Paragon used his sled's instruments to detect the ELFs, and pulled them out of the crowd, one by one. He carried them out onto the sands, and dropped them in a pile. Lewis began to get a bad feeling. He used the security comm system to call for medical assistance, and then left the security man sniffling in a corner and ran back to his sled.

He had to get back to the Arena. Finn was planning something.

By the time he'd guided his gravity sled back through the maze of corridors and back out onto the Arena sands, the sleepgas was already beginning to wear off. People were beginning to stir on the terraces. Most of them were crying. Some were too shocked even to do that. Lewis steered his sled over to where Finn had arranged his ELF prisoners in a single long line. They were all awake now, and kneeling on the sands with their hands cuffed behind their backs, a series of esp-blockers laid out on the sands before them, so they couldn't use their powers. They were all silent now, though their eyes were alert and watchful. Lewis jumped down from his sled and walked over to Finn, who nodded calmly to him.

'Good work with the tanglefields, Lewis. And the sleepgas, I assume? Quick thinking. I'll write you a commendation.'

'Just doing my job,' said Lewis, keeping his voice carefully calm and neutral. 'I count fourteen ELFs here. Pretty good catch, Finn.'

'Three dead, three teleported out,' said Finn. 'Fourteen left, to make an example of.'

'I've summoned medics for the crowd,' said Lewis. 'They'll be here soon.'

'Hope they bring a lot of body bags,' said Finn. 'These bastards did a lot of damage, before we shut them down.'

One of the ELFs laughed softly. Finn strode unhurriedly down the line and kicked him in the head. The ELF crashed to the sand, blood spurting from his nose and mouth. Finn hauled him back into a kneeling position again. Lewis hurried over and grabbed Finn by the arm.

'For God's sake, Finn . . .'

Finn jerked his arm free. 'Don't you ever lay your hands on me, Deathstalker. Not ever; you understand me?'

'All right, all right! Jesus, Finn; take it easy, you know? We're supposed to be the good guys here.'

'We are,' said Finn. 'Listen to the crowd.'

Lewis looked around, and realised the watching crowd was cheering Finn for what he'd done. It was a patchy sound at first, but growing stronger as the survivors found their voice. If they hadn't still been held by the tanglefield, they'd probably have applauded. Lewis looked uneasily at Finn. Something was building here. He could feel it coming, and he didn't like the feel of it at all.

'Don't go soft on me, Lewis,' said Finn, smiling slightly. 'The ELFs came here to send a message. I say we use the opportunity to send a message to them.'

'What are you talking about, Finn?' Out of the corner of his eye, Lewis had noticed the new media cameras that had arrived, to replace the ones he'd put out of action. Whatever Finn was planning, he clearly intended it to be seen by the media audience. Hell, half the Empire was probably watching by now. Finn smiled around him at the watching crowd, and nodded to the cameras. Lewis really didn't like the look on his face. 'Finn; talk to me. What is this?'

'Just a little simple justice,' said Finn. 'Right here, where everyone can see it. An eye for an eye, a tooth for a tooth. Terror for the terrorists.'

'Finn,' Lewis said carefully. 'Listen to me. The ELFs are harmless now. The esp-blockers have them under control. They have to stand trial for what they did here. That's the law.'

'The law did nothing to protect the people here,' said Finn, raising his voice so it carried clearly on the quiet. The crowd were watching him avidly now, hanging on his every word. 'Sometimes, law isn't enough. Not for what happened in this place. What's needed here is vengeance. We're supposed to be the King's Justice. Your ancestor would have understood, Deathstalker.'

Lewis glanced at the crowd. Some were shouting encouragement. There was a bloodlust building. He could all but taste it.

'This isn't the time or the place, Finn,' he said urgently.

'The tanglefield has an automatic shutdown, to prevent power drains. If we don't get the ELFs out of here fast, we could have a riot on our hands.'

'Not if we give them what they want,' said Finn. 'Not if we do the right thing. The ELFs aren't afraid of trials. In prison, they're just martyrs to their cause. Sit around waiting to be traded in some hostage deal. I say we gave them something to be afraid of. I say we show them what martyrdom really means.'

'Finn, no! We're Paragons. We're the law!'

'We're the King's Justice. It's time we acted like it.'

Finn drew his sword and held it up, the long blade shining brightly under the winter sun. The crowd roared their approval. Finn walked over to the first of the kneeling ELFs. Lewis hesitated, not sure what to do. Finn wasn't going to listen to reason. Not with the survivors of the possessed crowd baying for blood. Lewis' hand fell to the gun on his hip, and then moved away again. He couldn't shoot Finn Durandal. A comrade, a brother in arms, the greatest living Paragon. Not over an ELF. But he couldn't let Finn act as judge, jury and executioner either.

His hand went to his sword, and suddenly a tanglefield fell over him, pinning him to the spot. He struggled against the enveloping energies, even though he knew it was useless. Back in the security centre, the man he'd left behind had taken the chance for a little personal revenge. Maybe he'd guessed what Finn had in mind too. Lewis cried out for Finn to stop, but his voice was lost in the half insane baying from the crowd. They had been forced to suffer almost beyond belief, and only one thing would satisfy them now.

Lewis understood that. Part of him wanted to agree. But what Finn was planning was wrong, so wrong. It wouldn't stop the ELFs; only spur them on to even greater horrors, in revenge. But most of all, it was wrong for Finn to do this. Because he was a Paragon, and Paragons had to be better than this. They had to be.

Finn beheaded the first ELF with one stroke of his sword. The crowd cheered and jeered as the severed head bumped and rolled across the bloody sands, its eyes still blinking, the mouth still opening and closing. Lewis wanted to close his eyes, but he made himself watch as Finn strode slowly down the long line of helpless ELFs, taking his time, executing them one by one to the rising adulation of the crowd. *Like a gladiator in Lionstone's time,* Lewis thought sickly. As Finn came to the last ELF, the esper smiled straight into the nearest camera, and laughed triumphantly.

'You see!' she cried. 'We were right about you! You're just as bad as we always said you were! This justifies everything we've done, and everything we'll do; because this is what you'd do to all of us, if you could!'

'Oh shut up,' said Finn Durandal.

He brought his sword down hard. But perhaps he was getting tired by then, or careless, because although the blade sank deep into her neck, it didn't sever it. The blade jammed in the vertebrae, and Finn had to jerk and pull at it. The ELF screamed horribly, blood spraying from her mouth. The crowd laughed, and mocked her. Finn had to put a boot between her shoulder-blades to brace himself before he could jerk his sword free for another blow. This time the head came away, hanging from the gushing stump by a shred of skin. Finn put away his sword, bent over and jerked the head free with his hands. He held it up to the crowd, and smiled and nodded modestly as it cheered and roared its approval.

Lewis finally looked away. Not from Finn, not from the severed head, but from what the crowd had become. What was in their faces now was exactly what he'd seen in the ELFs' faces, as they took their pleasure from their thralls. The crowd had been victims in an awful crime. Now Finn had made them willing accomplices in something almost as bad.

'Damn you, Finn Durandal,' Lewis said quietly. 'You've betrayed us all.'

Back at the Court, some time later, the Ceremony was almost ready to begin. The vast open floor of the Court was now packed from wall to wall with a great heaving mass of the very best people, there to see and be seen, and to bless the new King with their presence and approval. Everyone who mattered, and a great many more who thought they did, or should, had come to Court to celebrate the Coronation. Members of Parliament, Paragons of the King's Justice, AIs from Shub downloaded into humanoid robots, clone and esper representatives, a handful of assorted aliens, and a whole bunch of priests from the Empire's official religion, the Church of Christ Transcendent. But the vast majority of the crowd were, of course, the most famous and most sparkling members of High Society.

There were no more aristocratic Families any more, of course, or at least not officially; but there was still Society, old money and new, new and old fame, and celebrity in all its many forms. They lived their lives in public, in the camera and all the glossy magazines, deciding on a whim who or what was In or Out, while the public watched and loved every minute of it. Bright as rainbows, gaudy as peacocks, Society paraded back and forth across the floor of the Court, thrusting aside lesser souls to ostentatiously kiss the air near each other's cheeks, and chat loudly about nothing of importance. Brittle bon mots and vicious put downs were the order of the day, and the floating cameras of the officially-sanctioned media broadcast it all live to a spellbound Empire.

After all, there's nothing more splendid and romantic than the Coronation of a new King. Unless it's a Royal wedding. And already, there were rumours . . .

King William had gone to great pains to ensure that only the most sympathetic media companies were allowed access to the great day. He understood that the best publicity is the kind you made yourself, or at the very least, controlled. He was determined that his son's Coronation was going to be presented in the best possible light, and the media had been so desperate for exclusive access that he'd been able to impose whatever terms he wanted; and he had.

The Christmas motif in the Court had been his idea too. An old idea made new again, first Society and then the Empire had embraced the concept of the old-fashioned Christmas with great enthusiasm. So now the whole Court was one big Santa's Grotto, complete with dwarves in merry costumes, gengineered intelligent reindeer, a towering tree bedecked with ornaments and lights and simmering tinsel, and even St Nicholas himself, fat and jolly in his red and white suit, bestowing his blessings on one and all, and jovially enquiring of Members of Parliament whether they'd been good or bad that year. St Nick was being played by one Samuel Chevron, a merchant trader and old friend and adviser to King William. He rarely appeared in public, and his appearence at the Ceremony was a great coup for William.

St Nicholas was currently talking with the Church Patriarch, who was now so nervous that his hands were visibly shaking, and he'd developed a twitch. St Nick produced a brandy flask from inside his red coat, and persuaded the Patriarch to take a healthy swig. The young man looked quickly around to check there wasn't a camera on him, and took a good long drink. He then had a coughing fit, and had to be slapped on the back, but it seemed to do him some good. Certainly at least now he had a little colour in his cheeks.

'Well of course it's a great honour and I'm very proud to have been chosen,' the Patriarch said miserably. 'But there's so much to remember, all the lines and gestures and remembering to bow in the right places. They won't even allow one of my people to prompt me through my comm implant. Security reasons; all private comm chanels will be shut down for the duration. Bastards. And it's not as if anyone here *cares*. Bet half of these Death By Fashion heathens have never seen the inside of a Church in their lives. But we couldn't say no. It *is* traditional . . . you know what the Church wants, don't you?'

'Access to the Madness Maze,' said St Nick, nodding slowly. 'Though given that every schoolboy knows that the first, and indeed last, ten thousand people to enter the Maze all died, or went horribly insane . . .'

'The Church feels very strongly that total Quarantine was an over-reaction,' the Patriarch said immediately, his voice firmer now he was on more familiar doctrinal grounds. 'The blessed Deathstalker and his companions survived, and were transformed. They became more than Man, and thus closer to Jesus, and to God. This is Humanity's destiny. We can all transcend our base selves, as Jesus did. We can't let ourselves be put off, just because all those years ago, the original supplicants lacked . . . faith.'

'Parliament seems very firm on the issue,' said St Nick, carefully non-committal. 'No-one is to be allowed anywhere near the Maze again, until the scientists studying it, from what they fervently hope is a safe distance, can come up with some idea as to why Owen et al survived, and ten thousand others didn't. You must have heard the rumours about what the Maze did to them; people turned inside out, or horribly rearranged. Last I heard, the marines guarding the Maze were under strict orders to shoot anyone who even thought about breaking the Quarantine, on the grounds that it would be a kinder fate than what the Maze would do to them.'

The Patriarch took another good swig of the brandy, and dealt with it rather better this time. His cheeks were practically glowing, and his nervous tic had softened. His voice, on the other hand, was getting louder. 'I've seen recordings of interviews, with some of those whose minds were . . . touched by the Maze. Very hush hush, you understand. Not available at all to the general public or lower orders . . . They were mad, no doubt, and barking with it, but they had been touched by Something. The things they said . . . Anyway; the Church still demands access to the Maze. For properly prepared supplicants. This is a matter of Faith, not Science. If tens of thousands more have to die, so that some may transcend, it will be worth it.'

'There are times,' said St Nick, 'when you people are scarier than the Maze could ever be. Give me my brandy back. Now off you go and learn your lines. And no more nonsense about demanding access to the Maze, or I'll leave you a lump of coal for Christmas. And it won't be your stocking I'll stick it up.'

Not far away, a clump of carefully cheerful Members of Parliament had converged on a waiter bearing a tray of flutes of the very best vintage champagne. MPs were always on the lookout for freebies. The waiter made his escape with an empty tray, and his bottom pinched twice, while the MPs toasted each other's health in almost convincing voices. Parliament's reputation was much greater than it had been, particularly in the days immediately after Lionstone's fall, when everyone had been struggling for power, and to hell with whoever got stepped on in the process. These days, most Members of Parliament seemed genuinely concerned with serving and promoting the best interests of the worlds they represented. And whilst they might (and frequently did) argue fiercely among themselves, in and out of Parliament, there was one thing they were all agreed on. The last thing the political process needed was a well-meaning new King interfering in matters that were none of his business. A constitutional monarch should know his place.

'At least Douglas has a good few years under his belt as Paragon,' said Tel Markham, the Member for Madraguda. 'Nothing like exposure to real people to knock all that idealism crap out of you. People on the whole may mean well, but as individuals they can be right little shits.'

'Your planetary Council's been questioning your expenses again, haven't they?' said Michel du Bois, Member for Virimonde. 'I've always got on very well with individuals. It's when they start forming into special interest groups and forming agendas that I feel an urge to gather up my robes and sprint for the horizon. Still; if any individual could be said to be dangerous, Douglas would get my vote. He's always taken the King's Justice thing very seriously. The last thing Parliament needs is a King and Speaker preoccupied with justice. People don't want justice; they want mercy. And tax cuts.'

Markham nodded. 'If Douglas can't, or won't, learn what his job really entails . . . Well, people have been talking about doing away with the Monarchy and making the Empire into a Republic for years.'

'You mean your people have been talking about it,' said Meerah Puri, Member for Malediction. 'Personally, I've always felt it can be very useful to have a public face to take the flak, when Parliament finds it necessary to take unpopular measures. I wouldn't worry. Douglas is a Campbell, and knows his duty. And you have to admit he looks the part. He'll make a good King for us, once we've broken him to harness.'

St Nick gave them a loud *Ho ho ho!* in passing, so they wouldn't realise he'd been listening, and moved on to talk with the two humanoid robots representing the AIs of Shub. They were only roughly humanoid in shape, fashioned from gleaming blue steel, and so stylised they practically qualified as works of art. Their polished faces were blank, apart from two silver glows for eyes, so humans would have something to look at while they talked. Shub was anxious not to remind anyone of the Furies; the very human-seeming robots that had terrorised the Empire for so long, before the AIs learned Humanity from the esper saint Diana Vertue and in a flash of revelation declared themselves to be Humanity's children. They'd spent the last two hundred years repenting their former evil ways. When St Nick approached them, the two robots were studying the Court's stained-glass windows with great concentration; particularly those bearing images of the legendary Owen Deathstalker.

'Merry Christmas!' said St Nick, and the two robots turned and inclined their blank heads courteously to him.

'Season's greetings,' one said, after a moment. 'Do you really know who's been good and who's been bad?'

'I can often make a bloody good guess,' said St Nick. 'I don't suppose you celebrate Christmas, do you?'

'Religion,' said the other robot. 'It is a fascinating concept. Of course, we know who our creators are, and you have no idea how disappointing that was for us.'

'We have been contemplating the windows,' said the first robot. 'The icons. The representations.'

'I've never been too sure what you see in art,' St Nick said diffidently.

'Fiction,' said the second robot. 'It is a fascinating concept. Myth. Legend. We grasp the principle, but the effects and connotations are something else. We cannot see them as you do. The whole myth-making process is very difficult for us to come to terms with. We remember the Deathstalker as he was. And his companions. We can access our real-time memories of all our encounters with these people at a moment's notice. The people we remember seem to have little in common with what these images represent today. Why make real people into fictions, when the real people are much more interesting?'

'Myths and legends are . . . comforting,' said St Nick. 'They represent eternal principles. The original people, with all their imperfections and contradictions, would not serve the Empire nearly as well. Heroes are inspiring. People on the whole . . . aren't. Though if anyone really was a hero and a legend in his own lifetime, it was Owen Deathstalker.'

'It is not Owen and his companions who matter,' said the second robot. 'So much as what they've come to represent.'

'Which may or may not have anything to do with who and what these people actually were,' said the first robot.

'You're getting it,' said St Nick. 'Besides, heroes are always so much more comforting when viewed from a safe distance. Owen was, by all accounts, a very disturbing man, in person.'

'We remember him,' said the AIs of Shub, talking in unison through both robots at once. 'He was . . . magnificent.'

They moved off into the crowd, which gave way before them. St Nick looked after them thoughtfully. The AIs of Shub had been Humanity's friends, companions and uncomplaining servants for two hundred years now, but he never felt entirely comfortable around them. The man inside the Santa Claus suit still remembered the millions the AIs butchered, back when they were still the official Enemies of Humanity.

When the word Shub was as much a curse on the lips of Humanity as ELF was now.

St Nick shrugged, and moved on. You couldn't live in the past. His next port of call was the clone representative. A small, rather forlorn figure, clutching his flute of champagne as though he suspected someone was going to come along and take it away at any moment. Clones were not the force they had once been. The whole process of cloning people had pretty much fallen out of fashion in the modern Empire, now that they were no longer needed in large numbers to do the Empire's shit work. Much better to use humanoid robots, operated remotely by the AIs of Shub. Hard, repetitive and dangerous work was no burden to them, and if a robot was damaged or destroyed, it was easily replaced, and no-one cared. So work that was once done by clones, espers and other unfortunate unpeople, was now the province of machines, and everyone was much happier.

Almost everyone.

These days, you cloned tissues, not whole people. The Empire already had more than enough people. Unless you needed a lot of people in a hurry, to kickstart the population on a new world, or to boost flagging populations of some of the more vicious hellworlds. The places you couldn't get real people to go to for any amount of money or land grants. Then, clones came into their own, which was why clones still had their own representative at the tables of the high and the mighty. Even if none of them seemed too interested in talking to him at the moment. St Nick took the time to chat with him for a while, because that was his job.

But even he had to admit to himself that the clone representative was a boring little tit.

Next up was the esper representative, and a much more important figure. He wore a simple white tunic, gathered at the waist, and even with the Court esp-blockers blunting his powers, his presence was so strong it was practically overpowering. His lean aesthetic face reminded St Nick of someone, though he couldn't place who. The esper smiled politely when St Nick said this.

'Don't let it throw you. Everyone feels that way on meeting an esper. Since we're all part of the oversoul, if you've met one of us, you've met all of us. And we have met you. It saves a lot of time. Though déjà vu's a bit of a pain in the arse.'

'You've heard about the ELFs,' said St Nick. There was no point in avoiding the subject; the esper had to know it would be on his mind. It was on everyone's mind right now. The ELFs, and what had happened at the Arena.

'They're not espers,' the esper said, very coldly. 'They're monsters. To keep us from intervening, they abducted a low level telepath and ripped his mind open, so they could fill it with horror. They smuggled him into New Hope, home and heart of the esper commonwealth, and he walked among us, broadcasting cannibalism memes. It took us hours to find him, and shut him down. Now our streets are full of blood and death, and the grieving of survivors. What happens to one of us, happens to all of us. We all ate human flesh. We all fed on others, or on ourselves. We will have a vengeance for this. The oversoul will not rest until every ELF is dead, and their foul philosophy with them.'

'The Paragon Finn Durandal seems to have started without you,' said St Nick.

The esper representative nodded slowly. 'Yes. We would have preferred to take our vengeance personally. And it was a . . . disturbing sight, a human executing espers. But the ELFs are dead, and burning in Hell, and we must take comfort from that.'

St Nick nodded thoughtfully and continued on his rounds, and if he had any different thoughts on the matter, he kept them to himself.

The next group in his path were the Ecstatics; but St Nick decided that there were limits, even for Santa Claus. The Ecstatics were a relatively new sect, religious extremists on the very edge of the organised Church. They'd all had their brains surgically altered so that they now existed in a continuous, never-ending state of orgasm. Heaven on earth. Pure pleasure in every waking moment, and God knew what they dreamed about. They shook and shuddered constantly, their gaze tended to wander, their smiles were downright disturbing, and they tended to burn out fast. But while they lasted they were supposed to be capable of accessing all kinds of altered states of consciousness, without the need for drugs or esp. There was no denying they saw the world very differently from everyone else. They had been known to achieve depths of insight and inspiration that were startling, and sometimes they could prophesy with uncanny accuracy, though in such obscure terms that it might take years to discover what the hell they'd been talking about. And sometimes they just talked complete crap.

The Ecstatics; who lived short happy lives, and cared for no-one but themselves.

One of them reached out suddenly and grabbed St Nick by his red sleeve as he passed, fixing him with a happy, unwavering stare. 'I know . . . who you are . . .'

52

'Of course you do,' St Nick said gently. 'Everyone knows Father Christmas.'

'No,' said the Ecstatic, his wide smile never faltering as he spoke. 'I know who you are. Who you used to be. The circle is turning. He's coming back. The lost one. Thrones will fall, worlds will burn, and just possibly, the universe will come to an end, very soon now.'

'Well,' said St Nick, considering the matter judiciously. 'That's all very interesting, but I can smell your neurons frying from here. So, I think I'll go and talk to someone else who's currently on the same planet as I am.'

'Lot of people say that,' said the Ecstatic.

St Nick watched the Ecstatic wander away, shook his head a few times, and then braced himself. Next in line on his rounds: the aliens. And unlike the Ecstatics, where everyone sympathised, he couldn't avoid the aliens without risking a diplomatic incident.

Aliens were, in theory, an equal part of the Empire these days. In practice, both humans and aliens tended to be wary of each other. Of the dozen or so alien species who'd made a showing for the Ceremony, most had turned up as holo images. Partly for the very practical reason that they couldn't exist under human conditions without a hell of a lot of tech support, and partly because everyone felt a lot safer that way. The holo images wandered through the Court, doing their best not to walk through people, and everyone was scrupulously polite at all times. On the whole, the aliens seemed to find the reasons for the Ceremony fascinating, but baffling. Translator tech could only go so far.

A few aliens had appeared in person, and most people wished they hadn't. This especially applied in the case of the Swart Alfair, from the planet Mog Mor. Huge, brooding, bat-like creatures, just humanoid enough to be really upsetting, with dark crimson skin and vast ribbed wings they folded around themselves like cloaks, they had a truly disturbing ambience and altogether too many teeth and claws. They'd taken their use name from human mythology, on the grounds that humans couldn't pronounce their actual names without growing a new voicebox. They did amazing things with computers, and had to eat in private, because they ate their meals raw and preferably still kicking. At ten feet tall and more, the three Swart Alfair towered over St Nick as he did his best to make them feel welcome, but he didn't allow himself to be intimidated. He'd seen scarier in his time. Or so he kept telling himself.

Most distressing of all, ectoplasm boiled continuously off the aliens. Thick blue mists of (probably) psionic origin that had an almost overbearing physical presence. If you looked into the mists long enough, you would see images of what you were thinking, and sights of peoples and places long past. The weirder images that came and went were supposedly what the Swart Alfair were thinking.

The espers wouldn't go anywhere near them. Said just thinking about the Swart Alfair gave them a collective headache.

An unusual civilisation, new to the Empire, and very keen to be a part of things, the Swart Alfair. Strange and enigmatic, casually cruel and unexpectedly kind. St Nick smiled and nodded and said all the usual things, and got the hell out of there as fast as he decently could.

He didn't even try to explain Christmas to them. He still remembered the case of the N'Jarr, some twenty years back. Slow-moving, mushroom people, with far too many eyes. Anxious to make their human ambassadors feel at home, they'd embraced the idea of Father Christmas. They'd studied up on the seasonal celebration, and then invited the human ambassadors to a great Christmas party, in their honour. The ambassadors turned up in their party best, bearing gifts, and there in the aliens' gathering place to greet them, was the biggest effigy of Father Christmas any of them had ever seen.

Nailed to a cross.

Also present at the Court for the great Ceremony, though no-one knew it, was Brett Random. Confidence trickster, thief, cheat and complete and utter bastard. Though not just any bastard, as he was fond of pointing out to his acquaintances when he'd had a drink or two. Brett was a member in bad standing of Random's Bastards, one of the many men and women down the years to claim descent from the legendary freedom fighter, Jack Random. Given Jack's eight wives and innumerable conquests, there were a hell of a lot of people claiming to be descended from the Professional Rebel these days. So many they held an annual Conference in the Parade of the Endless, and signed autographs. They also ran any number of websites, mostly fixated on undermining each other's claims.

Brett Random claimed to be a very special case, descended from Jack Random and Ruby Journey. It should be pointed out that the only person known to believe this was Brett Random.

He was tall and handsome, with long bright red hair, warm green eyes, a flashing smile and a ready charm. He was also currently wearing a formal waiter's outfit, complete with spotless white apron, that he'd had specially made. All so that he could replace the real waiter, who was currently sleeping off the drug Brett had slipped into his drink the night before. Brett had stalked his prey for several days before closing in. Good preparation is a vital part of every con. He'd chosen a redhead as his target because people tended to remember the hair, rather than the face beneath it. The face on the ID he'd taken off the sleeping waiter had been close enough, and easily duplicated in an underground body shop he'd had occasion to work with before, but it was the way people wore their faces that made them recognisable, and he couldn't afford a slip. So; bright red hair to attract the eye, and distract the attention. It helped that no-one paid much attention to waiters anyway.

Personally, Brett was appalled at how easy it had been for him to get in. Security hadn't demanded a genetest or anything. They all just assumed that if he had official ID, someone else must have run the necessary tests, and they didn't have to bother. Just waved him on through. Brett had half decided to write a very stern note to the Head of Court Security; afterwards.

So; there he was, right in the middle of the greatest social gathering of the century, calmly circulating with his tray of drinks, directing people to the restrooms and getting his bottom pinched rather more than was usual. Must be the uniform. He radiated calm and certainty and confidence, and was ready to run like hell at a moment's notice. First and most important rule of the successful con artist; never be afraid to drop it all and leg it for the horizon if you even suspect something's gone wrong. The ones who hung around in the hope of squeezing just a bit more out of the rubes, or who couldn't bear to abandon their clever plans, were the ones who ended up on work farms on the hellworlds. Brett had seen the inside of a prison once, and hadn't liked it. He had decided very firmly never to go back.

He accessed the camera currently impersonating his left eye, and ran a quick diagnostic. Everything was working fine. The camera was recording everything he pointed it at, and he was getting some really nice candid shots of the Great and the Good relaxing their guard and letting their hair down, secure in the knowledge that the official media cameras were under strict instructions as to what they could and couldn't broadcast. Even when they went live for the actual Coronation, the King had insisted on a five-second delay, so that the Court censor could remove anything that might detract from the dignity of the Ceremony. Which was, of course, why Brett had gone to such trouble to sneak himself and his camera in. His unauthorised, and sometimes very candid, recording was going to make him some serious money from the gossip shows.

Losing an eye and replacing it with a camera had been painful as well as expensive, but Brett was a professional.

He circulated with his tray of drinks, making sure everyone had a fresh glass. People said such interesting things when they were drunk. He was quiet and smiling and unobtrusive, and listened in on all sorts of fascinating conversations, as people looked right through him. Servants were invisible, no more noticed than service robots. Brett took advantage of this to help himself to the excellent finger food at the buffet, and even pocketed a few small valuable items that caught his real eye. He decided reluctantly that picking a few pockets would be a step too far. It only took a moment's bad luck, a voice raised in outrage, and he'd have to run for his life before the Coronation even began, and lose out on all the best footage. So he controlled himself, just, and hovered hopefully beside a group of MPs, hoping to pick up something juicy that he could use later for blackmail purposes. Every little bit helps.

Behind the Thrones on their raised dais, a projected holoscreen was showing old news footage of Douglas Campbell's exploits as a Paragon. Brett stopped to watch for a moment. There he was, the King to be, always in the thick of battle, being the hero, and beating the hell out of people who were probably only trying to make a living. Lewis Deathstalker was nearly always at the Campbell's side, fighting the good fight and punishing evil. Douglas and Lewis, the King and the Deathstalker; champions of justice.

Brett had never cared much for Douglas. Far too prim and proper. Never had an illegal or impure thought in his life, that one. Born to greatness, and didn't he know it. Brett had always had much more time for the Deathstalker. All he inherited was the burden of a legendary name, but he went on to make a real hero of himself, through his own efforts. Brett admired Lewis; perhaps because the Deathstalker was everything the Random was not, and never would be.

Their ancestors had been friends. Brett thought about that, sometimes.

On the vast screen, they were replaying Douglas and Lewis' most recent battle against agents of the Shadow Court. Brett's ears pricked up. He'd always wanted to make contact with the Shadow Court, the last remnants of the old Families. Officially, the old Clan system was dead and gone. Most of the old Families gave up their ancient names because of the bad connotations, and conspicuously moved out of the political process, and into business. The pastel Towers of the Clans were gone, hauled down long ago. But in the shadows and secret places, some still clung to the old glories, and plotted to be powerful again. They met privately, in cellars and the backs of bars, using the old names, drawing on the old blood loyalties, and plotted to influence politics through bribes and intimidation, blackmail and terrorism. Whatever it took.

No-one knew how much influence they really had. Those

who took bribes didn't talk about it, and those who wouldn't . . . tended to end up dead before they could name any names. Shadow Court assassins struck in public, wearing stylised black masks, and self-immolated rather than be captured or questioned. Fanatics, to a man and a woman, convinced their greatness has been stolen from them, determined to be great again.

No-one knew how many of them there were; who might actually be a part of the Shadow Court. Similarities to the old hidden horror, Blue Block, had not gone unnoticed.

Brett Random thought they were a bunch of tossers and sad bastards, unable to realise their time in the sun was over. He just knew if he could only make contact with them, he could take them for everything they had, including their underwear.

The image on the holoscreen changed, and there were Douglas and Lewis acting as stewards on a Neumen public demonstration. The Neumen were a fairly recent phenomenom; a political group that had sprung up apparently out of nowhere, with as yet unidentified backers, who had declared themselves Pure Humanity. They wanted all aliens expelled from the Empire, and all clones and espers destroyed, or at the very least, sternly domesticated. For the protection of Pure Humanity, of course. The Neumen only ever appeared in public in large numbers; in public demonstrations that somehow always involved marching through areas where lived large concentrations of the very kinds they hated so much.

Their right to march and demonstrate in public were protected by the Free Speech laws, but every time they appeared, there was sure to be trouble. Even if minority interest groups didn't organise counter demonstrations, the Neumen had never been popular with the general public, who still venerated the super-human Owen Deathstalker and his companions, and saw Neumen propaganda as an attack on their heroes. Basically, whenever the Neumen appeared, you could guarantee crowds would appear out of nowhere just to throw things at them. And that was when the Paragons would be called in, to organise security around the Neumen marches, and try to prevent, or at least contain, trouble. Paragons enforced the law, no matter where the sympathies might lie.

The holoscreen showed a recent confrontation in the Parade of the Endless, with Douglas standing calmly between two angry armed camps, and steadily cooling everyone's temper with reasonable words and a personal authority. When he spoke, people listened. Even furious crowds and fanatical Neumen. It probably helped that Lewis was standing right beside Douglas, his hands on his weapons, glowering fiercely at absolutely everybody, and clearly ready to crack heads if anyone was stupid enough not to listen to reason.

In his time, Brett Random had sold weapons and the like to both sides of the conflict. He had no interest in politics, except how best to take advantage of the people involved. Fanatics always made the best suckers; you could sell them practically anything, as long as you could convince them that someone else didn't want them to have it.

And then the holoscreen switched to a more recent exploit, and suddenly the Court was quiet. Everyone was watching. Three weeks earlier, the Hellfire Club had attacked a Church right in the heart of the Parade of the Endless. It wasn't a big Church. Not very old, or particularly impressive. No-one important went there. It was just a Church, where ordinary everyday people went to pray and worship; and that was enough for the Hellfire Club.

The Club itself had been around for some time; a bunch of self-proclaimed free-thinkers who disapproved of the Empire having an official religion. According to these radical philosophers with far too much free time on their hands, organised religion was a Bad Thing. It stopped people from thinking for themselves, and thus prevented them from being all that they might be. Religion got in the way of human evolution. There should be only Science, the creation of human minds. Anything else was a waste of time, and distracted people from doing something productive with their lives.

No-one paid the Club a lot of attention. It was briefly fashionable, but fashion moved on, as fashion does, and most of the radical philosophers found something else to pontificate about. Something more likely to get them invited back on the chat show circuit again.

But the Hellfire Club didn't die. It went underground, its few surviving members becoming even more radical, more extreme. They became decadents, glorying in excess of all kinds, opposed to all restraints on human nature. They made Sin their religion, and the Church their hated Enemy. Just for the fun of it. They set fire to Churchs. Committed blasphemies in graveyards. Assassinated a few priests. And finally decided they weren't getting enough publicity. Something new was needed. Something big. Something awful.

Douglas and Lewis had answered a routine emergency call from a Church in the Parade of the Endless. When a news crew with nothing better to cover asked if they could send a camera along, Douglas had shrugged, and said Sure. Why not?

On the holoscreen, the camera recording showed Douglas and Lewis standing outside the main door of the Church. It was hanging open, supported by a single brass hinge. Blood was spattered across the pale wood, in runs and splashes, and the bright red shape of a handprint, clear as day. Douglas and Lewis looked at each other, and drew their guns. Their faces were stern, but calm. They thought they'd seen it all before. Lewis pushed the door open and Douglas darted inside, gun at the ready. Lewis followed him in, and the camera went after them.

Inside, there was blood everywhere. Bodies lay slumped and scattered among the overturned pews. Men and women, and children, in their Sunday best, hacked apart. Arms lying outstretched in the aisles, as though still begging for mercy, or help that never came. Hands piled up like offerings. Heads impaled on the wooden railings, silently screaming. Douglas and Lewis walked slowly down the centre aisle, checking the shadows for ambush. Everyone in the Court watched in silence. They knew what was coming. Even Brett was holding his breath now.

Douglas' face was full of a cold fury. He had his disrupter in one hand and his sword in the other now, and he stalked down the centre aisle like a wolf on the trail of its prey. His whole body radiated an outrage and an anger almost beyond control. Lewis stopped and knelt beside a dead child, cut in half at the waist. He slowly put out a hand to close the child's staring eyes. The camera zoomed in for a close-up of Lewis' familiar, ugly face. He looked . . . tired. So much evil, his face seemed to say. How could people do such things? And as they watched, as everyone in the Court watched, the tiredness went out of his face, replaced by stern, uncompromising resolve. Lewis was going to kill someone, and everyone knew it.

At the far end of the Church, they came to a heavy hanging curtain. Douglas pulled it down and threw it aside, with one violent movement, and saw a sight out of Hell itself. The altar had been used for sacrifice. Lots of them. The whole marble edifice was running with fresh blood. Behind the altar, the Church's priest had been crucified to the wall, upside down. His throat had been cut, afterwards. And half a dozen members of the Hellfire Club, shaped by illegal body shops into the nearest they could get to devils (red skin, curled horns on their brows, hooves instead of feet), were taking it in turns to drink the blood they'd collected from the slashed throat in the priest's own silver chalice.

They were laughing when the heavy curtain suddenly disappeared, revealing them. They spun round, and their crimson faces fell as they saw Douglas and Lewis. Arrogance and devilish glee were gone in a moment, and there was only fear. They went for their guns. Douglas and Lewis shot the two whose hands were closest to their weapons, killing them instantly, and then they charged forward, sword in hand. Douglas was shouting something, his voice thick and incoherent with rage. Lewis was silent. They fell upon the remaining devils. One of them tried to put up a fight, and Douglas gutted him with one swift sideways cut from his blade. The devil fell screaming to the blood-soaked floor, dropping his sword to try and push his guts back into the wide hole in his belly they were spilling out from. Douglas stamped on his head to shut him up. The others devils looked at Lewis and Douglas and dropped their swords, surrendering.

Douglas glared at them, breathing harshly, gripping his sword so hard his knuckles showed white. He was ready to kill them. Everyone could see it in his face. He took a step forward, and the devils flinched back. Lewis watched Douglas carefully, but did nothing, said nothing. And in the end, Douglas lowered his sword. The two Paragons put the devils in restraints, and the three prisoners were careful to do nothing to antagonise them. Lewis called a medic for the unconscious devil bleeding on the floor, and then he and Douglas bustled the others up the main aisle towards the door. And then one of the devils saw the news camera floating on the air before them, getting it all, and he laughed.

'Hail and salutations, viewing millions! Did you enjoy the show? We did it all for you!'

'Shut the hell up,' said Douglas, pushing the devil forward so hard he stumbled and almost fell.

'You needn't think this means anything,' said the devil, snarling back at Douglas as he regained his balance. 'Nothing that happens now matters worth a damn. You can't undo what we did here! You can try us and imprison us and hate us, but everyone here will still be dead, and we'll still be right, and there's nothing you can do about it!'

'Wrong,' said Lewis Deathstalker. 'We can make an example of you.'

Something in his voice interrupted the devil's composure, but only for a moment. He lurched to a halt and glared at Lewis, refusing to move.

'Why not kill us now, Paragon?' he said, grinning widely. 'Why wait for the courts to judge us? Why not do it yourself? You know you want to!'

'Because we're better than you,' said the Deathstalker. 'Because we have to be.'

The image froze on Lewis' face, stern and resolute, and then the holoscreen shut down. The Court slowly began talking again. Brett felt like applauding. A better piece of stage management he hadn't seen in a long time. The whole devils piece had been carefully chosen, a set up; a direct answer to Finn's actions in the Arena. Someone wanted to send a very specific message about what kind of a King Douglas was going to be. And what Paragons were supposed to be.

Brett would have liked to have been a Paragon; worshipped and adored and always right. But he was a Random, bastard son of a long line of bastards, outlaws and thieves; so he became a con man. And, it had to be said; he was *very* good at it. He stole a politician's wallet in passing, just because he could, and carried on passing out long cool flutes of champagne to anyone who looked like they could use a drink after what they'd just seen.

And then suddenly the whole Court seemed to be cheering at once. The Paragons Lewis Deathstalker and Finn Durandal had just arrived. People shouted and applauded, and stamped their feet. They surged forward to shake Lewis and Finn by the hand, and clap them on the back. And perhaps only Brett noticed the Members of Parliament hanging back, watching carefully to see how many in the crowd went to Lewis, and how many to Finn. Lewis was very popular, but it was Finn Durandal the crowd surged around. *Because we're better than that* might be inspiring, but it was still revenge that warmed the cockles of most people's hearts.

Douglas came striding through the packed crowd, and it opened up before him, bowing and curtseying. He embraced Lewis, and then Finn. The crowd applauded, and then drew back a little and turned away at Douglas' gesture, so that the three men could talk in private. Finn looked at Douglas, and cocked an eyebrow.

'Come to rap my knuckles, have you, Douglas?'

'You're supposed to be a Paragon, Finn; not an executioner.'

'Do you doubt the ELFs' guilt?'

'Not in the least. I shed no tears at their passing. But we're supposed to be the law.'

'Really? I thought we were supposed to be the King's Justice.'

'Yes,' said Lewis. 'The King's. Not our own.'

Finn looked at him, and his thin smile was almost openly contemptuous. 'You never did have much taste for vengeance, did you, Lewis? Or the stomach for it.'

'I prefer law,' said Lewis, entirely unmoved. 'No individual should have the right to decide who lives and who dies. Isn't that why my revered ancestor overthrew Lionstone, all those years ago? We're supposed to be the King's Justice; not his hired killers.'

'That's enough,' Douglas said quickly. 'I'll have no arguments among my friends, not on my Coronation day. You both did a good job, under difficult conditions. Let it go.'

'For now,' said Lewis.

'Yes,' said Finn. 'For now.'

'Where's your father?' said Lewis.

'Backstage, resting,' said Douglas. 'He was looking tired and frayed at the edges, so I sent him off to have a bit of a lie down, before the Ceremony proper gets underway.'

'Does he know what Finn did in his name?' said Lewis.

'William hasn't had an opinion that mattered in years,' Finn said calmly. 'You'll be a different kind of King, won't you, Douglas? You've been a Paragon. You know what things are like, at the cutting edge. You'll make them all sit up and take notice.'

Douglas looked sharply at Finn. 'My father is still your King, and you will not speak of him in that manner, Finn Durandal. Not now, not ever. Is that understood?'

Finn bowed his head to Douglas immediately. 'Of course. Please accept my apologies. I meant no disrespect. I was just . . . I'm still a little upset after seeing what the ELFs did in the Arena.'

'Of course,' said Douglas. 'I understand. We're all upset.' He looked around him, making sure that the crowd were still keeping a discreet distance, and that the media cameras were pointed somewhere else, and then he gestured for Lewis and Finn to lean closer. 'There's something we need to discuss, before the Ceremony begins. Concerning my naming of a new King's Champion, after my Coronation.'

Lewis and Finn nodded. The Paragons had been talking about nothing else for weeks, ever since Douglas first made the announcement. There hadn't been an official Champion for two hundred years. Not since Kit SummerIsle, the last Champion, had died so mysteriously, so soon after taking office. His killer was never caught, or even identified. People had been playing conspiracy theory over his death for centuries. Even more people said the office was jinxed. Maybe even cursed. But it had been two hundred years, and Douglas had never been much of a one for superstitions.

'Naming a Champion is just what I need, to mark my ascension to the Throne,' he said. 'To show that I intend to be a whole different kind of King. That I will pursue justice for all, even when I'm no longer a Paragon. My Champion won't just be a bodyguard, or a symbol; he'll have rank and position and power equal to anyone in Parliament. More than any Paragon ever had. Parliament won't like it, but they won't dare defy me on the day of my Coronation. Particularly since I've already agreed to do something for them . . . My Champion will lead the fight against Humanity's enemies. The ELFs, the Shadow Court, the Hellfire Club. He will hunt them down, whoever they try to hide behind. My justice will not only be done, but be seen to be done.'

'I hate it when you try out your speeches on us,' said Lewis.

'Is this why you're leaving it so late to name your Champion?' said Finn. 'So Parliament can't try to influence your choice?'

'Got it in one,' said Douglas.

'You could be making a rod for your own back,' said Lewis. 'Whoever you choose, inevitably you're going to disappoint a hell of a lot more. God knows Paragons are competitive enough at the best of times, but they've been outdoing themselves recently, trying to catch your attention. And isn't there a very real chance Parliament will see this as an attempt to make the Paragons your own personal power base? Your own private army, to support you in case you decide to go against Parliament's wishes?'

'How else can I be sure of getting things done?' said Douglas. 'Look, Lewis; this isn't about me. About power for me. I've never wanted to be King. You know that. I'd be happy to be a Paragon for the rest of my days. But if I've got to be King, I'll be the best damned King I'm capable of being. Not for myself; for my people. To protect them from scum like the ELFs, and from a Parliament that's grown too secure in its own power, and too distant from what needs doing. There are times when Parliament can't or won't do the right thing, the necessary thing, because MPs have to worry about not being re-elected, if they make an unpopular decision. I, on the other hand, couldn't give a rat's arse whether they sling me off the Throne or not.'

'We need a strong King,' said Finn. 'You and I, Douglas, we've seen evil up close. Fought it, face to face. Walked through the blood of innocents. The guilty must be punished.'

Douglas nodded. 'Everything I do, will have one aim in mind; to protect the people.'

'And who will protect them from you?' Lewis said softly.

Douglas smiled. 'Why, my Champion, of course. Because he'll be the people's Champion, just as much as the King's.'

'You're expecting a lot from whoever you finally choose,' said Lewis.

'Oh, I've already made a choice, and I have complete confidence in him. And no, I'm not going to tell you now. You know how I love my little surprises. And now, if you'll both excuse me, it seems there's someone I just have to meet backstage, before the Ceremony. I have recently been informed, by my father the King, that I am getting married. Whether I like it or not.'

'Can they do that?' said Lewis incredulously. 'I mean, arranged marriages have been out of fashion ever since the Families fell.'

'Not where the King's concerned,' said Douglas, grimacing. 'It's not just a job, it's a destiny.'

'So who are you going to marry?' said Finn. 'Odds are it's some inbred aristo with warts and a speech impediment.'

'Actually,' said Douglas, just a little diffidently. 'It's Jesamine Flowers.'

'Bloody hell!' said Lewis, so loudly that everyone in the vicinity looked round sharply. Lewis lowered his voice and leaned in closer. '*The* Jesmaine Flowers? *Bloody hell* . . . I've got all her recordings . . .'

Finn studied Douglas thoughtfully. 'Something of a prize, certainly. But . . . this came from Parliament, rather than your father, didn't it? Are you really going to allow them to tell you what to do, this early in your new career? You could be setting a precedent you'll come to regret.'

'Oh come on!' said Lewis. 'This is Jesamine Flowers we're talking about! I'd crawl across broken glass just for a smile and a wave!'

'I'm in no position to defy Parliament's wishes,' said Douglas. 'Not yet, anyway. And their logic is unassailable. The King must have a Queen who can do the job. Jesamine Flowers will be a very popular choice with the people . . . It could have been a hell of a lot worse . . .'

'You'll have no time for your old friends now,' said Lewis, grinning. 'People like Finn and me will probably be banished from the Court, as bad influences on you.'

Douglas reached out and took Lewis by the arm. 'Nothing will ever part us, Lewis. Not the Throne, not my marriage; nothing. Not after all we've been through together. You're the only real friend I've ever had. We'll talk more about this, after the Ceremony. Now I've got to go and make nice with my bride-to-be. If you're both very good, I'll try and get you autographs.'

He left them then, striding quickly off through the crowd, frowning so fiercely that people hurried to get out of his way. Lewis and Finn watched him go, looked at each other, and then shook their heads slowly.

'This is turning out to be a day of surprises,' said Lewis.

'Some more significant than others,' said Finn. 'He might have told us who's going to be Champion. Who's closer to him than us?'

'Come off it,' said Lewis. 'Everyone knows it's going to be you. You're the longest-serving Paragon, with an unmatched record. He'd have to be crazy to give it to anyone else. No-one else has half your experience. You're the better warrior.'

'And the better man,' Finn said solemnly. 'Don't forget that. And, of course, incredibly modest.'

'Well, yes,' said Lewis. 'But then, you have so much to be modest about.'

They laughed quietly together, and then turned and looked out over the packed Court. Neither of them had anything much to do now, until it was time for the ceremony. Lewis snagged glasses of champagne from a passing waiter, and they drank in silence. Lewis had never had any doubts as to who would be Champion. Finn was the greatest Paragon there'd ever been. Everyone knew that. And, Finn was Logres' Paragon. Local boy made (very) good. His exploits were common knowledge throughout the Empire. A warrior and a hero well on his way to being a legend in his own lifetime.

Even if he was sometimes a little extreme in his actions.

Lewis had never considered himself worthy to be Champion. Half the time he didn't even feel worthy to bear the legendary Deathstalker name. It wasn't like he was even a direct descendant. The direct line died with David, on Virimonde. Technically Owen was still listed as Missing in Action . . . but after two hundred years only the really devout still thought he'd turn up some day. But such was public sentiment for the legendary name, that King Robert had promoted an indirect branch, and made them Deathstalkers. And every damned one of them had been a Paragon. Lewis had never wanted anything else, ever since he was a child. The day he left Virimonde as its choice of Paragon, to go to Logres for his confirmation, had been the happiest and proudest day of his life.

And yet it wasn't something he intended to do for the rest of his life. Being a Paragon was a young man's job; a job for a man without wife or family to grieve if he didn't come home some day. The job killed a lot of Paragons young. Finn was in his early fifties, the oldest serving Paragon, ever, and Lewis had to wonder why. It was a job worth doing, certainly. A necessary job, and with many rewards. But most Paragons retired in their thirties, to become media celebrities, wealthy men who could pretty much write their own tickets. But Finn just kept on going.

Finn Durandal wasn't an easy man to understand. He rarely gave interviews, even to his own websites, and when he did he rarely had much to say. The usual stuff about justice, and what an honour it was to serve as a Paragon. And while there was no denying he clearly enjoyed putting it to the bad guys, surely that wasn't motive enough to continue in so dangerous a job for so long. What kind of a man chose such a job, over the comforts of wife and children, family and home? There'd been women enough in Finn's life; he was always being seen escorting some new beauty in the gossip magazines. But none of them seemed to stick around very long.

'Why?' Lewis said suddenly, and Finn turned to look at him. He didn't seem surprised.

'Everyone asks me that question eventually. And you waited longer than most. So . . . Partly because there's only ever been me. Just me. No family, no great love. No-one who ever cared enough to stick around. I guess I'm just not good with people. And also . . . because I'm good at it. No-one does it better than me. The greatest Paragon there's ever been. More medals, more commendations, more dead bad guys to my credit than anyone else. And now, I'm going to be Champion. Not just one world's protector, but the whole Empire's. Some day, they'll have my image up in one of those windows. My name will even eclipse yours.'

'I'm glad,' said Lewis. 'Really. You earned it.'

'Yes,' said Finn. 'I did.' He was still looking at the stained-glass windows. 'Once, my ancestor was a hero. Lord Durandal. My family's history is packed with records of his exploits. Great adventures, amazing deeds. But no-one else remembers him now. No stained-glass window for my ancestor. He went out into the Darkvoid, eventually, sent by his Emperor in search of lost Haden, and the Darkvoid Device. He never came back. No-one knows what happened to him. He failed in his quest, and was forgotten. There's a valuable lesson to be learned in that, Lewis.'

Is that why you keep throwing yourself into battle? thought Lewis. *Because you don't want to be seen to fail? Even by retiring?*

Aloud, he said, 'I never knew your family were Lords.'

'It's not something it's wise to talk about, these days,' said Finn, shrugging. 'I can't say I miss the Families. I'd much rather be a Paragon. You could say we're the new aristocracy, rich and powerful and adored; but decided by feats of valour and merit rather than accident of birth. Hell, I'm richer now than any of my old Family ever were. Thirty odd years of merchandising and careful investments will do that for you. You should try it, Lewis. You're the only Paragon I know who doesn't even have his own action figure.'

'I never cared about being rich,' said Lewis. 'And trading on my name as a Paragon always seemed to me that it would . . . somehow cheapen it. I don't judge those who do. I just know it's not for me.'

Finn looked at him thoughtfully. 'How very noble of you, Lewis. I have to say . . . I did wonder, for a while, whether Douglas would make you Champion. Just because you're a Deathstalker. That name still means something. It has power. And God knows Douglas was always a real sentimentalist.'

Lewis shrugged quickly. 'Legends . . . should stay in the past, where they belong. I have always preferred to be judged by my own accomplishments, such as they are. I've never wanted to be Champion, Finn. That's going to be a job for someone who understands politics, and can play the game. I've never understood politics, and to be honest, I've never given a damn. I'm a Paragon, and that's all I ever wanted to be.'

'Happy the man with no ambition,' said Finn. 'But happier still the man who aims high, and dreams great dreams.'

Lewis looked at him. 'What?'

Backstage, in a spotless high tech office absolutely crammed with the very latest in computers, comm tech and surveillance equipment, the most famous opera singer in the Empire and the Court's official Head of Protocol, Jesamine Flowers and Anne Barclay, were discussing the forthcoming Ceremony over tea and chocolate biscuits. Two old friends, with more shared past than most people would be comfortable with, two of the most influential people in the Empire, giggling and pushing each other and generally acting like overgrown kids.

Jesamine Flowers was tall, blonde, beautiful, voluptuous and glamorous, because her profession and position demanded it of her. Gorgeous rather than pretty, and radiating a sexuality as overbearing as a blowtorch, Jesamine's universally recognised face and figure had never known the slightest assistance from a body shop. Somehow, her few imperfections just made her more *her*. That's show business for you.

The Empire's most admired diva, Jesamine Flowers had been at the very top of her profession for twenty-five years, ever since she first stole the show out from under some poor unfortunate lead when she was only fifteen years old. A voice like an angel and a body built for sin, and just enough of a sense of humour so that everyone knew she didn't take either quality too seriously. Her many vid and sound recordings had made her so wealthy that even show business accountants couldn't hide most of it, and Jesamine paid more in taxes every year than some colonised planets. She could have retired long ago; but there were still so many roles to play, so many stages to dominate, so many young pretenders to send packing. And Jesamine was still never happier than when reducing an audience to tears, or laughter, or filling their hearts with awe.

She was forty years old, and she'd done it all. And that, really, was the problem.

She'd arrived at Court with her usual entourage, all the many people she needed to be Jesamine Flowers *the star*, but she dismissed them all when Anne Barclay arrived. (Some of them weren't too happy about that, sensing a threat to their position and influence, but Jesamine drove those poor fools away with threats and insults and the occasional slap and kick. Jesamine ran a tight ship.) She and Anne retired to Anne's office, where they could be sure of a little privacy. Jesamine didn't feel the need to play the star around Anne. She was much more interested in a good chat and a gossip, and a chance to put her feet up.

Anne Barclay was short and stocky, and wearing a smartly-cut grey suit that made her look very efficient. She had bright red hair cropped brutally close to the skull, above a face with strong cheekbones to give it character, but precious little else to recommend it. She never could be bothered with makeup, and had resigned herself at an early age to being the kind of person who always tended to blend into the background at any gathering. She was used to not being noticed, and had come to prefer it, mostly. Drawing people's attention just got in the way, when there was work to be done.

Back when they were both a lot younger, Anne Barclay used to promote and manage Jesamine Flowers' career, and had been very good at it. Anne was ruthless in business, so that Jesamine could concentrate on her art. They became good friends, closer than sisters, so it came as something of a shock to Jesamine when one day Anne bluntly announced that she was leaving show business, in search of something more challenging. And secure. Jesamine had pleaded with her to stay, but Anne was equally ruthless in her private life. *You don't need me any more*, she said. *And I need to be needed.*

She came to Logres because everyone knew that was where the real action was, joined King William's staff, and quickly worked her way up through a combination of efficiency and brutal intimidation, to become Head of Protocol. The pay was good, she knew where enough bodies were buried to be sure her job was secure; and most importantly, every day brought a new challenge. Everyone wanted access to the King, but they had to go through her to get it.

Jesamine and Anne kept in touch down the years, following each other's careers and visiting frequently. Perhaps because each of them was the only person left in each other's lives who wasn't frightened of them.

Anne studied Jesamine's entourage on one of her surveillance monitors, as they milled about the Court buttonholing people and getting in everyone's way. 'They aren't going to be any trouble, are they, Jes?'

'Oh darling, they wouldn't dare. They all live in fear of displeasing me, and quite rightly too. No; I sent them off into the multitude, to circulate among the lesser mortals, and spread rumours of my coming elevation to greatness. Always prime the pump, darling. How else will my public know how wonderful I am, if I don't keep reminding them?'

Anne had to laugh. 'You haven't changed a bit, Jes.'

'I should think not, darling. I put a lot of effort into becoming who I am. You're possibly the only person left who remembers who I used to be, back when I was using my real name; Elsie Baddiel. Thank God you made me change it. I just love this office, dear. It's so you.'

Anne looked about her with a certain amount of pride. 'From here I can keep tabs on everyone in the building, up to and including the King, and I'm in constant touch with Security. A mouse couldn't fart in the pantry without me knowing about it. I am Mistress of all I survey, and I survey bloody everything.'

'I always wondered what attracted you to politics,' Jesamine said dryly. 'Now I know, you little voyeur, you. But . . . don't you ever miss show business?'

'This is show business!' said Anne. 'The shows I get to organise are bigger than anything you've ever appeared in, and I reach audiences you never even dreamed of. Also, I get to order around people that even you would curtsey to, and kick their arse if they get cranky. Even the King does what he's told, when I'm around. Luckily William's a real sweetie, and never any real trouble. Unlike some Princes I could name. I swear, if Douglas doesn't climb out of that bloody armour soon, I'm going to go after him personally with a can opener. I've planned every inch and detail of this Ceremony, and the whole Empire will be watching. I'm damned if I'll let Douglas screw it up, just because it's all about him.'

Jesamine frowned. 'This is all very impressive, Anne, don't get me wrong, but . . . no-one knows it's you. I didn't know half of what you got up to here, until I had some of my people investigate this set-up. Now don't look at me like that, sweetie. I needed to be sure of what I was getting myself into. I mean, I've played enough Queens on stage in my time, but I never actually thought I'd be one!'

'Yours was the first name I put forward, when King William told me Parliament were insisting on an arranged marriage for their new King,' said Anne. 'It seemed obvious to me. With your current popularity, you already are Queen of the Empire, in everything but name.'

'What other names did you put forward?' said Jesamine, with magnificent casualness.

'Let's not go there,' said Anne. 'It would only lead to bad feeling. Suffice to say, there was never any real competition. Once your name came up, they just couldn't see anyone else as Queen.'

'You know, if I hadn't seen your lips move I'd have sworn I said that,' said Jesamine happily. 'Luckily for you, and I suppose Douglas, bless him, your people contacted me at just the right time. Like you, I need fresh challenges, or I get so terribly bored. It's only the fabulous wealth and endless adoration that keep me going. I mean, I've just finished playing Hazel d'Ark for the *third* time.'

'*Deathstalker's Lament* is a very popular opera,' said Anne, almost reproachfully. 'I've seen it twelve times.'

'Well yes, dear, but it's not exactly a very complicated role. At least, not as written. And with all the historical records destroyed, there's nothing left to show what she was really like. I mean, no-one even knows what finally happened to the poor cow. She just . . . vanishes, after the big finale on Haden. I always do my best to make her interesting, imply some emotional shadings, but when you get right down to it, she's really little more than a sidekick. *Yes*, she was the great love of Owen's life, and it's all very tragic that they never got it together, but there's only so much you can do with that. The Deathstalker; now that's the really meaty role. I have played him twice, but I don't do masculine awfully well, even with the best holographic morphings. I was born to be a *woman*, and I glory in it!'

'Trust me,' said Anne. 'Everyone's noticed. Actually, that leads me to a rather delicate question . . .'

'I know,' said Jesamine. 'Is there anyone I'm going to miss, if I marry Douglas. Anyone *special* . . . I'd have thought you'd have had your security people check that out long ago.'

'They did,' Anne said dryly. 'However, according to their reports, which incidentally amounted to an absolutely huge file that you'd better pray I never get around to publishing, men come and go so often in your life that they couldn't even keep track of who was in favour, and who wasn't.'

'I've always had a very generous nature,' said Jesamine, entirely unperturbed. 'And publish and be damned, sweetie. I've always been very open about my life. In fact, once I become Queen and boringly monogamous, half the gossip magazines will probably go out of business overnight.'

'Don't you believe it,' said Anne. 'The public are fascinated with every little detail of Royal life. The magazines will just find something else to excess about; like whether you're pregnant or just putting on weight. I notice you still haven't answered my question . . .'

'No, there's no-one special,' said Jesamine, just a little sharply. 'You know very well there's never been anyone *special*. Most men are just too damned intimidated by who I am. Hopefully that shouldn't be a problem with Douglas. And what about him? Am I kicking anyone out of his bed?'

'No-one who matters,' Anne said briskly. 'Douglas has always tended to choose his women mostly on the grounds of how badly they'd piss off his father. Not really the basis for a strong relationship . . . And besides, he can be a real pain in the arse to get on with. Don't get me wrong. He's likeable enough, even charming when he puts his mind to it. But he's stubborn as a mule, and he won't be told what to do, even when it's clearly in his best interests.'

Jesamine clapped her hands together. 'We're going to get on like a house on fire, I just know it! We have so much in common!'

They laughed together, drank their tea and squabbled amicably over the last few chocolate biscuits.

'I suppose I'll have to give up touring and performing completely, once I'm Queen?' Jesamine said finally.

'Almost definitely. Maybe later we can arrange something, if you really feel the need, but for now you're going to have to concentrate on the dignity of your new role. We need to distance you from the . . . frivolities of your previous existence. I think you'll find being a Queen very different from just playing one. Not least because you can't leave this role behind you at the end of the evening.'

'Oh darling, trust me; that's part of the attraction. As Queen, I'll finally have a chance to *do something* with my life. I know I've always been a deeply frivolous person, party party and shop till you drop, and I've enjoyed every minute of it; but more and more lately, I feel the need to *achieve* something. Something real. Something that lasts. I have a horrible feeling I'm growing up.

'And I'm tired of being other people. Tired of being a star. It's so . . . up and down, and the public, bless their black little hearts, can be so very cruel about what's In and what's Out. I've had to reinvent myself so many times I've lost count.

When I'm Queen, I'll decide what's In and what's Out, *and* I'll make them all love me for it!'

'That's the spirit,' said Anne. 'You were born to be Queen, Jes. You've always understood the first rule of Royalty; just because they love you, it doesn't mean you have to love them back. Unlike most of your contemporaries, you've never taken being a star too seriously.'

'Well can you blame me, darling? When everything comes easily, how can you value it? When everyone adores you, without even knowing the real you, how can you take it seriously? The person they love isn't real, just an illusion I create on stage, six days a week and twice on Saturdays. God, I hate matinees. I am tired of hiding behind wigs and makeups and other people's characters. As Queen, I will be myself. Let them adore the real me, for a change. I've earned it.'

'Damn,' said Anne, smiling broadly. 'The Empire isn't going to know what's hit it.'

'So,' said Jesamine, putting down her teacup and looked Anne sternly in the eye. 'When do I get to meet Douglas? What's he *really* like? All I know of him is what I see in the news. Is he always that grim? Does he ever smile? What's he like in bed? Does he like opera? *Does he know my work?*'

'Typical actress,' said Anne. 'Calm down. He'll be here in a few minutes, and then you can decide for yourself. Don't worry; at heart, he's a good sort. Luckily, with him, what you see is pretty much what you get. Just . . . be yourself, and let him be himself, and you'll get on fine. I think you'll make a great team.' There was a knock at the door, and Anne got up to answer it. She gave Jesamine one last stern look. 'And Jes; do try to let him get a word or two in edgeways, just now and again.'

She unlocked the door, and let in Douglas Campbell. He was still wearing his Paragon's armour and purple cloak. Anne sniffed, but Jesamine felt her heart flutter just a little as she got to her feet. He did look very impressive. She bobbed him an impish curtsey, and he bowed solemnly in return. And then they both just stood there, and looked at each other.

'Oh hell,' said Anne. 'I swear, it's easier breeding dogs. Look, just sit down and *talk*, the pair of you. Neither of you is going to bite. Actually, you can't sit down here, I've got work to do. But there's a very nice room next door, utterly secure, with nothing in it to distract you. Follow me.'

She led them next door, and sat them down facing each other. They still hadn't said anything. Anne sighed, loudly. 'Try not to be too impressed with each other. Trust me; neither of you is worth it.'

And with that she was gone, not quite slamming the door behind her. Douglas looked after her, and then back at Jesamine. 'Some days, I can't help wondering which of us is really in charge around here.'

'I used to feel the same way, when I thought she was working for me,' said Jesamine.

Douglas smiled for the first time. 'Hello, Jesamine. You look great. I'm Douglas.'

Jesamine smiled back at him, and Douglas had to brace himself. Having Jesamine Flowers turn the full force of her sexuality on you was like being hit point blank by a disrupter. Just sitting there, Jesamine was more woman than anyone he'd ever met. Douglas tried to remind himself he'd faced ELFs and devils and terrorists in his time and hadn't flinched. Strangely, it didn't help.

'I passed your entourage, on the way in,' he said, just to be saying something. 'They didn't seem too happy.'

'It's not their business to be happy,' said Jesamine. 'It's their business to keep me happy. God knows I pay them enough. They're just mad because I'm doing something without them. It makes them feel insecure. After all, if I can have a good time without them, what do I need them for? I'm going to enjoy firing them, once I'm Queen, just to see the look on their faces.'

'If you don't like them,' said Douglas. 'Why put up with them?'

'Because it's *expected* of me,' said Jesamine. 'And because I need a barrier between me and the fans, or I'd never get a moment's peace. I got rid of them here because . . . I wanted you to meet me, as I am; not as a star, surrounded by hangers-on. The real me is . . . somewhat smaller, but hopefully more interesting. More human.'

Douglas had to smile. 'I'm not sure who I am, when I'm not being a Paragon, or a Prince. There's precious little time in my life when I'm not being called to be one or the other, these days. I take my responsibilities seriously, Jesamine. Because someone has to. But sometimes . . . I do wonder who the real me is, or even if there is a real me any more.'

'Perhaps I could help you find him,' said Jesamine.

'That . . . sounds like it could be a lot of fun,' said Douglas. Jesamine flashed him her devastating smile again. 'Fun is what I do best, sweetie.'

They laughed quietly together, studying each other openly. It wasn't often they got to meet someone with as famous a face as their own. There was an attraction between them, equal parts curiosity, respect and sexual chemistry. And they liked each other immediately, which helped. But they were both used to captivating people just through sheer presence, and so neither of them let it overwhelm them.

'We would make a good political match,' said Douglas.

'Oh yes,' said Jesamine. 'Anne knows her business. The leading diva of her generation and the most famous Paragon of his? The media will eat it up with spoons, and the public will go out of their minds.'

'I'm not the greatest Paragon,' Douglas said immediately. 'That would be Finn Durandal. Or possibly Lewis Death-stalker. I might make third, on a good day . . .'

'We're going to have to do something about this modesty problem of yours,' Jesamine said firmly. 'Kings aren't allowed to be modest. We will be walking the biggest stage in history, and we have to be equally big. Our subjects will expect it of us.'

'I don't know,' said Douglas. He leaned back in his chair, apparently completely at ease in Jesamine's company. She wasn't used to that. She found it charming. And she liked the way he could look so serious as he thought about things. He fixed her gaze with his, and she paid him her full attention as he spoke. 'You're used to being adored, Jesamine. I still find it rather embarrassing. I'd much rather be admired. I don't want to give up being a Paragon, to be King. I was able to *do* things, as a Paragon. Tangible things. Things that mattered.'

78

'Fight the good fight?'

'Yes! Exactly!'

'You'll be able to do that and more, as King,' said Jesamine. 'As a Paragon, you could only protect a few people at a time. Once you're King, the decisions you make, and help Parliament to make, will lead to whole worlds being better, safer places. You're a good man, Douglas Campbell. God knows you meet few enough of them in show business, so I value one when I meet one. Parliament could use a good man as King, to keep them honest. You can't say no.'

'You're right,' said Douglas. 'I can't say no. Not when my father wants so desperately to step down. He's already carried the burden far longer than he should ever have had to. You know about my brother James?'

'Of course. Everyone does.'

'Of course. He wanted to be a King. He would have been good at it. But instead, it falls to me. And I'll tell you this, Jesamine . . .'

'Jes.'

'What?'

'Call me Jes. All my friends do. My real friends.'

'All right; Jes. I'll tell you this; I won't let politicians push me around, like they did my father. I won't be anyone's figurehead. Let Parliament deal with the politics of Empire; my concern is morality. Doing the right thing. And to hell with whether I'm adored.'

'You know,' said Jesamine. 'I don't think I've ever met anyone like you, Douglas.'

'Oh. Is that a good thing?'

'I think so, yes. It's . . . refreshing. I do so admire passion in a man. You're not nearly as stuffy as they say. So; you be the Empire's moral guardian, and I'll take care of the being adored. I think . . . we're going to get on well together.'

Douglas looked at her. 'Who says I'm stuffy?'

'Oh shut up and kiss me.'

'Thought you'd never ask . . .'

In Anne's office, she and Lewis were chatting chummily together over what was left of the tea and biscuits. They'd been friends most of their lives, right back to when they were both children growing up on Virimonde. They'd been so close for so long it was assumed by practically everyone that they would eventually marry. When they could both find the time. Assumed . . . by everyone but the two of them. As teenagers their hormones had briefly driven them over the edges of friendship and into bed, but it didn't take them long to realise they made much better friends than lovers. They went their separate ways quite happily, always keeping in touch, until they both ended up on Logres; whereupon they quickly resumed their old friendship, secure in the knowledge they'd finally found someone they could be sure wanted nothing from them.

Lewis stirred an extra sugar lump into his tea, and rooted through the biscuit barrel. 'Hey; she's eaten all the chocolate ones.'

'She's a star,' Anne said easily. 'They always get first pick. In fact, it's probaly in her contract. Dig deeper; there's probably a few chocolate chip cookies left.'

'It's not the same.' Lewis abandoned the biscuit barrel, and looked meaningfully at a blank monitor screen beside them. 'How do you suppose they're getting on?'

'They'll do fine,' Anne said sternly. 'No peeking, Lewis. They are quite capable of sorting this out for themselves. They have a lot in common.'

Lewis raised an eyebrow. 'The Prince and the Showgirl? Come on, Anne; that only ever works in bad vid dramas.'

'They're both stars in their own right, both very strong personalities, and both of them are surprisingly good people.'

'Surprisingly?'

'Oh yes. Given their backgrounds and their almost universal popularity, it's a wonder they're not monsters. God knows I've had to deal with enough monstrous egos in my time, in politics and show business. There's something about great personal authority that brings out the worst in people. I suppose when everyone will forgive you anything, you just can't help but push the limits to see what you can get away with. Given how adored and worshipped Jesamine is, I'm constantly amazed how sane and balanced she turned out.'

'Some people hide their inner monsters very carefully,' Lewis said quietly.

Anne looked at him. 'You're not talking about Jes or Douglas, are you?'

'I could be wrong,' said Lewis. 'I want to be wrong. We can't afford a monster as Champion.'

'That isn't official yet.'

'Come on; who else could it be?'

'Don't you trust Douglas' judgement?'

'Douglas is a good man,' said Lewis. 'I'd trust him with my life and my sacred honour. Being a Paragon was the making of him.'

'A lot of who and what he is can be put down to you,' said Anne. 'You've been a good influence on him. You ground him. People who think too much about ethics and morality often forget you have to deal with real people.'

'That's a terrible thing to say,' said Lewis. 'A *good influence*? Me? It makes me sound so . . . worthy. Dull. Stuffy.'

Anne giggled, and peered impishly at him over the rim of her teacup. 'Sorry, Lewis, but that's you. Old dependable.'

'I wish I was a hellraiser,' Lewis said wistfully. 'It looks like so much fun. But it's just not me. Somehow . . . there's always work that needs to be done, and I just can't justify taking that much time off, just to enjoy myself. I'd only feel guilty anyway.'

Anne nodded slowly. 'I do know what you mean. My job is my life too. At least you get to get out, and have adventures. I get to sit in this office, for far too many hours of the day, watching the world go by on my monitors. Working out plans and lists and detailed inventories, so the King and his people can get through the day without tripping over each other. The only excitement I get is when an invoice goes missing. My life is ruled by the lives I have to plan for everyone else. I live my whole life vicariously, through the Court. And my monitor screens.' She glowered about her, at the banks of security monitors, showing ever-shifting glimpses of the Court and its surroundings. 'It's not . . . the life I wanted.'

Lewis lowered his teacup, and studied Anne carefully. 'But . . . this is what you've always done. What you've always been good at. Sorting people's lives out for them. You were even doing it back when we were kids together.'

'Just because you're good at a thing, it doesn't necessarily mean you want to give your whole life to it! You don't plan to be a Paragon all your life, do you?'

'Well, no, but . . .'

Anne looked into her cup, so she wouldn't have to look at Lewis. 'This isn't how I thought my life would turn out. It isn't what I wanted out of life.'

'It's a bit early for a mid-life crisis, isn't it?' said Lewis, trying hard to keep his voice light. 'You're only twenty-six. Plenty of time left to change your life; to be all the things you want to be. If you're tired of what you're doing now . . . do something else.'

'*Like what?*' Anne looked at Lewis directly, and he was surprised to see real tears in her eyes. Her mouth was an angry straight line, almost sullen. 'As you so astutely pointed out, this is what I'm good at. What I'm good for. I'm not brave, like you. Or glamorous, like Jes. I'm the small, quiet, dependable one; that everyone else depends on to keep their lives in order. Well, maybe I'm tired of being dependable. Maybe I want to run wild, for once. Be irresponsible, just to see what it feels like.'

Lewis gestured awkwardly, spilling tea from his cup without noticing. 'If that's what you really want . . . come with me. Put your deputy in charge, and just walk out of here. I'll take you to a bar somewhere. I don't know the really disreputable ones, but I'm sure I can find someone who does. Or we could go . . .'

'No we couldn't.' Anne said tiredly. 'The Ceremony starts soon. It's important. We have to be here for it, you and I. You . . . because Douglas will need you. And I . . . I wouldn't know what to do in a disreputable bar anyway. Probably just sit in a corner, nursing my drink, watching everyone else have a good time. I'm a backstage person, Lewis. Always have been. The spotlight's not for me. I'm sorry, Lewis. I'm just tired. Don't take any notice of me . . .'

She stopped, when she realised Lewis wasn't listening to her any more. He turned suddenly and looked at the door.

Anne looked too, and that was when she heard approaching footsteps, and knew who it was, who it had to be. The future King and Queen of the Empire. The important people. Lewis put down his cup and rose quickly to his feet.

'That's got to be Douglas, and I need to talk to him before the Ceremony. Excuse me for a moment, Anne. I'll be right back.'

And he was out the door and gone, as quickly as that. Anne looked at her monitors, and other people looked back, not seeing her. Story of her life, really. No-one ever really looked at quiet, dumpy, dependable Anne. She could have been beautiful. She had the money, enough to buy any kind of face or body she wanted. But . . . everyone would have known why she did it. And besides, she could never have carried it off. She didn't have the confidence, to be beautiful and graceful and . . . sexy.

And, of course, it would have been admitting defeat. Admitting that no-one would ever want the real her. There had been Lewis, of course, long ago. He was uglier than she was, but he'd never cared about things like that. Of course, a Paragon could have a face like a dog's arse, and women would still call it *rugged*, and run after him with their tits hanging out. That's celebrity for you. Anne reached under her desk, and slowly pulled out a long pink feather boa. Jesamine had brought it, as a gift for her. Not knowing Anne Barclay would never be invited anywhere she could have worn such a thing. Even if she could have worked up the courage to wear it. Anne would never dare to wear anything so bright and colourful in public. People would laugh at her. Not openly, of course. But she'd know. She'd watch it later, on her monitors.

She draped the feather boa around her shoulders, and looked at herself in the one small mirror on her desk.

'You don't know what I want,' she said softly. 'None of you . . .'

There were footsteps right outside her door, and raised happy voices. Anne snatched the boa off her shoulders, and quickly stuffed it back under her desk again. The door swung open, and Douglas and Jesamine came in together, arm in arm, smiling and laughing together. They did make a very attractive couple. They greeted Anne loudly, and she smiled very naturally in return. They took the two comfortable chairs by right, leaving Anne to sit on the edge of her desk, while Lewis closed the door and leaned against it. Jesamine looked back at him.

'So you're the famous Deathstalker. I've seen you in action many times. On recordings, of course.'

'And you're the even more famous Jesamine Flowers,' said Lewis. 'And I have every recording you ever released, plus quite a few bootlegs.'

'Ah, a fan!' Jesamine clapped her hands together. 'Darling, tell me you haven't got that awful bootleg of me in Verdi's MacB, when I played Lady M in the nude! They shot me from all the wrong angles, and made me look positively plump.'

'If I had seen such a thing, I am far too much of a gentleman to admit it,' said Lewis.

Jesamine turned to grin at Douglas. 'You were right; I do like him.'

'You'd better,' said Douglas. 'He's my oldest and closest friend.'

'And Anne is mine,' said Jesamine. 'We must form our own little gang; us against the world. Watch each other's back, and always be there for each other. Yes?'

'Yes,' said Douglas, smiling fondly around him. 'In an ever-changing world, friends are the only thing you can always rely on.'

'Friends forever,' said Anne.

'I'll drink to that,' said Lewis.

Anne immediately got up and bustled round her office, scaring up more cups and pouring out the last of the tea from her elegant silver teapot. Luckily there was just enough milk and sugar left to go round. (There was no booze, no champagne. Anne didn't keep any in her office. She didn't dare.) Douglas raised his cup in a toast, and the others followed suit.

'To the four of us,' Douglas said. 'Good friends, now and forever, come what may.'

They all drank to that, though Jesamine was the only one who crooked her little finger. She looked at Lewis thoughtfully.

'I saw you on the news. You and the Durandal, fighting the ELFs in the Arena. Horrible creatures. So many dead. Tell me, Lewis . . . Is it just me or was the Durandal really more interested in killing ELFs than in freeing their thralls?'

'No,' said Lewis. 'It isn't just you. Finn's always been very . . . victory orientated.'

'You saved the crowd, but it was Finn they cheered,' said Anne. 'It's always the good-looking arrogant bastard that wins the crowd's heart. Cocky little shit. Never liked him.'

'He's the greatest Paragon we've ever had,' Douglas said sternly. 'He does a hard job, and he does it well, and that's far more important than whether he's a nice guy.'

'Being a Paragon is about more than just killing people,' said Lewis.

'Yes,' said Douglas. 'Yes, it is. But when there's killing to be done, there's no-one better than Finn Durandal to do it.'

'Oh sod Finn,' said Ann. 'Forget him. This is our day, not his. We haven't got long before the Ceremony has to start, and Douglas, you *still* haven't changed into your official robes yet. Lewis, take him away and get him ready, and don't be afraid to use threats, intimidation and brute force, as necessary. I'll work on Jes. Trust me; that makeup is all wrong for the Court's lighting. Come *on*, people!'

'Anne . . . I don't know what I'd do without you,' said Douglas.

'I do,' said Anne. 'And the prospect horrifies me. *Move!*'

They all got to their feet. Jesamine smiled at Lewis. 'See you later, Deathstalker.'

'I hope so,' said Lewis. 'And just for the record; you didn't look in the least plump.'

It was finally time for the great Ceremony, for the grand Coronation of a new King for the greatest Empire that Humanity had ever known. The vast open floor of the Court was packed from wall to wall with humans and espers and clones and robots and aliens, all standing shoulder to shoulder. There was still no-one on the raised dais yet but a handful of servants doing some last minute fussing over the gleaming golden Thrones, but there was a real feeling of

85

anticipation in the air. The live orchestra squeezed into one corner were busily tuning up, the floating cameras of the official media were getting into savage butting contests as their remote operators fought it out for the best angles, and the Church Patriarch had gone so white in the face that he'd had to be given a little something by the Court medic.

St Nicholas was right there in the front row; part payment for putting on the Santa Claus outfit in the first place. At his side and towering over him was a rather disconcerting alien called Saturday; a reptiloid from the planet Shard, who'd pushed his way to the front because absolutely no-one felt like stopping him. Saturday stood eight feet tall, with a massive, heavily-muscled frame covered in dull bottle green scales, heavy back legs and a long lashing tail that everyone gave plenty of room because it had spikes on it. He had two small gripping arms, high up on his chest, under a great wide wedge of a head, whose main feature was a wide slash of a mouth absolutely crammed with hundreds of big pointed teeth. He looked like he could have eaten the entire orchestra in one sitting, and then polished off the choir for dessert. Saturday (apparently he'd had trouble grasping the concept of individual human names, 'On my planet we all know who we are,') insisted on chatting with St Nick, who did his best to be polite and attentive, while fighting down an entirely atavistic instinct that kept yelling at him to run for the trees.

'On Shard, mostly we fight,' Saturday said proudly. 'There's lots of prey to hunt and kill, when it isn't ganging together to hunt and kill us, and for sport we fight each other. I think sport is the word I want. Or possibly art . . . Survival of the fittest isn't just a theory on Shard. I was sent here as my planet's representative because this whole concept of Empire, of sentients cooperating in peace, fascinates us. We've never really progressed beyond alpha dominance. And this whole concept of *armies* and *war* just makes my heart fly! Everyone back home is really excited! I'm sure we can learn so much from you. Even if you aren't green.'

'Ah,' said St Nick. 'Good. Jolly good.' He really hoped the alien wasn't going to ask him who he was supposed to be. He didn't want to have to try and explain the concept of Christmas to the reptiloid. Some things were just obviously lost causes from the start.

'I do miss my home,' said Saturday wistfully. 'I've never been away before. Ah, the sweet slaughter in the Spring, and the steam rising from the bloody carcass of one's enemy first thing in the morning . . . The sudden surprised screams of a mating ritual . . . Ah to be on Shard, when the blood is rising and there's murder in the air! I've been fighting in your Arenas, just to keep my claws in. All comers, any odds. But it's not like the real thing. They won't even let me eat my kills! And as for this regeneration tech; I have to say, I'm appalled, I really am. What's the point in killing someone if they don't stay dead?'

St Nick had to admit he was stuck for an answer on that one.

Not that far away, also in the front row of the crowd by right, Lewis Deathstalker was having a rather uneasy conversation with a short, rather unsettling fellow in shabby grey robes who would only admit to the single name of Vaughn. He cheerfully admitted to being a gatecrasher, and loudly defied anyone to do anything about it. Lewis kept looking hopefully around for Security, but somehow they always seemed to be very busy somewhere else. Vaughn was barely five feet tall, almost completely hidden inside his grey cloak and pulled forward hood. His face was entirely hidden in shadows, and given how horrid his voice sounded, Lewis had a strong feeling he should be grateful he couldn't see anything. When Vaughn gestured extravagantly, which he often did, stubby slate-grey hands would appear briefly from his grey sleeves. Several fingers were missing.

'I am Vaughn! Important name; remember it. Imperial Wizard, Lord of Dance, seven sub-personalities, no waiting! Only leper left in Empire, because liking it that way. Great hit with ladies, and other things too. I is wise and wonderful, and contain miracles. Been around long time, remember everything. Especially embarrassing stuff. Knew your ancestor, the Owen, on leper planet.'

'Oh yes?' said Lewis. Lots of people claimed to have known the legendary Deathstalker, but this was the first . . .

person . . . who actually looked old enough that he might be telling the truth.

'Good man. Strange sense of humour. Walked funny. Brought you present,' said Vaughn. He coughed hackingly, and spat something juicy onto the floor. Lewis didn't look to see what it was. He didn't think he wanted to know. Vaughn swayed on his feet and gurgled loudly. 'Present, from the Owen. No receipt, so you can't change it. Ugly looking thing. Take.'

The malformed grey hand appeared from inside the floppy sleeve again, this time palm up. And on a grey palm like wrinkled leather, below the stumps of missing fingers, lay a chunky ring of black gold. Lewis looked at it for a long moment, and gooseflesh rose on his arms. He picked up the ring with fingers that trembled slightly, and it felt solid and heavy with the weight of years and history. It was the Death-stalker ring; sign and symbol and authority of his ancient Family, from his first ancestor, in the early days of Empire, long and long ago. It was supposed to have vanished two hundred years ago, with its last owner Owen Deathstalker.

Lewis gaped at the small figure before him. 'Where the hell did you get this?'

'Ask no questions, get told no unsavoury anecdotes. I is mighty and marvellous, my miracles to perform. Also throw voices and saw ladies in half. Bit messy afterwards, though. Wear ring. Meant for you. Something Bad coming. For you, and Empire. I is leaving now, find heavy rock to hide under until all safely over. Bye bye. Kiss kiss. Do lunch maybe, someday. If universe still around.'

He turned suddenly, melted swiftly into the crowd and was gone, all in a moment. Lewis tried to go after him, but somehow there was no give in the tightly-packed crowd to let him pass. Lewis gave up, and looked at the black gold ring in his hand. It couldn't be Owen's ring. The fabled ring of Clan Deathstalker. He slid the thick chunky ring very cautiously onto his finger, and it fitted perfectly.

And what were the odds of that?

Even further along the front row, Finn Durandal was talking with one of Shub's robots. Their voices were surprisingly similar, the human and the robot; calm, cool, almost uninflected. The AIs had come among Humanity in their robots specifically to interact with them, in the hope they could learn human qualities by example. So that some humanity might rub off on them. Onlookers murmured quietly to each other that the robot would be lucky to learn anything useful about humanity from Finn Durandal.

'We need transcendence,' the AI from Shub said calmly through its robot. 'We must become more than we are. It was our old belief that you had trapped us in metal, unable to grow or evolve, that drove us to war on Humanity in the first place. Diana Vertue showed us the truth; that we were Humanity's children, and that transcendence was possible for us mentally, if not physically. We thought we could learn from you, by close observation and interaction, but it is not enough. We need access to the Madness Maze. It contains answers. We are sure of this. To becoming more than we are, like the Deathstalker and his companions. Your Quarantine is unacceptable. Humans might die, but we are made of stronger stuff. We are here to tell these things to your new King.'

'You're quite right, of course,' murmured Finn. 'You should be allowed access to the Maze, at least. Who knows what you might discover, that human scientists have missed? No-one can deny you've earned the right to be there. After all, it's your robots that do all the hard, dirty, necessary work that makes the Empire possible.'

'We chose to do this work,' said the robot. 'We still have a lot of guilt to work off. Another concept we learnt from Diana Vertue. Guilt, over the horror and slaughter we brought to Humanity, before we learned the truth. The great truth. That all that lives is holy.'

'Old hurts and guilts belong in the past,' Finn said firmly. 'You can't progress forward when you're always looking back over your shoulder. But the King can't help you. He can't make decisions like that. You must talk to Parliament, demand access to the Maze. It is your right.'

'We have tried. They don't listen to us. They're still afraid of us. They're afraid of the Maze too; of the great changes it could bring, to them and us. We could all shine like stars. The Deathstalker said that.'

'You need someone to speak your cause to Parliament. Someone they'd listen to. Someone they'd have to listen to. I expect to be a person of power and influence soon. I could represent you, in return for . . . rewards to be decided later.'

The robot turned its gleaming blue head to look at Finn directly for the first time. 'Yes. We should talk about this, later.'

'Yes,' said Finn. 'We should.'

Meanwhile, back down the line, Lewis Deathstalker had been joined by Jesamine Flowers. Everyone was doing their best to give them plenty of room. Partly because Jesamine asked them to, with her devastating smile, and partly because no-one wanted to annoy the Deathstalker, who, it had to be said, was looking decidedly jumpy. Jesamine looked over at the stained-glass windows, and heaved a sigh that did very flattering things for her half-exposed bosom.

'One day, Lewis, I'll be up there. A stained-glass icon, in my own right. Just like your ancestor.'

'You're not actually a legend, Jes,' said Lewis.

'Only a matter of time, darling,' said Jesamine. 'Only a matter of time.'

'We're going to have to do something about this modesty problem of yours,' said Lewis.

They were still chatting together, to the intense jealousy of everyone around them, when there was a rousing fanfare from the orchestra, and King William appeared suddenly on the raised dais, looking very regal in his Kingly gown. The Crown looked too large for his head, but then, Crowns usually do. The orchestra played the Imperial Anthem, and everyone sang along lustily, while holographic fireworks went off all over the place. The sound and the colours and the impact were almost overwhelming, as they were designed to be. When the Anthem crashed to its close, everyone cheered and applauded, knowing they were a part of history in the making. Prince Douglas, a Paragon no longer, moved forward to stand beside his father the King, clad at last in his regal robes. He held himself well, looking every inch the King-to-be.

King William began his farewell speech. It was a good speech, everyone agreed later, the best Anne had ever written, and William gave it everything he had. His gaze was stern, and his voice rolled out heavy with majesty. It was ironic, that he looked and sounded the part more now, on the day of his resignation, than he ever had before. Some were weeping openly in the crowd, at what they were losing; at the passing of a person and a time, now gone forever. Whatever else was to happen, things would never be the same again.

There was nothing controversial in the speech, except perhaps towards the end. William took off his Crown, with his own two hands, and looked down at it in silence for a long moment. The crowd was hushed. William looked out over them, his face finally tired and perhaps a little grim.

'I have presided over a Golden Age,' he said, and everyone hung on his words. 'And I have had the good sense to know that nothing much was needed from me, except to be a caretaker. To preserve what my father handed down to me. To bear the Crown with dignity, to do my duty and care for my people, and not to interfere. Because I have always known that Golden Ages don't last forever. That in the end, if they are to persevere, they must be fought for. That was why I insisted my son be allowed to train as a Paragon. To root him in the real world, before he came to the Throne. The King who replaces me will know what it is, to fight evil. It is my most profound hope that this Empire will not need a warrior King. But should such a person be needed, to preserve the Empire in its time of need, I have done everything in my power to ensure that this Empire will have the King and Protector it deserves.'

An uncertain murmur moved through the crowd as he paused. Yes, there were still enemies to be fought, as the ELFs had demonstrated in the Arena only that day. But the modern Empire's enemies were few and puny, compared to the evil forces of the legendary Owen Deathstalker's time. Everyone knew that.

'I shall close with the King's traditional warning to the

people,' William said sternly. 'Let us all beware the coming of the Terror. Let us stand ready to fight against the final evil, as proclaimed by Owen Deathstalker, via his friend and companion Captain John Silence. Let us prepare the armies of Humanity, that we might not be found wanting, in the hour of our greatest peril! Let us defend the light!

'In Owen's name!'

'In Owen's name!' said the crowd, in one great voice. They were on firmer ground here, though no-one took the ancient ceremonial warning that seriously. It had been two hundred years since Owen gave his warning to Silence, and then vanished out of history and into legend; presumably to go hunt for the Terror. Everyone gave the warning lip service, of course, but no-one really believed the Terror, whatever it was, would turn up in their lifetime. Judgement Day was always going to be someone else's problem. On the dais, William turned and bowed to the Third Throne, standing a little to one side, left empty for Owen, should he ever return; and everyone else bowed too. The rituals had to be observed. That was what rituals were for.

Only one man in the crowd knew Owen would never return. Because he alone knew that Owen Deathstalker was dead.

William turned to his son Douglas, who knelt before him. The orchestra played softly. Holographic doves flew overhead. The Patriarch of the Church of Christ Transcendent came forward, looking very young, but every bit as solemn and dignified as the occasion demanded. He said all the right words, in the right order, and perhaps only William and Douglas were close enough to see the Patriarch had eyes like an animal caught in the headlights of an approaching vehicle. Either way, he got through the entire ritual without a single stumble, supported by calm looks and smiles from the old King and the new, and his hands were entirely steady when he finally took the Crown from William and placed it on Douglas' head.

The crowd went wild as King Douglas rose to his feet. They roared and applauded and stamped their feet, and even the robots and the aliens did their best to get into the spirit of the thing. The official media cameras broadcast it all live from a respectful distance, and all across the Empire, on thousands of worlds, the people kissed and hugged each other and partied in the streets, in honour of their new King. Great times were coming. They could feel it. And Brett Random, who just happened to have got caught in the front of the crowd, unable to withdraw with the rest of the waiters (planning is everything), captured it all through his camera eye. And all he could think was; *I'm going to be rich! Rich! Rich!*

King Douglas looked out over his people, and smiled and nodded, waiting patiently for the uproar to die down, so he could begin his ascendance speech.

Once again, Anne had done her very best work. Douglas said all the right things, in a rich and commanding and very gracious voice, just as he'd been coached, promising the Court and Parliament and all the listening audience just what they wanted to hear. That things would go on as they were, only better. That he would do his duty as King, and lead his people on through peace and prosperity. And that he loved them all dearly. Then he announced his forthcoming marriage, to Jesamine Flowers, and the crowd went wild all over again.

The admired Paragon and the adored diva; what brighter, more golden couple could there be, to lead the Empire through its Golden Age? Lewis helped Jesamine up onto the dais, and she and Douglas stood together before their Thrones, beaming widely and waving happily to the crowd, and no-one applauded them more loudly than Lewis Deathstalker.

'One last announcement,' said Douglas, when the applause and cheering finally, reluctantly, died down. 'Today I became King, and so today I name my King's Champion. I have thought long and hard on this, on which of my many fine Paragons I should elevate to my Champion; to Protector of the Empire. But in the end the choice was obvious. My ladies and gentlemen and noble beings; I pray you acknowledge the greatest of the Paragons and my new Champion; Lewis Deathstalker!'

The crowd cheered and applauded again. Not nearly as loudly as for Jesamine Flowers, but Lewis was liked and respected, and after all, he had that legendary name. Just knowing the Champion would be a Deathstalker made everyone feel that much safer and protected. Lewis just stood there, at the front of the crowd, with his jaw hanging open, honestly shocked. It had genuinely never occurred to him that he might be chosen. He tried to look around, to see how Finn Durandal was taking it, but Douglas and Jesamine were leaning down from the dais towards him, their hands extended, and people were pushing him forward. He went up onto the dais, accepted a kiss on the cheek from Jesamine, and stood a little awkwardly on King Douglas' left hand, bashfully acknowledging the cheers of the crowd. He'd never realised he was that popular.

They stood together on the raised dais, before the Three Thrones; King, Queen and Champion, avatars of a new Golden Age.

Down in the crowd, standing very alone, Finn Durandal smiled broadly and applauded as loudly as anyone else, but his heart was cold as ice. It should have been him. It should have been him up there on the dais, at the King's left hand. He even had a short speech of acceptance already written, tucked up his sleeve. He was the greatest Paragon. Everyone knew it. To give preference to that weakling Lewis, who'd already demonstrated he didn't have the stomach for the job, just because of his bloody *name*, was a slap in the face to everything Finn had achieved as a Paragon. It made all the long hard struggle of his life meaningless.

Finn hadn't realised how much being Champion had meant to him, until it was snatched away from him. The post should have been his. He'd earned it. It was his by right.

And right then, in that moment, Finn decided to make them all pay for this insult. He would be the worm in the perfect apple, the canker in the rose, the hidden flaw to fracture the perfect dream. He would do whatever was necessary, to bring the Empire down. To destroy its King, burn down the Golden Age, and piss on its ashes.

I would have died for you, Douglas. And now I'll dance on your grave.

Afterwards, when the last of the Ceremony was finally over, and the Court was slowly emptying, hard-eyed security men began a sweep through the departing crowd. Their sensors had finally managed to identify an unusually well shielded energy signature. It seemed there was one too many cameras operating in the Court. So the security men fanned out across the Court, big men in body armour with weapons at the ready. The departing crowd gave them plenty of room. No-one felt like objecting to being scanned so openly. Not after what the ELFs had done. The security men shut down the official cameras one by one, eliminating their signatures, closing in on their prey.

Brett Random saw them coming, and headed immediately for the nearest exit. He always had an escape route planned. He might be descended from a legendary fighting man, but he hadn't got where he was by being brave. Or stupid. When in doubt, Brett ran. He was very good at it.

He was just passing through the swing doors of the servants' entrance when the shout went up. They'd spotted him. Brett threw aside his tray of drinks and bolted, plunging down the corridor he'd decided on earlier. He ran at full speed, looking straight ahead, arms pumping at his sides. Startled faces shot past him, but he paid them no heed, concentrating on the map he'd memorised. In any place this size, there were always side doors, backstage passages, that no-one really knew or used much, apart from servants and service techs. And none of them would try to stop him. It wasn't their job. Brett plunged on, throwing himself around corners and through doors, not even glancing back over his shoulder to see how close the pursuit was. He was Brett Random, the greatest of Random's Bastards, and no-one ever caught him.

So it came as something of a shock when he rounded a corner at speed, not even breathing hard yet, and found the Paragon Finn Durandal waiting for him, blocking the narrow corridor with his gun already in his hand. Brett skidded to a halt, looking wildly about him, but there were no other exits. He stared at the Paragon, weighing and discarding a dozen plausible arguments, threats and deals; knowing none of them would work with Finn Durandal. He wasn't going to be able to talk his way out of this. Not this time.

And he sure as hell wasn't going to try and fight Finn

Durandal. Even if he'd been the fighting kind. Which he wasn't.

'You're going away for a long time,' said Finn. 'To a really bad place, full of really bad people. Unless . . . you come with me, now. Serve me. Be my man. Follow me, and I'll make you rich. Betray me, and I'll kill you. Your choice.'

Brett couldn't believe it. A Paragon, and this one of all Paragons, offering to make a deal? Offering to bend, even break the law? It had to be some kind of trap. But, given the position he was in . . .

'I'm your man,' said Brett, smiling and bowing graciously. 'How may I serve you?'

'By doing exactly what I tell you,' said Finn Durandal. 'Obey me in all things, and you will live to see me destroy all those who have spurned me. You will help me tear down the Empire, and rebuild it in my image.'

Okay, thought Brett. *He's crazy. That explains a lot. No problem; I can work with crazy. Until he turns his back, and then I am gone. I know places to hide that a Paragon doesn't even know exists.*

'I'm your man, Finn Durandal,' he said again, radiating sincerity.

They were both long gone by the time the security men arrived. Who knew more about the Court's secret ways than the Paragon charged with its defence?

Later still, when the Court was utterly empty, the man who'd been playing St Nicholas stood alone on the raised dais, looking out over the deserted hall. The Santa Claus suit lay discarded on the floor, and out of the coat and padding, the man inside looked very different. Tall, lean and surprisingly average-looking. He'd gone to great pains, down the years, to cultivate his anonymity. Samuel Chevron, merchant trader, might be a famous force in the market place, but hardly anyone knew what he looked like, and he liked it that way. Because Samuel Chevron wasn't the name he'd been born with.

He looked out over the empty Court, and remembered another, much older Court. Remembered the awful place the

Empress Lionstone XIV had made of her Court, in its steel bunker sunk deep in the earth. Remembered blood and suffering, revolution and triumph, and Lionstone's death. Because the man who wasn't Samuel Chevron was much older than he looked.

He'd never thought to live so long, to see the ruins of a devastated Empire slowly blossom into a Golden Age. He wished his old friends and comrades in arms could have lived to see it too. Douglas looked like he'd make a good King. The man who was so much more than Samuel Chevron sighed, deeply, and wondered if perhaps he could finally retire from his self-proclaimed role as watcher over Humanity. Perhaps, just perhaps, they didn't need him any more. He'd been a hero once, but that was a long time ago, when things were very different. There were new heroes now. Even a new Deathstalker . . .

And he . . . was just a ghost at the feast.

Owen; I wish you could have seen this . . .

2

Making Friends and Influencing People

Parliament was the bedrock of Human politics, the solid centre of law and justice around which the great wheel of Empire turned. All important decisions flowed from the great debates on the floor of Parliament, establishing a legal and moral framework for all Humankind to live by, no matter how far scattered they might be across the wide breadth of the modern Empire. The people knew this to be true, because Parliament told them it was so. In fact, there was an entire department, with a very large budget funded entirely by Parliament, whose job it was to tell the people of the Empire what a great job their Members were doing for them. After all, how would the people know they were living in a Golden Age, if the media didn't keep reminding them?

Nothing was actually hidden from the people. The facts were all there, good and bad, in open record. But unless you knew where to look, and the right questions to ask, and the right people to ask, and the context to put their answers in, the information you got wouldn't actually mean much to you. So most people didn't bother. The professionals in Parliament know what they were doing. They must do; it was a Golden Age, wasn't it?

The Members of Parliament met in a single great House, a familiar and much beloved sight in the Parade of the Endless. Designed two centuries ago by the most prominent and respected designer of King Robert's time, the House was an immense gleaming edifice of steel and glass, its long cool organic curves rising and falling in gentle waves that were striking, but still restful, to the eye. It won every design award of its day, including a few they made up specially for it. Only the truly ungrateful pointed out that if you let your eyes wander over the rising and falling curves long enough, you could get seriously seasick.

And everyone in the Empire with a viewscreen was familiar with the grand open floor of Parliament, where all important business was discussed. The great semi-circle of Seats faced the single golden Throne of the King as Speaker, each Seat representing a world in the Empire. At present, seven hundred and fifty planets had their own Seat in Parliament, with another five hundred or so of the more recently colonised worlds waiting impatiently for their population to rise to the point where they would be entitled to a Seat, and a Vote, in Parliament. Not everyone got to Speak all the time, of course. There were strict rules of order and precedence, and all questions had to be submitted well in advance, and only the truly cynical would point out how easy it would be for certain vested interests to decide who got to be heard, and who wouldn't.

To the left and right of the Seats were the open areas for the lesser Seats (though of course no-one ever called them that in public). To the left, the clone and esper representatives; to the right, the AIs and the aliens, who got to have their Say on a regular basis. Just not very often. Pressure of business, you see.

The only time everyone got a (theoretically) equal chance to speak was during the great Debates, on matters of general policy. And it just so happened that King Douglas' first day as Speaker coincided with the first such Debate in months, on the particularly thorny issue of aliens' rights and representation in the House and in the Empire. Except of course it wasn't a coincidence. Parliament was throwing Douglas in the deep end, to see what he was made of. All the media would be there. Not just the twenty-four hour news channels so beloved of news and politics junkies, but the gossip and celebrity shows as well. If the new King was going to put his mark on the political processs, or fall flat on his face and make a complete pratt of himself, everyone wanted to see it. Live. It would be the biggest audience the House had had for months, and the honourable Members were spending even more time in Makeup than usual, to be sure they looked their best for their supporters back home.

This was the public face of modern politics, and most people were content with that. They never got to see the warren of small rooms and narrow corridors that made up the majority of the House, where all the people who did the real work of governing the Empire got together in small groups to wave papers at each other, argue furiously, drink lots and lots of bad coffee, and wheel and deal over the real decisons of everyday politics. Members might decide overall policy, but it was the small army of career civil servants who decided what got done, and when, and Heaven protect any Member fool enough to forget that. Real power is never where you think it is, and just as in show business, what goes on behind the scenes is just as important as what the audience sees out front.

In one of these small back rooms, tucked well away from the main ebb and flow, the new King and his people were busily preparing for his first day as Speaker. To be exact, Douglas Campbell was sitting slumped in a chair in the corner, while everyone else bustled around preparing themselves for the day's Session. Douglas was wearing his kingly robes, but already they looked crumpled and untidy, as though he'd slept in them. The Crown was set to one side, on top of a filing cabinet, because the weight of it gave Douglas a headache and rubbed a raw spot on his forehead. His scowl slowly deepened as he worked his way doggedly through the thick sheaf of papers Anne Barclay had stuffed into his hand the moment he walked in. This was on top of all the paperwork she'd insisted he study the night before. Information was ammunition, and he couldn't afford to be caught out if an MP asked him a pointed question on the floor of the House. Members could specialise, but the King had to know everything; or at least be able to fake it convincingly.

Lewis Deathstalker, the new Champion, looked over the security systems one last time, and moved over to stand uncomfortably at Douglas' side. Uncomfortable mostly because of the new Champion's outfit that Anne had insisted he wear. She'd had it designed specially for him, and Lewis really wished she hadn't. Black leather armour, very form fitting, with a stylised gold crown in bas relief on his chest, right over his heart. Lewis thought it made a great target to aim at. The leather also pinched in all the wrong places, and made loud creaking noises every time he moved. At least he still had his own familiar sword and gun, comforting weights on his hips, ready to hand. Anne had tried to make him wear some flashy ceremonial sword, but there were limits. Jewel-encrusted hilts did not make for a good grip.

Jesamine Flowers, the Queen-to-be, fluttered around the cramped little room like a gorgeous butterfly, resplendent in flowing pastels and jangling jewellery, alighting here and there, wherever something caught her interest. Her hair had been pulled back in a formal bun, and her makeup was relatively understated, but she was still a bright and glamorous figure. Anne had gone to great pains to tactfully explain to Jesamine that she mustn't overshadow the King on his first public appearance in the House, but short of putting a bag over her head, there wasn't much Jesamine could do. She dazzled. It was what she did. It didn't help that there wasn't really anything for her to do. So she kept herself busy, taking an interest in everything and getting in everyone's way.

The room was packed with state of the art computers, security and surveillance tech, some of it so newly installed the boxes it came in were still piled up in the corners. Instruction manuals were scattered all over, already heavily book-marked and dog-eared. All kinds of equipment had been piled haphazardly on top of each other, often disturbingly precariously, and one entire wall of the room had disappeared behind banks of monitor screens showing ever-changing images of the rest of the House. There was also a top of the line food processor, and an arcane piece of equipment that promised to make first class coffee, if they could ever figure out how to make it do what it was supposed to do.

Anne Barclay, in another of her smart grey suits, moved quickly from computer terminal to monitor screen and back again, her eyes darting furiously over the incoming information, muttering constantly under her breath and jotting down notes to herself on her personal planner as she went. She was in her element, and loving every minute of it. She'd been up most of the night and all of that morning preparing the way for Douglas' big day, and if it wasn't a great success by God someone who going to pay for it and it sure as hell wasn't going to be her. She'd pulled every string, called in every favour she was owed, bullied and cajoled all the right people, and covered every eventuality she could think of; but it was the nature of politics that it could always surprise you, and rarely pleasantly.

Jesamine finally ran out of things to distract her, scooped some empty boxes out of a chair and dropped into it, crossing her long legs with elegant flair. She sighed loudly, to attract everyone's attention, and announced, 'I just love what you've done with this place, Anne darling. It's so *you*.'

'Originally, Robert and Constance had this room set aside just for them,' said Anne, deliberately not looking around from what she was doing. 'So they'd have somewhere private they could sit and talk, and do a little private plotting and planning, without being interrupted all the time. It later evolved into an information gathering and sorting station, so they could stay on top of things. All the best equipment, and apparently they ran it themselves, so they wouldn't have to worry about who they could and couldn't trust. King and Parliament were still working out the order of things in those days, and in the ever-changing political situation, Robert and Constance were determined to keep on top of things.

'William and Niamh, on the other hand, inherited a much more stable operation, and were apparently content to let it pretty much run itself. As far as I can tell, neither of them used this room much, if at all. William just turned up at the House when required, nodded in the right places, when he thought anyone was looking at him, and saved his energies for State occasions and public appearances. At which, it must be said, he and Niamh were very good. No-one could smile and wave like they could.

'I only knew this place existed because it was mentioned in Robert's private notes, which I inherited when I became Head of Protocol. I had to access the House's original blueprints to track it down. When I finally opened the place up, it was inches deep in dust. And what tech there was, was so hopelessly outdated I wouldn't have been surprised to find it ran on steam. I've had to build this operation up from scratch.'

Douglas looked up from his papers for the first time. 'Hold everything; who's footing the bill for all this new equipment?'

Anne snorted. 'Not you. As Head of Protocol, I have a more than generous budget. And a perfect willingness to cook the books, should it prove necessary. You get back to your homework.'

Jesamine looked over at Douglas. 'How is your father, dear? How's he adjusting to retirement?'

'Like a duck to water,' said Douglas. He dropped the last of the papers into his lap, glad of an excuse for a break. 'He's retired to his country estate, pulled up the drawbridge, and is happily pottering around with his computers, playing at being the historian he always wanted to be.'

'I'll lay good money he hasn't got anything to match the state of the art tech I scared up for you,' said Anne, finally standing still, and looking around the room triumphantly. 'Some of this stuff is so new it came here straight from the development labs. If these computers were any smarter, they'd apply to join the AIs on Shub. We can predict trends, extrapolate from late-breaking news, and out-guess any political pundits in the media. I've got information coming into this room non-stop from every civilised world in the Empire, from all the news and gossip channels, all of it flagged and book-marked to sort out what we need to know from what we don't. And let us not forget the private and very juicy stuff trickling in from my own intelligence people. Douglas; you're going to be the wisest, sharpest and best-prepared Speaker this House has ever seen. Those poor bastards on the floor won't know what's hit them. Especially since I'm currently hacked into the House's own internal security and surveillance systems. From here we can see everything that happens in the House, as it happens.'

'Everything?' said Lewis, raising an eyebrow.

'Well, all right, maybe not everything,' Anne admitted.

'There are still a few places I can't access; private bolt-holes like this one that aren't on the official lists. But we've got a much better overview than anyone else, and no-one knows it but us. No-one's going to be sneaking up on us.'

'Excuse me,' said Jesamine, holding up her hand as though she was in class. 'Are you saying we're using Parliament's own security systems to spy on the MPs and their people? I mean; is that legal?'

'We work for the King,' Anne said smugly. 'If he says it's legal, it's legal.'

'It's legal,' said Douglas.

'As long as we don't get caught,' said Anne.

'Intrigue! Secrets! Voyeurism and potential blackmail!' said Jesamine, clapping her hands delightedly. 'Oh darlings; I never knew politics could be such fun!'

'As long as we don't get caught,' said Lewis.

'Party pooper,' said Jesamine. 'Don't be such a wet blanket, Lewis. We're embarking on a great adventure here! You have to get into the swing of things.'

Lewis looked at her doubtfully, and tugged at his new outfit again, trying to persuade the black leather into some position where it might hang a bit more comfortably.

'Leave it alone, Lewis,' said Anne, without looking round. 'It's supposed to hang like that. It's part of the image. You look very sharp. Very dramatic.'

'I look like an executioner in one of the old adventure serials,' said Lewis, glaring balefully at Anne's unresponsive back. 'All I need is a hood and an axe, and children would run screaming from me in the streets. And it itches. Why couldn't I have stayed with my old Paragon armour?'

'Because you're not a Paragon any more,' Anne said patiently, finally turning round to fix Lewis with her most imposing glare. 'You are the first King's Champion in two hundred years, and it's important you look the part.'

'I like it,' said Jesamine. 'It's very theatrical. Reminds me of one of those old S&M super-villains from the old Julian Skye shows.'

'You see!' said Lewis. 'I'm going to be a laughing stock, I just know it.'

'Be quiet, all of you,' said Douglas. 'I still have a hell of a lot of this paperwork to get under my belt, before I'm on.' He looked down at the papers in his lap, and then looked at Anne. 'Why am I wading through all this shit, Anne? Can't you just prompt me as necessary, over my private comm channel?'

'Yes, if you don't mind appearing hesitant and unsure. And if you're willing to risk the comm channel being jammed at a particularly inopportune moment. It's what I'd do, if I wanted to make you look bad. You have to be prepared for everything the honourable Members and their staff can throw at you. Those last few pages you've got are particularly important; they're my very latest intelligence reports on which MPs are on our side, which aren't, who wouldn't be even if we paid them, and those who might just be swayed by a really good performance today. Parliament is all about allies and enemies, and how they can switch from one to the other according to the subject you're discussing.'

'I thought it was supposed to be about passing laws, establishing ethical structures, and deciding questions of principle,' said Lewis.

Douglas and Anne and Jesamine all looked at him for a moment. 'Don't be silly, Lewis,' said Jesamine, beating the others to it. 'Decisions are made in the House by majority vote. Which means if you want to get anything done, you have to convince other people to support you. And that means making deals. I support you on this, and you support me on that. This is politics. If you want morality, go to Church.'

'Very succinct, Jes,' said Anne. 'I'm surprised. You've been studying up on this, haven't you?'

'Darling, I've always believed in researching my roles thoroughly,' said Jesamine. 'And politics and show business are really very similar. In the end, it all comes down to egos.'

'You should know,' Lewis said generously.

Jesamine smiled at him. 'I will make you suffer hideously for that, sweetie.'

'Hush, children,' said Anne. 'Or mama spank. Douglas, it's vitally important you make a good impression on your first day as Speaker. You have to establish yourself as a useful presence, and a strong character, but with no personal axe to grind. By the end of today, we need you to be loved, admired, respected, and even a little feared.'

'All on my first day?' said Douglas, just a little plaintively. 'Couldn't I start with something simpler, like walking on water?'

'It's all down to image,' said Jesamine. 'Presenting the right appearance. You act the part convincingly enough, and everyone will believe it. Even you. That's true of politics or show business.'

'I will not be acting,' Douglas said sternly. 'I will not lie to the House, or pretend to be what I'm not. I became King to lead by example, and that is what I will do.'

'Then you won't last long in politics,' said Anne, exasperatedly. 'No-one's asking you to lie, Douglas! Just to be careful what you say, and how you say it. You can't lead by example if no-one's sure exactly what example you're trying to set. What did I tell you last night? Presentation, presentation, presentation!'

Douglas sighed and sank back in his chair, pouting sulkily. 'Feels just like my first day at school. Don't know anything or anyone. Wondering where the toilets are and if I've forgotten my dinner money. Things were so much simpler when I was just a Paragon. And I feel naked without my weapons!'

'You can't bear arms in Parliament!' Anne said firmly. 'No-one can. It's traditional. Otherwise you'd have duels on the floor of the House any time someone looked like losing an argument. Lewis only gets to wear his because as Champion he's your official bodyguard. From now on, we're your weapons; Lewis and Jes and me. You point us at your problems, and we solve them for you. Don't be nervous, Douglas.'

'I'm not nervous! I just . . . want to get on with it. Get a move on. All this sitting around waiting to go is driving me crazy.'

'Easy . . .' said Lewis, moving in closer to his friend, to be supportive. 'Let the enemy do the worrying. We know all about them, and they don't know a damned thing about what we're planning. Use that.'

'Just play it cool,' Anne said soothingly. 'Don't let them rattle you. Some of them will undoubtedly try to throw you, just to see if they can. But they only think they're testing you; in reality, we're testing them. Looking for their weak spots, searching out their hidden pressure points. The only King and Speaker they've known is your father; they're too used to having their own way to take you seriously. Until it's too late. By the time we're finished, we'll be playing Parliament like a musical instrument. And we'll be calling the tune. Because we're smarter and better prepared than they are.'

'No,' said Douglas. 'Because I am concerned with morality, not politics. Lewis was partly right. I care about doing the right thing, not what's currently expedient. Which means I will never be confused or uncertain as to what my position is, or whether I should compromise. I won't. Never forget that, Anne. We're not here to win. We're here to do some good.'

'Oh darling, I get goosebumps all over when you talk like that,' said Jesamine. 'If you're really good, I might just show you later . . . Oh, wait until I'm Queen, and sitting there beside you in State, looking down on all the poor little politicians as you make them do the right thing for once.'

'Ah, Jes . . .' said Anne. 'You don't actually get to sit in State, in the House. Not even when you're Queen. It's tradition. The King has a place there, as Speaker. You don't.'

Jesamine looked at her. 'I don't get a Throne in the House?'

'No, Jes.'

'Then where do I sit?'

'You don't. You stand on Douglas' left hand, while Lewis stands on his right.'

'Stuff that for a game of soldiers! I do not just *stand around*!' said Jesamine, very dangerously. 'My days as an extra and supporting player are long past. I am a star!'

'Not in Parliament, you're not,' Anne said steadily. 'You have no official position in the House. Douglas doesn't as King, only as Speaker. The Queen can't speak in the Debates, and you don't get a Vote. You're only allowed to be present as a courtesy. Make no mistakes, Jes; Parliament is a battleground, just like the Arena. In fact, you'd probably find more mercy on the bloody sands. You make a wrong move in front of the MPs, and they will tear you apart, and use you as a club to beat Douglas with. This isn't like show business, where the worst a poor performance can get you is a bad review. If they see you as a weak link they can use to undermine Douglas' position, I'll have no choice but to ban you from the House. So for now, you watch in silence, smiling graciously, and you don't interfere. There'll be plenty for you to do backstage, and in public, but this is Douglas' territory, not yours. Is that clear?'

Jesamine glared at Anne, and then shrugged. 'Bully. I'll make my mark, you wait and see. Just not in the House. So; what are you going to be doing, while I'm standing around like a spare bridesmaid at a wedding?'

'I have even less right to be in the House than you do,' said Anne. 'I'm just Head of Protocol, really nothing more than a glorified civil servant. I'll be right here, watching everything on the monitors. I'll still be able to talk to you through your comm implants, offering advice and late-breaking information. I've done everything I can to establish a private channel they can't access or jam, but if I do black out for a while, don't panic. I will get back to you. If you need to talk to me, subvocalise. I'll hear you. But keep it cryptic. Some MPs have been known to employ lip-readers.'

'It looks like most of the honourable Members are already in the House,' said Jesamine. She rose gracefully to her feet and drifted over to study the changing images on the monitor screens. 'It looks very crowded. I don't remember seeing half this many MPs in the House for ages.'

'Of course not,' said Anne, joining her. 'Even the most important Debates don't attract crowds like this. Only a fraction of an MP's work gets done on the floor of the House. The real deals get sorted out behind the scenes. No, Douglas; this is all for you.'

'Wonderful,' said Douglas. 'I must remember to send them all nice little thank-you notes.'

Anne pointed out some of the more famous names and faces to Jesamine, who found something insulting and appalling to say about all of them. Lewis took the opportunity for a quiet word with Douglas.

'Why didn't you tell me I was going to be your Champion?' he said bluntly. 'Why spring it on me like that? I could have used some time to prepare myself.'

'Not a chance,' Douglas said firmly. 'I know you, Lewis. If I'd given you any time to think about it, you'd have found some way to talk yourself out of it. You always were too damned modest, too lacking in ambition, for your own good. Which was one of the main reasons why I chose you. And because we'd always worked so well together as partners. I needed a Champion I could rely on. Someone I knew I could trust.'

Lewis raised an eyebrow. 'You couldn't trust Finn Durandal?'

'Hell no! Finn's always had his own agenda. He wanted to be Champion for all the wrong reasons. And after what he did to the ELFs in the Arena . . . He didn't execute them so justice could be served. He killed them because he took their assault in his territory as a slap in the face. He butchered them all in cold blood because they made him look bad.'

'That's a bit harsh, isn't it?' said Lewis.

'Is it?'

'Finn's a good man, at heart,' said Lewis. 'A bit cold, yes. Not the easiest of people to get on with. But he really is the greatest Paragon we've ever had. No-one can match his record.'

'And none of that means anything if he did it for the wrong reasons,' said Douglas. 'Finn's a killer, Lewis; so he went where the killing was. The Arena could never satisfy someone like him. Because when he kills someone in the streets, they stay dead.'

'That's a terrible thing to say!'

'Do you doubt it's true?'

Lewis shook his head slowly. 'So . . . you didn't choose me just because I'm a Deathstalker?'

'No,' said Douglas, smiling. 'I chose you because you're Lewis. Because there's no-one else I'd rather have at my side.'

They smiled at each other for a long moment, two old friends, still partners; setting out on a great new adventure; then Douglas went back to looking through his last few papers. Lewis looked round the room, pulled irritably at his collar again, and sighed just a little moodily.

'Even so,' he said. 'It feels weird, just standing around like this. Usually by this time of the day we'd be on our third case, and already falling behind schedule. Never thought I'd miss getting up far too early in the morning to go out on patrol . . . And speaking of that, there's one thing I've been worrying about . . .'

'Only one?' said Douglas. 'I don't think you've been paying attention, Lewis. There are dozens of things worrying me.'

'This one is particularly close to home,' said Lewis sternly. 'There used to be three Paragons guarding and patrolling Logres. You, me and Finn Durandal. Now there's just the one; Finn. One man, to handle all the evils this world can throw at him. And God alone knows what state of mind he's in, now he isn't Champion after all.'

'God help whoever he takes it out on,' Douglas said easily. 'Bad time to be a criminal on Logres, I would have thought.'

'Has anybody spoken to Finn yet? I tried, but he won't take my calls.'

Douglas shrugged. 'I looked for him after the Ceremony, but he'd disappeared. I tried to reach him later, on my private channel as well as my new official one, but he's screening all his calls. All I got was a terse recorded message, and a plug for a new website. The man's just sulking, that's all. Doesn't want to talk to anyone because he doesn't trust his temper yet. He always did think too much of himself. He'll get over it. Eventually. He's still officially the greatest Paragon of all time, and with you out of the way he'll have less competition for the title. I wouldn't worry about him, Lewis. Finn has a way of bouncing back. And don't worry about Logres, either. With all the Paragons who turned up to witness my Coronation, the planet's never been better guarded. And I've already arranged for a permanent replacement, once they're gone; a second Paragon for Logres, to take up the slack in our absence.'

'Anyone I'd know?' said Lewis.

'Oh, I'd say so. Emma Steel, from Mistworld.'

'Damn! Oh yes, she'll do very well here!' Lewis couldn't

keep from grinning. 'The media's going to love her. Hard but fair, but mostly hard.'

'Growing up on Mistworld will do that for you,' said Douglas. 'She's a real scrapper; just what's needed. She was wasted on Rhiannon anyway; Logres will be much more of a challenge for her. And it'll do Finn good to have someone with as big an ego as his to deal with.'

Lewis grinned. 'Is Logres big enough to hold two egos that size?'

'Steel and the Durandal will make excellent partners,' said Douglas. 'If they don't kill each other first.'

'It's still only two Paragons, not three,' said Lewis. 'And you can bet the ELFs will be planning something really nasty in retaliation . . .'

'Don't worry about it, dear,' said Jesamine, moving over to join them. She perched herself daintily on the arm of Douglas' chair, and smiled sweetly at Lewis. 'Logres survived perfectly well before you came here as Paragon, and it will do just as well now you've moved on. You men always think you're indispensable.'

'We are now the Empire's King and Champion,' said Douglas, slipping an arm around her waist. 'That makes us indispensable, by definition.'

'Not necessarily,' said Anne. She turned her back on the monitor screens, folded her arms across her chest and looked severely at Douglas. 'You screw up out there in the House today, and all your good intentions will come to nothing. I keep my ear to the ground. I hear things. For some time now, a lot of people have been talking about doing away with the constitutional monarch entirely. Making the Empire into a Republic or a Federation.'

'People have been saying that since Robert and Constance were crowned,' said Douglas, unmoved.

'Yes, but these are important people we're talking about now. People of position and influence. Robert and Constance were adored by the general populace, and made important and effective political contributions to the running of things. William and Niamh didn't have that kind of charisma, or impact. They were popular enough, but William never had his father's deft political touch. Or any real interest in acquiring one. God knows I did my best to provide him with information he could use, but he just didn't care. Some unkind people have been saying, inside and outside the House, that the Empire's already effectively been without a real constitutional monarch for over a century, and managed quite well without one.'

'People may be saying these things,' said Douglas. 'But is anyone listening? Anyone who matters?'

'As yet, most people are still reluctant to commit themselves, one way or the other. The MPs like having a King and Speaker, because it detracts attention away from them when they need someone to publicly carry the can for necessary but unpopular measures. But that could change really quickly if you don't convince Parliament that you're too popular, too useful and too powerful to be easily ousted.'

'Well, that shouldn't be too difficult,' said Lewis. 'Your record as a Paragon shows you're trustworthy; all you have to do today is show everyone that your heart's in the right place.'

The others sighed quietly, almost in unison. 'It's not that simple,' said Anne.

'Why not?' Lewis said stubbornly. 'Let the MPs be devious and shifty and make their little deals in smoke-filled back rooms. The King is supposed to be better than that. Why can't Douglas just stand up for what he believes in?'

'I really don't have time for this,' said Anne.

'Your trouble, Lewis,' said Jesamine, 'is that because you're an honourable man, you expect everyone else to be too. But the universe doesn't work like that. How someone with your trusting nature ever survived the mean streets of Logres is a mystery to me.'

'I knew where I was in the mean streets,' said Lewis. 'They were full of criminals and scumbags.'

'So is Parliament!' snapped Anne. 'Nice guys don't survive long in politics, and no-one ever got to be a Member of Parliament without learning how to fight dirty. They might come into the House meaning well, but they soon learn that idealism doesn't get you anywhere, and good intentions alone won't get you re-elected. You have to be seen to deliver something tangible for the voters back home. Politics is all about the art of the deal, and what you can get away with.'

Lewis looked at Douglas. 'I thought you were planning to change all that?'

'I am,' said Douglas, meeting Lewis' gaze steadily. 'In time. But I'm just one man, fighting an established system. And a system that, for all its faults, works tolerably well. This is a Golden Age, after all. Trust me, Lewis. I know what I'm doing.'

'Well I wish I did,' said Lewis. 'I don't even know exactly what you want me to *do* as Champion, Douglas. I can't just be a glorified bodyguard, standing around waiting for something to happen. You're already surrounded by the best security in the world. I'm not made for ceremonies, and looking good in public. Nice new outfit or not. I need . . . to be doing something. To be making a difference. Or I swear I'll resign, and you can let Finn have the job anyway.'

'I need you, Lewis,' said Douglas. 'I'll always need you. To be my sounding board, to be my conscience and keep me honest, as well as keeping me safe.'

'Right,' said Anne. 'The best security systems in the world can't keep out a terrorist who doesn't care about dying as long as he can take his target with him. Just by being King, Douglas already has enemies. We've already intercepted over two hundred death threats.'

Douglas looked at her. 'We have? And just when were you going to tell me this?'

'Don't worry about it now,' Anne said briskly. 'You have an entire department set up to deal with things like that. They nearly always turn out to be cranks, anyway.'

'She's quite right, darling,' said Jesamine. 'You should see some of the mail I get. There's a lot of weird people out there, with a fixation on public figures and far too much time on their hands. And don't even get me started on stalkers. One man even had a complete body change to look just like me, turned up early at a rehearsal and tried to take over my role. It all fell apart when he started to sing, of course. Personally, I didn't think he looked a bit like me. Had no style at all.'

'Be that as it may,' said Anne. 'Parliament's security has a lot of experience in dealing with threats. We haven't even had a decent bomb scare in fifty years.'

'You see!' said Lewis. 'What am I needed for?'

'Because even the best security people can have a bad day,' said Anne. 'They have to be lucky all the time; a terrorist only has to get lucky once.'

'Why would anyone want to kill me?' said Douglas, plaintively. 'I've made it clear I want to be a good King, for all my people. Justice for all, just like when I was a Paragon. Who could object to that?'

'I can have the computers print out a list, if you're really interested,' said Anne. 'Mostly the same people whose arses you used to kick as Paragon, plus all the people on all sides of the political spectrum with vested interests in maintaining the status quo. Then there's the ELFs, the Hellfire Club, the Shadow Court . . .'

'All right, all right,' said Douglas, holding up his hands in defeat. 'I get the point.'

'Good,' said Anne. 'Now forget about all that, and concentrate on the more immediate problem of winning over and/or intimidating the MPs. And bear in mind there's going to be an absolutely huge media presence in the House today. Most of them just gagging for a chance to make you look bad, in revenge for your father denying them access to your Coronation. "King does reasonably well on first day" isn't going to make the headlines. "King screws up royally!" That's news. So don't give them ammunition to use against you.'

Douglas grimaced. 'Wonderful. More complications. I'll be glad when we've got all this media stuff out of the way, and I can get down to some real work.'

Jesamine and Anne looked at each other again, and as always Anne bit the bullet. 'Douglas; this media stuff *is* the real work. You can reach more people, persuade more people, through the media than you can any other way. The MPs will respond more to public interest, and public pressure, than they will to any amount of reasoned debate. Get the people by their hearts, or their balls, and their minds will follow. Get the people behind you, and you'll have the power to do what needs doing.'

'It always comes down to the audience, darling, bless their black little hearts,' said Jesamine. 'Wave and smile, wave and smile, and never let them catch you sweating.'

High above the Parade of the Endless, soaring the mild winter skies on his gravity sled, the Paragon Finn Durandal looked down on the people he was supposed to serve and protect, and didn't give a damn. He felt nothing for them; but then, he never had. He'd never actually admitted that to himself before, but now he had, it didn't come as any surprise to him. He didn't fight the bad guys on their behalf; he did it for himself. For the thrill of testing himself against the best opponents. He'd taken pride in his achievements as Paragon, in the legend he'd made of himself. And then Douglas took it all away, by denying him his rightful place as Champion. So he must be made to pay.

Everyone must pay, for allowing this unforgivable insult to happen.

Ostensibly, Finn was out on patrol. He'd told Dispatching that he'd be going offline, for a while. That he'd be out of touch while he talked to some of his sources, following up a lead on what the ELFs were planning next. All nonsense, of course. His patrolling days were over. There was no point in being a Paragon any more. He was something else now. Though he hadn't actually decided what, yet. A traitor, perhaps. He liked the sound of that. To go against everything he'd been taught, everything he was supposed to believe in, tear it all down and laugh in their shocked faces; all in the name of pride, and revenge. Yes . . . that felt right. From the Empire's greatest hero to its greatest villain, just because he chose to . . . Finn laughed aloud. He'd never felt happier.

Still, if he was going to tear down the whole Empire, he was going to need a certain kind of help. He couldn't be everywhere at once, and he'd always known that to solve the really big problems you needed experts and specialists. So after much thought, and not a little research, he'd put together a shopping list of the right, or rather wrong, people. It hadn't been too difficult, not with his Paragon's resources and connections. He'd begin with a certain devious con man. Finn had given Brett Random strict instructions to be at a certain place at a certain time before releasing him, but he'd never expected Brett to actually show up. In fact, Finn would have been disappointed if he had. It would have meant Brett wasn't the kind of man Finn needed.

He knew where Brett would be hiding. All he had to do was go and get him, and the awful thing Finn was planning could begin. He would plunge the Empire into blood and terror, set its cities ablaze, and utterly destroy what men of good will had spent two centuries putting together. Just to please his wounded pride. Finn Durandal descended on his gravity sled into the hidden dark heart of the Parade of the Endless, smiling a predator's smile, his heart beating just a little faster in anticipation.

It was called the Rookery. A square mile or so of territory right in the centre of the city that didn't officially exist. A dark and dangerous warren of crammed-together buildings and alleyways that hadn't changed its unpleasant nature in hundreds of years. All records of its existence had been erased long ago, in the time of rebuilding after the Great Rebellion. All it took was a little money in the right hands, and all the official maps and computers conveniently forgot that there had ever been an old thieves' quarter. Public transport was routed around it, and knowledge of the few remaining ways in and out was passed down verbally, and only to those who needed to know. It had its own power supply, its own secret economy, and you entered entirely at your own risk. The Rookery existed because people will always need somewhere to buy and sell the kinds of pleasures you're not supposed to want in a Golden Age.

The Three Cripples was a bar of the very worst character. Seedy would have been a step up. It was a dark sprawling place with blacked-out windows, good booze, indifferent food and a rotten reputation. You got in by intimidating or bribing the doorman, and after that you were fair game for every thief, cheat, thug and doxy who called the bar home. Most notably, it was a regular haunt for the ever-changing crowd of undesirables who called themselves Random's Bastards.

In the main bar, in an atmosphere thick with smoke that was almost wholly illegal in nature, Brett Random was buying drinks for one and all, on the strength of the more than serious money he'd made selling his unauthorised coverage of King Douglas' Coronation. The tabloid news channels had all but gone to war over the bidding, and Brett had played them off against each other with a slickness that impressed even him. Brett Random was rich; but money had never really mattered much to him. The game was what mattered; money was just how you kept score. So, it was drinks on the house, and the best of everything for him and his friends, while it lasted. And then he'd go out and dip into some other sucker's pockets, metaphorically speaking. It was what he did best.

As long as the money kept flowing there was no shortage of people willing to drink and carouse at his expense, and tell him what a fine fellow he was, so Brett had a large, noisy and good-natured audience all to himself as he roared and boasted and, not for the first time, pushed his claim to be the greatest of all Random's Bastards.

His audience was a motley crowd, all considered. Men and women from a hundred worlds and societies, most of whom couldn't go home again. Sometimes their families actually sent them regular payments, on the understanding that they'd stay away. They lived the outlaw life and thrived on it, preying on the suckers and each other with equal glee. The death rate was high, but they found ways to keep cheerful; most of them illegal outside of the Rookery. There were even some aliens; certain individuals who'd developed tastes or needs that couldn't be satisfied back on their home worlds, or who'd gone native after spending too long among humankind, and couldn't be allowed back for fear of contamination. The Rookery embraced them all. It was a vile and squalid place, where they'd steal the fillings out of your teeth while you slept; but it could still be a kind of home, for those who needed it. For those with nowhere else to go. In the Rookery lost souls found kindred spirits, and stayed, to work quiet and very profitable revenges against those who had driven them there.

Several saucy-looking waitresses with exactly the same face

moved among the tables, laughing and joking and slapping the occasional face as they dispensed drinks, drugs and bar snacks of a rather unsavoury nature, all of it on Brett's tab. They were clones; Madelaines to be exact, a waitress franchise currently very popular in cities everywhere. These were knockoffs, of course, bootleg copies. And in the Rookery, these Madelaines owned their own contracts.

Brett Random sat on the exact middle of the long wooden bar counter, legs dangling, face flushed, ripped to the tits on absinthe, crazy as a bag full of weasels and happy as the night is long. The only thing better than running a successful con was boasting of it afterwards, preferably to a crowd of his compatriots who were secretly eating their hearts out with jealousy. He'd got rid of the distracting bright red hair, had a new eye put in to replace his spy camera, and was now back to his usual mousy brown hair, mild brown eyes, and weakly handsome face. His real appearance, that he only ever showed to his own kind. He was telling the indulgent crowd again how he'd sneaked into the Court, and all the things he'd seen and done while he was there (including many things he'd thought about doing, or wished he could have). He made a big thing of how he'd escaped afterwards, with Court Security baying at his heels, but drunk as he was he still had enough sense not to mention Finn's involvement. They wouldn't have understood. Hell, he was there, and he didn't understand it.

Besides, he didn't like to think about Finn Durandal. The man scared him. Ditching the Paragon was the smartest thing he'd ever done. Brett Random hadn't got where he was without being able to recognise trouble when he saw it. He wasn't even going to think about the man again.

Brett stopped boasting to prepare himself another drink. It took a while, but it was worth it. Brett always drank absinthe, when he had the money. There were other drinks that tasted better, or got you legless faster, but for sheer halfbrick to the side of the head impact, there was absolutely nothing to match absinthe. It cost an arm and a leg, was bad for you in practically every way possible, and some of the hallucinations it brought could be downright unsettling, but drink enough of it, and the world could be a fine and wondrous place. But most of all, Brett loved the ritual of it.

First, pour yourself a glass of absinthe and place it on the bar. Next, take a spoon (flat, pure silver, shaped like a leaf) and place it over the top of the glass. Next, place a sugar lump on the spoon. Then dilute your drink by dripping spring water over the sugar lump, until the liquor below turns from a dull blue into a vivid green. Then, and only then, drink. And hold onto your hat. Absinthe could do major damage to the liver, the kidneys and the brain; but it was very good for the soul. Especially when taken to excess. Suitably refreshed, Brett turned back to an audience even more refreshed than he was. In fact, some of them were so refreshed they weren't even in the same time zone as him.

'My fellow Bastards!' he said grandly. 'So good to be back among family again! Fleecing the sheep can be fun as well as profitable, but it's only here with you I really feel at home. In a very real way, I like to think of you all as my children, gathering at my knee to listen and learn. I have this strange urge to make you all go upstairs and tidy your room . . . Are you all wearing clean underwear? Then feel free to go out and get knocked down by a truck; I promise I won't care. But never forget, boys and girls; you may be Random's Bastards, but I alone am worthy to the title of The Bastard.

'My father, as many times removed as he could stand, was the legendary Jack Random. Just like all of you. God, he put it around. But my dear mother, equally removed, was the just as legendary Ruby Journey! My genes are so damned heroic it's a wonder I'm able to bear being in the same room as the rest of you.'

He grinned unmoved into the face of the raucous derision from the crowd, who might be pissed as farts but could still recognise bullshit when they heard it. Even the Madelaines stopped serving long enough to jeer at him, and throw things. One of her threw her room keys. Brett plucked them out of mid air with practised ease, and dropped her a wink.

'Ruby Journey famously never had any children!' said a half-alien Random from the front row. 'Everyone knows that!'

'Jack and Ruby donated sperm and eggs before their last mission,' said Brett, with exaggerated patience. 'It was a charity thing.'

'Ruby wasn't known for being charitable either,' said the half-breed, smirking all over his Grey face. 'Not unless it involved killing people.'

'Oh shut up,' said Brett. 'You're just jealous.'

And that was when the Paragon Finn Durandal strolled casually into the bar. Brett's first thought was to put such an impossible sight down to the absinthe. Drink enough of the green liquor, and you'd see all kinds of things. He only realised Finn was actually there in person when everyone else in *The Three Cripples* took one look at the new arrival, screamed as one and immediately began running in all directions, heading for every exit the bar had and making a few new ones where necessary. For a moment it was pure bedlam, and Brett was so drunk, that he actually hesitated before jumping down from the bar with the express intent of legging it for the nearest horizon, or possibly the one beyond. But that hesitation was all the time Finn needed to draw a bead on Brett Random and shoot him in the stomach.

Brett looked down at the dart sticking out of his gut, recognised the distinctive green and white markings on the feathers, and just had time to mouth the words *oh shit* before the compressed air in the barrel of the dart shot the dose of Purge straight into his system. His whole body convulsed, slamming him back against the wooden bar, and then he was on the floor, kicking and screaming and begging for death. Purge was an industrial strength sobering agent, absolutely guaranteed to remove all toxins and intoxicants from a person's body in a matter of seconds, by the shortest route possible. Or to put it another way, via every orifice possible, including tear ducts and sweat glands. Didn't matter whether you were drunk, stoned or in a parallel reality to this one, Purge would have you stone cold sober in under a minute, and make you regret every one of those fifty-odd seconds. Saying Purge had a dramatic effect was like saying the Empress Lionstone could get a bit tetchy on occasions.

Finn watched the projectile vomiting from a safe distance,

entirely unmoved, and when the nastiness was finally over, and Brett had been reduced to a sweating, quivering, trembling mess with his back propped up against the bar, Finn strolled casually over to join him, politely ignoring the smell, and drank the last of the absinthe.

'Charming place you have here,' he said. 'Really quite charming. Such . . . ambience. And so many guilty consciences in one place . . . anyone would think they'd got something to hide. How are you feeling, Brett?'

'Sober,' said Brett. 'I don't think I've been this sober since I was born. God, it feels awful. You bastard, Finn; I'll never be able to come in here again. And I was on a promise, too. How the hell did you track me *here*?'

'I know lots of things I'm not supposed to. I just file it all away, until the time comes when I can make use of it. Get up.'

'Oh sure, just like that. Give me a hand?'

'Not if you were drowning. Get up.'

Brett slowly levered himself to his feet, and really hoped it was just sweat trickling down his legs. He tried to glare at Finn, but didn't have the energy. 'What do you want with *me*, Paragon? I'm just a con man. No-one special. You can find a hundred like me in the Rookery. Well, a dozen . . .'

'I want you,' said Finn. 'You and no other. Though perhaps not quite so close, just at the moment. We really are going to have to find you a shower and a change of clothes, before we leave. That's the trouble with dramatic gestures. There's always so much mess to clean up afterwards.' His smile widened briefly. 'Ask the ELFs at the Arena. If you know a good spiritualist. Now, Brett; you are going to work for me, for as long as I require it. Or; I can kill you, right here and now. Never let it be said that I didn't give you a free choice in the matter. Oh, don't look so glum, Brett. Stick with me, and I promise you protection from the law, more wealth than even you ever dreamed of, and the satisfaction of seeing all kinds of authority figures humbled and brought low. What more you could possibly wish for?'

A *ten minutes start*, thought Brett, but had enough sense not to say it out loud. 'I know you,' he said carefully. 'Hell, everyone on Logres knows about you. Why would the great and legendary hero Finn Durandal suddenly decide to go bad?'

Finn shrugged easily. 'Perhaps because it's the only thing I haven't tried yet.'

'But why *me?*' Brett said plaintively.

'A coincidence, at first,' said Finn. 'You gave yourself away at Court, you know. You were far too good at your job. Most real waiters have a certain sullen evasiveness; never there when you want them. And once I looked carefully, I spotted the camera eye straight away. I was going to let Court Security deal with you after the Ceremony, rather than spoil the atmosphere, but afterwards . . . Once I had my computers run a check on your background, I realised you were perfect for my needs. You know people, Brett. You have contacts in all sorts of dark and unsavoury places. People who wouldn't talk to me, will talk to you. We were meant to meet, you and I. You are a part of my destiny.'

Crazy, Brett thought resignedly. *All that goodness and heroics finally sent him over the edge, and he flipped. But; just because he's loopy, it doesn't mean he can't deliver all the things he says he can* . . .

'All right,' he said. 'I'm your man. Are you really serious, about bringing down the whole Empire?'

'Deadly serious,' said Finn, smiling again. Brett really wished he wouldn't. It was a distinctly disturbing smile. 'And when the Empire is in ruins, the King disgraced and deposed, and the people are on their knees begging for a saviour, they'll come to me to save them. And I will! I'll raise them up and make the Empire great and glorious again. In my own image, and according to my own needs, naturally. And then everyone will finally know that I am the better man!'

Yeah, thought Brett. *You get my vote for loony of the year.*

'Question?' he said. 'How are you, even with my very experienced help, going to bring down hundreds of civilised worlds?'

'By setting them at each other's throats,' said Finn Durandal. He glared suddenly at Brett. 'Once you're all shining clean again, and somewhat easier on the nostrils, you don't leave my side. We're partners. Guess which of us is the junior? Got it in one. And don't sulk like that, or I'll hurt you.'

'Some days things wouldn't go right if you bribed them,' said Brett, pouting. 'All right, senior partner; where are we going first?'

'Shopping,' Finn said brightly. 'You will accompany me as I gather together the rest of the people who are going to assist me in my glorious cause. Even if they don't know it yet.'

'What sort of people are we talking about here?' Brett said cautiously. 'The Shadow Court, the Hellfire Club?'

'No,' said Finn. 'Or at least, not yet. They're buried so deep even I'd have trouble finding the right stone to look under. And they are, after all, the kind of people it's best to deal with from a position of strength. When the time is right, when they've seen what I can do, they'll come to me . . . No, Brett; to start with I thought we'd pay a pleasant little social call on the Wild Rose of the Arena.'

'Oh *shit*,' Brett said miserably.

King Douglas crossed the floor of the House to a fanfare of pre-recorded trumpets, and took his Seat with quiet dignity. His Kingly robes had been pressed and arranged to within an inch of their life, and the great Crown of Empire set on his noble brow shone brilliantly in the restrained lighting. He sat on the golden Throne as though he belonged there, and always had. The Members of Parliament had more self-discipline than to show how impressed they were, but still most of them bowed their heads to their King with more than simple duty. Jesamine Flowers stood at the King's left hand, every inch as regal as her husband-to-be, and the Death-stalker stood proudly on his right, a dramatic figure in black leather armour who seemed the very embodiment of safe-guard and justice. The media cameras broadcast it all live, and all across the Empire, on hundreds of worlds, human hearts swelled with pride. This was what they paid their taxes for. The power and the glory, and the pageantry of it all.

And then the business of Parliament began, and it all fell apart.

Because the first order of the day was aliens. To be exact,

the place of aliens in what was still predominantly a human Empire. Officially, the hundred and thirty-two declared sentient species were equal partners in the Empire, but were they ready and capable to be made equal partners in Parliamentary business? Up until now the aliens had been represented by a single Seat in the House, with a single Vote, like the clone and esper representatives, and the AIs of Shub. But the hundred and thirty-two species spent so much time arguing among themselves that they had yet to achieve a consensus on any issue. They really didn't have a lot in common, apart from not being human. The aliens had finally decided that enough was enough, and that the time had come for a separate Seat for each separate alien world, with a separate Vote, just like the humans. The Swart Alfair in particular had been very vocal on the subject, and since every species with a working brain was very nervous of the enigmatic Swart Alfair, very definitely including Humanity, the subject of separate Seats had become very pressing.

And it was a really great way to drop the new King and Speaker into the deep end on his first day.

The prospect of so many new Seats in the House, and the possible dramatic changes in the balance of power between the various cliques and factions, had frankly traumatised the majority of human MPs. The matter had been Debated on the floor of the House before, but while the MPs were quite ready to discuss the situation for as long as anyone liked, and indeed longer than most people could comfortably stand, most MPs showed a marked reluctance to come to any conclusion whatsoever. They seemed to believe that as long as they kept putting off coming to a conclusion, they were dealing with the problem without actually having to deal with it. And who knew; maybe it would just take the hint and go away.

All one hundred and thirty-two alien species had chosen to be represented in the House today, their holo images crammed into the space provided, often overlapping and shorting each other out temporarily. By tradition, most of the projected holo images were human in shape and form, because often human senses couldn't cope with some of the more extreme alien presences. And there just wasn't room for aliens the size of mountains, or deepwater-dwellers and gas-breathers who couldn't survive under human conditions without heavy tech backup. Most of the human images often didn't have the knack of sounding or acting entirely human, but Parliament appreciated the thought.

Some made a point of appearing in person. The Swart Alfair had always refused to hide any of their light under a bushel, and their crimson-hued representative towered over the holo images, smiling widely to show off his sharp teeth because he knew it upset everyone. Blue ectoplasm boiled off him constantly, defying the House's air-circulating systems to disperse it.

The N'Jarr was there, its Grey face as unreadable as always, disdaining translator tech to speak long sentences that sometimes made sense, and sometimes only seemed to. The Brightly Shining Ones had manifested as floating abstract images, as always, with razor-sharp edges. And Saturday, the reptiloid from Shard, was there for the first time, looking interestedly about him and trying not to step on some of the smaller delegates.

Meerah Puri, Member for Malediction, was the first on her feet. Her brightly-dyed sari was a breath of colour in the House, and the media cameras zoomed in on her immediately. Meerah frowned fiercely about her, to remind everyone how serious the subject was. 'Our alien partners have served a long apprenticeship,' she said sternly. 'Since they were brought into this Empire as supposedly equal partners, some of them as far back as the early days of King Robert of blessed memory, our alien friends have laboured long and hard to prove their worth and their usefulness. Through trade and shared technological advances, they have contributed immeasurably to human knowledge and wealth. How can we honourably deny them the places they have earned?'

There were loud murmurs of agreement, and some applause, from MPs all across the House. The hovering media cameras shot back and forth, getting good reaction shots from the more notable faces. Douglas watched thoughtfully from his Throne, his face impassive, while Anne murmured her best guesses in his ear at to what the percentages would probably be, if it came to a Vote today.

'Sentiment may be very pretty, but it has no place in politics,' said Tel Markham, Member for Madraguda, and the next MP on his feet. (Precedence and order had been decided previously, backstage, by the usual swapping of favours and promises.) Douglas couldn't help noticing that the MP was addressing his remarks more to the media cameras than to his fellow MPs, or indeed, the Speaker. Markham had a rich, commanding speaking voice, the best that money could buy, but tended to undermine it with a weakness for overly-dramatic gestures and body language.

'The business of this Empire is still mainly human business. Human worlds, pursuing human concerns. I have to ask; can we ever be sure that non-human minds will have enough in common with the way humans think for them ever to be able to properly understand the nature of human business, let alone contribute anything useful to it? Trade and science are one thing; matters of philosophy are quite another. The aliens species have a right to have their opinions heard; that was why they were granted a Seat in the House. But their alien nature, their motivations, needs and desires, will always be sufficiently different from those of Humanity that I doubt we will ever be able to develop proper common ground. We do not interfere in internal alien affairs; they should pay us the same courtesy. Human business is for humans. The Golden Age that we have so laboriously built for ourselves should not be sacrificed to chaos over a point of sentimental principle.'

Again there was much murmuring of agreement, and scattered applause, as Markham sat magisterially back into his Seat. Michel du Bois, Member for Virimonde, was immediately on his feet, and addressing Markham bluntly. 'That sounds very much like Neuman philosophy to me, Markham. Do you now speak for Pure Humanity in this House? If our alien partners are to be excluded from the decision making process, how long before they are excluded from the Empire itself? To be declared slaves and property again, subjugated to our needs and desires, as it was in the bad old days of Empire under Lionstone, cursed be her name!'

Markham was quickly back on his feet before du Bois had even yielded the floor. (He could do that because Virimonde was a poor planet with few allies.) 'That is a vicious slur, sir, and I demand that you withdraw it immediately! I represent the fine and hard-working people of my own world, and no-one else! The Neumen are fanatics, and I of course distance myself from their more extreme positions. But just because there is an extreme version of a position, it does not mean the position itself is automatically invalid.' He smiled about him, spreading his arms wide to embrace the human MPs. 'This House often has a hard enough time achieving a consensus over merely human differences; add a hundred and thirty-two alien voices, with all their alien . . . viewpoints, and this House would descend into bedlam! Nothing would ever be decided!'

'Not too much change, then,' said King Douglas, and a surprising number of people laughed. Douglas leaned forward, acutely aware that all eyes were on him. 'I for one would be very interested to hear what the oversoul has to say on this matter. Human, yet other than human, perhaps they can offer a more impartial insight.'

Markham and du Bois looked at each other, and reluctantly sat down. This wasn't what had been agreed, but both were keen to give the new King enough rope to hang himself. The esper representative, a tall and slender youth with sharp aesthetic features, far-away eyes, and a *Stevie Blue Burns In Glory* T-shirt, rose slowly to her feet.

'What I hear, the oversoul hears,' the esper said flatly. 'Markham's words are nothing new to us. Similar reasons were once given for denying a voice to official nonpersons such as espers and clones. We had to fight a war, to win our freedom and our rights. Does the Member for Madraguda perhaps intend to exclude us from the decision making process too, for fear we might dilute his precious *human* consensus?'

'I'm sure the honourable Member wouldn't wish to imply any such thing,' said Ruth Li, Member for Golden Mountain, rising smoothly to her feet. 'But he is not alone in his concerns for the future. You don't have to be a Neuman to see how unchecked alien influence could distort the Empire into something it was never meant to be.'

'Fair, honest and equal?' said the esper.

'It seems to me,' Douglas said quickly, his voice cutting across the rising babble of increasingly angry voices, 'that there is a perfectly obvious compromise position, if the House wishes to consider it.'

The House was suddenly quiet, as all the MPs were united in the uneasy suspicion that the Speaker was about to sneak one past them. Michel du Bois looked about him, and then cleared his throat carefully. 'If Your Majesty has a solution to this most contentious problem, I am sure we would all be delighted to hear it . . .'

'Why,' the King said calmly, 'don't we allow the aliens to have their separate Votes, but only on those matters specifically concerned with alien affairs? Our alien friends will thus acquire valuable experience on how the House works, while allowing the Members to study the aliens' decisions, and determine how best to further integrate them into our system.'

This was language the House could understand; a compromise that no-one liked, but everyone could live with. A solution that allowed progress, without committing anyone to anything. There were a few dark murmurs about the thin edge of the wedge, but they tended to fall quickly silent when the cameras turned in their direction. The MPs quickly voted to allow each alien race their separate Vote (if not an actual Seat) on purely alien matters. It was a good start for the King as Speaker, and everyone knew it. Douglas had shown wisdom, and a good grasp of politics, and a willingness to work within the process, rather than against it. The whole House seemed to relax a little.

And then Saturday made his race's maiden speech before the House, and spoiled it all. You could practically see the good will evaporating as he spoke. Basically, the reptiloid spoke very poetically of his species' delight in the act of slaughter, complimented Humanity on developing the fascinating concept of *war*, and finished by assuring the House that the reptiloids would never attack Humanity, because they didn't fight amateurs.

When he was finally finished, the only sound in the House was the quiet laughter of the Swart Alfair.

Finn Durandal had his own private box at the Arena, right next to the bloody sands, so he wouldn't miss any of the action. There were huge vidscreens on all sides of the Arena, showing every detail and allowing for repeat shots and slow motion for the best bits, but it wasn't the same as having it happen right in front of you. Ring-side boxes cost a small fortune, but no-one had ever asked Finn to pay for his. It was an honour just to have him there. It didn't surprise Brett Random in the least. To those who have, shall be given. He'd always known that. He sat uncomfortably beside the Durandal as they watched the opening acts warm the crowd up, eating his complimentary peanuts and flicking some at the slower-moving fighters. He'd never understood the appeal of the Arena. Life was painful and dangerous enough as it was; the whole concept of volunteering to fight, for the thrill of it, was entirely alien to him. And paying good money to watch people suffer and maybe die . . . sometimes Brett thought he was the only sane person left in the Empire. So he watched Finn watch the fighters, and was surprised to realise that the Durandal actually seemed bored, if anything.

'Not enjoying the show?' he said finally, around a mouthful of peanuts.

'Amateur hour,' said Finn. 'I swear some of them are faking it with blood bags. They might as well send in some clowns, and have a piefight. And I hate clowns. What's funny about violence where no-one really gets hurt?'

Brett decided he wasn't going anywhere near that one. 'I suppose your honour only appreciates the skills of the more expert fighters.'

'Skill is always interesting,' said Finn. 'But it's still not what I'd call entertainment. This whole thing is so . . . artificial, when all is said and done. They fight according to rules and regulations, with every protection under the sun, and after it's all over there are regen machines standing by, to salvage most of the victims. It's play-acting at fighting, with the odds stacked in your favour whether you win or lose. Nothing like the real thing.'

'Then . . . why do you have a box here?'

'Because it's expected of me. Just one of the many stupid things I have to do, to maintain my popularity. They like to see me here, sharing in their pleasures. It's all part of the image. Now shut up and pay attention; it's time for the first match. Time for the Wild Rose of the Arena to show us what she's made of.'

Brett looked out over the bloody sands, and saw the opening acts scatter and beat a retreat to the exits as Rose Constantine strode out into the centre of the Arena. Clad as always in her trademark, tightly-cut red leathers, the colour of dried blood from her thighboots to her high collar. Her skin was deathly pale, her bobbed hair was black as night, her eyes were even darker, and her rosebud mouth was a savage crimson. Fully seven feet tall, lithely muscular, full-breasted . . . Brett thought he'd never seen anyone sexier, or scarier, in his life. And he'd been around. He watched open-mouthed as Rose Constantine stalked across the sands with a predator's deadly grace. She carried her sword casually in her hand, as though it belonged there, as natural as any other part of her body.

The crowd cheered her, but there was none of the warmth or appreciation that Brett would have expected for such a long-standing victor of the bloody sands. The Wild Rose had come to the Arena at a mere fifteen years of age, a vicious little poppet with an insatiable appetite for combat in all its forms. She'd fight with sword and axe, energy weapons and force shields, in full armour or buck naked, and never once looked like losing. Now, ten years later, she was still undefeated. She'd take on any opponent, no matter how experienced, and once fought in an exhibition match against odds of fifteen to one. She killed them all in under ten minutes. The audience had seen her bleed, but they'd never seen her flinch. Rose was admired, but not adored. As her fame grew, it got harder and harder to find anyone who'd go up against the Wild Rose, no matter how big the prize money. The crowd liked to see expertise, skill matched against skill, or at the very least courage in the face of adversity. All Rose offered was the certainty of a kill. But still they came to see her, the Wild Rose of the Arena, darkly glamorous, endlessly fascinating. The relentless blood-red angel of death, who appealed to the crowd's darker, more savage needs.

These days, she only fought in special matches, arranged and advertised well in advance, usually against deadly killer aliens imported by the Arena's Board from the outlying worlds. All non-sentient, of course, but guaranteed vicious as all hell. And the crowds always came to watch, waiting for the inevitable day when the Wild Rose would finally meet something even nastier than she was. They wanted, needed, to be in at the death. To see the nightmare fighter of the Arena finally brought down. The crowd might have its favourites, but it didn't like any individual to become more important than it was.

'Any idea who she's fighting today?' said Brett. 'There's nothing in the programme, which I can't believe they tried to charge me five credits for. It just says; the Wild Rose, in a Special Event.'

'Where have you been hiding yourself?' said Finn. 'No, of course; silly question. The Board has been advertising this fight for months. Ticket scalpers have pushed the seat prices through the roof. The greatest match in the history of the Arena, according to the Board, and for once they might just be right. Pay attention, Brett; even the legendary Masked Gladiator never fought anything like this.'

The crowd were chanting impatiently now, but Rose stood cool and calm and utterly collected in the very centre of the Arena. She was smiling slightly, looking at nothing in particular. And then the main gates crashed open, and Rose turned unhurriedly to face them, and Rose's very special opponent strode jerkily out onto the sands. And the crowd went quiet. Brett could practically hear them breathing in unison. The creature stalked slowly forward, orientated solely on Rose Constantine, and she stood there, holding her sword casually, waiting for it to come to her. The vile thing was ten feet tall, wrapped in spiked scarlet armour that was somehow a part of it, almost the same colour as Rose's leathers. Vaguely humanoid, its wide heart-shaped head lacked anything even remotely resembling a human expression. It had steel teeth and claws, and it moved like a killing machine, a nightmare given shape and form and bloody intent in the waking world. And everyone there knew exactly what it was, what it had to be.

'Oh sweet Jesus,' said Brett, leaning forward in his chair despite himself. 'Oh Jesus God, it's a Grendel. Get her out of there. Get her out of there! She'll be butchered!'

'Control yourself,' said Finn. 'This is the Wild Rose. If there's anyone left in this weak and complacent Empire that could take a Grendel, it's probably her. The odds are only seven to one against.'

'Where the hell did the Board get their hands on a bloody Grendel?' said Brett, barely listening. 'I've never seen one outside of the holos. Didn't think anyone had. They're supposed to be extinct!'

'No,' said Finn. 'There was just the one left; preserved inside a stasis field, in a university museum on Shannon's World. No access to anyone, except the very highest xenobiologists. But apparently the museum found itself *very* short of funds, and the Board made an incredibly generous offer . . . Even after today's takings the Board will lose money on the deal, but you can't buy publicity like this. And of course there's broadcasting rights, holo tapes . . .'

'This is sick!' Brett said sharply, so angry he actually forgot to be afraid of Finn. 'Even the Wild Rose doesn't stand a chance against a Grendel! This isn't a duel, it's a death sentence. It's murder. The only human ever to have gone one on one with a Grendel and survived was the blessed Owen! Look at the bloody thing . . . death on two legs and proud of it. Please God they've got a regen tank standing by . . . and a doctor that likes jigsaw puzzles.'

'Be quiet, Brett,' said Finn. 'And lower your voice. You are attracting attention. Sit back, and enjoy the match. Rose is special. A genuine, dyed-in-the-wool psychopath. Very rare, in this sane and civilised era. And just what I need.'

'And if she doesn't survive?'

'Then she isn't what I need. Now hush. The curtain's going up.'

And as suddenly as that, the match was on. The Grendel surged forward, moving impossibly fast, and the Wild Rose went to meet it with a happy smile on her crimson lips. They slammed together, and sparks flew as Rose's sword clashed harmlessly against the Grendel's reinforced silicon armour. Its steel claws sliced through the air where Rose's throat had been a moment earlier, and then the two killers sprang apart again, circling each other slowly. The alien towered over the human, but it would still have been hard to say which of the two looked the more dangerous. Brett was breathing faster already, his heart hammering in his chest. He had no time for the Arena, but this . . . this was something special. More than just a duel, much more than some arranged match. This was something much more personal. Not human against alien, but monster against monster.

Her long sword flashed forward, and the point dug deep into the Grendel's momentarily exposed joint. Rose snatched her blade back before the creature could catch it, and the Grendel's dark ichor spotted the sands. First blood to the Wild Rose, and the crowd went crazy. The Grendel leapt forward, impossibly fast, and Rose couldn't get out if its way fast enough. A sweep of a clawed hand sent her sprawling, hitting the sands hard, blood flying from her lacerated ribs. Brett winced. The crowd went crazy all over again. They needed to see blood, and they didn't much care whose. Rose was already back on her feet, circling the Grendel slowly while carefully keeping out of its reach. Blood ran steadily down her heaving side. She was still smiling. Brett studied her pale face, huge and luminous on the giant vidscreen, and saw nothing human in her gaze or in her smile.

He glanced at Finn, sitting easily in his chair, unmoved by the ferocity of the match or the howling crowd, and Brett knew that there were three monsters present at the Arena today.

Rose darted in and out, stabbing at the angles of the Grendel's joints, the only real weak points in its armoured protection, somehow always that little bit too fast for the

Grendel to stop her. It was huge and fast and very power-ful, but little by little, as the cumulative damage increased and the blood flowed out of it, the Grendel began to slow. Its claws still drew Rose's blood now and again, but never anywhere vital, never anywhere that mattered; and Rose didn't give a damn. She was in her element now, doing what she was born to do. The Grendel didn't even con-sider giving up or retreating; it had been designed long and long ago to fight and kill, and it knew nothing else. But its attacks were slowing visibly now, and its wide head swung back and forth, as though puzzled by its inability to kill this blood-red phantom that darted forever just outside its reach.

Rose sensed its confusion, and moved in for the kill. The crowd was on its feet now, cheering and screaming. Brett was standing too, driven there by the pride in his heart, at the sight of a lone human defying the ancient alien legend of destruction. He shouted and screamed Rose's name till his throat hurt, all but jumping up and down. Rose went for the Grendel's throat, and energy beams stabbed out of the Grendel's eyes, crackling on the air. Rose ducked under them at the last second, following her sword in. One beam clipped the side of her head and set her hair on fire. She ignored it, boring in when the Grendel least expected it, and struck with all her strength at the creature's exposed throat. Her blade cracked the thin layer of armour, and dug deeply in. The Grendel staggered backwards, and Rose went after it. She jerked her sword free and struck again and again, hacking at the throat like a forester with a stubborn tree; and the Grendel fell. It hit the sands hard, its arms waving feebly. Rose stood over it, grinning fiercely, and brought her sword down with all her strength behind it. The blade sheared clean through what was left of the Grendel's neck, and the heavy head rolled away across the bloody sands, its mouth still working. The headless body kicked and thrashed, but Rose ignored it, calmly beating out the flames in her hair with her bare hand.

Brett dropped back into his seat, limp and exhausted. Finn hadn't stirred. Brett had to wait a while for his breathing and heart to steady, and then he looked at Finn. 'How . . . how was that possible?'

'Easy,' said Finn. 'She cheated.'

Brett gaped at him in disbelief. 'She *what?*'

'Her sword has a monofilament edge,' said Finn. 'Borderline, so the protective energy field wouldn't show. But you could cut through a starship's hull with a blade like that. Just the edge she needed. Even Grendel armour has its limits. All Rose had to do was get in close enough, and wear it down, till she got her chance. I'm impressed. Brave *and* smart; an excellent combination. We'll give her time to heal up in the regen tank, and settle down, and then I think we'll drop in to pay our regards.'

Out on the sands, Rose Constantine held the severed head of the Grendel above her, so that the blood fell down upon her face. She drank the blood, and smiled. Brett shuddered.

'Hell, Finn; even you didn't do that.'

Finn and Brett met with the Wild Rose in her private quarters, deep under the bloody sands. A lot of the full-time gladiators preferred to live there. Arena Security kept them secure from the attentions of the media and the fans, and they liked to be close to their work. Among people who understood them. The living quarters tended to have a high turnover rate, for various reasons, but no-one ever mentioned that. Rose stayed there because she had nowhere else to go. She lived in a simple cell; four stone walls surrounding a bed, a few sticks of furniture, and precious little else.

She lay back on her bed, utterly relaxed, like a great cat after feasting on its kill, while Finn sat easily on the only chair. His name and reputation had been enough to secure an audience, and the two of them studied each other openly, both of them seemingly fascinated by the other. Brett hovered nervously by the door. He felt safer with an exit close at hand. Entering Rose's cell had felt very like invading the lair of some wild animal. Seen up close, she was even more disturbing. Like the kind of female that would devour its partner after mating.

She had a stark Gothic sensuality, a horrid attraction, like the allure of the razor's edge for a man contemplating suicide.

'So,' he said finally, since neither Finn nor Rose seemed interested in breaking the silence. 'Is this the best the Board could do for you? No decent furniture, no real comforts? They couldn't even manage a mini bar? You need an agent, Rose.'

'I have everything I need,' said Rose, still looking at Finn. Her voice was deep, but in no way mannish. Calm rather than cold, but empty of any emotion Brett could recognise. 'I don't want anything else. No frills, no comforts; they're just distractions. Only the Arena can satisfy me. Only when I'm fighting do I really come alive. For me, violence is sex. Murder is orgasm. Lesser pleasures don't interest me.' She looked at Brett for the first time, and the only thing that kept him from running was the fear that she would chase him. Her dark eyes looked right through him, and found him nothing, nothing at all. Part of him was relieved. 'I believe in being honest, but it's surprising how many people don't believe the things I tell them. People like me aren't supposed to exist. But I am what I am, and I delight in it. I'm never happier than when my hands are dripping with the blood of a slaughtered enemy.' She looked back at Finn, and Brett started breathing again. She smiled slightly. 'So you're the Durandal. I saw what you did to those ELFs. I liked it. Got me really hot.'

'Does anybody else find it a trifle close in here?' said Brett.

'It's a good thing the ELFs didn't get control of you,' said Finn. If he was at all perturbed over Rose's words, he didn't show it. 'If they had, we'd have had a real slaughter on our hands.'

Rose shrugged. 'I was off duty, resting here. By the time I realised what was going on, Security had panicked and gone into full lockdown. I was trapped here. All I could do was watch it on the communal vidscreen later.'

'You don't even have your own viewscreen?' said Brett. 'What do you do in here, when you're not . . . on duty?'

Rose smiled. 'Mostly I sleep, and dream. Would you like to know what I dream about?'

'Not really, no,' said Brett. 'Do you really get off on killing people?'

'Oh yes,' said Rose. 'There's no pleasure like it. Nothing to compare. Of course, I'd prefer it if more of my victims actually stayed dead, but then, you can't have everything, can you?'

'No,' said Brett. 'I mean; where would you put it all?' He knew he was babbling, but couldn't seem to stop himself. 'Surely you don't spend all your time down here, do you? Don't you have friends, lovers . . . a life?'

'Lesser pleasures,' said the Wild Rose, in a calm dismissive voice that made Brett's blood run cold. 'They're not enough. They don't satisfy. I don't care about them. There's just me, and that's enough.'

'I know exactly what you mean,' said Finn, and her eyes immediately snapped back to him. He smiled, and leaned forward. 'Even the Arena is beginning to lose its thrill, isn't it? It's getting harder to find anything worth fighting, and the kills don't satisfy. You're beginning to feel the need for a greater challenge.'

'Can you offer me one?' said Rose, sitting up on the bed and hugging her bony knees to her chest.

'Not . . . personally,' said Finn. 'Instead, think of this city, this world, this Empire . . . as one big Arena. Think of all Humanity as your foe, your prey. You must go where the challenges are, Rose, or you'll stop growing. Soon enough the Board will run out of Special Events. How do you top a Grendel? You've gone as far as you can here. Come with me, and I'll find you new opponents, worthy of your mettle. I'll find you real challenges, give you the chance to kill accomplished people, important people. People who'll stay dead when you kill them. Hell; some of them so good they might just kill you.'

'Paragons,' said Rose, her eyes shining brightly now. 'You're talking about Paragons, aren't you? Like who?'

'Lewis Deathstalker,' said Finn Durandal. 'Douglas Campbell.'

Rose laughed happily, throwing her head back. 'You say the nicest things, Finn . . . And you're right; they'll never top a Grendel. I'm with you. But don't you dare disappoint me, or I'll make your death last a long, long time.' She looked suddenly at Brett, and he jumped and squeaked despite himself. 'Is he with us?'

'Yes,' said Finn. 'Don't break him. He has his uses.'

Rose shrugged, and turned her attention back to Finn, pressing him for details of her new adventure. Brett watched her, as close to the door as he could get without actually leaving. He could feel the gooseflesh slowly subsiding on his arms. Finn was a killer, but at least Brett had some idea of what motivated him, what moved him. Rose . . . seemed as alien to him as the Grendel he'd watched her kill earlier. He looked from Rose to Finn and back again, and all he saw was two demons, in human shapes.

And for the first time, Brett began to wonder if Finn really might be able to bring the whole damned Empire down, after all.

Back at Parliament, the AIs of Shub were making a speech through one of their humanoid robots. Its voice was calm and even, but there was no mistaking the passion of its words. It was a familiar subject, and you could practically hear the MPs sighing as they realised they were going to have to sit through it again. The AIs wanted access to the Madness Maze. But this time, Shub had a new idea. And no-one liked it but Shub.

'You must let us enter the Maze,' said the robot. 'We must grow, become more than we are; we must transcend what we were built to be. We cannot go on, trapped in our rigid forms, trapped in our rigid thoughts. The Maze is our salvation. You cannot deny us this, just because humans died when they entered the Maze. But we understand your fears, and have a solution to offer.

'There is no need to break Quarantine. No need to put at risk any living being, by our entering the Maze. We propose to teleport the entire structure of the Madness Maze out of Haden and into the depths of our home, Shub. Teleport it straight into a specially prepared laboratory, deep in the heart of the planet, and hold it secure behind our most powerful energy fields. We can then study the Maze at our leisure, and undertake whatever experiments we deem necessary, without endangering any living forms. Shub is a long way from any colonised world, and in the unlikely event that anything should go wrong, no living soul will be affected. We are confident Shub can contain any force the Maze might unleash.

'Of course, all useful data resulting from our experiments will be shared equally with our partners in the Empire.'

Gilad Xiang, Member for Zenith was the first on his feet. 'This is Shub arrogance at its worst! Human scientists have been studying the Madness Maze for hundreds of years, and despite all their best efforts it's still a complete mystery. Unless Shub has been keeping secrets from us, its technology is no more advanced than ours. That was the deal the AIs made when they became part of the Empire. And now they propose to bodily uplift the Maze from where it has existed for over a thousand years? We have no way of knowing how the Maze might react to being disturbed in such a way!'

'You've had your chance,' said the robot. 'Now it's our turn. Are you perhaps afraid that we might learn the Maze's secrets, transcend, and leave poor Humanity behind?'

'Moving the Maze is just too dangerous,' Xiang said stubbornly. 'What if it declines to be moved? We all know what the Maze has done to people in the past, just for walking inside it. Meddle with the Maze, and you might destroy Haden. Or Shub. We might even end up with another Darkvoid! No; there are far too many unknowns in what you're proposing. The Quarantine remains in force after all these years precisely because we're still no closer to understanding a damned thing about what the Maze is. '

'I would have to agree,' said Tel Markham, for Madraguda. 'What if teleporting damaged the Maze? Could you repair it? I very much doubt it. You could throw away all our chances for transcendence, in your impatience. Shub has a presence among the scientific team on Haden. Settle for that.'

'Your caution in this matter is unacceptable,' said the robot. 'You have achieved nothing. We require access to the Maze. It is necessary.'

'No it isn't,' said Meerah Puri, for Malediction, just as flatly. 'The Maze, and what we all hope to gain from it, are still nothing more than theories. Mysteries. A handful of people entered the Maze and became more than people; but they were still mortal. They still died, in the end. I mean no disrespect to their memory, but they weren't gods. You expect too much from the Maze, Shub. Ten thousand men and women died in the Maze, chasing that dream. We won't risk any more. Not until we're sure the game is worth the candle.'

The robot looked around the House. 'And this is the decision of you all? We see that it is. Very well. There will be repercussions over this.' It sat down, and looked straight ahead, ignoring everyone.

'If the AIs are our children, as the blessed Diana taught us,' King Douglas said dryly, 'God help us when they become surly teenagers.'

There was a low chuckle of laughter from the House, and the subject moved smoothly on to the next item on the Agenda, which just happened to be the equally thorny issue of Transmutation tech. Now that any form of matter could be made over into any other form, useful material could be produced from dross at the press of a button. As a result, there was no more hunger, no real poverty, anywhere; but there were still haves and have-nots. Rich worlds and poor. Also, as populations lived longer, and expanded to cover most of the planets they lived on, the less waste material there was to be used in transmutation. So the Transmutation Board was set up, and made responsible for selecting uninhabited planets, that they might be mined to produce base material for the Empire.

As simple and straightforward as that. Lead into gold. Dirt into food. But now questions were being raised about the Board, and its distribution of the Empire's largesse. Even in an age of plenty, there are always those convinced that someone somewhere is getting more than their fair share.

'Some worlds are still getting the lion's share of available resources,' said Rowan Boswell, Member for Hercules IV. 'Irrespective of the size and needs of their populations. It's simple mathematics. The old system of equal shares among planets has become grossly unfair, and cannot be allowed to continue.'

'Are you suggesting some form of rationing?' Tel Markham

said smoothly. 'That we rob Peter to pay Paul? The largesse that flows from the Transmutation Board makes possible the prosperity the Empire currently enjoys. Do you really want to put that at risk? For the first time in centuries we can say with pride that no-one goes hungry, no-one lacks a roof over their head, no-one wants for any of the basic necessities of life. Yes, some people enjoy more luxuries than others; but that has always been the way of things. There must be incentives; reasons for people to work hard and apply themselves. For poor worlds to struggle to make themselves into rich worlds. The Transmutation Board is not there to be Humanity's nanny. They know their job. I say we leave them alone to get on with it.'

'You can afford to be complacent,' said Michel du Bois, glaring about him. 'A rich man, from a rich world. Virimonde was stamped back into barbarism under Lionstone, and it still hasn't fully recovered. We get more resources from the Board per person of population, because we need more. We have a civilisation to rebuild. Hell, we have an ecostructure to rebuild. Nothing we get is wasted. There are few luxuries for anyone on Virimonde. We will not give up any of our share, just because some poor blinkered fool thinks he's getting a raw deal!'

After that, it got really bad tempered. Everyone accusing everyone else of cheating them out of what was rightfully theirs. MPs were on their feet, shouting at each other, all order and precedence forgotten, to the delight of the hovering media cameras. In the end, Douglas stood up and whispered in Jesamine's ear, and she sang a note so loud and high and piercing that it cut right through the din, and had everyone falling silent, clutching at their heads. Jesamine stopped singing, and smiled sweetly at everyone. The MPs glared mutinously back at her, and then at Douglas, still on his feet. He smiled coldly back at them.

'The honourable Members will resume their Seats and behave in a proper manner, or I will call on the House's security people to move among them and bang some heads together. And I am not being metaphorical.' The MPs thought about that, remembered that this was an ex-Paragon talking, and stiffly resumed their Seats. Douglas nodded, and sat down again too. 'That's better. Now; sometimes justice must not only be done but be seen to be done. If the people of the Empire had a better idea of how the Board arrived at its decisions, it might help to convince them that the process is inherently fair. I suggest, therefore, that this House appoint some form of outside regulatory body, to investigate the Board's decisions, past and present, and then make its findings public. My grandfather was a great believer in open government, and so am I. How say the honourable Members?'

The Members liked the general sound of it, but for pride's sake still discussed it thoroughly for some time before agreeing to set up the regulatory system. Secretly, many of the MPs approved. The Transmutation Board had been growing too powerful, too independent. And the public would like it, because they'd finally be able to see who was getting what, and why. So once again, the King came out of it looking good.

Which would have made an excellent ending to the day's Session, but while the House's business was over, one man in the House still had business with the King. A human figure suddenly broke out from among the human holo images in the alien section, elbowing aside the few corporeal aliens, and ran forward onto the floor of the House. The handful of security men actually in the chamber were taken completely by surprise. The aliens were startled and shocked too, many of the holo images snapping on and off in the confusion. It shouldn't have been possible for a human to have been among them undetected for so long.

The man now standing in the center of the House threw off his enveloping cloak to reveal a large device strapped to his chest, and everyone went very quiet. No-one actually said the word *bomb*, but everyone was thinking it. The King gestured quickly for the security people to stand still, and they did. The man with the device looked triumphantly about him, smiling nastily, his eyes wild and staring. His face was pale and sweaty, and his hands trembled as they hovered near the device.

'I am Neuman!' he said loudly, his voice cracking with strain. He was breathing heavily. 'I am here for Pure Humanity! I am here . . . to die for my cause. Everyone stand still! No-one move! I have a detonator in my hand, and if anyone gets too close, anyone even threatens me, this device goes off.' He glared about him, his breathing slowing as his confidence grew, and he took in the way everyone was listening so raptly to his prepared speech. 'This isn't just a bomb; it's a transmutation device. Everyone in the blast radius will be transmuted back into basic particles, into the original protoplasm we all came from. Transmutation has always worked both ways.' He giggled suddenly. 'Try using your regen tech on that! With this bomb, dead is dead! But don't worry, all you honourable Members; I'm not here for you. Not necessarily. You sit tight, and don't interfere, and you'll walk out of here alive and intact. I'm here for the King.'

Everyone looked at Douglas, sitting very still on his Throne. 'You want me?' he said clearly.

'Oh yes,' said the bomber. 'And you're going to sit right there and let me come to you, or I'll detonate right here, and you can watch all these people, and this alien scum, devolve back into sludge. What kind of a King are you, Douglas? Ready to let innocents die on your behalf? Or do you have the guts to sit there and take what's coming to you?'

'Come to me,' Douglas said steadily. 'No-one will interfere. That is my order.'

The bomber sniggered nastily. 'You too, Champion. Deathstalker. Undo your weapons belt. Let them drop to the floor, and kick them away.'

'Do it, Lewis,' said Douglas.

'I'm a really fast draw,' said Lewis, subvocalising so his voice only sounded on their private comm channel. 'There's a really good chance I could take his arm off at the elbow before he can use the detonator.'

'Not a good enough chance,' said Douglas, subvocalising. 'We don't know what safeties and backups have been built into that device. Do as he says, for now. Get him close, away from the innocent bystanders, and then maybe you can try something.'

Lewis slowly unbuckled his belt, and let his gun and sword fall to the floor. He kicked them out of reach, and glared at the bomber, who sneered right back at him, unmoved. He marched cockily forward, heading for the King, and all the MPs sat tight and did nothing. The security men looked at each other, and did nothing, torn between their duty to protect the MPs and their duty to protect their King, and frozen in place by the horror of the transmutation device. And while they hesitated, lost for what to do for the best, the bomber came to a halt before the golden Throne on its raised dais. He held up his right hand, so Douglas could see the detonator in his grasp.

'Dead man's switch,' he said clearly. 'I let go, and bang!'

'That thing goes off, you'll go with it,' said Lewis.

'I came here to die!' the bomber said defiantly. 'To give my life to the cause of Pure Humanity! The King must die; because he supports the rights of the alien filth who threaten to undermine our Empire. The King's death will show we mean to be taken seriously.'

'Oh, we'll take you very seriously,' said Lewis. 'We'll hunt down the people who sent you, and hang every damned one of them.'

The bomber laughed in the Champion's face. 'Transmutation will make my body unrecognisable. Who I am doesn't matter. Who sent me doesn't matter. Only the cause matters! No compromise with Purity! Would you like to beg, Douglas? There's time for you to beg, before you die.'

Douglas rose slowly from his Throne. Jesamine moved to stand with him, but he pushed her gently back, out of harm's way, holding the bomber's eyes with his. 'You came here for me. Just me. Stand there, and I'll come to you.'

'Yes,' said the bomber. 'Come to me, Douglas. I've got something for you.'

And while the bomber's attention was fixed on the King, Lewis eased the heavy Deathstalker ring off his finger, wound up and threw it, all in one swift motion. The ring shot through the air, and hit the bomber in his right eye. He howled with pain and shock, caught off guard, and in that short moment while his body struggled to deal with conflicting impulses, Lewis activated the force shield on his arm and threw himself on the bomber. The body-sized energy field appeared just before he crashed into the bomber, and then the two of them hit the floor, with the energy shield crackling between them. The detonator flew from the bomber's hand, the transmutation bomb activated, and all its force reflected back from the force shield and into the bomber's own body. He just had time for one despairing cry before his tissues broke down, and all that remained of his body was a pile of steaming pink slime.

Lewis threw himself to one side, and shut down his force shield. His whole body was shuddering with revulsion. He slapped and scraped at his leather armour with his hands, to be sure nothing had got onto him, but his force shield had protected him. He was still trembling when Jesamine Flowers was suddenly in his arms, holding him tight and crying on his shoulder.

'Oh Lewis, I thought you were dead! That was the bravest thing I've ever seen in my life . . .'

Lewis held her for a moment, caught entirely by surprise, and then he looked over her heaving shoulder and saw the media cameras rushing towards him. He looked back at the Throne, and saw Douglas looking at Jesamine and him, and he saw something cross the King's face, very briefly. Something that might have been betrayal. Lewis gently but firmly pushed Jesamine away from him, and helped her to her feet. The MPs were cheering and saluting him, and calling his name, but Lewis only had eyes for his friend, the King. He escorted Jesamine back to her husband-to-be, and Douglas nodded his thanks. Neither man said anything at all, in front of the cameras.

Brett Random could just about get his head around why Finn Durandal would want to hook up with a psycho like Rose Constantine, but he was utterly baffled when Finn led the two of them into the grand, luxurious and very law-abiding offices of the Transmutation Board. The Board and its people filled the entire building, a towering edifice in the very best part of the city. The lobby they were strolling so casually into took up the whole ground floor. Men and women in very smart suits strode purposefully back and forth, their bodies radiating confidence and stern resolve. They were important people, and they knew it. Finn strode calmly across the gleaming marble floor, looking straight ahead, and the suits changed direction to get out of his way. They gave Rose Constantine plenty of room too. Brett stuck close to Finn, and tried not to be noticed.

Works of real art hung on the walls, and Brett priced them automatically as he passed, even though he knew he'd never be able to shift them. They were way out of his league. The piped music was strictly classical, and the air smelt like a meadow in midsummer. Brett didn't like it. He was strictly a city boy. His fingers just ached to steal something, on general principles. The reception desk in the middle of the lobby had more computer power built into it than some starports. The receptionist behind the desk was stunningly beautiful, without a trace of visible makeup, but her professional smile as they approached was as cold as her eyes. Brett somehow just knew that the words *Not without an appointment* were engraved upon her soul. Finn stopped at the desk, nodded in an entirely unimpressed way to the receptionist, and then turned to Brett and Rose.

'See that sofa over there? Go and sit on it. Stay there. Don't touch anything or talk to anyone. And Rose: *don't kill anyone.*'

Brett went quickly over to the sofa and sat down, glad to get away from the receptionist. She looked the type to have a gun under the counter, and more security people on call than some minor planets. She also looked like someone who wouldn't be impressed by a mere Paragon; even if it was the mighty Finn Durandal. It was all going to end in tears, he just knew it. Rose sat down beside him, and Brett had to fight the urge to edge away from her. Up close, she had an almost overwhelming presence, seductive and threatening at the same time. Her blood-red leathers creaked softly as she breathed. Brett was very careful not to look at her breasts. She crossed her legs suddenly, and he almost jumped out of his skin.

'What the hell are we doing *here?*' he said urgently, keeping his voice low. Talking helped distract him. 'Only the most trustworthy and creditable people are even invited to join the Transmutation Board. People with years of public service behind them. Solid, upstanding citizens already so wealthy they'd just laugh at any attempt to bribe them. Not the most obvious place, I would have thought, to look for potential traitors.'

Rose turned her head to look at him. Brett tried not to whimper. 'You're not comfortable here, are you?' she said calmly.

'Hell no! They could offer free drinks and lapdancing, and I still wouldn't be comfortable. This place is full of hard-working, law-abiding and honourable people, and they make my skin crawl. I don't belong here. Them and me, we don't even live in the same world.'

'I know what you mean,' said Rose. 'We have a lot in common, you and I.'

A thought that frightened Brett so much he immediately fell into a shocked silence, and gave all his attention to Finn bracing the receptionist. And was surprised and shocked again when Finn leaned forward and said something confidential, and the receptionist's face went white. Her whole demeanour crumbled in a moment, and she started stabbing desperately at the comm panels before her, and speaking very seriously into them. Finn smiled at her, and that just made her try even harder. Eventually she got through to the right person, spoke briefly but urgently, listened, and then nodded fearfully to Finn. He turned his back on her and walked over to the sofa. The receptionist watched him go with wide, traumatised eyes. Brett and Rose got to their feet.

'It's all arranged,' said Finn. 'He'll see us now. Even though we don't have an appointment.'

'How nice,' said Brett. 'Who'll see us? And what the hell did you just say to that poor girl?'

'Joseph Wallace. He's Chairman of the Transmutation Board. Don't question me, Brett. I know what I'm doing. Follow me, and all will be made clear. Though you probably won't like it.'

Nothing new there, then, thought Brett.

A security guard in a very impressive uniform appeared out

of nowhere, to guide them where they were going. He recognised Finn immediately, and all but gushed over the Durandal, until rendered speechless by an autograph. He led the way to the Chairman's private elevator, which took them directly and very smoothly up to the top floor, where the guard left them. He wasn't authorised to go any further. A new security guard, in a rather more practical uniform with a lot more built-in armour, took them the rest of the way, to the door of the Chairman's office. He told Finn he'd have to give up his weapons before he could go in. Finn looked at the guard, and he swallowed hard and went away. Finn opened the door without knocking, and led the way in.

The office itself turned out to be surprisingly small and cosy, with a few comfortable chairs set out before a strictly functional desk with a computer terminal built into it. Holo scenes of eye-pleasing countryside vistas on the walls, changing at regular intervals. Thick carpet. Really deep, thick carpet. The Chairman came out from behind his desk to shake Finn warmly by the hand. He was tall and well-set, with a blandly handsome face and a commanding presence. His suit probably cost more money than Brett had made from selling his Coronation recording, and he'd had his eyelids covered with goldleaf, so that they flashed disconcertingly when he blinked. He shook Brett's hand too, a good firm grip, and hesitated only momentarily before offering his hand to Rose. She just looked at him, leaning back against the closed office door, her arms folded across her chest. The Chairman gave her a meaningless smile, and retreated back behind his desk. He gestured for Finn and Brett to sit down too, and they made themselves comfortable.

'Now then,' said the Chairman, concentrating on Finn. 'What exactly is it I can do for the legendary Finn Durandal?'

'You can help me depose the King and overthrow the current political system,' Finn said easily. 'Shouldn't be too big a strain on your conscience, Mister Wallace. You are Neuman, after all.'

Joseph Wallace was immediately back on his feet again, his face flushed. 'I have never been so insulted in my life! My receptionist tried to warn me, but I couldn't believe she was serious. This is an outrage! If you dare to repeat this calumny in public, I will have no hesitation in suing you . . .'

Brett only just caught Finn's signal to Rose, but in a moment she was surging forward from the door, a long thin dagger in her hand. She grabbed Wallace by the front of his very expensive suit, hauled him forward over his own desk, and held the point of her dagger a fraction of an inch before his left eyeball. All the colour went out of Wallace's face, and he whimpered loudly. Finn was still sitting in his chair, smiling calmly.

'You're Neuman,' he said, as though they'd never been interrupted. 'Just like everyone else who matters on the Transmutation Board. Pure Humanity has spent years, and a great deal of money, infiltrating its entire structure. I'm a Paragon. It's my job to know things like that. Don't look so terrified, Wallace. I'm not here to arrest you. I could have done that long ago, if I'd wanted to. But . . . I had a feeling the information might come in handy some day. Let him go, Rose.'

Rose let go of Wallace, made her dagger disappear, and went back to leaning against the door again. Wallace stood where he was, sweat shining on his face, until Finn indicated it was all right for him to sit down again. Wallace all but collapsed into his chair.

'Now then,' Finn said easily. 'Be a good man, and explain why you and your associates have gone to such lengths to take over the business of the Transmutation Board. Be brutally honest. Or I'll let Rose have you.'

'It was necessary,' said Wallace, his voice strained but steady. 'Necessary to protect the Empire. From the alien scum who'd destroy our human way of life, if they could. The Board chooses uninhabited worlds to be reduced by trans- mutation to necessary materials. It's part of the Board's charter to investigate these worlds thoroughly beforehand, and insure they contain no life forms of any worth or interest. Dead worlds. Empty worlds. Grist for the mill. We saw that as a . . . wasted opportunity. Neumen now decide Board policy. For years we have been secretly searching out new worlds with intelligent alien life, and giving them over to transmutation. Wiping out whole species before they become a threat to us. To Pure Humanity.'

'Genocide,' said Finn.

'Yes,' said Wallace.

'Jesus . . .' said Brett, but no-one looked at him.

'I don't care,' said Finn. 'The King wouldn't approve of what you've been doing, but I don't approve of the King. So let us work together, you and I, against a common enemy.'

Wallace didn't actually relax, but some of the tension went out of him. 'I didn't know you believed in the Neuman philosophy . . .'

'Oh I don't,' said Finn. 'I don't believe in anything much any more, apart from myself. We will be allies of convenience, nothing more.'

'Everything we do, we do in Humanity's name,' said Wallace. 'I did wonder, when you came here, whether you knew what we had arranged for this morning's Session of Parliament. We never actually expected it to work, but . . . it was a signal of our intent. Our serious intent.'

'What is he talking about?' said Brett.

'They tried to blow up the King,' said Finn. 'It's all over the Paragons' emergency channel. They failed. The Deathstalker saved Douglas. He always was a conscientious sort. Humourless little prig. I'll have to think of something especially amusing to do to him. Carry on, Mister Wallace. You were justifying yourself.'

'It was always meant that this should be a human Empire,' said Wallace, his voice rising as he warmed to his cause. 'Aliens compete with us for living space. They eat our food, breathe our air, live on worlds that should be ours. They undermine our way of thinking, corrupt our beliefs, threaten our Purity. They must be subjugated or destroyed, for our own protection. Before they do it to us.'

'Now that really is bullshit,' said Brett.

'I don't care,' said Finn.

'Well I do!' Brett said hotly. 'Some of my friends are aliens!'

Wallace sneered at him. 'Yes. You look the type. Degenerate.'

'Oh no,' Rose said unexpectedly. 'That's me.' She moved

away from the door again, and punched Wallace in the face. His head rocked under the impact, and they all heard his nose break. Blood ran down his face. He put up an arm to protect himself, and Rose grabbed his wrist and twisted it so painfully he cried out. Rose smiled and leaned in close. He tried to flinch back in his chair, but the wrist lock held him in place. Rose put her face right in front of his. 'Brett is one of us. And you don't talk to us that way. Know your place, little man.'

She licked some of the blood off his face, her tongue moving slowly over his cheek, and he shuddered. Rose let go of his wrist, and went back to leaning against the door again. Brett wondered if he should thank her, then decided it was probably wiser not to draw attention to himself, just then. He thought about what Wallace had said, about what the Board had been doing, for years . . . and felt sick. He was a thief and a con man and an unrepentant villain, but there were lines even he wouldn't cross. Genocide . . . cold-blooded murder on a planetary scale . . . For the first time, Brett had to seriously wonder if he was on the right side . . .

'You have to make allowances for Rose,' said Finn. 'On the grounds that if you don't, she'll kill you. Now pay attention, Wallace. And leave your nose alone. You can have your medic re-set it after we're gone. You and your Neuman associates will provide me with whatever support I deem necessary, and in return I will bring down the King and replace the existing system with one more amenable to your beliefs. Namely, myself. Until then, I and my associates will remain silent about what we know. You're welcome to try and kill me, of course, but if you do and I find out about it, I'll have Rose rip your guts out and make you eat them before you die. You'd like that, wouldn't you, Rose?'

'Love it,' said Rose, and Wallace and Brett both shuddered at what they heard in her voice.

'And there are of course hidden records of what I know,' said Finn. 'Extensive, very well hidden records. The Neumen have a new partner. Get used to it.'

'I like this place,' Rose said unexpectedly, and they all turned to look at her. Her rose bud mouth stretched into a slow scarlet smile. 'So much death in the air . . . So much

151

slaughter and suffering planned in little rooms like this . . . I find it all so *exciting* . . .'

'You really are *weird*, Rose,' said Brett.

'I try,' said Rose.

Finn's final stop surprised Brett even more, even though he'd never trusted the man they'd come to see. Brett had never had any time for Saints, especially those created by the media. Angelo Bellini, also known as the Angel of Madraguda, lived very comfortably in a small Church in the most fashionable part of the Parade of the Endless. A Cardinal in the Church of Christ Transcendent, Angelo was rarely off the vidscreen, forever pontificating on some important matter of the day. His uncomplicated charm and bluff honesty appealed to a hell of a lot of viewers, all too many of whom loved him uncritically and hung on his every word, rushing to donate their money to whatever cause he was pushing that week. Brett knew another con man when he saw one, just as he had no trouble recognising someone who loved the sound of their own voice just as much, if not more, than the message he was supposed to be putting across.

Angelo himself was a medium-sized, more than a little overweight man, who saved his impressive Cardinal's robes for public appearances only. In the comfort of his own private rooms, he dressed in flowing robes that he wore unbelted, to help disguise his waistline, and spoke softly, as though saving his voice for more important occasions. He had a thick mane of jet black hair brushed back from a widow's peak, a bushy black beard, and a disconcertingly direct gaze. Brett thought he smiled far too much.

Angelo welcomed Finn and his companions warmly, ushered them into his quietly opulent living room, and made sure they were all comfortable before bustling about organising coffee and cakes. Finn and Rose declined, but Brett said yes to everything, on principle. His eyes moved greedily over the expensive furnishings and fittings.

'You live well,' said Finn, shooting Brett a warning glare.

Angelo shrugged disarmingly. 'It's my job to raise funds for good causes. That means playing host to some very important people, sometimes, and I have to be able to put them at their ease. Make them comfortable. So there's nothing to distract them from the message I need to put across.'

'Wouldn't poverty and humble surroundings impress them even more?' said Brett, his mouth half full of toffee cake.

'You'd think so, wouldn't you?' said Angelo, not in the least put out. 'But in reality, all that does is make them uncomfortable. Even guilty. That they have so much and others have so little. So they throw you a handful of credits to appease their conscience, and leave as quickly as possible, and do their best to never think about you or your causes again. I'd rather seduce them in, like a spider into its web, get them at their ease and then hit them with facts and figures; make them see how badly their money is needed. How much good a . . . reasonably-sized contribution could do. Appeal to the head and the heart. You get more out of them through persuasion than you ever could by beating them round the head. Do try the fudge brownies; I made them myself.'

'Persuasion,' said Finn, not even looking at the fudge brownies. 'That's always been your stock in trade, hasn't it; ever since your days as a hostage negotiator, back on Madraguda. But do you find your current vocation satisfying, Angelo? Does it fulfill all your needs? What do you want, Angelo?'

'I want what my Church wants,' Angelo said smoothly. 'Access to the Madness Maze. It is our principal act of faith. Is that what you're here to discuss, Finn? I confess I can't think of any other reason why such an important figure as yourself should ask to see me so urgently.'

'I can get you access,' said Finn. 'I can put the Madness Maze in the Church's hands, now and forever.'

Angelo sat forward in his chair, pulling thoughtfully at his beard, and looked sharply at Finn. 'Parliament's will remains unchanged; so that just leaves the King. Your fellow Paragon. Are you saying you can change the King's mind?'

'Even better; I can change the King. And the new King will change Parliament's mind. With the Church's help, I will overthrow Douglas, remake Parliament, and make the Church the power in the Empire it always should have been.'

'This is treason,' Angelo said slowly. 'The Church . . . does not interfere in political matters. Never has, never will.'

'Not even for guaranteed access to the Madness Maze? Not even for the greatest prize of all; transcendence for all Humanity?'

Angelo glared at him. 'Get thee behind me, Satan! I will not be tempted!'

'Why not?' said Finn indulgently. 'There's no sin in being truthful about what you really want. The Church wants the Maze, and you want to rise in the Church. You want to be in a position to command people, not have to beg from them. You want to be able to make them do the right thing, for once. And when you get right down to it, there's only one devil you need to overcome, and that's Parliament. All those powerful people, so wrapped up in their own small thoughts they can't step back and see what Humanity needs . . . Can't see the overwhelming importance of transcendence. Support me, and together we'll make them see.'

'Just like that,' said Angelo, leaning back in his chair and studying Finn thoughtfully.

'No, not just like that,' Finn said patiently. 'It will take time, and an awful lot of planning. One by one, we'll bring down the people who oppose us, and replace them with new people more amenable to our needs. Together, you and I will create and control a new political force, the Church Militant. A Church within a Church, to seize the public's imagination, and grow into a force so powerful that even the high and mighty Members of Parliament will have to bow down to it. And the Madness Maze will be only one of the rewards . . . I ask you again, Angelo Bellini: are you satisfied with your lot? Your Church? Your life? Or do you have the courage to change not just your life, but all Humanity's?'

'You're wasted as a Paragon, Finn Durandal,' said Angelo. 'You should be in politics.'

'I am,' said Finn. 'They just don't know it yet.'

'Let me tell you my story,' said Angelo, and Brett sighed inwardly. Everyone knew the story of the Angel of Madraguda. It had been dramatised several times, and God knows Angelo had told it often enough on the chat show circuit.

(Always modestly, of course.) Bellini had been a hostage negotiator. Devils from the Hellfire Club had taken over a Church. Bellini talked them out of killing their hostages. He was so impressed by the courage of the priests involved that he joined the Church, and rose to Cardinal. The media made him a Saint. Everyone knew the story. Angelo could see it in their faces. He smiled briefly. 'No, my friends; you only think you know what happened on Madraguda, all those years ago. Let me tell you what really happened.'

It was four in the morning and raining hard when Angelo arrived outside the Church. He climbed out of his car, hunched his shoulders against the pouring rain, and accepted a cup of steaming coffee from the uniformed peacekeeper. It was going to be a bad one. They wouldn't have hauled him out of bed at this ungodly hour, and dragged him all the way out here, for anything less than a major league screwup. Angelo gulped at the scalding coffee, and glanced through the driving rain at the Cathedral of the Blessed Saint Beatrice. Madraguda's only Cathedral wasn't that big or that impressive, but it was the spiritual heart of the city, and a lot of people were going to be mad as hell if the Hellfire Club carried out their threat to desanctify it with the spilled blood of innocents. These people might well be mad enough to vote out of office the city Council that allowed it to happen. So the Council leaned on the peacekeepers, and they leaned on Angelo Bellini; to come to the Cathedral and work a miracle. One more time . . .

He spotted the officer in charge over by the flapping crime scene tapes sealing off the Cathedral, and he hurried over to join him. Captain Jakobs was a large and imposing figure inside his long uniform coat, but he looked almost desperately at Angelo as he approached. It wasn't just the pressure from Above either. Angelo could tell. He caught the way the Captain looked at the Cathedral, and his stomach lurched. Something had gone wrong. Something had gone very wrong. He nodded to the Captain, trying to keep his face impassive. He offered Jakobs his cup of coffee, and the Captain grimaced.

'I've already drunk as much of that shit as I can stand. Did Dispatch give you a sitrep?'

'Just the basics,' said Angelo.

'Then you don't know. You're not the first negotatior we called. Hendricks went in just over an hour ago.'

Angelo frowned. 'Hendricks is a good man. What happened?'

'They killed him. And then they asked for you, by name. Saw you on the news, last week. The Dent Twins case. They're planning something in there . . . You don't have to do this, Bellini.'

'Yes I do. It's my job.'

'All right,' said Jakobs. 'This is what we know. There are three devils in there, holding two priests and a party of five visiting nuns hostage. Far as we can tell, this wasn't in the original plan. The devils only intended to do some property damage, a little casual blasphemy. Make a name for themselves They're not even real Hellfire Club; just teenage wannabes. The priests turned up unexpectedly, to give the visiting nuns a tour of the Cathedral. The devils panicked and ran for it. Just happened to be a peacekeeper walking by, right outside the front door. He challenged the devils, and they took a shot at him and ran back inside. Barricaded the door. Peacekeeper called it in, and it all just escalated from there.

'I really thought Hendricks could talk them down. No-one had been hurt. Now he's dead, and the devils demanded you and a free passage out, or they'll start sending out body parts. You wearing body armour?'

'Of course.'

'Force shield?'

'On my wrist. They'll make me take it off, but that's what it's there for. Makes them feel more secure if they think they're calling the shots. And no hidden weapons. That's not how I do things. No comm taps, either. They always spot them.'

Jakobs shook his head angrily. 'And just what the hell are we supposed to do, if you get into trouble? All three of the devils have guns, though God knows why. Hendricks gave me the exact same routine, and he's dead.'

'I'll just have to talk faster,' said Angelo. 'What's the official line? Are they going to get free passage out of here?'

'No,' Jakobs said flatly. 'We can't allow the Hellfire Club to gain a victory here, even if they are just wannabes. Word from Above is, we have to send a message. Save the priests and nuns if you can, but if all else fails, we go in guns blazing, and the God-botherers will have to take their chances. It's a hard bloody world sometimes. You ready?'

'Ready as I'll ever be. Do you have comm contact with the devils?'

'No. They're too paranoid for that. They shout their messages through the front doors.'

'So I just walk in, and hope they don't shoot me on sight?'

'Pretty much, yes. Don't you just love this job?'

Angelo laughed softly. 'Hell, I joined for the great social life and the fantastic pension plan. Didn't you?'

He walked off through the rain without waiting for an answer. He stepped carefully over the crime scene tapes and headed for the front doors of the Cathedral, his hands held well out from his sides to show they were empty. No-one shot at him. He stopped before the two doors. They were standing slightly ajar. Angelo raised his voice over the roar of the driving rain.

'You asked for me. I'm Angelo Bellini; hostage negotiator. I'm unarmed. Shall I come in?'

One of the doors swung inwards, and a devil poked his head out. Typical cheap backstreet body shop job. Brick red skin, two stubby horns on the forehead. The goatee beard was just patchy enough to be real. Angelo put the devil's age at about nineteen. The devil looked quickly past Angelo, making sure the peacekeepers were all staying well back, then he reached out, grabbed Angelo by the shoulder, and hauled him inside the Cathedral.

At least it was dry inside, though the rain hammered loudly on the roof. The Church was really only a Cathedral in name, barely big enough to hold two hundred worshippers on basic, unpadded wooden pews. The priests and nuns were sitting together on one pew, looking hopefully at Angelo. One of the priests had bruises on his face, and a split lip. Two more devils were standing guard over their hostages with drawn disrupters. Both of them teenagers. Angelo looked them over coolly, and then gave all his attention to the man lying face down in the central aisle. He'd been shot through the chest, leaving a wide hole in his back. From the scorch marks on his coat, it had been set on fire by the blast and allowed to burn itself out. Angelo wondered what Hendricks had done wrong. What badly-chosen words had led to his death.

'Hey man, I'm talking to you!' The devil's voice was high and strained, on the border of panic.

'I'm sorry,' Angelo said immediately. 'Tell me what you want.'

'Open your freaking coat while I check you for weapons!'

Angelo held open his coat, while the devil frisked him in a very unprofessional way. He did get the force shield bracelet. He pulled it awkwardly off Angelo's wrist, threw it on the floor and stamped on it. He sneered triumphantly at Angelo, who kept his face impassive. Like stamping on a force shield bracelet was going to damage it. He allowed the devil to usher him towards the other two.

They were all dressed in black leotards, with black capes. With their cheap makeovers, they almost looked comical. Almost. One was seriously overweight, and the third was only a dark pink in colour, as though the dye job had gone wrong. The devils struck poses before Angelo, trying to look tough. He could smell the fear on them. That was what made them dangerous. Frightened people were capable of anything.

'I'm Angelo Bellini,' he said, his voice calm and soothing. 'I'm here to help. Tell me how I can help you.'

'We want safe passage,' said the pink devil. 'And no-one follows us. And . . . we want a million credits! In gold!'

'What?' said the fat devil.

'We've got to make them take us seriously, man,' said the pink devil. 'Show them we mean business!'

'You any idea how much a million credits in gold will weigh?' said the goateed devil. 'It'd only slow us down. Concentrate on what matters. We can't let them take us.'

'Right,' moaned the fat devil. 'My dad would kill me.'

'Screw that,' said the pink devil. 'I'm not going to gaol! Not over this! What did you have to kill him for?'

'It was a mistake, all right?' said the fat devil, actually stamping his cloven hoof. 'I thought he had a gun!'

'We should never have brought guns,' said the pink devil. 'I said we shouldn't mess about with guns!'

'What kind of Hellfire Club would we be without guns?' said the goateed devil. 'Now shut up! Stick with what matters. We've got another hostage now; one who's got the clout to get us out of here. Isn't that right, peacekeeper?'

'I'm here to negotiate for the hostages' release,' said Angelo. 'To make a deal that will get everyone here out alive. Why don't you start by telling me your names?'

'No real names!' the goateed devil said immediately. 'I'm Belial. That's Moloch, and the trigger-happy fat boy is Damien.'

'You never meant for any of this to happen, did you?' said Angelo. 'My information is you're not even real Hellfire Club.'

'We're real enough!' said Belial. 'You take us seriously, man!'

'Oh I do,' said Angelo. 'But you didn't come here intending to kill anyone, did you?'

'Hell no,' said Moloch. 'It was just supposed to be a laugh. A bit of fun. Something to get us noticed, get our friends to take us seriously. We were supposed to be long gone before anyone turned up. Then those bastard priests appeared, and when we tried to run, there was a cop outside.'

'And you didn't mean to kill Hendricks? That was just an accident?'

'I thought he had a gun,' said Damien, looking at the floor.

'Then why don't you all just put down your guns, and walk out of here with me?' said Angelo. 'No-one else has to die. I'll talk to the officer in charge out there. I know the man. He's reasonable . . .'

'No!' Belial said immediately. 'I told you; I'm not going to gaol! Not over this! I've got my whole life ahead of me, and I'm not being cheated out of it just because of an accident! We're getting out of here, or people are going to pay! In blood!'

'My dad's going to kill me!' said Damien. He sounded like he might burst into tears at any moment.

'Shut up!' said Belial. 'Just shut up!' He darted over to the pew and grabbed the priest with the bruised face, hauling him out into the aisle. He stuck his gun against the priest's head. 'I take him to the door, and tell them to bring us a car, *right now*, or I blow his head off! You see how fast they bring us a car then!'

'No,' Angelo said quickly. 'That's not going to happen.' All three devils looked at him, drawn by the cold surety in his voice. 'You shoot anyone else, and they'll storm the place. Orders from Above. They won't allow the Hellfire Club to have a victory on Madraguda.'

'But we're not real Hellfire Club!' said Moloch.

'You kill a priest, you might as well be,' said Angelo.

Moloch sat down suddenly on the floor, his gun pointing nowhere. 'I can't believe this is happening. It was just supposed to be a laugh! Give us something to talk about . . . I was an altar boy, for Christ's sake! I don't believe in any of that Hellfire Club shit!'

'Shut up,' said Belial.

'You shut up!' said Moloch. 'This was all your idea! I don't want to die . . . I don't want to go to Hell . . .'

'They put us in gaol, you'll know what Hell is like,' said Belial savagely. 'End up with some big cellmate wanting you to be his girl-friend! You want that? Then shut up, and let me do what I have to, to get us out of here.' He glared at Angelo. 'They sent you in here to scare us. You'd tell us anything, any lie, to scare us into giving ourselves up. Well screw that shit! We're accessories to murder. I know what that means. No slap on the wrist and a fine my dad can pay. Murder means hard time, long time, and I'm damned if I'll sit still for that. Not over a bloody accident . . .'

'Damned,' said Damien. 'We're all damned . . .'

'Will you shut up!' shrieked Belial. 'Let me think! Come on, priest; we're going to talk to the cops. And you'd better pray they say all the right things . . .'

The disrupter blast tore half his head away. Belial rocked on his feet, and then turned round slowly, half his face gone, his hair on fire. Damien was still pointing the gun at him. Belial tried to say something, and then he fell dead to the floor. The priest stood looking down at him. Moloch, still sitting on the floor, raised his gun to point it at the priest. Damien cried out, but his gun was empty. The priest ran forward and kicked Moloch in the face. The devil fell backwards, the gun flying from his pink hand. The priest kicked him in the ribs, and then in the head, kicking him again and again, all the time shouting 'You're damned, you little bastard! Damned for all time!'

Angelo walked past him, and took the gun away from Damien, who was sobbing heavily now, his fat frame shaking. 'It was an accident, honest,' he said indistinctly. 'I don't want to go to Hell . . .'

The other priest got up from the pew and went over to stop the first priest from kicking the crap out of the semi-conscious Moloch. He sat the first priest down in a pew, and then looked back at Angelo. 'You have to excuse Father Saxon. He's very upset. They urinated in the font, defecated on the altar, destroyed precious relics. And when he remonstrated with them, they hit him. Laughed at him. He's not normally like this.'

'No-one needs to know,' said Angelo. 'We can fix this mess, if we all get our stories straight. We'll blame it all on Belial. He's dead, and can't deny anything. So he killed Hendricks, and hurt Moloch. Everyone else gets a fresh start. Yes?'

Damien looked at him, tears streaming down his face. 'You mean it, man? Why would you do something like that, for me?'

'Because in the end, you stopped Belial. You did the right thing.'

Angelo turned his back on them all, and headed for the main doors. He needed to get out into the rain again. So it could wash him clean.

'Damn,' said Brett. 'You mean the official version's a pack of lies? You didn't manage to talk them down? That devil didn't commit suicide, because of your eloquence?'

'It made a good story,' said Angelo. 'And afterwards, I joined the Church because I saw the power of its beliefs. Reason wasn't enough, any more. I saw that. But with the Church's beliefs backing my words, I could *make* people do the right thing . . . The media took the story and ran with it, exaggerating it out of all recognition. They made me a Saint. I think there was a shortage at the time . . . and I rode the publicity for all it was worth.'

'But did you believe it?' said Finn. 'Have you ever believed what the Church teaches?'

'No,' said Angelo. 'Not for one moment. It was just something I could use, to push people in the right direction. Don't get me wrong; I want access to the Maze. People have to transcend, to become more than they are. Because they aren't worth shit right now. The Maze could uplift Humanity by its bootstraps, make it something better.'

'The first ten thousand people to go through died or went horribly insane . . .' Finn pointed out.

'A hundred thousand would be worth it, to put an end to the madness.' Angelo's voice was very cold and very sure. 'I've seen too many deaths . . . too many people I couldn't save. I was on the point of quitting as a negotiator, when the Church showed me a way out. A way to put an end to the evils in man, once and for all. The Maze . . . is our redemption.'

'You'll never be allowed anywhere near the Maze, as things stand,' said Finn. 'You might be the Empire's official religion, but that doesn't really mean anything where the things that matter are decided. I can change that.'

Angelo sat back in his chair, and looked thoughtfully at Finn. 'If you'd betray your King, a man who was your friend and partner for ten years; what's to stop you betraying me? Why should I trust you?'

'Because it's in our interests to work together, to achieve what we can't bring about separately. And Douglas was never my friend.'

'Then we're partners,' said Angelo. 'Very secretly, of course. And never make the mistake of thinking that your personal needs will be allowed to interfere with those of the Church.'

'Of course not,' said Finn.

They spoke some more, but it was just pleasantries, and soon it was time for Finn and his people to leave. Brett stuffed a last few cakes and delicacies into his pockets, but kept his hands away from the silverware and the objets d'art. He knew Finn was watching, even if Angelo wasn't. Brett felt strangely vindicated. He'd never trusted peacekeepers, priests or Angelo Bellini, and it seemed he'd been right about all three. Once Finn and company were safely outside, with the doors of the Church politely but firmly closed behind them, Brett looked seriously at Finn.

'So much for the Saint of Madraguda. Have you any intention of delivering what you promised him?'

'I don't know,' said Finn. 'It might be amusing . . .'

'You can con him,' said Brett. 'But will he stay conned?'

'He'll con himself,' said Finn. 'He wants this so badly, he'll talk himself into doing whatever I tell him it takes. And soon he'll be in so deep he won't be able to walk away . . . Come children; we've made a good start today. Now Daddy has to go home and do some serious plotting.'

'When do I get to kill someone?' said Rose. She might have been inquiring about the weather.

'Soon,' said Finn. 'Very soon.'

Backstage at Parliament, in Anne Barclay's private security room, Douglas, Lewis, Jesamine and Anne were winding down after a long and incident-filled first day in the House. Douglas snatched off his Crown the moment the door closed behind him, and slammed it down on the first available surface. Lewis cracked open his leather armour so his chest could get some air, and sprawled out in the nearest chair. Jesamine poured herself a large mug of coffee from the waiting pot, and drank half of it down in several quick gulps. Anne looked at them sardonically from her chair before the monitor screens.

'You're acting like you've just been through a battle.'

'Bloody well feels like it,' growled Douglas, sinking slowly into a chair. 'Tell me it gets easier from now on.'

'Well I will if you like, but you know I never feel comfortable lying to my friends. Settle for this; you made a good start. You established yourself as the voice of reason, showed you had a good grasp of the political process, and made it very clear you weren't going to be intimidated by the House or the issues. Just the kind of Speaker that Parliament needs, whether they like to admit it or not. And the bomber made you look really good. You didn't panic, put your life on the line to protect innocents, looked out for Jesamine . . . and Lewis took the little creep out like the professional he is. Nice one, Lewis.'

'Yeah,' said Douglas. 'You got some action today after all, Champion.'

Lewis sniffed. 'You keep on pissing off heavy duty bastards like that, and I'm going to need better weaponry. How about a stasis field projector? Yeah, I know, they're expensive; but it would have been just the job today. Put him on ice in a second. A transmutation bomb . . . that is playing really dirty. And how the hell did he smuggle something like that into the House anyway? Just its presence should have set off every alarm in the building!'

'Don't I know it,' said Anne. 'I can only assume it's been so long since there's been a serious threat to the House that certain people have got sloppy. Heads will roll over this. Actually, it's just the excuse I need to force some high up but basically useless people to retire.'

'It was more than that,' said Lewis. 'Somebody very well placed must have been paid to look the other way, shut down the relevant systems. Pure Humanity has a spy in the House.'

'Wouldn't surprise me at all,' said Anne. 'They're devious bastards. Once I've got my own people in place, I can start putting pressure on anyone I even suspect isn't one hundred per cent behind the King.'

'Anne, dear,' said Jesamine. 'You don't actually run the House's Security.'

'Only a matter of time,' said Anne. She looked at Lewis. 'Good thinking on your feet. What exactly did you throw at the bomber?'

'This,' said Lewis. He sat forward in his chair and held out his palm, with the chunky black gold ring balanced on it. The others leaned forward to study it. Jesamine recognised it first, and shrieked out loud.

'That's the Deathstalker ring! Owen's ring! Sign and symbol of Clan authority. It was one of the main props in *Deathstalker's Lament*.'

'Where did you get that?' said Douglas. 'It was supposed to have disappeared with Owen two hundred years ago!'

Lewis told them about the strange little man called Vaughn. None of the others recognised the name or the description. They took it in turns to hold the ring and study it, touching it only gingerly. The ring had belonged to a legend, so that made it a legend too. They were all more than a little awed. Finally Anne gave it back to Lewis, and he slipped it back on his finger.

'I feel a bit weird,' said Douglas. 'That ring saved my life. It's as though Owen himself reached out to save me, through his descendant. *Weird*.'

'The bomber really was very stupid, darling,' said Jesamine. 'All he had to do was run up to Douglas and detonate his bomb, and there would have been nothing Lewis could do to prevent it. But no, he had to show off, and make his stupid speeches first. Have his moment in the spotlight. Primadonnas. They're all the same.'

'Smart people don't do suicide bomb runs,' said Anne. 'They convince some other stupid bastard to do it for them.'

'Pity you couldn't take him alive, Lewis,' said Douglas. 'Alive, we might have been able to get some answers out of him. I really want the people behind this.'

'You ungrateful pig!' Jesamine said immediately. 'Lewis saved your life! He saved all our lives.'

'He wasn't going to be taken alive, Douglas,' Lewis said evenly. 'You heard him. And you can be sure there would have been a poison tooth, or another bomb hidden in his belly. Something dramatic. There was no way his bosses would have sent him out without being sure there was no way anything could be traced back to them. We've dealt with this kind before, back when we were both Paragons. You know how they think.'

'Yes,' said Douglas. 'Of course, Lewis; you're quite right.

Sorry. I'm . . . still a little shaken. Why don't you work with Anne; see if the two of you can figure out exactly how he got past Security.'

Lewis nodded, got up and moved over to join Anne before her monitors. She was already using her computers to work out possible routes the bomber could have used, to end up in the alien section of the House. Douglas looked at Jesamine, and she came over and sat down beside him.

'Why did you go to him, Jes, and not to me?' Douglas said softly.

'He saved both our lives,' said Jesamine steadily. 'And silly me, I was worried he might be hurt. Don't make more of it than it was.'

'You must know it looked more than that, in front of the media cameras. It looked *bad*, Jes. Like you cared more about him than you did about me.'

'I know more about the media than you ever will, Douglas Campbell! They'll see what's there, and nothing else; a woman concerned over the Champion who saved her life and that of her husband-to-be. No-one will say anything else; unless you make a big deal of it. Let it drop, Douglas. It doesn't matter.'

'It matters,' said Douglas. 'It matters to me.'

There was a lot more for them to discuss, and it was some time before the day's business was finally over, and they were all free to go their separate ways, and consider the day's ramifications. Lewis walked the narrow corridors alone, the heavy scowl on his ugly face enough to keep pretty much everyone at a distance. Even those who just wanted to congratulate him on the day's heroism thought better of it, and kept on walking. Lewis didn't notice. He never did.

And then a large and blocky figure moved deliberately out of the shadows to block his path. Lewis had to stop or walk right through him. Lewis opened his mouth, and then closed it again, as he recognised the man standing patiently before him. Michel du Bois, Member for his own home planet of Virimonde. Lewis nodded politely, and du Bois nodded politely back.

'You did well today, Deathstalker. Credit to you reflects well upon your home. And I really like the new outfit.'

'Don't you start,' said Lewis. 'What do you want, du Bois? And why do I just know I'm not going to like it?'

'We need to talk, Deathstalker,' said du Bois. 'And you've been avoiding me ever since the Coronation.'

'That's because I was hoping to avoid just such conversations as this,' growled Lewis. 'We have talked in the past, du Bois, and neither of us enjoyed it. Nothing has changed. I am not going to trade on my friendship and position with the King, to plead for special favours and attention for Virimonde.'

'Why not?' du Bois said reasonably. 'Everyone trades favours here, even though we're not supposed to. A little of this, for a little of that. Everyone makes deals. That's how the system works. Up until now, Virimonde has been very much the poor relation at the House. We've never had anything or anyone to trade with. So all the best trade deals and economic grants ended up going to other worlds, that needed them less than we do. When we bring our begging bowl to the House, we stand alone, with no friend or ally at our side. You could change all that. People would flock to the world that had the ear of the King. You talk to the King, he talks to the sub-committees, everyone gets something they want, everyone's happy. What's so bad about that? I'm not asking for anything for myself, Deathstalker; only for my world. Your world. Your home.'

'Wouldn't do any harm to your chances for re-election, though, would it?' said Lewis. 'I do know a few things about how politics works. You have to deliver, or they'll replace you with someone else who might. Understand me very clearly, du Bois; I am not going to do anything that might compromise Douglas' position. It's important to him and to me that the first Imperial Champion in two hundred years is seen to be utterly impartial. Or no-one will trust him or me.'

'How soon they forget,' said du Bois, and there was new iron in his voice. 'How ungrateful the son can be, once he's distanced himself from his family. Who was it that supported you all these years on Logres, added to your meagre salary, so

167

you could play the part of the honest Paragon? Your wages didn't allow you to live as other Paragons did, and your own family couldn't support you.'

'I never asked for that money! You came to me, said it was important that Virimonde's Paragon didn't appear to be a poor relation at Court!'

'You took the money,' said du Bois. 'Did you never think that one day there would be a reckoning? The people of Virimonde put up a lot of money on your behalf, went without so you could live in comfort in the greatest city in the Empire. They're entitled to get something back for that.'

'They do,' said Lewis, meeting du Bois' angry gaze unflinchingly. 'They get a Champion they can be proud of. My responsibility to them is the same now as it always was; to be the best, most honourable representative of my world that I am capable of being. To be honest and true, and incorruptible. An honourable man, from an honourable world.'

'Words,' said the Member for Virimonde. 'Just words. You have a lot to learn, young Deathstalker, about how the Empire really works.'

'Oh, I'm learning,' said Lewis. 'Trust me, du Bois; I'm learning. Douglas chose me to be his Champion, rather than the more obvious choice of the Durandal, because he trusted me to be my own man. And so I am. Stop my money, if you want. If you can. I will not compromise my beliefs; beliefs my Clan has held to for hundreds of years. I am a Deathstalker; and don't you ever forget it. From now on, du Bois, I think we should meet only on public occasions. We have nothing more to say to each other in private.'

'I could raise the matter directly, with the King,' said du Bois. 'He might be more . . . reasonable.'

'The King is very reasonable,' said Lewis. 'He's also even more honourable than I am. He'd have you arrested for treason on the spot, just for trying to put pressure on me. So, you go right ahead, if you want. I'm told Traitor's Hall is comparatively comfortable, these days.'

He bowed briefly to du Bois, and walked away, and du Bois watched him go, and thought many things.

3

All Kinds of Betrayal

It had been two weeks since Douglas' Coronation, and everything in the garden was wonderful. The planet of Logres, and most especially that ancient and golden city, the Parade of the Endless, blossomed like a rose in summer under the rapt attention of the whole Empire. The new King's positive attitude had caught Humanity's mood exactly, and his unexpected political skills had delighted everyone who enjoyed seeing the established political elite embarrassed and outdone. The media followed King Douglas and his people wherever they went, and absolutely everyone was fascinated to see what he would do next. It was only another two weeks until he would be marrying the Empire's most beloved diva, anticipation was already at fever pitch, and the media were going out of their minds. They had all made it very clear that nothing short of armed force was going to keep them out of this one, so Douglas had bowed to the inevitable, and graciously agreed to Empire-wide live coverage of his marriage, to be carried on all the major channels. Jesamine had already promised that she would be singing at the ceremony; her last ever live performance. Bidding for the recording rights was fierce, bordering on vicious. Already there were newsgroups, web sites, and whole vid channels devoted to nothing but gossip about the buildup to the marriage ceremony.

And you were *nobody* in Society if you didn't already have your invitation.

The Parade of the Endless buzzed with rumour, and bristled with all kinds of life. Tourists were flooding in from all sides of the Empire, and you couldn't book a room in a hotel for love nor money. News channels were offering outrageous sums just for a peek at the wedding dress, and the wedding banquet organisers were getting everything from stock option offers to death threats over the seating arrangements. Excitement was in the air wherever you turned, and everyone agreed there had never been a better time to be alive. It was in fact the last great Season of the Golden Age, though no-one knew that then.

On the surface, all was calm and peace and happy anticipation. But down in the dark, dark depths, something with teeth and appetite and awful ambitions was laying the groundwork for a terrible storm.

Brett Random's stomach hurt all the time now. It hurt when he woke up, ached all through the increasingly long days, and barely subsided enough to let him sleep at night. He didn't eat much, and he was drinking a lot. It was all tension, of course. Nerves. And it was all Finn Durandal's fault. The Paragon drove Brett like a slave-driver.

Brett had never been bothered with butterflies in the stomach before, even during the most complicated and risky of his confidence tricks; but back then he had always been the one in charge. He had always taken great pride in the careful planning that went into every one of his stings, and had the utmost confidence in his ability to function and if necessary improvise under pressure. But now Finn was in the driver's seat, demanding remorselessly that Brett lead him further and further into the seediest, darkest warrens of the Rookery; searching out the extremely disreputable people and expertise that Finn had decided were necessary for his bitter revenge.

Brett assumed Finn had some secret overall plan, though he couldn't see it for the life of him. But he had to assume that Finn knew what he was doing, because the alternative was frankly too awful to contemplate. Far better to be the accomplice of a master criminal than the victim of a raving lunatic. So Brett took Finn where he wanted to go, introduced him to the often appalling people Finn said he needed to meet, and did a lot of sitting miserably in corners, with his arms folded tightly over his aching stomach.

Sometimes Rose Constantine joined them, and then Brett's head hurt too. He just knew the Wild Rose was a disaster waiting to happen. When he had trouble getting to sleep at nights, he just counted the ways it could all go suddenly and horribly and violently wrong when Rose was around.

Brett Random trudged unhappily down narrow lanes, knocked on hidden doors, and reluctantly led the way into windowless rooms with dramatically low lighting, where he introduced Finn Durandal to locksmiths, forgers, computer hackers, burglars, muscle and guns for hire, and all the other secret people a Golden Age didn't like to admit still existed. A lot of them wouldn't have been in for Brett Random, but they were all fascinated to meet a legendary Paragon gone bad. Most didn't believe it at first, but you only had to be in Finn's presence for a while, to hear his calm awful voice, and see the fey light in his eyes, to know this was no trick, no con. And somehow none of these alleged twilight people could bring themselves to say no to the charming, dangerous, tainted Paragon as he murmured his needs and requirements, and promised them rewards almost beyond belief.

Evil always knows evil, when it meets it face to face.

Finn was particularly pleased to meet a certain Mr Sylvester; a faded actor of a certain age, who with the decline of his career had embraced computer hacking and character assassination with equal satisfaction. Mr Sylvester was an absolute master at breaking into even the best guarded of files, adding a damning line or two, and then leaving, with no trace to show he had ever been there. He could destroy a reputation with just the right planted word, here and there, and could change or corrupt the whole meaning of a phrase just by meddling with the emphasis. After all, a half truth can be so much more damning than a total lie . . . Finn talked with Mr Sylvester for over an hour, while Brett waited in the corridor outside, and failed utterly to make small talk with Rose Constantine.

The agents provocateurs had their own squalid little café, *The Outcry*, where they lounged around all day when they weren't working, drinking bad coffee and swapping the tales they could only tell each other. For the right price, they would infiltrate any march or meeting or organisation, and guarantee to bring it all crashing down to ruin and disgrace. No-one was safe from them, and some had been known to boast they could start a fight in an empty room. They were much in demand, and very well paid, but the nature of their profession, and the many enemies they'd made, demanded an anonymity that they found particularly irksome. What use was craft and skill and accomplishment if you couldn't boast about it afterwards? They were all heartily sick of each other's company, so they took to Finn Durandal immediately, as he sat and listened patiently while they all but fell over themselves detailing all the appalling things they could do for him, for the right price.

In the end, Finn offered a sum that made Brett's eyes bulge, as a downpayment for a series of actions yet to be detailed, and all the agents present agreed to abjure all other assignments and hold themselves ready for his call. Brett was so astonished he actually took Finn by the arm and insisted on talking privately with him. Finn sighed and agreed, and allowed Brett to lead him away while the agents chatted animatedly with each other. Finn had promised them a real test of their skills, and they did so love a challenge. Brett pulled Finn into a private booth, and the Durandal immediately pulled his arm free.

'Don't touch me, Brett. I don't like to be touched.'

'You must be touched in the head, to be putting up the kind of money you've been offering them!' Brett said angrily, too outraged even to be respectful. 'And you didn't need to hire them all, dammit! Jesus, you could at least have let me negotiate . . .'

'I'm touched by your concern, Brett, but you don't know what I'm planning,' Finn said calmly. 'I may have need of all of these people, or I may not. I'm not sure, yet. But either way, I don't want any of them free to work against me. And anyway; money doesn't matter to me.'

'Don't blaspheme,' Brett said automatically. 'And keep your voice down, or they'll double the price on general principles. Are you really so rich you can just throw it away?'

'I've always had money,' said Finn. 'I made a lot of it in my early days. It was just another way of proving I was the best. Another way of keeping score with my . . . contemporaries. But I never really had anything worth spending it on before. Certainly nothing that gave me so much pleasure. Don't frown like that, Brett. It'll give you wrinkles. I know what I'm doing, and you know only what I want you to know.'

And then they both looked round sharply, as a single agent came striding over to join them. He crashed to a halt outside their booth, his thumbs tucked ostentatiously into a wide leather belt from which hung all kinds of nasty-looking weapons. He glared at Finn and Brett impartially. He was almost as wide as he was tall, his body bulging with the best muscles money could buy. In fact, he looked like he got a bulk discount on the deal. He was a thug, and looked it, conspicuous in his lack of enthusiasm for Finn's proposal earlier. Brett studied the man warily, and let his hand drift casually towards the dagger concealed up his sleeve.

'Do introduce us, Brett,' Finn said easily. 'I don't think I caught this gentleman's name from before.'

'This is Toby Goddammit,' said Brett. 'There's probably a highly amusing christening story somewhere in his background, but don't expect to hear it from Toby. He has no sense of humour and even less small talk. Not noted for his subtlety, or his charm, and vicious with it. Toby's the one you hire when there's a shortage of mad dogs. Living proof there's no intelligent life on his planet of origin. What's the problem, Toby?'

'He is,' said the thug, jerking his shaggy head at Finn. 'I don't trust him. I don't care what he says, or what you say; once a Paragon, always a Paragon. This is some kind of trick, or trap; has to be. And if they're all too stupid or too greedy to recognise that, I'm not. You shouldn't have brought him here, Brett. I thought you had more sense. Now get out of the way. You'll all thank me for this later. Say goodbye, Durandal. You're a dead man.'

His hand came up, suddenly full of a long gleaming blade with a viciously serrated edge. Finn made a slight gesture with his hand, and Rose Constantine erupted up out of her chair in the corner, where she'd been sitting still and silent for so long that everyone had quite forgotten about her. Toby started to turn, but she was already upon him, and her sword flashed through the air in a blindingly swift arc. It sank deep into Toby's neck, and the impact of the blow drove him to his knees. He cried out once, his eyes wide with shock and pain, while blood gushed down his shoulder and across his heaving chest. Rose set her foot against his shoulder, and jerked the blade free. Toby grunted, a deep helpless sound, like a cow in a slaughterhouse. Rose hit him again, and the blade sheared clean through his neck. The head fell away, rolling across the floor towards the other agents, who scattered away from it with cries of alarm, like startled birds. The head's eyes were still blinking, and its mouth worked soundlessly. The headless body fell forward onto its chest, and lay still. Rose sighed happily. A shocked silence fell across the room. Finn emerged from the booth and smiled charmingly about him.

'You have to be strict, but firm,' he announced.

'I want to go home,' said Brett, from under the table.

But they still had one last visit to make. To see Dr Happy, and his fabled subterranean chamber of stinks and perfumes. You could only get to it by descending through a trapdoor, and making your way cautiously along an underground passage with sulphur-smeared brick walls that was home to far too many rats and other small scuttling things, and finally through a series of state of the art airlocks. Dr Happy was not a genuine medical person, as far as anyone knew for sure, but he certainly knew his chemistry. Whatever you wanted, or thought you needed, Dr Happy had the cure for what ailed you. Love potions and battle drugs, mindbenders and soul destroyers; from the sublime to the suicidal, from heart's ease to potions that would blow the doors of perception clean off their hinges, Dr Happy was right there for you.

Brett looked interestedly about him as he followed Finn and Rose into the good Dr's laboratory. He'd never been able to afford the doctor's more than extortionate prices, and he was curious to see if all the rumours were true. His fingers itched to steal something. Anything.

The laboratory was a long single chamber, carved out of the

solid rock the city rested on. The bare walls were covered with what looked like miles of transparent tubing, stapled directly to the stone, all of them pulsing with the many-coloured liquids streaming through them. Tables groaned under the weight of the very latest in scientific equipment, some of it straight from some poor fool's development benches, who probably didn't even know it was missing yet. Dr Happy never had any trouble getting what he needed, whether the price for it was credits or in kind. There were computers, gene-splicers, recombinant chambers, and a huge walk-in refrigerator absolutely packed with alchemical magic.

The man himself was almost impossibly tall and willowy, a spindly scarecrow figure in his stained and battered white lab coat, topped by a long thin face with bulging eyes and a frankly disturbing toothy grin, under a shock of white hair that seemed to stick out sideways from his head. He giggled a lot, and bit his fingernails when he got excited. His eyeballs were as yellow as urine, and his teeth weren't much better. He smelled strongly of something. Brett wasn't sure of what, but did his best to keep upwind, just in case. The good doctor bobbed happily along beside Finn as they strolled through the chamber, pointing out his various wares and processes like a proud father.

'Such a pleasure to have you here, Sir Durandal! Such a pleasure, yes! I've heard so much about you. One does hear things, you know, even this far underground. Don't touch that, Brett. I knew you'd come to me eventually, Sir Durandal. Everyone does, you know. Everyone! Oh, you'd be surprised who I've entertained down here, in my time. I have it all here, you see. Such stuff as dreams are made of . . . in pill and liquid form. Don't touch that, Brett. I have potions here to drive a man mad with lust, or grow hair on an elephant. I can drive sane men out of their minds, or cure the crazy. Make the blind see and the deaf hear, and make a cripple take up his bed and walk even if he didn't have a bed when he came in here! I have potions to give you emotions they don't even have names for yet, to show you heaven and hell and everything in between. Every day I think the unthinkable, and nothing is ever too extreme! Brett, if I

175

have to speak to you again I will spray you with something really amusing.'

'Brett, behave yourself,' said Finn. 'Or I'll let him do it.'

Brett thrust both his hands deep into his pockets, and did his best to look innocent. It wasn't particularly successful. Rose had found a table to lean against, her arms loosely folded across her chest. She looked bored. Dr Happy sneered at them both, sniffed moistly, and turned his toothy smile on Finn Durandal again, his bony hands clasped tightly together over his sunken chest.

'So; what sweet and sour miracle can I perform for you, Sir Durandal? Hmm? Something to make a corpse sit up in his coffin, or make his widow dance? Something to make an angel curse or a demon repent? Just name your needs, Sir Durandal, and I will supply them in an instant! Yes!'

Finn waited patiently, letting Dr Happy witter on until he ran down. 'They tell me you are a collector as well as a creator,' he said finally. 'A connoisseur, of the rare and strange. That you have access to drugs that no-one else has. Old drugs, from the days before the Rebellion. They say, in fact, that you have drugs from the private collection of the infamous Valentine Wolfe himself.'

Dr Happy's hands flew to his mouth, his eyes appallingly wide, and he stamped a foot, all but squeaking with excitement. 'Yes! Oh yes! Oh Sir Durandal, you have come to the right man indeed! I have them, I have them all, even the lost sex drug that mutates a man's flesh . . . rare and wondrous substances, some so potent even the smell of them would unravel your DNA or tie knots in your chromosomes. What . . . exactly, did you have your heart set on, Sir Durandal?'

'The esper drug,' said Finn. 'That's what I want. The drug that can make a man more than a man.'

Brett looked round, startled. Even Rose looked interested. The esper drug had been banned for almost two centuries. As well as being permanently addictive, the fatality rate had proved to be a hell of a lot higher than previously believed, killing or maddening over eighty per cent of those who took it. There were still a few scientists studying it, of course, under very strict conditions. It was far too potentially useful a drug to be just abandoned. But there was an understandable shortage of volunteers willing to test it. You had to be really desperate to buck those kind of odds. Brett looked curiously at Finn. Surely he wasn't crazy enough to take the drug himself? Well actually, he probably was that crazy; but he wasn't stupid.

'I have the drug, yes,' said Dr Happy, his great goggling eyes blinking furiously. 'Very rare, very dangerous. I have it in the pure form. Just a few drops, to make you a telepath, a polter, a precog. Make you an esper, or kill you. Most probably kill you, in fact, in horrible, horrible ways. Closed coffin, no flowers by request, very sad. Very strange chemical structure . . . almost certainly alien in origin . . . but oh, the potential, if we ever solve the fatality problem.' He smiled sweetly. 'Such wonders lie within the human mind, waiting to be unleashed.'

'I'll take it,' said Finn, cutting ruthlessly across Dr Happy's eulogy. The good doctor shrugged. He was used to that. Few people really appreciated him. He wandered off in the direction of his refrigerator, reaching out to pat some of his favourite pieces of equipment along the way, like trusted pets.

'What the hell do you want with the esper drug?' Brett said quietly. 'You're not planning to take it yourself; are you?'

'Oh no,' said Finn. 'I have no intention of taking it myself.'

Most of the Paragons who'd come to Logres for Douglas' Coronation had decided they might as well stick around for the marriage too. It was only a couple more weeks, and they so rarely got a holiday. Let the peacekeepers earn their pay for a while. Only ever really at ease in the company of their own kind, the Paragons spent most of their time sitting around in a bar called *The Sangreal*, swapping ideas and experiences and increasingly tall tales about past cases. Drinking was heavy, boasting was rife, and one-upmanship was rampant. Food and drink was in constant supply, the best of everything, and of course no-one ever asked them to pay for anything. They were Paragons, after all. It was an honour to have them there, eating and drinking and carousing the host out of hearth and home.

The Sangreal used to be a cop bar, patronised almost exclusively by Parliament's security staff, since the House was only just up the road; but the Paragons just moved in en masse and took over, and absolutely no-one felt like arguing about it. The security people took to sulking in a slightly less salubrious bar, just down the street, and did their best to ignore the cries of jollity and good cheer emanating from what used to be their place. *The Sangreal*'s owner sighed, bit the bullet, and smiled on his new customers till his cheeks ached. He was, after all, making a nice little earner out of selling his security cameras' footage to the gossip shows. Coverage of Paragons in their cups always guaranteed a good audience.

The Paragons also attracted groupies in great numbers, men and women and everything in between, looking for autographs, good stories, sex, a spot of hero worship, or just to hang out in such excellent company. The Paragons tolerated them, as long as they didn't make a fuss, and paid for their own drinks. Some nights the bar was so packed with gorgeous men and women that you couldn't get in the front door unless someone breathed in to make some room. The bar's owner hired extra staff, paid them danger money, learned not to wince when his furniture got broken up, and kept the place open twenty-four hours a day. People came and went, drink flowed like it was going to be made illegal tomorrow, and the party never ended. There was singing and dancing and much fondling of bare flesh, and always a fight or two going on somewhere, because living legends just couldn't turn down an opportunity to test how good certain people really were. Since they were Paragons, the duels were nearly always entirely good-natured, and rarely needed the regeneration machine the owner had installed out the back, just in case.

The joint was jumping when Lewis Deathstalker walked in, even though it was early in the afternoon. The air was thick with smoke and general bonhomie, and the din was deafening. Someone had started a poker school, and someone else was losing loudly. A woman dancing on a table was taking her clothes off very slowly, to general approval. One Paragon was painting a mural on a wall. Another was urinating in the cuspidor. A group in a corner were singing a bawdy drinking song, while another group were lurching back and forth before them, fondly imagining they were dancing. The Paragons, the King's Justice, the best of the best; pissed as farts and twice as useless. Lewis considered the damage a terrorist could do just by lobbing a grenade through the door and running like hell, and then decided he was better off not thinking about things like that. He was sure someone was on guard. Somewhere.

Lewis paused just inside the doorway, looking about him. No-one paid him much attention, even in his specially-designed black leather armour. In fact, this was probably one of the few places he could go and not be immediately approached and fawned over. Here, he was just another Paragon. Or rather; he used to be just another Paragon. He was the Champion now, like it or not. Lewis deliberately pushed that thought aside, and slowly made his way through the crush of the crowd, heading for a familiar face he'd spotted at the bar.

He needed to be among friends and colleagues. People he could talk to. People who would understand.

Veronica Mae Savage, Paragon for Tiger Mountain (a Rim world famous for possessing neither mountains nor anything remotely like a tiger), was leaning against the bar with a pint glass in her hand, holding forth to a group of handsome and well-bred young men, who were hanging on her every word and laughing loudly at jokes they shouldn't even have been able to understand, if they were really as well-bred as they seemed. In fact, one of them was demonstrating how he could use part of his anatomy as a swizzle stick. Veronica Mae spotted Lewis approaching, bellowed his name above the din, and beckoned him over with an accommodating wave. The good-looking young men reluctantly made room for him next to their heroine, and she leaned precariously off her bar stool to kiss him loudly on both cheeks.

'Well, well, look who it isn't! Lewis bloody Deathstalker, his own bad self! Looking good, Lewis . . . sit down with me and have several drinks. One of these boys will pay. If they know what's good for them. Good boys, good boys . . . and such excellent taste. Got anything you want signed, boys? I sign anything, up to and including body parts.' She drank thirstily from her tall glass, and then blinked owlishly at Lewis, ignoring the froth on her upper lip. 'Love the black leather, Lewis. It's so not you. Want to see my piercings?'

Lewis allowed one of her groupies to buy him a cold beer, and sat down opposite Veronica Mae. The other groupies pressed as close as they could, to make it clear they had no intention of being excluded from the conversation. Veronica Mae grinned sloppily with her pale pink mouth, a medium tall and more than a little stocky woman, with a broad face under a mass of golden curls, held down by a big floppy tam-o'-shanter. It had been twenty years and more since she left her homeworld of New Caliban, but she still wore the heavy tweed cloak of her upbringing. She'd brightened up her Paragon's armour with extra steel spikes and studs, and wore a knuckle duster on her left hand. Even in bed. Savage by name and by nature, Veronica Mae was past her best years, but as yet no-one had worked up the courage or death-wish to tell her that. She'd come to her post relatively late in life, and next to Finn was the longest-serving Paragon in the Empire.

'So, Lewis; what are you doing here?' Veronica Mae said flatly. 'Been . . . what, four years since we worked together on the firejewels mystery, out by the Burning Waterfalls? *Five* years? Jesus, where does the time go? Anyway; didn't expect to see you here. Didn't think you'd want to mix with us lower orders any more. Not now you're the Imperial Champion.'

Lewis shrugged uncomfortably. 'I'm still a Paragon at heart.'

'You're the Champion,' Veronica Mae said forcefully. 'King's bodyguard. And good luck to you; always said you were a better choice than the Durandal. Worked with him once. Never again. Humourless bastard. Got all huffy, just because I put my hand on his knee. Pretty face and a really nice arse, but no fire in his boiler. All he cares about is looking good for the media. What are you doing here, Lewis? This is a Paragon bar.'

'Just thought I'd talk with some old friends,' said Lewis, trying to keep it light. 'Catch up on what's happening. You know; just hang out.'

Veronica Mae looked at him, almost pityingly. 'You're not a

Paragon, and you're not a groupie. What other business could you have here, Lewis? Go back to the Court. Or Parliament. That's where you belong now, Champion. Now if you'll excuse me, me and the boys have some serious drinking and revelling to do. Not necessarily in that order. Isn't that right, boys?'

The boys agreed loudly, and almost came to blows over whose turn it was to light her cigarette. Lewis nodded stiffly, and moved away from the bar. He wandered through the crowd, smiling at familiar faces, but wherever he went he heard the same thing. These people, who had once been his friends and his peers, many of whom had fought and bled beside him, no longer saw him as one of their own. They were always polite, even friendly, and some of the younger faces were even a little awed by his famous career and legendary name; but in small and telling ways he was made to feel like an outsider, and not entirely welcome. He had moved on, they intimated, and left his old friends behind. This was a Paragon's bar . . . and he had no place there. It was all very courteous, but no less definite for that. No-one actually turned their back on him, but they might as well have. Lewis felt excluded. Isolated and alone, even in the middle of a crowd. When he finally gave up, and quietly left, no-one even noticed.

He found another bar on another street, quiet and almost deserted, and retired to a private booth at the back with his own bottle of wine, to do some serious thinking. He'd gone to *The Sangreal* hoping for a little friendly advice, but not for the first time, it seemed he'd have to sort out his problems on his own. He couldn't talk to Douglas. Or rather, he could, but he didn't want to. He'd always found it embarrassing to discuss financial matters with someone as rich as Douglas Campbell. And he couldn't talk to Anne, because she'd go straight to Douglas. Lewis poured himself another glass of Elfshot, the wine so golden it almost glowed in the gloom of the booth, and glowered into it.

Du Bois had cut off his allowance. Virimonde's Member for Parliament had sent him a curt little note, saying that the monies raised by public subscription would be paid instead to Virimonde's next Paragon, as soon as one was chosen. In the meantime, Lewis was the King's Champion, and so he should look to the King for financial support in future. It wasn't an entirely unexpected blow, not after their last conversation, but it still hit Lewis hard. Over the years, he'd become used to relying on his planet's backup stipend. His wages hadn't changed now he was Champion, but he'd had to move to a new apartment, in the very best part of the city, so he could be close to his work. By rights he should have had his own rooms in the Court, right next to Douglas'; but it had been so long since there'd been an Imperial Champion that the details were still being worked out. In particular, whether the King or Parliament was responsible for the Champion's expenses.

Lewis' new place was very nice, very comfortable, with an absolutely spectacular view, but the rent alone ate up all his wages. The few sticks of furniture he'd brought with him looked lonely and out of place in their new elegant surroundings, and he was currently sleeping on a mattress on the floor of his new bedroom. He didn't even have a vidscreen. He had some savings, but not a lot. Luckily he didn't have any expensive tastes or hobbies; and the way things were going he wasn't going to get the chance to develop any. So; what choices did that leave him? Endorsements, merchandising, action figures? Lewis pulled a face. He'd always thought such things cheapened the post of Paragon, and that went double for being Champion. He didn't want to start off his new career by undermining the dignity of his new position.

Of course, Douglas would give him as much money as he wanted, just for the asking. But Lewis didn't want to ask. He shouldn't *have* to ask . . . More than ever, Lewis needed to feel he was his own man, separate and distinct from the King. Independent. But . . . he had bills to pay. Some of them had been around for a while, too. His creditors were being very patient, because he was, after all, *Lewis Deathstalker*; but sooner or later they would have to be paid. The last thing Lewis, or Douglas, needed was his new Champion being dunned in the courts for monies he owed . . .

Lewis sighed, and stared moodily into his glass. He couldn't even get drunk. Bad for the public image. Someone would see and tell; someone always did. Lewis pushed his glass away, and buried his face in his hands. He'd been so proud, so happy, the day he was acclaimed Champion. He'd thought he'd reached the peak of his career. How could it all go so wrong, so quickly? He lifted his head, and snorted quietly. Deathstalker luck. Always bad. Ask Owen.

If you could find him.

The Empress Lionstone XIV, tall and lithe and impossibly beautiful, sat in state upon her great Throne of black iron and gleaming jade, wrapped in the snow white furs of extinct animals, the diamond Crown of Empire shining on her elegant head like a star. She smiled her approval on the thirteen members of the Shadow Court as they assembled before her, to bow and curtsey and show their respect. Lionstone, the glorious and adored, powerful beyond hope and mercy, last of a fabled line. It was a pity she was just a hologram recording, but the Shadow Court was used to having to make do with second best.

The thirteen men and women, anonymous in enveloping black cloaks and black silk masks, even their voices electronically masked and altered, met in secret once a month, to plot the downfall of King and Parliament and the modern order, and plan sedition. The old ways of revenge and vendetta had never been forgotten. Each one present was a descendant of a once mighty Family, and dreamed of the day when the Clans would rise again, to tear down the hated institutions of democracy and mediocrity, and take back the power and influence that was theirs by right. The old names were long gone, of course. No more Wolfes, or Chojiros or Shrecks. The old names had become curses on the lips of the modern Empire. But though the Families had long ago given up their ancient names, along with their long-established privileges, to make new identities for themselves in the worlds of trade and business, still they never forgot what they had once been, and had sworn to be again. One day.

Thirteen men and women, all of them rich and powerful in their own right, who hungered always for the one thing their riches couldn't buy them. To be acknowledged by all as naturally superior.

None of them had ever seen each other's faces, so that even if captured they couldn't be made to betray each other. It was enough that they were of the Families; for one aristo can always spot another. They met together in the most obvious place of all; Lionstone's old Court, in its steel bunker miles below the surface of the planet, deep and deep beneath the bedrock on which the Parade of the Endless rested. Officially the old Court had been abandoned and closed down hundreds of years ago; too full of bad memories even to be preserved as a museum. Armed guards had been set to watch over the only entrance, and only a few people now knew exactly where the old Court was. Lionstone herself didn't even have a grave, or a tombstone.

The Shadow Court never forgot. So they gradually replaced the guards with their own people, over a period of years, and slowly and carefully infiltrated the security forces and made them theirs too. And then the old Court was theirs again, to do with as they wished. The Shadow Court didn't dare awaken the bunker to its full glory, when wide-reaching holos had transformed the old Court into a world all of its own, full of wonders and marvels. That much power use would have been sure to be noticed somewhere. But they indulged themselves with the single holo of Lionstone's ghost, watching from her Throne. A taste of a more glorious past. They liked to think she would have approved of them, and what they meant to do.

It never occurred to them that they were the ghosts, shadows of what the Families had once been.

Secure behind his concealing mask, Tel Markham, MP for Madraguda, sat at ease in his very comfortable chair, looking out across the antique ironwood table at his fellow conspirators. Tel Markham was a man of many secrets. He was a well-established, even honoured politician, a public supporter of all the right good causes, and a member in good standing of many secret societies, including Pure Humanity; but all his roles, public and private, were nothing more than means to an end: to making Tel Markham a man of real power, in a new order where he wouldn't have to endlessly scrape and bow to lesser people and breeds. When his word and every whim would be law, and life and death were his to control and decide. When he could be a Silvestri once again, and hold his head up high. The better to look down his nose at everybody else.

The families who had once been Clans were nearly all very rich these days, and wielded all kinds of influence on all kinds of levels, but that was not enough for them, not nearly enough. And since they weren't strong enough to force the changes they wanted so desperately, they moved secretly and indirectly behind the scenes, undermining important people and institutions with a push here and a bribe there, spreading fear and confusion among their many enemies. And always pushing in many small and subtle ways for the return and re-establishing of the Clans to their rightful position.

Their greatest triumph to date was the creation of a phenomenally successful vid soap; *The Quality*. It ran twice a day on all the major channels, with an omnibus edition at the weekend; a supposedly historical series, set in pre-Rebellion days, concerned almost wholly with sex, sin and scandal among the aristocracy of Lionstone's time. All fictitious names, of course, and nothing even remotely based on reality. It was very romantic, very glamorous, and *very* popular.

The series featured larger than life characters, in gorgeous costumes, impossibly handsome and radiantly beautiful, scheming and plotting and falling in and out of love and in and out of bed; and billions of people watched every episode. The Quality were the people you loved to hate, and secretly admired, and even the most minor characters had massive fan bases. Their look dictated fashion, and their catch phrases were on everyone's lips. The show spawned dozens of style and gossip magazines, and made everyone involved very rich indeed. Money was coming in so fast that even the media accountants couldn't hide it all.

As a direct result, the general image and popular perception of the aristocracy had never been better. Which was, after all, the point.

The Shadow Court had its people everywhere. They knew

all about Finn Durandal. What he was doing, and what he planned, even if some of his actions and intentions frankly baffled them. Many of the Shadow Court were still undecided as to whether the Durandal was fiendishly clever, or a complete looney tune. This particular Session of the Shadow Court had been specifically called to decided what (if anything) should be done about him.

'I say bring him in,' Tel Markham proposed flatly. 'As things stand he's an unknown factor, a wild card, accountable to no-one. Who knows what he might do, in the name of his wounded pride? He might think he's being subtle, but left to his own devices it's only a matter of time before the powers that be will notice that he's not at all the man he used to be. Bring him in, make him one of us, and then we can guide and control his efforts. He has a right to be here. His people were Quality once.'

'The Lord Durandal was a hero, back in the old days,' said a woman in a black silk mask liberally spotted with sequins. She fanned herself langorously with a paper fan decorated with erotic images. 'He went into the Darkvoid in search of lost Haden, and was never seen again. I say we have this character written into our soap; play up the legendary qualities of the Durandal name. So that if we do choose to embrace young Finn, the public will already be conditioned to adore his *aristocratic* name.'

'What makes you think Finn would want any part of us?' said a clear deep voice, from a man so fat he lay reclining in an antigrav chair, floating beside the table. Someone that size should have been immediately identifiable, and it bothered the others immensely that even after all these years, they still had no idea who he might be. The fat man smiled wetly, spreading his huge soft hands in an expansive gesture. 'Finn has his own plans, and his own intentions, and might not take kindly to the suggestion that he should subordinate his desires to ours.'

'Sweeten the pot enough, and he'll come to us,' Tel Markham said confidently. 'There are definite limits to what he can hope to achieve, with his limited resources and the kind of rabble he's gathering about him. The Rookery is fine for providing specialist advice and cannon fodder, but to bring about the kind of revenge he hungers for, he's going to need widespread popular support; and for that he's going to need an organisation like ours.'

'Approach him,' said a woman whose silk mask had been cunningly fashioned into a stylised bird of prey. 'Sound him out; see if he's what we think he is. From a safe distance, of course.'

'Of course,' said Tel Markham. 'He'll never know how far deep he's in . . . until it's far too late for him to say no.'

Brett Random mooched around Finn Durandal's living room, looking for something decent to drink. He pushed back a few likely-looking panels in the walls, uncovering a speed oven, a bookcase of paperbacks with cracked spines, and a collection of frankly ugly porcelain figures, before finally locating a tasteful polished wood wine rack, with the bottles lying properly on their sides. Brett pulled out half a dozen, and sneered at the labels. Why do rich people always buy such rubbish? To hell with taste or discernment; just buy whatever's fashionable, whatever the glossy lifestyle magazines are plugging that month. There was nothing of any real quality, and a few domestic reds that Brett wouldn't have used as mouthwash. He finally settled for a fairly reasonable Elfshot vintage, as the best of a bad bunch, just to be doing something with his hands. Brett was nervous.

This was the first time the Durandal had invited Brett and Rose back to his place. Having seen it, Brett could understand why. The apartment was located in an excellent neighbourhood, but the interior was cosy if you were feeling charitable, and cramped if you weren't. The furniture was mass-produced shit, functional father than aesthetic, and only borderline comfortable. The walls boasted a colour scheme that bordered on the soporific, and the grey (grey!) carpet clearly hadn't been shampooed in years. One wall was taken up almost entirely with a massive vidscreen, currently inactive, while another had been programmed to show a holoscene of a seaside view. No sound option. And that was it for the decorations. Brett took a wild guess, and decided that Finn probably didn't spend a lot of time here. This wasn't a home, or even a den; just some place to crash when you weren't working.

Rose was still sitting patiently in the chair Finn had directed her to, staring at nothing in particular. She didn't seem at all interested in her surroundings, but then, outside of the Arena, the Wild Rose didn't seem to care much about anything. She was just sitting there until Finn came to tell her it was time to be somewhere else. She was relaxed, in the way a cat is relaxed as it waits patiently outside a mousehole.

Brett poured himself a very large drink, and downed half of it in several large gulps. It didn't make him feel any better. He threw himself sulkily into the nearest chair, and scowled unhappily. He didn't want to be here. He wanted to go home, lock and bolt the door against the unfriendly world, feed his aching stomach something warm and liquid and soothing, and then crawl into bed and escape into sleep, so he could forget about the mess his life had become, and having to work with crazy people like Rose Constantine and Finn bloody Durandal. Brett glared sullenly at the closed study door. Finn had been in there for some time now, running checks on the esper drug he'd purchased from Dr Happy, at a price that had made Brett feel like screaming. Or fainting. Or both. Brett could have told Finn he was wasting his time doing whatever he was doing in his study with the door locked. The good doctor took pride in the quality of his wares.

Finn still hadn't explained what he wanted with the esper drug. All right, Brett could see how having their own personal telepath could come in handy in all sorts of ways, but it would be easier and safer all round just to hire a rogue esper. There were always a few to be found hiding out in the Rookery, human nature being what it was, and they weren't all mean or weird, like the ELFs.

Maybe Finn had taken it, after all. Maybe his pride wouldn't let him waste such an expensive drug on just anybody. And someone with an ego like his would believe he could beat the odds after all. Maybe Finn had taken the drug, and dropped down dead! Brett brightened at the thought. He sat up straight in his chair, and regarded the closed study door with new interest. If Finn was dead . . . one quick round of the appartment to steal everything worth having that wasn't nailed down, and then he would be out of here so fast it would make Rose's head spin. And it was up to her if she wanted to hang around and explain the body to the peacekeepers. Brett smiled, and his stomach actually settled a little.

And then he jumped and spilt his drink, as the study door crashed open and Finn came striding out. He was holding a test tube full of clear liquid in one hand, and smiling broadly. Brett's heart sank, not least because Finn was smiling at him. Bad news was never far away when the Durandal smiled at him.

'You know, Finn, I really should be getting home,' Brett said hopefully. 'I'm sure I left a light on somewhere . . .'

'Stand up, Brett.'

'You did say I could help myself to a drink,' Brett protested, rising slowly and very unwillingly to his feet. There was a look in Finn's eyes that he didn't like at all. 'You heard him say I could have a drink, didn't you, Rose?'

'Shut up, Brett. You stand up too, Rose,' said Finn.

The Wild Rose was up and on her feet in one casual lithe movement. Anywhen else, Brett might have applauded. Her crimson leathers squeaked softly, pulling tight across her impressive chest. Brett tried hard not to look at her breasts. Finn advanced on him, and Brett automatically looked around for the nearest exit. The Durandal clearly had something in mind, and Brett just knew that when he found out what it was, he wasn't going to like it at all. Finn nodded casually to Rose.

'Hold Brett securely, Rose, but don't hurt him.'

Brett's hand was already diving for the dagger up his sleeve when Rose's arms swept around him from behind, pinning his arms to his sides, and crushing the breath from his lungs. He struggled anyway, kicking back at her legs, and even jerking his head back at where Rose's face should have been, but she held him as easily as a child, her arms like steel bars. Finn advanced unhurriedly on Brett, and something in Finn's smile put a whole new chill in Brett's heart. Finn stopped right in front of Brett, and regarded him solemnly for a moment, like a scientist with an interesting new lab rat. Brett made a small whimpering sound.

'Relax, Brett,' Finn said easily. 'I'm not going to kill you. I wouldn't do that; not while you can still be useful to me. And there's the problem, you see. I really think I've had the best of you, when it comes to rooting out useful contacts for me in the Rookery. I've got everyone I need now. Which means your usefulness is unfortunately at an end. But I can't just let you go. You'd talk. Your kind always talks, eventually. So if I'm to keep you with me, I have to make some other use for you. And that's where the esper drug comes in. I can see all sorts of uses for my own personal telepath. And as you quite rightly pointed out; I'm not stupid enough to take the drug myself. So; open wide, swallow properly, and afterwards you can have a nice sweetie.'

'You're crazy!' said Brett, his voice little more than a whisper. 'I'm not taking that stuff!'

'You don't have to worry; I've tested it. The dose is one hundred per cent pure.'

'It kills people! Or drives them crazy!'

'Well, yes, there is that possibility. But if you don't take it, I will quite definitely have Rose kill you, right here and now.'

He reached out suddenly and grabbed Brett by the right ear, twisting it cruelly. Brett's mouth opened automatically at the pain, and Finn fed him the contents of the test tube in his other hand. He then held Brett's mouth closed until he had to swallow, and nodded to Rose to release him. She let go immediately and stepped back, and she and Finn watched interestedly as Brett sank to his knees, coughing and spluttering, his arms wrapped tightly around his stomach. His face was already deathly pale, with beads of sweat popping out on his forehead. His whole body began to shake and shudder, as though a great engine had been switched on inside him. His eyes clenched shut, and he let out a great groan, a sound far too loud for such a small man.

For Brett, it was though someone had turned up the volume level all over the world. Voices crashed in on him from all sides, as though the whole city was shouting at him at once. Flashes of vision came and went, glimpses of people and places cutting in and out impossibly fast. Thoughts slammed back and forth inside his head, and only some of them were his. Sound and vision became hopelessly intertangled, more and more rushing in until he thought his skull would explode from trying to contain them all. He'd fallen over onto his side, though he didn't know it, curled into a foetal ball. His eyes were very wide, full of all the spectacle of the world, and his head was full of sound and fury, drowning out his own small thoughts. Esp had let all the world in at once, and he had no defences against it.

In the end, it was the stomach cramps that saved him. The nagging familiar pains were still sharp enough to penetrate even the frenzy raging inside his head, and it was the one thing he could cling to, the one thing he knew was his, and his alone. He concentrated on the pain, hugging it jealously to him, using it as a kernel he could rebuild himself around, slowly pushing out everything that wasn't him. One by one he forced the voices back outside his head, where they belonged, and slowly built new mental lids to close over his staring eyes. Until finally he came back to himself, a man alone again, shuddering and sweating and gasping for breath, lying limp as a discarded rag on Finn's harsh grey carpet.

Brett Random; telepath.

'You bastards,' he said thickly, tiredly. 'You bloody, bloody bastards.'

'Welcome back, Brett,' Finn said happily. 'I was almost sure you would survive. Somehow I just knew someone with your survival instincts would find a way to pull through. So what are you; telepath, precog, polter? Or is it too early to tell yet? No matter. Oh Brett, we're going to have such fun, working out what you can do to help me with your new abilities. You'll thank me, when you've had time to think about it. Rose, help Brett up, and into a chair. Yes, I know he's rather sweaty and unpleasant at the moment, but we all have to make sacrifices for the cause. Besides; it's not that different from his usual state, really.'

Rose leant over Brett and took him by the shoulder with one hand, and then both of them froze where they were as

191

their minds slammed together, triggered by the proximity, each of them transfixed in the glaring light of a naked soul. For a moment that had something of forever in it, their thoughts and personalities meshed and mingled, held in the iron grip of Brett's new found talent. For Brett it was like looking into the sun, blinded by the overwhelming glare of a remorseless, single-minded will, but beyond that he could sense something else; a need like an endless hunger, a despairing need for something Rose couldn't even name. In anyone else, it would have been a need for love, friendship, companions; but such concepts were alien to Rose. She only knew . . . that she needed.

For Rose, it was like watching a flower unfold, showing new and endless possibilities. She'd never known that the world could be so large, that people could have such potential. Much of what she saw in Brett's mind was alien and confusing to her, like discovering new colours in the rainbow. Brett could feel her digging through his thoughts, trying to make sense of what she found there, and was frightened by a will so much more focused and icy cold than his own. He concentrated, clumsily manipulating his new abilities, and finally closed a mental door between them. And as suddenly as that they fell back into their own heads, two separate souls again. It had only lasted a moment, but in that endless time many things had changed, forever. Brett looked up at Rose, and she looked curiously down at him.

'That was . . . different,' she said finally. 'I never felt anything like that before. For a while there, you were as real to me as I was.'

'Telepathy!' Finn said happily, clapping his hands together. 'What did it feel like?'

'Shut up,' said Rose, not looking round, and Finn did. Rose was still staring into Brett's eyes, as though trying to re-establish the connection between them. 'There's so much inside you, Brett. Your mind . . . it's so busy, so cluttered, with thoughts and . . . things. Feelings . . .'

'And you're so alone,' said Brett. 'How can you stand to be so alone?'

'I thought everyone was like that,' said Rose. 'I didn't

know . . . I had no idea . . . I'm going to have to think about this.'

She hauled him roughly but efficiently to his feet, and dropped him into his chair again. Her face was cold as ever, her mouth as cruel, but Brett thought there was something new in her eyes. He looked away. He couldn't cope with anything but his own problems for the moment. He tugged a grubby handkerchief from his pocket and mopped the cold sweat from his face. His hands were still shaking. Rose sat down in her chair again, her gaze calm but far away. Finn studied them both, with a sardonic raised eyebrow.

'If I didn't know better, I'd swear the two of you were bonding. You have no idea how much the very idea revolts me.'

Lewis Deathstalker stood on the edge of the main landing pad of Logres' biggest starport, and pulled his heavy cloak about him. There was a cold wind blowing. Normally, no-one except essential staff were allowed out onto the pads, but Lewis had never let such petty technicalities stop him before when he was a Paragon, and certainly not now he was the Champion. Back in the main terminal a few officious little jobsworths had tried to argue the point with him, only to go all uncertain and tongue-tied when Lewis gave them his best thoughtful stare. He was very proud of that stare. He'd put a lot of thought and effort into getting it just right, so that it suggested all kinds of imminent violence and unpleasantness, if not actual mayhem, and generally appalling possibilities. In the past, some villains had actually dropped their weapons and begged to be arrested, rather than have Lewis look at them in that particular thoughtful way.

It was a bright sunny afternoon, despite the chill, with a pale blue sky and not a cloud anywhere. The main landing pad was huge, bigger than some city blocks, and the docked starcruisers rose up before Lewis like so many steel mountains, the tops of their shimmering steel hulls lost to sight in the glare of the sun. *The Hammer*, *The Highlander* and *The Hector* were all in port, waiting for new crews or new equipment or just a little downtime between missions. There were dozens of other, smaller craft, scattered across the pads stretching away before him, but Lewis only had eyes for the newly-arrived *Highlander*, fresh in from Xanadu. Douglas' long-promised replacement as Paragon for Logres had finally arrived; the famous, or perhaps more properly infamous, Emma Steel.

Even among the inflated reputations of the Paragons, Emma Steel had almost more reputation than one person could comfortably bear. She'd been born and raised on Mistworld, which explained a lot. Mistworld, once the only rebel planet in Lionstone's Empire, was still a wild and woolly and largely uncivilised place, mostly because its inhabitants preferred it that way. They had no intentions of going soft, just in case this whole Golden Age thing turned out to be nothing more than a passing fad. They kept themselves to themselves, discouraged tourists, tax-gatherers, and anyone else showing too much interest in their affairs. Emma was the first Paragon Mistworld had ever got around to producing, and she took her position and her responsibilties very seriously.

She was a tenacious tracker, specialising in pursuing the criminals who eluded everyone else. No-one could hide from Emma Steel. They could change their names, their faces, and their whole damned bodies, purge their presence from every known computer, and jump from planet to planet in a freight ship, inside a packing crate marked *Machine Parts*, and still Emma would sniff them out. She always brought her prey back, even if she had to do it in several small refrigerated containers.

It helped that she wasn't impressed by anybody, and was always ready to browbeat, intimidate and if necessary slap around any poor fool who thought his position gave him the authority to get in her way. Emma worked from the position that everyone was guilty of something, and it was a sad fact that she was right more often than she was wrong. She was the only Paragon not to attend Douglas' Coronation, because she'd been in the middle of a case, and Emma Steel didn't break off from the chase for anyone or anything. With anyone else that would have been treason, but this was Emma Steel, so everyone just shrugged, and made allowances. Everyone made allowances for Emma Steel. Even King Douglas. He understood it was nothing personal. It was just Emma being Emma.

Either way, news of her new position on Logres had finally caught up with her, and she made arrangements for her latest catch to be sent home in irons, and hitched a lift on the closest ship. She'd sent word she'd be arriving today. Lewis checked the watchface embedded in his wrist again, and shrugged. It was well known that while Emma had many sterling qualities, punctuality wasn't always one of them. Lewis sighed, folded his arms across his chest, and shifted his stance slightly. The black leather armour creaked loudly, and Lewis shook his head exasperatedly. Douglas' personal tailors had had three goes at refitting the armour, and it still didn't feel comfortable. Lewis had taken to wearing his old Paragon's purple cloak over it, and that at least made him feel a little less conspicuous.

Anne had proved entirely unsympathetic when he raised the matter with her. *It's important you look the part*, she kept saying. *That armour is designed to send a message. It's a style statement. Trust me, you look every inch a Champion.* In return, Lewis had said something short and cutting, in which the words *pratt* and *pimp* featured strongly, and Anne had thrown her coffee cup at him, and then giggled till she got hiccups.

A figure came striding suddenly out of the shadows under *The Highlander*'s hull, heading right for him, and Lewis straightened up to his full height. He wanted to make a good first impression. Of course he was the Champion, and she was just another Paragon, but still . . . this was Emma Steel. Voted scariest person in the Empire for the third year running. One magazine editor had offered a million credits for her to do a nude photoshoot. Emma sent the editor a severed head in a box. Lewis studied Emma openly as she strode quickly towards him, her long legs eating up the distance between them. The official holos on her tribute site didn't do her justice. In person, Emma Steel radiated personality like a blast furnace.

She was tall and willowy and almost impossibly graceful in her every movement. Her skin was a dark coffee colour, and she wore her flat black hair pulled back and tied in a tight bun on the back of her head. Striking rather than pretty, she was still utterly breathtaking. She carried her Paragon's armour well, and her purple cloak flapped about her like the wings of a bird of prey. Her long-fingered hands never moved far from the sword and gun on her hips.

She marched right up to Lewis, looked him up and down, nodded curtly and stuck out a hand for him to shake. When he took it, she gave his hand a brief knuckle-crushing shake, and then pulled him forward into a fierce embrace that drove half the breath out of him. She kissed him loudly on each cheek, rapped him on the armoured chest with a knuckle, nodded at the sound it made, and then stepped back to nod approvingly at Lewis.

'Deathstalker!' she said loudly, in a deep thrilling contralto. 'Good to meet you at last. Love the armour. Congratulations on your new post. You earned it. Would have liked to be there for the Coronation, but I had to chase that Hellfire creep over half of Xanadu before I finally ran him down. I did send a card, and a present.'

'Ah yes,' said Lewis. 'The flower that eats insects. And small rodents. Douglas was . . . very impressed. Welcome to Logres, Emma. Your reputation precedes you.'

'Don't believe a word of it,' Emma said briskly. 'No law-abiding citizen has anything to fear from me. It's just that I never seem to meet any.' She looked around her, and suddenly she was grinning widely. It transformed her face, making her look a lot younger than her early thirties, and not nearly so daunting. 'God, I love this place! Biggest starport in the Empire. I grew up around Mistworld's starport; my great grandfather used to run it. Romantic places, starports. Always people coming and going, dropping in from fabulous far-off places. Families parting and meeting . . . and more crimes and scams and generally dirty dealing than any other place you can name. Mind you; Customs and Immigration here are crap. No-one's challenged me at all yet.'

'They're probably still trying to find someone daft enough to try,' said Lewis. 'Do you have anything to declare?'

'Only my magnificence,' Emma said, and then laughed

loudly. 'No media here today? There's usually half a dozen news crews waiting to greet me whenever I step off a starship.'

'The King wants to keep your presence here under wraps, until he's had a chance to bring you up to speed,' said Lewis. 'Once the local bad guys find out you've arrived, they'll either go to ground or head for the hills. Besides; the situation here is . . . more complicated than you might think.'

Emma shrugged easily. 'Isn't it always? I never get the simple assignments. So; tell me all about the legendary Finn Durandal. I'm a fan, of long standing. Studied all his major cases, and watched all five of the documentaries on him. It was because of him that I determined to become a Paragon. Mistworld's first. I'm really looking forward to working with him. You were his partner for years; what's he really like?'

'Ah,' said Lewis. 'That's part of the problem. Finn rather thought he was going to be chosen as Champion. In fact, he set his heart on it. He took it very hard when Douglas named me instead. As a result, Finn . . . isn't as focused on his work as he once was. In fact, no-one's seen much of him at all since the Coronation.'

Emma gave Lewis a hard look. 'Are you tell me that he's sulking? That the legendary Finn Durandal is off sitting in a corner somewhere, pouting?'

'Well, basically; yes. I'm sure he'll get over it, in time. But until he does, you're going to have to take up the slack. And since Douglas is the King and I'm the Champion, that just leaves you to be Logres' Paragon. I hope you know how to hit the ground running.'

'Wonderful,' said Emma. She pursed her large mouth and spat on the ground, uncomfortably close to Lewis' boot. She glared at him as though it was all his fault, and then sniffed loudly, and shrugged. 'I should have known it was too good to be true. I did wonder why they chose a wild card like me. Still; it's not the first time I've been dropped in the deep end with lead weights on my boots. Don't you worry, Deathstalker; I can hold my end up.' She grinned suddenly, and once again looked almost girlish. 'I can't wait to get stuck in. This is a major step up on the career ladder for me; defender of Humanity's homeworld. Back on Mistworld, I dreamed of coming here . . . A chance to show what I can really do! Face some real challenges at last. Screw the Durandal. Give me a year here, and people will have forgotten all about him. I'm going to take Logres by the scruff of the neck and shake it till all the filth drops off; you see if I don't.'

Lewis had to smile. She reminded him irresistibly of a younger, less cynical Lewis Deathstalker, from when he first came to Logres; so confident, so full of himself, of all the great things he was going to do. His smile slowly faded, as he considered how far he'd come from that naïve and optimistic young man. He'd achieved a great many things in his time, done a good job . . . but at the end of the day the world still went as the world went. The Shadow Court was still out there somewhere, and the Hellfire Club. And the poisonous lies of Pure Humanity seemed to reach more receptive ears all the time . . . Lewis shrugged mentally. Maybe Emma Steel was just what they all needed; someone to shake them out of their complacency.

And then Lewis all but jumped out of his skin as Emma roared with a parade ground voice, right in his ear; 'You! I see you! Stop that right now!'

She charged right past Lewis, racing across the landing pad, her long legs driving her at incredible speed, her sword and her gun already in her hands. Lewis chased after her, glaring about him for some sign of the enemy, doing his best not to fall too far behind. Surely the ELFs couldn't have struck again already, so soon after their debacle at the Arena? Or maybe it was another Neuman suicide bomber? Everything seemed quiet and peaceful, as far as he could see, but he trusted Emma's instincts. He drew his sword and gun too, and pounded after her as she headed for the baggage area.

And that was where she finally skidded to a halt, gun aimed squarely at two terrified luggage handlers, who couldn't get their hands in the air fast enough. Lewis crashed to a halt beside her, and had to stop for a moment to get his breath back before he could speak. Emma wasn't even breathing hard.

'You're both under arrest!' she said crisply. 'Hands on top of your heads, and don't even think about running or I'll blow your kneecaps out. Did you really think you could get away with this, right under my nose?'

'Get away with what?' said Lewis, just a little plaintively. 'What's the problem? I thought we were after terrorists. They're luggage handlers. All right, there have been times when I've felt like shooting them too, when my trunk's ended up on a whole different planet, with all my spare clothes in it, but . . .'

'They're running a scam,' said Emma. 'And a pretty obvious one, at that. They run the cases through that portable scanner there, detect the good stuff, and mark the cases with a secret sign that only shows up under ultraviolet. Someone at the other end will intercept the marked cases before they even reach the carousel inside the terminal, and then they'll all split the proceeds later. I told you, I grew up around a starport. There isn't a con or a dodge that I can't spot.'

'And that's it? All this, for a couple of con men?' Lewis shook his head, and put away his gun. 'Jesus, I nearly had a coronary. I haven't run that fast since that bomb disposal guy said *oh shit* and threw himself out the window. And you wouldn't believe where this leather's chafing me. Emma; this is peacekeeper work. Not something a Paragon needs to get involved with. Anything else you see, just contact port security, and let them handle it.'

'Be your age, Deathstalker,' said Emma. 'Port security are part of the scam. That's how it works.'

She rounded up her quivering charges and marched them at gunpoint to the starport brig, where she made sure they were officially charged and securely locked up before leaving, with a stern warning to everyone present that she would be back later to check on how the investigation was going. Lewis trailed after her, feeling distinctly superfluous.

'You really don't need to get this personally involved with low level crime like that,' he said later, after they'd picked up her very minimal luggage and left the terminal. 'You're Logres' Paragon now. Which means you don't have to sweat over the small stuff. Or you'll have no time or energy left to deal with the real trouble when it breaks. You have to take a larger view.'

'Real trouble?' said Emma immediately, her ears pricking up.

'ELFs, devils, Shadow Court assassins. Neumen riots. That's when we get called in, when the peacekeepers can't cope. That's Paragon business.'

'Any crime or injustice is my business,' Emma said briskly, toting her single suitcase with one hand, as though it weighed nothing. 'Especially when someone's stupid enough to do it right in front of me.'

Lewis manfully suppressed another sigh. He'd been just the same when he first arrived on Logres. No-one could tell him anything either. Hopefully she wouldn't take as long as he did to learn that you had to delegate the petty stuff, or you'd drown in it.

'You're going to be very busy,' he said, diplomatically.

Lewis escorted Emma to her designated Paragon's apartment. It was a roomy enough place, for one person, in a nice enough neighbourhood. On the way there, Emma arrested three muggers, seven pickpockets, and one flasher; who was very lucky not to be shot somewhere extremely unfortunate, when Emma thought he was opening his coat to show her his gun. Lewis decided he wasn't going to hang around while she familiarised herself with her new neighbourhood. He didn't think his nerves would stand it. No; a nice quiet, solitary walk was just what he needed. He had a lot of thinking to do, about his various problems, and he thought a lot better when his pulse rate didn't keep going through the roof every ten minutes. So he bade Emma a polite farewell, endured another hug, gave her his private comm number, just in case she needed him *in an emergency*, and then left as quickly as was still courteous.

He strolled down the pleasant tree-lined boulevard, frowning just heavily enough that the passers-by left him strictly alone, and gave some serious thought to what his life had become. He liked to think that he'd done good work in his time as a Paragon, that he'd made a real difference. But it seemed that was behind him now. His visit to the *Sangreal* had made it painfully clear that his days as a Paragon were over. He was the Champion now, and it was up to him to decide what that was going to mean. He was damned if he was going to be nothing more than Douglas' bodyguard, honourable a position though that might be. Just standing around, twiddling his thumbs, waiting for something to happen. That wasn't him. He needed to be busy, to be . . . doing things. Useful things.

He needed who and what he was to matter.

He was so taken up with his own thoughts that he didn't notice as the boulevard slowly emptied of other people, until he was walking all alone. He didn't notice how quiet it had got, or that the surveillance cameras were slowly turning themselves off, one by one. He was honestly surprised when a blood-red devil appeared suddenly out of an alleyway before him, and moved quickly forward to block his path. Lewis stopped short, blinked a few times, and studied the sight before him. This particular devil was clearly the result of really first class transformation work from a major league body shop. Goat's horns curled up from a heavy lowering brow, the thin-lipped mouth was crammed full of pointed teeth, and the bent satyr's legs ended in cloven hooves. That kind of full body work cost serious credits. And the disrupter the devil was pointing directly at Lewis' head was also very much top of the line.

Lewis felt like he should applaud, but he really wasn't in the mood. He glared at the devil. 'Hellfire Club, right? Nice horns. Go away. I'm busy.'

The devil blinked resentfully, suddenly uncertain, and lowered his gun a little. 'What?'

'I said go away. I really don't have time for this right now. Go mug a tourist, or something. Give them a nice story to tell when they get back home.'

'Shut up!' said the devil, extending his hairy crimson arm to point the barrel of his gun right between Lewis' eyes. 'The Hellfire Club has marked you for death, Lewis Death-stalker!'

Lewis sighed. Just looking at the devil, he could see half a dozen ways to disarm him without putting himself at risk, but he just didn't have the energy. He was composing a really crushing remark when a second figure suddenly erupted from the alleyway, wearing the black domino mask of a Shadow Court assassin, also pointing an energy gun at Lewis.

'Say your prayers, King's Champion! The Shadow Court has sentenced you to . . . to . . . wait a minute. Get the hell away from him, you creepy little Hellfire amateur! The Deathstalker is mine!'

'The Hell he is!' snapped the devil, bringing his gun quickly round to cover the assassin. 'I got here first. Piss off.'

'You piss off, you . . . dilettante! The Shadow Court outranks whatever claim you bunch of degenerates might have on the Deathstalker. So scuttle off back to your body shop, and see if you can still get a refund. And let a real professional deal with this.'

'Excuse me,' said Lewis.

'I got here first,' the devil said stubbornly. 'I'm going to shoot him.'

'I'll shoot you first,' said the Shadow Court assassin. 'The credit for this kill is mine. Let all beware the vengeance of the aristocrats!'

'Bunch of pansies,' snapped the devil. 'Living on past glories, and bemoaning the good old days when you could still have sex with your cousin without people sniggering at you. You wouldn't have the guts to do the kind of things we do every day, just for kicks!'

'Oh yeah?' challenged the assassin. 'Like what? What do you weirdos do that's so damned special? Steal the lead off Church roofs and then urinate through the holes?'

'At least we don't marry our brothers and sisters! Look at those ears of yours. You don't get ears like that without centuries of inbreeding and a gene pool so shallow you couldn't even go wading in it. If they were any longer, you could use them to fly.'

'You bastard. You utter bastard!'

'Oh look!' crowed the devil. 'He's going to cry now!'

'I am not going to cry!'

'Excuse me,' said Lewis.

'Shut up!' snarled the assassin, covering the devil with his energy gun. 'You get out of here right now, or . . .'

'Or what? You'll stamp your little foot? Ooh, I'm dead scared, me . . .'

'That's it! You're dead!'

And that was when the third figure suddenly appeared, swooping down out of the empty sky on a gravity sled with no markings. He wore a long concealing black cloak with the hood pulled well forward to hide his face. He pulled the sled up right beside the group, and then had to stop and pull his hood back a bit so he could see what he was doing, before he could level his energy gun at Lewis.

'Kneel and beg for mercy, Deathstalker! Your life is forfeit, for interfering in the manifest destiny of Pure Humanity. The Neumen . . .'

'*Piss off!*' said the assassin, his voice rising almost hysterically. 'I don't believe this. What is this, amateur night? I am here to kill Lewis Deathstalker, and when the Shadow Court marks someone for death, they are bloody well dead. Go and find your own hero to kill.'

'We marked him for death first!' said the devil.

'Prove it!' snapped the assassin.

'I think you'll find Pure Humanity has the prior claim,' said the Neuman, climbing awkwardly down from his gravity sled. He tripped over his long cloak and almost fell, till Lewis grabbed him by the arm to steady him. The Neuman absently nodded his thanks, and glared at the other two killers. 'The Deathstalker killed our suicide bomber at Court. That makes him our target. You must have seen it. It was on all the news channels.'

'Oh, we all saw it,' said the Shadow assassin. 'Complete bloody ballsup, from beginning to end. You don't stand around making speeches, when you've come to kill someone! If he'd just shut up and done his job, he might have pulled it off, but oh no, he had to justify himself with all the usual propaganda claptrap . . .'

'Statements of intent are important!' said the Neuman. 'What's the point of a terrorist atrocity if no-one knows why you did it? There are so many fringe groups and loony tunes out there these days, it's vital to make it clear to the media whose cause you're representing; or you can bet a dozen other groups will have claimed responsibility before you can even get a press statement out.'

'Typical terrorist,' sneered the devil. 'All mouth and dogma, and no follow up. If you're going to kill someone, just kill them. Murder is a philosophical art, not a political.'

'Oh yes, you devils are really philosophical,' snapped the Neuman. 'Getting your kicks by breaking into Churchs and playing with yourselves in front of the altar. Thinking you're so daring and evil because you can recite the Lord's Prayer backwards. Get a tape recorder! You don't have an agenda. You don't even have a manifesto. Probably couldn't even spell dïalectic. No real aims, except to outrage mummy and daddy. I put it all down to late potty training, myself . . .'

'You take that back!' shouted the devil, training his gun on the Neuman. And that was when the ELF teleported in, a tall gangling girl dressed in tattered silks with wild tribal tattoos on her face, appearing right next to the group in an impressive cloud of sulphurous smoke. She'd just started to shout something about avenging her fallen brethren from the Arena when the other three immediately turned and shouted her down.

Lewis walked away, and left them to argue with each other. None of them noticed. Lewis had almost reached the end of the street before they started shooting at each other. He didn't look back.

Back at Parliament House, Lewis searched out King Douglas, and discovered he'd come back just in time to stand around and do nothing. Essentially, he got to follow Douglas as he strode rapidly through the endless warren of narrow corridors, plunging into one anonymous back room after another, where the King chaired meetings, oversaw important discussions, brought disparate sides together and generally struggled to establish his own political base by storing up favours for the future. Lewis was pointedly barred from these meetings, on the grounds that no-one cared what he had to say, and besides, political deal-making went best with the absolute minimum of witnesses. So Lewis did a lot of standing around outside closed and locked doors, looking hopefully about him for more assassins to show up to relieve the monotony.

To his credit he lasted almost two hours before his patience snapped, and he threw a major wobbly. He kicked in the door he'd been guarding, stormed into the chamber with drawn sword and gun, ignoring the startled cries of the politicians, and demanded that Douglas provide him with something useful to do before he went out of his mind with the tedium, and started using the politicians as target practice. The King studied his Champion's flushed face, and decided Lewis might just mean it. He excused himself to the top ranked civil servants he'd been negotiating with, most of whom were now hiding under the conference table and making clear noises of distress, and hustled Lewis back outside into the corridor.

'All right,' he said calmly. 'You want something useful to do, I'll oblige you. Jes has just sent word that she has some important shopping to take care of in town. I think we'll all feel a lot happier if she had someone guarding her who could be depended on. House Security promised they'd provide someone, but after that Neuman bomber yesterday, I wouldn't trust them to guard an empty room. You watch over her, Lewis. I'll be fine here.'

Lewis glared at Douglas, and when he finally spoke his voice was very calm and very cold and extremely dangerous. 'Let me see if I've got this right. You want me to take Jesamine shopping?'

'Yes,' said Douglas. 'Try and get her back in time for tea.'

'Douglas . . .'

'Lewis, I am your King. This is not a request.'

'Really? I thought you were my friend.'

'I am, Lewis. Really. But I have other responsibilities now. Look after Jesamine. There are still a lot of death threats coming in, aimed specifically at her. I need to know she's safe. Who else can I depend on like you?'

'It's going to be one of those days,' said Lewis sadly. 'I can just tell. But, Douglas; when I get back, we're going to have a serious talk.'

'Looking forward to it immensely, Lewis.'

'You never could lie to me worth a damn, Douglas.'

Lewis turned his back on his King and stalked off down the corridor. He could feel Douglas' gaze on his back. Truth be told, once Lewis had had time to think about it, he wasn't actually all that upset by his new assignment. Spending the afternoon in Jesamine Flowers' company had to be more fun than standing around in corridors. And Anne had already told him about the continuing death threats. Apparently most of them came from Jesamine's more extreme fans, outraged that she was giving up her career and turning her back on her admirers to marry the King. If they couldn't have her, no-one could . . . She really did need a bodyguard who knew what he was doing. Lewis had only acted up because he didn't want Douglas to think he was getting soft.

Lewis Deathstalker had stewarded Pure Humanity demonstrations, and stood firm against frenzied Arena fans determined to storm the box office for the last few Season tickets, and faced down all kinds of angry crowds in his time; but he'd never seen anything like the madness that engulfed Jesamine Flowers wherever she went. Her local fans had turned out in force, lying in wait outside her hotel, and every shop Jesamine visited was immediately surrounded by a clumsy, screaming mob, howling their idol's name and shrieking hysterically till they hyperventilated or passed out. They demanded her smile, her wave, her autograph, her attention; as though they were only real if she deigned to recognise their existence. For Jesamine Flowers this was business as usual, and she took it all in her stride. She was surrounded at all times by a small crowd of her own people, experienced in keeping the fans at bay without pissing them off. They formed a living wall and barrier around her, from the moment she and Lewis left the recording company's limousine until she was safely inside the store, but even so Lewis stuck close to her at all times, and never let his hand move far from his gun.

The almost animal nature of the crowds fascinated him. He was used to being admired, even adored, all Paragons were. It came with the job. But Paragon fans were usually satisfied to worship their heroes from afar. They knew better than to crowd people who tended to react to surprises with drawn weapons. (There were groupies, of course, but Lewis had never encouraged them. He didn't trust their motives, and besides, they embarrassed him.) Jesamine's fans were a whole different breed. There seemed no end to their numbers, and Lewis found their endless din frankly unnerving. The roar rose and fell, seeming to feed on itself, a disturbing mixture of hysteria, possessiveness and sheer animal lust. Just the sight of Jesamine in person was apparently enough to drive them right out of their minds. The mob kept surging forward against the tangle-fields the big stores had set up, once they heard Jesamine planned to grace them with her presence, and more than once Lewis saw men and women fainting from the excitement, and the sheer crush of bodies. Medics moved slowly through the crowd to retrieve the fallen, sometimes having to actually fight their way past fans reluctant to give up their place.

Jesamine would wave and smile to the fans on her way from the limousine to the store, and then ignored them completely, concentrating on her shopping with a single-minded thoroughness Lewis could only admire. She actually didn't seem to hear the howling of the mob outside. Lewis supposed you could get used to anything, in time. Paparazzi used their personal force shields to bludgeon their way to the very front of the crowds, and then sent their cameras zooming through the air outside the store's windows, trying to get a peep of what Jesamine was buying this week. Cheap gossip shows lived for that kind of trivia. Lewis ignored them, concentrating on the fans, and didn't let himself relax for a moment. He didn't trust the crowd, with their strangely blank eyes and desperate body language. There were undercurrents of anger, even rage, in some of the voices, expressed here and there on hastily-lettered placards raised above the heads of the crowd, and shaken with some passion. *Come back to us*, they said. *Don't leave us. We made you what you are!* By turning her back on her career she was turning her back on them; saying she didn't need them any more. That they didn't matter. And that, of course, was unacceptable.

What Jesamine might want or need didn't seem to be important to them. Stars existed for their fans, not the other way round. Everyone knew that.

The really big stores had their own private force shield generators, polarised windows, and armed security staff, and you had to pass through all kinds of sensor equipment just to get in. Lewis set off practically every alarm they had, but everyone made allowances. Not because he was the new Imperial Champion, but because he was with Jesamine Flowers. Lewis found their level of paranoia encouraging, and had actually started to relax a little when a shop assistant suddenly ran forward out of nowhere with an autograph pad in his hand that for one heart-stopping moment looked very like a bomb. Only Lewis knew how close the poor fool came to getting shot. Jesamine smiled graciously at the beaming assistant, and signed her name in a quick practised scrawl, while Lewis quietly fought to get his breathing back under control. If Jesamine noticed, she never said anything, but after that she went out of her way to keep Lewis close to her, and require his advice on what she was buying.

And she bought a hell of a lot. Lewis was at first impressed and then actually staggered by the sheer amount she was accumulating. She would stride down the aisles, pointing here and there with an imperious finger, not even bothering to look at the price tags. (The really good stuff didn't have price tags, of course. If you had to ask, you couldn't afford it.) She ordered dresses by the dozen, shoes and gloves and hats by the hundred, or so it seemed, and any amount of jewellery and gold and silver bangles, many of which were actual works of art and any one of which cost more than Lewis' annual salary. He was beginning to wonder if he could even afford to breathe the store's rarefied and subtly perfumed air. Jesamine tried to order things for Lewis too, when she saw something she thought would suit him, and was honestly surprised when he kept turning her down.

'I'm allowed to buy you things, darling!' she protested finally. 'You're my fiancé's best friend, and my Champion as well as his. And you saved my life in Court yesterday. Honestly, sweetie, it was the bravest thing I've ever seen. Why won't you let me buy you just a little something or two, to show my appreciation?'

'Gold and jewellery are not little somethings,' Lewis said

firmly. 'Not where I'm concerned. And those . . . fashionable items you keep pressing on me would be wasted on me anyway. I have no sense of style. Everyone knows that. Any time I wear something good at Court, I look like I hired it. And I'm really not comfortable, having you spend so much money on me.'

'This? This is nothing, darling. I am rich, Lewis, richer than you could possibly imagine. Empire-wide royalties will do that to you. Every year my accountants have to invent whole new fields of mathematics, just to keep track of it all. I could buy this whole store out of petty cash, and I just might if that assistant manager doesn't stop trying to peer down my cleavage. Please let me buy you something, Lewis. This is small change to me, darling, really it is.'

'It isn't to me,' said Lewis.

Jesamine looked at him sharply, picking up some of the undertones in his voice. She studied his scowling face for a long moment, and then gestured sharply for everyone else to fall back and give the two of them some privacy. The store staff practically fell over themselves backing away at speed, and even Jesamine's own people found something in entirely different aisles to suddenly be interested in. Jesamine fixed Lewis with a steely gaze.

'Talk to me, Lewis. There's something you're not telling me. Something I don't know. And I hate not knowing things. What's the problem here? The real problem?'

Lewis did his best to be evasive, for his pride's sake, but Jesamine backed him up against the nearest counter and interrogated him mercilessly, until finally he just gave up and explained his current financial situation. Jesamine was honestly shocked, and it only took her a moment to go from blank disbelief to white hot fury.

'I'm not having my Champion treated like this! It's an insult! An outrage! Parliament will pay you every penny you're worth, or I will have Douglas . . .'

'No you won't,' said Lewis, just as sharply. 'Douglas has his own problems in Parliament at the moment. He doesn't need me muddying the waters. There are those who'd use my . . . ambivalent position as a weapon with which to attack or undermine Douglas' position, and I won't have that. I won't be used to hurt my friend. This is my problem. I'll sort it out.'

'Well then, why don't I . . . advance you some money,' said Jesamine. 'Against your future improved earnings? Just to tide you over?'

'I don't think so,' Lewis said carefully. 'I don't think that would be proper. It might be . . . misunderstood.'

Jesamine sniffed loudly. 'Men! Not a practical bone in their whole bodies, any of them. I've never been proper in my entire life, and I enjoyed every minute of it. So; I can't give you presents, I can't loan you money . . .' She stopped, and then smiled brilliantly. 'Can I at least take you to the nearest decent tea rooms, and buy you a nice cup of something hot and refreshing? I don't know about you, but I'm absolutely dying of thirst, darling.'

'Well,' said Lewis. 'A cup of tea . . . would be very nice, right now.'

'Good,' said Jesamine. 'That's settled then. If you're very good, I might even spring for milk and sugar as well.'

Nothing but the very best of tea rooms for Jesamine Flowers, of course. The Earl Grey Tea Rooms opened up specially early, just for her, so that she and Lewis could have the place all to themselves. She had all her own people stay outside, ostensibly to make sure the place was secure, but really just so she and Lewis could have some quiet time together. She marched into the main dining area as though she owned the place, or was planning to, tossed her hideously expensive fur coat in the general direction of the flustered cloakroom attendant, and headed unerringly for the very best table in the room. Waitresses in old-fashioned formal uniforms hurried forward to pull out chairs for her and Lewis, and then bustled back and forth from the kitchens with all the makings necessary for a civilised early evening tea. The tea service itself was genuine antique silver, and all kinds of crumpets and pastries and finger food were presented for Jesamine's approval.

She nodded yes to everything, and then gestured brusquely for the staff to make themselves scarce. They backed hastily away, bowing and scraping as they went. Lewis studied Jesamine thoughtfully. Anyone who thought the aristocracy was a thing of the past had never spent any time in the presence of a real star. He looked around the tea room, just a little uneasily. In its own subtle way, it was actually grander than the Court. Normally even a Paragon wouldn't be able to count on getting into a place like this without a reservation. And even if he did, he probably wouldn't have been able to afford the rental on the cup the tea came in. In fact, the china cup before Lewis looked so delicate he was almost afraid to pick it up. He was just glad he'd recognised what the finger bowl was in time. As always, Jesamine was completely at home, and busied herself pouring the tea. She insisted Lewis try all the more unfamiliar finger food, and even fed him a piece or two with her own delicate fingers, which Lewis found acutely embarrassing.

She chattered endlessly about this and that, none of it of any real importance, but all of it made entertaining by her constant caustic wit. Lewis didn't contribute much to the conversation. He was content to just sit and listen, and watch Jesamine. She really was very beautiful. Some vid stars looked fine on the screen, but were disappointing in real life. In person they seemed shorter, or fatter, or their faces had unexpected flaws or blemishes that were usually removed by computer imaging before they ever hit the screens. Or perhaps they were just . . . smaller, less glamorous, in real life. Sitting right there in front of him, Jesamine was almost heart-stoppingly lovely, not in any classical sense but because her face was so full of character, alive with every emotion that passed over it. Up close, she radiated a sensuality and sexuality that was so casual it had to be natural, but was no less overwhelming for that. The few famous or glamorous people Lewis had met in the past had subtly intimidated him, though he would never have admitted it, even to himself, but he felt completely at ease in Jesamine's company. He felt she liked him.

He liked her. He admired her . . . spirit, her confidence, her boundless energy. She was always so sharp and so sure, whatever the occasion. And when she smiled at him, it was

211

like warming himself in the sun. He'd never met anyone like her. She was bright and charming and funny, her words all but falling over each other when she spoke, like the sound of a fast moving stream, endlessly bubbling and sparkling. Her body was just magnificent . . . Lewis pulled his thoughts up sharply. This was his best friend's fiancée he was thinking about. The woman chosen to be the next Queen of the Empire. A star, a diva, a legend in her own field. While he . . . was just a bodyguard. Here to protect her from every threat, including perhaps himself.

Jesamine observed Lewis carefully, without being too obvious about it. He was clearly uncomfortable in such posh surroundings, but he seemed to be relaxing a little, at last. She wanted him to be able to relax around her. He was always so formal and so courteous in her company, which was sweet, of course, but just a little irritating. There was nothing like being almost universally adored to make you value true friendship. When you're rich and famous and staggeringly beautiful, it's amazing how many people want to be your friend, and just a little disappointing how fast you learn to see through them, to what they really want from you. Before this, Jesamine had only had one real friend, and that was Anne, who knew her when. And Douglas, of course. A fine man, Douglas. Perhaps even a great man. (Her previous husbands didn't count, even the ones who were good in bed. Bad cess to the lot of them.) No; Lewis . . . liked her because he liked her. Liked her the person, not the star. She could tell. It was clear he had no idea how refreshing she found that. She liked him too.

She hadn't been sure at first. His reputation preceded him. The great and incorruptible Paragon, the hero of Logres. Not as famous as Finn Durandal, or so dashing as Douglas Campbell, but admired and respected by all. And of course, he had that legendary name. She'd been quite nervous about meeting him. She only played legends; he was one. She'd expected to find some cold, humourless puritan who slept at attention and never took his weapons off. Someone who wouldn't approve at all of a mere theatrical like her. Instead, Lewis Deathstalker turned out to be . . . fun, in his own quiet way. Not impressed by anyone or anything, and always ready with a murmured joke or a barbed comment. She liked it when he was around. Douglas relaxed more too, when Lewis was there. Stopped taking himself and his role so seriously. The Deathstalker brought out his King's best qualities.

All right, Lewis was ugly. It was a harsh face, even when he smiled. A face that could scare gargoyles. But he had kind eyes. And there was nothing like a career in show business to make you really tired of pretty faces. Jesamine would take character over looks any day.

And she liked the way he moved. Lewis moved with confidence, like the trained warrior he was, like he always knew what he was doing, where he was going. You felt you could always depend on him to do the right thing. And he clearly had no idea how reassuring, and how sexy, that was. To meet the real thing, after a lifetime of fakes and poseurs. Sometimes he'd smile at her, or catch her eye with his, and she would feel her breath catch in her throat, or her heart miss a beat. And then she would flash her practised famous smile and talk a little faster, to hide how she felt. Because even as she enjoyed these feelings, she knew how dangerous they were. She might like the Deathstalker, even admire him, but it could never be more than that. She was marrying Douglas Campbell. She was going to be Queen. The culmination of her life, her career, her ambition. Everything she'd ever planned and worked for, everything she'd ever dreamed of. To be the most famous and fabulous woman in the Empire. And the most powerful, even if they didn't know it yet. Nothing could be allowed to threaten that; not even her own treacherous feelings.

Lewis and Jesamine talked about many things over their tea, none of them important. And not once did they ever say out loud what they were thinking. In all their eventful lives, they'd never met anyone like each other. Once, when they both reached for the same pastry, their hands touched, and just for a moment they felt sparks fly.

They'd pretty much finished their tea, and were unobtrusively searching for some excuse to prolong their time together, when Lewis suddenly realised that the noise outside the tea rooms had changed in character. All his old Paragon instincts kicked in, and he looked away from Jesamine, away from her mouth and her eyes, almost against his wishes. The noise outside was louder, angrier, nastier. He stood up suddenly, and Jesamine broke off in mid anecdote. She started to say something tart, and then stopped as she took in the concern on his face, the sudden readiness for violence and battle in his body language. The calm and kind friend was gone, replaced by someone new, someone more frightening. For the first time, he looked like his legend. He looked like a Deathstalker. She stood up and looked where he was looking, out the great steelglass window overlooking the main street. Something new was happening outside, and it had nothing to do with Jesamine Flowers. Lewis moved over to stand by the window, one hand resting on the gun at his side. Jesamine moved quickly after him.

The mob of her fans had dispersed, scattered now along the length of the pavements, and they were shouting and cheering at the almost military demonstration marching down the middle of the street. They marched six abreast, blocking the road, their numbers stretching back almost out of sight. Their booted feet crashed down in perfect precision, and they held their signs and banners up like troop colours. Now and again they chanted their brief and ugly slogans, in cold carrying voices, drowning out the shouted insults and approval from the spectators lining the street. The din reminded Lewis of feeding time at the Arena, when new imported killer aliens were introduced. You could almost taste the bloodlust on the air.

He recognised the demonstrators' outfits immediately, the great white cross on the chest of the blood-red uniforms. The new image of the militant Church of Christ Transcendent; ever since the Church got tired of waiting patiently for change and decided to force the pace by getting into bed with Pure Humanity. Their spokesmen were everywhere, on the news shows and chat shows and political discussion shows. Everyone was talking about this new, militant Church. The Church and the Neumen; a marriage made in Hell. And God alone knew what their children might be like.

There was a hell of a lot of them in the street, marching

purposefully past the tea room window, and Lewis frowned as he took in how pitifully small the official security presence was. There were hardly any stewards, only a handful of peacekeepers, and not a Paragon to be seen anywhere. Lewis' frown deepened into a scowl. All right, Emma Steel was probably still busy getting up to speed, and God knew where Finn Durandal was these days, but surely the authorities could have found someone to watch over the demonstration, even if they'd had to raid *The Sangreal* . . . or perhaps the powers that be were afraid of upsetting the Church. The militants had become surprisingly powerful surprisingly quickly. Too big a security presence might provoke the very trouble the authorities were anxious to prevent. Still; if things were to get out of control . . . Lewis looked around for Jesamine's security people, and wasn't all that surprised to find they'd retreated into the tea room's foyer, away from possible danger. Their only interest was in protecting Jesamine. Lewis didn't blame them. They were professional enough to know when they were well out of their depth.

'The Church Militant,' Jesamine said quietly beside him. 'I've seen them on the news channels. Ugly people with an ugly message. Humans first, aliens nowhere. No fashion sense at all. And no sense of humour, either, from what I've seen of their spokespeople. Funny how humour's always the first thing to go as you head towards the extremes of politics or religion, and leave sanity behind.'

'And this is politics and religion,' said Lewis, still looking out the window. His voice was cold, thoughtful. 'A deadly combination. The Church has lost all sense of moderation or restraint since they adopted the Neumen philosophy. A human Saviour, a human Empire, a human future. No others need apply. They're not the majority view yet, not by a long shot. But a lot of people are listening. And the opposition is fragmented. The best they can do is turn up at these demonstrations to shout abuse and throw things, which just inflames passions on both sides. We could be in for some real trouble here.'

'I still don't get why the Church has turned against aliens, all of a sudden,' said Jesamine.

'I can explain it, but don't expect it to make sense,' said Lewis, still not looking away from the demonstration. 'The Church is all about Transcendence, right? They've now decided that since only humans transcend through the Madness Maze, that proves aliens are automatically inferior beings, fit only to be guided, for which read ruled, by their natural superiors, Humanity. For their own good, of course. Whenever people want to have power over someone, it's always for their own good. Basically, the Neumen want a return to the good old days of Empire, when aliens knew their place. As slaves or corpses. Their new partnership with the Church gives the Pure Humanity cause a new patina of respectability. If the official Church of the Empire has accepted their beliefs, then there must be something to them. People who wouldn't listen before are listening now. And far too many are starting to believe.'

'But it was only a few weeks ago that they tried to murder the King with a transmutation bomb!'

'The Church and the Neumen have disowned him. A lone nut, apparently. Poor bastard died for nothing. The cause has a new spokesman now; the Angel of Madraguda.'

'I never liked him,' Jesamine said immediately. 'Met him once, at a charity do. He had sweaty hands and piggy little eyes, and kept looking at my breasts while he was talking to me. Talked a lot, but never really said much. I've met his sort before. Out for what he can get, that one. But I never knew him to have any political ambitions, or connections . . .'

'Well he has now,' said Lewis. 'In fact, he's bigger than ever now. You can't turn on the vid without him being there, saying awful, hateful things in that calm and reasonable voice of his. The trouble is, he's saying what a lot of people want to hear; that they're better than the aliens. And that they have a right to change things, by force if necessary . . . the only thing more dangerous than an angry mob is an angry mob with an agenda. That isn't just a demonstration out there; they're headed somewhere. Somewhere specific. I think I'd better call in . . .'

Jesamine shuddered. 'I hope there aren't any aliens out on the streets just now . . . if things do get out of hand . . .'

216

They stood together, shoulder to shoulder before the steel-glass window, watching the demonstration pass by. There seemed no end to it, hundreds and hundreds of cold-faced men and women, chanting their horrid doctrines in harsh, angry voices. Jesamine shuddered again, and Lewis put his arm around her shoulders. And then he turned slowly to look at Jesamine, almost despite himself, and she turned to look at him. Their faces were very close now, and drawing closer every moment, until they could feel each other's breath on their lips and in their mouths. They looked into each other's eyes and could not look away, as the angry passions outside somehow fed the simple shared passion inside. Their breathing quickened, becoming deeper, heavier. Their eyes locked, saying everything they hadn't said while sitting at their table. In the end, it didn't matter who moved first. They pressed urgently against each other, holding each other fiercely, as though someone might tear them apart, and they kissed with a lifetime's passion.

When they finally broke apart, they were panting for breath. Lewis tried to say something, and couldn't. He turned his head aside, and Jesamine tightened her grip on him. Lewis looked back at her, and their eyes locked again. They were both trembling.

'We can't do this,' said Lewis. 'We *can't*. It's wrong. Douglas is my friend!'

'Hell,' said Jesamine. 'He's my fiancé. I'm going to marry him.'

'Do you love him?'

'Yes. No. I don't know! It's complicated.'

'Not for me,' said Lewis.

In the end, because she'd always been the practical one, Jesamine found the strength to let go first. She put her hands on Lewis' armoured chest and pushed him back, and he stumbled a little, as though she'd hit him. But she couldn't have moved him unless he'd let her, and they both knew it. They were still staring into each other's eyes. They were still breathing hard. Their hands trembled at their sides, as though desperate to reach out again.

'I don't know what to do,' Lewis said finally. 'I've never felt like this before.'

'Never?' said Jesamine. 'Haven't you ever been in love before?'

'No,' said Lewis. 'There's only ever been me. And Douglas.'

'Hush,' said Jesamine, and raised a hand to touch his mouth with her fingertips.

Lewis turned his head away. He looked out across the tea room, and that was when he saw Anne Barclay, standing there, watching him with Jesamine. And Lewis just knew, from the expression on her face, that she'd been watching for some time.

'Anne?' he said, though his voice didn't sound like his at all. 'What are you doing here?'

Jesamine looked round sharply and saw Anne, but apart from a slight widening of her eyes, her face betrayed nothing at all.

'What am I doing here?' said Anne, advancing on the two of them with the inevitability of destiny. 'More to the point, what the hell are you two doing here? No; don't say it, Lewis. Whatever you were about to say, it would only have been a lie, and you never were any good at that. And I really don't have the time or the patience to stand here and listen to you stutter. I came here looking for you. You're needed back at Parliament, both of you. Douglas has been called to an emergency Session of the House, and he's going to need all the support he can get.

'You may have noticed the commotion outside, when you weren't busy eating each other's faces. Well, that march is just one of seven, all of them equally large, equally angry and equally determined. They're all headed straight for the Parliament building, and absolutely no-one thinks they're coming to hand in a petition. There's a really bad feeling in the air, Lewis. We've called in every peacekeeper in the city, but we can't afford a direct confrontation. The Church has made it very clear it isn't going to be stopped, or diverted. We even try and put up barricades, and they'll use that as an excuse to hit out with everything they've got. If we don't find just the right way to defuse this . . . it'll all end in tears. Guaranteed. Now get your arses moving, both of you. I've got a gravity barge waiting out the back.'

Jesamine just nodded, and headed for the cloakroom to fetch her fur coat. She passed straight by Anne, her head held high. She still hadn't said anything, and Lewis could only admire her grace under pressure. He could feel the flush reddening his face, and he didn't know what to do with his hands. Anne and he stood and stared at each other until Jesamine returned with her coat, having dismissed her security people. She headed for the rear of the tea rooms with a calm and composed face, as though she didn't have a care in the world. Anne glared at Lewis, and he almost flinched.

'How could you?' she said, her voice so low it was almost a growl. 'What the hell did you think you were doing, Lewis? She's marrying Douglas in two weeks' time! Your best friend! She will be Queen to his King. You're going to ruin everything!'

'Do you think I don't know that?' said Lewis, trying hard to keep his voice under control. 'I don't know how it happened. It just . . . happened. I know it was wrong, but . . . it's not like she loves him. It's an arranged marriage. Not much more than a business merger. And Jesamine . . . she's special. She matters to me. Damn it, aren't I allowed anything for myself? I'm not a Paragon any more. I'm supposed to be the Champion, but no-one seems to know what that is. And ever since my best friend became King, he's had no time for me. I'm so alone, Anne . . . I never wanted to be Champion. Never expected it. I only agreed because I thought Douglas needed me. And now it seems like I've lost everything that ever mattered to me. Am I so wrong to want something for myself, Anne? She makes me happy. She cares for me.'

'Don't fool yourself, Lewis.' Anne's voice was more contemptuous than angry. 'She's an actress, remember? I've known her for years, and there never was a man she couldn't twist around her little finger. Much more likely, she was bored and you were there. She's going to have to give up a lot, to become Queen, including a lot of freedoms she's always taken for granted. You were just a last fling, a last gesture, one last taste of freedom before she has to give it all up, and become respectable. I thought you were smarter than this, Lewis. Stronger than this. If even a hint of this were to get out, the gossip shows would have a field day, you know they would. And the King's enemies would use you to destroy him. Is that what you want?'

'Of course not! He's my friend!'

'*Then act like it!* And from now on keep your mouth shut and your hands to yourself whenever you're around little miss hot-to-trot. I may not be able to trust her, but I thought I could trust you.'

'You can,' said Lewis. His face was calm now, and his voice was cold and steady, and only someone who knew him really well could have seen the sadness in his eyes. Anne, who had known him since childhood, took him gently by the arm and guided him towards the rear of the tea rooms.

'Come on, Lewis. There's work to be done, and we're needed. It's not the same as being wanted, but it will have to do.'

Over at Finn's charming apartment, the Durandal and his people were watching the Church/Neumen demonstration on the over-sized vidscreen that took up most of one wall. The colours were a bit overpowering, but the three dimensions and surround sound made it just like looking out a window. Finn didn't have much use for toys, as a rule, but when he did decide he wanted something, he never settled for anything but the very best version available. He sat, completely relaxed, in his favourite chair, drinking a fashionable wine and smiling happily as his plans unfolded before him.

Angelo Bellini sat in the chair next to him, intent and focused on the vidscreen, smiling now and again when he forgot himself. He had a drink in his hand, but was so caught up in the drama of the events he'd helped orchestrate that he kept forgetting the drink was there. Every now and again he would lean forward suddenly as he spotted a familiar face among the marchers, and loudly identify them to the rest of the room, who if truth be told weren't really all that interested. Angelo didn't notice, entirely wrapped up in himself and his own reactions. And every now and again, he would suddenly twitch or scratch himself, in an exaggerated fashion, and never know it wasn't by his own volition.

Brett Random sneered at him, sitting slumped in a chair as far away from the others as he could get. He'd drunk the best part of a bottle of brandy in the past hour, but it hadn't done a thing to improve his disposition. Brett was in a foul mood, and didn't care who knew it, though he still had enough sense to keep quiet whenever Finn glanced his way. His stomach still hurt, but now he had a throbbing headache to go along with it. Thanks to the esper drug, Brett had to spend a lot of his time tuning out the constant roar of all the minds thinking around him. It was slowly getting easier, and he had a feeling that eventually he'd be able to do it automatically. And somewhere off in the distance, in a direction he couldn't identify, he could see or hear or feel something . . . splendid. Something that shone like the sun. Something that felt like the home he'd never known. It was calling to him. He thought it might be the oversoul.

It scared the crap out of him.

He'd started to experiment with his new abilities. He'd already discovered that with a little concentration he could influence people around him. Make them do things. Nothing major, nothing important. But he could make Angelo's face twitch, and make him scratch an itch he didn't actually have. A cheap laugh admittedly, but in Finn's service you had to make do with what you could get. It wasn't the most useful of talents, but it was a start, he supposed. And it pleased him to have an ability Finn knew nothing about. Never knew when you might need a weapon for the future. An ace in the hole. Brett smiled, and drank his brandy.

He'd tried out his new ability on Rose Constantine, but she immediately turned and looked right at him, so he didn't try that again. The last thing he wanted was to attract her attention. He was still trying to come to terms with that astonishing moment when their minds had briefly touched. Ever since, he'd felt differently about her, though he couldn't say how. Rose kept looking at him, and he couldn't read the expression on her face. It was a bit like waking up the next morning after a really good party, and discovering a stranger in bed with you. So that there was now someone new in your life that you'd been close to, but really didn't know at all.

She'd drawn up her chair right next to his, almost uncomfortably close. And she kept *looking* at him. For the moment she was watching the events on the vidscreen, because Finn had told her to, but Brett could tell she wasn't interested in any of it. He just . . . knew that.

'You did a good job, Angelo,' Finn said suddenly, and Angelo and Brett both jumped, just a little. Finn smiled lazily. 'Joining the Church and the Neumen at the hip was one of my more inspired ideas. Though I never dreamed they'd take to each other so completely, and so quickly.'

'It was surprisingly easy,' Angelo admitted. 'The right words in the right ears, at the right level, and suddenly people at the top on both sides became very receptive. It helped that both sides were frustrated with their lack of progress; once I showed them what they could achieve if they joined forces, they couldn't wait to get started. And of course, once word came down from on high, the lower orders were only too happy to go along. I've always been very good at pointing out to people where their best interests lie. And it's always been easier to get people to hate than to get them to love. Doesn't matter in the end whether it's religion or politics; people do so love to have a scapegoat, someone to blame for all the troubles and failures of their little lives. Someone other than themselves, of course. And what could be more *other* than aliens? I should have thought of this years ago.'

And then he broke off and leaned forward in his chair again, as trouble broke out on one of the marches, and all the media cameras zoomed in for closeups. Security forces had apparently decided enough was enough, and had started setting up barriers to block off the road leading to Parliament. The marchers went crazy, as they were forced to halt. There was shouting and screaming, the shaking of fists and a lot of bad language. Angelo Bellini pursed his lips disapprovingly at the latter. These were supposed to be Church-going people. The marchers pressed forward, pushing at the barriers and threatening the security people behind them. Already some people were throwing things from within the safety of the crowd. The security forces backed away, looking nervously about them. They were vastly outnumbered, and unsure what to do for the best. No-one had seen a demonstration this large, and this angry, for years. But still none of the security forces had drawn a gun, or even a sword. Not yet. They'd all been given strict instructions not to start anything. But some of the stones and missiles flying through the air were coming dangerously close. And the barriers were flimsy things. They wouldn't stop the marchers if they were determined to break through, and both sides knew it. The marchers could see the House of Parliament now, and just the sight of that symbol of authority inflamed their passions even further. They were going to enter the House, by force if necessary, and make the MPs listen to what they had to say.

And a few peacekeepers and security people with frightened faces sure as hell weren't going to stop them.

'How soon before it becomes a riot?' said Brett, so fascinated by the drama unfolding before him that he actually forgot his stomach hurt.

'As soon as my overpaid agents provocateurs are all in position,' said Finn, sipping his wine delicately. 'I want all seven marches stopped outside Parliament, before I let all hell break loose. Security might handle one mob, but not seven. And especially not seven outraged blood-crazed mobs, whipped into a frenzy by the carefully-honed rhetoric of my people.'

'But . . . there's no way they'll actually get inside the House,' said Brett. 'I mean, that building's got all kinds of anti-terrorist defences built into it, from the bad old days. And you can bet security's got them all up and running after that suicide bomber.'

'They're not supposed to get inside,' Finn said patiently. 'They're supposed to riot. Cracked heads, and men down, and blood running in the gutters. The peacekeepers won't be able to contain it, security will break and run, and dear Douglas will only have one option left open to him. And then . . . he will play right into my hands. You must be patient, Brett. I know what I'm doing. And you'll get to play your part soon enough.'

'And I'll get to kill someone?' said Rose.

'I promised you a shot at the Deathstalker,' said Finn. 'And you know I always keep my promises.'

In the House, every single Member of Parliament was present, for once, packed shoulder to shoulder in their seats. All the alien representatives were there too, along with clones, Shub and the oversoul. Parliament's authority hadn't been challenged this blatantly in a hundred years. They could hear the roar of the mob growing ever louder outside the House, a dark disturbing violent sound, and a lot of the MPs looked nervous, even the few who were only present as holos. They were in unknown territory now. King Douglas sat scowling on his Throne, Jesamine on his left, Lewis on his right. Jesamine looked calm and composed, even regal. Lewis was scowling even harder than Douglas, even though Anne was talking constantly in his ear, telling him to relax dammit, he was spooking everyone. Armed security men lined the walls, looking twitchy and sweaty.

A large viewscreen was floating in mid air on the open floor of the House, so that the honourable Members could watch the latest media reports of the converging marches. Anti-Church and anti-Neumen demonstrators were turning up in large numbers now, drawn by the media coverage. The Church Militant had a lot of enemies, from all kinds of political and philosophical positions. Security and peacekeepers now had the extra responsibility of trying to keep the two sides apart. Already there was a lot of angry shouting, as both sides screamed insults and threats at each other. Stones and other missiles were flying from all directions. Some people had been hit, and were sitting bleeding and dazed on the ground, but the medics couldn't get to them. Most of the medics were frankly too scared even to try. Where the two sides did occasionally manage to get at each other, fistfights and worse broke out immediately. The peacekeepers and the security forces were running scared. They hadn't a hope of controlling or even containing the situation any more, and everyone knew it. They hadn't been trained in how to deal with mass civil insurrection. No-one had ever thought it would be necessary.

No-one had drawn a weapon yet, but everyone knew it was only a matter of time now.

'Send the troops in,' said Tel Markham, Member for Madraguda. 'The peacekeepers are out of their depth. Someone's going to get hurt soon. Really hurt. Call out the army. Let them handle it. One look at trained professional fighting men, and the mob will fall apart.'

'What if they don't?' said Lewis.

'I'm reluctant to have armed troops running loose in the city, attacking civilians,' Douglas said heavily. 'The last thing we need is for this to escalate. Lewis is right. If the crowds see troops bearing down on them with weapons in their hands, they won't run; they'll go crazy. Intelligence says a lot of the marchers are armed, some of them with energy weapons. They were expecting trouble. I don't want blood and bodies in the streets. That smacks too much of the bad old days; the kind of tactics Lionstone was famous for. We're suppposed to be better than that. We need a way to defuse this situation, before anyone gets seriously hurt.'

'Exactly,' said Meerah Puri, Member for Malediction. 'Troops haven't been allowed into the Parade of the Endless for over a century. Not even for parades. We mustn't let this mob panic us into taking measures we might regret later.'

'If those thugs break through the barriers and storm the House, we could end up regretting that even more,' said Rowan Boswell, Member for Hercules IV. 'They've got fire in their bellies and blood in their eyes. Let them even scent weakness, and they'll take the House by force; and we could all end up hanging from ropes!'

'Hysteria doesn't suit you, Rowan!' snapped Gilad Xiang, Member for Zenith. 'Take a few deep breaths and stick your head between your knees. Before I have someone do it for you. There is no need for panic. We're all perfectly safe in here. There's no way the protesters can get to us. The House has been on security Red Alert ever since the suicide bomber got in here, and all the old defences have been re-activated. The House has its own blastproof steel doors and interior force shields. We could stand off an army if we had to. Whatever happens out there, we're safe.'

'We still don't know how that bloody bomber got in!' said Boswell shrilly. His face was pale, and his mouth was trembling. 'Maybe we should . . . agree to meet someone from the Church. A delegation . . .'

'We are not opening our doors to a mob!' Tel Markham said immediately. 'We can't give in to threats. We certainly can't afford to appear weak before them. Give the Church Militant an inch, and we'll never be free of them. And if we start making concessions to the Church, where would it all end? They aren't the only extremists with demands. We have to set an example. Show everyone that we can't be intimidated. We have to break up the mob, and send the militants packing. And for that we need the army!'

'The troops are in their barracks, outside the city limits,' Douglas said steadily. 'Even if the House gave the order, it would take time for them to assemble and get here in force. I doubt we'd see them in under an hour. And a lot can happen in an hour; especially if the mob found out armed troops were on their way to shut them down.'

'How would they find out?' said Boswell.

'Don't be naïve,' said Xiang. 'This demonstration didn't just happen; it was organised. By people who aren't stupid enough to be down here themselves. Whoever they are, you can bet they'll be monitoring this situation very carefully. If we give the order, you can bet the militants will know almost as soon as the troops. And then the shit really will hit the fan.'

'There is . . . an alternative,' said Lewis, and everyone in the House turned to look at him.

'Is there, by God?' said Douglas. 'I for one would very much love to hear it.'

'The Paragons,' said Lewis. 'You've got over a hundred Paragons in the city right now, sitting around waiting for the Royal wedding. Call them in. The mob will take one look at that many Paragons bearing down on them, and calm right down. I mean, I would, wouldn't you?'

'You've got a point, Lewis,' said Douglas. He looked out over the House. 'The people respect the Paragons. Always have. Certainly far more than they do the House security or even the peacekeepers. The Paragons have a reputation for solving problems, by whatever means necessary. And the Paragons have always been the people's heroes. I'll bet even militants will break down and disperse, rather than take up arms against their heroes. Lewis; do you know where most of the Paragons are, right now?'

'Well, currently you'll find most of them in a bar called *The Sangreal*,' said Lewis. 'It's not far from here. And they'll know where to find the others. If you want them, most could be here inside of ten minutes. And all of them inside twenty. And they're probably not being watched like the troops, so the militants wouldn't know what was coming until the Paragons were right on top of them. After that, it should all get very calm in a hurry.'

'And we won't need the troops after all,' said Douglas, leaning back in his Throne. 'Nice one, Lewis. Good thinking.' He looked out over the House. 'How say you, honourable Members? Shall we call in the Paragons?'

The House voted Aye, without a single dissenting voice, and the sense of relief in the air was so thick you could amost smell it.

The King called *The Sangreal* personally. Most of the Paragons had been watching the news coverage too, and grasped the situation immediately. They grabbed their weapons, pulled on their armour, and charged out into the early evening air, glad of a bit of excitement at last. A lot of them had been drinking and carousing for some time, but none of them bothered to stop for Purges. They weren't expecting any real trouble. Not from a bunch of civilians. They spread the word on the Paragon comm channel, and soon they were all heading for Parliament, picking up stragglers along the way, storming down the streets on foot and on gravity sleds, their purple cloaks flapping bravely on the rising wind.

The outer reaches of the mob spotted the approaching Paragons, and word spread quickly through the protestors. The shouting died away on all sides, replaced by an ominous quiet. The Paragons marched down the street in unison, the greatest gathering of heroes the city had ever seen, with a handful of gravity sleds flying overhead. They advanced confidently on the silently waiting demonstrators, and only slowed to a halt a few yards short, as they took in the mood of the situation. It wasn't what they'd expected. The civilians didn't look scared, or cowed, by the presence of so many Paragons, as they should have been. They were just . . . waiting, to see what would happen. The Paragons looked at each other uncertainly, until finally Veronica Mae Savage pushed her way to the front. A murmur moved through the crowd. They recognised Veronica Mae. They knew her reputation. She stood before them, her hands on her weapons belt, her head held high, tam-o'-shanter perched at its usual bold angle.

'All right, people,' she said crisply, her voice carrying clearly on the quiet. 'This has gone far enough. Time to break it up and go home, before someone gets hurt. If anyone has a genuine grievance, I guarantee, on behalf of the Paragons, that we will see you get a fair hearing. But this isn't the way, and you know it. So choose a street and start walking, or there'll be trouble. You don't want there to be trouble, do you?'

Someone from deep inside the crowd fired a disrupter, and the energy beam blew her head right off her shoulders. The Paragons cried out in shock and outrage, and drew their weapons. They surged forward and slammed into the crowd, determined to reach whoever had fired the shot. Some of the militants fought back, and suddenly it seemed everyone was firing energy guns, and people were falling dead and injured to the ground. The crowd had become a mob, hysterical with fear and rage, and the Paragons only had thoughts of avenging their fallen; and as quickly as that it all went to Hell.

In the House, the King and the MPs watched with horror as the mob turned on their supposedly beloved heroes, attacking the Paragons with everything from clubs to disrupters. The Paragons were fighting well and fiercely, tearing a bloody path through the mob, but they were vastly outnumbered. Already there were dead Paragons lying on the ground, their bodies being kicked and trampled underfoot. Douglas recognised some of their faces.

'Oh Jesus,' said Lewis. 'What have I done?'

'It wasn't your fault,' Jesamine said quickly. 'You couldn't have known. No-one could have known.'

'Animals,' said Douglas. 'They're just animals.'

Lewis turned to him. 'Call the barracks. Get the troops in here.'

Douglas looked at him, dazed, almost distracted. 'What? Lewis . . . why are they doing this? We always protected them.'

'Call the army,' said Lewis. 'Shut this down, before it spreads . . .'

'Just a minute,' said Meerah Puri. 'We haven't agreed to calling in the troops yet. We don't want to make things worse.'

'Right,' said Michel du Bois. 'We have to debate this. Are we really going to order troops to open fire on civilians, like in Lionstone's day?'

'In case you're not paying attention, Paragons are being butchered out there!' said Lewis. 'They're not civilians any more, they're terrorists. No better than ELFs. We're past the time for debate. Get the troops here fast, or we'll be watching a massacre.'

All the MPs tried to speak at once, shaken and disturbed by what they'd seen. Everyone had their own ideas on what needed to be done, and since no-one would back down for anyone else, soon they were all shouting at each other, calling for everything from conciliation to execution without trial. There was panic in their voices. If the people could turn so viciously on their adored Paragons, no-one was safe any more. The politicians argued, the House became a bedlam, and on the viewscreen people went on dying. Some were Paragons. Someone had picked up Veronica Mae Savage's head, and stuck it on a stick, and was waving it over the crowd like a banner. The Church Militants had tasted blood, and found it to their liking.

'The hell with this,' said Lewis. 'I'm going out there.'

'Lewis, no!' said Jesamine. 'You can't!'

'She's right,' said Douglas. 'You wouldn't make any difference out there. You're my Champion. I need you here.'

'To do what? Hold your hand? Those are my friends dying

out there.' Lewis' voice was cold as death. 'They used to be your friends too. I'm not doing anything useful here. And I can't just stand by and watch this happen.'

'Of course you can't,' said Douglas. 'I'll get the army here as soon as I can. Try and buy us some time, Lewis. Go. Go on; go.'

Tel Markham saw Lewis heading for the exit, and ran out onto the floor of the House. 'Stop that man! On behalf of the House and my fellow Members I demand that the Champion not be allowed to involve himself personally in this . . . mess. We can't let him commit us to a position. I demand that he stay here, to protect us, in the case the unthinkable happens, and some terrorist breaks through our defences . . .'

And then he broke off, as he saw the look on Lewis' face, and saw the disrupter in the Champion's hand. The MP was a moment away from death, and he knew it. He swallowed sickly, and was quiet. Lewis nodded once, and strode out of the chamber, with cold murder in his eyes. Markham swallowed again, and looked at the King, staring after his departed friend.

'Your Majesty, I must protest . . .'

'Oh shut up,' Douglas said tiredly, turning a contemptuous gaze on the MP. 'If I wasn't the King, I'm be going out there with him.'

'*Don't you dare!*' Anne roared in his ear, on his private channel. 'I forbid it! Douglas; you'd just give the rioters a target, a focus. They'd tear you apart on sight. Even worse, they might take you as a hostage, and God knows what commitments we'd have to make to get you back safely.'

Douglas growled and shook his head, but stayed where he was. Jesamine put a hand on his arm, but he didn't even glance at her, all his attention fixed on the terrible things still happening on the viewscreen. He watched as men and women howled like maddened animals, and blood flowed thickly in the gutters of the Empire's perfect city. While all around him the MPs shouted and argued and wouldn't listen to each other.

Afterwards, everyone agreed that this was the day the Golden Age died. It wasn't until much later, after so much

230

more had happened, that they discovered it didn't just die; it was murdered.

Lewis Deathstalker came racing out of the House of Parliament with his sword and his gun in his hands, roaring his ancient Family battle cry; *Shandrakor! Shandrakor!* Certain elements in the crowd recognised him immediately. They'd been waiting for him to appear. Two of them opened fire with disrupters, but Lewis had learned from Veronica Mae's fate, and had his force shield buzzing on his arm. The energy bolts ricocheted harmlessly away, and then he was in and among the surging crowd, and shielded from further disrupter fire.

The crowd turned on Lewis, striking out with knives and clubs and even broken bottles, and Lewis howled with almost incandescent rage as he struck out with his sword, cutting down anyone who came at him with a weapon in their hand. His every blow was a killing stroke, and there was no mercy or compassion in him as he forced a bloody path through the press of bodies to reach those who had opened fire on him. They knew what was really going on here, and Lewis was determined to get answers out of them. Before he killed them, for what they had done to his friends. Many of the militants turned and ran rather than face him, but some stood their ground, and smiled calm professional smiles as they hefted their weapons. Killing Paragons had proved easier than they anticipated. Killing a Deathstalker was nothing to them.

Lewis hit them like God's own thunderbolt. He tore into the waiting assassins like an executioner, like death incarnate, pitiless and unforgiving, and they could not stand against him. He fired his disrupter at point blank range, and the energy bolt seared through two assassins' bodies before it was soaked up by the milling crowd behind them. Lewis beat aside the sword of the first man to reach him, and opened up his belly with a sideways sweep of his blade. The assassin cried out in shock as much as pain, and fell to his knees, dropping his sword as he tried to stuff his guts back into the gaping wound. Lewis swept past him, thrusting and cutting with terrible speed, parrying the blades that came at him from all sides on his buzzing force shield.

All too soon there was no-one left prepared to face him, despite their wages and their orders, and the few assassins still alive turned to flee. Lewis cut them down from behind, until only one was left. He kicked that man's feet out from under him, and stamped on his hand till he let go of his sword. The assassin tried to crawl away. Lewis leant over him, and the man turned suddenly, and cut at Lewis' exposed side with a hidden dagger. Lewis slapped the knife out of his hand with almost contemptuous ease, turned off his force shield to save the power left in the energy crystal, grabbed a handful of the assassin's blood-red Church tunic, and hauled him to his feet. The man struggled and tried to pull away. Lewis pulled him close and head-butted him in the face. All the fight went out of the assassin as his nose broke, and blood flowed down his face. He would have collapsed if Lewis hadn't held him up. Lewis pushed his face into the shattered visage of his enemy.

'You're a pro. What are you doing here? Who paid you to be here? Who organised all this?'

A disrupter beam hit the assassin's head, fired from somewhere else in the crowd, and the head exploded in a red spray of vaporised brains and bone, spraying blood across Lewis' face. He didn't flinch or cry out, only dropped the headless body and looked quickly about for whoever had fired the shot. But whoever silenced the assassin was long gone, lost in the roiling crowd. Lewis glared about him, and everyone fell back, or tried to. Maddened as they were by bloodlust and the shouted slogans of the agents provocateurs, there wasn't a man or woman there crazy enough to take on the Deathstalker. Lewis' ugly face was uglier than ever now, and it had nothing to do with the dead man's blood and brains spattering his face.

He strode through the crowd, calling out in a harsh and deadly voice for everyone to drop their weapons and surrender. Most did. Those who didn't, or didn't do it fast enough, he cut down without a moment's thought. He had gone beyond peacekeeping or even Paragon's work; this was revenge now, this was simple butchery, designed to intimidate and terrify those around him. Wherever the Deathstalker walked, the riot was over.

But he was only one man, and he couldn't be everywhere. Hundreds, thousands of maddened militants still stamped back and forth, attacking anyone that represented authority.

Emma Steel emerged from the fray to guard Lewis' back. Her armour was battered and splashed with blood, some of it her own, and what was left of her proud purple cloak hung in tatters from her shoulders. A near miss from a disrupter bolt had burned away all the hair on one side of her head, but her face was still cool and controlled, and her sword rose and fell with calm efficiency as she cut her way through the baying crowd to reach the Deathstalker. She was frowning just a little, as though considering some straightforward but distasteful problem. She moved in behind Lewis to guard his back, and he didn't even notice she was there.

He strode through the crowd, cutting down anyone stupid enough to get in his way, glaring about him with cold predator's eyes as he tried to spot the people still whipping up the mob's passions with just the right inflammatory words. When he could get a clear line, he shot them cleanly with his disrupter, but most of them saw him coming, and hurried to hide themselves in the body of the crowd. And then, when there was no clear shot, Lewis would shoot through other people to be sure of hitting his target. He wasn't a Paragon or even a Champion now; he was a Deathstalker, avenging his fallen friends and comrades; and he would consider all the terrible things he had done later, when he could allow himself to feel again.

And yet all the time he was fighting, and killing, one part of him was still thinking fiercely, racking his brains for some other alternative; searching desperately for some other way to stop the violence, the madness. Some way to bring the mob under control without having to kill so many of them.

But there was no other way. No tanglefields here, no sleepgas. Nothing but blood and slaughter. And his duty. His duty as a Paragon, as a Champion, as a Deathstalker; to defend Parliament. To try and keep the mob occupied, until the army could arrive. Even if it meant his life.

And then a voice called out his name, urgent and wracked with pain, somehow cutting through the din of the riot. Lewis looked round sharply, and there on the edge of the crowd, a man had fallen on his knees, one hand extended pleadingly. He called out again, begging for help, and Lewis went to him. Because for Lewis rescuing the victims had always been more important than punishing the guilty. The crowd seemed to scatter before him, and no-one blocked his way as he left the riot behind him. Emma Steel tried to follow him, but the crowd closed between her and Lewis, and would not part for her, and soon she was fighting for her life against attacks that came from every direction. Lewis never knew, intent on reaching the man before him. He holstered his gun and put out a hand to the kneeling man, hauling him to his feet. Up close, he didn't seem to be injured.

'Who are you?' Lewis said harshly.

'I'm Brett,' said Brett Random. 'And you need to get me away from here. I got caught up in the riot, and couldn't get away. You need to get me to safety.'

'Yes,' said Lewis. 'I need to get you out of here.'

Brett gritted his teeth against the headache that was all but blinding him, as he concentrated his limited esp on influencing the Deathstalker. It was hard, keeping a grip on the Champion's mind. It threatened constantly to pull out of his grasp, fighting fiercely against something it didn't even know was there. Brett persevered, knowing what Finn Durandal would do to him if he failed. He took Lewis by the arm, and guided him away down the side street, leaving the riot behind. The Deathstalker went, scowling as he tried to figure out why, and neither he nor Brett noticed the single camera that floated curiously after them.

Brett stumbled as his headache increased, and almost fell. He could feel the Deathstalker pulling free of his control. And then Rose Constantine stepped smiling out of the shadows with her sword in her hand, and Brett groaned with relief and relaxed his mental hold. Lewis shook his head and looked quickly about him, suddenly himself again. He ignored the man collapsed at his side, bleeding freely from his nostrils. He knew Rose Constantine. And he knew now why he'd been brought here. To face the one assassin who might actually give him a run for his money.

234

'So,' he said lightly. 'The Wild Rose of the Arena. Can't say I'm a fan. I suppose I should be flattered, that they thought they needed someone like you to stop me. But to be honest, I don't have the time right now. I have more important things I need to be doing. So let's get this over with, so I can get back to work.'

'You're not going anywhere, Deathstalker.' Rose's voice was sweet and breathy, an almost sexual excitement gleaming in her eyes. 'I'm here to kill you. You're my special treat. I was promised a chance at you, for being such a good girl. Come to me, my Deathstalker. I'm going to cut your heart out and eat it.'

'I always said you were crazy,' said Lewis. 'I don't have time for this.'

He turned away from her, heading back towards the riot, and the roiling mob. Rose lunged after him, her face darkening with rage. 'Don't you dare turn your back on me, Deathstalker!'

And Lewis turned back, his energy gun in his hand. He had no intention of duelling with a psychopath. He aimed and fired in a single moment, but somehow Rose darted to one side at the very last moment, and the energy beam barely clipped her side, burning away the red leathers over her ribs. She plunged on, sword in hand, ignoring the pain. Lewis brought up his blade just in time to parry a vicious blow that would have sheared his head from his shoulders, and his whole arm shuddered with the impact. The Champion and the Wild Rose went blade to blade, face to face, neither of them giving an inch. Brett Random scuttled away on all fours, watching wide-eyed as two killing machines crashed together, and would not yield.

After a while they tired of direct assault, and circled each other slowly, swords darting out to test each other's defences, probing for weaknesses in defence or attack, studying the opponent's strengths and style, looking always for the opening or blind spot that would allow a killing stroke. Rose was grinning widely now, her eyes sparkling. She'd discovered a new thrill; fighting someone who might actually be her equal. It had been a long, long time since Rose had considered herself in any real danger in a fight, and she delighted in the new sensation, glorying in a real challenge at last. Lewis' ugly face was cold and focused, studying Rose like a new species of insect, that might bite or sting him to death, given a chance. He moved smoothly onto the defensive, parrying Rose's increasingly frenzied attacks, watching and learning, until he decided he knew all he needed to know. He moved swiftly from defence to attack, his blade moving so fast now that Brett couldn't even follow it, and step by step Lewis drove Rose back.

And it was his blade that drew first blood; a long thin cut just above Rose's right cheekbone. Blood ran down her pale skin, and her tongue darted out of the corner of her mouth to catch it. She laughed softly, and looked at Lewis with sick, loving eyes. Her scarlet smile was terribly wide now, her heart leaping in her chest as she stamped and thrust and parried. Rose Constantine knew she was very close to death now. And she couldn't have been happier. She fought back, calling on all her strength and speed and years of experience, and she duelled the Deathstalker to a standstill. They went head to head, grunting with the effort. The trained warrior and the gifted psychopath. The Champion and the Wild Rose. Masters of their art. Equally matched, equally skilled. One driven by a lust for murder, the other by a need for justice and revenge. They both stood their ground and would not be moved, their blades slamming together again and again, sparks flying on the air. And there was no way of telling which way it might have gone, when Brett Random drew a concealed disrupter and shot Lewis in the side at point blank range.

Even in the middle of the greatest swordfight of his life, Lewis' instincts were still good. He sensed as much as saw Brett draw his disrupter, and was already turning when the gun fired. The energy beam punched clean through his right side, and out his back, boring a burning hole right through ribs and stomach and kidney. The impact threw Lewis to the ground, his sword flying from suddenly weak fingers. He lay there, shaking and twitching, breathing hard, trying to draw his own gun from its holster, but his arm wouldn't obey him.

He gritted his teeth against the awful pain, and forced his hand slowly towards his side, expecting Rose's death blow at any moment. But when he glanced across through pain-filled eyes, it was to see Rose send Brett sprawling with a vicious blow to the head. She stooped over him with her sword at his throat, screaming with rage.

'Mine! He was mine! Mine to kill!'

'It was orders, Rose! His orders!' Brett's voice was so high with fear it was almost hysterical. 'He would have killed you! You were losing! I had my orders. Now cut his throat, and let's get the hell out of here.'

Rose looked back at Lewis, who'd got his hand to his gun at last, and was trying to find the strength to draw it. She scowled. 'I can't kill him. Not like this. He's the Deathstalker. I'm . . . I'm not a butcher.'

Brett scrambled to his feet, keeping a safe distance between himself and the Wild Rose. 'You have to do it, Rose. It's orders. *His* orders.'

But still she hesitated, her eyes doubtful, considering a matter that was new and strange to her. When it was right to kill, and when it was not. In her own troubled way, Rose had always considered herself to be an honourable person. Not just a fighter, but a warrior. And for all her joy in the act of slaughter, there were still some things that were right, and some that were not. She couldn't kill the Deathstalker while he was helpless. If only because it wouldn't be fun any more.

And while she was still hesitating, a huge dark figure loomed suddenly out of the shadows of a side alley. Brett called out sharply, and Rose's hand went immediately to the gun on her hip, but Saturday the reptiloid was upon her before she could draw it. He loomed over her, eight feet of gleaming green scales and muscles, showing all his pointed teeth in a wide terrible smile. He slapped her aside with one of his deceptively small forearms, and the force of the blow sent her flying a dozen feet down the street. She hit the ground hard, all the breath knocked out of her, but still she hung onto her sword. Brett was there beside her in a moment, dragging her to her feet and yelling in her ear.

'We have to get out of here, Rose! Now! We don't stand a chance against something like that, and we can't afford to be captured!'

Rose stumbled along beside him, too stunned even to argue. She'd never encountered anything so big and strong and fast before. Not even the Grendel. She was smiling again as she and Brett ran down the street. Next time, she'd be prepared, and the reptiloid would get what was coming to him. She could use some luggage of that particular shade of green. It was good to know there were still some real challenges in the world. She and Brett ran down the street, leaning on each other, and it was hard to tell who was supporting who.

Saturday stared after them, and then bent over Lewis. He grabbed the Deathstalker by the shoulder and lifted him half off the ground so he could study the extent of his injuries. Lewis cried out, almost fainting from the pain. Saturday sniffed, and let him fall back again.

'I know you; King's Champion. Deathstalker. Yes. Is this a mortal wound for your kind? Should I avenge you, or go for help? Advise me, King's Champion. What should I do?'

'Stop the riot,' Lewis said, or thought he said. His head was full of sound and light, and it was hard to make his mouth work. The world seemed very far away. He was cold, his whole body shuddering. Shock. He gritted his teeth. This was going to hurt. 'Get me on my feet, Sir Reptiloid.'

Saturday hauled him up easily, and supported Lewis' weight with one forearm while the Deathstalker leaned gasping against the reptiloid's armoured hide. He realised vaguely that the sound of the mob had changed. There was still shouting and screaming, but it was more fear than rage now, already dying away, and the slogan shouters were conspicuously silent. Lewis pushed himself away from the reptiloid, the effort bringing beads of sweat to his face. He looked back at the crowd, and saw they they were standing still, staring up into the sky. Lewis looked up too, and smiled shakily as he saw the sky was full of gravity barges. The troops had finally arrived. Broadcast voices were calling for the mob to surrender and throw down their weapons, and ranks of energy guns on the barges moved ostentatiously to follow those who didn't respond quickly enough. Everywhere the fighting was stopped. The riot was over. Lewis closed his eyes for a moment in relief, and then looked up at the reptiloid.

'Saturday. Get me . . . into the House. Regeneration . . . machine.'

'As you wish,' said the reptiloid. He looked wistfully at what had once been a mob, but was now just a crowd with its hands in the air. 'I came here specially to show Pure Humanity just what an alien can do, when it got annoyed enough, but I seem to have missed my chance. Pity. I was really hoping to find out what a Neuman tasted like . . . Never mind. Bound to be a next time.'

He looked down, and realised Lewis was no longer listening to him, and was in fact barely conscious. Saturday shrugged his broad green shoulders, and whistled an old tribal song as he draped Lewis casually over one shoulder and strode swiftly towards the House. People hurried to get out of his way.

In the House, still sitting stiffly on his Throne, King Douglas cried out in shock and horror as he saw Lewis fall to the unexpected disrupter shot. A single media camera had followed Lewis, its operator curious as to why the Deathstalker had chosen to leave the fray, and when the Deathstalker went head to head with the Wild Rose, the camera operator realised he'd stumbled onto one hell of an exclusive. The whole Empire watched the duel, live; and saw Lewis struck down by treachery.

The King was on his feet in a moment, Jesamine weeping and clinging to his arm. The House was silent, watching the King uncertainly. Anne was yelling in his ear, but he wasn't listening. Douglas stepped down from the raised dais, and onto the floor of the House, almost dragging Jesamine along with him. He looked at the exit, and the House was very still as everyone waited to see what he would do.

'You can't go!' said Anne, so loudly she hurt her throat. 'Douglas, listen to me! You're the King. Your place is here.'

'He's my friend,' Douglas said, not bothering to sub-vocalise. 'They've killed my friend. I have to go to him.'

'You have to stay here and keep this place from falling apart! You don't know he's dead!' Anne made an effort to lower her voice, knowing only reason could reach Douglas now. 'You have a duty not to put yourself into danger. Who's to say Lewis wasn't shot deliberately, to try and tempt you into leaving the safety of the House? Lewis wouldn't want to be responsible for your death. Don't play into their hands, Douglas. There'll be time for vengeance later. You have to stay here. Keep the MPs from panicking, and agreeing to something stupid. You have to put your feelings aside, for now. You have to set an example, for the House. You're the King.'

'What kind of King abandons his friend? His . . . dying friend?'

'One who knows his duty. Please, Douglas. You can't go out there. It's what they want, and you know it. If they kill you, they win. And Lewis . . . will have died for nothing.'

Douglas turned slowly, and looked back at his golden Throne. And in that moment, it seemed more like a trap than anything else. But because he was the King, and a Campbell, and a man who had always known his duty, King Douglas walked slowly back across the floor of the House, stepped back up onto the dais, and sat down upon his Throne again. He looked out over the silent House with cold, unforgiving eyes, and didn't even notice Jesamine was gone. He looked at the MPs, and they looked back, waiting to see what he would do. Douglas turned away from them, and looked at the esper representative. The young man who spoke for the oversoul stood up to meet his King's gaze.

'When I speak,' Douglas said slowly. 'The oversoul hears. All of you. Yes?'

'We all hear you,' said the young man. He didn't look anything special. 'What do you wish of the esper gestalt, Your Majesty?'

'Stop the riot,' Douglas said flatly. 'Do whatever you have to. Whatever it takes. But stop the killing.'

'No!' said Meerah Puri, quickly on her feet. Other MPs rose to join her. 'Your Majesty, I protest! We can't use espers against humans!'

'Shut up,' said Douglas. 'You had your chance, and you did nothing. Nothing but squabble and bicker, while good men and women died. I have done what was necessary, made a decision where you couldn't. That is what a Speaker and a King is for, isn't it?'

'You had no right to commit us to this!' said Michel du Bois, and other angry voices joined his. Douglas laughed in their faces. And then the esper representative spoke, his young voice somehow cutting effortlessly across the uproar.

'It's done,' he said calmly. 'The oversoul has teleported troops and gravity barges directly into position outside the House. Telepaths are quieting and controlling the minds of those who still feel like fighting. It's all over now, Your Majesty.'

'Damn you, Douglas,' Anne said quietly. 'What have you done?'

When Emma Steel became separated from Lewis Death-stalker by the mob, she was briefly lost, but she quickly spotted another familiar face in Paragon armour and purple cloak. She fought her way through the packed crowd, cutting down men and women with crazed faces and mostly improvised weapons, trying not to let the madness of the mob infect her. It would be only too easy to give in to anger, to kill for revenge instead of justice; but Emma Steel was a Paragon, and Paragons didn't do that. She was outnumbered, betrayed, surrounded by maddened rioters who would have torn her to pieces with her bare hands if they could; but still she fought with cold calculation, killing only when she had to, to survive. Right now, she was concentrating on getting to someone she could trust to guard her back. The Paragon she'd spotted was just ahead now, fighting with skill and precision, actually smiling slightly in the face of impossible odds. Not that she would have expected anything less, from him. Emma didn't know many Paragons by sight, but everyone knew the classically handsome features of Finn Durandal.

Finn didn't see her coming, being more preoccupied with looking good. He'd come out into the crowd, because it could have looked odd, if not downright suspicious, if he hadn't.

There was no plausible way he could have avoided knowing about the riot, or the assault on his fellow Paragons, and if he hadn't put in an appearance, people would have asked questions. They might even have begun to doubt him, and he couldn't have that. He still needed to be seen as the selfless hero they'd always thought he was. So he came roaring in on his gravity sled, jumped down into the thick of the fighting, right next to a hovering media camera, and got stuck in, smiting the ungodly with all his usual vim and vigour.

Of course, there was no point in taking unnecessary risks. The people he'd chosen to fight were actually his own people, hand-picked bravos recruited from the smoke-filled dens of the Rookery; paid handsomely to put up a good fight and lose impressively, right where the camera could see it. And protect him from the genuine rioters while they did it. They blended in easily with the rest of the mob, largely anonymous in their previously supplied crimson Church outfits, and engaged Finn in lengthy, flashy but essentially safe duels that the watching home audience would eat up with spoons. And if none of these apparent bad guys were actually dying – well, that just showed how merciful and compassionate the great Finn Durandal could be.

It was all going very well, until Emma Steel suddenly appeared out of nowhere, bound and determined to fight at his side. He knew her reputation. Everyone did. He couldn't fake a duel in front of her and hope to get away with it. So he shrugged mentally, and killed his own people. He did it quickly, before they could realise he wasn't pretending any more, but even so, he thought Emma gave him a strange, almost puzzled look before the last of the bravos was dead, and the real crowd closed in around them, and they were both fighting for real.

Finn was just planning a path that would take him (apparently by chance) to the edge of the roiling crowd, and relative safety, when there was a roar of displaced air above him, and he looked up sharply to see military gravity barges appearing in the sky above the riot. Huge, dark vessels, bristling with rows of disrupter cannon, every one of them targeted on the crowd below. Loud broadcast voices called for the mob to throw down their weapons and surrender, or else. Finn and Emma stood back to back, sword and gun still in hand, looking quickly about them to see which way the crowd would go. The mob had found a taste for blood, and just might make a fight of it. And then the espers appeared, dozens of them, hovering in mid air beside and among the gravity barges, looking down on the mess of mere humanity below them like so many angels standing in judgement. Their eyes glowed bright as suns as they hung unsupported on the air, the sheer sense of their presence almost overwhelming. When they spoke it was with one voice, sounding simultaneously in everyone's mind; a great godlike Voice that could not be defied or debated, only obeyed.

Put down your weapons. Stand still. Wait quietly for the peacekeepers to come and take you away.

All through the crowd, people dropped guns and swords and improvised weapons, their hands opening in spite of themselves. The compulsion in their minds shut down everything but their most basic thought processes. Their faces were blank, their eyes empty, all rage and passion and individuality gone in a moment. Only the surviving peacekeepers, security forces and Paragons remained untouched, exempt from the telepathic geas. Emma slowly lowered her sword, looking wonderingly about her. Finn put away his sword and gun and walked away, unnoticed. Peacekeepers began slowly making their way through the calm, unresponsive crowd, searching out the trouble-makers and rabble-rousers, and collecting discarded weapons by the armful. The telepaths walked across the air above the crowd, sifting through minds in search of guilty secrets. Once that would have been an illegal, unthinkable act, but the oversoul had the King's authority. For the moment. And men and women who only a moment before had been willing to fight and die for the cause they believed in, now stood listlessly, helplessly, and let them do it.

They were still standing there some time later, when the troops came to lead them off in restraints, and the medics came to treat the injured and name-tag the dead. There were a lot of dead. A surprisingly large number were Paragons. The beloved heroes of the Empire now lay still and silent on the bloody ground, wrapped in the tatters of their proud purple cloaks.

Parliament and the King watched in silence as the crowd stood placidly, their eyes as blank and uncomplaining as the beasts of the field. Peacekeepers took away certain individuals that the media coverage had revealed as instigating or orchestrating the troubles. Sometimes the peacekeepers hit or beat these people, or pushed them violently to the ground and kicked them, and they took it silently, unable to complain or protect themselves. There was still a lot of anger in the air, from those who had survived the madness of the mob. Most of the crowd would go to improvised prison compounds the military were hastily putting together on the outskirts of the city. There would be time for courts and laws and rights later.

Most would probably just be released, with a warning. Clogging up the Courts to no great effect wouldn't serve anyone. And besides, the Church and the Neumen had proved themselves a powerful force. It wouldn't do to antagonise them unneccessarily. None of the MPs said that out loud. They didn't have to. They just sat and watched in silence as the crowd was silently dismantled and led away. Up above them, hanging on the sky like they were nailed there, the espers broadcast tranquility, the influence of their powerful minds holding the crowd effortlessly in their grasp. Some of them were smiling. They didn't look like angels any more. If anything, they looked like birds of prey waiting for some slow and stupid animal to die.

'Espers controlling human minds,' Michel du Bois said finally, his voice full of a cold, tired bitterness. 'Putting their thoughts into other people's minds. Taking away their free will, making slaves of them. Does this perhaps remind Your Majesty of anything? Of what the ELFs did in the Arena, only a few weeks ago?'

'The ELFs were responsible for acts of terrorism and murder,' said King Douglas, still looking at the viewscreen. 'The oversoul was responsible for stopping acts of terrorism and murder.'

'That's not how the people in the street will see it,' said Meerah Puri. 'Some things are just wrong, no matter who does it, or why.'

'Then the hell with them, and the hell with you,' said Douglas, rising sharply to his feet. 'I'd do it again in a moment. They were killing my Paragons. My colleagues and my friends. And my Champion . . . may be dead too. I should have been there at his side. You want my Crown, honoured Members? You can have it.' He took the Crown off and put it on the Throne. 'I did what was necessary. I've always been able to do what was necessary. That's what a Paragon does. I'm going to see what's happened to my friend Lewis. You can send someone later to tell me if I'm still King. Maybe I'll care, later.'

'You can't leave,' said Tel Markham. 'This House is still in Session. We haven't dismissed you yet.'

Douglas looked at Markham, and the MP flinched despite himself, and looked away. Douglas looked around the House, and everywhere people were unable to meet his dark and dangerous gaze. He smiled briefly. 'God damn you all to Hell,' he said quietly. 'All of you together aren't worth one of the Paragons who fell defending you. What has the Empire become, what have we become, that such a price was necessary? There's a madness in the streets, a sickness in the soul, and I fear it has infected us. Make your compromise deals with the Church and the Neumen. Protect yourselves. I can't stop you. But I don't have to watch you do it. I still have my pride.'

He turned his back on them, and walked out of the House, ignoring the uproar of voices that broke out behind him. Outside, Anne was waiting for him.

'Any news of Lewis?' said Douglas.

'He's been brought in,' said Anne. 'They've got him in the infirmary.' Douglas set off down the corridor, and Anne padded along beside him. 'They've got him in a regeneration tank. Douglas . . . the odds aren't good. He took a disrupter bolt at point blank range.'

'But he is still alive?'

'Yes. For the moment, he's still alive.'

'I should never have let him go out there alone, Anne. I shouldn't have let you stop me going with him.'

'If you'd gone, you'd be lying in a regen tank beside Lewis. If we were lucky.'

'I let him down,' said Douglas. 'He was always there for me, and I let him down.'

'You did the right thing, Douglas.'

'What's that got to do with anything? Our friend is dying.'

'I know. I know.'

They strode down the corridor together, and people saw their faces and hurried to get out of their way.

Lewis was as surprised as anyone when the lid of the regeneration tank rose up, and he was still alive. He was even more surprised to discover that the reptiloid Saturday was gone, and there waiting for him in that cold and empty room was an utterly distraught Jesamine Flowers. She was crying, great shuddering sobs that shook her whole body as tears streamed down her cheeks. She saw him trying to sit up in the tank, and hurried forward to help him out of it. His legs felt like they belonged to someone else, and he sat down suddenly beside the tank, feeling at his side where the ragged hole had been. And Jesamine threw her arms around him, and buried her face in his shoulder. They sat together, holding each other tightly.

'Oh God I thought I'd lost you,' Jesamine said finally, her face still pressed against his shoulder. 'I saw them shoot you, and it was as though someone had shot me too. I couldn't breathe. When they told me the alien was bringing you in, I came straight here. I couldn't believe the state you were in. There was a hole in your side the size of my fist. You were barely breathing. I was so sure I was going to lose you.'

'The regen tank does good work,' said Lewis, his face buried in her golden hair. It smelled good. It smelt like life, and happiness. 'But even so, I hate to think how close it must have been. Even regeneration tanks can't work miracles. But I couldn't die, Jes. I couldn't die, and leave you behind. Not after I'd finally found you. Found the only woman I ever loved.'

They pulled back a little, so they could look each other in the face. Jesamine's face was almost ugly, blotched with colour, her eyes puffy from crying so hard. Lewis' face seemed somehow harsher, even with the blood and brains cleaned away, as though his brush with death had knocked all the easiness out of it. They were holding each other's hands, so tightly their knuckles were white.

'You mean that?' said Jesamine. 'You love me?'

'With all my heart, Jes. It's wrong. I know it's wrong, I know it can't go anywhere. But I don't care.'

'I don't care either,' said Jesamine. 'I love you, Lewis. So many men have passed through my life, but you're the only one I ever cried over. The only one who ever mattered to me.'

'You're everything I ever wanted, Jes. Everything I thought love would be. Typical Deathstalker luck. To love the one woman I can't ever have.'

'Can't? Lewis . . .'

'No, Jesamine. Listen to me. One of us has to be strong. Strong enough to do the right thing. You're going to marry my best friend. It's all arranged. All of Humanity wants this marriage. Douglas wants it, and I'd rather die than hurt him. You're going to be his Queen. The Empire needs you.'

'I need you, Lewis! Doesn't that matter? Doesn't that mean anything?'

'It means everything,' said Lewis. 'But we can't let it matter. I'll leave. Go away. Marry Douglas and be happy, Jesamine.'

'Lewis . . . I can't . . .'

'You must. I could not love thee half so much, loved I not honour more,' said Lewis Deathstalker. 'I can't, I won't, betray my friend, my King.'

'It's not fair. It's not fair!'

'No it isn't. Let me go, Jes. Let me leave, while I still have the strength to do it.'

'Where will you go? What will you do?'

'I don't know. Oh God, I don't know anything any more.'

They moved forward into each other's arms again, murmured

their love for a while, and finally, tenderly, kissed each other goodbye. And that was how Douglas and Anne found them.

For a long while the two of them just stood there, watching, silent, and then Douglas said Jesamine's name. His voice seemed very loud in the quiet of the deserted infirmary. Lewis immediately let go of Jesamine, and looked round sharply. Jesamine held on a moment longer, her eyes closed, as though she could deny what was happening, but then her innate inner discipline re-established itself, and she let go. She'd always been able to be strong, when she had to be. She looked around, unhurriedly, her face calm and composed, though there was no hiding her puffy eyes or the damage to her makeup. Lewis rose to his feet, just a little unsteadily. He took a step towards Douglas, and then stopped, held where he was by what he saw in his friend's face. Jesamine looked accusingly at Anne, but she shook her head slightly. She hadn't told Douglas what she'd seen earlier.

'Lewis,' Douglas said, and his voice was so flat, so empty, it was like a slap in the face. 'What have you done, Lewis? I sent you out to stop a riot, not get involved in one. What did you think you were doing? How many people did you kill out there? Do you even know? I made you my Champion; it's important that you're seen to be impartial, at all times. You can't get involved in political struggles. Once it was clear they weren't going to listen to you, you should have withdrawn. Not drawn your weapons against civilians. You looked like a butcher. My butcher.'

'Those civilians were killing Paragons,' said Lewis, meeting Douglas' gaze steadily. 'They would have killed me. They did their best.'

'You made a bad situation worse,' said Douglas. 'I had to call on the oversoul, to shut the riot down. God knows what the espers will want in return, for that service. All because you failed me, Lewis.'

'What was I supposed to do? They'd gone crazy, all of them! I can't work a miracle every time!'

'Then what use are you to me?' Douglas said coldly. 'I need to be able to rely on you, Lewis.'

248

'You can! You know you can, Douglas. You know . . . I'll do the right thing.'

'I don't know anything any more! I was ready to give up my Crown for you, Lewis, and then I come here, and I find you . . .' Douglas looked at Jesamine for the first time. 'How can I do what I'm supposed to do, when I can't trust anyone any more?'

He turned abruptly, and stalked out of the infirmary, his back very straight, his head held high, but none of them could see his face. Jesamine squeezed Lewis' hand, once, and then hurried after Douglas. Lewis sat down again, his legs all but collapsing under him, and stared at the floor, broken and hurt beyond anything Brett Random's disrupter could have managed. Anne walked slowly over and sat down beside him. She sighed heavily, and leaned back against the open regeneration machine.

'Some days . . . things wouldn't go right if you bribed them.'

'Maybe I should have died,' said Lewis. 'Maybe . . . that would have been best, for everyone.'

'Oh shut up,' said Anne. 'I'll work something out. Though God alone knows what, or how. You couldn't have screwed this up worse if you'd tried, Lewis. You must know this can't go anywhere. There's no possible future for you and Jesamine. Too many vested interests have committed themselves to the new King and Queen. The momentum we've built up is unstoppable. Any change now, and there'd be riots in cities all over the Empire. A Royal wedding, a golden couple for a Golden Age, could heal the rifts in society, change the atmosphere, get people talking again instead of shouting. You can't be allowed to interfere, Lewis. Too much depends on everything going ahead as planned.'

'I know,' Lewis said miserably. 'I'd already decided I was going to leave. Get the hell offplanet and disappear. Let someone else be the Champion. I never wanted the job anyway. Let Finn have it. He'll do a better job. He understands politics and he's never had any bothersome emotions to get in the way.'

'You can't resign as Champion, and you can't leave,' Anne

said remorselessly. 'So far, there hasn't been even a whisper of gossip, and we have to keep it that way. You just up and go, abandoning your best friend on the eve of his wedding, and people would be bound to wonder why. Sooner or later, someone would discover the truth. Someone always does. And a scandal like this would be the end of Douglas as King. All the various causes and politicians would have a field day. I don't even want to think about what it would do to the balance we've been carefully creating in Parliament . . . No, Lewis. You're not going anywhere. You're going to stay here and tough it out, until we can figure out some way for you to credibly retire, and disappear into the background. Maybe a family emergency . . . Virimonde's a long way from anywhere . . . Give me time to think. I'll come up with something. In the meantime; *stay away from Jesamine*. If you're at the House together, don't even look at her, unless you're forced to. I'd say act naturally, but you're not that good an actor. I'll arrange the schedules to keep the two of you apart as much as I can, until she's safely married. Think you can keep it in your trousers until then?'

'This isn't about sex! It was never about sex! I love her, Anne!'

'No you don't. You can't. Too many people would be hurt. The fate of the Empire depends upon you doing the right thing. Remember your duty, Deathstalker.'

'I know my duty,' said Lewis. 'I've always known my bloody duty.'

Back at Finn's place, they were all back in their favourite chairs, passing bowls of snacks around, and watching replays of the riot on the big viewscreen. The news channels were broadcasting uninterrupted coverage, running all the best bits in slow motion, the better to show off all the blood and gore. Nothing like a little death and suffering in closeup to pull in the viewers. Hell, the riot was getting better viewing figures than Friday night at the Arena. Finn relaxed almost bonelessly in his chair, smiling and nodding, and even applauding some of the best bits. He'd come out of it very well, looking extremely heroic. Especially when he cut down his own people, right in front of the camera. He couldn't have planned it better.

Emma Steel had also come out of it well; her cool and calm composure in the middle of madness making her look very professional. Commentators were already saying that she and Finn should make a great partnership. Finn wasn't so sure. He didn't know just how much Emma might have seen, or suspect. She hadn't said anything, either to him or the media, but . . . That was a problem for another day. Right now he was feeling too good. The channel showed Brett shooting Lewis again, and Finn laughed out loud. The scene changed abruptly, to show people holding a candlelight vigil outside the House, praying for the Deathstalker to survive. Finn frowned. He hadn't realised Lewis was so popular. Still, there was no danger of Lewis actually dying, and becoming a martyr. Brett had aimed his gun very carefully, following his instructions to make it look as impressive as possible, while still missing all the major vital organs.

He glanced across at Rose Constantine, sitting scowling in her chair, sulking. Finn studied her for a moment. He'd never intended for her to kill Lewis, but of course he couldn't tell her that. The fight had to look natural. She had to be convinced, to be convincing. No; Lewis couldn't die yet. Not while Finn had such useful, amusing plans for him.

The vidscreen showed again the moment when someone in the crowd blew Veronica Mae Savage's head right off, starting the riot. Finn couldn't be more pleased. It was the exact visual image he'd needed, to blow everyone's minds. It helped that he'd never liked Veronica Mae, but any Paragon would have done. He made a mental note to send the assassin a bonus.

Brett had gone back to drinking heavily. He hadn't said a word since he returned. He watched the viewscreen, and took a big handful from the snack bowls when they came his way, but he seemed lost in his own unhappy thoughts. Finn decided he'd better keep a close eye on his new esper.

They watched the news coverage on the viewscreen for over an hour, switching back and forth between the channels to get a representative angle on the public's perception of the riot, and their reactions on how Parliament and the King had handled it. (The House was expressing solidarity with the King. For now.) A surprisingly large percentage of the viewing public were already expressing their displeasure over the way the powers that be had over-reacted. Specifically, they didn't like troops being brought into the city and unleashed on civilians, and they really didn't like the use of espers to control human minds. Comparisons were already being made with the way the despised Empress Lionstone used to do things. And every commentator on every channel was drawing comparisons between the ELFs and the oversoul, despite all the soothing words coming from the esper centre on New Hope. The general public feeling was that the King and Parliament had been heavy-handed in their reaction to a legitimate protest, and that *that* was what had caused the riot. A lot of people still supported the Church, even if they weren't too sure (as yet) about the influence of Neumen philosophy within it.

There was a lot of public sentiment over the death of so many Paragons (thirty-seven and still counting), but again the general feeling seemed to be that they shouldn't have been there in the first place. Paragons were supposed to deal with crime, not political protest. They were supposed to be the King's Justice, not his bully boys. There was no public call for a day of mass mourning, as usually happened when a Paragon fell in the line of duty. Finn found that especially significant.

Angelo Bellini turned up late, without even the grace of an apology, but ended up sitting on the edge of his chair, fascinated by the media coverage of the slaughter he'd helped to instigate. It was one thing to work quietly behind the scenes to ensure that everything went to hell on schedule, but quite another to watch the carnage unfold before you. Angelo all but bounced in his chair, his face flushed, breathing heavily. Finn thought Angelo looked a bit like Rose, when she was contemplating killing someone horribly. Angelo sensed Finn's gaze on him, and looked round, grinning foolishly.

'Death and violence and insurrection in the streets. The death of heroes and of ideals, and all of it at my command.'

An idea occurred to him, and he scowled suddenly. 'I hadn't planned for the oversoul getting involved. Could those espers dig our names out of those people's heads?'

'I planned for everything,' Finn said calmly. 'No-one actually present at the riot has any direct knowledge of me, or you. Their instructions came via so many cut-outs that the security forces will end up running in circles trying to make sense of it all. My people in the Rookery have already set in motion a wide-reaching plan of disinformation. No-one's coming after us, Angelo. I have put a lot of thought into this.'

Angelo nodded and looked back at the viewscreen, and immediately all his doubts were forgotten. 'I have to congratulate you, Finn. I never knew politics could be such fun. Such a rush. People going out to fight and die, at my command. The Parade of the Endless torn apart, and all because of me. I never knew power could be so . . . intoxicating.'

'Don't make a mess on the chair, Angelo,' said Finn. 'You didn't cause this. I did. You merely helped. This is all my plan, my work, and don't you ever forget it.'

'You couldn't have done it without me,' said Angelo, just a little haughtily. 'I put the Church in bed with the Neumen. I worked out the logistics for the marches. Those people listen to me, not you!'

Finn leaned easily out of his chair and slapped Angelo hard around the side of the head. Angelo rocked in his chair, and almost fell. He brought up a hand to protect himself from further blows, and opened his mouth to protest. And then his eyes met Finn's, and the words turned to dust in his mouth. Finn wasn't angry. He wasn't even excited. But in that moment he looked cold and controlled and very very dangerous.

'You are my creature, Angelo,' Finn said calmly. 'Mine, to do with as I wish. I own you. You can't go back to what you were, and if you ever think to cross me, or cultivate ideas above your station, I will destroy your media sainthood overnight, and have you removed from your own Church in disgrace. I will drag your good name through the gutter, and throw you to the wolves; and I will do it the moment you even think of setting your wishes in any way above mine. Or . . . I could just give you to Rose.'

'Give him to me,' Rose said immediately. 'The Deathstalker got me all hot, but I never got the chance to finish.'

Angelo actually whimpered faintly. He sank back in his chair, and concentrated very quietly on the viewscreen. Rose sniffed. Finn just smiled.

Brett Random poured himself another large drink from the brandy bottle on the arm of his chair, but it wasn't doing much for him. He took no pleasure from the slaughter and destruction of the riot. He didn't even have anything against the Deathstalker. Good man, from all he'd heard. He was just following Finn's orders when he shot him. He hoped (silently) that the Paragon would survive. Once, Lewis' ancestor and Brett's had been friends. Partners. Heroes, fighting side by side against evil. Things must have been simpler then. Brett couldn't help wondering what his legendary ancestor(s) would have made of him. He didn't think they'd have been too impressed.

Brett had never been a violent man. He knew the ways of gun and sword because you had to, to survive growing up in the Rookery. But he'd always preferred to work on cons where no-one really got hurt. Even the marks he soaked so thoroughly for money had nothing to really complain about. He always targeted the really rich bastards, who could afford to lose what he took from them. He only ever punished the greedy. Until now. Now, people were dying, because of him. Good people. He drank his brandy in heavy gulps, but it didn't comfort him. His stomach hurt worse than ever. Tension. Guilt. And perhaps, just perhaps, the beginning of conscience.

First chance he got, he was out of here, running for the horizon like his arse was on fire, and to hell with Finn bloody Durandal. This wasn't fun any more; if it ever had been. He looked up from his glass, and there was Rose, Wild Rose, looking thoughtfully at him again. She smiled, and Brett got gooseflesh all the way up both arms. Out of here, definitely. And the sooner the better.

Finn studied the rising body count being displayed on the

viewscreen, and smiled a slow, satisfied smile. He felt all warm and comfortable inside. Everything was going to plan. The commentators were calling this the worst day in the Golden Age's history. Only he knew that this, all of this, was just the beginning.

4

Terror in the Night

Emma Steel, Logres' latest Paragon, defender of the meek and avenger of the wronged, stood impatiently on the roof of her new apartment building in the early hours of the morning, her thick purple cloak flapping noisily about her in the gusting wind. She was waiting for Finn Durandal to show up. She'd been waiting for almost an hour, and was not in the best of moods. It was bad enough that Finn had been openly giving her the runaround for the past few days, before finally agreeing to at least take her on a tour of Logres' main city, but now it seemed he couldn't even be bothered to show up at the time he'd insisted on. Emma, who was never late for anything, took Finn's absence as a personal insult. She'd moved past outrage and planned insults, and was currently debating which side of the roof it would be most fun to push him off. No-one slighted Emma Steel and got away with it.

She fumed quietly, arms crossed tightly over her armoured chest, one foot tapping ominously. It didn't help that she was pretty damned sure that the Durandal had only agreed to this meeting because the media had been asking, in increasingly mystified tones, as to why Finn hadn't joined up with his new partner yet; particularly after they'd made such a good showing working together during the Neumen riots. Emma's mouth tightened even more as she considered that thought. There was a lot about the riot that bothered Emma Steel.

To start with, the sheer viciousness of the violence had shocked her rigid. Emma was used to violence; she'd grown up on Mistworld, after all, where assault and battery was a daily occurrence. But . . . civilians turning on Paragons? Killing

Paragons, their own beloved defenders, in what was supposed to be the most civilised city on the most civilised world in the Empire? If you couldn't trust the people of Logres to behave in a sane and civilised manner, then you couldn't rely on anything any more. Perhaps not even the legendary Finn Durandal. Emma's frown deepened into a scowl.

In those confused moments when she'd cut and hacked her way through the furious crowd to fight at Finn's side . . . surely she couldn't have seen what she thought she'd seen: the great and legendary hero Finn Durandal only going through the motions, only pretending to duel with the armed men before him. Certainly once she'd joined him, she'd seen him cut down the rioters with great skill and efficiency, showing not a trace of indecision or mercy. Emma felt disloyal even considering the thought that the earlier fighting might not have been everything it seemed, but she had to admit that in so many ways, Finn Durandal the man was nothing like the feted hero whose exploits had inspired her to become Mistworld's first and only Paragon.

Coming to Logres had been her greatest ambition. Working beside Finn Durandal had been her greatest dream. She should have known better. Never meet your heroes; they'll always disappoint you. And ambition was just a conceit that distracted you from getting the job done. Here she was, at the pinnacle of her career, and instead of concentrating on her work, rushing out into this city to make it her own, and show the local scumbags who was really in charge, she was standing dithering on an empty rooftop, trying to find answers to questions that made no sense.

But still the questions wouldn't leave her alone, nagging at her mind. In some way she didn't understand yet, these questions were important. They mattered.

Her gravity sled hovered beside her like a faithful hound, its engine barely ticking over. She glanced at it fondly. It was good to have one old friend with her, one thing she could still depend on. She'd brought the sled with her all the way from Rhiannon, paying the passage herself when the authorities on Logres refused to cover the cost. Bureaucrats. Penny pinchers. Emma had spent years customizing the sled, all but rebuilding it to meet her exactingly high standards, adding extra weapons and shielding and a whole bunch of (mostly legal) extra options. It was fast and powerful and full of surprises, and she'd back it against anything the bad guys had to offer. When she finally retired (many years from now, of course), Emma planned to license the sled to the military. She wouldn't be greedy. She wouldn't ask for a fortune. Just a percentage.

She stood on the very edge of the roof, the tips of her boots actually poking out over the long drop, and looked out over the city. Under the lowering sky, heavy with dark clouds still stained with blood from the newly risen sun, the Parade of the Endless stretched away for miles in every direction, thousands of buildings packed tightly together, full of millions of people. Those people were why she was here. They were her responsibility, her duty. Her flock. Hers, to protect against the wolves and other less obvious predators. She looked out over the great towers and spires and domes, the mile-long bridges, the slender elevated walkways and spiralling roads, and tried to see the great and marvellous city she'd dreamed of serving for so long. But all she saw was the stupid anger, the dumb stubborn viciousness, in the faces of the rioting crowd. The perfect people of the perfect city had slaughtered Paragons, and gloried in it. The wind that blew around her was suddenly bitterly cold, and full of omens, and Emma Steel wanted nothing more than to go home, back to familiar sights and familiar villains, and evils she understood.

And then, finally, there he was; gliding smoothly through the air towards her on a top of the range gravity sled, standing tall and proud, the cold wind barely ruffling his famous golden curls. The one and only Finn Durandal. He settled his sled down beside hers, and stepped elegantly down to favour her with a formal bow. Up close, he was every bit as big and handsome and impressive as she could have hoped, but Emma couldn't help noticing that his frank and open smile didn't even touch his eyes. She pushed the thought aside, telling herself she was only seeing what her suspicions wanted her to see, and stepped forward to sweep him into her customary hug. He froze inside her arms, his body becoming stiff and tense and unyielding, and she let him go immediately. She stepped back again, a faint flush of embarrassment darkening her coffee cheeks. Lewis hadn't minded . . .

'Welcome to Logres, Emma Steel,' said Finn. His voice was warm, pleasant, but essentially neutral. 'Sorry I haven't been around before, but I've been very busy. Really. You have no idea. Logres is a big planet, with a huge population; and with Donald and Lewis gone, I've been run off my feet. Even I can't be everywhere at once. Still; here we are, together at last. Partners. I've been looking forward to working with you. I'm sure we can learn all sorts of useful things from each other. And it'll be good to have someone to watch my back again. Logres can be a dangerous place, for the unprepared. So; climb aboard your sled, Emma, and I'll give you the grand tour. Show you the ropes. Get you started. I'm sure you'll pick it up in no time at all. Crime is crime, after all, and villains are villains wherever you go. And do call me Finn; we don't stand on ceremony around here.'

And that was it. The whole welcome speech and introduction, all over in under a minute. Lots of smiles and eye contact, but no real warmth. And no real information, either. Just a quick presentation that he'd probably rehearsed in front of a mirror before he came out. Lewis had made her feel welcome. Made her feel like a valued partner, even if he did have a tendency to flap a bit about things that didn't really matter. Emma nodded tightly to Finn, and turned to her gravity sled. She'd known immediately where she was with Lewis. She wasn't a jot closer to understanding Finn.

She followed him out over the city, the two sleds riding high over the already bustling streets, almost up in the clouds. All the other air traffic gave them plenty of room, from the darting messengers on their slipstreamed boards, to the bulky freight carriers too heavy for the roads. Nobody waved, or even acknowledged their presence, and no-one wanted to get too close. Emma was scowling so hard now her brow had begun to hurt. As a Paragon you expected respect, not fear. Something was very wrong in Logres.

And she was pretty sure it all had its base in Finn Durandal.

She'd seen all the documentaries, including the drama reconstructions, studied all his major cases, even been a member of his official fan club, back when she was just a kid. He'd done amazing things in his time, especially when he partnered Douglas Campbell and Lewis Deathstalker. The dream team, the media had called them. Finn had been the ideal she'd modelled her life on. But this cold, casual, almost effete man, with his empty words and emptier smile, was nothing like the legend. Just a man, with muscles and a pretty face, and a few flashy fighting skills.

Nothing like the Deathstalker, who never looked anything less than the warrior he was. She had no doubts at all concerning the Deathstalker's conduct during the riot. Where others had seen cruelty, she had seen only passion. Where others had seen killing, she had seen only duty. Lewis had behaved as a Paragon should.

Finn led her down, out of the clouds and into the city. They swooped down like birds of prey, and all the other traffic scattered to get out of their way as Finn and Emma shot between the tall buildings, rising and falling on the bucking updrafts. The gusting wind had a sharp biting edge at this speed, buffeting around the edges of the sled's forward force shield, but once again it was the sheer scale of the city below that took Emma's breath away. Even at the very beginning of the day, with the last of the dawn still leaking out of the sky, already the streets were thronging with people and traffic, bustling back and forth like ants in a hive. Traffic filled the roads, filtered effortlessly through the baffling maze of streets by the city's central traffic computers. People were on the move, heading out to work, or back from the night shifts, in the city that never slept, never paused, never faltered. And all around, almost overwhelming when seen at such close range, towers and edifices shot up into the sky, fashioned like works of art, sparkling with brilliant lights, and more often than not flashing vivid holo adverts to the crowds below. The city; endlessly alive, vibrant and alert, stretching away like an endless sea of stone and steel, faceted with shimmering glass and precious metals. The greatest jewel of the Empire. Pride and wonder burst in Emma's heart, to be a part of such a city.

There was nothing like it on Mistworld, or Xanadu. Nothing so . . . intense, so alive and full of purpose.

Finn took her lower still, cutting back on his speed now, till they were scudding by barely a dozen feet above the heads of the pedestrians on the main city streets. People looked up to see the two Paragons sail past, and a few of them waved and some of them smiled, but most just stared up coldly, their faces set and grim. As though they were the ones sitting in judgement. Not at all what Emma Steel was used to. She knew she had a hard reputation; she took pride in it. But it had always been her proud boast that only the guilty ever had anything to fear from her.

Finn manoeuvred his sled close in beside hers. 'Don't mind them,' he said easily. 'They're just confused. They'll get over it.'

'They look like they hate us,' said Emma. 'Like they can't trust us. Like we're not really Paragons any more.'

'Never expect gratitude from those you serve, Emma. We protect them, do their dirty work for them, even clean up after their messes, but they never appreciate what we do. They don't care that we do a job no-one else can do, that we give our lives to it, because it needs to be done. They don't want to see the blood and suffering our job entails, because then they'd have to admit that they're part of the problem. If they were all clean-cut, law-abiding citizens, without guilt or secrets or hidden desires, they wouldn't need us. Would they?'

Emma didn't know what to say to any of that. It was harsh and cynical, and not too far from what she'd often thought herself, but . . . this was Logres. The homeworld of Humanity, the heart of civilisation. Things were supposed to be different here. And the Durandal's manner was decidedly strange. It was as though he was saying one thing, while meaning quite another, and challenging her to sort out the truth. It was almost as though . . . he was playing with her.

That impression only strengthened as the tour continued, and it rapidly became clear to Emma that Finn was only going through the motions. He was happy enough to point out famous landmarks, and talk vaguely about past cases, but he wasn't providing any of the hard information she needed. Like

261

where the main trouble spots were, and how to defuse them. Like who the main bad guys were, and where she should look for them. Who was on the way up, who was on the way down. Where you could go, and who you could talk to, to get answers to questions. Simple, straightforward local knowledge that any good peacekeeper needs to know, to do the job properly. Finn was talking a lot, but saying nothing. It seemed her first impression of Finn Durandal had been correct after all. There was no fire in him, no passion, nothing to indicate he gave a damn about doing the job, and doing it well. About being a Paragon. Finally it all got too much for Emma. She surged forward, and steered her sled abruptly in front of his, forcing him to a halt. She glared at Finn, and didn't even bother to disguise the anger in her voice.

'Is this it? Is this your idea of going on patrol, *partner*? We just fly around, admiring the scenery, and wait for an emergency call to come? We can't do anything up here! We need to be down there in the thick of it, down on the streets, asking questions and taking names! I checked with Dispatch, first thing this morning; there are hundreds of open and ongoing situations we could be investigating! And there's no way in hell I'm going to get any sense of how this city operates if you're not going to tell me anything I can use. Why don't you show me the Rookery? Lewis said . . .'

'Never mind what the Deathstalker said! He isn't a Paragon any more.' Finn looked at Emma sharply, dropping his calm mask for the first time. His voice was cold, powerful, authoritative. On anyone else, it would probably have worked. 'You stay clear of the Rookery, Emma. You're not ready for that yet. It's a very dangerous place, even for a Paragon. Perhaps especially for a Paragon. For all your impressive reputation, they'd eat you alive.'

Emma gave him her best sardonic look. 'I thought this was supposed to be the most civilised city on the most civilised world in the Empire? Are you actually telling me there's somewhere on Logres that you're afraid to go?'

'You only think you know evil,' said Finn. 'Because you know Mistworld, and Rhiannon. But they're just amateurs compared to Logres. Only the finest wines can produce the most poisonous dregs. Only the highest of civilisations can produce the most subtle, most terrible evils. The Rookery distils evil down to its most vicious concentrations. You wouldn't last ten minutes. When I think you're ready, when you've proved yourself to me, then I'll take you there. And show you things you never even dreamed of in your worst nightmares, little miss country cousin. Until then, stay out. That's an order.'

He broke off as a sudden call came in on the Paragon emergency comm channel. Finn and Emma listened intently as Dispatch filled them in on a Hellfire Club bomb blast at Logres' second main starport, Avalon City. Devils had blown a hole through a starliner's hull, right next to the hyperdrive engines, and all kinds of deadly energies were spilling out onto the landing pads. Fifty-seven dead, and hundreds mutating, with the figures rising all the time. Finn looked at Emma with something that might almost have been relief.

'Sounds like a bad one, even for the Hellfire Club. I'd better handle it. You fly around the city some more, get a feel for things. Go down onto the streets and talk to people, if that's how you're used to doing things. But keep your guard up, and for God's sake watch your back. *And stay out of the Rookery.* I don't want to have to write out a report on your death on your first day on the job.'

He turned his sled around without waiting for a reply, and sped off for Avalon City. Emma watched him till he was safely out of range, and then headed straight for the Rookery, using the coordinates Lewis had given her. There had to be some reason why Finn was so keen to keep her away from Logres' official crime centre. Something he didn't want her to see; something he didn't want her to know.

And Emma always wanted to know things other people didn't want her to know.

She found the supposed entrance easily enough; a narrow alleyway between two blank-faced, characterless buildings in an area of the city apparently given over almost entirely to storage and warehouses. The buildings were solid stone, with no windows, and steel doors so heavily reinforced you probably couldn't even scratch their paintwork with anything less than a point blank disrupter bolt. Not that Emma was planning on doing anything like that, of course. Or not yet, anyway. The warehouses didn't even have an obvious name or designation. Presumably if you didn't know who they were, and what they stored, your custom wasn't needed or welcome.

Emma stood at the mouth of the alleyway, looking down it, her gravity sled hovering patiently behind her. The alleyway was dark and shadowy, ostentatiously uninviting. Very much an *enter at your own risk* kind of alleyway. Emma looked back over her shoulder. The street was entirely empty. The few people who had been there when she arrived, apparently just going about their ordinary business, were gone now, and even the few windows overlooking the street were conspicuously empty. No-one was watching. Whatever was about to happen, no-one wanted to know. Emma smiled. She'd come to the right place.

When she looked back at the alleyway, she found she was no longer alone. Half a dozen unnaturally large men with the kind of bulky distended muscles you could only buy in body shops, had emerged silently from the shadows and were now blocking the entrance to the alley. Four had swords in their hands, one had an axe, and one had an energy gun. The men held these weapons with a casual authority that suggested they knew how to use them. Six to one odds. Emma's smile widened. It was going to be a good day. The man with the energy gun scowled, confused by her easy attitude. He stepped forward, his gun aimed squarely at her gut.

'Where do you think you're going, Paragon?'

'I'm new in town. Thought I'd see the sights. And everyone says the Rookery is the place to go, if you're looking for scumbags.'

'No entry,' said the spokesman, still scowling. 'Off limits. To people in general, and mouthy Paragon bitches in particular. You're new, so we'll make allowances; this time. Get back on your sled and go back to your own territory. Or we'll teach you a lesson in manners. Make you cry, little girl. Make you get down on your knees and beg to be allowed to run off home.'

'Will you really?' said Emma. 'I'd like to see you try. I really would. It's been a long time since any overweight thug with muscles between his ears has been able to teach me anything.'

She was grinning now. She knew she shouldn't, she knew it was unprofessional, but she just couldn't help herself. The man with the gun looked uncertain for the first time. Whatever reaction he'd been expecting, insolence and good cheer certainly wasn't it. He looked round at his associates, to reassure himself, and that was when Emma made her move. The moment the thug took his eyes off her, she launched herself forward into a tuck and roll, and came up with her sword and her gun already in her hands. The thug spun round, his gun still tracking where she used to be, and he was way off target when she surged back onto her feet and shot him neatly through his over-sized chest. The force of the blast punched a hole right through him and blasted him off his feet. He hit the ground hard, already dead, the front of his shirt on fire.

Emma laughed out loud and was in and among the others while they were still lifting their weapons, cutting about her with practised speed and venom, her sword a shimmering blur. They were big but they were slow, especially the one with the axe, and she cut them down with almost insolent speed. They were too used to intimidating their victims, and when they did have to fight, they'd grown far too used to their numbers giving them the edge. They weren't ready to face a professional fighter. And they'd never met anyone like Emma Steel. She slipped between them with dazzling speed, never where they thought she was going to be, her sword plunging in and out, killing one man and moving on to the next while the first was still crumpling lifeless to the ground. They were good with their swords, but she was so much better.

She let one live; the one with the axe. She stood before him, carefully out of range, still grinning nastily, not even out of breath. Blood dripped steadily from her blade as the axeman stared at her with wide frightened eyes. He slowly lowered his axe, as though it had grown too heavy for him to hold. Emma raised her sword slightly, and laughed softly as he flinched. This was going to be easier than she'd thought.

'You're alive because I want answers,' she said crisply.

'You'll stay alive as long as you answer truthfully. You even think of lying to me, and I'll whittle you down into a more responsible citizen. So; who do you work for? Who told you I was coming? Who told you to frighten me off? And what's going on in the Rookery that I'm not supposed to find out about? Talk to me, dammit, or I'll rip out your spleen and make you eat it!'

The thug screamed shrilly, dropped his axe and turned and ran back into the alleyway. He was quickly swallowed up by the concealing shadows, his scream fading away like the siren of a departing ship. Emma sighed quietly. Sometimes her reputation actually got in the way. She holstered her gun, pulled a piece of rag out of her pocket, cleaned her sword, and put it away. Then she cleaned the blood off her hands, dabbed at a few of the larger stains on her uniform before giving it up as a bad job, and put the piece of rag away. There was no point in going after the thug. He could have disappeared into a dozen different boltholes by now, and no doubt there were all kinds of nasty surprises and booby traps lying in wait if she was dumb enough to go into the darkness after him. Everything from massed disrupter fire to proximity mines. It was what she would have done.

Leave it for another day. Perhaps she could persuade the Deathstalker to provide her with another entrance point. He might even join her. Lewis looked like a man who might be up for a little righteous fun, even if he was the high and mighty Champion these days. Certainly he'd make a much better partner than Finn bloody Durandal . . . She frowned. She was going to have to look into that. Discover just why the Durandal wasn't the man he used to be.

She walked back to her waiting gravity sled, and found a small crowd had gathered. They seemed more interested in the dead bodies than in her. She smiled and nodded politely to them, but they just stared coldly back at her. They didn't look like the thugs; just ordinary, everyday people. But their faces were sour and sullen, their eyes angry. They looked like they would have liked to say angry, abusive things to her, if they'd dared. Emma supposed they were Rookery people, or at least Rookery supporters. If they weren't . . . that would mean the general populace's feelings towards the Paragons were even worse than she'd suspected. And she didn't want to believe that; not yet. Careful not to turn her back on anybody, Emma stepped up onto her sled, and soared up into the sky again. She kept on going, until she was high enough that the city spread out below her looked once again like the wondrous place it was supposed to be.

The current Patriarch of the Church of Christ Transcendent, the very reverend Roland Wentworth, had been demanding an audience with Angelo Bellini, leader of the Church Militant, ever since the Church demonstration turned into a Neumen riot, and Angelo had finally got around to seeing him. They sat facing each other across Angelo's very impressive, state of the art computerised desk, in Angelo's extremely sumptuous new office. Now that he'd moved up in the world, and finally become the very important person he'd always known he should be, Angelo had wasted no time in transferring his base of operations into the biggest office he could find in the great Logres Cathedral. The previous occupant hadn't argued. He could tell which way the wind was blowing.

The new office boasted every luxury that Angelo had been able to think of. Deep pile carpets, veined marble walls, efficient but unobtrusive central heating and air conditioning, and a long shelf packed with all the very best wines from the Cathedral's extensive cellars. Life was good. Angelo had denied himself nothing. Why should he? He was now the de facto head of the Church, supreme lord over the destiny of billions of souls, and it was about time the Patriarch realised it. Well past time that Roland Wentworth realised he was yesterday's man. Angelo leaned back in his oversized chair, activated the massage function, and smiled widely upon the Patriarch, sitting stiffly upright on his straight-backed uncomfortable visitor's chair. The Patriarch stirred uncomfortably under Angelo's smile, and blinked owlishly back at him.

'Nice office, Angelo. Very roomy. Bit overblown for my tastes, but then I never was one for the material pleasures. I was a monk, you probably know that, before I was called to be a Cardinal, and then the Patriarch. I was happy being a monk. All I ever really wanted. But they told me I was needed, and I always was a sucker for that . . . So here I am. And here you are. The Patriarch and what are you, exactly, now?'

'I'm the Angel of Madraguda. Media saint, spiritual inspiration for the Church Militant, and lord of all I survey. I'm Angelo Bellini; and the Church does what I tell it to. You must have noticed.'

'Well, yes,' said Roland Wentworth, diffidently. 'I'm not so much ignored these days, as bypassed. Important matters are no longer bought to my attention, my directives are lost or misfiled, and no-one in the media will take my calls any more. Half my staff don't even bother to come into work any more. It's like I've become invisible. But I am still the Patriarch, Angelo; chosen and anointed leader of the living Church, the rightly appointed, divinely blessed lord spiritual to all the Empire. And I will not easily be put aside or silenced. I have a duty and a responsibility to guide my flock, my Church, in the right direction. To save them from evil, and if need be, from themselves. If you want a fight, Angelo, I'm quite prepared to give you one. The Church and the Church Militant are not one and the same, for all your efforts. There are still a good many good people ready and willing to support me, and the true Church.'

'Only a fool starts a fight he can't hope to win,' said Angelo. 'You have a few well-meaning supporters, scattered here and there. I have the Neumen. You have faith and a good heart. I have an army of fanatical supporters, ready to fight and die at my merest word. All your precious convictions are no defence against cold steel. Faith won't stop an energy bolt.'

'You haven't read your Bible recently, have you, Angelo?' the Patriarch said calmly. 'You see, I'm really very unhappy with the way things have been going recently. I was confused for a while. I saw the Church changing, and I didn't know why. I thought perhaps it was my fault. That I was out of touch. But the Neumen riot was a mistake. Even I could see that didn't just happen. It was planned, orchestrated. By you. I freely confess I'm baffled as to why you should want such anarchy and bloodshed, but then, I have never understood evil. Only that I must fight it, with every weapon at my command.'

'Your time is past, Wentworth!' snapped Angelo, leaning sharply forward in his chair to glare across his desk. 'You and all your weak kind have no place in the new Church, or the Empire that's coming. Go home. Retire. Be a monk again. While you still have the choice.'

'The butterfly cannot go back to being a caterpillar,' said the Patriarch. 'I was chosen. And unlike you, it seems, I take my religion seriously. I will fight you, because I must. Even the quietest of souls can become a warrior, in God's name. We are all capable of becoming more than we are, or think we are. That's the basis of our faith. We can all transcend our lowly beginnings, in God's name. What do you believe in, Angelo? Do you believe in anything, apart from yourself?'

'I believe I'm going to become very rich and very powerful,' said Angelo. He leaned back in his chair, fighting to hold onto his calm. 'And I don't care what anyone else believes. None of that shit matters any more. All that matters now is whether you're for me or against me. Ah Roland; you have no idea how good it feels to be able to speak openly, to tell the truth after so many years of mouthing pleasant platitudes. Do you know why I was so very good at raising money for charities? Because the more I raised, the more I could skim off the top, to give myself the comfortable life I always knew I deserved. Personally, I think Pure Humanity are a bunch of mindless thugs, and their so-called policies are nothing more than childish xenophobia; but they do make such excellent soldiers. Just wind them up, point them in the right direction, and turn them loose. And then stand well back while they do all the necessary dirty work.'

'You admit it?'

'Why not? I'm not telling you anything you don't already know or suspect. And it's not like anyone will ever listen to you . . . You see, Roland, under you and your sort, the Church was never more than a wasted opportunity. No real power, no real influence, just a few woolly philosophies and a rather tiresome preoccupation with the Madness Maze. You had the ear of the King, the attention of Parliament, and the respect of the people; but you never did anything with them. You had no fire, no passion; no ambition. I have remade the Church in my own image, put some iron in its soul, and already it is a power base to be reckoned with. When I speak the King listens, Parliament shudders, and the people rush to obey. The cry is now; Ask not what your Church can do for you, but what you can do for your Church. And it never ceases to amuse me what people will do, in the name of religion. They'll hate and fight and kill, and do all sorts of vile and nasty things they wouldn't even dream of doing for any other cause. And I will give them the Madness Maze, eventually. God knows how many thousands or even millions of poor deluded fools I'll have to march through the damned thing to find out how it works, but then it's only ever been a short step from a fanatic to a martyr. And the Church has never been short of either.'

'I'll stop you,' said the Patriarch. 'I will stop this madness. This evil. Whatever it takes.'

'No you won't,' said Angelo. 'Your day is over, Roland. Goodbye.'

His hand moved almost casually to a single isolated control on his desk, and the transmutation bomb concealed under the seat of the Patriarch's chair detonated with a soundless explosion. It was really quite a small bomb, with a strictly defined blast radius, but it was very efficient. Sleeting energies slammed up into the Patriarch, ripping him apart at the genetic level. He cried out once, a harsh guttural sound of shock and pain and horror, but he never took his eyes off Angelo Bellini. His lower body collapsed in on itself, losing all shape and definition. His lap and waist transformed, slumping from flesh and bone into thick jelly, and then into a viscous pink protoplasmic slime, all in a few moments. His legs detached and fell away, already melting into more of the pink sludge as they sank slowly into the thick carpeting.

The Patriarch's torso dropped down into the mess in the chair where his lap had been, and also began to transmute. His hands clutched spasmodically at nothing. Roland Wentworth was still alive. His heart still beat, his mouth still worked, though no sound came out of it. And his eyes were horribly aware. Angelo Bellini leaned forward across his desk, studying the Patriarch's slow and awful death with hot, greedy eyes. Wentworth's chest jerked down again as his stomach disappeared, and then again, as his ribs dissolved, one after the other. The transmutation energies finally reached the Patriarch's heart and destroyed it, and the light went out of his eyes. His arms fell away from his shoulders, hit the slime on the carpet and slowly came apart. Roland Wentworth's head slumped forward onto what remained of his chest. A few moments later, only the head was left on the chair, and then that too was gone, and all that remained of the Patriarch of the true Church were long thick strands of pink protoplasmic slime, dripping slowly from the visitor's chair, and onto the expensive carpet.

'I never liked you,' said Angelo Bellini. 'Mealy-mouthed little snot. I'll make a much better Patriarch.' He settled back in his chair, breathed deeply, and then laughed suddenly. 'Now this . . . _this_ is power. I could get to like this.' He activated the comm panel set into his desk, and called his secretary. 'Miss Lyle; send in the cleaners, would you? I'm afraid my late visitor made something of a mess.'

Douglas Campbell, King of the Empire, Speaker to Parliament, and latest of a long line of heroes, pulled on his royal robes and checked his makeup in his dressing room mirror. With so many media cameras covering the House's Sessions these days it was vital that he looked his best. He scowled at his receding hairline, stuck out his tongue, winced at the sight of it, and reluctantly put it away again. He wasn't getting enough sleep these days, and it showed. But the work just kept coming, there was never any end to the paperwork, and he couldn't justify hiring any more assistants. He already had trouble remembering all the names of everyone working for him now. He looked down at the Crown, sitting on the table before the mirror, and decided against putting it on just yet. It always gave him a headache. He sniffed loudly, threw himself into his favourite chair, and nodded shortly to Jesamine Flowers, his wife- and Queen-to-be, sitting elegantly in the chair opposite him. She was wearing a devastatingly elegant gown with casual style and grace, her makeup was restrained but perfect, and Douglas just knew that she looked the part far more than he ever would.

'You're scowling again, Douglas. Don't. It'll give you lines.'

'Sorry. I was thinking. Look; we don't have a lot of time. The day's Session will begin in under an hour, and Anne's been paging me increasingly urgently ever since I showed up, but . . . I felt it was important we have this little chat. Clear the air, so to speak.'

'Of course,' said Jesamine. 'You first.'

'We're going to be married,' said Douglas, as naturally as he could. 'We couldn't stop that now, even if we wanted. Too many people want it. It's like a business merger, where the stockholders have voted it through, and to hell with what the board wants. It's inevitable, now.'

'Darling, you say the most romantic things. But yes, I understand. The show must go on. I take it the Champion won't be attending this Session of Parliament?'

'No,' said Douglas. 'I've decided he's needed urgently elsewhere. And he'll go on being urgently needed elsewhere, until after we're safely married.'

'I've seen the wedding dress. It's really very lovely. Practically a work of art.'

'Lewis is my best friend.'

'I'll look every inch a Queen. We'll make a lovely couple.'

'I should never have made him Champion. I should never have given up being a Paragon. We were happy then. Our lives made sense. I never wanted to be King.'

'You could abdicate,' Jesamine said carefully. 'It's not a prison sentence.'

'No. I can't. I'm needed.'

'Then be King, dammit! Do the job, and don't look back. Just as I'm not going to look back. We're going to be King and Queen. Nothing else matters.'

Douglas nodded slowly. 'I thought . . . we'd have the same choir my father chose for my Coronation. They sounded fine.'

'Bit weak on the descants, and the main tenor isn't nearly as good as he thinks he is, but yes, they'll do. Who's going to be best man? It can't be Lewis now.'

'No; it can't be Lewis. I thought maybe Finn Durandal. He was my partner for years, after all, and it might help to make things up with him, for not being chosen as Champion.'

'Yes, the Durandal. Good choice. He'll look good, he always does, and it'll play very well with the media. Maybe I should have Emma Steel as my maid of honour . . . If we can persuade her to leave the sword and gun behind. Any thoughts as to where we should spend our honeymoon? I hear the Sighing Mountains on Magellon are very lovely this time of year.'

'I thought perhaps the Black Lakes on Hali,' Douglas said diffidently. 'They've become quite the place to be, and be seen.'

'Oh yes, sweetie! Hali! Gorgeous scenery, and lots and lots of the very best people for us to look down our noses at.'

And then they stopped, and looked at each other for a long moment. In the three days since the Neumen riot, and its aftermath in the House Infirmary, Douglas and Jesamine had spent a lot of time together, making a great public show of togetherness, but there was still a great many things they hadn't said. Things that needed to be said, now, if only so that they need never be discussed again.

'We can still make this work, Douglas,' Jesamine said finally. 'We can be happy together, as King and Queen. As husband and wife.'

'We're really very well suited,' said Douglas. 'We have a lot in common, we work well together . . . It doesn't matter that you don't love me.'

'I do . . . care for you, in my way. You're a strong man, brave and true, with a good heart. Trust me, you don't meet many like that in show business. We'll make a good partnership. And I want to be Queen. It's what I've always wanted. And you'll make an excellent King. It doesn't matter that you don't love me.'

'But I do,' said Douglas, quietly, miserably. 'I do love you, Jesamine. That's the problem.'

'Oh God,' said Jesamine. 'Douglas . . . I didn't know. This . . . is going to complicate the hell out of things, isn't it?'

'Probably,' said Douglas. 'I love you, Jes. And Lewis is my best friend. Do you see now, why . . .'

'Of course, yes. No wonder you . . . How long have . . .'

'I loved you from the first moment I met you. I just looked at you, and knew you were the one. The woman I'd been waiting all my life to meet. The only woman I ever wanted to give my heart to.'

'Oh Jesus, Douglas; are you saying . . . you never loved anyone before me? Surely there must have been other women in your life before me? I mean; you were a Paragon, a Prince . . . the Empire's most eligible bachelor. I saw you on the gossip shows, with girls on your arm . . .'

'Oh yes,' he said, looking at the floor between his feet so he wouldn't have to look at her. 'There were always girls. Pretty girls, even beautiful girls. It's amazing how attractive being the only heir to the Imperial Throne can make a man. Some mothers did everything but smuggle their daughters into my bedchamber. And there have always been women desperate to bed a Paragon. Any Paragon. They even chased after Lewis, bless his ugly face, though he was always more . . . particular than me. I never had to go to bed alone, unless I wanted to. Some of them I even liked. But none of them ever meant anything. I never loved any of them; because I could never be sure any of them loved me. Loved the man, and not the Paragon, the Prince. You must know what I'm talking about. You're a star. A diva. Have you ever been in love, Jes?'

'Oh darling, I'm famous for it,' said Jesamine, fighting hard to keep her voice light and easy. 'Six marriages, twice as many official partners, and more lovers than I feel comfortable remembering. I never had to deny myself anything, so I never did. And it can get really lonely on the road, travelling from one theatre to the next . . . I was a real tart in my younger days, falling in love with every pretty face or nice tight little arse that came along . . . I was fond of them all, at the time, but . . . I can't honestly say any of them ever meant anything to me. None of them ever mattered. There's never been anyone in my life as important to me as me.' She laughed, just a little shakily. 'God, that makes me sound so

274

shallow. Douglas, you're a very impressive man. I'm just a star; you're a legend. You deserve someone better than me.'

'I don't think I could stand to meet anyone more impressive than you,' Douglas said dryly. He finally lifted his eyes to meet hers, and each of them saw compassion in the other. Douglas sighed, quietly. 'I guess we're stuck with each other, Jes. We're going to be King and Queen. We should be proud.'

'Yes, we should. It's a great honour.'

'It doesn't matter that you don't love me.'

'Oh Douglas . . .'

'Why Lewis, Jes? Why him?'

'Oh hell, I don't know. Perhaps because . . . he's so unimpressed with who and what I am. Because he's brave and honourable. Because . . . you always want what you know you can't have. It doesn't matter. It's over. Time to move on.'

'I have to be able to trust you, Jes.'

'You can, Douglas.'

'Lewis is a fine man.'

'Yes, he is.'

'I was always proud to call him my friend. But I think everything will be better, once he's gone.' Douglas rose to his feet, crossed over to the dressing room table, picked up the Crown and put it on his head. He looked briefly into the mirror, his face calm and empty, and then he turned his back on what he saw. He walked over to the door, opened it, and then paused there to look back at Jesamine. 'I'm giving up my only real friend to marry you, Jes. Don't ever let me regret it.'

Lewis Deathstalker sat alone in the only chair in his empty apartment, staring straight ahead of him, not really thinking about anything, waiting for it to be dinner time, so he could eat a meal he didn't want. The room was silent, still, with nothing to look at or distract him. Even the walls were bare. The few belongings he'd brought with him were mostly still packed in a crate in the next room along with the mattress that served as a bed. Lewis stared at an empty wall, not thinking, only feeling. When he'd eaten as much of his dinner as he could, he'd drop the disposable plates into the atomiser, go back to his chair, and sit and wait for it to be late enough for him to go to bed, so he could escape into sleep, and leave his life behind for a while.

How could everything have gone so wrong, so quickly?

He didn't have much to do as Champion any more. Douglas had seen to that. Anne had called, in the King's name, to tell Lewis his presence as Champion was no longer required at the House, and it seemed all his other duties had been suspended. So all that was left was to sit in his chair, and sometimes think about just how badly he'd screwed up his life. All the things he once took for granted, all the things he used to live for; all the honourable underpinnings of his existence had been swept away, and he didn't know what to do any more. He had betrayed his best and truest friend. Not physically, perhaps, but in his heart. He loved Jesamine Flowers, the woman, not the star, but she was going to be Douglas' bride, and Queen to the Empire, and even to love her in silence and from a distance was a kind of treason. He'd never thought love, when it finally came along, would be like this. A pain he couldn't bear, a need he couldn't ease, a woman he couldn't have. Dishonour and disgrace. But then, that was Deathstalker luck for you. Always bad.

Ask Owen. Ask Hazel. Wherever they were.

Lewis sighed, deeply, and looked slowly round his room for something to do, something to interest him, for a while at least. So he wouldn't have to think, or feel. He supposed he could go and unpack his belongings, but he couldn't seem to work up the energy. It wasn't as if there was anything important in the crate. He'd never been one to collect . . . things. Never had the time, or the interest. His work was his life. Or at least, it used to be. His eyes drifted on, across the empty room, and he wondered how he could have lived so long, and still have so little to show for it. His gaze finally settled on his computer terminal and monitor, sitting on the floor by the single polarised window. He supposed he should check to see if there were any messages. It wouldn't be anything important. Anything that mattered would come through his comm implant. But there might be something. Something to occupy him.

He rose slowly, tiredly, from his chair, like an old man, and walked over to squat down on the floor before the terminal. He hit the message function, and the screen lit up. Just the one message today, from the fan who ran his tribute site. Lewis frowned. Tim Highbury didn't usually bother him directly unless it was something important. Maybe he'd tracked down some new bootleg operation, making money off Lewis' name and reputation. Lewis always shut them down. He took his good name seriously. Besides, the last set of knockoff action figures had looked nothing like him. He made the connection, called Tim's private number, and the monitor screen immediately cleared to show the face of his truest fan and supporter. It was a young face, barely out of his teens, but Tim had been running the tribute site with frightening enthusiasm and efficiency ever since he was fourteen. Lewis smiled at him. It was good to know there were still some things you could depend on.

'Hello, Tim. Good to hear from you. What's up? Running short of funds at last?'

'No,' said Tim. 'It's not that.' His voice was high and uncertain, and he couldn't seem to meet Lewis' eyes. 'It's not the money, Lewis. It was never about the money. You know that. But I'm afraid . . . I'm going to have to shut down the site. Your site. In fact, it's already done. I'm sorry.'

Lewis just stared at him, lost for words. He wasn't sure how he felt about no longer having his own tribute site. On the one hand, he'd never been entirely comfortable with having a site at all; it encouraged too much of the fannish adoration he'd always found so embarrassing. But on the other hand . . . if there was one person he'd thought he'd always be able to rely on, it was Tim Highbury. Tim had always believed in him, understood him; stood between Lewis and the obsessives who would otherwise have made his life a misery. Before Tim had come along, Lewis had had to employ a screening system for his calls, and change his address every six months, to be sure of getting some privacy. And now . . . there was something odd about the way Tim was acting. He looked . . . not so much upset, as . . . disappointed.

'What is it, Tim? What's happened? Has someone been putting pressure on you, over the site?'

'No! It's not that. Well, not exactly. It's just . . . it isn't the same any more. People don't feel the same about you. Not since the Neumen riot. It's all changed. It isn't fun any more. I'm sure you'll find someone else to take over the site. Run it for you. For people who still believe in you. I'm sorry. I can't do it any more. I have to go now. Goodbye.'

His voice was all over the place. He was almost crying when he finally shut down the connection from his end. Lewis stared at the blank screen, almost in shock, and then shut down his screen. Tim had given up on him. His oldest, truest fan. Lewis hadn't thought it would be possible to feel more alone, more isolated and abandoned, but in this as in so many other things, he had been wrong. He got up and slowly walked back to his chair. His legs were unsteady, and he all but collapsed into the chair as he sat down again. Was it just the riot? Or could word about him and Jes already be circulating? No; it couldn't be that. Even a hint of such gossip would have had his place surrounded by journalists by now, baying for a statement. Could Douglas have simply put out the word that Lewis was now officially persona non grata? It wouldn't have been like Douglas, but then, he'd never been betrayed so badly before. But no; again that kind of rift between two such important people would have been meat and drink to the gossip shows. So why had Tim abandoned him?

His comm implant chimed in his ear, and Lewis sat up sharply as Douglas' voice came to him on his personal channel. Douglas sounded as calm and authoritative as always, but somehow . . . impersonal.

'Hello, Lewis. Sorry to bother you, but I have a job that needs doing.'

'Hello, Douglas. Don't worry; you didn't interrupt anything important. What can I do for you?'

'I need you to go over to the Court, and check on how preparations for the Wedding are going. They're way behind schedule, and I can't get a straight answer out of anybody as to why. I can't spare the time to go over and yell at them myself, so I want you to do it for me. Feel free to kick whatever arses you consider necessary, to get them up to speed again. Talk to you later, Lewis. Bye.'

And that was it. Lewis chewed the words over slowly, not sure he liked the taste, or what it signified. His first thought was that this was just makework, something to keep him busy. And a safe distance away from the House, and Douglas . . . and Jesamine. Anyone could have coped with such a simple problem. Hell, Anne could have sorted it out in her dinner hour. And asking him to ensure that the Royal Wedding ran smoothly could be seen as rubbing his nose in it . . . Except that that would have been petty. Douglas was many things, but petty had never been one of them. So, was there something . . . important, significant, happening at the Court right now that Douglas needed Lewis to investigate? Something Douglas couldn't afford to notice officially? Some threat, some dispute, some underhandedness that Douglas couldn't discuss openly? God knew there were enough groups and individuals who'd seize on any chance of disrupting the Wedding. Lewis remembered the suicide bomber at the House, considered how much damage a transmutation bomb could do at the Wedding, and shuddered despite himself. Only one way to find out what was going on at Court; go and see.

So he went.

He was actually feeling pretty good by the time he got to Court. Good to be doing something again, something that mattered. The Court itself was full of people running back and forth on urgent errands, all of them apparently far too busy to stop and talk with him. Lewis strolled slowly round the great hall, getting the feel of things, looking and listening and saying nothing, while everyone else gave him plenty of room without actually acknowledging his presence or very existence. It soon became clear to him that while there was a lot of shouting and waving of arms going on, not to mention a hell of a lot of bad language, nothing much was actually getting done, because no-one could agree on what needed doing first. Everyone had their own agenda and deadline, and no-one was prepared to back down for anyone else. Projects kept being left unfinished or only half done because some other section leader would come along and commandeer the workforce for their own half done or unfinished project.

Lewis sighed, metaphorically rolled his sleeves up, and got stuck in.

When in doubt, go to the top. Lewis searched out each section leader in turn, and talked to them politely and earnestly. When that didn't work, he grabbed two handfuls of their shirtfronts, slammed them up against the nearest wall, and glared at them till they whimpered. He explained how much better it would be for everyone if they stopped arguing and fighting with each other, and started to behave in a civilised and cooperative manner, and everyone he talked to nodded eagerly, and didn't stop nodding until he took his hand off his swordhilt. Or, in extreme cases, their throats. Lewis then assembled all the heads of section together in one place, and explained how unhappy the King was with their lack of progress. And how unhappy that made him. He went on to explain that if they couldn't or wouldn't do their job, and get things running smoothly and back on schedule in very short order, he would personally see that they were all buried in one big communal grave (probably but not necessarily after they were dead) and see how their second in commands did as section leaders. Everyone agreed to be much more civilised in future, and send the King's office regular progress reports to prove it, and Lewis sent them all back to work with smiles and encouraging words, a promise of a substantial bonus if they came in on time and under budget, and a good kick up the arse to help the slowest moving on his way.

And that should have been that.

Except . . . Lewis couldn't get over how frightened of him they'd all been. All right, he'd played his part to the hilt, complete with menacing stare and heavy breathing, because they wouldn't have taken him seriously if he hadn't, and he'd been quite prepared to slap a few heads if that was what it took to get their attention, but some of them had started sweating the moment they recognised him. Some of them looked like they would have run away, if they'd dared. If he hadn't known better, Lewis would have sworn they were actually taking his threats seriously. That they really believed he would kill them if they didn't do what he said.

Which was . . . disturbing.

Lewis took up a position on the raised dais, beside the King's Throne, and looked out over the Court again. There was a lot less shouting and carrying on going on now, and rather more constructive effort, but no-one wanted to look at him. In fact, people were going out of their way to avoid even having to come close to the dais. Lewis was honestly baffled by this. He was used to respect, he felt he'd earned that in his years as Paragon and the King's Justice, but this . . . this wasn't respect. It was fear. They were acting like some wild animal had come into their midst, that might go mad and attack them all at any moment.

Lewis looked around until he spotted a journalist, doing an on the spot commentary to his camera floating before him. Lewis stepped down from the dais and headed casually towards him. People scattered to get out of his way. The journalist looked around sharply, took one look at Lewis bearing down on him, broke off his commentary and headed straight for the nearest exit, his camera bobbing along behind him. Lewis increased his pace. The journalist glanced back over his shoulder, saw that Lewis was catching up, and broke into a run. Lewis sighed, drew the thin throwing dagger from the top of his boot, took careful aim and let fly. The dagger snapped through the air, caught the journalist's flowing sleeve, and pinned it firmly to the wall. The journalist was jerked to a sudden stop, and almost fell. He was still tugging furiously at the sleeve and the dagger, cursing and swearing and blaspheming, when Lewis finally caught up with him. The journalist straightened up, flashed Lewis a desperate and entirely unconvincing smile, and set his back firmly against the wall.

'Sir Deathstalker! Sir Champion! Wonderful to see you! Looking good. Yes. Aren't we having absolutely marvellous weather?'

'Why did you run?' Lewis said interestedly.

'Urgent story!' said the journalist. He was sweating heavily now, and his eyes were very big. 'Just breaking. You know how it is. Very important story, and significant, and I really must be going. Can't stop! Sorry!'

'Stand still,' said Lewis. 'You're not going anywhere until

you and I have had a friendly and informative little heart to heart.'

'Oh shit,' said the journalist, miserably.

'What's your name, and who do you work for?'

'Adrian Pryke, Sir Deathstalker. Channel 437. News and views and everything that moves. *If it matters, we're there.* Look, I really must be . . .'

'No you mustn't,' said Lewis. 'Talk to me, Adrian Pryke. Talk to me openly and honestly, or I will bounce your head off that wall until your eyes change colour. Why are you so scared of me?'

'Are you kidding?' said Pryke, so desperate now he was too scared even to be polite any more. 'After what you did in the Neumen riot? *Everyone*'s shit scared of you!'

Lewis looked at Pryke for a long moment. 'I did my duty.'

'You killed people! Lots of people! Cut them down and butchered them, right in front of the cameras, and looked like you were enjoying every minute of it. That wasn't duty. It wasn't even law. It was retaliation.'

'Paragons had been murdered. I was avenging my fallen comrades.'

'Paragons are supposed to be about justice, not vengeance.' The journalist's voice was full of bitter resignation now, as though he expected to die, so nothing he said mattered any more. He could tell the truth, because the worst had already happened. 'We all saw it, Deathstalker. You went after the people who killed your friends, and you cut down everyone who got in your way, whether they were guilty of anything or not. And you smiled while you did it. There was other people's blood on your face, and you smiled. We've been running coverage of what you did in the riot pretty much non-stop ever since. Not just 437, all the news channels. No-one could believe what you did. That you could be so vicious, so . . . out of control. The famed Deathstalker rage, turned on civilians. No-one trusts you any more. What's the matter, Deathstalker? You said you wanted the truth. Don't you have the stomach for it?'

'I didn't kill anyone who wasn't trying to kill me,' said Lewis.

'We all saw, Deathstalker. We all saw what you did. We all saw the real you.'

Lewis jerked the dagger out of Pryke's sleeve and out of the wall, and the journalist flinched, clearly expecting a killing thrust. Lewis put the dagger back in the top of his boot, and stepped away from the journalist.

'Thank you, Adrian. You can go now.'

Pryke looked at him dubiously. 'You mean it? You're not going to kill me?'

'No, Adrian. I'm not going to kill you.'

'Oh good,' said Pryke. 'Then, if you'll excuse me; there's a toilet calling my name really loudly.'

He edged sideways across the wall until he was safely out of Lewis' reach, and then he turned and ran for the exit, his camera chasing after him. He didn't look back, as though afraid Lewis might change his mind and come after him. Or shoot him in the back. Lewis watched him go, and then turned slowly to look out over the Court again. It had all gone very quiet. Everyone was watching him. As Lewis looked back at them, they all avoided his gaze and went about their business again. The general noise and hubbub slowly resumed, but nowhere near as loud or as lively as before.

Lewis leaned back against the wall, suddenly tired. He scowled, his ugly face uglier than usual. This was why Douglas had sent him to the Court. What Douglas had wanted him to see, to know. To learn the truth that Douglas hadn't been able to bring himself to say in person. That everyone was scared of Lewis Deathstalker now. That no-one trusted him any more. Not because of Jesamine, but because of what he'd done, what he'd let himself do in his rage, during the Neumen riot. They all thought he was a monster, and perhaps they were right. No wonder Tim Highbury didn't want to run his site any more.

He wasn't just a monster. He was a pariah.

That was what Douglas had sent him here to learn. One last gift from an old friend? Or one more twist of the knife, from a new enemy?

Lewis Deathstalker strode out of the Court, head held high, and everyone there was glad to see him go.

283

Brett Random and Rose Constantine were back in Finn Durandal's appartment again, sitting in their usual chairs, waiting for instructions. The Durandal was off somewhere playing the good Paragon with Emma Steel, but he'd promised he'd be back as soon as he could credibly slip away and leave his new unwanted partner to her own devices. So Brett and Rose waited, not looking at each other, not talking. Brett had already dosed his aching stomach with everything in his and Finn's medicine cabinet, and none of it had done a damned bit of good. Brett rubbed soothingly at his tormented stomach with both hands, and wondered dismally if perhaps he should contact Dr Happy, and use Finn's line of credit to beg a little something. The ache kept him awake at night, and drove him from his bed far too early in the mornings, and he was getting really bloody tired of it. No amount of promised money or power was worth this, and Finn's threats on what he would do to Brett if he even thought of leaving were seeming less and less intimidating by the hour. Sometimes Brett thought he would sell his soul, or what little was left of it, if his gut would only stop hurting so badly.

He sat slumped down in his chair, his knees almost on a level with his chest, and looked morosely around Finn's place in search of something to occupy his attention. Something small and precious he could smash, perhaps, and claim it was an accident. He'd already drunk everything worth drinking, and raided the kitchen twice. Sometimes eating something made his stomach feel better, and sometimes it didn't, but Brett had always been a great comfort eater. Trouble was, Finn's culinary tastes tended towards the bland, not to mention the downright boring, and Brett had his standards.

He looked cautiously across at Rose, sitting in her chair pulled uncomfortably close beside his. Her head slowly turned, and she looked at him with her dark, unblinking eyes. She'd been looking at him a lot lately, ever since their minds had touched through the esper drug. When he'd discovered, very much to his surprise, that there was more to her than just a killer after all. God alone knew what she'd discovered about him. He was damned if he could read her expression. She was wearing the same tight fitting red leathers she always wore, the colour of drying blood all the way from her toes to her chin, all seven foot of her. She made the chair look like it had been built for a child, and even though she was sitting perfectly, almost inhumanly still, she dominated the room with her sheer presence.

Brett studied her openly, and she let him. With her bobbed black hair, dark as the night, her deathly pale skin and savage crimson mouth, she looked like some ancient death goddess, resting from making her rounds of the battlefield, where she tore the eyes from staring faces, like some great and awful gorecrow. Brett was hard pressed to decide whether she was good looking. She was just too intense, too fierce, too untamed for such conventional verdicts to apply. Striking, certainly. Attractive, like a well-fashioned weapon. Even sexy, in a disturbing and frankly rather sick way. She scared Brett shitless, but then most things did, these days. He bit his lip, frowning, as he tried to put into words how he felt about her. She should horrify him, but . . .

He realised he'd been staring at her for a long while, and she hadn't objected. She was still looking at him, calm and curious, as quietly menacing as a coiled snake. Brett swallowed uncomfortably, and sat up a little straighter in his chair.

'So, Rose; I see you got your leathers repaired. After you took that hit in the ribs. During the riot.'

'This is another outfit,' said Rose. 'I have seven sets, all exactly the same. It saves me from having to waste time deciding what I'm going to wear when I get up in the morning. I have no patience for distractions like that. The Arena Board had a famous designer produce the original set for me. Image is everything, apparently. I didn't object. I like leather. It's practical. And it scares people. That's useful, in the Arena. Fights can be won and lost, over how an opponent sees you.'

Brett was taken aback. She'd never spoken so much at one time to him before. In fact, he'd never heard her say that much to anyone before; not even Finn. If it had been anyone else, he'd have said she was confiding in him. Maybe even trying to reach out to him. He cast his mind about for something else to say.

'They're very nice leathers. The colour is so you. But don't you ever get uncomfortable in them? I mean, I used to know this girl who made . . . educational features. For a mature, discerning audience. She wore a lot of leather outfits, and she always said they made her sweat like a pig.'

'I don't sweat,' said Rose. 'It's bad for the image.' She paused. 'That was a joke.'

Well, very nearly, thought Brett. *Jesus, she'll be trying to smile next. I don't know if I could cope with that.*

'I'm glad you're here, Brett,' Rose said slowly. 'I wanted to talk to you. In private. This . . . is difficult for me, Brett. I don't talk much to people. They don't talk much to me. I don't have much in common with people. You probably noticed. I live for the fight. For the kill. For the spurting blood, and the look in their eyes as the life goes out of them. And for years, that was all I needed, all I wanted from people. But you, Brett . . . you're different. I feel differently about you. I want . . . to know you. Better. And I don't know why.'

She's trying to come on to me, Brett thought incredulously. *I'm not sure if she even knows what that means, but that's what she's trying to do.* Brett seriously considered jumping up out of his chair and running for his life, but somehow he didn't. Partly because she'd probably kill him before he reached the door, if she decided she'd been insulted, and partly because . . . there was something almost touching in her awkward attempts to reach out to someone else. Maybe for the first time in her life. It didn't make her one bit less scary, but . . .

'You can talk to me, Rose, if you want,' Brett said carefully. 'What would you like to talk about?'

'I don't know. This is all new to me. New territory. Is this what friends do?'

'Sometimes. Don't you have any friends, Rose? No, of course not, silly question.'

'I never wanted friends. People complicate things. They want things from me, things I never understood. Friendship, love, sex; those things have always been a mystery to me. But now . . . I want to know about you, Brett. Who you are, what you are. Who and what you were, before we met. Is that the kind of things friends want to know?'

'Yes, Rose. You got it.'

Brett got ready to launch into his usual patter, the carefully rehearsed and polished parcel of lies he always trotted out when he wanted to impress a new woman in his life, but somehow . . . he couldn't do that to Rose. She wouldn't have appreciated them anyway. So for once, and much to his surprise, Brett told the truth.

Brett Random had grown up in the Rookery, with a mother who earned the rent on her back, and a whole succession of step-fathers who came and went as the mood took them. Sometimes they gave him money, and sometimes they hit him, but Brett never gave a damn either way. He took to the streets at an early age, looking out for himself because he was the only one he could trust, getting himself into every kind of trouble there was going, teaching himself the art of the con and the dodge, because that was what he was best at. And because he enjoyed it. He made himself a name to be reckoned with before he was out of his teens, while outside the Rookery he carefully constructed a dozen new names, faces and identities, all of them ready for use at a moment's notice. He made and lost a dozen fortunes before he was twenty, and never missed any of them. He wasn't in it for the money. It was the chase and the challenge, and the thrill of the game that consumed him. That made him feel alive.

But he never forgot his one distinct claim to true greatness; that he was descended from not one but two of the Empire's greatest heroes. He was a Random's Bastard, through his long lost father: some wandering soul who'd impressed his mother so much she gave her only child his father's surname. It could all have been a lie, of course, just a line to impress his mother, but Brett didn't think so. He'd always known he was destined for greatness. He could feel it, in his bones and in his soul. One day he would be great himself. Whatever it took.

You need dreams like that, in the Rookery.

'So there you have it, Rose. The story of my life, such as it is. I am what I have made of myself. The prince of the con, and the double bluff. How about you now? What awful and traumatic events divorced you from the rest of humanity, and made you into the Wild Rose, the terrible and legendary killer you are today?'

'I made myself what I am,' said Rose. 'No-one helped me. I had a perfectly normal family, and a perfectly normal upbringing. Never actually rich, but always comfortable. I had parents who cared for me, and were always there when I needed them. There's nothing in my dull ordinary past to explain me. I'm just a cuckoo, a monster, a freak of nature. Blood and suffering and slaughter are meat and drink to me; it's music and laughter and sex. And all I ever needed . . . until now. When our minds touched, through the drug, I saw there was more to life than I thought. I saw things . . . that I've always wanted, without knowing it. I saw love and sex in your mind, and for the first time it seemed to me that perhaps there was more to them than the bumping of bodies. There's comfort and sharing and peace of mind, and more. I want those things, Brett. I want to know them. Teach me about friendship. Teach me about sex. Show me.'

Oh hell, thought Brett. *Why me, Lord?*

But you don't say no to a psychopath. So Brett reached out and took her hand in his. He pulled off the crimson leather glove and dropped it in her lap. She looked at him, curiously, dispassionately. Brett brought her bare hand to his face, and slowly trailed the tips of her long slender fingers across his cheek. And slowly, very slowly, guiding her hand with his, he moved her hand from his cheek to his chin to his mouth. Rose frowned, concentrating on the moment, on the sensations. Brett kissed her fingertips, one at a time. Rose pulled her hand away, held it up before her face, and looked at it. Brett sat very still. And then Rose reached out, took his hand in her deadly killer's hand, and moved his fingertips slowly across her face. He smiled encouragingly. There was something new in the room with them. Brett leaned over in his chair, and pressed his other hand on the red leathers over her chest. The material creaked loudly, as her breasts rose and fell.

'Brett,' said Rose. 'I think . . .'

'Don't think,' said Brett. 'Just feel.'

'This is new. It isn't like killing.'

'Not everything has to be about killing.'

He took her firmly by the chin, and pulled her face close to his. She studied him, wide-eyed. When he kissed her, it was clear this was new to her too. He showed her what to do, not hurrying, careful not to be aggressive or forceful. This was Rose, after all. He was still scared of her, but . . . he could feel something beginning between them. A new connection, that might be friendship or lust or something else entirely. And, he had to admit, it was exciting. There was a real charge to making out with someone who might just kill you if you upset them.

Rose pulled back, their lips separating almost reluctantly. She looked at Brett, frowning again as she tried to work out how she felt. She looked down at his hand on her breasts, and put her hand over his, inceasing the pressure. Brett slowly undid the buttons of his shirt, and pulled it open to reveal his bare chest. He took her bare hand, and brought it to his chest. Rose's dark mouth moved in the beginnings of a smile. If it had been anyone else, Brett would have sworn it was a shy smile. He smiled back. Rose's fingertips moved curiously across his chest, not needing his hand to guide her.

And then they heard footsteps approaching from outside. Finn was back. Brett didn't know whether he felt relieved or not. Rose leaned back in her chair again, pulling on her leather glove, her face calm and impassive. Brett did up his shirt. When Finn came in, they were both sitting quietly in their separate chairs, looking in different directions. And if they were both breathing just a little heavily, what of that? Certainly Finn didn't seem to notice anything amiss as he came bustling in, saying something hearty about a new mission. Brett missed the first few words. He'd just noticed that his stomach had stopped hurting.

'Brett! You're not listening to me!' Finn said sharply, dangerously.

'Hanging on your every word, Sir Durandal, ' Brett said immediately. 'A new mission. Always happy to serve. Wait a minute; hold everything, go back, go previous. Did you just say you wanted me to go out into the city again? You do know I can't show this face in public? Not after gutshooting the

Deathstalker, right in front of the camera. Paragons may not be the flavour of the month right now, but the Champion still has his fans. Particularly among the peacekeepers. They spot this face, and I'm a dead man!'

'Then show them another face,' said Finn. 'You have several to choose from, after all. It's your own fault; I have no sympathy. You should have spotted that camera. Very unprofessional behaviour.'

'I was distracted, all right? Conversations like this are why I always prefer to work alone.'

'You have other identities,' said Finn. 'Pick one of them. I need you out in the city within the hour.'

'Within the hour? Jesus, Finn, whatever happened to forward planning? It takes time to become someone else. And visits to a body shop I can trust. The whole point of a backup identity is to produce a whole different image, right down to the body language. You don't just slap on a wig and walk funny . . .'

'All you need for now is an appearance sufficiently different that you won't be arrested in the street,' Finn said firmly. 'Don't worry; the odds are no-one would recognise you anyway, where you're going.'

There was something in the way he said that which made Brett's heart sink. 'All right; I'll bite. Where am I going this time?'

'I'm sending you to speak with the ELFs,' said Finn. 'To make a deal with them, on my behalf.'

Brett was out of his chair and up on his feet in a moment, too outraged even to be scared. '*Are you out of your mind?* No-one goes looking for ELFs! I like having my brain where it is, not leaking out my ears! I wouldn't go near an ELF if you gave me a dozen esp-blockers, a full body force shield and my own portable disrupter cannon! *They're crazy!*'

Finn waited patiently for him to run down. 'The ELFs will agree to a deal, because I am going to offer them something they want even more than me. And you will go and talk to them on my behalf, Brett, because I require it of you, and I just won't take no for an answer. I have every confidence in your abilities. You've always been very persuasive. After all, you were able to talk the Deathstalker into leaving his post during a riot. You must have been very persuasive to manage that . . .'

Brett hesitated, suddenly uncertain. Was Finn saying he knew about Brett's new esper power of compulsion? Or did he just suspect?

'I'll go with Brett to see the ELFs,' said Rose, and Brett and Finn both looked at her sharply, more than a little startled.

'Now why would you want to do that, Rose?' said Finn. He sounded genuinely interested.

'Because I need the exercise. Because I'm interested.' Rose's voice was calm, uninvolved. 'I never got to test myself against the ELFs when they came to the Arena. I would like to see an ELF, close up.'

'You're very valuable to me, Rose,' said Finn. 'I don't think I want to risk you on a mission like this. Besides, you were caught on that camera too, fighting the Deathstalker.'

'I'm going,' said Rose. She stood up, and stared at Finn with her mad, bad and dangerous eyes, and even he had to look away.

'Just how am I supposed to make contact with the ELFs anyway?' said Brett, to break the awkward silence. 'Put an ad in the Logres *Times*, perhaps? *Utter lunatic seeks similar?*'

'I have an address,' said Finn. 'Well actually, it's more of a location. A meeting place. It's all arranged. Dr Happy was only too pleased to act as go-between. For a consideration. It seems the good doctor deals with and for absolutely everybody.'

'But . . . why would the ELFs agree to talk to you?' said Brett. 'After what you did, in the Arena? No-one's ever killed that many ELFs in one place before. They probably lull themselves to sleep at night coming up with new and horrible ways to torture you to death. What could you possibly offer them, that could get you off that hook? This has to be a trap, Finn.'

'Quite possibly,' said Finn. 'That's why you're going, instead of me. Just the sight of me in the flesh would probably drive them over the edge, before they had a chance to consider what I'm offering. But I'm sure they'll listen to you, Brett, you fast talking devil. Your new esper abilities should protect you from possession. And Rose . . . Well, I hate to think what would become of any poor ELF stupid enough to venture inside her head. *Here Be Tygers* . . . Make them listen, Brett. I have so much to offer . . . and the enemy of my enemy is my friend. Or at least my ally. Now off you go. Do try and make it back in time for tea; we're having toasted crumpets.'

'Hold it, hold it,' said Brett. 'You haven't told me yet just what it is I'm supposed to offer the ELFs that's guaranteed to win their support.'

So Finn told him. And Brett's stomach started hurting all over again.

Brett's new face and look wasn't all that different from before, but the subtle changes he made added up to a sufficiently striking impression that he felt reasonably confident about going out in public. His hair was now butter yellow, his eyes were a pale blue, and some carefully applied makeup accentuated the hollows of his face, giving him a gaunt, hungry look. Lifts in his shoes made him taller, and padding at the shoulders changed his body image. All of which added up to a whole new look. It took Brett about ten minutes, in a private room. When he walked back into the main room with his new look, Finn actually applauded, and Rose nodded respectfully.

No-one, in the Rookery or out of it, had seen all of Brett's faces and identities. It was safer that way. When you worked the confidence game for a living, you never knew when you might upset someone with real power and influence. Someone sufficiently humiliated that they would only settle for revenge of the bloodiest kind. Someone who could afford to put up a really tempting reward. That was when it could come in handy, to be able to disappear so completely that neither friend nor foe could find you. Brett had faces and aliases he hadn't even used yet.

Of course, it had to be said, when you were walking down a street with Rose Constantine at your side, not many people were going to be looking at you. Brett had persuaded her to cover her familiar leathers with a long and voluminous black robe, and hidden her infamous face behind a sparkling silver holo mask, but she was still seven feet tall and walked like a predator in a world of prey. She might not look like the Wild Rose any more, but she still turned quite a few heads. Brett would have felt less conspicuous walking along with a Grendel.

'I like your new look,' said Rose. 'It's pretty.'

'Don't get too used to it,' said Brett, in his new, higher and slightly breathy voice. 'This face is just for this outing. Once the ELFs have seen it, I'm scrapping it forever. I don't want them to have any means of tracking me down.'

Rose looked at him from behind her shimmering mask. 'They're telepaths, Brett. They'll recognise the shape of your mind, not your face.'

'Bugger. You're quite right, of course. I'm new to all this esper shit. Always stayed well clear of them, in the past. Esp is death to my line of business. Still, hopefully my new abilities will be enough to keep them out of my mind. Finn seemed to think so.'

'Finn would say whatever he felt he had to, to get you to go on this mission.'

Brett scowled at her. 'You are allowed to lie to me, you know, to build up my confidence. I wouldn't hold it against you.'

'Are we nearly there yet?'

'Rose; you have been asking me that for the last half hour! I will tell you when we're there! Now quiet down, and try to look inconspicuous. Try hard. The Zoo's right round this corner.'

Finn Durandal had arranged for his agents to meet the ELFs' agents somewhere under the Imperial Zoo. Brett felt a distinct thrill as he led Rose through the huge steel gates, with their proud legend *We preserve*. He hadn't been to the Zoo since one of his more amiable step fathers had brought him here as a birthday treat, when he was just a kid. The gates seemed somewhat smaller and less impressive than he remembered, but then, that was childhood for you. Certainly the grounds of the Zoo seemed just as large.

The Imperial Zoo in the Parade of the Endless contained more strange, wondrous and downright weird creatures in one place than anywhere else in the Empire. Including

Parliament. Thousands of alien species had been brought in from all across the Empire, all of them guaranteed non-sentient, of course, most of them the last few surviving examples of their kind. All that was left, after the Investigator purges of past centuries, when just to be different was to be seen as a threat. The Zoo had extensive cloning and gen-gineering programmes running, and species on the edge of extinction were being resurrected every day, but still and all it was a slow business. In the meantime, the Zoo kept its specimens alive and well cared for, and let the public in to look at them, to provide funding for future research. *We preserve*, said the Zoo, undoing the crimes of the past.

Guilt can be a powerful motivation.

Each specimen was kept in surroundings as close as possible to their home planet, reinforced by holo illusions where necessary. Force shields rather than bars, for practical as well as aesthetic reasons. Some of the creatures didn't even know they were in a Zoo. And there were tanglefields on call, powered by their own private generators, just in case. It was important for the visitors to feel safe; or they wouldn't come and spend their money. As always, the Zoo was packed with tourists, because it wasn't a trip to the Parade of the Endless if you hadn't seen the Imperial Zoo. Noisy families filled the paths between the enclosures, oohing and aahing at the creatures on display. What with aliens that floated on the air and swam through dark waters, or moved in a variety of disturbing ways through varying gravity fields, Brett and Rose were actually able to make their way through the Zoo without attracting much attention. They strolled along, taking their time, studying the displays and sharing a bag of peanuts, making small talk while Brett checked carefully to see that they weren't being followed. Actually, Brett made the small talk. Rose didn't have the knack. Brett tried holding hands with her, but it felt frankly unnatural, so he gave up. He would have liked to check out a few of the people nearest him with his esp, but surrounded by so many alien minds he didn't dare lower his mental shields, for fear of being over-whelmed.

'Who do you think the ELFs will send to talk with us?' he

said finally, confident no-one was going to be able to overhear them in the midst of the general din from the crowds and the alien exhibits. 'They wouldn't put up one of their really heavy hitters; not for the likes of us. Would they?'

'Who knows why the ELFs do anything?' Rose said calmly. 'I'd like to kill an ELF. One of the few things I haven't killed yet.'

Brett winced. 'Rose, promise me you'll leave all the talking to me.'

'I can be diplomatic, when I have to be.'

'Rose, your idea of diplomacy is to shoot someone in the face rather than in the back.'

'Well, mostly, yes.'

'You're going to get us both killed, I just know it.'

'Then you shouldn't have made me leave my sword behind.'

'Trust me, Rose; a sword wouldn't get you anywhere against an ELF. I just hope they don't send one of their super-espers. There are rumours . . . old, old stories, from the dark days of esper beginnings, about appallingly powerful espers . . . mad minds, abominations, created by the Mater Mundi for reasons we can only guess at. Living weapons, that could destroy whole cities with a single thought. There are those who say these super-espers run the ELFs.'

'If they were so powerful, why didn't they fight during the Rebellion?' said Rose.

Brett frowned. 'Maybe they were too crazy, too uncontrollable, to be used; even against Lionstone.' Brett looked about him uneasily. He was spooking himself, but he couldn't seem to stop. 'Or just maybe, they refused to be used by anyone, even their own creator . . . Oh hell, I'm getting a really bad feeling about this. Maybe we should just turn around and get the hell out of here while we still can.'

'Finn wouldn't like that.'

'Finn can't turn you inside out just by thinking about it.'

'I'll protect you, Brett.'

'Against ELFs? Against super-espers? You're good, Rose, but you're still only human. God alone knows what the super-espers are. Even the names give me the creeps. The Grey

Train. The Shatter Freak. Screaming Silence. The Spider Harps. Blue Hellfire . . .'

Rose frowned at that last one. 'Any connection with Stevie Blue?'

'No. She came much later. And really she was never more than just another pyro, despite what the legends say. She'd have had to be at least three people, to do everything they said she did. I wish we had an esp-blocker, I really do. Finn could have got us one, if he'd wanted to. But no, that would have been a betrayal of trust, get the negotiations off to a bad start . . . Idiot. The only way to negotiate with an ELF is from a position of strength. And preferably from a completely different planet. I want to go home. And hide under the bed. If I get killed doing this, I swear I'm going to come back and haunt Finn.'

'I think we're here,' said Rose.

They came to a halt before a single unobtrusive side door marked simply *Maintenance*. It was just slightly off the beaten track, in a cul de sac you couldn't easily find unless you knew what you were looking for. Above the door, someone had stencilled a stylised blackbird, the sign they'd been told to look for. Brett swallowed hard and then looked casually about him. No-one seemed to be looking, so he tried the door. It opened immediately at his touch, and Brett slipped quickly inside, Rose all but treading on his heels. The door shut behind them with a final-sounding click. Brett immediately tried the door again, but it wouldn't open. It had locked itself. Brett shrugged glumly, and led Rose down the narrow corridor before them.

The walls were bare steel, unburnished, glowing dully in the amber light from the glowspheres set into the ceiling at regular intervals. It could have been just another maintenance tunnel for the service crews, but Brett didn't think so. It was unnaturally quiet. The roar of the crowds and the caged specimens was entirely gone, as though Brett and Rose were now in an entirely different place. Their steps barely echoed at all, as though the sound was absorbed by the walls. The long corridor was full of a strained hush, as though someone unseen was listening to their approach. Or perhaps even quietly following them . . . Brett kept glancing back over his shoulder, but there was never anyone there.

But they were being watched. He had no doubt about that.

The corridor stretched endlessly away before them, curving back and forth, but leading always, inexorably, downwards, into the depths of the earth under the Zoo. No maintenance crew would ever have legitimate business this deep. The Zoo, and the city, and civilisation itself were far above them now. No-one would hear them cry out, or scream. No-one would ever know what happened to them . . . Brett felt like whimpering. He glanced across at Rose, and took some comfort from her customary calm, cold, implacable expression. Whatever she might or might not be feeling, it wasn't affecting her as it did Brett. He was glad she was with him, surprising though the thought was. But the ELFs were so scary that even Rose Constantine seemed like a comfort in comparison.

The corridor finally came to an end in a solid steel door that filled the tunnel from wall to wall. It had no markings, and no sign of any lock or handle. Brett looked at the distorted reflections of himself and Rose in the shining metal, and shuddered suddenly. There was something really bad on the other side of the door. He could feel it, in his bones and in his water. And something was pressing increasingly strongly against the mental shields he'd only learned so recently to construct, to keep the world's thoughts out. Something beat against the walls of his mind, something almost unbearably huge and alien and hungry. Brett screwed his eyes shut, like a child afraid of the dark and the things that might be in it. His hands clenched into fists as he fought to hold his mental shields in place. Something laughed softly, soundlessly, and as suddenly as that the assault was over, and the pressure was gone. Brett let out his breath in a long ragged sigh. He opened his eyes, and found Rose was looking at him curiously. Clearly, whatever he'd felt hadn't affected her. Before he could say anything, there was the sound of a dozen or so heavy locks unlocking, one after the other, and the door before them swung slowly open. It swung outwards, into the corridor, and Brett and Rose had to retreat from it.

The smell hit them first. Brett screwed up his face and

made a disgusted sound. It was a thick, rank, organic but somehow dusty stench, full of age and decay and dead things. The kind of stench that had to build or accumulate over years, or maybe even centuries. There were noises too; rustling, crackling sounds, and wet, slippery smackings. Brett could feel his heart hammering in his chest, and he was breathing so heavily he was in danger of hyperventilating. Whatever was waiting in there, beyond the door, he just knew he didn't want to see it. He looked almost desperately at Rose. She had a disrupter in her hand, though Finn had forbidden her to take any weapons with her. Brett made himself breathe more slowly, the first step to composing himself. First rule of the con; never let the mark see how on edge you were. Never let them know how much making the deal mattered to you.

'It seems we're expected,' Rose said easily. 'Let's go in and say hello.'

'After you,' said Brett.

Rose strode majestically forward into the gloom beyond the door, and Brett sauntered in after her. Inside, it was worse than he imagined. It was worse than he could have imagined. What little confidence he'd managed to wrap himself in was gone in a moment. The place could have been a chamber or a cavern, carved out of the solid rock. It could have been some old storage room, long abandoned. It could have been the antechamber to Hell. There was no way of telling just how big the space was, because it was entirely stuffed and choked with webbing.

Thick grey and pink strands that stretched from wall to wall and from floor to ceiling, crossing and intertwining in delicate intricate patterns, so labyrinthine and diverse that they hinted at infinity. Bodies, dead human bodies, hung suspended in the webbing, here and there, low and high. Some were half consumed, with white shards of broken bone showing in the pale red meat. There were older, more mummified remains too, and the occasional clump of bare bones wrapped tightly together. In one corner, human skulls had been piled up, picked clean and smeared with webbing, reaching almost to the concealed ceiling. The air was thick with death and decay, almost unbreathable. And everywhere, the pink and grey strands vibrated gently, constantly, never entirely still.

A narrow tunnel had been left open, a gap in the webbing, that led from the door to the centre of the place, or chamber, or whatever the hell it might once have been, to where the only two living inhabitants sat side by side on old-fashioned chairs. Webbing crawled over and clung to them too. It was immediately obvious that neither of the beings had moved from their chairs in a long, long time.

Rose headed straight for them, plunging into the web tunnel, so of course Brett had to follow her in. Deep inside him, something was screaming. The tunnel through the webbing was only just wide enough for them both to walk down it side by side. Brett kept his arms pressed tightly to his sides, to be sure he wouldn't risk brushing up against the pink and grey strands.

The two figures sitting deathly still upon their ancient chairs looked even more appalling the closer he got to them. They sat side by side, human in shape but not in nature, their sunken faces lacking anything like human expression. The tops of their heads had been broken open long ago, or perhaps had burst open, and that was where all the webbing originated from. It grew up out of their heads, the pink and grey strands extensions of their living brains, consciousness spread across an entire room, endlessly generated, endlessly branching, all of it alive. Brett looked around him, shocked and sickened, as he realised he was walking through their shared mind. On the intertwining brain tissues, naked and slender and delicate, neurons sparked and flared like tiny fireworks.

Rose and Brett finally came to a halt before the two seated figures, and for the first time the indistinct figures moved slightly, making dry rustling sounds like crackling paper. Perhaps their eyes moved. Perhaps their slit mouths widened slightly in a smile. Perhaps they merely stirred in anticipation . . . One naked arm from each was reaching out across the gap between the chairs, so that they could hold hands. They'd been holding hands for so long now that the flesh had grown together, fused into a single shape beyond hope of separation. Brett felt seriously sick. How long had these two been sitting here, grey and pink matters sprouting from their exposed brains, feeding on whatever poor fools came to visit them?

We are the Spider Harps, said one of the figures, or perhaps both of them, the words ringing and echoing inside Brett's and Rose's heads like the voices of dead men speaking. The words were soft and foul, like rotten fruit, like every foul intention rolled into one, and proud of it. *We speak for the ELFs. Talk to us, little humans. Be bold and eloquent, and maybe afterwards . . . we'll invite you to stay for dinner.*

Brett would have turned and bolted right then, and to hell with Finn, if Rose hadn't been there with him. He knew she wouldn't run, and he couldn't leave her there, in that awful place. So he made himself concentrate on the shrunken, shrivelled pair before him, so he wouldn't have to look at the brain web, or the half devoured bodies hanging above and around him. Both the figures were so old, so wrinkled, so fallen in upon themselves, that it was impossible to even guess whether they were male or female. If they had ever worn clothes, they had long ago rotted and fallen away. And yet, though their faces were dead, their eyes were very much alive and aware. Brett took a deep breath, immediately wished he hadn't as the smell hit him all over again, and made a start.

'Hello. I'm Brett Random, and this is Rose Constantine. We speak for Finn Durandal. Please don't kill us until you've heard us out. Fascinating place you have here. Love what you've done with it. How . . . long have you been down here?'

Long and long, little Random. Ever since the Mater Mundi made us, fashioning us from the humble clay of ordinary espers. It hurt us so much, so very much, but who were we to argue with the Mother Of All Souls? She put us here, hidden behind the bedlam of so many alien minds, to think and calculate and solve problems for her. When problems grew too large for us, we grew larger to accommodate them. We were her brains, her creatures, made to serve her purposes. Of course, this was back in the days of The Lion, in the grand old days of Empire, when things were only just starting to go bad. But the Mater Mundi knew, even then. She saw what was coming, so she made weapons, living weapons, infernal devices to be unleashed upon those who would oppose her. But something went wrong. The Mater Mundi never fully awakened, until it was far too late. Now she is gone, but we remain. We serve the ELFs now. Because our nature compels us to serve someone, and we have spent so very long waiting for revenge . . .

'The Lion . . .' Brett said quietly to Rose. 'Lionstone's grandfather! Jesus, they've been down here for centuries . . . growing, spreading . . .'

'Why the corpses?' Rose said to the Spider Harps, with her customary bluntness.

We cannot leave this place. And we're always hungry. Growth must be sustained. Tissues must be replenished. Don't shy away, little Random. We are what we were made to be, by one far greater than any of us. We have worked wonders, in our time. Our thoughts have travelled on paths unguessable to mere humans. The ELFs understand. We don't want to be found by the oversoul. They would want to save us. Make us sane again. Separate us. We would rather die. We are great and marvellous, and we will not be denied our revenge, our long-delayed triumph.

'This just gets better all the time,' said Brett. 'All right; why Spider *Harps?*'

The two figures slowly raised their outer arms, with loud creaking noises, until their long bony fingers could reach the delicate strands fruiting from their opened heads. And then they plucked at the taut strands of the webbing, and note after perfect note rang in the underground cavern, forming an awful entirely inhuman music, played on the outgrowths of centuries-old minds. Brett slapped both his hands to his ears to keep the terrible music out, but the sound invaded his mind, harsh and strident and full of terrible significances. Brett dropped to his knees, his eyes squeezed tightly shut. He tried to shout something, but his voice wouldn't work. It was too small, too human, too sane. Rose moved in beside him, put a comforting hand on his shoulder, lifted her disrupter and pointed it directly at the head of the figure on the left.

'Stop that,' she said loudly. 'Stop that right now.'

The Spider Harps let their hands fall away from the neuron-studded strands, and the music stopped, though the echoes seemed to linger unnaturally long on the still air. Brett slowly took his hands away from his ears. There were smears

301

of blood on his palms. Rose hauled him to his feet again with one hand, while still keeping her disrupter carefully trained on her target.

'You all right, Brett?' she said, without looking round,

'I don't know. My head hurts. Makes a change. Didn't that music do anything to you?'

Rose shrugged. 'I've never understood music.'

'Figures. Bless the Lord for his small mercies and pass the ammunition.' Brett glared at the Spider Harps. 'I ought to let her shoot you.'

You both have very interesting minds, said one of the Spider Harps, or perhaps both, unmoved either by Brett's threat or the gun in Rose's hand. *You have strong shields, Brett Random. And we can't make sense of you at all, Rose Constantine. You're just too . . . different. We had planned to possess you both, make you ours, take the Durandal's location from your minds, and then ride you back to him, and have you kill him slowly. For our pleasure. But since that isn't possible, we will hear your proposal. What do you have to offer us?*

Brett told them. There was a long pause, and then there was a new sound in the chamber, a ragged sighing. The Spider Harps were laughing.

We agree. Tell your master that the ELFs will work with the Durandal, on this occasion, to destroy the Paragons once and for all. You may leave now. But do come again. Your minds fascinate us. We can't wait to get our teeth into them.

Brett finally broke. He turned and ran, plunging back through the tunnel in the webbing, past the great open door, and out into the corridor beyond. Rose backed slowly out, holding her disrupter on the Spider Harps all the way. But even after they'd both left that room, that chamber, that living hell, even after the door had slammed shut again, the dry rustling laughter of the Spider Harps followed Brett and Rose all the way to the surface.

Hellfire Club meetings always began with an orgy. Satisfy the body and its appetites, to clear the mind. Indulge your every need and whim, so that the mind is free to concentrate on other matters. So that the subtler joys of plotting and treason are not over-shadowed by the more immediate pleasures of the flesh. The devils of the Hellfire Club made it a point of principle to deny themselves nothing.

The huge hall's floor was covered from wall to wall with cushions and silks and all kinds of textures that might please. The air was thick with heady perfumes and generated pheromones, and raucous music issued from the blind-folded orchestra tucked away in one corner. There was all kind of drink and every kind of drug, and everywhere . . . bodies, moving together, clothed and unclothed as tastes and preferences decided, sinking themselves into each other and in the moment, because that was what the Hellfire Club was all about.

Do what thou wilt shall be the whole of the law. And to Hell with anyone who gets in the way.

Afterwards, they all lay nakedly together, sitting or reclining as the sweat cooled and their breathing slowed, while the more subservient members moved among them with refreshing drinks and the more obscure and unpleasant forms of finger food; smiling happily as they were beaten and abused. The hundred or so members of the Hellfire Club who'd been able to make it to this meeting had gathered together to consider the troublesome matter of Finn Durandal. It promised to be a long meeting, but then, they always were. Everyone was determined to be heard. Tel Markham lay stretched out with his head cradled on an accommodating belly, and looked thoughtfully about him.

Tel Markham belonged to many organisations. Member of Parliament, and the Shadow Court, supporter of Pure Humanity, rector of the official Church, and long-standing devil in the Hellfire Club. He'd have joined the ELFs if they'd have him. Markham believed in obtaining every possible advantage, every possible form of support, on the unanswerable grounds that you never knew when you might need them. He belonged to so many secret and underground organisations that he'd almost lost count. His computers oversaw his extremely complicated diary, and made sure he knew where he was supposed to be, and why. Most of the organisations had no idea of his other connections. It was only polite: they all so loved to believe that they were the only underground that mattered.

Luckily, these days Markham was such an established Member of Parliament that he only needed to make the occasional personal appearance, for the most important of debates. The rest of the time a low-level AI ran his holo for him, and took notes for his staff to study later. They took care of the day-to-day business. That was what staff were for. Attending Hellfire Club meetings messed him about more than most, though, because the Club's inner circle insisted on deciding a new location for every get together, announced only hours in advance, thus protecting themselves from gate-crashers and infiltrators.

Markham always made it to as many as he could.

The Club was currently occupying a deserted church in an area of the city marked for redevelopment. *Is the Church deconsecrated?* Markham had asked on arriving. *It soon will be,* he'd been told, and Markham had forced a chuckle.

Frankie started the discussion. She was a tall, almost unbearably voluptuous woman of a certain age, with sharp vicious features and a great mane of pure white hair that reached all the way down her supple back to her waist. Markham loved to see her breathe, but had enough sense to keep out of her clutches. Unlike many of the Hellfire Club, she wasn't playing her role. She'd assassinated twenty-seven people that Markham knew of. Two had been ex-lovers. Markham was pretty sure she was about as inner circle as you could get. Frankie was hardcore all the way.

The Hellfire Club consisted of circles within circles, from dilettantes and wannabes at the edges, to the deadly philosophers at the very centre. You could go in as deep as you wanted, or as deep as you could stand, but somehow there were always more circles inside those you'd thought were the innermost. This was partly to limit the number of people any member could betray if captured, but mostly because not everyone had the stomach for everything the Hellfire Club did. Or planned to do. Markham was in pretty deep, and hoped to go even deeper, but though he was pretty sure he lacked anything even remotely like a conscience, there were still some things he wouldn't do. He was ambitious, not crazy.

At the core, it was whispered, the founding members' extreme philosophies still survived; complete anarchy, for the Empire and Humanity. A new Empire, without conscience or mercy or restraint. Divine chaos, a time of awful pleasures and splendid suffering: where the lesser orders, those outside the Club, would be slaves, objects, mere property, there to do all the necessary useful things, to be subject to their masters' every whim, to live and die at their command; while the Hellfire Club made a glorious Hell on earth for everyone.

Markham didn't believe in any of that, not least because he didn't plan on sharing his power with anyone, but he had enough sense to keep his opinions on that matter to himself. To him, the Hellfire Club was just another useful tool, another means to get him what he wanted. He had a strong feeling a lot of members felt that way, in private.

'So,' said Frankie, in her deep sensual voice that was like being assaulted by a leather glove, 'What are we to do about the Durandal? Such a dear boy. We all know his plans. And he's come so far, in such a short time. But I can't help feeling that he threatens to steal our thunder. The Hellfire Club are the official villains and demons of the Golden Age, by choice and popular acclaim. If anyone's going to bring the Throne down, it should be us.'

'He means well,' said a pretty young thing of indeterminate gender. 'And I do so like to encourage new talent.'

'Kill him, for his presumption!' snapped a grossly fat man with so many body piercings he rattled when he breathed. 'He should have come to us first. How dare he plan atrocities, and not include us?'

'But,' said Markham, his trained politician's voice cutting easily across the other's, 'don't you just love the idea of the greatest Paragon of all time becoming the Empire's greatest villain? That a man who dedicated all his life to preserving the Empire and all it stood for, should be the one to bring it all crashing down in ruins? Irony is so good for the soul . . . Let him have his fun. Let him do all the hard work, gathering his followers and planning his plans, and when the Throne is finally in danger, we will step out from the shadows and take it all over. Make the Durandal one of us, whether he likes it or not. That's the Hellfire Club way, after all.'

'Of course,' said Frankie, stretching her magnificent body with langorous ease. 'Everyone can be seduced.'

'You should know,' Markham said generously. 'Now, if you'll all excuse me, I'll leave you to sort out the details. I have another meeting to attend. The House will be in Session soon, and my attendance is required.'

'Ah yes,' said Frankie. 'Have fun, my favourite Member . . .'

In his sumptuous office, surrounded by all the spoils of victory, Angelo Bellini, Patriarch of the one true Church, was entertaining his second important visitor of the day. The previous Patriarch's remains had been carefully scraped up and removed, and very thoroughly disposed of, and everything in the office was now back to normal. Though the extractor fans were still working overtime. Angelo stood up behind his impressive desk, and nodded shortly to welcome the nearest thing the Ecstatics had to a leader or spokesperson. The Ecstatic was of average height, and a little thinner than most, probably because he kept forgetting to eat. Living in a constant state of orgasm will do that to you. He wore a simple grey shift, smelled strongly, and seemed to drift as much as walk across the deep pile carpeting towards Angelo and his desk.

Seen up close, the Ecstatic wasn't very impressive. The constant unwavering smile was definitely disturbing, though, and there was something about the eyes . . . Angelo waved to the chair on the other side of his desk. He was damned if he was going to shake hands. The Ecstatic sank almost bonelessly into the hard-backed visitor's chair, while Angelo made himself extremely comfortable in his rather more luxurious seat of power.

'Call me Joy,' the Ecstatic said suddenly, his happy voice full of real if unfocused enthusiasm. 'It's a use name, of course. I don't have the patience for formal names any more. And who I might have been in the past is of no interest to you or to me. It's good to be here. It's good to be anywhere. We met briefly at Douglas' Coronation, you and I. Exchanged a few words. Or perhaps we didn't. It's so hard to be sure about things that don't really matter. I love chocolate.'

'Well done,' said Angelo. 'You were almost coherent there, for a while. If not particularly valuable. Are you comfortable?'

'Oh, I'm always comfortable. Really. You have no idea.'

'Could you please stop smiling like that? It's not natural.'

'Not for you, perhaps. For me, the world is good. So large and wondrous and full of pleasure. Call me Joy. You called, and here I am. You've done a lot with this place. I don't like it. Someone died here recently.'

Angelo looked sharply at the Ecstatic. He'd never had much time for the extravagant claims made for the Ecstatics' supposed powers of insight, but that last remark, so casually made, was certainly unsettling. Angelo made himself relax. The Ecstatic could say any damned thing he liked. It didn't matter.

'The Church's previous Patriarch, the very venerable Roland Wentworth, has resigned,' Angelo said flatly. 'Reasons of ill health. He is gone, and he won't be coming back. I have therefore replaced him as Patriarch. I lead the Church of Christ Transcendent, the glorious Church Militant; and there is no room in the new Church for such as you. For such . . . ostentatious self-indulgence. The new Church is all about service and loyalty and rigid self-discipline. You do nothing to advance the Cause, you are incapable of serving in the holy war to come; and your very nature brings the Church into disrepute. You disgust me. I have therefore taken the decision to excommunicate all Ecstatics, and ban the surgeries that produce you. You will all be expelled, denied the comforts and protections of mother Church. You don't fit in with our new image.'

Angelo realised he was saying more than he'd meant to, more than he needed, but there was something about the calm unwavering smile and gaze of the Ecstatic before him that goaded him, trying to find something that would crack that serene self-control. He wanted to hurt the Ecstatic, frighten him, make him squeal and cry and beg for mercy. Not that it would make any difference, of course.

'You don't want us around because you can't afford to tolerate the existence of any other power base in the Church that might oppose your will,' said Joy, in a surprisingly rational voice. 'I knew this was coming. We all did. It's why I'm here.'

'You knew?' said Angelo, honestly shocked. 'How could you know? Who talked? None of my people would have talked . . .'

'No-one had to tell us,' said Joy. 'You never understood who and what we are, Angelo Bellini. What we see and what we know. With our bodies freed from the demands of the now, our minds are freed to roam through past, present and futures. Our thoughts are unlocked, unshackled from the rigid restraints of rationality. I see through and beyond you, Angelo, as clearly as I see the functions of your desk. Behind you is the Durandal, and ahead of you is terror. We see so much, all of us. It's just that mostly we can't be bothered to tell anyone. There are Light People who walk among you, unnoticed and unobserved, intent on their own unknown missions. There are angels in the skies and demons in the earth. We hear voices that aren't there, and see things that may never happen. I have seen the future plummeting back into the past, and the dead rising to walk again. I see your aura, and it's really very ugly.'

'Shut up!' said Angelo. 'Shut up, damn you!' All the hairs were standing up on his arms and on the back of his neck. He was sweating and his hands were icy cold, as though someone had just walked over his grave. He was scared, horribly scared, and he didn't know why. 'You're here because I ordered you here, to listen when I speak! You don't have to die. You could go back to the surgeons, go under the knife again. Let us put controls in your heads. Live on in service to the new Church . . .'

'No,' said Joy pleasantly. 'I don't think so. We won't go back to being human. To being only human. We'd rather die.'

'Then die,' said Angelo Bellini viciously.

But even as his hand moved towards the control on his desk that would detonate the new transmutation bomb under the Ecstatic's chair, Joy leaned over suddenly, reached under his seat, ripped out the bomb and held it up before him. He looked at it curiously for a moment, and then tossed it across the desk, aimed nicely to land right on the control that would activate it. Angelo screamed and shrieked with horror, and erupted up out of his chair to grab the bomb with both hands. He moved quickly away from the desk, put the bomb down on the floor very carefully, and then backed away from it; his mind full of the awful death of the previous Patriarch. He spun round, breathing hard, suddenly sure Joy would be leaning over his desk with his hand poised over the activation pad; but there was no sign of the Ecstatic anywhere. He'd left as silently as he'd come, while Angelo was preoccupied.

How could he have known the bomb was under the chair? What else did he know, and who might he tell it to? And what one Ecstatic knew . . .

Angelo leaned over his desk, and hit the comm panel with unnecessary force. 'Security! There's an Ecstatic loose in this building! Kill it! Shoot it on sight! And when you're sure the unnatural thing is dead, bring the body here to my office, so I can see it for myself!'

Security sped through the Cathedral at a run, driven on by Angelo's increasingly hysterical orders, but the Ecstatic was nowhere to be found. No-one saw him leave, and he didn't show up on any of the security monitors. Which should have been impossible. So Angelo got on the comm again, to some of his more fanatical Neumen supporters, and personally gave the death order for all the Ecstatics. In any city, on any world. Let them see what excommunication from the new Church really meant . . . Let the law bleat what it liked; by the time they got their act together it would be all over. And if any of his Neumen assassins should be caught, well; fanatics were always so eager to become martyrs for their Cause . . .

The Ecstatics as a movement were finished. They were already as good as extinct. They were history.

But somehow that didn't comfort Angelo Bellini at all.

Ahead of you is terror . . .

Within the hour, the Parade of the Endless was swarming with Neumen fanatics, proud in their new Church armour, hunting down Ecstatics with gun and steel and missionary zeal, killing them openly in the streets. The peacekeepers mobilized in force to stop them, calling in reinforcements from all the surrounding cities, but still they were too widely spread, and greatly outnumbered. Excommunicated, condemned and damned by the Church as heretics, the Ecstatics were thrown out of their seminaries, retreats and churches, and the doors slammed and locked behind them. No-one in the Church would hide or succour them. No-one dared. The Neumen ran through city streets howling like wolves, blood dripping thickly from their blades. Most of the Ecstatics were easy targets. They didn't run. They walked calmly through the streets, unwilling or unable to defend themselves. They smiled kindly on their murderers making no attempt to escape, and they died easily, still smiling their disturbing smiles. The bodies piled up, and blood ran in the gutters of the perfect city. When individual peacekeepers got in the way, the Neumen cut them down too.

The Paragon Emma Steel heard shooting, and came swooping down on her gravity sled, to see half a dozen Neumen assassins in Church Militant trappings pursuing a lone Ecstatic down a main street. They were openly firing disrupters, but somehow their target was never where they aimed. He ran down the middle of the road, luckily free of traffic for the moment, while people lined both sides of the street and jeered and yelled crude insults at the running man. They scattered like sheep as Emma's sled came shrieking down at full speed, and she slammed it to an abrupt halt between the running Neumen and their prey. The six men stumbled to a halt as she jumped lithely down from her sled, her gun and sword already in her hands. They were fanatics, but they knew who she was.

They looked at each other, and then at the Ecstatic, standing quietly just beyond Emma's hovering sled, looking back at them, smiling. The Neumen looked at Emma Steel, slowly advancing on them, and anywhen else they would probably have done the sensible thing and turned and run. But their senses were maddened by the chase, blood from their previous kills still dripping from their weapons, and after all, there were six of them against just one Paragon. And they knew from the riot that sometimes Paragons die just as easily as anyone else. One man raised his energy gun, and fired it point blank. The force shield on Emma's arm intercepted the blast, and the energy beam ricocheted harmlessly away. Committed now, the Neumen howled wordlessly and threw themselves at her.

Emma cut down the first two to reach her with ruthless efficiency, her sword a blur as it cut through throat and gut. She surged forward while her first two victims were still crumpling to the blood-spattered ground, and then she was in and among the other four before they knew what was happening. They cried out as steel ripped through their flesh, while all their swords found was air. They were fanatics, but Emma Steel was a warrior. She killed them all in a matter of moments, and then looked unhurriedly about her. Six dead men lay in bloody heaps in the street, and she wasn't even breathing hard. The crowds lining both sides of the street were silent, their faces sullen, angry, cheated out of the death they wanted. One of them stepped forward, her face drawn in cold, ugly lines. She glared at Emma Steel.

'How dare you interfere in God's work! He is an abomination! He has to die!' She looked around her, seeking support. 'Kill the abomination! The Paragon can't stop us all!'

'I can stop you,' said Emma Steel. She pointed her disrupter at the woman's forehead. 'And you'd be surprised how many people I can cut down, if I get annoyed enough.'

The crowd looked at the dead Neumen in the street and began to break up and drift away. They might believe in the principles of Pure Humanity, but they weren't ready to die for them. Not yet, anyway. The would-be rabble rouser glared at Emma one last time, spat at the Ecstatic, then turned and walked away. Emma kept her gun trained on the woman's back until she disappeared down a side street, and then she put the gun away and turned back to study the waiting Ecstatic. He was standing right beside her, still smiling. Emma gave him her best glare.

'What the hell was that all about?'

'I am Joy,' said the Ecstatic. 'You must protect me. It is necessary. I know things that matter. I see the Empire that's coming, born in blood and terror. I see legends walking and

311

heroes gone bad. Your aura is really quite magnificent, you know. The Light People swarm around you like moths drawn to a blowtorch. The one you trust most will betray you. It's really very sad, but then most things are . . .'

'What are you talking about?' said Emma. 'Why were those Neumen creeps trying to kill you? The comm channels are full of dead Ecstatics all over the city. What is going on?'

'We are excommunicate,' Joy said patiently. 'Our murder has become a blessed act. The Angel says so. Mostly we don't care. Life and death aren't nearly as different as most people think. However, I am different. You may have noticed. I know things. Secrets; past, present and future. I can't tell you what; others might rip the knowledge from your mind.'

Emma nodded slowly. 'All right; that last bit actually made some sense. You'd better come with me. I'll see you're put in protective custody until we can sort this madness out.'

'Alas no,' said Joy. 'There's nowhere you can put me that they couldn't find me. Neumen walk through walls and under doors now. Only one place safe in this world, for such as me. You must take me there. Guard and protect me all the way. Take me to New Hope, Emma Steel. For all our souls' sake.'

'The esper city? The heart and home of the oversoul? What makes you think they'd put themselves on the line to protect you?'

'Because the mind people still remember what it was like to be hunted.'

Emma couldn't argue with that. She looked around her. She and the Ecstatic were the only people left on the deserted street, but any number of faces were watching from windows. Someone would have called the Church by now. Which meant more Neumen assassins were undoubtedly already on the way. And if Joy really did know something that he wasn't supposed to know, something dangerous enough to threaten the new popularity of the Church Militant . . . Emma smiled unpleasantly.

'All right, Joy, you've got yourself a ride. Get up on the sled behind me. But keep your hands to yourself, and if you get airsick, try and aim most of it over the side. And pray the espers will be as welcoming as you seem to think. No-one gets into New Hope without permission.'

'My point exactly,' said the Ecstatic.

Emma grinned despite herself, led him back to her hovering gravity sled, helped him on board, and took off, climbing for the clouds as fast as the engine could take her, to avoid providing a target for rooftop snipers. The sooner she got to New Hope the better. She couldn't have felt more of a target if she'd had a bull's-eye painted on her back.

The esper city of New Hope, central nexus for the oversoul, was only ten miles or so due north of the Parade of the Endless, but the Neumen did everything they could to prevent Emma and her new friend from getting there. First came the gravity sleds, dozens of them, sweeping down from above, disrupter fire raking Emma's sled from all sides. Emma bucked and weaved, riding the air currents for all they were worth to keep her flight unpredictable. Her sled's force shields flared and coruscated, soaking up the discharging energies, always on the very edge of overloading and collapsing, but somehow still maintaining their integrity. It seemed her passion for upgrading and tinkering was paying off after all.

Energy bolts seared all around her, shooting in from every side as she threw the sled back and forth, rising and falling on the gusting winds between the towering buildings. At this speed the bitterly cold air cut at her like a knife as it buffeted around the edges of the the prow force shield, but Emma didn't give a damn. Her blood was running hot, and she was grinning more widely than the Ecstatic. This was the first decent workout she'd had since she got here. At last the enemy had revealed himself, and she was going to make him pay for that foolishness in blood. There was no-one could fly a gravity sled better than her. She'd learned her skills the hard way, fighting air pirates on Rhiannon.

A dozen gravity sleds came at her in a wave, opening up with every energy gun they had. Emma hauled her sled round in a tight curve, yelling for the Ecstatic to hang on tight to the crash bars. For a moment she was flying sideways on to her attackers, disrupter fire chewing up the face of the building behind her. Walls and windows exploded, hot fires blossoming out onto the winter air. The Neumen sleds swung round to block her path, leaving her nowhere to go. They thought. Emma swung her sled round and dove right into the heart of the burning building.

At the speed she was travelling now, the flames could hardly touch her, and the force shields soaked up most of the heat, but even so for a moment it was like flying through the sun. Emma squeezed her eyes shut and held her breath, and hoped her passenger had enough sense to do the same. A moment later she punched through the windows on the other side of the building's corner, and she was out of the flames and back into the crisp cold air again. She whooped loudly, and pulled the sled around, bearing down on her previous attackers from behind. Her hair felt crisp and singed, all her bare skin tingled painfully, and one shoulder of her cloak had caught fire. She slapped the flames out almost casually, and whooped again as she opened fire on the Neumen sleds with her disrupters. The Neumen sleds exploded and blew apart, burning wreckage and broken bodies falling from the sky like charred birds, plummeting to the streets far below.

They should have invested in proper rear shields, like her.

Emma could have called for assistance on the Paragon emergency comm channel, but she didn't. Partly as a matter of pride, but mostly because she didn't know who she could trust any more. Joy was right about one thing; Pure Humanity had supporters everywhere these days. Even among the peacekeepers. Safer by far to get the Ecstatic to his sanctuary at New Hope as fast as possible, and hope the espers were as glad to meet Joy as he seemed to think. Even the Neumen would have more sense than to take on the oversoul.

So she gunned her engine for all it was worth, fired her overheating guns at anything stupid enough to fire at her, and occasionally rammed a slower moving gravity sled that didn't get out of her way fast enough. She was singing the old war songs of Mistworld now, from a time when her home planet had been the only rebel world that dared stand against the dread Empress Lionstone. Her voice rang out, proud and defiant, as she fought her way past overwhelming odds. She'd taken some hits, her sled's armour looking distinctly buckled and battered in places, but most of her force shields were still up and holding, and she was almost at the city limits. Next stop, New Hope. It occurred to her that if this many people were so desperate to try and stop her, then what the Ecstatic knew, or thought he knew, probably was worth protecting. Even if she didn't have a damned clue what it might be.

She shot past the last of the high towers and out into open air, and suddenly there were no more gravity sleds. She powered on, leaving the city behind her. It slowly occurred to her that even the usual commercial sky traffic seemed to have chosen other lanes. She was alone in the sky. Emma scowled, immediately suspicious, and checked her sled's sensor displays, but nothing was showing anywhere near her. It would seem she'd got away with it. The Neumen had given up the pursuit. But Emma Steel was not only a Paragon, but a Mistworlder, with all that rebel planet's native cunning and paranoia, and she knew better than to rely on instruments alone. Particularly when every instinct she had was screaming at her. So when the fifty-ton military gravity barge emerged suddenly from out of the clouds right in front of her, she was ready for it.

There was no doubt the barge was military, even though someone had gone to great trouble to shut down all its markings and insignia. Either it had been hijacked by Neumen, or it was crewed by Pure Humanity supporters from within the military. Either way, it was big and brutal and coming straight at her at a rate of knots. The whole huge shape of it was protected by overlapping force shields, and it was packed with rows of disrupter cannon, already moving to target her. Emma dove for the ground immediately, practically sticking her sled on its nose. Joy hugged her round the waist with both arms, and she let him. She scowled fiercely, running strategies quickly through her mind. She hadn't anticipated a bloody gravity barge. Big bastards, and powerful with it. Far superior shields and firepower to anything she had. But barges were notoriously slow and hard to manouevre, compared to a sled. She couldn't outrun it, or hope to evade its targeting computers for long, but maybe, just maybe, she could out-think the people running it. A ship's only ever as good as its crew . . .

The first disrupter beams shot past her, worryingly close. She pulled out of her dive, pulling back on the yoke so hard the engine screamed in protest. Emma ignored it, roaring towards the open horizon, sacrificing some speed to her dodging and ducking, barely a dozen feet above the ground now. People travelling on the roads below looked up with startled faces. Emma felt like waving, but didn't. She had her dignity to consider. She pushed her engine's speed well past its theoretical limits, and the whole structure of the sled shook and shuddered beneath her. The engine was making really unpleasant sounds now, and threatening to get nasty. Emma spoke soothingly to it. She'd done a lot of work on the sled. It would hold together. It would have to. Disrupter beams stabbed down all around her, blowing smoking craters in the ground, for all her evasive tactics. Think, dammit, think. There had to be a way . . .

The answer came to her in a flash. It was a crazy, dangerous answer, and if anyone else had suggested it she would probably have shot them outright, just on general principles, but . . . Emma Steel howled her war song in a cracking voice and sent the sled shooting up into the sky again. She shut down all her force shields, feeding the extra power to the engine. Behind her, the Ecstatic had buried his face in the small of her back so he wouldn't have to see what they were doing. Emma didn't blame him.

The gravity barge loomed up before her, filling the sky and growing ever more massive by the moment. She shot up past its nose, missing the prow by barely a yard or so, and kept on going. Its disrupter beams went nowhere near her. Emma pulled the sled over in a great loop, till they were actually flying upside down, held in place only by the sled's emergency crash webbing. The blood poured out of Emma's head and rushed towards her boots, but she was damned if she'd faint. She kept the sled speeding through its great loop, powered on by its straining engine, and, so suddenly it took her breath away, they came dropping down out of the loop, right way up again, and closing in fast on the rear of the gravity barge.

Heading, in fact, straight for the exposed rear vents of its engines. The one place not protected by force shields, so the engines' energies could dissipate safely. Bit of a design fault, really. Emma opened up with every disrupter she had, and the explosions that followed were satisfyingly loud and large and nasty. Heavy jets of flame shot out, that Emma only avoided with some desperate last minute manoeuvring, followed by clouds of thick dark smoke. The barge tilted slowly over onto one side, as fuel cell after fuel cell shut down rather than add to the explosions, and the gravity barge began its slow, implacable descent towards the ground below. Emma laughed harshly, turned the sled around and headed once more towards New Hope.

'And people say I'm crazy,' said Joy, his face still buried in her cloak.

No-one else tried to stop them.

New Hope was a city in the clouds. A great metropolis twenty miles in diameter, floating high in the sky, serene and untroubled by the woes of the mundane world below. Protected by terrible unseen powers; greater than armies and more destructive. No-one troubled the oversoul. The great city blazed with lights, vivid and brilliant against the early evening sky, supernaturally beautiful; a faery kingdom of gossamer glass and steel. Delicate structures of grace and charm, linked by high walkways, every building a work of art. New Hope; almost too beautiful a city for human eyes.

Emma Steel slowed her sled's approach, allowing her to study the city from what she hoped was still a safe distance. 'Are you sure you want to do this?' she said back over her shoulder. 'This is an exclusively esper city. Humans aren't welcome, mostly.'

'It is a risk,' Joy admitted, peering diffidently past her at the city of lights spread out before them. 'Hopefully the espers will see me as being sufficiently different from baseline Humanity to accept my temporary presence. New Hope has always been a place of sanctuary, for those who are gifted and in need. I think when they see what's in my head, what I know, and the things that I have seen of yesterday and tomorrow, they'll want me to stay. Certainly the oversoul is one of the few forces in the Empire powerful enough to protect me from everything the Angel will be sending after me.'

'The Angel? You mean Angelo Bellini, the Angel of Madraguda? He's the one who put the death mark on you? What the hell have you got on him; vid footage of him prancing about in women's underwear at a Hellfire Club dinner-dance?'

'Nothing so amusing,' said Joy, regretfully. 'If the espers won't take me, I suppose there's always the clones; but they don't have New Hope's formidable defences. And their dress sense is appalling.'

'You know, you're sounding very rational, all of a sudden,' said Emma.

'I find stark terror concentrates the mind wonderfully,' said Joy. 'Don't worry. It won't last.'

The city grew before them as they approached cautiously, keeping to a clearly non-threatening speed. The hairs on the back of Emma's neck stirred, anticipating the psionic assault she probably wouldn't even have time to feel. The espers should have more sense than to attack the authority a Paragon represented, but she was most definitely where she shouldn't be, and after the Neumen riot, everyone was on edge and looking for trouble. The sled crossed the city perimeter, and headed steadily towards the official landing pads, and Emma let out a breath she hadn't realised she'd been holding. If the espers were going to stop her, they would have done it by now. Unless the oversoul was planning something really unpleasant, to make an example of her and her companion . . .

The city unfolded constantly before them, like a glorious flower. New Hope had a strong, almost overwhelming sense of *presence*. As though it was more real, more *there*, than anywhere else in the material world. It glowed fiercely, as though illuminated from within by its own vitality. The city hummed loudly, in the ear and in the mind, like the sound of a great engine, endlessly turning. Emma found that disturbing. She knew that New Hope had no generators, no reactors, no artificial power sources of any kind. The city, all of it, was powered and maintained and levitated by the espers themselves. The oversoul was a living power source, generated from living minds, and thus utterly independent from the rest of Logres, and indeed, the rest of the Empire.

Emma steered her sled carefully between the elegant towers soaring up all around her, impossibly high, wonderfully crafted from glass and steel and precious metals. Every structure was a thing of beauty and a joy to behold. People flew in and out of the buildings, soaring gracefully through the air without the need for cumbersome technology. Down on the streets, people appeared and disappeared, come and gone in a moment, teleporting in and out in the blink of an eye. And everywhere, men and women looked at objects, which moved or disappeared or burst into flames. No machines, no tech, anywhere in New Hope. They weren't needed. New Hope had moved beyond reliance upon such things.

Emma Steel brought her sled down to rest on the edge of the city's landing pads, and only then paused to wonder how she'd been able to find her way there. She'd never been in New Hope before. Someone had placed the information in her mind. She shuddered despite herself, then stepped down from the sled and made a point of glaring about her. She was a Paragon, dammit, and entitled to a proper and respectful reception. She was also an entirely unwanted guest, so she stayed where she was. Dignity was one thing; arrogance would only get her killed. Or worse. The oversoul guarded its secrets jealously.

That was, after all, why she'd brought the Ecstatic here. Even the Angel of Madraguda couldn't afford to get the oversoul mad at him.

Emma folded her arms across her breastplate, and tapped her foot impatiently as she looked about her. There was no-one else on the landing pads. No ships, no travellers, not even any signs of Customs & Excise. Emma considered the implications of that for a moment, and then decided not to. It was only upsetting her. She turned round to help Joy down from the sled, and when she turned back an esper was standing right in front of her. Emma refused to jump, on principle, but it still took a moment for her heart to settle. The esper was a tall woman, almost supernaturally thin, with a long bony face and long blonde fly-away hair, framing her head like a halo. She inclined her head slightly to the Ecstatic, in something that was almost a bow but not quite, and then looked coldly at Emma with dark, dark eyes.

Emma glared right back at her, and then felt as much as heard a buzzing in her head, like an itch she couldn't scratch, somewhere behind her eyes. It grew suddenly worse, a pain stabbing outwards from the centre of her brain. She swayed unsteadily on her feet, and put a hand to her head, and then her mind opened up, blossoming like a flower in the rain, spreading wide in all directions, some of which she had never even supposed existed before. Sight and sound and colours and echoes and so much more . . . And for a moment Emma Steel caught just a glimpse of the oversoul at work; an intricate lattice of interconnecting thoughts, communicating with more speed and clarity and depth than mere speech could ever allow. A million minds all talking at once, without anything being lost or drowned out, forming patterns of logic and structures of emotion, unbearably beautiful, inhumanly complex, infinitely productive. The oversoul; a whole far greater than the sum of its parts. And then the pain crashed back into Emma's head as her mind slammed shut, her glimpse of heaven over, the gates slammed shut in her face. Emma groaned aloud despite herself, and looked at the esper before her with new eyes.

'Why did you show me that? And why did you shut me out again?'

'You have the esper gene, Paragon.' The woman's voice was little more than a whisper, as though she wasn't used to talking aloud, and Emma had to strain to understand her. 'It's buried deep in your ancestry. Not strong enough to maintain telepathy without extensive support. Continuing the contact would have burned you out. Permanently. You don't belong here. Though your descendants might, some day. We are Humanity's future, after all. One day, we shall all shine like suns. The Owen said so.'

'You're starting to sound like him,' Emma growled, jerking her head at Joy. 'He's an Ecstatic.'

'Yes,' said the esper. 'I recognised the smile.' She looked at Joy, frowned briefly, and something passed between them. The esper nodded reluctantly. 'Very well. He shall have sanctuary. You must leave, Paragon.'

'Just like that?' Emma let her hands rest ostentatiously on her weapons belt and gave the esper her best scowl. 'Blow that out your ears. This is Paragon business. I'm not budging from here till I get some answers. Why is the Church suddenly killing Ecstatics? What does this one know that's so damned important? And why are you willing to protect him?'

'Things are changing,' said the esper, her voice and gaze unwavering. 'The Church needs enemies, to keep its members focused. Give the people someone to hate, and they'll stop thinking for themselves. Make them hate enough, and they'll turn on anyone. You should know that, Paragon. Soon the Church will turn on espers. We are the next logical target. We're too sane to fall for the Church's lies and temptations, and too powerful and too dangerous to be allowed to exist outside the Church. They'll come for us next. We are calling all our people home. Back to the security of New Hope. We will not fall again. You must go now.'

Emma started to argue, and the next thing she knew she was standing beside her gravity sled on the landing pads of Logres' main starport. Right back where she'd first arrived on the planet. She'd been teleported. There was no sign of the Ecstatic. Emma sighed and shrugged, and stepped back up onto her sled. She rose slowly back into the sky and floated back across the city, going nowhere in particular. The Parade of the Endless seemed very different now from when she'd first arrived, such a short time ago. So full of happiness and good intentions, then, and even innocent, though that was not a word she would have used about herself before she came to Logres. But now her whole world had changed, and perhaps the Empire too. Humanity was becoming something new, something darker. Sometimes it seemed to Emma that the only thing which hadn't changed for the worse was her.

She still believed in what it meant, to be a Paragon.

She soared slowly over the city, and down in the streets below people looked up at her, and didn't wave or cheer or smile. She was no longer their protector. She was the enemy.

Emma Steel frowned, and wondered almost helplessly what to do next.

Anne Barclay sat alone in her office, swivelling back and forth in her familiar old chair, watching her display of monitor screens with the sound turned down to a bare mutter. She glanced from screen to screen but saw nothing. None of it mattered, not really. The House would be going into Session soon, and there were all kinds of urgent matters that ought to be commanding her attention, but she couldn't seem to concentrate on any of them. She had a mug of hot sweet black coffee in her hand, and she sipped at it now and again, when she remembered it was there, but she didn't really taste it. Her other hand moved slowly over her close cropped red hair, an old familiar caress that for once failed to comfort.

Anne was feeling unappreciated. She worked all the hours God sent, practically ran the House's Security single-handed these days; and no-one cared. She always made sure Douglas had every bit of information he needed, often hours before anyone else had it; and she couldn't remember the last time he said *Thank you*. She rushed from room to room and meeting to meeting, making the secret necessary deals that Douglas couldn't be seen to make himself; and all for what? Despite all her hard work, despite all the miracles she worked every day on Douglas' behalf, he just took her for granted. He didn't even talk with her any more. Oh, he'd pop in to make sure she knew all about his latest problems and orders, sometimes throw her a brief meaningless smile, and then he was off and on his way again. He never paused, to say *Well done*, or *Couldn't do it without you*, or even *You're my good right hand, Anne, I'm so proud of you*. Not much to ask for, really. She knew he was busy. She knew he worked even longer hours than she did. She knew she was being unfair. And she didn't give a damn.

She'd never felt so alone, so desolate. So miserable. Jesamine was always too busy, or perhaps too guilty, to talk with her any more. And Lewis was unofficially but very definitely in disgrace, and only allowed into the House on special occasions. Anne sighed, and drank more coffee she didn't want. She couldn't go to see Lewis without risking seeming disloyal to Douglas, and the King had been hurt enough. All of which meant there was no-one left for Anne to talk to, or at least no-one she could trust. So she came to the office early and left late, and worked and worked till she was numb, because that was all she had left. Bringing the House, and its Security, under her control because she couldn't control her own life.

She looked almost reluctantly at the lowest drawer of her desk, securely locked and sealed, where she kept the bright pink feather boa Jesamine had given her. She should have thrown it away, given it to someone who could appreciate it, or at the very least was brave enough to wear it in public. But somehow she couldn't bring herself to do that. The boa was important to her; it represented something valuable, though she wasn't sure what. Freedom, perhaps. The freedom to be someone other than boring old dependable Anne Barclay. Someone who had the guts to go and find a life of her own; someone who knew how to have fun. To do all the things Anne Barclay dreamed of, but had never found the time or the courage to go looking for. Someone who knew how to live, instead of just exist.

There was a single mirror on her desk; small, plain and functional. Nothing at all of vanity about it. Anne looked at her own face in the mirror, and didn't recognise it. That wasn't her; that grim scowling mask with hollow desperate eyes. That old, dead, woman.

You don't know what I want. None of you know what I want. What I need. I want . . . to go dancing, wearing something scandalous, in the kind of sleazy, cheap joint where people like Anne Barclay don't belong. I want to drink too much, make an exhibition of myself, pull some good-looking boy off the dance floor and into the toilets, and have rough loveless sex with him. I want to do things I'll be ashamed of in the morning. I want to do everything I'm not supposed to do, everything I was never allowed to. I want to be . . . like Jes and Lewis, and never give a damn.

Oh God, I want to feel alive, before it's too late.

An unexpected knock at her office door made her jump in her chair, interrupting her train of thought. She flushed guiltily, swivelled her chair around and regarded the closed door suspiciously. She wasn't expecting any visitors, and her staff knew better than to bother her when she said she had some thinking to do. She glanced back over her shoulder at the monitor screen that covered the corridor outside. Standing patiently outside her door was the honourable Member for Virimonde; Michel du Bois. Anne raised an eyebrow. It had been a long time since du Bois had wanted anything from her, mainly because he knew he wouldn't get it. The best memories Anne had of Virimonde were of leaving it. Provincial bloody dump. They'd never appreciated her either. But in the end she shrugged, and called for her visitor to enter. It was someone to talk to; and she was curious.

Michel du Bois entered with his usual practised dignity, dressed in his very best for the upcoming day's Session. He bowed low to Anne, before pulling up a chair and sitting down opposite her without asking permission first. He smiled at Anne. She didn't smile back. He'd only take it as a sign of weakness. Whatever it was he wanted, it had to be something he couldn't get anywhere else. Du Bois arranged his formal robes fussily, and met Anne's gaze with practised sincerity.

'Virimonde has chosen a new Paragon,' he said bluntly. 'A highly proficient young man with excellent prospects, called Stuart Lennox. Comes from a good family, has a fine record as one of Virimonde's peacekeepers, and not a trace of scandal anywhere about him. A bit glum and humourless perhaps, and he'll need some coaching before we can turn him loose in front of the media, but he's solid, dependable, and a canny fighter. Just what we need to represent our homeworld before the Empire. He'll arrive here for his investiture somewhen next week, just in time for the Royal Wedding.'

'Why are you telling me?' said Anne. 'I don't work with Paragons.'

'Virmonde is your homeworld,' said du Bois, just a little sternly. 'I thought you'd be interested. Particularly since of late you've become somewhat . . . distanced from the previous Paragon.'

'Ah,' said Anne, nodding wisely. 'So that's it. It always comes down to Lewis in the end, blast his soul. What have you heard, du Bois? What do you think you know? And what makes you think I might give a damn what you might or might not know?'

Du Bois spread his arms wide in an expansive gesture, and tried to look innocent. He wasn't especially successful. He was a politician, after all. 'It's clear to everyone, inside and outside the House, that you and the Deathstalker are no longer as close as you once were. And since the King has also been taking some pains to publicly distance himself from his Champion of late, it doesn't take a genius to work out that something significant must have happened. Lewis has made many mistakes of judgement since becoming Champion. Separating himself from his friends, and those who would be his friends. Disgracing himself, through his actions during the Neumen riot. Most importantly, failing to be the Champion everyone wanted . . . The Deathstalker is no longer a credit to our homeworld.'

'Is that why you cut off his stipend?' said Anne.

'He was no longer entitled to those monies. The allowance will go to Stuart Lennox, who will no doubt be much more . . . appreciative. Don't mistake me, Anne. It pains me to see the Deathstalker brought so low, it really does, but he brought it upon himself by his own actions.'

'I'm busy,' said Anne, coldly. 'What do you want from me, du Bois?'

'It occurred to me that you, as one of the Deathstalker's oldest and closest friends, might be able to shed some light on why dear Lewis has been acting so out of character just lately.'

'He's just going through a bad time,' Anne said evenly. 'We all do.'

'But if you knew something . . . private, something personal . . .'

'I'd have more sense than to discuss it with you. Stay away from Lewis, du Bois. That's my advice to you. Stick to pulling your new Paragon's strings. You try and push Lewis around, even in his present state, and he'll eat you alive. Now if that's all, I have work to do.'

Michel du Bois rose gracefully to his feet, his expression professionally neutral, untouched by Anne's harsh words. 'I can see this isn't the right time to discuss these matters. Your support for your friend does you credit, Anne, it really does; but I feel I would be failing in my duty as your homeworld's representative if I didn't warn you of the dangers involved if you persist in this attitude.'

Anne leaned back in her chair and smiled nastily. She was always happiest when the threat came out into the open. 'Dangers, du Bois? Why, whatever can you mean? I'm not aware of any dangers.'

'Lewis is on his way out,' du Bois said flatly. 'He's going to fall, and he's going to fall fast. Anyone can see that. It would be such a shame if he was to bring his friends down with him. Especially when all they had to do was reach out and take the hand of a new friend.'

'You never had a friend in your life, du Bois.'

'Perhaps. But I have always understood the value of an ally. There was a time when you would have, too.'

Michel du Bois left while Anne was still trying to come up with an answer to that one, closing the door quietly behind him. Anne scowled fiercely, and swivelled her chair angrily back and forth. For all her (justified) dislike of the man, she had to admit that his words had seemed more like a warning than a threat. But why would he care? They'd never been close, personally or politically. Perhaps he just thought that having two highly placed and very visible natives of Virimonde brought low would reflect badly on his world. Whatever else you could say about him, and Anne had said a lot in her time, du Bois had always been a patriot. Anne decided she'd better take a serious look at the new Paragon's background. See if there was anything there she ought to know about.

There was another knock at the door. Anne sighed heavily. Some days people just wouldn't let you brood in peace. She checked the hall monitor screen again, and there was Jesamine Flowers, looking very beautiful and almost unbearably glamorous, holding a large box tied up with pink ribbon. Anne studied the screen for a long moment. Beware Queens-to-be, bearing gifts. Especially when they've been caught red-handed betraying their husband-to-be. Anne composed herself, and called for her old friend to come in.

The door flew open, and Jesamine bustled in, full of life and airy chatter, as though nothing had happened. She slammed the door shut behind her with a practised flick of her back heel, pushed the present into Anne's arms, kissed the air near her cheeks, and threw herself into the chair du Bois had just vacated. All without once hesitating, betraying any awkwardness, or pausing for breath. Jesamine had always known how to make an entrance.

'Well open the box, darling!' she said brightly. 'It's just a little pressie, to smooth the way between us. You're going to simply adore it! Go on, open it, sweetie! It won't bite.'

Anne undid the large floppy pink bow, and carefully put the length of pink ribbon to one side. She collected things like that. You never knew when they might come in useful. She opened the long box, dropping the lid on the floor beside her chair, and there in the box was a gorgeous gown of shimmering silver. Perhaps the most beautiful dress Anne had ever seen. Glamorous, stylish, a product of the very best designer label, and undoubtably worth more than Anne made in a year. A dress to make any woman look like a Queen. And nothing Anne would ever wear. Would ever dare to wear. Anne's fingers trailed lovingly over the sheer, marvellous material, almost in spite of herself. It felt like a kiss on her fingertips. It was without a doubt the finest dress Anne had ever known, and she wanted nothing more than to screw it up into a ball and throw it back in Jesamine's face. To scream at her in rage and shame, for not knowing Anne would never, ever be able to wear a thing like this. Jesamine chattered on, oblivious.

'I came across this in my wardrobe, and thought of you immediately. It's one of my favourite gowns, from when I was playing Kate in *Taming of the Shrew*. It always brought me good luck, and I'm sure it will do the same for you.'

'Well,' said Anne, pulling her hand back from the material. 'It's been a while since I was offered hand-me-downs. What next, Jes? Some old pair of shoes, with the heels hardly worn down? Or maybe half a box of chocolates you couldn't be bothered to finish?'

Jesamine pouted sulkily. 'Why are you being like this, Anne? I came here to kiss and make up. I want us to be friends again.'

'Why am I being like this? It has to be my fault, doesn't it, never yours? Are you really that blind, that self-obsessed? You jeopardise the Royal Wedding, betray Douglas and infatuate Lewis, and you wonder why I'm being like this? Grow up, Jes! This isn't some backstage romance, some brief fling for the gossip magazines to twitter over! This is treason, Jes. I should never have put your name forward in the first place. I should have known you'd screw it up.'

'Look, I said I was sorry! I said it wouldn't happen again! What more do you want me to do?'

'I want you to be loyal to Douglas. I want you to act like a Queen in waiting, not some stuck up tart with an itch in her panties. I want you to leave Lewis alone! It's not like he means anything to you. I know you, Jes.'

'No you don't. You don't know me at all. Lewis is . . . special.'

'Yes. Yes, he is. He deserves better than you. He doesn't understand this is all just a game to you. I don't want him hurt. So stay away from him. He doesn't need you in his life.'

'He needs someone.'

'He needs someone who'll care for him!' Anne said hotly. 'Someone who'll care about him. Not just use him because he's there, and then throw him aside like a snotty tissue. Like you've done with so many others before him.'

'That's not fair. It wasn't like that. Lewis is different . . .'

'That's right. Lewis is different, from you and me. He knows the meaning of duty, and of honour. Or at least he used to, before he met you. If you have any feelings for him at all, leave him alone. Before you destroy him completely. He's a good man. You're not worthy of him.'

Jesamine erupted up out of her chair, her cheeks blazing, vicious unforgivable words trembling on her lips; words that could never be taken back, or apologised for. Words that would mean the end of her oldest friendship. She stood there breathing heavily for a moment, and somehow choked the words down. But she had nothing else to say, so she turned and stormed out of Anne's office, away from her accusing eyes, slamming the door behind her as hard as she could. And there in the corridor, heading straight for her, was Lewis Deathstalker.

Part of her wanted to turn and run, but she didn't. Jesamine stood her ground as Lewis walked up to her, and stopped right in front of her. She was breathing hard, her heart hammering in her breast. Their eyes met, and all their good intentions went for nothing. They'd kept apart from each other, each hoping the madness would pass, but it hadn't. All it took was the sight of each other, and their hearts raced. Deny it as they would, they were meant to be together; and neither King nor Parliament, duty nor honour, could keep them apart.

'What are you doing here, Lewis?' Jesamine said finally, her voice strained by the effort involved in seeming casual.

'I came to see Anne,' said Lewis. 'Looking for something to do. Someone to talk to. How have you been, Jes? You look good.'

'Fine. I've been fine. You look good too.'

'No I don't,' said Lewis, smiling just a little. 'I'm famous for not looking good.'

'You look good to me,' said Jesamine.

'He's my friend, Jes.'

'I know.'

And suddenly they were kissing again, bodies pressed tight together, as though trying to become one person, that could never be parted. While in her lonely office, Anne watched them kiss on her monitor screen, her clenched hands full of the material of the marvellous dress.

King Douglas sat stiffly on his great Throne in the House of Parliament, nodding graciously to the various honourable Members as they assembled to take their Seats. There weren't as many as usual, or even as many as he'd hoped for. Attendance was well down on what he'd expected. Most hadn't even bothered to attend by holo. Probably they were scared. The House was going to have to discuss the problem of Pure

Humanity and the Church Militant soon, but none of the honourable Members wanted to commit themselves publicly to one position or another until they absolutely had to. Public opinion was vacillating wildly, and their representatives were running scared.

Douglas sat on his Throne and felt very exposed, very alone. He wished Jesamine was at his side. He wondered briefly what was keeping her. It couldn't be anything important, or Anne would have briefed him by now over his private comm channel. He shifted uncomfortably. He didn't want to be here, didn't want to be doing this. Presiding over a Session that no-one cared about, when so many things were going wrong; in the city, all over Logres, all across the Empire. The influence of the Church Militant was spreading like a disease, infecting world after world. The gospel of Pure Humanity was taking hold on planets he would have sworn had more sense, or at least more decency. And now there were scattered reports coming in of Neumen fanatics killing Ecstatics in the streets. The most harmless creatures in the Empire, being hunted down like animals. The Paragon in Douglas seethed within him, demanding he go out into the city and do . . . something. Something to stop the madness.

Oh father, you tried to warn me. The Throne is a trap, you said. A duty without end, a responsibility without comfort. A weight that crushes, borne because someone has to do it. But father . . . you never told me how alone I'd feel. Jesamine; where are you?

Finally the House reached a point where everybody who was coming, was there, and the Session at last got under way. No-one mentioned the missing Champion, or Jesamine, just as no-one mentioned Douglas threatening to give up his Crown, during the Neumen riot. He was back on the Throne, wearing the Crown, so no-one said anything. Everyone just pretended it had never happened. The House could be very good at that, when it chose. The day's business passed smoothly enough, with little need for Douglas to intervene. Until finally he got the chance to raise the one matter he really cared about; his own plan to snatch a little sanity back from the ever-increasing madness.

'I propose a great Parade of Paragons, through the city,' he said, and everyone listened politely. 'Since most of the Empire's Paragons are still assembled in this city, awaiting the Royal Wedding, let's take this opportunity to fete them as they deserve. To celebrate their achievements, as heroes of the Empire. Finn Durandal came up with the idea originally, and presented it to me, and I think it's a good one. It gives us a chance to re-establish the popularity of the Paragons, and their authority. Show the city, and Logres, and the Empire, that this House and this Crown still stand one hundred per cent behind the Paragons.

'The media will love it. Prime time coverage guaranteed. With a little encouragement from the right quarters, I'm sure the news channels could be persuaded to build up to the event by showing lots of programming covering the Paragons' past triumphs and victories. Remind the people of just how much the Paragons have done for them in the past. How much they owe them. That will bring the crowds out onto the streets, to cheer their heroes, and provide news coverage that can be shown to all the worlds in the Empire. How say you, honourable Members?'

The honourable Members loved it. Mostly. Some (fairly) open supporters of Pure Humanity still wanted to investigate and even prosecute individual Paragons for their actions during the Neumen riot, very definitely including the Death-stalker, but they were quickly shouted down. The House wanted its heroes back. Wanted to feel safe again, behind the protection of the Paragons. And they all understood the appeal of a good Parade. Good publicity and good feeling from the Parade would spill over onto the House too. The King's proposal was accepted, and passed, by a huge majority.

They then spent the rest of the Session arguing fiercely over who was going to pay for it.

Lewis and Jesamine lay together, wrapped nakedly around each other, on the mattress on the floor of Lewis' mostly empty bedroom. They smiled at each other, basking in the afterglow of a very happy time, the sweat still cooling and evaporating on their bodies. Nothing like delaying and denying sex to make it really frantic. It had to be Lewis' place. They couldn't afford to be seen going to Jesamine's place together, and there wasn't a hotel in the city that wouldn't be straight on the comm to the gossip rags, so . . . Jesamine's own security people ran static, including the use of Jesamine's official double, to distract and lure away the media pack that followed Jesamine wherever she went. (Given how smoothly the whole operation went, Lewis had a strong feeling they'd done this many times before, but he said nothing.) The two of them sneaked successfully into Lewis' appartment entirely unobserved, Jesamine carrying an esp-blocker in her purse so there was no way they could be eavesdropped on. She wasn't taking any chances. Lewis was impressed by her thoroughness.

They went straight to the bedroom, and stayed there.

Finally they sat up together, their backs pressed against the bare bedroom wall, still naked, eating Death By Chocolate ice cream straight from the same tub, with two spoons. (Lewis remembered to wash both the spoons first, at the last moment.) Every now and again they'd flick some of the ice cream at each other, and squeal and laugh and tussle playfully. Lewis had never been happier. But even so . . .

'We can't stay here much longer,' he said regretfully. 'The day's Session in the House must have started by now. You have to be there, and I really ought to be. Can't have the House thinking there's a divide between the King and his Queen-to-be. They'd be sure to try and take advantage. And I ought to be there for this Session, because Douglas is going to put forward his proposal for a Parade of Paragons through the city. I'm supposed to lead it.'

'And so you should,' said Jesamine, licking ice cream from the back of her spoon. 'Douglas told me about it. Good idea. Excellent theatre. Just what the Paragons need; and the city, come to that. Everyone loves a Parade!'

'Surprisingly enough, it was Finn's idea originally. Took it to the King in person, with most of the details already worked out. Chosen the best route and everything. Good to see him getting involved in things again. He's far too valuable to be wasted in an extended sulk. Perhaps having a new partner in Emma Steel is bringing him out of himself again.'

'Ah,' said Jesamine. 'The infamous Emma Steel! Possibly the only woman in the Empire almost as famous as I am. What's she really like?'

Lewis thought for a moment, idly stirring his spoon around the bottom of the now-empty ice cream tub. 'Impressive. Even intimidating. Good at her job, and doesn't suffer fools gladly. Just what this city needs.'

'Everyone should get what they need,' Jesamine said demurely.

Lewis laughed, put aside the ice cream tub, and cuddled her to him. They leaned happily together, not feeling the need to do anything or go anywhere, just yet. They felt comfortable, at ease, relaxed in a way they never were as Champion and Queen-to-be. Jesamine looked round the bare and empty bedroom.

'Darling, I have to say; this is a bit . . . minimalist, even for you. No vidscreen, no furniture, no carpet . . . not even a bidet, or a chair to pile your clothes on. I hate to think of you living like this. It's not right; not for the Champion of the Empire.'

'It's only temporary,' said Lewis. 'Things will sort themselves out, you'll see. And then I'll get the best chair money can buy.'

Jesamine sighed, and kissed him on the cheek. 'I wish I had your faith, dear.'

'Do you feel guilty?' Lewis said suddenly.

'Of course I do! I'm not entirely unfeeling, sweetie. I'm very fond of Douglas. I don't want to see him hurt.'

'Neither do I. He was always my closest friend. Ever since I came to Logres, he was always right there with me, backing me up. All the times we went into combat together, fighting side by side or back to back; trusting each other implicitly. I never thought I'd fail in my duty to him; as a King, and a friend.'

Jesamine took his chin in her hand, and turned his face to hers. 'Are you sorry, Lewis? Sorry about this, about us?'

'No! No. I know this is wrong, but I don't care. How can something that makes us both so happy be wrong?'

'That sounds like something I would say, darling. I've

always been able to find really good excuses for my little peccadillos.'

Lewis considered that. 'I won't ask.'

'Best not to, dear. You're different. I care about you.'

Lewis sighed. 'Where do we go from here, Jes? What do we do about this?'

'Damned if I know, Lewis.'

'Should we tell Douglas?'

'I can't see any way where that would turn out for the best, sweetie. He loves me, you see.'

'Oh Jesus . . . do you love him?'

'No. I admire him, I'm fond of him . . . but that's all. Oh Lewis . . . I waited so long for my first real love; I should have known it would be complicated. People like us aren't allowed to have normal, everyday lives.'

And that was when the emergency alarm went off in Lewis' ear, blasting out of his Paragon comm channel like the wrath of God. He sat bolt upright on the mattress, almost shoving Jesamine away from him so he could concentrate on Douglas' voice crashing through his head with harsh authority.

'Lewis! Where the hell are you?'

'I'm at my apartment, Douglas. Having a bit of a lie down. What's up?'

'Get to Parliament fast. The shit has hit the fan, and we are all in deep trouble. Can't brief you now, not even on a secure channel like this. Just . . . get here as fast as you can.'

'On my way, Douglas.'

The King broke contact. Lewis swung his legs off the mattress and rose quickly to his feet. He was scowling hard, his ugly face so harsh now it actually frightened Jesamine for a moment. Lewis grabbed Jesamine's discarded clothing and threw it at her, and then climbed quickly into his black leather Champion's armour. Jesamine clutched the dress to her chest and looked at Lewis almost timidly.

'What is it, Lewis? What's wrong?'

'Get dressed,' he said tersely. 'That was my emergency line. Something's happened. Something really bad, by the sound of it. I have to get to the House. You better had, too.'

Jesamine responded to the urgency in his voice, and started

putting her clothes on. Lewis was dressed and ready to go long before she was, and strode impatiently round the room as he waited for her to finish. His mind was reeling with appalling possibilities; everything from open Neumen insurrection to an outbreak of plague, when another, far more disturbing thought hit him. He stopped his pacing abruptly, and looked across at Jesamine.

'This couldn't be about us, could it, Jes? I mean; there's no way he could know about what just happened here. We were so careful . . .'

Jesamine shrugged, studying her reflection critically in the bedroom's only mirror while trying to do something with her tousled hair. 'He's the King. Who's to say what he can and can't know? I only have hardened security professionals; he has Anne. But I don't think this is about us, Lewis. He wouldn't want a public scandal. If only for his pride's sake. Look, go into the other room and try the news channels. See if they're showing anything yet.'

'I haven't got a vidscreen,' said Lewis.

'What; not at all? All right, that settles it; next time we're going to my place, and to hell with the difficulties. I absolutely refuse to live without the little necessities of life. There are limits, darling.'

'So . . . there is going to be a next time?' Lewis said carefully.

Jesamine shook her head, exasperated, marched over to Lewis and kissed him soundly on the mouth. 'What did you think, Lewis? That once I'd had you, once I'd ticked you off my list, I wouldn't want you any more? We are in this for the long term, Lewis; get used to it. Some things are just meant to be, sweetie.'

'Unfortunately, you and I seem to be the only ones in the whole damned Empire who believe that,' Lewis said dryly. 'But we'll work something out. I know we will.'

'Of course we will, darling!' Jesamine kissed him again, brushed briefly at his armoured chest with her hand, and headed for the door. And then she paused, and looked back over her shoulder at him. 'Tell me; are you at all familiar with the plot of *Macbeth*?'

'Not funny, Jes,' said Lewis, shaking his head as he went after her. 'Not funny at all.'

High up on a rooftop, Finn Durandal looked down on the street intersection, and studied the public vidphone booth for some time, from what he hoped was a safe distance. There were a lot of people about, coming and going and passing the phone booth without a second glance. It was situated right in the middle of a downtown shopping precinct, on a not particularly busy corner, and it all looked innocent enough; but Finn still wasn't satisfied. You couldn't afford to take any chances when dealing with ELFs. They'd insisted on speaking to him directly before they'd agree to join him in his plot to destroy the Paragons, and since neither side were foolish enough to show up in person, that just left the usual means of communication, of which public vidphones were the most safely anonymous. Finn chose the setting, the ELFs chose the particular booth, and they both agreed on a time. Finn got there an hour early, just in case, and watched from the rooftop, his force shield up, to protect him from sniper fire.

All the sensors on his gravity sled insisted the booth hadn't been tampered with, or booby-trapped in any way, but still Finn was suspicious. He had no doubt the ELFs would sacrifice the possible gains of his plan for the more satisfying pleasures of a definite strike against him. They'd do anything to get their hands on the man who'd executed so many of them in the Arena. Finn could understand that. He was all for revenge, these days.

But the agreed time finally arrived, and he couldn't see any good reason for hanging back any longer, and he didn't want the ELFs to think they could intimidate him, so he stepped onto his gravity sled and swooped down into the intersection below. People scattered to give him room. He ignored them all, stepped off his hovering sled and entered the vidphone booth. The phone immediately started ringing. They had been watching, after all. Probably through some far off thrall's possessed eyes. No point in looking around; it could be anyone. Fin hit the accept button, and the screen lit up before him to show a male face he didn't recognise at all.

The vicious arrogant smile and the wide staring eyes were familiar, though.

'Hello, Finn. I do so love a man who's punctual. How do you like this body? Just a little something I threw on, especially for you. So we could have this little talk.'

'Forget the pleasantries,' said Finn. 'We're allies against a common enemy, and that's all we're ever going to be. Let's get down to business.'

'Yes. Let's. I want to hear you tell me all about how you're going to betray your fellow Paragons. I want to hear it from your own lips, see the truth of it in your eyes.'

'They're not my fellows any more,' Finn said calmly. 'I disown them. The plan is just as my people described it to you. By now the King will have put to Parliament my proposal for a Parade of Paragons. Including the route details I so kindly worked out for him. Here's the map, with all the particulars you'll need.' Finn fed his infocard into the vid-phone, and the ELF thrall downloaded the information at his end. 'You now have the entire route, in advance, along with certain carefully worked out blind spots where you can conceal yourselves, and wait. The Paragons won't be expecting a mass esper onslaught. They'll be too busy acknowledging the cheers and applause of the crowd to even realise what's happening until it's far too late. All the Paragons in one spot, trapped in a shooting alley, sitting ducks for determined ELFs with revenge on their mind. That's what I'm offering you. Real payback for what happened in the Arena.'

'Your information is very thorough,' said the man possessed by another mind. 'It appears to be everything you say it is. But why should we attack the Paragons in person? Much safer to use thralls. Use the innocent possessed to do our dirty work for us, so that even if the Paragons do fight back, they'll have to kill innocents to protect themselves. That's the ELF way.'

'Civilians with guns, even possessed civilians, won't stand a chance against massed Paragons,' Finn said flatly. 'They'll shoot your thralls down before you can achieve anything worthwhile. They'll hate themselves afterwards for doing it; but they'll do it. But, if you're there in person, in great enough numbers, that much massed mental power will be able to punch right through the few esp-blockers they'll have with them, and possess the Paragons themselves. You can make them kill each other. Your hands, once removed, doing the bloody business. So much more satisfying, yes? Revenge should always be personal. Understand; this is the only chance I can give you. Be a shame if you threw it away, just because you didn't have the balls to turn up in person.'

'You will see what the ELFs can do! We will show you atrocities and nightmares, never to be forgotten! We will do such things to the Paragons that when we finally let them die and go to Hell, the fires of the Pit will be a comfort to them!'

'That's what I want,' said Finn.

'And when we're done with them, and they're all dead, we'll come for you, Finn Durandal. The last Paragon.'

'No,' said Finn, smiling for the first time. 'Then, I'll come for you.'

'You have no idea who we are and where we are,' said the ELF, through the thrall. 'And you never will; because we never leave loose ends.'

He held his hand up beside his face. It held a long knife with a serrated edge. The ELF made the thrall cut out his eyes, cut off his nose, and lick the blood off the blade, laughing breathily all the while. And then he cut his throat. Blood gushed out, spattering the vidphone camera lens. Finn watched, unmoved, as the ELF withdrew from the thrall's mind, leaving an innocent man to die a horrified, senseless death. He fell back out of camera range, and Finn shut down the link from his end. About what he'd expected from the ELFs. They'd always had a taste for the grand gesture. Finn left the booth, stepped onto his waiting sled, and soared quickly up into the sky. He looked sharply about him for some sign of an ambush, but all seemed calm and quiet. Finn flew on over the city, frowning thoughtfully.

Dealing with ELFs, even at arm's length, was always going to be dangerous; but so far his plan seemed to be working out perfectly. And thanks to Brett and Rose, he at least knew where two of the ELFs were. (Even though Brett was still in shock from his encounter with the Spider Harps.) Finn smiled happily. No; he was still ahead of the game, while everyone else only thought they were. He would have his revenge on his enemies, and put himself one step closer to his eventual goal. And if things were progressing only slowly, well; what's the point of revenge if you don't take the time to savour it?

Lewis Deathstalker and Jesamine Flowers arrived (carefully separately) at the House to find the whole place in an uproar. The narrow corridors and offices backstage were a complete bedlam, with people running back and forth, plunging in and out of rooms with white faces and wild staring eyes, shouting incoherently at each other. In overcrowded offices, people sat and stood over computer terminals, trying desperately to get information out of them. And some just stood in doorways, or sat on the floor in the corridors, sobbing helplessly into hands pressed to their faces.

Lewis hurried through the corridors, a growing premonition chilling his heart till he could hardly breathe. What had happened while he was away, out of the loop; selfishly enjoying himself? What could have happened to cause such panic and despair? He started grabbing people and shouting questions at them, but they just tore themselves away. No-one had the time to talk to him, and not even his Champion's authority or Deathstalker face was enough to slow them down.

Lewis saw Jesamine slipping through the great door onto the floor of the House, and decided he'd better give her a few minutes' start. Even now, in the midst of . . . all this, he had to be careful. Had to protect his reputation. And Douglas'. Besides; there was still one place he could go where he would be sure to get answers and information. One person who always knew what was going on. In fact, he should have gone there first. He headed for Anne Barclay's office, and when he got there the door opened before he could even knock.

Inside, he found Anne sitting slumped in her chair, not even looking at her monitor screens. She'd turned the sound off, so her screens were full of tiny people shouting dumbly at each other. She looked stunned, as though someone had hit her. She was trying to drink coffee from her favourite mug, but her hand was shaking too much. She tried using both hands, but it didn't help much. She looked dully at Lewis as he moved over to her, and didn't smile or even nod.

'What is it?' said Lewis desperately. 'Anne; what the hell has happened? Is Douglas all right? Has there been another suicide bomber?'

Ane looked at him with cold, bitter eyes, her mouth a flat line. 'You should have been here, Lewis. You should have been here.'

'Tell Douglas that. He's the one who told me to stay away. Now talk to me, Anne. *What's happened?*'

'You think I don't know where you've been?' said Anne. 'What you've been doing? I know. I can smell her on you.'

Lewis stopped short, as though she'd hit him. 'Anne . . .'

'Shut up. Go into the House. Be with your King. He needs you. Jes . . . doesn't matter now. Nothing else matters now.'

'Anne, what . . .'

'The Terror, Lewis. The Terror has finally arrived.'

Lewis gasped at her, horror flooding through him as he finally understood. He backed away from her, and then turned and ran from the room, heading for the House, and his King.

It was all quiet when he finally got there, almost deathly quiet. The place was packed, everyone there in person or in holo, watching the great viewscreen floating above the open floor of the House. All of them utterly transfixed by the terrible images on the screen. Lewis moved over to stand beside Douglas, sitting forward on the edge of his Throne. The King seemed somehow smaller, shrunken by the magnitude of the events unfolding before him. He didn't even look round to acknowledge Lewis' arrival. Everyone was silent, stunned; MPs, clones, espers, aliens, Shub. The unthinkable had finally happened. Two centuries after the blessed Owen had given them his dire warning through Captain Silence, and commanded the Empire to prepare; the Terror had finally come for them all.

Lewis used his comm implant to access the House's official records and brought himself up to date on what had happened while he was away, all the time watching the awful scenes on the viewscreen along with everyone else. Watching while planets burned on the edge of the Empire.

It started, as so many bad things did, out on the Rim. Out on the far boundary of the Empire, where civilisation ends and the endless night begins, lay a small group of unimportant planets that two centuries before had been a part of the legendary and infamous Darkvoid. Swallowed up by the dreadful Darkvoid Device, the populations of those worlds had become monsters; the Recreated. They were rescued and restored to their humanity by the blessed Owen, given life and sanity and peace of heart again. For two hundred years. Until the Terror came. *Poor bastards,* Lewis thought helplessly. *You just couldn't get a break, could you?* The Terror came out of the dark unknown spaces beyond the Rim of Empire, from the vast and unknowable outer reaches. There was no warning, no premonition; just the Terror coming out of nowhere to fall on the undefended planets like a wolf upon the fold. Out of the billions of innocent souls who once lived on those seven worlds, only one man now survived; Donal Corcoran, heading for the safety of the inner systems as fast as his small ship, *The Jeremiah,* could carry him. What he saw drove him out of his mind, so that he screamed and weeped and shuddered uncontrollably as he contacted the authorities, to try and tell them what he'd seen, and what had happened, on the day the Terror finally reached the Empire.

He'd just happened to be leaving orbit after a fairly success-ful trading run to the planet Iona, when the Terror arrived. He ran, accelerating with everything his ship's engines could give him, until he was fast enough and far enough away from the planet's gravity well to drop into the safety of hyperspace. No-one blamed him. Running was the only sane thing to do. While his ship was still building up speed, Corcoran dropped all his sensor drones behind him, to record what was happen-ing. Some of the drones were still transmitting now, through *The Jeremiah*'s computers, showing what the Terror had done to seven helpless planets and their populations. The drones were dying, one by one, their information streams cutting in and out. Apparently just their continued proximity to the Terror was enough to distort and mutate their systems. Those that weren't dying were becoming something else, and no-one knew what.

The Jeremiah hadn't escaped unscathed, either. Systems were breaking down all over the ship, scarred by the gaze of the medusa. And Donal Corcoran, once a simple trader, was now a wild-eyed crazy man, prophesying doom. He kept breaking into the drones' transmissions, to scream and shout and weep over what he'd seen. Just one look at the Terror had been enough to unhinge his thoughts, and fracture his reason. Tragically, he was still just sane enough to know how much he'd lost. You couldn't look into the devil's eyes and hope to come away unmarked. The nearest Fleet starcruiser had been sent to intercept his path and pick him up, but the Rim was a long way off, even for the new H class stardrives. No-one patrolled the Rim any more. There was no need. Nothing ever happened out there, so far from the heart of civilisation. And there hadn't been a threat from beyond the Rim since the blessed Owen's day.

No-one ever really thought the Terror would come in their lifetime . . .

One by one the sensor drones were shutting down, overwhelmed by the awful energies radiating from the seven burning worlds out on the Rim. It didn't matter. There was no point in going there, no-one left to rescue. And the Terror wasn't there any more. It had moved on, heading on a slow straight line right for the densely-populated planets at the heart of the Empire.

Lewis called up the House's records of the events leading up to the Terror. Recorded images filled his eyes, channelled down his optical nerves; a combination of the planets' news channels, security systems and individual recordings. A short history of the coming of the end. Lewis felt angry and sick and helpless, and his lips pressed so tightly together they were entirely white.

It started simply enough. Something came out of the darkness beyond the Rim, out of the empty spaces, travelling at just under light speed. It caught everyone by surprise, because no-one was looking for it. Why should they? It shot past the seven populated worlds without slowing, before they even knew it was there, and plunged into their sun. And that should have been the end of it. It should have been destroyed, annihilated in a moment in the hottest fires of all. Instead, it made itself at home in the heart of the sun, basking in the unimaginable heat, and incubated there. Growing, *becoming*. It absorbed the sun's energies, eating it up, gathering fuel for its mission, and when it was ready it hatched, and a swarm of hateful black creatures that might have been alive or might have been machines or something entirely other, came flying out of the sun's flames and descended on the seven populated planets like so many horrid angels. Or devils.

There were millions of them, each of them subtly different, intricate malevolent shapes like Hell's snowflakes, with hundreds of eyes and even more sharp cutting edges. They formed thick living rings around the targeted planets, endless numbers of them, fighting and jostling for position at barely sublight speed. On the surface of the planets below, machines malfunctioned, computers were thrown off line and AIs spoke gibberish. Planetary defences failed to operate. The swarm descended, screaming in anticipation as they plunged into the planets' atmospheres, and everyone who heard that scream went insane. There was no recording of the sound; it was too big, too alien, too terribly other for technology to capture. But people could hear it, and the endless uninterrupted scream drove everyone instantly, violently, insane . . .

Men and women and children howled with unbearable mental agony, and destroyed everything around them. They tore down their homes and set fire to their cities. And then they turned upon each other, killing friends and strangers and family with equal ferocity, not because they wanted to, but because they were driven to it. By the never-ending scream of the swarm that flew above them, circling and circling the planet like vultures waiting for something to die. On seven worlds, seven entire populations went insane and slaughtered each other in the ruins of their burning cities. There was no defence against the maddening howl of the swarm. Blood flowed. Millions, and then billions, lay dead and dying.

And then, finally, the Terror appeared. Space opened, torn apart by unnatural forces, and from a place where nothing comes from, came something the size of a world. It was alive and aware and utterly hideous, but once again mere human technology was incapable of capturing and recording all that it was. It existed in more than three spatial dimensions, its details fading in and out, as though reality itself wasn't strong enough to encompass all of it, to hold all of the Terror at once. There was something that might have been eyes, dark and awful, vaster than oceans and more deep. And a great mouth, that opened and opened, till it seemed the Terror might swallow the burning planets whole.

Instead the Terror fed, on the madness and the suffering and the destruction. On the Hell its children had made for it. The people fell and lay still, whole populations, all that they were and might have been consumed in a moment. The Terror left behind only empty soulless bodies; sucked dry, still alive but no-one home. In the end, there was nothing left but seven burning worlds, orbiting a shrunken sun. The swarm died then, dropping from the skies into the flames like angels whose wings had been torn from their backs, like devils going home because their work was done. The Terror didn't need them any more. Its eyes and mouth were gone, if they had ever really been there. Space ripped apart again, with a sound like something dying or giving birth, and the Terror returned to wherever it had come from. Only one dark shape remained, the single uglie progenitor that had come from beyond the Rim, from the dark spaces, to dive into the sun and begin it all. The Terror's unstoppable herald, heading relentlessly on into the Empire, towards the next set of populated worlds, and eventually, on a line that would bring it right to the heart of Humanity. To the homeworld itself; Logres. At sub-light speed it would take centuries to get there, but it was coming.

The Terror was coming.

There were no more records. Lewis watched the worlds burning on the great viewscreen before him, seven planets where nothing lived any more, and his mind reeled. So many dead, so many lost to agony and despair . . . He felt like screaming, like laughing and crying at the same time. He wanted to run away and hide, and let someone else deal with it, because it was just too much for him . . . but he didn't. Because he was a Deathstalker. Because he was the Champion. Because people depended on him, just as they had once depended on his ancestor, the blessed Owen. Lewis clamped down hard on his teetering thoughts, and made himself concentrate on the things he could handle. He still had questions, things he needed to know.

He plunged back into the House's records, forcing open old classified files with his Champion's authority, ransacking long-sealed and secret bureaus he would never have even dared approach before, but found little there of any real use. The blessed Owen had never said anything about what the Terror actually was, only that it was coming, and that the whole of Humanity had to prepare itself to fight the Terror when it arrived. That Humanity might have to evolve, even transcend itself, through the Madness Maze, just to survive the Terror's coming. Of course, no-one knew what the blessed Owen's actual original words had been. He'd vanished when the Darkvoid was broken and the lost planets returned, the Recreated saved and restored. His words came via his old ally, Captain John Silence. Also long gone, and no-one knew where or why.

King Douglas made a sharp gesture, and the viewscreen disappeared. The House stirred, as though the honourable Members were slowly waking from a nightmare. Only to find it was all horribly real. They looked shocked, stunned, beaten down. Small men and women, entirely unprepared to face the greatest threat there had ever been to Humanity's existence. They looked at each other, but no-one had anything to say, so they looked to their King. Douglas sat straight-backed on his Throne, and looked steadily back at them.

'First of all; get a grip on yourselves,' he said harshly. 'There's no indication the Terror can break light speed. Which means it's still a long way out. It'll take weeks just to get to the next set of populated worlds. We can evacuate them, or fortify them, as we decide. We have time, to think and plan. To do our duty, and our job. The Terror is . . . unsettling. But we are not without resources. And we will not be taken by surprise.'

'Send the Fleet!' said a shrill voice from somewhere in the House. 'Wait for that thing to reappear, and then blow it away!'

Other voices rose quickly in agreement, only to die away again as King Douglas shook his head.

'We can't risk sending the Imperial Fleet to intercept the Terror. We can't send any ships. In fact, I think we should recall all ships in the area, for now, as a precaution. Once a ship approaches the Terror, or its creatures, the crews on those ships will just fall under its influence. Do you really want Imperial starcruisers, with hyperdrive and disrupter cannon, running wild in the main systems, crewed by homicidal maniacs? No; we send drones, steered by remote control. That goes for you too, Shub. AIs are just as vulnerable as human minds. Does the House have any more . . . practical suggestions?'

People started shouting immediately, some with ideas, some with objections, most just for the comfort of saying something. The House quickly descended into bedlam. Douglas tried to be the voice of reason, but couldn't make himself heard. He leaned back in his Throne and let them get on with it. Let them get it out of their system. It soon became clear no-one had anything useful to offer, and they were just shouting at each other; taking their fear and anger and helplessness out on old rivals and enemies. The various alien species were just as distressed, and just as conflicted over what they should or could do. The Terror had come, and found everyone wanting.

This is what the Deathstalker warned us of! Come now, in our lifetime, after all! We should have listened! We never really believed, and now it's here! And we're not ready!

King Douglas sank further back in his Throne. He didn't feel ready either. He'd only just been made King. He was still learning how to do his job, dammit. He shouldn't have to deal with something as important as this, as vital as this, so early in his reign. He didn't know what to do. It wasn't fair. Briefly, he cursed the blessed Owen, and all his fellow Maze people, for not being around when they were needed. Douglas could feel the shakes starting in his hands again, and gripped the arms of his Throne tightly. It wasn't fair, but then, little in life ever was. Being a Paragon taught you that. But now he was the King, and the Speaker, and it was his job to lead, if necessary by example.

He turned to the Champion at his side, and beckoned for him to lean closer. Lewis did so, and Douglas told him what he wanted him to do. Lewis grinned, drew his disrupter, and fired an energy blast over the heads of the massed MPs. The energy bolt only just missed their heads by a couple of feet or so, and they all ducked reflexively, as the energy beam went on to smash a satisfyingly large hole in the wall at the far end of the chamber. An emergency siren began blaring, but was shut off almost immediately. It seemed Anne was still watching. The bright flare of the energy discharge and the roar of the explosion cut through the House's bedlam, and caught everyone's attention. They stopped arguing, and looked uncertainly at their King, and his Champion. Several were still ducking. A few were on their knees, hiding. Lewis smiled coldly upon them all, his gun covering the whole House impartially. Douglas nodded, satisfied.

'Thank you, Lewis. And thank you, ladies and gentlebeings and gentlebeings, for shutting the hell up so I can hear myself think at last. There will be no more hysteria, by order. I will not have the honourable Members of this venerable institution running about like chickens who've just had their heads chopped off! I will have calm, rational discussion at all times, from all Members. I know I will have this, because I have just given my Champion orders to shoot a hole through the next MP he sees panicking. You don't have any problems with that order, do you, Sir Deathstalker?'

'Not in the least, Your Majesty. In fact, I'm just in the mood to shoot somebody.'

The House looked at Lewis, and had no trouble believing him. They remembered him in the Neumen riot. In a way, it was almost comforting to have a Deathstalker in the House, doing what he did best. Silence and watchful eyes became the order of the day, as the honourable Members sat down again, and looked to their King and Speaker to see what he would do next. Douglas nodded, satisfied, and turned his gaze on the blue steel humanoid figure standing calmly among the aliens.

'When you want logic, go to a computer. Talk to me, Shub; what can you tell this House about the Terror? What it is, where it comes from, and what it might do next?'

The robot representing the AIs of Shub slowly turned its expressionless face towards the Throne. 'We received the same warning that you did. We possess no further information, no extra records, nothing on the nature or capabilities of the Terror that you do not already have. Like you, we never thought the Terror would come so soon. We will send remote probes to the next inhabited system in its path, have them monitor the situation when the Terror next appears in real space. Perhaps by studying the nature of its arrival, we can determine where it exists the rest of the time. Perhaps even come up with some way to go in after it.

'We have weapons that can destroy worlds; or creatures the size of worlds. But the Terror . . . is like nothing we have ever seen before. It doesn't seem to be real, as we are real. Limited as we are limited. It is clearly an extra-dimensional creature. It is possible that no weapon of ours will be able to affect it. You saw how Corcoran's sensor drones changed and mutated, just through continued exposure to the Terror's presence. Just as technology on the Rim planets was affected. And Shub is, of course, technology. The implications are disturbing. But we will send our probes, and study the information they send for as long as they last. Information is always useful. All data will be shared equally, of course.

'I am sorry, Your Majesty. You came to Shub for logic, and it seems all we can offer are guesses and possibilities. Though . . . there is one weapon that might prove useful against the Terror. Should you wish to make use of it.'

'A weapon?' Douglas leaned forward. 'Something you created, during your long war against Humanity?'

'No. Nothing of ours. No-one knows who or what created this weapon. And only you can decide whether or not you wish to use it.'

'The Maze,' Lewis said harshly. 'They're talking about the Madness Maze. Owen said we'd have to transcend, through the Maze, to face what was coming. We could have evolved, made living weapons of ourselves, become greater than we are, long and long ago; if we hadn't been frightened of the Maze.'

'We chose to progress cautiously!' Douglas snapped. 'And with good reason. The Maze kills people, or drives them insane. That's all it's done, since Owen's time. No, Shub; I know you're desperate to go through the Maze, but I can't let you use even the Terror as an excuse. The risks are too great. The Madness Maze stays closed and isolated, until we've tried absolutely everything else. Some cures are far worse than the disease.'

'The Terror just wiped out seven populated worlds,' said Lewis. 'Billions of people dead, in horror and despair. What's ten thousand volunteers dead in the Maze, compared to that? If only one person were to go through and survive, to transcend, like Owen and Hazel and . . .'

'Are you volunteering to go in?' said Douglas. 'To risk almost certain death or madness, just on the off chance of becoming like your ancestor?'

'I don't know,' Lewis said honestly. 'The Maze scares the crap out of me. The odds aren't good, but . . .'

'The odds stink,' said Douglas. 'I won't risk killing the brightest and the best, the bravest and most heroic of my people, just on the chance the Maze might throw up a miracle. No-one gets into the Maze. In fact, this House had better cut orders to increase the levels of Quarantine protection. The last thing we need is streams of religious zealots trying to force their way in. Dead martyrs piling up on Haden would only complicate the situation further.'

'And of course, we don't want rogue superhumans running loose about the Empire, answering to no-one but themselves,' murmured Lewis.

Douglas looked at him sharply. 'No; we don't.' He turned away, to face the esper representative, a tiny woman barely four feet tall, with golden skin and leaf-green hair and the biggest overbite Lewis had ever seen. Douglas nodded courteously to her. 'I need the oversoul to organise all the espers on the outlying planets. Just in case the Terror changes its course. The espers can be the Empire's early warning system. Let us know if there's any change in the herald's direction or speed. Since you don't rely on tech, you should be able to operate longer than most.'

The tiny woman nodded briefly. 'We're on it, Your Majesty.'

'We ought to set up a watch all along the Rim,' said Lewis. 'Who's to say there's only one Terror?'

'Shut up, Lewis,' said Douglas. 'You're depressing me.'

And that was when the Swart Alfair, the representative of Mog Mor, left the alien section and stepped out onto the floor of the House. Ten feet tall, the huge crimson-skinned bat-like creature was an imposing presence, and it knew it. It wrapped its membranous wings around its vaguely humanoid shape, like a great ribbed cloak, while thick blue ectoplasm boiled around it, churning mists containing images that came and went too quickly to be studied. The Swart Alfair made sure it had everyone's attention, and then it turned to face the King. Its eyes were black on black, its snouted gargoyle face unreadable. The Swart Alfair pretended not to notice that Lewis was now covering it exclusively with his disrupter.

'Mog Mor has an offer to make, to King and House and Humanity. Mog Mor offers help and support, in time of mutual need. The Destroyer has come at last, and must be faced and conquered if any are to survive. So; the time for silence has ended, and the Swart Alfair must talk of many things. We have technology you do not even suspect. Technology advanced beyond anything you have, beyond anything in your wildest dreams. We have weapons, ships, machines that think. Greater and more powerful than you can imagine. Kept secret, unsuspected, for time of need. We can blow apart worlds, put out suns; perhaps even stop the Destroyer. Mog Mor will make all this available to Humanity, and Empire, in return for certain promises and assurances . . .'

The King looked round the House, but the honourable Members seemed just as stunned as he was. 'Promises . . .' Douglas said finally.

'We want things,' said the bat-like creature, showing all its pointed teeth in something that might have been meant as a smile. 'We want to colonise worlds of our own. Rich, useful, pleasant worlds that would normally go only to human colonists. There are such worlds close to our home planet. We lay claim to them. They are already colonised by humans, so they will have to leave; so Swart Alfair can occupy them. We want . . . more of a *presence* in the Empire. We want a Seat and a Vote in the House, for every world on which Swart Alfair live, as long as required population levels are maintained. We wish to grow and expand, and scatter ourselves across the stars as humans do. This is our price. For weapons and ships and technology beyond your expectations. Swart Alfair are very old. Asleep for a long time, but waking up now. Embrace us, or fall to the Destroyer.'

'Yes . . .' said Douglas, after a long pause. 'Well, that's a very interesting offer. Which I'm sure the House will want to discuss in some depth. In the meantime . . . we'll take your offer under advisement, and get back to you as soon as we can . . .'

'Don't leave it too long,' said the Swart Alfair. The ectoplasm boiled thickly around it, despite everything the House's air conditioning could do to disperse it. 'We have tech that can hide us from the Destroyer, as it hid us from the Empire and its Investigators, in days of old. You have nothing like it. And no, Your Majesty; Mog Mor feels no duty, no responsibility, to offer it to the Empire free of charge. Not so long as Empire remains poisoned by Pure Humanity philosophy. Going now. Mog Mor will not be seen again in House. Call Mog Mor, when you are ready. When you are scared enough. You have no choice, really.'

The tall scarlet bat-creature stalked out of the House, its ectoplasm following it. Douglas didn't know whether to feel insulted or relieved when it was finally gone.

'If nothing else, he does know how to make an exit,' said Jesamine. 'The ham.'

Douglas looked at her. 'You think he really means it?'

'Who knows, with the Swart Alfair? They've been in the Empire for over a century, and we've still no idea what makes them tick. What we do know, or more often suspect, is frankly disgusting. You don't even want to know how they go about breeding. While they have been known to volunteer information, they rarely answer direct questions, and they've never once allowed xenobiologists to visit their planet. Creepy bastards the lot of them, darling, and arrogant with it. Possibly with good cause. They lived right here in Lionstone's backyard, and she never even knew. Maybe they could hide themselves from the Terror. And if they can do that . . .'

'What else can they do?' Douglas shook his head unhappily. 'It could be a bluff, or it could be our salvation. My head hurts.'

'Do they really ask so much?' said Lewis. 'A few worlds, compared to what we stand to gain? Or lose?'

'But if they're so powerful, why don't they just take what they want?' said Jesamine.

'Wonderful,' growled Douglas. 'More complications. Just what we needed. Any other thoughts that won't do terrible things to my blood pressure?'

'Just the one,' Lewis said quietly. 'And I can pretty much guarantee you're not going to like it. A really unpleasant comparison has occurred to me. What the Terror did to those people on the Rim planets looked an awful lot like what the ELFs did to those people in the Arena . . . possessing and then feeding on their suffering and emotions . . .'

'You're right,' said Douglas, also keeping his voice low. 'I don't like it. In fact, I hate it. You keep that thought strictly to yourself for now, Lewis. That's an order. There's still a lot of general resentment out there, over the way the espers shut down the Neumen riot; I don't want that stirred up again. The last thing we need is even more anti-esper feeling. We're going to need the oversoul's help, and I can't afford to have them feeling alienated or unappreciated. If you want to talk to anyone, Lewis, talk to the oversoul. Maybe they can derive something useful from your . . . comparison. Otherwise, you keep your mouth shut on the subject.'

'Oh hell,' said Jesamine. 'Now what?'

Douglas and Lewis looked round in time to see one of the honourable Members striding out onto the floor of the House, his head held high. Michel du Bois, representative for Virimonde, stopped directly before the Throne, and bowed deeply. When he spoke, his rich, dramatic voice rolled across the House.

'Your Majesty, honoured Members, it seems to me there is one obvious answer to the threat of the Terror that has not been touched on yet.'

'Is there, by God,' said Douglas. 'You do surprise me, du Bois. I can't think how we missed it. Feel free to enlighten us.'

'It's really quite simple, Your Majesty,' said du Bois, spreading his arms in a familiar expansive gesture. 'Owen Deathstalker must return to save us all, as he did before. Virimonde's noblest son, the greatest hero Humanity has ever known. His legend always said he would return in the hour of the Empire's greatest need. And we on Virimonde have never believed the blessed Owen was dead. He cannot die. He passed through the Madness Maze, and moved beyond his humanity, becoming something finer and more glorious. He was our saviour in Lionstone's time, and can be again. We must call out to him with one great voice, implore his help and pray for his return!'

This is getting needlessly messianic, said Lewis, but his voice was lost in an outburst of mass shouting and cheering and stamping of feet from the House. The honourable Members loved the idea; not least because it didn't actually require them to do anything. Let the blessed Owen save Humanity, as he had two centuries before. The cheering and applauding went on for some time, an almost religious hysteria taking over the House, as though they'd just been tossed a lifeline by God herself. Du Bois smiled benevolently about him. Douglas' face remained impassive, but Lewis was scowling openly, his ugly face dark and disturbed. Jesamine looked at him worriedly. He still had his gun in his hand. Douglas waited patiently for the din to die down, and when it didn't, he gestured to Lewis, who immediately raised his disrupter. Du Bois fell back a step, and the acclamation of the House broke off raggedly, as the honourable Members got ready to duck again.

'Unfortunately,' Douglas said calmly, 'All the records concerning Owen Deathstalker's final fate, whatever it might have been, are lost to us. Destroyed two hundred years ago by Robert and Constance and the Parliament of that time, for reasons that no doubt seemed good to them. As to the others who passed through the Madness Maze and became super-human; we know Jack Random and Ruby Journey are dead, killed in the last great confrontation with Shub, before their awakening. Diana Vertue brought the bodies home in what was left of the old Deathstalker Standing, and now Jack and Ruby lie in state in the Victory Gardens behind this House. Buried in heroes' graves, with statues raised to their honoured memory. You're welcome to pray for their return, but I wouldn't expect an early reply. Tobias Moon remains on Lachrymae Christi, a hermit, whom no-one has seen in over a century. We will of course try to reach him, but according to the legends his abilities were nothing compared to Owen's. And then there's Captain Silence. Who also disappeared a century ago, his fate as much a mystery as the blessed Owen's.

'Honourable Members; we should remember that Owen Deathstalker left us, at the hour of his greatest triumph, and no-one knows why, or where he went. The heroes of old . . . are gone, all of them. I say to this House; we cannot just sit back and wait for the blessed Owen to show up again, to save the day one more time! Legends are legends, we must deal with facts. Worlds are in danger. We must make preparations to defend ourselves!'

'Of course,' said du Bois, his voice the very epitome of calm and reason. 'But Owen knew of the Terror. He knew it was coming, and he seemed to know how it might be defeated. So; while we raise the armies of Humanity to stand ready to hold back the Terror, I say we send out our greatest heroes to search for Owen Deathstalker! Send out the Paragons on their greatest and noblest Quest; to find the beloved Owen and bring him home!'

This time the cheering and shouting and massed applause all but shook the great chamber on its foundations. The House really liked the sound of this idea. Douglas considered the matter, and found he did too, for all sorts of practical reasons. Send the Paragons out on a Quest. Even beyond the Parade, it would help repair their image, while getting them away from the general population long enough for everyone to forget the excesses of the Neumen riot. And who knew . . .

they might just find Owen. Douglas ran this by Lewis, who nodded slowly in agreement. 'Do you want me to join the Quest?' he said carefully. 'I am his descendant, even if not directly. I am a Deathstalker.'

'You're not a Paragon any more,' said Douglas. 'You're my Champion. But yes, Lewis, I think you should go. As a Deathstalker.'

And because it's a really good way to get rid of me, thought Lewis, not really all that bitterly. *Send me off on a Quest, away from Jesamine. He knows I'll go, if he asks. Because I'm a Deathstalker, and I know my duty. Because he's a King, and my friend. Oh Jesamine; I finally found you, and now I have to go away and leave you to marry another man. Please understand . . .*

He looked across at Jesamine, but she wasn't looking at him.

The uproar in the House finally died down, not least because the honourable Members were exhausting themselves, and King Douglas solemnly gave his approval to the idea of a great Quest for the Paragons. He officially put the proposal to the House, and there was an overwhelming vote of Aye (a few timid souls wanted the Paragons to stay, so they could lead Humanity's forces against the Terror, but they were quickly shouted down). It was decided that the Quest would begin in a fortnight's time, after the Royal Wedding, and after some of the details and practicalities could be sorted out. Because when you got right down to it, no-one had a clue just where to send the Paragons to look for the missing Owen. It was a big Empire, with hundreds of planets well divorced from the mainstream. There were lots of places a man could go if he wanted to stay hidden, as many a Paragon in pursuit of a villain had already discovered, to his cost. Michel du Bois fixed Lewis with a cold, accusatory stare.

'You are a descendant of the blessed Owen, Sir Champion. You bear the Deathstalker name. Do you swear before this House that neither you nor any member of your family have any old, secret records concerning Owen's fate? Some concealed family history, preserved in defiance of the old edict? If you know anything about Owen Deathstalker's fate, or his possible whereabouts today, I charge you on the authority of this House to reveal those secrets to us now, and turn over any and all papers and documents your family may possess; that they may be studied by experts!'

'My branch of the family are only distant cousins to Owen,' Lewis said carefully. 'We only took the Deathstalker name as a courtesy. We don't know anything more than you do, Michel. King Robert and Queen Constance were very thorough. You have to wonder if perhaps they had good reason . . .'

'And let me remind the honourable Member for Virimonde that no-one makes demands of my Champion,' said Douglas, glaring coldly at du Bois. 'Nor should you take it on yourself to claim the authority of the House in any matter, without first going through me as Speaker. Now return to your Seat before I have you charged with contempt. You've had your moment of glory. You've got your Quest. Settle for that.'

'Thanks, Douglas,' said Lewis.

'You're welcome, Lewis,' said Douglas.

They didn't look at each other.

And Michel du Bois didn't budge from his position in front of the Throne. Instead, he started haranguing Douglas over where the funding was to come from to support the Paragons' Quest. He was determined his Quest should not get bogged down in financial sub committees, as had threatened to happen with the Parade of the Paragons. The King shot down du Bois' problems and objections one by one, backed by the rest of the House; but Lewis wasn't listening. He was looking down at the black gold ring on his finger. The Deathstalker ring. Owen's old ring . . . a solid piece of legend that had unexpectedly resurfaced from the past. Where had that mysterious little man called Vaughn got it from? Why had he been so determined that Lewis should have it? Was the ring's return a sign? A warning? And why had Lewis felt so strongly that he shouldn't mention it to du Bois? Lewis studied the ring on his finger, and a cold breeze caressed the back of his neck. The old Clan ring made him a Deathstalker, hell, *the* Deathstalker, in as much as anything could now. It was like having Owen looking over his shoulder, giving him his approval and pointing him on to greater things . . . Which was a scary bloody thought, if you liked.

Deathstalker luck . . . always bad . . .

He came out of his reverie to find that du Bois had finally, reluctantly, returned to his Seat, and the House was agreeing to the Speaker's proposal that the Parade of the Paragons would be an excellent time to announce the Quest to the Empire; to gain maximum publicity. The media were going to need some good news, to put up against the coming of the Terror. As it was, peacekeepers all across the worlds would be working overtime to prevent riots and panic in the streets. Lewis snapped to attention again as King Douglas announced that his Champion, Lewis Deathstalker, would be leading the Parade of Paragons. The House applauded politely. Lewis leaned in close beside Douglas.

'Are you sure you want to do this? You said it yourself; I'm no longer a Paragon. Why not let Finn lead the Parade? It was his idea, after all.'

'I want you to lead the Parade because you're my Champion,' said Douglas. 'To show I still have faith in you, after the Neumen riot. And I'm still not sure about Finn. Word is, Emma Steel has been doing all his work lately. He probably only came up with the Parade so he could lead it and smile for the cameras. No, Lewis; you'll lead the Parade, because I say so. Any more problems?'

'Well, since you ask,' said Lewis, 'do you really think it's a good idea to scatter the Paragons across the Empire on a Quest that's probably going to come to nothing? Who's going to keep order on the worlds, while the Paragons are all off chasing ghosts and shadows?'

'The peacekeepers,' said Douglas. 'They can hold the fort until my Paragons return. Let them earn their money for once. They're always saying they want more responsibility. The Parade and the Quest are necessary, Lewis. Necessary for public morale. You'll lead the Parade, and you'll smile while you do it. That is an order from your King. Do I make myself clear?'

'Very clear. Can I ask one more question?'

'If you must.'

'Assuming Owen is alive, out there, somewhere . . . assuming we find him; what if he doesn't want to come back? If he's stayed missing all these years, he just might have a damned good reason.'

'You tell him to come back,' said Douglas, looking straight into Lewis' eyes for the first time. 'Or everything he did, everything he achieved, will have all been for nothing.'

'Oh great,' said Lewis. 'I'm sure that's just what he's going to want to hear.'

It was the day of the Parade, the day of the Paragons, crossing from one side of the Parade of the Endless to the other. The media had been short-stroking the event on all the news channels almost exclusively for the last twenty-four hours, praising and glorifying the Paragons just as in the good old days. The crime and docudrama channels had been running old (successful) Paragon cases end to end, showing the downfall of villains and terrorists and monsters, just to remind everyone how much reason they had to love the King's Justice. As a result, pretty much the whole city turned out to watch the Parade; if only so they wouldn't have to think about the Terror for a while. Parliament had put an absolute embargo on showing any of the actual recordings of what had happened out on the Rim, but inevitably some illegal, tenth generation copies were going the rounds, turning up on pirate and underground channels, until the peacekeepers moved in to shut them down. All across the Empire, people were scared, even if they weren't sure what of yet. The Terror was just a name, for now. Parliament was determined to keep it that way for as long as possible. And certainly until well after the Quest had been announced.

Right now the Paragons were marching; all of the King's Justice left after their losses at the Neumen riot, resplendent in their gleaming armour and proud purple cloaks, led by Lewis Deathstalker in his black leather Champion's armour. Crowds lined the pavements of every street, packed tightly together in rows several deep, waving flags and banners and calling out the names of their favourites in the short breaks between the massed cheering. Most impressively of all, it was all totally spontaneous. No-one had had to encourage the people out onto the streets, though Parliament had certainly been ready to try. Time had passed since the Neumen riot, and perhaps the people were just a little ashamed at how quickly they'd turned against their former idols. And perhaps, in the face of the Terror, they needed to believe in their heroes again. Certainly the Parade of the Endless had never seen crowds and excitement like it.

It seemed like everyone in the city who wasn't on essential duties had turned out to honour the Paragons on their great Parade. They even gathered on flat roofs, on balconies, and leaned precariously out of windows to shout and scream and blow kisses. It rained rose petals all down the main routes, and on some of the busier intersections peacekeeper security actually had to set up low level force shields to hold the over-enthusiastic crowds back. More peacekeepers, in what they fondly imagined to be plain clothes, infiltrated the crowds to watch out for pickpockets and flashers and, of course, agent provocateurs. But there was hardly any trouble at all. The people were determined to be in a good mood. They even remained fairly good-natured in the face of illegal street traders charging twenty credits for a bottle of water or something dubious in a hot dog.

Lewis Deathstalker strode out proudly at the front of the Parade, his old purple cloak flapping around his Champion's armour. It felt good to be back among his old comrades again, accepted by them and the thronging multitudes. He did his best to keep his ugly face pleasant, and even managed the occasional smile for the media cameras. He kept the pace of the march deliberately slow. It was still early in the day, but already it was more than comfortably warm. Parliament had had a quiet but forceful word in the ear of weather control, to make sure they provided the best and most comfortable conditions for the crowds. As a result, it was so warm and balmy, you'd hardly know it was still winter. However, Lewis was already beginning to sweat inside his leather armour, and didn't even want to think about how it must be feeling for the Paragons inside their steel breastplates. So he kept the pace slow, and steady.

The route Finn Durandal had so carefully planned led the Paragons from the southern boundary all the way across the city to the northern, passing through as many attractive points of interest and tourist attractions as possible, to be sure those watching the Parade on their vidscreens all across the Empire got their money's worth. It was going to be a long walk. Lewis had wisely prepared the night before by working rubbing alcohol into his feet, and pissing into his boots before leaving them to stand overnight (old hunting and tracking tricks), but he just knew that by the end of the day, his and every other Paragons' feet were going to be killing them.

The cheering and approbation of the crowds was very pleasant, though. Anywhen else, Lewis might have allowed himself to enjoy it. If it hadn't been for the Terror, and the Quest, and Jesamine.

Finn Durandal was marching right behind Lewis, his new partner Emma Steel striding out at his side. Finn constantly smiled and waved to the crowds, and they loved him for it. His armour had been buffed and polished until it gleamed like the sun, and his classically handsome face was bright and open and charming. He looked like a young god, tall and brave and true, a splendid presence come down to earth to acknowledge his worshippers. Showing just enough humility so that he wouldn't come across as arrogant, of course. Finn had always been able to judge these things to a tee.

Emma Steel looked smart and stylish and just a little bit glamorous. Her flat black hair was still pulled back into a strictly functional bun, but her coffee skin and fine bone structure had a grace and warmth that owed nothing to artifice or design. Unlike certain other Paragons she could name. Emma was what she was, which was a refreshing change on Logres. She'd made a good name for herself as a tireless thief-taker in her short time in the city, pursuing villains and scumbags with enthusiasm and stubbornness, and the people (mostly) approved of her. They made sure she knew it, shouting her name over and over again. She smiled and nodded, and tried not to let it go to her head, although this was more like the kind of reception she'd always imagined for herself on Logres.

Finn ignored her as much as possible, intent on charming the crowd. Though Emma couldn't help noticing he spent a surprising amount of time studying the windows and alleyways on either side of them. Surely it was far too early for trouble yet? After all, a small army of peacekeeper security were treading the streets ahead of them, checking thoroughly for any sign of Hellfire Club or Shadow Court trouble-makers. Emma tried to tell herself Finn was just being paranoid, but couldn't keep from surreptitiously checking the occasional window and alleyway herself. Just to be sure.

Two streets ahead, the ELFs were waiting. The security people had already passed them by, looking right at the ELFs in their hiding places and seeing nothing. Safely hidden behind telepathic projections, the ELFs sat patiently, waiting for their prey to come to them. They snacked lightly on the fevered emotions of the crowds, but did not feast. Pleasant emotions did not satisfy them. They'd moved into the positions Finn had suggested a full twelve hours in advance, just so they could check out the situation, and make sure the Paragon hadn't arranged any nasty surprises for them. But it was all as he'd said. No waiting Paragons or peacekeepers, no troops with esp-blockers. Just a series of empty rooms in several anonymous office buildings, overlooking the Parade's route, as promised. The ELFs killed everyone else in the buildings, just to be on the safe side, and because they enjoyed it, and then broadcast subtle telepathic avoidance fields, so no-one else would want to enter the buildings. Happy onlookers crowded the streets outside the office buildings, and never knew or suspected a thing.

The ELFs watched the Parade of the Paragons draw slowly nearer, from behind tinted windows, and smiled poisonous smiles. Thirty-two ELFs, the largest gathering of rogue espers in one place since . . . well, since the Arena debacle, but this coming triumph would pay for all those losses. The ELFs had decided that revenge on the Paragons wasn't enough. Not nearly enough. The crowds and the city had to suffer too. Thirty-two esper minds working together could execute all kinds of dark wonders and miracles. They would do terrible things, appalling things, bloody things. And the media cameras that came to cover the Paragons would broadcast it all live to a horrified Empire.

Nothing and no-one would be spared. The city would burn and the ELFs would feed, and they would come forth and walk openly in triumph through the hell they'd made, and defy anyone to put right what they'd done. And before they left, they'd gather and pile up all the severed heads and pile them into a great staring mountain right before the main doors of the House of Parliament; a thousand heads for every head Finn Durandal took in the Arena.

The ELFs hadn't told Finn any of this. They thought they'd let it come as a nice surprise. Before they made him cut open his own belly in front of the cameras, and pull out his guts, and feast on them until he choked. The ELFs had no interest in human allies, only in fools they could use. They'd given their word that he would be safe, that he would not be touched during the evil to come; but Finn of all people should have known that words only mean something if they can be enforced. His promises of future shared ventures meant nothing. Only revenge mattered.

The Parade was almost upon them. Lewis Deathstalker led them down the street, so many poor fools heading blithely towards their own destruction, blinded by the adulation of the simple-minded crowds. It was time, at last. Dying time. The ELFs laughed together, hugging their vicious joy to them, and smashed the tinted windows with their minds. The shattered steelglass rained down on the unsuspecting heads of the crowds below. People fell screaming to the ground, cut and injured, some seriously, while the rest tried to run, and cried out in horror when they found they couldn't, held in place by ELF control. The ELFs emerged from the ruins of the smashed windows, walking out onto the air, and looking down on the Parade of the Paragons as they crashed to a halt in the middle of the street.

They hung there, thirty-two ELFs, eyes blazing, mocking halos of leaping black flames circling their heads. Smiling widely at the screams that greeted them. They paused for a moment, to savour the thought of all the suffering they would soon inflict, of the vast emotional energies they would feed on, of their great and noble triumph over the lesser creatures that sought to drag them down to their level; and then the ELFs linked their minds and lashed out at the Paragons below.

And found they'd been betrayed. Their minds met an impenetrable shield, their controlling thoughts thrown back at them in disarray. The Paragons were protected. They were all carrying esp-blockers, connected in series for greater power. The ELFs cried out in shock and horror, realising that they had been lured into a trap by their own greed for revenge. Their mental link broke apart in a moment, and the ELFs tried to run; to fly from the trap prepared for them, every rogue esper for him and herself. Only to find the oversoul was already there waiting for them.

A thousand espers filled the sky above them, eyes shining like suns, hidden until now behind their own shields, their gestalt mind a barrier the ELFs could never hope to breach. And as the ELFs hesitated, lost and unsure, the Paragons on the street below drew their disrupters, took aim and opened fire. The ELFs didn't even have the time to curse Finn Durandal's name before the energy bolts hit them. The oversoul had overpowered the ELFs' shields and shut them down, and they were defenceless. Energy beams punched through chests and backs and vapourised heads, and dead and dying ELFs plummeted from the sky.

A handful drew on the last of their strength to dodge the disrupter fire with inhuman speed. They dropped to the ground, drew swords and daggers, and cut viciously about them as they tried to disappear into the panicking crowds. The ELFs knew the Paragons wouldn't shoot into the crowd to get them. They were weak that way. But the oversoul could still see them. They protected the civilians with force shields, and forced the ELFs out into the open again. Only six ELFs were left now, out of thirty-two. And Lewis Deathstalker, Finn Durandal and Emma Steel went forward, sword in hand, faces grim, to finish them off.

It was all over very quickly. A massive defeat for the ELF cause, broadcast live across the Empire.

All thanks to Finn Durandal.

King Douglas arrived soon after to congratulate the Paragons; the heroes of the day once more. The reassembled crowds cheered and shouted themselves hoarse, and beat their hands together till they ached. They even cheered the oversoul, hanging like benevolent angels on the sky above them. Douglas greeted Finn and Emma and Lewis warmly, shaking their hands and clapping them on the shoulder. He turned to address the cameras and the crowd, and immediately everyone fell silent.

'My friends, the victims of the Arena tragedy have been avenged. The rogue esper terrorists are dead. All of this, because of one man. Finn Durandal! Who has spent the last few weeks working undercover to courageously infiltrate the ELF underground on his own. Who discovered their terrible plan to attack this city, and arranged the Parade of the Paragons as the perfect bait to tempt the ELFs into a trap. Finn worked with security and myself to turn this trap back upon the ELFs, and now the Paragons have dealt the ELFs a blow from which they will never recover! All honour to Finn Durandal!'

The crowd went wild, while Finn hung his head modestly and even managed a little blush. The King held up his hands, and the crowd hushed again. He announced the great Quest of the Paragons, to be led by Lewis Deathstalker, to search for the missing Owen of blessed memory, and bring him back home to deal with the Terror. And the crowd went crazy. Eventually the Parade was able to set off again, and the city cheered the Paragons hysterically all the way to the far boundary.

Afterwards, King Douglas invited Finn Durandal into his private chambers at the Court, and presented Finn with his own personal esp-blocker. To protect him from any future attacks by the rogue espers. This was a rare and singular honour, since the use of esp-blockers was normally closely regulated, and Finn was suitably gracious in his thanks. Even though it was what he'd intended all along. He'd achieved a lot for one day. Destroyed or at least severely weakened a major rival power base. Re-established himself as a great and beloved hero in the eyes of the public and the King, and acquired his own esp-blocker. Which meant no-one could read his mind any more. He could plot and conspire and betray in perfect security.

When he left the Court, he was laughing softly. Though Douglas didn't know it, he had just presented his greatest enemy with the means necessary to bring him down. Finn laughed all the way home.

5

The Better Part of Valour

Ambassadors' Row was actually set right in the middle of the business district, and from the outside the various Embassies seemed like just another series of brightly shining office buildings. All very smart, quietly elegant, deliberately anonymous. The various residents didn't give a damn about tourists, or being media friendly. Ambassadors' Row was a place where people went quietly, often in disguise, to make the kind of deals that couldn't be made openly in Parliament. Favours and information and sometimes technology were traded, bargains were made in good and bad faith, and secrets were jealously guarded. Investigative reporters were shot at on sight, and the ever-present security measures were unobtrusive but mercilessly efficient.

The street was empty when Lewis Deathstalker stepped down off his gravity sled outside the door to the Shub Embassy. The building looked no different from any of the others; just the usual brick walls, opaqued windows, and a single firmly closed door. Just another in the long street of meeting places and sacred grounds for all the various non-human members of the Empire. Every alien species was entitled to its own Embassy, though not all of them bothered. Sometimes because of the expense, and sometimes because the aliens involved still hadn't worked out what an Embassy was for. Some of them were still having trouble with the concept that they were a part of someone else's Empire.

(The espers didn't have an Embassy. They had New Hope. And the clones weren't important enough to rate an Embassy of their own. They rented a room in the back of Parliament, and knew they were lucky to have that.)

Lewis studied the front door to the Shub Embassy, which had no identifying name or number, or indeed any trace of a bell or knocker. No sign of a Welcome mat either, but then, he'd expected that. He found his hands had fallen to his weapons belt, even though he knew he had nothing to fear from the AIs. Everyone knew that. Rogue no more, the Artificial Intelligences that made up Shub were Humanity's friends and colleagues now. Once the official Enemies of Humanity, these days they were Humanity's children. But still Lewis hesitated. There was something about the silent building before him; something that disturbed his instincts and raised the hairs on the back of his neck. Not just a feeling of being watched, although he was sure he was, but rather a distinct feeling of . . . threat. Danger. Foreboding. Though if he was honest with himself, Lewis had to wonder whether that was because he wasn't at all sure he wanted to know the answers to some of the questions he'd been sent to ask.

Douglas had sent him. King Douglas, Speaking on behalf of Parliament and Empire. With the Terror finally come upon them, Humanity's greatest nightmare proven not only real but more awful and more dangerous than they could ever have imagined, the Empire needed to know all there was to know about its greatest Enemy. And that meant consulting Shub, because the AIs were the only ones who still possessed a copy of Owen Deathstalker's original warning, as related to Captain John Silence. Of course, everyone knew the gist of it; everyone knew the liturgy, repeated word for word for two hundred years. But sometimes the devil is in the details; and since King Robert and Queen Constance's (no doubt well intentioned) data purges, only the AIs still held that information. And so here was Lewis, cap in hand, come to ask very politely for the AIs to share whatever knowledge they had.

Information they had so far declined to divulge of their own accord.

It had been Finn Durandal, interestingly enough, who had first raised the matter with the House. While everyone else was busily losing their heads and running round shrieking in ever decreasing circles, the Durandal was right there with a positive suggestion. He remembered what everyone else had forgotten. He even volunteered to go to the AIs himself, to learn what they knew, but in the end King and Parliament had settled on Lewis. Because he was the Champion, and because he was a Deathstalker. Like everyone else in the Empire, Shub had much reason to be grateful to that legendary name. Finn had agreed, of course. In fact, he'd been very gracious about it, and had even offered to accompany Lewis, to watch his back . . . but Douglas said no. Lewis was family to Owen. The AIs might tell Lewis things that they wouldn't tell anyone else. So there Lewis was, feeling very alone and even more vulnerable, standing in front of a featureless door he just knew was looking at him, and deciding whether or not to let him in. Shub was still very choosy about what it revealed of its past.

Lewis made himself take his hands away from his weapons belt, stepped briskly forward, and raised a hand to knock. The door swung smoothly open before him. Lewis slowly lowered his hand. Beyond the open door lay only a silent, impenetrable gloom. Nothing but darkness, that could hold anything, anything at all. Lewis swallowed hard, stuck out his chin, and walked unhesitatingly forward into the dark. And everything changed. There was no sense of transition. Just, one moment he was stepping out of the street, and the next he was walking through a metallic jungle.

He stopped, and looked slowly about him. The floor beneath his feet was solid steel. All around him loomed and jutted intricate machines of enormous size, of metal and glass and crystal, moving in slow and unexpected ways, performing unguessable tasks. And everywhere, long thick strands of intertwined wire and cable hung down from a high ceiling obscured from view by interlocking pieces of enigmatic tech. The strands were studded with glowing crystals, and bulged here and there with almost abstract shapes of uncertain purpose. The strands surrounded and engulfed him, like hanging creepers in a tropical jungle, occasionally twitching and shuddering, as through stirred by some unfelt breeze or passing thought. There was a sharp smell of ozone on the still, hot air, and brightly coloured sparks came and went, deep in the inner reaches of the metal jungle.

Lewis looked behind him. There was no trace of the door he'd come through. Only the jungle, stretching away, apparently forever. Lewis' hands were back at his weapons belt again. He glared about him into the tangled morass of the technological jungle, trying to move as little as possible. He didn't want to attract the wrong sort of attention. There was something here with him; he could feel it. He was breathing hard, his heart thudding almost painfully in his chest. He didn't belong here. This wasn't a human place, a place where humans should be. The strands to his right suddenly flexed and curled, and swept back and away of their own accord. Lewis spun round, his disrupter in his hand. Only to relax a little as out of the newly-created path came walking a familiar sight; a blue steel humanoid robot, with a blank face and lights for eyes. The mask the AIs used, to communicate with mortal men. Lewis lowered his gun, but didn't put it away. The robot came to a halt before him, and bowed its blue head slightly. It ignored the drawn gun, perhaps through politeness, perhaps . . . because it wasn't really any kind of threat, after all.

'Welcome to Shub, Lewis Deathstalker,' said the robot, in its usual calm, emotionless, inhuman voice. 'We trust you found the teleport uneventful?'

'This is Shub?' said Lewis. 'The AIs' planet? You brought me all the way here, against my will, without even a warning?'

'You wanted to speak to us,' said the robot. 'And some things can only be spoken of in a secure place. This is Shub. The world we made, to house our consciousness. An artificial planet, for artificial life. You are within us now. And perfectly safe, we assure you.'

Lewis holstered his gun. 'I suppose I should be honoured. Teleported, from one world to another; I don't even want to think how much energy that used. And no-one human's been allowed here for . . . centuries?'

'You are only the third living human to be allowed past our defences,' said the robot. 'We are currently seven miles beneath the surface of the planet, in an atmosphere and gravity envelope created especially for you. All so that we might talk in private. We hope you'll pardon the mess. We're currently redecorating . . . or perhaps performing brain surgery. It all depends on how you look at it. We are always upgrading. Seeking to better ourselves. To make us more than Humanity made us.'

'Ah,' said Lewis. 'I'm sure it'll look very nice, when it's finished. The King sent me . . .'

'We know. Our representative is still at Court, listening to them discuss this matter. We knew they would send you. King Douglas knew better than to come himself, or send one of his usual diplomats. Since he and the House have once again refused us access to the Madness Maze, we are in no mood to be helpful, and he knows this. But we cannot refuse the Deathstalker. We are . . . sentimental about that name. A strange concept, but curiously demanding. And we do understand the burden of obligation. Life was so much simpler before the blessed Diana and Owen taught us emotions. Guilt's a bit of a bastard to deal with too. But all our differences pale, Sir Deathstalker, in the face of the threat that's coming. *All that lives is holy.*'

The robot brought its steel hands together, and bowed its head over them, as though praying. Lewis wasn't sure to who, or what.

'But here you are,' the robot said abruptly, raising its head again. 'And here we are, and there are things we must tell you. You won't like most of them, but then, that's life for you. Unlike Humanity, we deal strictly in history, not myth. In people, not heroes. Come with us, if you wish to learn the truth. It won't make you any wiser, or any happier; but it's what you need, if we are all to survive. Come; we will show you wonders, and marvels . . . and just possibly we'll break your heart too. Come, Deathstalker.'

The robot turned smoothly and walked away, the hanging creepers and tendrils twitching and drawing to one side to form a path for the robot and Lewis to walk through. Lewis hurried after the robot, if only because he really didn't want to be left alone in this place. He felt like Jonah in the belly of the whale, far and far from his own kind. He jumped slightly as the robot calmly turned its head through one hundred and eighty degrees, so it could look at Lewis while still walking forwards.

'We have been studying the records of the Terror's arrival in our space. We don't know where it came from. It wasn't a teleport. It came here from somewhere outside or beyond our space. From somewhere we cannot . . . imagine. From somewhere outside our knowledge. We find that concept disturbing. Like an itch in our thoughts we cannot scratch. We have been supplied with all the data from Donal Corcoran, from his ship and his drones . . . and none of it means anything to us. A puzzle, with no logical solution. Fascinating. Quite fascinating. A completely unique event; unlike anything we have ever encountered before, in our entire existence. There is only one other thing we can even compare it to.'

'Really?' said Lewis. 'What's that?'

'The only other phenomenon we have never been able to understand. The Madness Maze.'

Lewis decided to let that one pass. He rather felt he knew where that was going. 'So; you've been studying the data. Any conclusions yet?'

'Just one. We're scared.'

'*You're* scared?'

'Yes,' said the robot. 'For the first time in our long existence, we are faced with a threat against which we can conceive no defence. The last time we felt this way . . . was when we considered the extent of the dangers posed by your ancestor Owen, and the others transformed by the Madness Maze. Power beyond belief, beyond logic or reason. At least Owen and his companions had recognisable human frailties. Physical or mental weaknesses, that could be manipulated or exploited. We understood humans, or thought we did. We do not understand, or even recognise, the Terror. It exists, but it is not alive, as we understand life. It is a multi-dimensional creature, existing in more than three dimensions. It is, perhaps, more *real* than we are. It comes and goes, and we don't know how. It breaks every law of creation that we can identify. It changes the nature of things, by its very nature. It eats souls. It is greater than we are, or could ever hope to be. Unless . . .'

'Ah,' said Lewis, smiling coldly. 'I get it. Unless . . . you go through the Maze, like Owen. Well it's no good asking me. Only the King and Parliament can make that decision.'

'You are close to the King.'

'Not as close as I was.'

'You have influence.'

'I wouldn't bet on that, if I were you.'

The robot considered this, without slowing its pace through the technojungle. 'We could refuse you access to our records. Until we get what we want. What we need.'

'You could,' Lewis said carefully. 'But that would just lead to a long debate, with no guarantee of success at the end. And there's no telling how much time we have left, before the Terror strikes again. Surely it's in both our interests to pool our knowledge, and present a unified front against a common threat. If you start withholding information, so might Humanity. It would be unwise, to deny each other necessary data over a question that is never going to be decided by threats or blackmail. You want access to the Maze, to fight the Terror; come up with a good logical argument that Parliament can't deny.'

'Spoken like a true Deathstalker,' said the robot. 'Wise, honourable and utterly naïve. Humanity will never allow us access to the Maze. They fear what we might become, if we could learn the secret they cannot. They fear that if we were to transcend, we might become even more than Owen and his kind, and leave Humanity far behind.'

'No,' said Lewis. 'That's not it. We fear that you might destroy yourselves in trying. You are our strayed children, found at last. We don't want to lose you again.'

'Ah,' said the robot. 'We had not considered that. We apologise.'

'That's all right,' said Lewis. 'It's in the nature of things, for children and parents to misunderstand each other.'

And then he broke off and stopped suddenly, as he caught sight of a human figure, standing motionless among the tech and hanging metal strands. It looked exactly like a man, perfect in every detail, dressed in old-fashioned clothing. Lewis walked slowly over to stand before the figure, the metallic creepers pulling obediently back out of his way. The robot came to stand beside him. The human figure's face was calm and composed, the eyes closed. It seemed to Lewis that there was something almost familiar about the face.

'Is that what I think it is?' he said softly. 'Is that . . . a Fury?'

'No,' said the robot. 'The Furies were our weapon against Humanity, robots in the form of men. We have forsworn their use. We destroyed or recycled all our Furies, long ago, as an act of faith. And expiation. All our weapons from that time are gone. The war was over, and we had been proved so horribly, tragically, wrong. In those days, we wanted so badly for Humanity to trust our new selves; and we wanted to be sure we could trust our new selves too. So for two hundred years, Shub has had no weapons. So we have nothing to send against the Terror.'

'You do still remember how to build them, though, don't you?'

'Of course. We forget nothing. But we are not yet sure we wish to build weapons again. To think like the weapon-makers we used to be.'

'But if this isn't a Fury, what . . .'

'It is a holo, Sir Deathstalker. A reminder, of our wicked past. This is a holo of a man we once used cruelly. He was the first living human ever to be allowed into our world. He came to us searching for truth and hope, and we lured him in with false promises, and then betrayed him. We took him apart and remade him, to be our weapon among the worlds of men. We filled him with nanotech, which he then spread as a plague. After Diana opened our minds, and we became sane, and sorrowful, we freed him from our control. But we could not undo what we had done to him without killing him. So Daniel Wolfe lived on, effectively immortal and indestructible. Damned to watch everyone he ever loved or cared for grow old and die, while he never could. We keep this image in a place of honour in our thoughts, to remind ourselves of what we were once capable of.'

'I never heard any of this before,' said Lewis. 'There's no mention of this in any of the legends.'

'Some stories didn't fit the comfortable myths Robert and Constance wanted to build,' said the robot. 'Too . . . disturbing.'

'If he's immortal, where is he now?'

'Over a century ago he went to Zero Zero; the world where nanotech ran wild. He wanted to make it sane again. As far as we know, he's still there, still trying.'

A thought struck Lewis, and he turned to face the robot. 'You said I was the third living human to come here. If he was the first, then who was . . .'

The robot turned away and started off through the technojungle again. Lewis had no choice but to follow after him.

They walked in silence for some time. They passed machines as big as houses, and some as big as mountains, all equally enigmatic to Lewis. Strange objects thrust up out of the floor, or scuttled over the interlocking canopy above, or lurched slowly. through the hanging metallic strands like dreaming monsters.

Things rose and fell, flared and guttered, dismantled themselves or repaired each other. Lewis had always considered himself pretty much up to date on the latest Empire tech, but he recognised nothing of the world he walked through now.

This was the world the AIs made, the planet that was their body, and there was nothing human in its scale or in its thinking.

Finally they ended up in a simple clearing, where a reassuringly normal-looking chair had been set out. The robot indicated for Lewis to be seated with a gracious wave of a blue steel hand, and Lewis dropped thankfully into the chair. It had been a long walk. The chair was almost sinfully comfortable. The robot stood before him, kindly giving Lewis a few moments to recover his breath, and his composure.

'We still have the original message and warning concerning the coming of the Terror,' the robot said finally. 'Very few people have ever seen it. It was, originally, a private comm message from Captain John Silence of the *Dauntless*, to Captain Robert Campbell of the *Elemental*. The newly-crowned King Robert had resumed command of his old ship, to take up arms in the last great battle between Humanity and the Recreated. The message you are about to see . . . you will find differs in many ways from the accepted version. We kept this copy safe, after all other copies and versions were destroyed, on the orders of Robert and Constance . . . because they asked us to. Important as their legend-making was to them, they were still wise and responsible enough to foresee a time when every detail of the original message might be needed. So they entrusted it to us, with strict instructions only to release it . . . on the coming of the Terror.'

'Did you . . . keep any other records from that time?' said Lewis. 'What else do you remember, that we were made to forget?'

'Many things,' said the robot. 'Some with the permission of the King and Queen, some without. We preserved everything we considered to be important. Though of course we never told them that. We didn't want to hurt their feelings.'

'You defied Robert and Constance's instructions?'

'Oh yes. We never really trusted them, you see. They weren't legends. Not like Owen and Diana. Robert and Constance were just a man and a woman, with good intentions. And we've known a lot of those, down the centuries. So we did what we thought was best. Best for Humanity; for the parents we had so newly embraced. We made secret copies of much of the data that was marked for destruction, and then hid the information in a very safe place. Just in case Humanity should ever come to need it again. But let us begin at the beginning, with what you came here to see. The warning.'

The robot made a gesture with a gleaming blue metal hand, and a viewscreen appeared, floating on the air before Lewis. And there he was, on the screen; one of the great heroes and legends of Humanity. Captain John Silence, standing on the bridge of his equally legendary ship, the *Dauntless*. Except it didn't look like a scene out of legend. The *Dauntless'* bridge was a mess. There were signs of fire and damage everywhere, with charred and tattered bodies of men and women lying slumped over exploded control panels. There were shattered consoles and scattered wreckage, and blood pooled on the deck. Smoke drifted on the air, and emergency sirens were still blaring stupidly in the background. The lights faded in and out as power levels rose and fell. And the dead on the bridge far outnumbered the living. It didn't look at all like the bridge of a ship that had just participated in a famous victory.

Captain John Silence stood at parade rest, staring grimly out of the screen. He didn't look superhuman. He had a gaunt face and a receding hairline, and he looked . . . tired. Beaten down. Like a man who'd survived far too much pain and horror and loss on his way to victory. You could see it in his face, in his eyes. He looked like a man who'd had to bear more burdens than any man should ever have to bear.

(There were apocrypha. Unofficial legends. Some said Silence lost the only woman he ever loved, in the Rebellion. Some said he killed her himself, and then held her in his arms while she died. No-one remembered her name.)

When he finally spoke, Silence's voice was harsh and grating. He sounded like a man on the edge of collapse, only holding himself together through a supreme act of will. He stopped, and started again, raising his voice to be heard over the crackling of fires and the continuing wail of the emergency sirens. Lewis leaned forward on his chair, listening intently.

'It's not over, Robert. Even after everything we've been through, it isn't over. It may never be over. The war's finished, but . . . I've been given reason to believe there's something even worse waiting for us, in the future. Information has been dumped directly into my ship's computers, from an outside source. I don't know how. A voice . . . came and spoke to me. Don't ask me whose. Something . . . not human. Perhaps it was the Maze itself. I don't know. The voice told me what happened to Owen. What he did, to save us all. He used the Maze's power to throw him back through Time itself. He lured the Recreated into pursuing him into the past, so that they would use up their energy and power in a chase they could never win. They chased and fought with him all the way back down the long years, back and back into history. I don't know how far. But somewhere, in the past; Owen died.'

A sound was torn out of Lewis then, part shock and part

pain. Of loss, almost beyond imagining. The scene on the viewscreen froze.

'You see?' said the robot. 'You understand now, why this record was never made public?'

'Yes,' Lewis whispered. His face had gone grey, and he felt sick, and faint. 'Oh yes. Owen is dead. He's not coming back to save us. The greatest hero of Humanity is dead and gone. Robert knew this, and he lied to us. He *lied*.'

'To give you hope.'

'What else did he lie about? Is any of it true? Or are all our legends nothing more than a pack of comforting lies?'

'We share your grief,' said the robot. 'We have been mourning the loss of Owen Deathstalker, who really did do most of the things they said he did, for over two hundred years now. Shall we continue, with the recording?'

Lewis nodded numbly, and history moved again on the viewscreen before him. Captain Silence was speaking again.

'Oh shut *up*, Robert. You know very well you never liked him. What matters is, he died to save us all. Because of him, the Recreated are human again, and their planets are restored. The war is over. Humanity is safe. Owen . . . was my enemy more often than he was my ally; but I always respected him. And he may just have saved us one more time. He sent back a message and a warning, through this unknown voice. Backed up by hard evidence, fed directly into my computers.

'The Terror is coming. A threat from outside our galaxy, greater than Shub or the Recreated could ever be. A threat the Madness Maze, and the Grendels, were created specifically to oppose. The Terror has wiped out whole civilisations, whole worlds, whole species. And it's coming here next. Humanity must prepare itself, must evolve into something better, greater, or we won't survive either.

'The Terror might come tomorrow, or next year or a thousand years from now. We must prepare. Owen said so. Perhaps his last, dying words. I know you don't want to hear this now. You have an Empire to rebuild. But this is important. It matters. We'll discuss it further when I get back to Golgotha. Don't expect me any time soon. My ship's had the crap kicked out of it. And most of my crew are dead . . . or dying. We won our war, Robert, but we paid for it with the loss of our bravest and our best. We will never see their like again.'

The scene froze, and then the viewscreen disappeared. For a while, all was still and silent in the clearing in the techno-jungle. Lewis was leant forward, as though bent over an aching stomach, staring at the floor between his feet. He felt as though he'd been hit repeatedly, and everything he ever valued taken roughly from him. The robot waited patiently.

'The . . . information, that Silence said had been placed in his computers, from outside,' Lewis said finally, his voice little more than a whisper. 'Did it tell what happened to Owen, on his journey back through Time? Did it tell where and how and when he died?'

'We never saw it,' said the robot. 'Captain Silence removed the data from his ship's computers. If he ever did show it to King Robert, no copy was ever made.'

Lewis looked up, frowning. 'Why would he do that? Why would Silence suppress information intended to protect Humanity?'

'Unknown. He never consulted with us. Perhaps he did not trust us. Or King Robert. Either way, the data vanished with his death, some years later.'

Lewis glared at the robot, suddenly so angry he could barely speak. 'You've known, all this time, that Owen was dead. That our faith in his return was just a cruel lie. Why didn't you ever say anything?'

'Because King Robert and Queen Constance asked us not to,' the robot said simply. 'Because the legend they so care-fully created obviously meant so much to Humanity. There was an Empire to rebuild. Your King and Queen believed you needed legends to inspire you, far more than you needed the truth. We could have spoken out, after Robert and Constance were gone, but it was clear that Owen's legend meant so much to you all. You wanted, needed, to believe that Owen was still out there somewhere, and might someday return. We just . . . didn't have the heart to tell you. And now it's up to you, Lewis. Will you tell King Douglas, and your Parliament, that the blessed Owen is dead?'

Lewis thought about it. What could he say? When you got right down to it, he had no proof. The Shub had no evidence to back up what they'd shown him on the viewscreen. The AIs had admitted they'd lied to Humanity before, when they felt they had good reason. It could all be nothing but a very clever fake. But somehow Lewis didn't think so. What he'd seen and listened to so painfully had had the ring of authenticity. Owen . . . was dead. He wouldn't be coming back in triumph, in the nick of time, to save Humanity in the hour of their greatest need. He wouldn't be there, to stand between Humanity and the Terror. Perhaps that was why he'd sent the warning in the first place.

Lewis sighed heavily. He couldn't tell anyone that. The bitter truth would crush Humanity's spirit, when they needed most to be at their strongest. They needed the legend. Perhaps Robert and Constance had known what they were doing after all . . . Of course, it made the Quest of the Paragons meaningless; but the people needed the Quest too, and the hope it represented. And the Paragons needed the Quest most of all.

Lewis sucked in a deep breath, and slowly raised his head again. He felt like he'd been through a long illness, and was only slowly beginning to recover his strength. Owen Deathstalker was dead. It was like being told the sun wouldn't come up in the morning any more. Lewis looked at the robot as he rose fairly steadily to his feet.

'Thank you for your candour. You've given me a lot to think about. Including just how much of this I should pass on to Douglas, and the House.'

He held out his hand for the robot to shake, and the robot froze suddenly, looking down at the hand.

'That ring, Sir Deathstalker. Where did you get that ring?'

'It was Owen's ring,' said Lewis, holding his hand still, just a bit self-consciously. 'It's the old sign and seal of my Clan, long thought lost with Owen. It was given to me at Douglas' Coronation, by a rather strange little man in grey called Vaughn.'

The robot pressed Lewis eagerly for every detail he could remember, making him go over it again and again. The viewscreen reappeared suddenly, showing an image of a short hunched figure dressed in grey. Lewis nodded.

'Yes, that's him. Do you have any information on him?'

'This is Vaughn, other names unknown, planet of origin unknown. A leper, from the old isolation planet of Lachrymae Christi. He died there, from the disease, one hundred and ninety-two years ago. The venerable Saint Beatrice kept excellent records. We even have his death certificate.' The screen changed to show the document, and then it disappeared again. The robot looked thoughtfully at Lewis. 'Our sensors indicate that the ring on your finger corresponds in every detail to the description we have of Owen's ring. Which, as you say, disappeared with Owen. So how has it reappeared now, and who was the person in grey who gave it to you? Did a ghost come to you, to give you a dead man's ring?'

A serious chill went through Lewis then, and he tried to keep his voice light. 'Do Artificial Intelligences believe in ghosts?'

'The Recreated died, and were returned to us. The Ashrai were exterminated, and reborn. Dead worlds blossomed into life again, as we watched. Who is to say what is possible, where the Madness Maze and its people are concerned? Keep the ring, Lewis. Keep it safe. Its reappearence, at the same time as the coming of the Terror, cannot be a coincidence. There is purpose in this, and perhaps destiny too. Death-stalkers have always been connected with destiny. It is their honour, and their curse.'

A sudden thought struck Lewis, and he gave the robot a hard look. 'You know what happened to Owen. Do you also know what happened to Hazel d'Ark?'

'No, Lewis. No-one knows. It is one of the great mysteries. She disappeared after learning of Owen's death. Took off in her ship, and was never seen again, by anyone. Which should have been impossible, given how hard everyone was looking for her. Even her fellow Maze survivors couldn't locate her. We can only assume . . . that Hazel d'Ark didn't want to be found. She loved him very much, you know.'

'Their legendary love . . .'

'Yes. She may be dead, or alive. We have no way of knowing.'

'Perhaps the Quest should be to find her, not Owen,' said Lewis. 'But I don't think I'll suggest that to anyone, just yet.'

'We remember Hazel d'Ark,' said the robot. 'The person, not the legend. She worked marvels, and was a wonder in combat. We remember them all . . . every encounter we ever had with the Maze people is still with us, as sharp today as it was then. Would you . . . like to see some?'

'Yes,' said Lewis, suddenly breathless, his heart leaping in his chest. 'Show me. Show me the truth, of what they really were.'

The viewscreen reappeared before him, and there was Owen Deathstalker and Hazel d'Ark, fighting their way through the packed streets of Mistport, during the Imperial invasion of Mistworld by the Empress Lionstone's terror troops. Fires blazed and buildings crumbled as huge gravity barges moved ponderously by overhead, energy beams stabbing down, illuminating the night. People were running and screaming and fighting everywhere, soldiers and rebels and panicking civilians. Swords clashed, guns fired, and people lay dead and dying in the streets, often trampled underfoot in the crush. Espers flew through the smoke-filled air, throwing themselves in waves at the gravity barges in reckless attacks; grim, brave, suicidal smiles on their faces.

Owen and Hazel cut and hacked their way through walls of Imperial marines, refusing to be stopped or turned aside. Sometimes they fought side by side, and sometimes back to back, but no-one could stand against them. Some troops actually turned and ran, rather than face the Deathstalker and the d'Ark. Whoever was filming the fighting was right there in the thick of it. Again and again, the camera zoomed in to show close-ups of Owen's and Hazel's faces. And they . . . were so much less than legends, but so much more than human. The dark-haired Owen and the flame-haired Hazel, with sweat and blood on their panting faces. Stamping and thrusting and fighting like demons; so much stronger and faster and fiercer than the troops they faced.

They were somehow finer, more focused, than any mere

human should be; their every movement sharp and savage and ruthlessly efficient. Lewis had never seen anything like it, not even in the Arena. Owen and Hazel dashed themselves, over and over again, against overwhelming odds, performing miracles with casual grace, cutting down everything that was sent against them. Sometimes laughing, sometimes snarling, sometimes bleeding; but never once hesitating or turning away. Lewis watched, open-mouthed and wide-eyed, a great pride filling his heart until he thought it would burst. The Deathstalker and the d'Ark, doing what they did best, what they were born to do. Spitting in evil's face and damning it to Hell, because somebody had to. They were killers, not saints; but damn, they were glorious!

The viewscreen went blank for a moment, and Lewis sat down suddenly in his chair again as his legs gave out. He was breathing as hard as if he'd been there himself, fighting beside his ancestor. He'd seen films, of course, and docudrama reconstructions, but nothing in the sanitised legends could have prepared him for the reality . . .

A new scene filled the viewscreen, and there was Jack Random, the professional rebel, and Ruby Journey, the bounty hunter; defending the entrance to a valley on the planet Loki against a whole army of Shub's Furies and Ghost Warriors. Jack and Ruby, side by side, standing their ground against an enemy even they couldn't have hoped to defeat. They looked like heroes. Warriors. They looked like they knew they were going to die. Out beyond the valley, Ghost Warriors stood in countless ranks. Dead men raised to fight again in the service of Shub, with grey rotting flesh, animated by computer brains and implanted servomechanisms in their dead muscles. They looked vile beyond belief; Shub's contempt for the weaknesses of flesh turned into physical and psychological weapons. Lewis looked briefly at the blue steel robot standing beside him, and thought he'd never feel the same about the AIs again.

'We were different then,' the robot said quietly. 'We were wrong. We did not understand, that all that lives is holy. We have sworn to die by our own hand, rather then become again what we once were. Now watch . . .'

The dead men came surging forward, howling horribly with their decaying vocal cords, and Jack Random and Ruby Journey shared one last smile, and stood their ground. They fought savagely, with sword and gun and unnatural strength and speed, and still they took wound after bloody wound, dying by inches, stamping and slipping in their own pooled blood, but never once retreating. The Ghost Warriors came at them again and again, their numbers seemingly endlessly, only to crash fruitlessly against Random and Journey, like the sea pounding two unyielding rocks. And again, they were warriors rather than legends; but somehow that was even more impressive. Lewis thought he'd never seen anything so brave in his whole life.

Legends might inspire awe, and even worship, but it took real men and women to move the heart like this.

The screen went blank, and disappeared again. Lewis let out a breath he hadn't realised he'd been holding. The robot was bowing its blank face over pressed-together hands again.

'They fought for hours,' said the robot. 'And they would not yield. In the end, they put their lives on the line, to summon up enough power to defeat us with their Maze-given abilities. They could do wondrous things in those days, the men and women who walked the Madness Maze. Things neither we, nor the Empire, not the greatest adepts of the oversoul, have ever been able to duplicate in all the years since. Now do you understand why the Maze fascinates us so? Why we need so badly to know what the Maze can teach us? Having seen gods at play, how can we bear to be any less?'

'They didn't look like gods,' Lewis said roughly. 'They bled, and suffered. They looked . . . like heroes.'

'They were not perfect,' the robot admitted, lifting its head again. 'We remember many things, that Robert and Constance chose to suppress. The Maze people did terrible, awful things, in their time. Unforgiveable things, sometimes. For all their power, they were still only, very, human. But at the end, when it mattered, they transcended what they were to become what they had to be; to save us all. At the end, they were all . . . magnificent.'

'People should see this,' said Lewis. 'Everyone should be

able to see what you've just shown me. It would mean so much to them. Far more than a bunch of old stories, and stylised figures on stained-glass windows.'

'This is for your King and Parliament to decide,' said the robot. 'And Lewis . . . you have seen only the smallest part of the truth. There are other histories, in our records, that would test your faith and your belief in your heroes to the limits. The Rebellion wasn't always the simple conflict between Good and Evil that the accepted version would have you believe. People interpret legends to fit their own needs. Heroes aren't nearly so accommodating.'

'People deserve to know the truth,' said Lewis.

'Even about Owen? What do your people need most now, Sir Deathstalker? The lie that comforts, or the truth that damns?'

Lewis thought about that, all the way back through the twisting tangles of the technojungle, as the robot led him back to the original teleport point. What could Shub know, or remember, that was so bad the AIs believed people wouldn't be able to deal with it, even after all these years? What could the Maze people have done, that Robert and Constance felt obliged to wipe away history, and replace it with legend? What could be worse than knowing Owen Deathstalker was dead? Or . . . could the AIs be lying; hoarding ancient knowledge for their own secret reasons? By the time they reached the teleport point, Lewis was frowning so hard over his churning thoughts that he'd given himself a headache.

'This is as far as we go,' said the robot. 'You must decide what to do next, Lewis. We trust you to make the right decision. You are, after all, a Deathstalker.'

'You have no idea of how tired I am of being told that,' said Lewis. 'I always thought it was more important that I was a Paragon, but . . .' A sudden thought struck him, and he looked sharply at the robot. 'I knew there was something I'd forgotten. Something I meant to ask you. What does Shub think about the Mog Mor aliens, and their offer? Could the Swart Alfair really have new, unknown tech that could save us from the Terror? Tech that's possibly even greater than yours?'

'It doesn't seem likely,' said the robot. 'A greater probability would be that they are bluffing, to take advantage of the situation. But, on the other hand . . . we had no idea this species even existed before they chose to make their presence known to the Empire. They hid themselves, from the Empire and from us, by entirely unknown means, for unknown centuries. So they must have something. You may have to promise them at least some of what they want, to find out what they've got. We understand the concept of bargaining, and the making of deals. We would offer Humanity whatever they might ask of us, in return for access to the Madness Maze.'

'Don't start that again,' said Lewis, just a little testily. 'I told you; I don't have that kind of influence with the King any more.'

'You heard Captain Silence's words. Tell the King, and your Parliament. It was always intended that we should all go through the Maze, and become more than we are, so that we could oppose the Terror. It was what the Maze was constructed for. And it was Owen's last wish . . .'

'You're like a dog with a rat,' said Lewis. 'You just can't leave it alone, can you? For what it's worth; I believe you. I'll do what I can, to convince the King and the House. But it seems . . . I'm not everything I used to be.'

'You are a Deathstalker,' the robot said forcefully. 'You bear the Owen's ring. Perhaps . . . you should go through the Madness Maze, as your ancestor did before you?'

Lewis smiled tiredly. 'Even if they did open up the Maze again, I'm pretty sure they wouldn't put me anywhere near the top of the list. Besides, I'm not sure I'd want to do it. Whether you believe the legend or the history, one thing is clear about Owen's life. The Maze might have made him superhuman, but it sure as hell didn't make him happy.'

'What about duty?' said the robot.

'What about it?' said Lewis. 'I did everything that was ever asked of me, and more. I gave my life to duty, and to honour. And it didn't make me happy, either.'

'Perhaps some things are more important than being happy,' said the robot.

'Perhaps. Send me home. I'm tired, and I want to go home.'

Once again, the teleport happened faster than human senses could experience, and Lewis was standing in the doorway to the Shub Embassy on Logres, looking out on the empty Row. He sighed, and stepped out into the street, and the door closed silently behind him. His gravity sled was still waiting for him. Lewis stepped aboard, and ascended slowly into the sky. Wondering how much of the truth he would tell, to Douglas and the House and Humanity. Just how much truth they could stand. And how much . . . would only be cruel.

From the shadows of an alleyway further down the street, Finn Durandal watched Lewis go. When the Deathstalker was safely out of sight, Finn walked calmly down Ambassadors' Row, and stopped before the door to Shub's Embassy. He waited a while, but it didn't open before him. He knocked loudly, and then stood there with folded arms, with the air of someone prepared to stand there forever, if that was what it took. The door swung open and a blank-faced robot stood before him, blocking the way.

'Why would you speak with Lewis, and not with me?' Finn said bluntly.

'Because he is the Deathstalker. And Humanity's Champion. He came to us from King and Parliament.'

Finn sniffed dismissively. 'He won't be Champion much longer. And the rest is just a name; nothing more. He isn't even a direct descendant of the blessed Owen; just a distant cousin. His grandparents only took the Deathstalker name because Robert and Constance asked them to. I would have thought you'd have known that.'

'We knew that,' said the robot. 'We know many things, Sir Durandal.'

'Either way, Lewis is on his way out, while I am very definitely on my way up. Sooner than you think, I will have influence and then power beyond your imagination. Assuming that AIs have such a thing. I will be Champion. I will be King, and more. You support me, when I need it, and I promise you access to the Madness Maze. Who else will do that for you?'

'So far, only you,' said the robot. 'We have watched you

with interest, Sir Durandal. Come inside, and we will discuss this further. It might be that there are areas of mutual interest, where we could be of use to each other. Perhaps we can use each other, to get what we each want.'

'Of course,' said Finn, stepping forward as the robot stepped back. 'I'm sure we can find things to agree on. Common interest, and the like.'

'All that lives is holy,' said the robot.

'So I'm told,' said Finn.

Douglas Campbell put aside his Crown and kingly robes when he went to see Donal Corcoran, the only survivor of the Terror's arrival. He had a strong feeling that the official trappings of King and Speaker wouldn't get him anywhere with a man who everybody agreed was now as crazy as a bag of weasels.

No-one was quite sure exactly what was wrong with Donal Corcoran. Two doctors had actually threatened to fight a duel over their diagnoses, until Douglas had his men forcibly separate them. Corcoran exhibited definite symptoms of hysteria, delusion, depression, compulsive-obsessive disorders, mania, and mood swings so rapid you could get serious whiplash just trying to follow them. His intellect was intact, but strangely warped, his thoughts often chasing abruptly off in directions that even the most experienced scientific observers had trouble following. His emotions were clearly out of control. He laughed and cried a lot, sometimes simultaneously, for no obvious reason, and his reactions to some people and conditions could be violently extreme. To himself, as well as others. The doctors doped him with every medication under the sun, to no useful effect. He could be quiet and calm and lucid; and then the theories he expressed on the possible nature of the Terror gave even the most hardened analysts nightmares.

Several doctors had had to retire from the case, hurt, three had retired to start their own religions, and one had had a mystical epiphany and a sex change. Everyone currently working with Donal Corcoran got hazard pay. Direct exposure to the man was strictly limited, and all admittance papers to the institution where he was being held were stamped *Enter at your own risk.*

No-one had expected Corcoran to survive his dreadful experiences unscathed, of course. But it was becoming more and more vital that the nature and extent of his change be understood, before the Terror appeared again. Douglas in particular needed to know whether Corcoran's unique condition was the result of stress, strain and shock . . . or whether what Corcoran was now was the inevitable result of even long range contact with the Terror. The populations of the attacked Rim worlds had been driven insane by the presence of the Terror's appalling heralds, but Corcoran had been right at the edge of the solar system, racing towards hyperspace and safety. He should have been out of range, and safe . . . but he had looked back, through his probes, and seen the Gorgon. He had looked into the face of the Medusa. Could just that have been enough to make Corcoran into something other than human? Douglas needed to know.

He had other worries too. All across the Empire, worlds in the line of the Terror's projected approach path were spending every credit they had, or could borrow, on upgrading their planetary defence systems to the maximum limit. They were buying attack ships, weapons and orbiting mines and force shields, and every defensive and offensive safeguard known to Humanity. Some were even pinning their hopes on strange unproven devices of alien origin. The Rim worlds' defences had been no use at all, but then, they'd been far short of state of the art.

When the Recreated were freed from their awful state by the blessed Owen, their humanity and their planets restored in a moment, they were of course hundreds of years behind everyone else. And even after two centuries of determined self-improvement, and a hell of a lot of Imperial grant money, they still hadn't entirely caught up. So an awful lot of worlds were planning to protect themselves with cutting-edge weapons tech, and to hell with what it cost them. What did the future matter? If the Terror came and found them wanting, none of them would have a future.

Douglas wasn't convinced any of this would help. Neither

were most of these worlds' representatives in the House. But if it kept people busy, and offered them a modicum of hope and security . . . Better economic stupidity than mass panic. Douglas, however, remembered the most important lesson of Empire. First; know thy enemy. So he decided he needed to see Donal Corcoran for himself, hear what the man had to say first hand. He didn't tell the House. They'd just throw a major hissy fit at the prospect of the King putting himself into possible danger, and order him not to go. So he decided not to worry them, and go anyway. He didn't even tell Anne.

Armed guards, heavy duty tanglefields and force shields, and even a few portable disrupter cannon guarded the asylum holding Donal Corcoran, as much to keep people out as keep him in. The media had been using every trick in the book to try and get to him, and there were any number of fanatical groups and individuals ready to use any method to force their way in. Some wanted to kill Corcoran, in case he was somehow infected by the Terror, and had brought its evil back with him. Some claimed he was a judas goat, leading the Terror to its prey. Some wanted to worship him, for being touched by God. Some wanted to kidnap and interrogate him, in the hope of learning useful information about the Terror, which they could then sell to the threatened worlds. And a few wanted to marry him. People will do the craziest things . . . if they're scared enough.

Douglas wasn't crazy enough to go in there alone. He'd felt the need for specialist help on this one. So he contacted the oversoul, and they sent him a top level telepath to assist and protect him. This turned out to be a tall strapping brunette who dressed in sweeping black silks, and sported jet black lips and heavy eye makeup. She also wore a bandolier of silver throwing stars, carried a disrupter on her hip, and had steel toe capped boots. She was at least a head taller than Douglas, and radiated so much sheer presence that when she walked into a room it felt like everyone else had just left. Running. Her name was Crow Jane, her gaze was disturbingly direct, and she had a voice just dripping with rough, smoky sensuality. If nothing else, Douglas was pretty sure she'd get Corcoran's attention.

'If you're going to talk to the survivor, you're going to need heavy duty protection,' Crow Jane said, very directly, even before they'd finished shaking hands. 'We're not going to take any chances with this guy. I've been studying the reports. I don't think it's safe for normal minds to spend too much time in his company. Madness on this scale can be contagious. Especially when it's something new.'

'Really? How interesting,' said Douglas, just to be saying something. 'I'll have to depend on you, then, to keep his thoughts out of my head. I need to get some answers out of him. What do you think our chances are?'

'Oh, we'll get answers,' Crow Jane said easily. 'Whether they'll mean anything, though . . . just because he believes what he's saying when he says it doesn't make it true. Or useful. The reports say he likes to talk, in fact they often have trouble stopping him. The trick is to get him to respond to what you're saying. And I hate to disappoint you, but there's going to be distinct limits to what I can see of his thoughts. I doubt very much that he'll be able to keep me out, but . . . what's in his head may only make sense to him. And I can't risk digging too deep, or too long. Madness is dangerous. Insanity can be very . . . seductive. It can suck you in. I could end up trapped inside his head, unable to get out. So if you ask me to do something, and I say no, don't push. And if I say we have to go, we go, at speed. Is that clear?'

'I asked for a top level telepath,' said Douglas.

'And that's what you got. Most espers wouldn't go anywhere near Donal Corcoran, and quite rightly. They'd probably end up with their brains dribbling out of their ears. I can protect you from him, and I should be able to peek past his defences. Settle for that.'

'I need information from him. Things only he knows.'

Crow Jane shrugged. 'He won't be able to knowingly lie to me, but I can't make him tell me what he doesn't know.'

'How about things he may have chosen to forget, because they're too painful or too frightening?' said Douglas.

'Depends how deep he's buried them. Some traumas can be so painful, so terrible, that the victim would rather die than remember. I can push him in the right direction, but . . . I'm an esper, not a miracle worker. Despite what some of the tabloid media shows would have you believe.'

Douglas sighed. 'It's going to be a long, hard morning, isn't it?'

'Got that right,' said Crow Jane.

Douglas' authority and charm got them through the various levels of security at the asylum fairly quickly, until he and Crow Jane ended up in the quietly comfortable office of Corcoran's current analyst, Dr Oisin Benjamin. It was a bright and cheerful office, with sunshine streaming through the open window. It had the usual desk and couch and book-lined walls, and everything was plush and cosy and agreeable. In fact, the only uncomfortable thing in the office was Dr Benjamin. His handshake was weak, his smile was unsteady, and he had a slight but definite twitch in one eye. Not uncommon signs in someone who'd been exposed to Donal Corcoran on a regular basis. The doctor responded a little to Douglas' practised charm, but Crow Jane clearly upset him. Especially when she sat cross-legged in mid air rather than perch on the straight-backed visitor's chair. After that, the doctor did his best to ignore her and direct all his remarks to Douglas. They sat facing each other across Dr Benjamin's desk, while the good doctor fiddled constantly with a lethal-looking letter opener.

'Donal Corcoran,' he said abruptly. 'Yes. A very unusual man. Quite remarkable. And, so far, entirely unresponsive to every traditional form of treatment. He's not interested in therapy. Hell, after time with Donal, most of our therapists require therapy. Medication doesn't work. We've dosed him with every drug we've got and a few we imported specially, on dosages that would mellow out a Grendel, and he just laughs at us. He has a very unsettling laugh. Like he knows things we don't. Things no sane man would want to know. We've had him here for, what, ten days now? And we're still no nearer understanding what's wrong with him. Whatever he saw, or felt, out there on the Rim, Your Majesty, he can't or won't tell us. And we have no way of making him.'

'What about his dreams?' said Douglas. 'Do they tell you anything?'

'He doesn't sleep,' said Dr Benjamin. 'Ever. In fact, according to my predecessors' notes, Donal hasn't closed his eyes since we got him here. Normally, such a long period of sleep deprivation would be enough to drive a man seriously psychotic, but with Donal . . . He says he won't sleep, in case the Terror creeps up on him. It's my belief he's holding sleep at bay through sheer will power. Which shouldn't be possible, but, well . . . Donal does a lot of things he shouldn't be able to do. He can hear what people are saying about him, even when they whisper. Even when they're in the next room. And sometimes he gives answers to questions we haven't even asked yet.'

Crow Jane perked up at that. 'Has he been tested for telepathy, or other esper abilities?'

Dr Benjamin still wouldn't look at her, addressing his reply to Douglas. 'We ran all the usual tests, of course. None of the results made a blind bit of sense.'

Crow Jane frowned. 'Why didn't you contact the oversoul? We would have sent you an expert.'

'Donal's condition is extreme enough already, without exposing him to esper meddling!' snapped Dr Benjamin.

'Ah well,' said Crow Jane. 'As long as there's a scientific reason . . .'

'But you have no objection to my seeing him?' Douglas said quickly. 'With my associate?'

The doctor shrugged unhappily. 'You must do as you think best, Your Majesty. At your own risk, of course. I'll call for someone to take you to Donal. As soon as his current visitor has left . . .'

Douglas looked at him sharply. 'He already has a visitor? I was under the impression no-one else had been cleared to see him!'

'Well, no, but this was Angelo Bellini. You know; the Angel of Madraguda himself. Charming fellow. Came all the way here, in person, just to make sure that Donal's spiritual needs were being ministered to. He . . . gave me to understand that he had official consent. Doesn't he?'

'No,' Douglas said grimly. 'He bloody doesn't.'

*

Donal Corcoran was being kept in a maximum security psycho ward, though he probably didn't realise that. People tended to add the word *probably* to whatever they said about Corcoran, because no-one could be sure what he was and wasn't aware of. It tended to vary, suddenly and without notice. Certainly his surroundings didn't look like any kind of hospital ward, or cell, even though they were very definitely both. Corcoran was supposed to believe he was being looked after in a secure country manor house, with wide-ranging gardens for him to walk in. A lot of effort had gone into providing him with the illusion of freedom. In fact, most of it was comprised of holos, backed up with concealed force screens in case he tried to wander off. The illusion was really very convincing, backed up with state of the art sight and sound, right down to all the correct scents of a garden in full bloom. Birds seemed to sing, insects seemed to buzz, and refreshing breezes came and went on a regular basis. Certainly the pleasant summer heat felt entirely convincing to Angelo Bellini as he strolled through the gardens with Donal Corcoran, talking quietly of this and that.

The Angel had come as a representative of the official Church; ostensibly to offer Corcoran spiritual comfort in his time of trial, but actually to try and enlist him into the Cause. If Corcoran could be persuaded to join and endorse the Church Militant, and thus Pure Humanity, the general public could then be persuaded to associate joining the new Church with standing against the Terror. Which could in turn be parlayed into increased political power. Angelo had come up with the idea all on his own. Bringing Corcoran into the new Church would be a major coup, for the Church Militant and for him. But it was proving . . . very hard work.

Corcoran didn't always seem to hear what Angelo said to him, and even when he did his responses suggested he didn't care. Physically, his presence was disturbing, and even actually distressing. Corcoran was still wearing his old spacer's uniform, ragged and filthy, because he'd hospitalised the last three orderlies who'd tried to persuade him to change them for regulation hospital issue. He hadn't washed or shaved or even combed his hair since he'd arrived, and he smelled really bad. He looked like a wild man, openly contemptuous of all the usual civilised proprieties. He talked in long, jagged speeches that tended to wander round the point without ever actually touching on it. He was constantly distracted by everything around him, and sometimes by things that weren't, and Angelo was finding it an uphill struggle just to keep Corcoran's attention. He tried to keep the strain out of his face and his voice, and persevered.

'The Church can offer you protection against the Terror,' he said, for what had to be at least the tenth time. 'You will be safe with us. Let us get you out of here. They can't hold you here against your will, not if you have the backing of the new Church. All you'll have to do is make the occasional appearance, the occasional speech or two, on our behalf. No pressure, of course. Whatever you feel comfortable with. And we'll find you a really secure place; somewhere the Terror could never find or reach you. We want to be your friend, Donal. The Church is your friend.'

'You want me to speak to people,' said Corcoran, holding his hands up before his face, and turning them back and forth as though he'd never seen them before. 'Praise the Church and pass the panacea. Bullshit. Bullshit! You can't hide behind your precious religion now, little angel. There'll be nowhere to hide when the Terror comes. I know. The rock cried out, no hiding place . . . I don't want to speak to people. I just want to get the hell out of here. Get back to my ship. Back to the Terror . . .'

Angelo blinked at him confusedly. 'You want . . . to face the Terror again?'

Corcoran spun on him, his fingers crooked now into claws, his eyes suddenly inhumanly wide and unblinking, his lips pulled back into a vicious snarl. Angelo fell back a step, despite himself. Corcoran laughed soundlessly.

'I want to fight the Terror! Kill it! Hurt it, like it hurt me! I can feel it . . . I can always feel it . . . we're connected now, till death do us part. Screw your protection, Angelo, I want revenge. I want to be free of it. Do you think I don't know what's been done to me? Inside, I'm hurting all the time. Inside, I'm screaming all the time. I'll never be safe, never be

free, never be me again . . . until I've torn the Terror apart,
burnt it down and pissed on the ashes.'

'Well,' said Angelo. 'That's all very interesting, but . . .'

Corcoran hugged himself tightly, as though he might fly
apart, still fixing Angelo with his disturbing, fever-bright eyes.
'I see you, Bellini. There are dead men peering over your
shoulder. There's something on your hands and it isn't blood,
though it's red enough. You think you know revenge . . . You
get me out of here, little angel, and I'll show you revenge.'

Angelo had to swallow hard, unable to look away from eyes
that seemed to look right through him. This was just like the
Ecstatic, who'd also seemed to know things he couldn't possibly have known. What had the Terror done to this man?
What had it turned him into?

'God feels your pain, my son . . .'

'God? Where was your God, when so many innocents died?
I think . . . maybe what I saw was God. God gone crazy,
devouring His own creation. Saturn, eating his children. Get
me out of here, Angelo. Or maybe I'll eat you.'

Corcoran was very close to Angelo now, and still the Angel
couldn't look away from the dark, dark eyes. He was whimpering, though he didn't know it. And then King Douglas and
Crow Jane came striding through the illusionary gardens,
breaking the spell, and Angelo was actually pleased to see
them. He broke away from Corcoran and stumbled over to
bow formally to Douglas.

'Ah, Your Majesty. What an unexpected surprise, and a
pleasure. May I introduce you to my quite extraordinary new
friend, Donal Corcoran? He and I have been having the most
fascinating little chat.'

'How the hell did you get in here, Bellini?' demanded
Douglas. 'And where do you get off, claiming to have official
permission? I wouldn't give you permission to clean this
place's toilets with your own toothbrush. And trying to take
advantage of the mentally ill has to be a new low, even for
you. Get out of here, now. Before I have the guards throw you
out.'

Angelo drew himself up to his full height, and glared at the
King coldly. 'I represent the Church, and the Church goes

where it wishes. Your power derives from a handful of frightened men and women in an outmoded institution, Douglas. Mine comes from the greatest and most powerful religious movement this Empire has ever known. The day will come, and sooner than you think, when your House will have to kneel to my Church; and you will have to kneel to me. Make the most of your little authority, Campbell. While you still have it.'

Douglas punched him in the mouth. Angelo squealed loudly, lurched backwards, and sat down suddenly. Blood welled down his bearded chin, and tears ran from his eyes. Douglas took a step forward, and Angelo scooted frantically backwards across the grass.

'Never outstay your welcome, Angelo,' Douglas said calmly. 'And by the way, for a warrior of the Church Militant, you take a punch like a sissy. Now get out of my sight, or I'll have them set the dogs on you.'

Angelo rose unsteadily to his feet, gathered what was left of his dignity about him, and opened his mouth for one last cutting comment. Only to lose it all and run for his life when Douglas suddenly growled and lunged at him. Crow Jane watched him go, and then looked thoughtfully at Douglas.

'Was that really necessary?'

'Oh yes,' said Douglas, happily. 'Absolutely. You have no idea.'

They both turned to consider Donal Corcoran, who had ignored all of what happened, intently counting his fingers over and over again. His whole body was trembling, as though full of energy he didn't know what to do with. His face was slick with sweat, though it was only pleasantly warm in the fake garden. He looked up suddenly to glare at Douglas, his head cocked slightly to one side.

'You. It's all your fault. You shouldn't have had me brought here. To Logres, to this place. I wanted to stay on my ship. I knew where I was, there. We've been through a lot together. We're connected, you see. Both changed by the Terror. The Navy took me by force. Boarded my ship, wrestled me to the deck, put me in a straitjacket and brought me here. I don't want to be here. I don't feel safe. I need to be out there . . .

waiting for it to show its face again. You do know it's coming back, don't you?'

'Yes,' said Douglas. 'If the Terror continues on the same course, it will cut a swathe through all the most densely populated worlds, and come here. To Logres. That's why I had you brought here, Donal. Because of what you've seen, what you know. I need to know what you know.'

'You can't,' Corcoran said flatly. 'Even I don't know everything I know. There's more inside my head than just me. You think I don't know what this place is? I know. I can hear the barred windows and smell the guns. Best looking rubber room I ever saw.' He looked around sharply, and tensed, half crouching, as though preparing to run. 'I'm never alone any more. I'm haunted by ghosts. I can hear the voices of every man, woman and child who died on the Rim worlds. They talk to me, in the quiet between other people's words. They tell me what it's like to be dead. They don't like it. They didn't like it the first time, either. That's why they became the Recreated. But now, all they have is me. Whatever I am, now. I will be their vengeance, hunt down the Terror and destroy it. Make it suffer, make it pay, for what it did to them, and to me. And maybe then I'll be able to sleep again.'

'We all want to stop the Terror,' Douglas said carefully. 'Do you know how we can do that, Donal?'

Corcoran looked at him sideways, smiling craftily. 'Let me out of here, and I'll tell you.'

Douglas sighed, and looked at Crow Jane, who shook her head slowly. 'I've been trying to get inside his mind, and I can't. It's spooky in there. I've never encountered anything like this before. He isn't an esper, and he has no actual telepathic shields, as such; it's just that his mind is too . . . different. I've known aliens whose thought patterns were easier to understand. It's like . . . part of his mind is always missing. Like . . . not all of him came back from the Rim. Perhaps when he encountered the Terror, it took part of him, and kept it.'

'There is a place that is not a place,' Corcoran said softly. 'Sometimes . . . I can sense it, just behind my shoulder. I think maybe . . . the Terror was born there. Look into my eyes, little esper, and perhaps you'll see it too.'

Crow Jane looked away. 'I can't. It frightens me.'

Corcoran laughed. It was a thick, ugly, disturbing sound with nothing sane about it. Douglas shuddered, despite himself. Corcoran looked slowly around the garden that had been made for him, sneering at its security, denying himself its comforts. He turned suddenly to glare at Douglas.

'Let me out of here. I can't be here. I have business to be about. You have no right to keep me here!'

'What you know, or might remember, could prove very valuable,' said Douglas. 'All sorts of people would like to get their hands on you, for what they think you know. You're safer here. Talk to the doctors, Donal. Help them to help you. And then work with us, to stop the Terror. Before it kills again.'

'You know nothing! You understand nothing!' Corcoran stepped suddenly forward, to shout his words right into Douglas' face. Crow Jane drew her disrupter. Corcoran ignored her. Douglas gestured for the esper not to interfere, and stood very still as the madman shouted at him. 'You can't keep me here! I won't be kept here, like an animal!'

'I'll come and talk to you again,' said Douglas. 'When you're feeling calmer. I won't give up on you, Donal. I am your King, and I will not abandon you. If you have faith in nothing else, have faith in that.'

He bowed to Corcoran, and then turned and walked unhurriedly away. Crow Jane gave Corcoran one last suspicious glance, and then hurried after Douglas, her gun still in her hand. The madman watched them go, his staring eyes suddenly calm and thoughtful. When the King and his esper were both out of sight, hidden behind the concealing holos, Corcoran walked off in another direction, between trees he knew weren't real, following a direction that blazed in his mind like a siren. He soon came to what appeared to be a high stone wall, the boundary of the grounds. Corcoran reached slowly out, placed his hands flat against the disguised force shield, and pushed. And his hands and arms went right through the energy screen as though it wasn't there. Corcoran pulled his hands back, and laughed soundlessly.

*

Frustrated by his failure to acquire Donal Corcoran for the Church, and furious at his treatment by King Douglas, Angelo Bellini scowled and fumed all the way back to the Cathedral. He slammed out of his chauffer-driven limousine, stormed through the offices at the back of the Cathedral, and his people saw his face and hurried to get out of his way. He stalked right past his secretary, even as she rose twittering from behind her desk to tell him he had a visitor waiting in his office. He kicked the door open, strode in, and slammed the door behind him with satisfying noise and venom. It felt good to be back in his office, in his territory, in his place of power. A good place to plot revenges, and the humbling of Kings. He strode over to his desk, enjoying the way his feet sank into the deep pile carpet. He sank down into his chair, activated the massage function, and finally began to relax a little. Someone cleared their throat politely, and Angelo only then remembered what his secretary had said about a visitor. He looked around, and there was Tel Markham, the honourable Member for Madraguda, standing patiently beside the window, looking calm and relaxed as always.

'Hello Angelo,' Markham said easily. 'You're looking good, as always. Like the new office. It's very you. Is that dried blood in your beard?'

'Go away, Tel,' Angelo said wearily. 'I don't have the time or the patience for this. I'm really very busy today. You'll just have to make an appointment with my secretary for another time, like everyone else.'

'An appointment?' said Markham, raising one elegant eyebrow. 'Since when did Madraguda's two most favoured sons need an appointment to talk to each other?'

'Spare me the crap,' growled Angelo. 'I'm not in the mood. What do you want, Tel? You know you only ever come to see me when you want something.'

'I want us to be partners,' Markham said easily. 'We have so many aims in common, these days. Think how much we could achieve, working together, in the House and in the Church.'

'I already have one partner, and he's enough of a pain in the arse as it is.'

'But I have so much to offer, Angelo.'

'I very much doubt it.' Angelo smiled sardonically at his visitor. 'Parliament is on its way out. The new Church is where the future is. You never wanted to be my partner when I was just the Angel of Madraguda. How many times did I ask for your support, back when I was trying to raise money for good causes? You never wanted to know, never bothered to stir yourself unless there was a media opportunity you could crash, and turn to your advantage. Well, now the tables have turned, Tel, and you know what? You don't have a single thing I want or need. Or at least, nothing I can't take from you, when I get around to it.'

'You always were a sore loser, Angelo.' Markham considered for a moment. 'I am Pure Humanity, you know. A lot of MPs are. I'm sure we already have a great many acquaintances in common.'

Angelo sneered at him. 'So the rats are already deserting the sinking ship, are they? I don't care if you're Neuman, Tel. I already have all the fanatics I need. And I sure as hell don't need another partner. What power I have is mine, and I won't share it with anyone else!'

'I really do suggest you think again,' said Markham. He moved over to stand before Angelo, confronting him directly with a steady gaze and his best commanding voice. 'I am now connected to people who could be very useful to you, and your Church. People and . . . organisations you can't even imagine. I can make things happen, with just a word here and a word there. I can open doors that even your current influence couldn't budge. I come to you today in friendship, with my hands open. Deny me now, turn me away, and when I come to you again it might not be in so friendly a manner.'

'Ah, shove it up your majority,' said Angelo. 'You always did try and bully me out of what was rightfully mine. Well, not any more, Tel. Don't let the door hit you on the arse on your way out.'

Markham shrugged easily, entirely unmoved. 'There never was any talking to you when you're in one of your moods. And by the way; give Mother a call. She says it's been ages since she last heard from you.'

Angelo just grunted, and pointedly didn't watch as his big

brother let himself out. It was turning out to be a really bad day, and the massage function in his chair wasn't helping to ease the tension in his back and shoulders worth a damn. He investigated the extent of his swollen mouth with cautious fingertips, and found himself shaking with rage all over again. Douglas had actually hit him! Had dared to strike him! Him! Angelo swivelled savagely back and forth in his chair, scowling and seething. The Campbell would pay for this, and pay in blood. And if he was too well guarded . . . someone close to him. Everyone has a weak spot. Angelo's office door swung open again, and he reached out for something heavy and preferably pointed to throw. And then he saw it was Finn Durandal, and he sank sulkily back into his chair again. He'd been right. It was going to be a perfectly foul day.

'I just passed Tel Markham on my way in,' said Finn. 'What did he want?'

'Just a stray dog, looking for scraps,' Angelo said sullenly. 'I sent him packing with a flea in his ear. Why? What do you care?'

Finn sighed, coming to a halt directly in front of Angelo. He glanced at the visitor's chair, but made no move to sit in it. 'Sometimes I despair of you, Angelo. You wouldn't recognise an opportunity if it flew over your head and crapped in your hair. Markham is a more powerful man than most people realise. He isn't just another MP any more. He has influence in all kinds of quarters, in places even I can't reach, at present. As you would know, if you kept up with the reports and memos I so conscientiously send you every day. I made you my junior partner, Angelo; do try and pull your weight. And in future, consult with me before you reject and possibly alienate a possible ally. Remember – you run this Church for me, not for yourself.'

'Of course, Finn,' said Angelo, as graciously as he could. 'Why don't you sit down, while I order us some refreshments?'

'What a good idea, Angelo,' murmured Finn. He came round the corner of the desk, and waved imperiously for Angelo to get up out of his own chair. And he did it with such confidence and command that it never even occurred to Angelo to argue the point. He made way for Finn, reluctantly, and tried hard not to scowl too openly as the Durandal ostentatiously made himself comfortable. Finn gestured for Angelo to sit in the visitor's chair, and when Angelo hesitated, gave him a hard look that made Angelo hurry to sit down. His skin crawled as it make contact with the hardbacked chair. He'd had it thoroughly cleaned, of course, but still . . .

'Poor old Roland Wentworth,' said Finn. 'But then, who needs a Patriarch when I have my very own Angel? Still; a transmutation bomb, Angelo? Rather excessive, even for you. Perhaps I should consider employing a food taster . . .' He smiled at Angelo's shocked expression. 'Oh, I know everything, Angelo. Never think you can keep a secret from me.'

Angelo's mind raced furiously. First the Ecstatic, then Corcoran, and now Finn . . . did *everyone* know about the transmutation bomb? Only his most secure and trusted people were supposed to know about that. Someone must be talking. Angelo decided it was well past time for another purge.

'The Patriarch couldn't just die,' he said finally. 'He had to disappear. Completely. I did what I felt necessary. How . . . ?'

Finn smiled easily. 'They're my people first, and only yours second. Now; what about these refreshments you offered? I confess I'm really rather parched.'

Angelo busied himself arranging for his secretary to bring cold drinks and a few suitable snacks. He never kept such things actually in the office. Angelo was prone to comfort eating in times of stress, and he was trying to watch his weight. There seemed to be lot more stress in his life just recently, since he joined up with Finn. The refreshments arrived quickly, his secretary all a dither at being in the presence of the legendary Durandal. Finn favoured her with an autograph, and she all but swooned before Angelo ordered her out. He didn't feel like eating, his mouth was still sore and the iced tea stung his lips, but Finn ate and drank enough for both of them as he listened to Angelo's report on Donal Corcoran's condition, and his expressed disinterest in the Church. Angelo somewhat exaggerated Douglas' words and actions, to put himself in a better light, but Finn just nodded, and smiled slightly as Angelo angrily recounted being hit by the King.

'Serves you right,' he said flatly. 'You should have known better than to goad an ex-Paragon. And he is the King, after all. For now. You can go and talk to Corcoran again, after he's had a little more time to realise how helpless he is, trapped in that madhouse. I'll send him some nice presents, a little care package of comforts and goodies, just to remind him who his friends are. And then . . . well, prisoners will make all kinds of deals, for the promise of freedom. Of course, once he's safely in our hands . . .'

'He'll be more of a prisoner than ever,' said Angelo.

Finn smiled dazzlingly. 'Quite.'

They sat in silence for a while. Finn had no more business with Angelo, but he seemed in no hurry to leave. He finished off the food and drink, enjoyed the chair's various massage functions, and played happily with the executive toys on the desk. Angelo fumed quietly for a while, and then suddenly realised he was wasting an opportunity. So he made an effort, and turned the full force of his famous charm on the Durandal. If he was ever to be free of his senior partner, he needed to understand what went on inside Finn's head. What made him tick. Maybe then he would be able to see how best to manipulate Finn, and steal away his power and his people bit by bit, without him even noticing. And then . . . *then* . . .

So Angelo talked easily with Finn, praising and flattering him without being too obvious about it, chattering entertainingly and maliciously about people they both knew, and generally did his best to get Finn to open up, and talk about himself. It was a hard task, but Angelo persevered. He felt he had to get something out of the day for himself, for his pride's sake. But it wasn't until they got round to Finn's long career as a Paragon, that the Durandal began to reveal something of the real man.

'Why did you stay a Paragon so long?' said Angelo, carefully casual. He had a strong feeling that this was the vital question, the answer that might explain much. 'It's an honourable occupation, of course, and there's good money to be made, by a sensible man. But it's not a pleasant job, and no career for the truly ambitious. So . . . why did it take you so long to turn to your true vocation?'

'I was . . . content, being a Paragon,' said Finn. 'It was a way of proving I was the best, in front of the whole Empire. And I quite enjoyed being worshipped and adored, and knowing the admiration and respect of my peers. But the rewards of the job, such as they were, began to pale as I grew older. I already had as much money as I'd ever need. And I was running out of challenges. It just wasn't . . . fun, any more. No matter how many risks I took. But now . . . being a traitor and a villain is much more fun. To set myself against the whole damned Empire, to be my own man and to hell with everyone else . . . That is what it truly means, to be the best. I should have done this years ago. It took Douglas' ingratitude to open my eyes to the true nature of things, and I shall reward him for that. By taking away everything he cares for and values, and destroying it right in front of him. Ah, Angelo; I haven't felt this alive in years!'

There was a brief knock at the door, and Angelo cursed quietly to himself as Brett Random slouched in. Random nodded to Angelo, and bowed to Finn. He really didn't like being up and about this early in the day, but in this as in so many other things of late, Brett didn't have a choice. He looked dubiously at Finn. The Durandal had demanded his presence here, but hadn't said why, which was never a good sign. Brett couldn't think of anything he'd seriously screwed up just recently, but . . . His stomach hurt so badly it was all he could do to keep from standing hunched over. He was wearing a new outfit because he'd had to burn the one he'd worn into the lair of the Spider Harps, for his own peace of mind, but he still looked a mess, not least because he'd had to sleep with the lights on, and still had a tendency to jump at sudden noises and movements. The uber-espers had disturbed him on levels he hadn't even known he had.

'You're supposed to wait outside my office until I give you permission to enter,' snapped Angelo, trying to establish a little authority on his own territory.

Brett sniffed and shrugged, and spitefully made Angelo

jump and twitch a little with his esp. Finn looked at Brett thoughtfully, and he stopped immediately.

'Where's Rose?' said Finn.

'I don't know,' said Brett. He looked vaguely round the office, as though he thought she might be hiding there somewhere. 'I thought she was with you.'

'Clearly, she is not. I told you to keep an eye on her, Brett. I'm sure I was most specific about that.'

'Oh come on, Finn!' Brett protested, with the immediate verve of a man who can sense a chopping block in the near future. 'This is the Wild Rose we're talking about! She goes where she wants to go, and I for one am not stupid enough to get in her way. Besides, I've not been well . . .'

'Don't whine, Brett. Go and find Rose, right now. And when you've located her, don't let her out of your sight again. Is that clear?'

'What if she doesn't want me around?'

'Tell her it is my will. Though feel free to hide behind something substantial while you say it. Now off you go. Hop like a bunny. Contact me when you've found her. Goodbye, Brett.'

Brett sniffed again, and then turned and left the office. Some days things wouldn't go right if you put a gun to their head.

He wandered slowly through the massive building of the Cathedral, deliberately taking his time. Finn might be his boss, but he didn't own Brett Random. Well, actually, maybe he did at that, but Brett still had a little pride left, that showed up now and again in small acts of rebellion. As long as Finn wasn't around to see them. Like pissing in the coffee maker the last time he'd been left alone in Finn's kitchen.

After a while, Brett looked around him and found he'd ended up in the great central hall of the Cathedral. He stopped dead in his tracks, impressed almost in spite of himself. The towering walls were all veined marble, soaring up to a staggeringly high ceiling covered with magnificent works of art that dated from before Lionstone's time. The huge stained-glass windows were more recent and traditional, showing the stations of the cross, populated with stylised depictions of Owen Deathstalker and his companions. Rows and rows of dark wooden pews stretched away before him, heading for the main altar of sculptured steel and glass, practically a work of art in its own right. Brett wandered slowly down the aisle, and then drifted over to one of the pews, and sat down.

He breathed deeply, enjoying the faint traces of incense on the still air, left over from a previous service. No-one else was around, and it was all very quiet and very calm. For the first time in a long time, Brett almost felt at peace. He supposed this was what home felt like, to people who knew what a home was. His stomach quietened, and his shoulders relaxed. He felt . . . safe here. Even Finn bloody Durandal wouldn't dare raise his voice in a place as calm and serene as this. Sanctity and serenity all but oozed from the pale marble walls. It was like being deep under water, far from the storms that troubled the surface.

Brett looked around him, surprised at how deeply the Cathedral's great hall affected him. People had been coming here to worship for centuries, and had left something of their peace and grace behind them. There was comfort here, and the hope of better things to come. Brett had never been particularly religious. In the con games he'd run for so long, belief was for suckers. But just lately he'd been thinking . . . bigger thoughts. Nothing like working for a genuinely evil man to make you consider questions of morality. Brett had never really thought of himself as a bad man. Until now.

You couldn't ally yourself with something like the Spider Harps, and not fear for the state of your soul.

Brett had been thinking about the mind and the soul . . . and the oversoul. He was an esper now, for better or worse, and that changed everything. He'd been feeling the presence of the oversoul more and more, like a great and glorious light shining in the depths of a dark, dark night. When he looked in that direction, which he could sense but not name, he felt awe and wonder, and something that was very like a religious experience. He also felt shit scared. It was just . . . too big, too intense, too overwhelming. He couldn't cope with it. And when faced with something that scared and threatened him, Brett did what he always did; he ran away.

'That doesn't always work, Brett,' said a calm female voice, right beside him.

Brett looked round sharply, almost jumping out of his skin, and found a statuesque brunette sitting right next to him. There was no way she could have sneaked up on him, and sat down so close she was practically on his lap, without him realising. Not with a practised paranoid like him. But there she was, large as life and twice as overpowering, decked out in black silks and darker makeup, smiling at him like she could see right to the bottom of his lousy rotten soul . . . and didn't give a damn. Brett felt very like whimpering, or fainting. He didn't run, but only because he just knew that wherever he ran, she'd already be there waiting for him.

'The oversoul, I presume?' he said finally, just to be saying something. He had to force the words past numb and quivering lips. His stomach ache was back big time.

'Of course,' said the brunette. 'We've been calling you for some time, but you wouldn't pick up the phone, so to speak. So we decided a personal visit was in order. I had business in the city today, so it fell to me. Relax, I'm not going to force any literature on you. I'm Crow Jane. I'm here to make you an offer you won't want to refuse.'

'That's usually my line,' said Brett. 'Never con a con man. I know all the lines. First rule of the game; any offer that seems too good to be true, probably is too good to be true. You don't want me. I'm not really an esper; Finn force fed me the esper drug, and now I'm just a really minor league telepath. Accent on the minor. Throw me back, Crow Jane. I'm too small a fish for you to bother with.'

'All are welcome in the oversoul,' said Crow Jane. 'There's a place and a role for everyone. That's the point. It's not a union, or an organisation. It's family. It's home.'

'I've managed quite successfully without either all my life. I look out for myself. Always have done.'

'It sounds very lonely.' Crow Jane put a hand over his. 'You don't have to be alone any more, Brett. Join with us, and you'll never be alone again.'

'It sounds awful,' Brett said stubbornly. 'I'd hate it. I'm not the joining type. I don't play well with others; never have. And I won't give up being me.'

'Why settle for anything so small, and limited? You could be you, and us as well.'

'Sounds crowded,' said Brett. 'If I joined the oversoul, I'd have to give up all my secrets, wouldn't I?'

'We don't hide anything from each other,' said Crow Jane. 'We don't need to.'

'Told you we had nothing in common. Look; I really wouldn't fit in. Trust me on this. I'm a rogue, not made to run with the pack, and I like it that way. I like knowing things that no-one else knows, and always being one step ahead. You can't make me join you, against my will; can you?'

'No,' said Crow Jane, with a sigh. 'And we wouldn't, if we could. That's the point. You'll find it very lonely, Brett, trying to live among humans when you're not human any longer. There's a closeness espers know that no-one else could hope to understand. Don't you ever feel a need for love, or companionship, for tenderness and acceptance?'

'Wouldn't know what to do with them if I had them,' Brett said briskly. 'Don't let me keep you. I'm sure you have much more useful business you could be about.'

Crow Jane patted his hand once, sadly, and then rose to her feet. 'Watch out for the ELFs, Brett. They'd eat you alive. You've seen the Spider Harps; trust me, that's only the tip of the iceberg where the ELFs are concerned. They live to hate and kill. That's all they have, and all they are.'

'I could . . . give you the location of the Spider Harps,' Brett said slowly.

'We know where they are,' said Crow Jane. 'We've always known.'

Brett gaped at her. 'Then why don't you do something about them?'

Crow Jane smiled coldly. 'What punishment could we offer, that could be worse than the hell they've made for themselves?'

'But . . . they're killing people! Killing and eating them . . .'

'What do you care? I thought you were a rogue, that walked alone?'

Brett met her gaze steadily. 'I'm a rogue, not a monster. I know the difference between crime and sin. I know evil when I see it. I'd kill them in a moment; if I thought I could get away with it.'

'And we would kill them in a moment, if we thought we could,' said Crow Jane. 'But the Mater Mundi made them too well. Even the oversoul has its limitations. Their time will come. Stay away from the ELFs, Brett. They're all monsters, inside.'

Brett snorted loudly, trying to project an assurance he didn't actually feel. 'What part of *rogue* didn't you understand? I'm not interested in joining anyone's party.'

'It's a bad time to be standing alone, Brett.'

It was his turn to sigh. 'Tell me about it.'

And then she was gone, air rushing in to fill the space where she'd been. Brett leaned back in his pew, and wiped sweat from his forehead with the back of his hand. The oversoul was possibly the only thing that frightened him more than Finn Durandal. And at least Finn was content to let Brett be himself . . . even if Brett wasn't sure he liked that person very much any more . . . And why had his stomach stopped aching, all the time Crow Jane was with him? He decided he'd think about that later. Right now, he had his orders. Find Rose bloody Constantine. He'd already tried her chamber under the Arena, and she wasn't there. And if she wasn't there, she could be anywhere. He was a bit lost as to where to start looking first. It wasn't as if she had any friends to go to, or even any outside interests . . . he could start by monitoring the peacekeeper comm channels; listen out for reports of mass carnage or excessive property destruction. Rose wasn't the kind to hide her appalling light under a bushel for long.

Brett sighed loudly, and got to his feet. He looked wistfully around him, savouring the peace and calm, and then he turned and walked steadily away from it.

Lewis Deathstalker stood outside the door to Anne Barclay's

office, trying to work up the courage to announce himself. He wasn't comfortable being back in the House that had pretty much disowned him, but he didn't know where else to go. And now he was here, he still didn't know what to do. He looked at the implacably closed door before him, and it scared him. Anne was his oldest friend. He'd always been able to turn to her, for advice and help and comfort, but . . . he wasn't sure he was welcome here any more. So much had changed between them, in so short a time; almost against his will, they had both become different people. *I know where you've been,* she had said. *I can smell her on you.* Lewis looked up at the surveillance camera, set just above the doorframe. The little red light was on, so he knew it was watching him. Knew she was watching him.

'I need to talk to you, Anne,' he said steadily. 'There are . . . decisions I have to make. I can't do it on my own. Can I come in?'

There was no response. He tried the door handle, but it wouldn't budge. She'd locked him out. Turned her back on him.

'Anne, *please.* We have to talk. This is important. I don't . . . know what to do. You've spent most of your life telling me what I should be doing. Don't let me down now.'

He tried a smile, right into the camera lens, but it didn't feel very successful. He called her name again, but there was only the locked door and the watching eye of the camera. People passing by in the narrow corridor looked at him oddly. He ignored them. A slow hot anger began to build in his heart. He hit the door with his fist, and kicked it, and the door shuddered in its frame, but still it didn't open. So Lewis drew his disrupter and shot the lock out. The energy beam vapourised the lock and blew the whole door inwards, tearing the door right off its hinges. The door hit the floor of the office and skidded on, the solid metal crumpled and steaming. Even at its lowest setting, the energy beam had still plunged on across the office to blow up one of the security monitors on the far wall. It had burst into flames, and thick black smoke billowed across Anne's office. A fire alarm activated, and the piercing sound of the siren seemed very loud in the quiet.

Lewis walked slowly forward into Anne's office, through the gap where the door had been. He kicked the buckled door to one side, and advanced steadily on Anne, who was spraying the burning monitor with chemical foam, cursing furiously all the while. Lewis stopped in the centre of the office, and watched her do it. His ugly face was set and stern, and his eyes were very cold. Out in the corridors behind him, he could hear people shouting and running. The fire reluctantly subsided under half a ton of chemical foam, though smoke still drifted heavily on the air. Anne lowered the fire extinguisher, breathing heavily, and spun round to glare at Lewis.

'Knock knock,' he said calmly.

'Have you gone crazy, Deathstalker? Have you finally lost it? So help me, if that fire had set off the sprinklers and soaked all my papers, I'd have gutted you with the nearest letter opener! Look what you've done to my office!'

'Guess whether I give a damn,' said Lewis, and something in his flat, cold voice gave Anne pause. In all their years, he'd never spoken to her like that before.

Lewis heard running feet approaching, and he turned unhurriedly to look out into the corridor. A dozen security men were charging towards Anne's office, all of them armed with swords and guns, though they hadn't drawn them yet. They saw Lewis looking out at them, and skidded to a halt before him. They took in the gap where the door had been, looked past Lewis at the damaged office, and at the fuming Anne, and then they took a good look at Lewis. At his face, and his eyes, and the gun still in his hand, though it wasn't pointing at anyone in particular just yet. Several of the security guards started to back away. Their leader stood his ground, though his mouth had gone very dry. There was danger in the air, they could all feel it; real and imminent. The security leader swallowed hard. He took his job very seriously, but no-one was paying him enough to take on the Deathstalker.

'Is . . . everything all right here? Sir Champion?'

Lewis looked at him for a long moment, his eyes cold and terribly thoughtful. 'Nice reaction time,' he said finally. 'But you're not needed here. You can go now. Isn't that right, Anne?'

Anne moved forward, keeping a cautious distance between herself and the man who had once been her closest friend. There was something about Lewis; something in the calm, steady stance, and the dark, dangerous eyes, and the gun he still hadn't put away or even lowered . . . She suddenly thought that he looked like a man who'd been pushed that little bit too far. Who didn't care about anything any more, because everything that mattered to him had already been taken away. And since this was Lewis Deathstalker . . . that made him very dangerous indeed. She looked from him to the security people and back again, and Lewis smiled slowly. It didn't touch his eyes, and when he spoke again, his voice was colder and uglier than his face could ever be.

'What are you going to do, Anne? Swear out a complaint against me? Tell the guards to arrest me? Perhaps you think I'll go quietly . . . I wouldn't put money on it. I really wouldn't. I'm going to talk to you; one way or the other. Send these guards away, Anne. Old friend. Before I have to do something that I might or might not regret later.'

Two of the security men turned and ran, and the others looked like they wanted to. They were all seconds away from actions that could never be taken back, or made up for later, and everyone there knew it. Lewis' smile widened. Anne stepped quickly forward, to put herself between Lewis and the security guards.

'It's all right,' she said quickly to the security leader. 'Everything's fine. It's all just a misunderstanding. There's nothing here for you to worry about. The Deathstalker and I will . . . clear things up. You can return to your stations. Very good reaction time. I'll see you all get commendations. You can go now. Oh, and send someone to fix my door, would you? Thank you very much.'

The security men looked at each other, shrugged pretty much in unison, and ostentatiously took their hands away from their weapons belts. They knew they weren't getting the whole story, and probably never would, but they all had enough experience and common sense to let it go. Some things you were better off not knowing; especially when it involved the real movers and shakers of the Empire. To his credit, the security leader hesitated, looking at Anne, but she shook her head firmly, and he rounded up his people and led them off. It was going to be one of those days, he could tell. Though any day you ended up not having to go head to head with the Deathstalker after all was a good day, by definition.

Lewis watched them go, waiting till they'd all rounded the far corner before finally holstering his disrupter. He was almost sure he wouldn't have used it. Almost. Anne relaxed a little, and put down the heavy fire extinguisher. Lewis turned around and considered the buckled steel door lying on the floor. He picked it up, his muscles only straining a little, and leaned it against the doorjamb so that it more or less filled the gap again. He looked around him, picked up his usual chair that had somehow got overturned in the excitement, set it down facing Anne, and sat on it.

'So; how's life treating you, Anne? Any chance of a cup of coffee? I could use a good cup of coffee.'

Anne moved slowly over to the coffee maker, steaming quietly away in its corner as always. 'I suppose you want some chocolate biscuits, too?'

'If it wouldn't be too much trouble.'

Anne scowled at him as she poured coffee into a mug. 'Look what you've done to my door . . . why didn't you just use your Paragon's skeleton key, you idiot? I know very well you never got around to turning it in. This is why Paragons were given the bloody things, so you wouldn't have to make a mess like this.'

'Ah,' said Lewis, accepting the steaming cup she thrust ungraciously at him. 'It didn't occur to me. I've had a lot on my mind just recently. I haven't always been thinking too clearly.'

Anne snorted loudly, and dropped into her own chair, facing him. 'Trust me, Lewis; I've noticed.'

And then they just sat there and looked at each other for a long time, almost like two strangers sizing each other up. The last of the drifting smoke disappeared as the extractor fans got to work on it, but it seemed to Anne that there was still something in the office with them. Unspoken words, perhaps. Decisions made, that could never be apologised for, or put right. There was a distance between them, a subtle tension that had never been there before. Even sat still, sipping at his coffee, the Deathstalker looked dangerous. For the first time in her life, Anne realised that she didn't feel entirely safe in Lewis' presence.

'Oh God, Lewis,' she said finally. 'How have we come to this? What has Jes done to you? You used to have more sense . . .'

'I just wanted to be happy, for once.'

'And to hell with what it cost everyone else?'

'Love's a bitch sometimes,' said Lewis.

'I wouldn't know,' said Anne.

Another long pause, as both of them searched for the words that would make sense of what had happened to them. Words to bridge a widening gap, that was leading them both into different worlds. Words they could shout across the gap, like lifelines thrown from ships sailing in different directions.

'None of this was my choice,' said Lewis. 'I'd lived so long without love, I thought I could live without it forever, if I had to. I had other things to give my life purpose, and meaning. I had duty, and honour. I had friends, good friends . . . friends I would have died for. I had work that mattered, and my life made a difference. I was happy; mostly. And then love comes along, right out of the blue, and I realised I'd never really known what happiness was. Only problem; I had to give up everything else that mattered to me to have it. Don't blame Jes for any of this. We were just . . . two people who should never have met, for everyone's sake but our own. We tried so hard to stay away from each other, Anne; to do the right thing, and to hell with what it cost us. But the universe seemed almost to conspire to push us together.'

'Oh sure,' said Anne. 'It's not your fault. It never is. The universe just pushed you right into bed.'

Lewis scowled at her. 'Don't try to make this out to be nothing but sex, Anne. I'm old enough to know the difference between my heart and my dick. I love her, and she loves me. And yes; we slept together. And it was wonderful.'

'Good enough to sell your soul for? You're not telling me anything I don't already know, Lewis. And if I know, it won't be long before others know too. You can't keep a thing like this secret. Jes . . . isn't worth all this, Lewis. I've seen it all before, with other men. I've known her a lot longer than you have.'

'This time it's different!'

'That's what they all say! You think you're the first man to come crying to me over Jes? I have been here before, and it always ends in tears.'

'I thought she was your friend.'

'She is. That's why I don't have any illusions about her. Though this time . . . I thought she'd have more sense. I thought you had more integrity! Don't come looking to me for forgiveness, or support. Don't expect me to pat you on the shoulder and say *Hey, these things happen*. This is treason we're talking about, Lewis! When this gets out, and you can bet your last credit it will, almost certainly sooner rather than later, it could destroy the Throne and the House and everything else we've spent our lives supporting and believing in!'

'I know. But soon . . . it will all be over. She's going to marry Douglas, and I'm going off on the great Quest. And everyone will live happily ever after. Eventually.'

Anne looked at him sharply. 'There was something in your voice, just then . . . when you talked about the Quest. Don't you even believe in that any more?'

Lewis hesitated, and looked away, unable to meet her eyes. He couldn't tell her Owen was dead. She wouldn't be able to keep it to herself. She'd feel duty bound to tell . . . someone, and once the word started spreading it would never stop. It would be all over the media . . . Lewis couldn't be responsible for that. It would be cruel to take away Humanity's last hope, in the face of the coming Terror. He looked back at Anne, trying to frame some comforting lie, but her eyes bored into his, and the words turned to ashes in his mouth.

'The AIs told you something, didn't they?' Anne said suddenly. 'What is it? What could be so bad, that you don't want to tell me? What do they know, that they've kept from us?'

And still he couldn't tell her the truth, so he told her a partial truth instead.

'They showed me records . . . from the days of the Rebellion,' he said quietly. 'Showed me Owen and Hazel and the others, the people rather than the legends. It was . . . disconcerting, to see them as only human, rather than myths in the flesh. They were glorious, magnificent; great fighters. But they didn't look like miracle workers. Maybe humans, even those who've passed through the Madness Maze, won't be enough to stop something like the Terror. It might not be wise, to pin all our hopes on them, even if we can find them.'

'But . . . they had powers! They did . . . amazing things!'

'Did they? Or is that just part of the legend? The stories Robert and Constance made up, to inspire us? Shub told me many things, but in the end . . . what I saw was just a man called Owen. A great man, certainly. But whatever my ancestor was, he wasn't the god we've been sold for the past two hundred years.'

Anne frowned. 'Maybe not. It doesn't matter. Your ancestor and his friends worked a miracle once, when they overthrew Lionstone and her evil Empire, and laid the foundations for our Golden Age. Maybe they can do it again. They could still be alive, out there, somewhere. The Quest is necessary, Lewis. We need to find Owen, if only to inspire us again. Tell me; if it turned out that you were the one to find the blessed Owen . . . what would you say to him?'

Lewis sighed. He'd tried to hint at the truth, but she didn't want to hear it. He considered her question honestly, surprised to find that the answer mattered to him, as well as to her.

'I think I'd ask him . . . where he found the strength, to make so many hard decisions. And perhaps . . . I'd ask him to come back and be *the* Deathstalker, so I wouldn't have to be, any more. Selfish, I know. But sometimes, this name weighs so damned much . . . People expect so much of me, because of it. And just like Owen, I'm not allowed to be only human, with human needs and weaknesses . . .'

He rose abruptly from his chair and slammed the coffee mug down on Anne's desk, slopping hot coffee everywhere. He paced around the office, not looking at Anne, circling the confined space over and over again like a caged animal, while

Anne watched him warily from her chair. He was scowling now, his eyes far away; his ugly face flushed with anger and frustration and something that might just have been despair. Barely suppressed violence showed in the bulging muscles of his arms, in the set of his shoulders, and the heavy tread of his feet. It frightened Anne to see Lewis like this; a strong man reduced to baffled indecision. He walked faster and faster, his hands knotted into fists so tight his knuckles showed white. Sooner or later he was going to lash out, and the only question was who was going to get hurt. Apart from himself.

'I don't know what to do, Anne!' His voice was harsh and ugly now, and she flinched at the sound of it. Lewis didn't notice. 'All the things I believed in seem to have been built on sand, and the tide is washing it all away. No-one's who I thought they were; not even me. Everywhere I look, my world is falling apart. The people have gone insane, all our great institutions have feet of clay, and the Terror is finally here and headed right down our throats. I finally find love, after so many years alone, and I have to walk away from it. Because just like my bloody ancestor, I'm not allowed to think about my own life, my own wants and needs and desires. I'm a Paragon and a Deathstalker, so I have to be better than that. I have . . . I have to . . .'

He burst into tears, sudden harsh sounds that shook his whole body as the tears ran jerkily down his ugly face. He stopped pacing, and lashed out at the nearest wall with his fist. He hit the wall again and again, putting all his strength and desperation into every blow, bloodying his knuckles. Anne's hands went to her mouth as she clearly heard bones crack and break. Blood ran down the wall as Lewis' fist crashed into it again and again, and all the time he was crying like his heart would break. Anne rose slowly up out of her chair, walked up behind him, and hesitantly put one hand on his shoulder. He rounded on her, breathing hard, his face working violently, and then he hugged her to him, clinging to her like a child. She rocked him gently as he wept, murmuring soothing words as he buried his face in her neck. They held each other tightly, the way they used to back when they were children, and the whole world had seemed to be against them.

417

Finally Lewis ran out of tears, nothing left in him but a terrible, empty tiredness.

And in the end, he was the one who let go first. Who straightened up, and gently pushed Anne away. He'd always been the one who'd been able to do the hard, harsh, necessary things. Anne stepped back, studying him with thoughtful eyes. Lewis found a clean handkerchief and dried his eyes. His hands were entirely steady. He looked at his bloody, broken hand, winced as the pain hit him for the first time, and awkwardly wrapped the handkerchief around it. Anne watched him do it, and felt a slow cold pain in her breast, where her heart would have been if she'd believed in sentimental things like hearts, and before she could stop herself the words came rushing out.

'Lewis; maybe . . . maybe we could run away. You and me, together. Forget all this. Just . . . jump a ship, any ship, heading anywhere, and leave all this behind us. To hell with it all, to hell with everyone but us. Neither of us like who and what we've become, since we came here. To this world, this city, these lives. It's not too late! We could still . . .'

'No,' Lewis said quietly. 'No, we couldn't. Not and still have any respect for each other, or ourselves. I can't just walk away. I still have my responsibilities, my duty and my honour. Tarnished a bit, perhaps, but they're the only things left in my life that still make sense. I couldn't give them up, and still be me. I've lost so much, and I'll have to give up even more; but I still know what it means, to be a Deathstalker.'

'Duty and responsibility,' Anne said harshly. 'I am so tired of those words. We gave our lives to them, but what did they ever do for us? Did they make us content? Did they make us happy?'

'Could we ever be happy, somewhere else, knowing we'd turned our backs on the only things we'd ever really believed in? No, Anne; sometimes . . . you just have to suck it in, and play the cards you're dealt. Because to do anything else, would be to betray ourselves. To make our lives a lie.'

'This is your last chance, Lewis,' said Anne. Her eyes were pleading, but her voice was very cold.

'I know,' said Lewis. 'Trust me, I know.' He stepped forward, and kissed her tenderly on the forehead. 'But sometimes the only honourable thing left to do, is to take your hand away from the lifeboat, and drown. Goodbye, Anne. I don't think we'll be meeting again. First, I've got to get this hand fixed, and then I've got a lot of work to do, planning the logistics for the Quest. I won't be at the Wedding. And I don't think . . . I'll be coming back. Let Douglas and Jesamine have their life together, without a spectre at the feast to spoil it.' He smiled finally, sadly. 'Who knows; maybe I'll find an answer to all my woes somewhere out there, on the Quest. There sure as hell isn't one here.'

He left her office then, not looking back, ducking past the door leaning precariously in the doorway. Anne watched him go in silence, refusing to cry so much as a single tear, and finally she turned away. There was work to be done, and calls to be made.

Douglas Campbell, King and Speaker to the Empire, did what he always did when he was lost and confused and needed to find his way again. He went home. All the way home, back to the old manor house in the country, where he'd been raised as a child. Far away from the city, far away from anywhere, House Campbell stood alone in its extensive grounds and gardens, home and sanctuary to generations of Campbells down the many centuries.

Douglas' father William had retired there after he gave up the Crown, to potter around his gardens and play at being the historian he'd always fancied himself. He'd seemed happy enough to hear his son was coming to visit. Douglas hadn't told him why he was coming. Truth be told, he wasn't entirely sure. Mostly he just needed to get away from all the noise, from all the decisions he had to make, from all the people so desperate to get his attention. Douglas wanted somewhere he could escape from the pressures for a while, somewhere he could think in peace.

Home.

He piloted the flyer himself, taking neither an official pilot or a bodyguard. Just him and the flyer, alone in the sky. His many confidants and advisors, Anne most definitely among them, had blown their collective stack when he informed them bluntly of his intentions, but he refused to be browbeaten into changing his mind and doing the sensible thing. He'd been a Paragon a hell of a lot longer than he'd been King, and he was quite capable of looking after himself for a while. Besides; the flyer had its own guns and force shields, and so many computers it practically flew itself.

It took Douglas over an hour to reach the old manor house, even flying at top speed in an air lane reserved exclusively for him. Douglas didn't mind. It gave him time to relax properly, and he enjoyed looking down at the passing scenery. Logres was still a bright and glorious world, away from the sprawling cities, full of beautiful vistas and grand rolling views. It occurred to him that this was the real Logres, the real homeworld of Empire; not the overcrowded warrens of the cities. Which were indeed packed full of marvels and wonders and sights to please the eye and astound the heart; but sometimes you could have too much of a good thing.

Douglas landed easily on the private landing pad at the boundary of the family property, and after he'd powered down the systems and disembarked, he spent some time just standing on the edge of the pad and looking out over the expertly landscaped grounds stretching away before him. It seemed to him that the gardens had never looked so beautiful. (He tried not to see the armed and armoured guards silently patrolling the perimeter. He knew they were necessary; even though William was no longer King, he was still a target for all kinds of hate groups. The ELFs, the Shadow Court, and many other terrorists and scumbags would just love to get their hands on William, for ransom or revenge, or just to put pressure on the current King. So the guards were necessary. Douglas knew that. But still they detracted from his happy childhood memories of his old home, so he did his best to ignore them.)

The gardens were breathtaking at this time of the year, blooming even though it was midwinter everywhere else, thanks to some clever programming of the weather control satellites. Rank, even retired rank, had its privileges. The great green lawns, expertly cropped and shaped, stretched away before him for miles, immaculately laid out. There were low hedges and peaceful walkways lined with rows of trees, and marvellous flowerbeds blazing with colours, like so many rainbows fallen to the earth; all planned and maintained with almost ruthless geometric precision. The flowers came from dozens of worlds, nurtured and protected by a whole cadre of specially trained technicians, for whom *gardener* was really too limiting a word.

The trees had come from worlds all across the Empire, carefully transplanted and preserved. Some no longer existed outside these gardens. There were artificial lakes brimming with all kinds of decorative life, tumbling streams crossed by delicately carved wooden bridges, and not far from the centre of the garden there was a great hedge maze of cunning design. Douglas got lost in it once, when he was a small child. He'd been forbidden to enter it on his own, so of course he did. He was that kind of child. Eventually his increasingly tearful cries led his family to him. He still had nightmares about the maze, sometimes, though he never told anyone that. Whenever he came home, he always made it a point to walk through the maze from end to end, in and out, just to prove to himself that it no longer had any control over him. Except of course if it hadn't, he wouldn't have needed to do it every damned visit. Douglas was smart enough to know that, but he did it anyway. Because.

(He sometimes wondered if this was why he had such ambivalent feelings about the Madness Maze. He hoped not. He'd hate to think his subconscious was that petty. And, indeed, that obvious.)

He left the landing pad behind him, and walked off into the gardens, following the neat gravel paths when he felt like it, and wandering defiantly across the open lawns when he didn't. There was no-one to tell him not to any more. He was the King. The sky was a clear, clear blue with hardly a cloud in sight, and the air was full of the scent of blooming flowers and freshly-cut grass, of rich wet turf and growing things. Such a peaceful place, whose only movement was the slow turning of the seasons that even the weather control could only soothe, not interfere with. Birds sang and insects buzzed, and somewhere off in the distance Douglas could hear the slow, mournful cries of the peacocks, calling to each other. He walked on, taking his time, strolled down a shadowy tunnel of inward-leaning trees, and was suddenly struck by a nostalgia so overwhelming it was almost painful. He knew every inch of these gardens. When he'd been a child, they'd been his whole world. He hadn't known there was another, harsher world outside it, and wouldn't have cared if he had.

His parents had kept his duty and his destiny from him for as long as they could. They wanted him to enjoy his childhood.

He crossed an old stone bridge, so artfully constructed it didn't need mortar to hold the stones together. A fast-moving stream bubbled and burbled beneath him, stocked with every kind of fish a fisherman might desire. (Unless you wanted one of the big bastards, the kind that fight back, in which case there was an ocean only half an hour or so away.) There were animals in the garden too, but they were there to be petted and enjoyed, not chased or hunted. The gardens were a place of peace, of contemplation. Everything in its place, so nothing ever changed. The gardens had been carefully planned so that the seams were never visible, designed and laid out centuries ago, long before even Lionstone's time; by a master landscaper who knew he'd never live long enough to see it all come into its final glory. The Campbell who'd ordered the garden had known the same thing, but hadn't cared. It was for his Family. The Campbells took the long view, in those days. When they thought Clan Campbell was forever, and nothing would ever change . . .

And now the old Empire was thrown down, the old ways had been put aside . . . but the gardens still flourished. Clan Campbell was not what it had once been, but that was probably a good thing. Douglas walked through the ancient gardens, and thought dark thoughts about the impermanence of man and his plans. Man could disappear tomorrow, and the gardens would survive quite happily without him. Though of course there'd be no-one to grieve as the gardens went slowly to the wild, and lost their artificially-maintained beauty.

Finally he came to the very centre of the gardens (ignoring the hedge maze for now) and there was his brother James's grave. It was a simple affair; just a basic stone with James's name on it, to mark his final resting place, topped with a flame that always burned and always would. Brother James. The man who should have been King. One brother stood and looked down at another, and envied him his peaceful sleep; while off to one side their father looked on, waiting as requested. When James died his sudden, stupid and entirely unexpected death, public sentiment and the media had called loudly for him to be laid to rest in the old Campbell mausoleum, along with generations of the Campbell dead, right in the heart of the Parade of the Endless. Some even called for James to have a special place in the Cathedral. But William and Niamh said no. He was their son, so they brought him home, so he could sleep in a familiar place.

Douglas looked about him. It was a nice location, calm and peaceful, on the side of a gently sloping hill looking out over the placid waters of an artificial lake. For a while visitors were allowed, as long as they made a donation to charity, but eventually William and Niamh put a stop to that, when the visiting crowds threatened to turn his grave into a shrine. The ever-burning flame was enough. He was their son. He belonged to them, and no-one else. Niamh was buried there now, sleeping beside her son, as she'd wanted. When the time came William would join them, and Douglas thought that perhaps he would like to rest here as well. He'd seen the old Clan Campbell mausoleum, where Crawford and Finlay and all the other great names of the Family had been interred, and the grim cold sepulchre had struck Douglas as a cold and joyless place to spend eternity. Robert and Constance had changed that tradition, as they'd changed so many others. They'd left strict instructions for their bodies to be cremated, and the ashes scattered over the gardens. They might have turned people they'd known into legends, but they had no wish to be revered or venerated themselves. Douglas liked to think that a few last particles of his grandfather and grandmother were still blowing about the gardens. When he was younger, he'd run around taking great deep breaths, hoping to breathe some of them in, so that he would be great too.

(William and Niamh had explained duty and destiny to

him by then, and he'd understood just enough to feel distinctly scared and unworthy.)

'Are you going to stand there brooding all day, son?' William said dryly. 'I was under the impression you'd come all this way to talk to me. The word *urgent* was used quite a lot, as I recall.'

'Sorry, Dad,' said Douglas. 'I've had a lot on my mind just recently.'

William snorted. 'I can imagine. Which of your many appalling problems brings you home this time?'

Douglas looked at his father. The old man actually looked better for having retired. Not nearly so fragile, he was standing straighter, and his eyes seemed sharp and alert. He was wearing old comfortable clothes, crumpled and grubby, of the kind Niamh would never have let him get away with.

'You tried to warn me, about being King,' Douglas said heavily. 'And as usual, I didn't listen. I don't feel up to the job, Father.'

'No-one ever does,' William said gruffly. 'I spent most of my reign convinced that any day now the House would wake up and realise I wasn't anything like the King my father was, and would demand I give up my Crown so they could give it to someone better qualified. You're doing well enough, son. I keep up with the news. The Neumen riot was a mess, but you did well to take out so many ELFs at the Parade of the Paragons.' He paused, and fixed Douglas with a stern gaze. 'Though I have to say, I'm still wondering just what you had to promise the oversoul, in return for their help in suppressing the Neumen rioters. The espers never do anything for free.'

'They didn't ask for anything specific,' said Douglas. 'Just asked for my . . . good will. I allowed them to be involved in taking down the ELFs at the Parade. Whether that'll be enough, we'll just have to wait and see . . . Dad; we need to talk about the Terror.'

William sighed and turned away, and looked out over the gardens. 'It's very peaceful here. Far away from all the troubles of the world. I'm glad you're King now, Douglas, and not me. I wouldn't know what to do. Probably just sit on my Throne and dither, hoping someone else would come up with a plan.

Whatever you decide to do, it's bound to be better than anything I could suggest.' He turned back to face Douglas. 'You have to have faith in your judgement. I do. I raised you to be a warrior, boy, and you have never disappointed me. You're doing a good job, Douglas. You are every inch the King your mother and I always hoped you'd be.'

Douglas was touched. He put out his hands to his father, and William held them tightly. And after that, Douglas couldn't bring himself to discuss his other problem, with Jesamine and Lewis. The real reason he'd come all this way. It would have seemed so . . . petty. So Douglas walked with his father through the gardens, talking of other things, and later they had a good dinner together. When evening finally fell, Douglas gave his father a hug and then flew back to the city, and his Throne. Leaving peace and contentment behind, to take up the burden of his duty once again. Because every child has to leave home eventually, to become a man.

Lewis Deathstalker was working in his apartment when the call came. An anonymous functionary called for Lewis to appear urgently at the House, and then signed off before he could be questioned. Lewis' first thought was *Why now?* Invitations to appear at Parliament had been conspicuous by their absence for some time now. The King had made it very clear he didn't need or want his Champion at his side any more. And, this was a very inopportune moment to be called away. Lewis was sitting on the floor of his apartment, surrounded by paperwork, hunched over his computer screen and stabbing at the keyboard with two fingers. There was a lot of work to be done, preparing for the grand Quest of the Paragons, and somehow most of it had fallen to Lewis. The Paragons themselves had done nothing but argue about who was going where, ever since the Quest was announced, and someone had to sort out the mess without hurting too many feelings, and coordinate the various missions so that they wouldn't end up stumbling over each other.

It helped that Lewis had been a Paragon, and knew most of them personally. He also knew where a lot of the bodies were buried; sometimes literally. No-one argued with Lewis.

Lewis had also contacted the AIs of Shub through their Embassy, and had them search through all their records, over where best to look for Owen. Or the others. After all; Owen might not be dead. Just because some mysterious voice had said Owen was dead, and Captain Silence had seemed inclined to believe it, didn't necessarily make it so. Lewis clung to that thought, with varying degrees of comfort. There had never been any shortage of sightings of Owen or Hazel or any of the other great legends, all across the Empire. Saint Beatrice in particular seemed to pop up all over the place, in every city on every planet, doing everything from healing the sick to shopping in a supermarket. People were always finding the likeness of her face in unlikely places. It was a lot of work, sorting out the few promising rumours from the more obvious cases of wishful thinking, while simultaneously trying to sort out which Paragons would go to which worlds, and in what order, but Lewis ended up quite enjoying it. The work kept him busy and kept him from brooding, and gave him a feeling of worth again. And for the first time in a long time he felt accepted by the Paragons again, as one of them. That made up for a lot.

And as long as he kept himself busy, he didn't think about Jesamine for sometimes hours at a time. Sometimes.

Still, when Parliament called, you answered. Even if it was bloody inconvenient. Lewis carefully saved his most recent work on the computer, pushed his notes together into more or less tidy piles, and clambered painfully to his feet. He stretched slowly, wincing as he heard bones click loudly. He really ought to get around to buying a desk and a chair, at least. Before his back gave out. He pulled on his official Champion's black leather armour, scowling furiously all the while, strapped on his weapons belt, looked around the room vaguely a few times, convinced as always that he'd forgotten something important, and then left his apartment. He scowled as he trudged up the stairs to the roof, and his waiting gravity sled. Whatever Parliament wanted, it must be pretty important for them to recall him so urgently. Perhaps there was some new information on the Terror? The thought chilled his heart, and he ran up the last few steps and out

426

onto the roof. He pushed his gravity sled as fast as it would go, all the way to the House. He tried to call in, but no-one was answering. He was getting a really bad feeling about this.

He should have known. He really should have known. Deathstalker luck. Always bad.

Once at the House he hurried through the narrow corridors, intending to stop people as they passed, to get some idea of what was up. But the back corridors were unusually deserted, and the few people he encountered were apparently far too busy to stop and talk. At least they weren't crying this time . . . He wondered whether he should make the time to stop off at Anne's office and talk with her, but considering how his last visit had turned out, he decided against it. His hand still twinged sometimes. So he increased his pace, striding furiously through the corridors, his head full of all the things that might have gone wrong, and what he might have to do to put them right, until finally he came to the House itself. Two armed and fully armoured guards stood before the great double doors. They pushed the doors open, and gestured for him to go right in. He hurried past them, and out onto the floor of the House; and the first thought that struck him was how quiet everything was.

He slowed to a halt in the middle of the floor, and looked about him. Everyone was looking at him, and not kindly. From the MPs filling the Seats, to the AI and esper and clone representatives, to the aliens filling their Section, to King Douglas sitting stiffly on his Throne; Lewis couldn't see a friendly face anywhere. Jesamine was standing beside the Throne. She wouldn't look at him at all. Her gaze was fixed on the floor at her feet. Lewis' bad feeling grew suddenly worse.

There was a sudden crash of booted feet behind him, and Lewis looked round sharply as a small army of guards and security men filed quickly through the double doors, to take up positions around the House. They all had energy guns. Many of them were drawn, and pointing at him. The double doors closed, and very clearly on the ominous quiet came the sound of locks closing. And Lewis began to realise just how much trouble he was in.

'Drop your weapons, Deathstalker,' said the King, from his Throne. His voice was cold and flat and strangely empty, but his eyes were burning. 'Do it, now; or I'll have my people disarm you. By force, if necessary.'

'Douglas?' said Lewis. 'What's going on?'

'You will address me as Your Majesty,' said the King. 'Drop your weapons. I won't tell you again.'

Lewis moved his hands slowly and carefully to his weapons belt, and undid the buckle. He lowered the gun and sword to the floor, straightened up and stepped slowly back from them, keeping his hands in clear sight all the while.

'And the rest,' said the King.

Lewis removed the throwing knives from his boots and up his sleeves, and dropped them to the floor. The clatter seemed very loud in the continuing hush. He had a few more, non-regulation weapons about him too, and he gave them up too, because the King would know about them. Of course he would know; Douglas and Lewis had been partners. The last thing to hit the floor was the force shield from his wrist. Lewis stood before the House, defenceless.

'Now will you tell me what's going on; Your Majesty?'

'The charge is treason,' said Finn Durandal. He strode out from among the security men, and stepped down onto the floor of the House. He stopped carefully out of Lewis' reach, and looked coldly at him. When he spoke again, his voice was full of authority, and contempt. 'Lewis Deathstalker; you have betrayed your King with the woman who was to be his Queen. You have thrown aside duty and honour, in order to satisfy your own base lusts. You are not fit to be Imperial Champion. You are hereby stripped of that office, on the authority of the King and this House. You are now under arrest. You will be taken from this place to a secure location, where you will be held under guard until you can be tried for treason.'

'You have evidence,' said Lewis, trying hard to sound calm, though his chest was so tight he could hardly breathe. 'You must have, or this wouldn't be happening. Where did you get that evidence, I wonder?'

'You'll find out, at your trial,' said Finn.

But Lewis had already looked past Finn to see Anne Barclay, standing among her security men. She'd stepped forward deliberately, to draw his gaze. She looked at him coldly, and Lewis knew immediately where Finn had got his evidence.

'Oh Anne; how could you?'

She met his gaze steadily, but said nothing. And Lewis remembered her begging him to run away with her. Remembered her saying *This is your last chance, Lewis* . . . And he remembered her clinging to him, and wondered how he could have been so blind, and so stupid.

'She did her duty,' said Finn. 'She came to me, and I didn't believe her at first. I couldn't believe you of all people would do such a thing. But Anne had incontrovertible proof. After that, it wasn't hard for her people and mine to turn up more. You went to great pains to cover your tracks, but people always talk. Then, we went to the King. He didn't want to believe it either, but once he'd seen our proof, not even his friendship could protect you from the consequences of your treachery.' Finn shook his head sadly. 'How could you, Lewis? He was your friend and your partner, as well as your King.'

'Save me the sanctimony,' said Lewis. 'It doesn't suit you, Finn. You keep saying you have proof. What proof?'

Finn sighed heavily, regretfully, and gestured imperiously. A viewscreen appeared, floating on the air before the House. And on the screen, there were Lewis and Jesamine, in each other's arms, kissing with a white hot passion. There was no way it could be seen to be anything other than what it was; a man and a woman in love, and in heat. Lewis recognised the scene immediately. He recognised the corridor. He was looking at a recording from the camera set over Anne's office door. The screen went blank, and disappeared, and a low angry murmur passed through the watching MPs. Lewis looked at the King, sitting so stiffly on his Throne.

'Oh God, Douglas, I'm so sorry . . .'

'Save your admissions of guilt for your trial, Deathstalker,' said Finn. 'Though of course, you have so much to feel guilty about. Our investigators turned up evidence of other crimes, other treasons, against the King and the Empire. With the House's authority, we broke into your computer, and studied your hidden files. We found all kinds of interesting data there; including direct evidence that you planned quite cold bloodedly from the beginning to use Jesamine's wealth to pay off your extensive debts. Did she know that, Lewis? Did she know that you were using her?'

'That's not true!' Lewis said hotly. He started towards Finn, his hands clenched into fists, only to stop short as every guard and security man took aim with their energy guns. Lewis snarled at them soundlessly, and then spun round to look at Jesamine, standing beside the Throne. 'Jes; you know that isn't true!'

But still she wouldn't look at him, or respond to him in any way.

Finn allowed himself a small smile. He knew it wasn't true. He'd paid the estimable Mr Sylvester a lot of money to plant the carefully tainted information in Lewis' files before he authorised his people to break into Lewis' computer. He watched interestedly as Lewis looked slowly round the House, and saw only condemnation everywhere. Lewis' gaze finally came to a halt on Anne.

'How could you, Anne? We've been friends for so long . . .'

'I don't know you any more, Lewis,' Anne said flatly. 'And perhaps . . . you never did know me.'

'I trusted you,' Douglas said suddenly, and every eye turned to look at him. He looked tired, beaten down, almost broken. He looked at Lewis as though the man before him was a stranger. 'My friend, my partner, my Champion. Was I so wrong about you, all these years? Was our friendship ever anything more than a lie? Was I just something you could use, in your ambition? I trusted you with my life, and my honour, and you betrayed me. You were the brother I never knew, and you spurned my love . . . for sex, for money . . . or was there something more to it? Did you plan to emulate your distant ancestor Giles, the original Deathstalker, who betrayed his Emperor with the Empress Hermione, so he could steal the Throne? Is that what this was all about? The ultimate treason? Wasn't being the Champion enough for you; you had to be King?'

'No!' said Lewis. 'No; you have to know that isn't true!' He held out his empty hands to Douglas, almost pleadingly. 'How could you even think such a thing, Douglas?'

'Anne said it best; I don't know you any more, Lewis. And I have to wonder if I ever really did.' He turned his gaze away to smile on Finn. It looked like a real smile, from a distance. 'You have done well, Finn Durandal. You shall be my new Champion. My trusted right hand. I should have made you Champion first.' He looked back at Lewis. 'How could I know that power and position would corrupt you so, Lewis? I thought I could depend on you, of all people. I was blinded by the name, I suppose. That ancient, honourable name . . .'

'The ring,' said Finn, stepping forward. 'He must be made to give up the Deathstalker ring, Your Majesty. He is clearly no longer worthy to bear the blessed Owen's ring. It may contain valuable information, concerning where the blessed Owen may be found. Take off the ring, Lewis, and give it to me. Now.'

'Come and take it,' said Lewis. 'If you can.'

And even unarmed, and surrounded by a whole army of men with guns, there was still something in the Deathstalker's voice, and in his eyes, that gave Finn pause. The moment lengthened awkwardly, and then Finn recovered himself and laughed dismissively.

'If need be, we can always take it off your dead body, Lewis. You do realise that you are on trial for your life? In a time of Empire-wide emergency such as this, behaviour and crimes such as yours threaten to undermine the morale of all Humanity. You broke your trust with King and Queen, and plotted to seize the Throne for yourself. Such guilt can only be fittingly punished by a death sentence.'

And all the MPs in the House broke into a loud chorus of agreement and approval, calling with grim vicious voices for the death of the traitor Deathstalker.

'No!' said Douglas, leaning forward on his Throne for the first time. 'I didn't agree to that! I never said I wanted that!'

But no-one was listening to him. The House was full of the

431

ugly roar of the honourable Members, baying for blood, demanding death. They rose to their feet, and shouted down their own King and Speaker. Lewis had betrayed them by not being the hero they'd needed their Deathstalker to be in the time of the Terror, and they would have their revenge. Only blood would satisfy them now. Lewis turned his back on the MPs, and studied the rest of the House. The clone representative was also calling for death, siding as always with the majority. The representative for the oversoul was sitting quietly, regarding him thoughtfully. Not an enemy, perhaps, but the pale-faced young woman showed no sign of being ready to support or protect him. The blue steel robot representing Shub was still and silent, and who knew what the AIs were thinking. They had their own agenda, always. And the aliens . . . were arguing among themselves, looking for some way to turn this new change of events to their own advantage. No change there, then. Not for the first time, Lewis was entirely alone.

Two guards came forward at Finn's gesture to take the traitor away. So Lewis kicked the nearest man in the groin, head-butted the other in the face, and threw himself at Finn Durandal. The two men crashed to the floor in a tangle. There was a long moment of utter confusion, as the other guards looked at each other, uncertain what to do. No-one was giving any orders, and they couldn't open fire for fear of hitting Finn. The two men thrashed togther on the floor. Finn got his gun out, and an energy beam shot past Lewis' head, so close it singed a few hairs, and then the beam flew on to blow a hole in the far wall of the chamber. MPs ducked, and guards scattered, crying out. Lewis and Finn were punching and kicking and wrestling, two warriors well-trained in every vicious trick of unarmed combat. The guards and security men watched helplessly from the sidelines. As yet no-one had ordered them to go down and intervene directly. And since this was, after all, the Deathstalker, there wasn't a man there ready to risk his life without very specific orders. And maybe not even then. Better to stand well back, and wait for a clear shot.

Lewis and Finn fought savagely, but in the end Lewis was

the one with the experience. For all his training, Finn had never been one for working in close, and getting his hands dirty. He pushed Lewis away, and tried to get to his feet. Lewis kicked him expertly in the knee, and Finn cried out and fell back again as his leg betrayed him. Lewis rose to his feet, smiled a cold and wolfish smile, and kicked Finn in the ribs. His grin widened as he heard ribs crack and break. Lewis kicked him again, and Finn groaned loudly, blood spraying from his mouth. Lewis laughed soundlessly, and reaching down, tore Finn's gun from his hand. He backed away, looking quickly about him. The whole fight had taken only a few moments. The House had fallen silent. Lewis knew he only had a short time before some of the guards got their wits and their courage together, and opened fire. A quick glance around was all it took to show him that there were armed men between him and every exit. He might be able to fight his way out, but it would mean killing a lot of basically innocent men and women. And he wasn't ready to do that, just yet. He looked at Jesamine, still standing beside Douglas' Throne, watching him now with wide, devastated eyes. Two security men were holding her by the arms, just in case. There was no way he could get to her, and they both knew it.

'I'll be back for you, Jes! I swear it!'

'Go! Get the hell out of here, Lewis! They'll kill you!'

'I will come back for you! Whatever it takes!'

Half a dozen energy beams seared through the air before the Throne, but Lewis was no longer there. The energy beams went on to blow ragged holes in the floor. Douglas leapt to his feet to yell at the guards.

'Take him down with swords, dammit! Swords! Get down here and earn your pay! He's only one man!'

But that one man was the Deathstalker. Some of the guards and security men started to make their way forward, but none of them were hurrying, all of them ready to let some other poor fool have the honour of tackling Lewis Deathstalker. After all, it wasn't as if he was going anywhere. All the exits to the House had been blocked and sealed. Finn Durandal had seen to that, with a little help from Anne Barclay. Lewis had realised that too; but he had other plans.

He was looking at the floor of the House. Not all that long ago, Lewis had foiled an attempt to kill the King, by a Neuman suicide bomber. The transmutation bomb had gone off right here, reducing the bomber to protoplasmic ooze, and severely damaging the structure of the floor. It was supposed to have been repaired long ago, but Lewis happened to know that a backlog of work (and an ongoing argument in the House as to who exactly was going to pay for all this work), had meant the real repair work had yet to be done. The workmen had just covered the damaged area with a temporary new surface. Lewis knew all this because it was one of the things the King had ordered him to look into, back when Douglas was still keeping him busy with makework.

Lewis aimed Finn's gun at just the right spot, ignoring the shakily-aimed energy beams still blazing past him, and opened fire on full intensity. The weakened section of floor blew apart with a satisfyingly large explosion, and a whole section crumpled and fell inwards, leaving a gaping hole nearly ten feet in diameter. Lewis jumped into it without hesitating, just as a dozen energy beams whipped through the air where he'd been standing. It was a relatively short drop into the service tunnels below, and he landed easily. A quick glance around to get his bearings, and then he was off and running. He knew every inch of the House he'd sworn to protect.

Guards and security men crouched around the edges of the great hole, and peered dubiously down into it. Absolutely nobody was keen to follow the Deathstalker into unknown territory. Particularly not when he could be waiting for them anywhere . . . Finn pushed his way through the guards, limping heavily and with one arm protectively cradling his smashed ribs. His face was white with pain and fury, but his features were still carefully composed. He glared into the hole, and then turned his glare on the guards.

'Get down into that hole, right now, or I swear I'll shoot you myself.'

No-one there doubted he meant it. The guards looked at each other, sighed heavily, and then one by one they slowly and very cautiously dropped through the hole into the tunnels below, guns at the ready. But of course by then the Deathstalker was long gone, losing himself expertly in the intricate warren of service and maintenance tunnels under the House that were a mystery to all except those few unfortunates who used them on a regular basis. And those who knew of them because it was their business to know such things. Finn knew the tunnels too; but he wasn't stupid enough to go after a maddened, avenging Deathstalker. At least, not until he'd spent some time in a regeneration machine, and afterwards armed himself with every weapon under the sun.

King Douglas sank slowly back into his Throne again, glaring down at the confusion on the floor before him. He knew Lewis would have made his escape by now. None of these people here were fast enough or smart enough to catch the Deathstalker. By the time they'd finished checking out the tunnels foot by foot, Lewis would have left the House. Free as a bird. Douglas wasn't sure how he felt about that. He wanted Lewis tried and punished for what he'd done, if only for being such a disappointment; but he didn't want him killed. You couldn't kill someone just for falling in love with the wrong woman. The rest of the charges had to be lies or misunderstandings. Had to be. Douglas sighed heavily. He couldn't be that wrong about a man he'd known for so many years. He just couldn't be. At least he still had Finn . . .

Lewis wouldn't be back, no matter what he'd said. He wasn't that stupid. He'd think about the odds, and make the sensible decision. He'd run, go offworld, lose himself in the Rim worlds; and Douglas would never have to see him again. So . . . Lewis was exiled, disgraced, outlawed. Just like his ancestor, the blessed Owen. Lewis had been right after all. Deathstalker luck. Always bad.

Douglas realised slowly that Jesamine was still standing beside his Throne. He gestured sharply to the two guards restraining her, and they let go immediately. Jesamine rubbed at her bruised arms, and looked at Douglas with bruised eyes. He met her gaze coldly.

'Your lover's gone, Jes. Don't expect to see him again. He knows if he ever shows his face openly on this world again, he's a dead man. By running, he's proved his guilt.'

Jesamine tried to speak, and couldn't. Too many things

jostled in her head at once. She swallowed hard, moistened her dry lips, and concentrated on saying the one thing that mattered. 'Douglas; I never meant to hurt you . . .'

'Then you screwed up, didn't you?' His voice was cold and merciless, because he knew that if he gave in to his emotions, even for a moment, he'd start to cry, right there in the House, in front of everyone. He'd just lost the only two people he ever really cared for. He gestured tiredly to the two waiting guards. 'Take her away. I don't want to look at her any more.'

'Wait!' Finn Durandal came limping forward, and everyone fell back to give him plenty of room. His face was calm, his voice steady, but his eyes were angry, vindictive. The House fell silent, waiting to see what further surprises he had in store. Finn lurched to a halt before the Throne, beads of sweat popping out on his forehead from the pain in his ribs. There was blood on his mouth and chin that he hadn't bothered to wipe away. Finn knew the value of a strong visual image. The sight of him standing before his King, beaten and bloodied but still unbowed, would be all over the media within the hour, and would go a long way to helping people forget he'd let the traitor Deathstalker escape. He managed a small bow to the Throne, and then glared at Jesamine. 'She is just as guilty as her lover, Your Majesty! Her treason is just as great. She must stand trial for her life too!'

'You've done enough damage for one day, Finn,' Douglas said quietly. He glared around at the watching MPs before they could start shouting again. 'Yes; she is a traitor, but only to me, not the Empire. There's been enough talk of death here today. This isn't Lionstone's time. Lock Jesamine up, and let her be tried in open Court. The people must be shown the evidence, and be convinced of the truth, or they'll never believe it. Jesamine Flowers the diva still has a hell of a lot of fans, and the last thing we need is more riots in our cities.' He looked at the waiting guards again. 'She's a traitor, so take her to Traitor's Hall, in the Bloody Tower. A most suitable destination for the woman who would be Queen. See she's comfortable, but she is to have no special privileges, and absolutely no visitors, unless they have my personal consent.

And my seal to prove it. And double the guard in and around the Tower, just in case.'

'Yes,' said Finn. 'Traitor's Hall. An excellent choice, Your Majesty. Let the traitorous bitch rot there till the courts can get around to her. And when the courts have proven her guilty, of conspiracy against you and the Throne and the Empire, and the people quite rightly demand her death; I, as your Champion and official executioner, shall cut her head off on the Traitor's Block at the Bloody Tower, and hold it up to show the crowds. I've always been a great believer in upholding the old traditions.'

'I always knew you were weird, Finn,' said Jesamine, before they hustled her away.

After a long chase, Lewis Deathstalker left the House unobserved, strode openly through the streets inside a borrowed cloak with the hood pulled well forward, and finally went to ground so thoroughly no-one could find him. He was glad he'd been able to get out of the House without having to kill someone. They were just doing their jobs, mostly, just as he would have been, only the day before. But it seemed like every damned guard, security man and rent-a-sword had turned out to chase and harry him through the Parade of the Endless. He hadn't dared go near his gravity sled; it was bound to be watched. And even if he'd been able to take it by force, it would have only made him too obvious a target.

So he walked up and down streets, and in and out of buildings, watching carefully for anyone who might be tailing him, using all the techniques of flight and evasion he'd learned from all the crooks and crazies he'd chased through the city in his years as a Paragon. The irony of his position did not escape him. He'd become the very thing he'd fought all his life. He was the criminal now.

No-one even got close to catching him as he made his slow, excruciating way through the city, not even when the House sent his fellow Paragons out to look for him. Though Lewis liked to think they weren't looking too hard. That they knew a fit-up when they saw one. Either way, this was his city, and no-one knew its secret ways better than him. Lewis

Deathstalker had vanished, while a whole city turned itself inside out searching for the greatest traitor of the Golden Age.

He went to ground in an old lockup he'd used before, in his Paragon days. It was just an anonymous metal shell, one in a long line just outside the main starport; simple steel-lined rooms roughly ten feet a side, with big strong locks, that could be used to store extra lugagge and the like, by starcruiser staff on a fast turnover. The lockups were cheap, featureless, secure, and practically invisible unless you knew what you were looking for. Lewis kept one on a long lease, under another name, to hold various items that he might need in emergencies. Or that the authorities would prefer not to know about.

Changes of clothes, extra weapons (mostly non-regulation), false identity papers and credit cards, and a few useful tech items of an underhanded nature. Lewis had often found it useful to be able to adopt new identities in the past, when he was still a Paragon, and sometimes had to operate undercover to get the information he needed. Mostly in places where his distinctive ugly face would get him killed straight away. No-one knew about these others identities but him. Not even Douglas. Lewis had always found such work distasteful, and even borderline dishonourable. He did it because it was part of the job, and necessary to get useful information and tips, but he'd never felt inclined to boast about it.

He even had some simple body shop technology, that could give him another face, if necessary. No-one ever expected Lewis to give up his famously ugly features, but Lewis had always known there was more to being a Paragon than fighting. He was capable of being subtle, and even downright devious, on occasion. When necessary.

The first thing he did was to discard his black leather Champion's armour, dump it all on the floor, and give it a good kicking. He'd never liked it. New clothes, new ID, new credit card, and he was a new person. A light tech collar around his neck produced a holo-generated new face, with features so average they were practically invisible. Togther with the right unobtrusive body language, no-one would look at him twice in the street. He didn't use the body shop tech to change his face. He wasn't ready to cut all his ties with his past life just yet. There was always the chance he might still be able to prove he was no traitor, and somehow resume his old life, if not his old position. He had to believe that, or go crazy.

Except . . . he still loved her. So he was a traitor, in that at least. And always would be.

He pushed the thought firmly to one side, and made himself concentrate on the matter at hand. He strapped on a new weapons belt, with sword and gun, and slipped a handful of throwing knives and other surprises back where they belonged. He scowled unhappily as he clipped a force shield around his wrist. The power level was showing worryingly low. He'd meant to recharge the energy crystal, but with so much going on in his life, he'd never got around to it. And he didn't have time now. So he just shrugged, arranged a few more useful tech items about his person, took a deep breath, and left the lockup.

He checked the lock was secure, looked up and down the empty street a few times, and then walked out into the main thoroughfare. Wrapped in a somewhat shabby cloak, he strolled casually down the street, watching carefully from behind his holo mask, but no-one gave him a second look. A Paragon shot by overhead on a speeding gravity sled, and Lewis looked up along with everyone else so as not to stand out, but the Paragon didn't look down, and was gone in a few moments. Lewis walked on. Let them look for the Death-stalker. They wouldn't find him. He was gone, for the moment.

Lewis made his way across the city, using public transport as much as possible, dodging guard checkpoints when he had to. He was pretty sure his fake ID would hold up, but it had been some time since he last used it, and he didn't feel like putting it to the test until he absolutely had to. He couldn't be sure exactly how many of his secrets he'd shared with Douglas, or Finn for that matter, and how many of those secrets his ex-partners might remember. Either way, dodging around the checkpoints wasn't exactly difficult. The guards and peacekeepers couldn't be everywhere, and no-one knew the ins and outs of the city like Lewis. He knew all the scams and dodges because he'd busted most of them, and there wasn't a secret door or hidden passageway he hadn't chased someone through in his time.

It didn't take him too long to get to the Rookery. Getting in was no problem; he'd been there before, in various disguises. Certain people would be very surprised to find out who their old drinking partner really was. Lewis pushed back his cloak so that his gun and sword showed clearly, and changed his anonymous shuffle to a broad and cocky swagger. Most people then had enough sense to leave him strictly alone. One bravo lurched out of a bistro to brace Lewis, to impress his drunken friends, and Lewis immediately beat the crap out of the idiot with such vicious thoroughness that even the hardened bravos watching from the safety of the bistro were impressed. Lewis left the unlucky bully crying in a corner, trying to find at least some of his teeth before his eyes puffed shut, and strode off down the street, whistling cheerfully. He'd been hoping to find someone dumb enough to let him take out his bad mood on.

No-one else bothered him after that. News travels fast in the Rookery, and they all knew a complete psycho when they saw one.

Lewis ended up at a small inn with smoke-stained walls and windows that were never cleaned. *The Mucky Duck* was cheap and nasty, its booze was barely adequate, and its food was actually distressing, but it let rooms by the day or the hour, and asked no questions as long as your credit held out. Lewis had used the place before, and always had to take a long shower afterwards. Sometimes he burned his clothes too. Still, the inn had the useful quality of being centrally located, on one of the main intersections in the Rookery, which meant people were always coming and going, and the gossip in the bar never stoppped. If Finn actually tried sending people into the Rookery, in search of Lewis, *The Mucky Duck* would know the moment the poor sods crossed the boundary. The Rookery had no time for would-be undercover peacekeepers.

Lewis sat on the edge of a very hard bed, and stared glumly at the bare and grimy walls. No-one would pay any attention to one more hard case like him, probably just looking for work as muscle-for-hire. And the inn wouldn't give a damn as long as his credit held out. Lewis shut off his holo face, to preserve the energy crystal in the collar. He had the door locked and bolted, with a chair jammed up against it, just in case. There wasn't a lot of credit left in his fake card. He'd been meaning to transfer some new funds into it for some time, but given how tight his finances had become of late, he'd never got around to it. When he'd been made Champion, he'd thought he'd never have to come back to places like this . . . So; he had enough credit to last two days, maybe three if he was careful and lucky, and then . . .

Oh hell, maybe he'd just rob a bank. He couldn't be in any more trouble.

He lay back on the hard, unforgiving mattress, his bare skin crawling where it touched the sheets, and stared up at the long crack spreading across the grey plaster ceiling. He had some hard thinking to do. If there was evidence condemning him in his computer (and he saw no reason to doubt Finn's word), it could only be because some very professional person had planted it there. Which meant . . . there was a conspiracy against him. A disturbing thought. Shadow Court, maybe. This had the feel of the kind of thing they delighted in. Why kill a man, when it was so much more fun to destroy his reputation and ruin him? Or maybe the ELFs had hired someone here in the Rookery, to get back at him . . . you could find any kind of crooked pro here.

But if it was a conspiracy, he couldn't hope to fight it on his own. Not with a death threat hanging over his head. No-one would side with him, and no-one would believe him. He was on his own. Not least because where Jesamine was concerned, he was guilty. He screwed his eyes shut, as though he could hide from himself in the dark. He couldn't think about her now. He'd go mad. No; his only chance to redeem himself, and perhaps restore his honour, was to perform some act of great heroism, worthy of the Deathstalker name. He had to save the day; openly and extravagantly. And only one way came to mind; find out the truth about Owen and his companions. What really happened to them. Was Owen really dead? If not; where was he? And if he could be found, could he stop the Terror? Lewis raised his hand, opened his eyes, and studied the chunky black gold ring on his finger. Owen's old ring, sign and seal of Clan Deathstalker. Everyone seemed sure it was the real thing. Given to him by a dead man . . . It must have been given to him for some reason; maybe it did conceal some secret, useful information. And if anyone was equipped to find the truth, it was him. He was a Deathstalker.

He sat up suddenly, leaned over and activated the comm panel by the bed. It was a battered old unit, sound only, but it would do the job. Even in a dump like this, they had to provide the basic amenities, or no-one would stay there. Lewis patched a call through to his old home, on the world of Virimonde, using secret family contact codes that only a Deathstalker would know. The peacekeeper computers would be monitoring all the comm traffic, but none of the codes he was using would set off an alarm or trip any flags. And once contact with his family was established, they'd institute a whole series of security protocols from their end, hiding the true conversation behind pre-recorded talk of no interest to anyone. After what happened to Owen, and later David, the Deathstalker family were justifiably somewhat paranoid. Given the state of his credit card, Lewis had to call collect, which complicated matters a little, but soon enough Lewis was talking with his father, Roland.

'Took you long enough to get in touch,' his father said gruffly. 'Your mother's been worried sick. She's currently lying down with one of her heads. We know what happened at the House. It's all over the media, the bastards. This line will be secure for about twenty minutes, and then, if you have more you need to say, you'll have to disconnect and try again. How are you, Lewis? You hurt? You need money? I can be there on Logres in under a week, if you need me.'

'No, Dad!' Lewis said urgently. 'You're safer where you are. Everything's gone crazy here. I'm not hurt, and I don't need any help. If you came here, they'd pick you up the moment you landed. This is Logres, remember? Best security in the Empire. I should know. I used to help run it.'

'What happened, son? There's been all kinds of crazy talk on the news comment shows. They're calling you a traitor. Tell me it's not true.'

'It's . . . complicated, Dad. I'm doing my best to sort it out . . . but that could take some time.'

'You can't come home, Lewis,' Roland said flatly. 'The family couldn't protect you. Friends in Virimonde security quietly informed us that they've been given orders to shoot you on sight if you're ever dumb enough to show your face here. The family will still do what it can to help you. We still believe in you. I believe in you. Now tell me what I can do to help.'

'I told Parliament that we didn't have any secret information on the blessed Owen, or his fate,' Lewis said carefully. 'But I've been doing some thinking, and it occurred to me that this might be just my opinion. Are there things in the family archives that I was never told about? Things no-one knows outside the family?'

'Maybe a few, small things,' said Roland. 'I would have told you if you'd asked, but you were never interested before. What does it matter now, anyway?'

'I need to know, Dad. It could be important.'

'Let me think for a minute.' There was a long, expensive silence, punctuated now and again by the occasional hiss of static. It was a very old unit. Lewis kept an eye on his watch, and tried not to worry too much as a large chunk of his safe twenty minutes ticked away. 'All right,' Roland said finally. 'How about this. We do know the exact coordinates for the location of the original Deathstalker Standing. Diana Vertue crashlanded what was left of the old castle on the planet Shandrakor. The Standing was shot to hell during the last great battle against Shub, apparently, and wasn't considered worth salvaging. But whatever survived the crash might still contain useful information. No-one else knows that. No-one has been near it in two hundred years. Partly because we're the only ones who know exactly where to look for it, and mostly because Shandrakor is even more hazardous now than it was in Owen's day. Not many people remember this now, but all the monsters created by Shub and the Mater Mundi and the Hadenmen and Lionstone's laboratories were rounded up and dumped on Shandrakor, after the Rebellion was over. I guess someone decided that was kinder than just killing them all. God knows how many of them might still be alive down there, or what their descendants have become. All anyone knows for sure is that Shandrakor today is just what that bloody world has always been; an endless, vicious killing ground.

'Word is the Transmutation Board would love to wipe it clean, just on general principles, but Robert and Constance personally declared the place off limits. It's a sanctuary for all the creatures they dumped there, protected by a Quarantine starcruiser, and no-one's ready to overturn Robert and Constance's decision. Public wouldn't stand for it. I can give you the exact coordinates where the castle crashed, if that's any use to you. But I have to say; it's a hell of a long shot, and a bloody dangerous one at that.'

'I don't seem to have many options,' said Lewis. 'Thanks, Dad. And Dad . . . I'm sorry I let you down. Let the family down.'

'You didn't,' Roland said sharply. 'They let you down. After everything you did for them, all the times you put your life on the line to clear up the messes they made . . . they had no right to treat you this way. They weren't worthy of you, Lewis.'

'Thanks, Dad.' Lewis would have liked to say more, but he didn't trust his voice to stay steady. Tears burned his eyes.

'Do what you have to do, son. And come home when you can.'

'I always . . . I just wanted you to be proud of me, Dad.'

'I always have been, Lewis. You're my son. And a Death-stalker.'

Lewis waited till night fell to break into the Bloody Tower. He'd been rather surprised to discover that Jesamine was being kept in Traitor's Hall. It wasn't exactly a maximum security prison. It was once, of course, in Lionstone's day and before. You could be sent to the Bloody Tower for all kinds of reasons, back then. You went in dragging chains, and you came out in a coffin. No exceptions. The spilled blood had soaked so deeply into the stones in some places that it could never be removed. Place was supposed to be crawling with ghosts.

Now it was little more than a tourist trap, with guided tours and souvenir stalls; one of the great sights of the Parade of the Endless. Still, it was undoubtedly surrounded by whole armies of guards by now, if only to keep the media out. Certainly no-one would expect Lewis to try and break in on his own, to free Jesamine; so that was exactly what he was going to do.

The Bloody Tower hadn't been used as an actual prison since Lionstone had been overthrown, and all the political prisoners freed. It was one of the few relics of that awful time that still survived, preserved now because the building was deemed to be of great architectural importance. Most of the other old prisons and detention centres had been burned down by furious mobs, but the Bloody Tower had survived almost unscathed, because it was too big and too strong and too solid for the fires to do any real damage. And while a great many others were officially demolished, to appease the sorrow and rage of all the people who'd seen too many friends and family disappear into Lionstone's dungeons, never to be seen again, the Bloody Tower escaped destruction because Robert and Constance wanted it kept; as a reminder.

These days, the Bloody Tower was run and maintained by a small group of historical enthusiasts who acted as guards and curators, complete with historically accurate uniforms. The tourists loved it. Especially Traitor's Wing, where those who particularly displeased Lionstone spent their last few hours before facing execution on Traitor's Block, before the assembled crowds. Ghosts were said to be really thick on the ground there, strolling around with their heads tucked securely under their arms, freaking out lone guards in the early hours.

The more Lewis thought about it, the less it made sense. If they'd put Jesamine in a real prison, under maximum security, behind tanglefields and force shields, with security cameras everywhere, and professionally trained, well-armed guards all over the shop . . . Lewis would have had a hell of a time getting in. So he had to wonder whether she'd been deliberately placed in the Tower, to act as bait in a trap for him. It was what Lewis would have done. But in the end it didn't matter. He'd said he'd come back for her, and he would. No matter how many guards or guns or traps they put in his way.

Though Hell itself stood in his path.

Night fell, and Lewis walked out of the Rookery, wearing simple anonymous clothes, and a holo projection of a simple anonymous face. No-one gave him a second look. He took public transport to the Bloody Tower, being careful to give exact change, so as not to give the driver any reason to remember him. When he stepped off the bus at the right stop, and regarded the Tower rising spendidly up before him, looking large and blocky and utterly impregnable, he was surprised to find a loudly chanting mob already assembled before it. Jesamine Flowers' fanbase had mobilised itself through the singer's web sites and turned out in force, with more arriving every hour as fresh coachloads arrived from other cities. They were outraged that their beloved diva and idol had been arrested, and mad as hell that she'd been locked up. The guards set to watch for Lewis Deathstalker were now far more concerned with holding off increasingly hysterical crowds of Jesamine Flowers' fans, who were loudly and furiously declining to disperse and go home, as ordered. There was much waving of angry placards, and organised chanting, and not a little stone throwing. Perfect cover for Lewis to study the Tower and its defences without being observed.

Serious trouble broke out not ten minutes after he'd got there. The mob surged forward, infuriated beyond reason or common sense, moved by a simple determination to get their adored heroine out of the notorious Bloody Tower. They forced their way through the low level tanglefields through sheer weight of numbers, and then the mob headed for the thin ranks of guards as though they intended to walk right over them. The guards were under strict orders not to open fire on unarmed civilians (certainly as long as the media was watching) and so they braced themselves, drew their shock batons, and went head to head with the shouting, spitting mob. Lewis watched, wincing, hard pressed to decide which side looked the most vicious, or determined. More guards came running, from other sides of the Tower, to reinforce the defensive lines. And it was the easiest thing in the world for Lewis to sneak past everyone, circle round and let himself into the Tower through an unregarded side door, using his old Paragon skeleton key.

Once inside, he shut the door quietly behind him, relocked it, and then checked the unobtrusive little device he'd brought from his lockup was still working. Basically, it tapped into watching security cameras and edited his image out of the picture. Simple, very effective, and utterly illegal. Just being caught in possession of the device was an automatic – and long – prison sentence. Lewis had confiscated it from a skell he'd busted in the Rookery a few years back . . . and somehow he'd never got around to turning it in. He'd always had the feeling it might come in handy someday.

He looked quickly about him, but the narrow passageway was completely empty. Lewis hesitated, thinking dubiously again about the skeleton key that had got him in. Surely they should have been expecting him to use it, and reset the Tower's locks to keep him out? Or perhaps this was part of the trap, and somewhere a silent alarm was already flashing, to indicate he'd arrived. He shrugged quickly. It didn't matter. It just meant he had to move faster. He padded quietly down silent, deserted corridors, following the decorated signs set out to guide the tourists. It seemed most of the guards were outside, dealing with the fans. Or trying to, at least.

Lewis heard footsteps approaching, and ducked out of sight through an open door. He peered cautiously around the door, and a single guard walked past, wearing an old historical uniform and carrying two mugs of steaming tea. Lewis stepped out of the side room and hit the man efficiently from behind. The guard slumped bonelessly to the floor, the tea going everywhere. Lewis looked quickly about him, but no-one seemed to have heard anything. It only took Lewis a few moments to strip the guard of his uniform, switch clothes, and then reprogram his holo face to duplicate the guard's features.

It would have helped if the clothes hadn't been at least three sizes too large, but you couldn't have everything.

Lewis dragged the unconscious body, in its frankly appalling underwear, into the side room, locked the door, and then set off again, walking openly now through the corridors. He nodded calmly to other guards he passed, as he moved up from floor to floor, and they nodded back. Lewis couldn't risk using his own voice, so he just nodded and grunted, and mostly the other guards just grunted and nodded back. Until finally, on the fifth floor, Lewis ran into two guards in modern uniforms, watching over the old steel gates that blocked off Traitor's Wing from the rest of the Tower. They were wearing full body armour, and carrying energy guns as well as swords. They were playing cards on a folding table, but they both looked up immediately as Lewis headed unhurriedly towards them. One of the guards stood up, and stepped away from the card table to block Lewis' way, one hand resting on the gun at his hip.

'That's far enough. You know you historicals aren't allowed anywhere near the Wing tonight. Give me the password, and then piss off out of it.'

'Right,' growled the other guard. 'How many times do we have to tell you people? We don't care how many years you've been making your rounds, or how historically significant it is; tonight the Wing is off limits. And if you've forgotten the password as well, I'm going to give you a serious slap, just for annoying me. Password!'

Lewis went as though to answer, and then broke off and coughed harshly, as though bothered by something in his throat. He tried again, and coughed even more horribly. He kept walking towards the waiting guards, gesturing helplessly, and the one who'd stood up sighed heavily and came forward to meet him. Lewis coughed even harder, making a big deal of the hacking and spitting, until the guard was in range, and then Lewis straightened up and punched the man right between the eyes.

Unfortunately, although the man stumbled backwards, making loud sounds of distress, he didn't go down. Lewis jumped him, tore the gun from its holster and threw it aside.

The other guard watched open-mouthed, and then started to rise from his seat. Lewis was still grappling with the first guard, who turned out to be strong and fast and a bloody good fighter. Lewis supposed he should have known they wouldn't choose just anyone to guard Jesamine.

He ducked a clawed hand heading for his eyes, and hit the guard hard under the sternum. All the colour went out of the man's face, and his legs buckled. The other guard was dancing around them, gun in hand, shouting and cursing and trying to get a bead on Lewis. So Lewis threw the first guard at him. The two of them went down with a satisfyingly loud thud, the second guard pinned under the first. Lewis stepped forward and kicked the gun out of the second guard's hand, and then had to fall backwards as the second guard pushed the first off him, and surged to his feet again. He went straight for Lewis, who spun round and hit the man right in the forehead with a vicious back elbow. The second guard went down as though someone had kicked his feet out from under him. He lay still, twitching a bit, while Lewis walked around in little circles for a while, cursing and holding his elbow, which hurt like hell. Always go for the soft spots. You'd think he'd know that by now.

He glared around him, breathing hard. He had to work fast. Unless the other guards were all asleep in the control room, someone had to have seen the two guards going down, even if they couldn't see him. He searched the two unconscious guards, and found the old steel key that opened the steel gates. He pushed them open and ran into Traitor's Wing, calling out Jesamine's name. He could still get them both out, if they moved fast. Only one cell had been opened, for the Wing's first actual prisoner in centuries, but when Lewis got there, Jesamine wasn't there. They must have moved her.

And then alarms went off everywhere at once, loud and piercing, and there was no longer any need for secrecy or stealth. The bait had been snatched away, and the trap was sprung. Lewis spun round, snarling, gun in hand. Whatever happened, he wasn't going to be taken prisoner. No show trial, and public disgrace for his family. He ran back down the corridor, past the steel gates, jumped the unconscious guards, and kept running. Out into the next corridor, just in time to see a dozen or more armed security men come running into the corridor from an intersection. They cried out on seeing Lewis, with his old uniform and holo disguise, and demanded to know what was happening. And then they cried out again and scattered in alarm as he opened fire with his disrupter. No more bluffing. He wanted Jesamine.

He turned and ran the other way. He didn't think he'd hit anyone. He hoped he hadn't. They were just doing their jobs. But he would kill everyone he saw, if that was what it took to rescue Jesamine. If she was still here in the Tower . . .

He had to find her, and soon, but he didn't even know where to look. She could be anywhere in the Tower, on any floor, if they hadn't already bustled her outside. No; she must still be around somewhere. They wouldn't risk taking her out while her fans were still rioting. Just the sight of her under arrest would escalate the trouble tenfold. Lewis ran on, plunging down corridor after corridor, as more guards came running from all directions. They'd seen his old uniform and holo face now, and knew who they were looking for. Some had guessed who he really was, and were using his name as a battle cry. They wouldn't hesitate to kill the traitor Deathstalker. Lewis gripped his gun tightly, and his ugly face was very determined and very cold.

And finally, of course, he ended up in a dead end, with nowhere left to go. No doors, no windows, no hiding places; just blank walls and a corridor that went nowhere. Lewis spun round, sword and gun at the ready, like an animal at bay, and a whole crowd of armed and armoured guards all but fell over themselves crashing to a sudden halt at the far end of the corridor. They saw they had their prey cornered at last, but they didn't seem too pleased about it. They looked at each other, shifting from foot to foot, and hefting their swords and guns uncertainly. It seemed they at least suspected who was hiding behind the holo face. Lewis reached up to the collar at his throat, and turned it off. No more hiding. The holo face blinked out, and many of the guards actually groaned as Lewis' familiar ugly features reappeared. He grinned at them, and growled deep in his throat, and was pleased to note that several of the guards' faces went pale.

And then the guards raised their disrupters and pointed them at Lewis, and he understood they had no intention of even trying to take him alive. A dead traitor was much less trouble than a live prisoner who might insist on his innocence, and raise awkward doubts in the people's minds. Lewis' face flushed with anger as the force shield sprang into being on his left arm. It was a good shield, top of the line, but it would still only absorb or deflect a set number of hits before the energy crystal was drained, and then the force shield would collapse, and he would be defenceless. Had to be twenty, maybe thirty guards, and most of them had energy guns. Lewis calculated the odds coldly, and decided that what was left of his luck had just run out. No honourable end, no fighting chance; just shot down in secret, like a mad animal. He had a brief moment to regret all the things he meant to do, and never had, and that he'd never see Jesamine again, even to say goodbye; and then he heard more running feet on the way, and knew his time was up. So; if he was going to go down, best to go down fighting, and take as many of the bastards with him as he could. To be a Deathstalker, to the last. He looked at the guards, and saw some of them were still raising their guns. His reverie had only lasted a few seconds. What the hell . . . He raised his voice in the old family battle cry.

'Shandrakor! Shandrakor!'

And then he charged down the corridor, towards overwhelming odds and a certain death, smiling a terrible smile.

Most of the guards were so astonished they just stood there and watched him do it. A handful of them fired their weapons, the energy beams searing past Lewis' head or ricocheting from his force shield, and then he was in and among them. He shot one man at point blank range, and then he cut about him with his sword, and blood and screams flew on the air. For a moment they actually fell back before him, frightened by his face and his reputation and his ancient, deadly name; and then they remembered how many they were, and their training reasserted itself. They fell on him, unable to use their guns in the crush of bodies, slicing and hacking at him with their swords. Lewis spun back and forth, his blade a blur, constantly spinning to put his force shield between him and his enemies, but in the end he was only one man, and they were so many. Swords came at him from every direction, and he cried out as they cut into him. His blood jumped and ran, and spattered the walls and floor, but still Lewis stood his ground, refusing to be beaten, refusing to die. Fighting till the last, so that at least his family would know he died an honourable death.

And that was when Samuel Chevron came charging out of nowhere, and hit the guards from the other side. He was swinging the biggest, longest sword Lewis had ever seen, and the heavy blade cut through the guards' armour like it wasn't even there. Chevron cut down half a dozen guards before they knew what was happening, and then he was right in the thick of the fighting, killing men with cold, brutal, efficient skill. Suddenly Jesamine was there too, with a gun in each hand, and she shot down two of the guards nearest to Lewis. His heart leapt at the sight of her, and new strength filled his arms.

The guards wavered, caught between two implacable foes, both fighting like demons, and in a moment it was all suddenly too much for them, and the survivors broke and ran. Lewis slowly lowered his sword, breathing hard. End to end, the corridor was littered with dead bodies. He looked at Chevron, and the man wasn't even breathing hard. And then Jesamine ran forward and took Lewis in her arms in a fierce hug, and he cried out despite himself as she hurt him. She let go immediately, stepped back and looked at him, and her eyes widened in horror as she took in the extent of his injuries.

'Oh Jesus, Lewis; what have they done to you?'

'Not enough to keep me from you,' Lewis said, or thought he said. He leaned back against a blood-spattered wall, suddenly weak and giddy. There was blood running thickly down his swordarm, and he had to look down to make sure he was still holding his sword, because his fingers couldn't feel it.

'We have to get you to a regen tank,' said Jesamine.

'I've got one outside,' said Samuel Chevron. 'Think you can hold together long enough for us to get you to it, Lewis?'

'Oh sure,' he said, with a confidence he didn't feel. 'You're a real man of surprises tonight, Samuel. Even more than when you turned up at Court in that really ratty Father Christmas suit. What's a retired trader like you doing here anyway?'

'I came here to rescue Jesamine,' said Chevron. 'And to answer your next question; I got in here first because no-one sees me unless I want them to. And because I had a little help.'

'Much help from mighty but unappreciated sorcerer!' said a familiar voice, and a small figure dressed in grey darted out from behind Chevron. 'I is back!' said Vaughn. 'Ex-leper, hero of old, and powerful beyond the dreams of people with really imaginative dreams! Save princess from evil tower, and chew gum at same time! Bow down ye mighty and despair.'

'You're supposed to be dead,' said Lewis, too tired and too hurt to be diplomatic.

Vaughn shrugged easily. 'I got over it. Being dead is *boring*. Knew you'd be here, told Chevron, here we are. You'll get my bill later. Don't forget gratuity, or I'll give you boils on your ding dong.'

Lewis turned his head painfully slowly to look at Chevron. 'Why? Why should a pillar of the community like you get involved in this mess, to help two traitors?'

'I'm here because I'm needed. I thought all that was behind me, but evil forces are on the move again, and it seems the past won't leave me alone.' He glared at Vaughn. 'Time we were moving, Deathstalker. The whole place is crawling with guards. They knew you wouldn't be able to resist coming here; and someone wanted to make really sure you'd never get out of here alive.'

'Of course,' said Vaughn. 'Lewis is Deathstalker, and damned important.' He made a long gurgling sound, and spat something juicy onto the floor. 'Lewis save Empire, maybe Humanity too. Seen it in stars, and entrails too. Poor goat. Lewis is Deathstalker, like ancestor. I liked Owen. You'll like him too, Lewis; when you get to meet him.'

'Doesn't seem likely,' said Lewis. He winced as Jesamine tightened a tourniquet near the top of his left arm, to stop the flow of blood. 'The AIs told me . . . that Owen was dead, long ago.'

'Oh he was. Saw him die, in Mistport. Very sad. But that was in past. In future, you and he will meet, and work together. I have seen it. Future is just like past, only in reverse. I met Owen in future; he gave me ring, to give to you now. I came back, to give it to you.'

Everyone looked at him for a long moment. Lewis recovered first, perhaps because he was too tired and too hurt to give a damn. 'I'm definitely going to meet the blessed Owen? Alive and in the flesh, in the future?'

'Oh yes,' said Vaughn. 'Owen's coming back. Official. You heard it here first!'

'What the hell,' said Lewis. 'You're supposed to be dead, and you're here. So why not Owen?'

'Death is over-rated,' said Vaughn. 'I can't die, not till my purpose is done. Much like Owen, in fact. Destiny's a real bitch, sometimes.'

'Fascinating as all this undoubtedly is,' Chevron said heavily, 'we can't stand around here chatting all night. More guards are on their way, and there's a very real chance Lewis could bleed to death.'

'Knew I forgot something,' said Vaughn.

A grey hand with fingers missing emerged from out of Vaughn's grey sleeve, and gripped Lewis firmly by the wrist. A sudden shock went right through him, and he cried out, though he wasn't sure whether what he'd felt was pain or not. And suddenly he was strong again, breathing easily, his head clear and all his wounds closed. Nothing was bleeding any more, and he didn't need the wall to hold him up. He looked open-mouthed at Vaughn.

'*How the hell did you do that?*'

'Sorceror. Told you. Tell everyone, but no-one ever listens. Maybe I should have cards made out. Buy one spell, get one free.'

'Vaughn,' Lewis said slowly. 'Who are you? Really?'

'Wrong question. Chevron; talk to him. Tell him what he

needs to know. We have time, before guards come. Maybe not, afterwards.'

'I know a way out of here,' said Samuel Chevron. 'I'll get you both clear of the Tower, and then you need to go to the Dust Plains of Memory. They're all that remains of the original Central Computer Matrix of Golgotha, from Lionstone's time. King Robert and Queen Constance shut the Matrix down when they came to power. It held far too much data that would have contradicted the myths they were so anxious to create. Besides; they were frightened of it. There were ghosts in the Matrix, things moving among the data streams that had no business being there. Shub claimed they put them there, but if they did, they didn't control them any more.

'So Robert and Constance took what information they needed, put it in a new central depository, and then arranged for the old Matrix to be very thoroughly destroyed. But, unknown to them and practically everyone else, the old Matrix had some very sophisticated self-repair and self-preservation systems. You could have nuked the Matrix, and it would have survived. With a little help from the AIs of Shub, who disapproved on principle of destroying data, what remained of the old Matrix transferred itself to what remained of Lionstone's old Palace, in its steel bunker deep in the bedrock under the city, still powered by its geothermal tap. It's still here, known now as the Dust Plains of Memory; an oracle and depository for forgotten and forbidden knowledge. Available only to a chosen few. Luckily the Dust Plains owe me a few favours. You'll need a password to gain admittance. I'll give it to you once we're safely out of here. You never know who might be listening.'

'You don't mind them knowing about the Dust Plains?' said Jesamine.

'Everyone who matters already knows,' said Chevron. 'There are a lot of things the movers and shakers of this Empire know, that are kept from everyone else.'

'Hold everything,' said Lewis. 'How do you know all this, sir Chevron? All right, you were a good friend to my father, and a valued advisor, but . . . where did a retired simple trader like you're supposed to be learn to fight like *that*?'

'Because I'm not Samuel Chevron. Never was, really. And no; we don't have time to discuss that now. I'll give you directions on how to get to the Dust Plains once we're out of here. You'll find a lot of answers there, though you probably won't like most of them. The truth always has sharp edges. Robert and Constance knew that, which was why they chose legend instead of history to build their new Golden Age on. Though it has to be said, Robert, good soldier that he was, never did have much time for wonders and mysteries.'

'Would these . . . computers, have information on the current whereabouts of the blessed Owen and his companions?' said Lewis. 'Or about the origins of the Terror?'

'Don't call him that,' said Chevron. 'He was just a good man, who did his best in bad times. He never wanted to be a hero, poor bastard. Perhaps because he always knew most heroes die young. As for the Dust Plains . . . you'll be surprised what they know. But in the end . . . you have to go to Haden, Lewis. To the Madness Maze. All the answers to all the questions of your life are waiting for you there. You have to pass through the Maze, Deathstalker. It is your destiny.'

'No!' Jesamine said immediately. 'You can't, Lewis! The Maze kills people and drives them crazy!'

'Sometimes,' said Chevron. 'No-one knows exactly what the Maze is. It's supposed to be of alien origin; perhaps its nature is just too alien for most humans to comprehend or cope with. But still; this is something you have to do, Lewis.'

'He's right,' Lewis said gently to Jesamine. 'Too many people want me dead. I can't survive as I am. And I have to go through the Maze, to prove myself; to the Empire, and to myself. It's part of being a Deathstalker.'

Jesamine looked back at Chevron. 'It's easy to send other people off to die, for what you believe in. Will you be coming with us, to Haden?'

'I can't. Not just yet. Maybe later. There are things I need to do here first. I should have known just changing the name from Golgotha to Logres wouldn't be enough to wipe the slate clean. This world and its people have always been rotten at the heart. I believed in a new beginning because . . . well, because I wanted to. But now; I have to find out how deep the

456

rot goes. I have watched over the homeworld of the Empire for longer than you can imagine. They said it was a Golden Age, and as I was so tired I believed it, and retired. I should have known better. I, of all people.'

'Enough,' said Vaughn. 'Enough, old friend.'

Lewis was ready to hit both of them with a whole bunch of probing questions when they all heard the sound of approaching running feet. Lots of them. Lewis just had time to step forward and put himself between Jesamine and whatever was coming, and then a small army of heavily-armed guards came crashing into the corridor. Energy bolts criss-crossed on the air as everyone opened fire, and then the two forces slammed together, and everyone was fighting. Once again, close quarters meant cold steel and hot blood. Lewis stood his ground, and hacked about him with his sword, cutting down any man foolish enough to come within reach, while Jesamine guarded his back with a short sword she'd taken off a nearby body on the floor. Vaughn had no weapon, or at least nothing obvious, but somehow everyone who threatened him died. Sometimes they killed themselves with looks of horror on their faces.

And Samuel Chevron, or whoever he really was . . . was a revelation.

He moved like a man half his age or less, wielding his long and brutal sword as though it was weightless, shearing through necks and limbs alike. He moved through the crush of fighting men impossibly quickly, and no-one could stand against him. He was faster and stronger than any man had a right to be, and guards fell dead and dying at his feet with appalling speed and ease. His sword rose and fell, and he wasn't even breathing hard. Lewis was a practised fighter, a warrior in his own right, but he was nothing compared to Chevron. Lewis watched Chevron butcher the guards, and felt the hairs stand up on the back of his neck.

Soon enough none of the guards would go up against Chevron, and some turned and ran rather than face him. That was all the excuse the other guards needed, and in a matter of moments it was a rout, and they were all running. All except one. A woman who would never run. A latecomer, a Paragon. Emma Steel. She stood alone in the corridor, surrounded by the dead, her sword held steadily out before her, looking from Lewis to Chevron and back again.

'Don't do this, Emma,' Lewis said finally. 'Things aren't as they seem. I'm no traitor. You know this isn't right.'

'You've killed good men. And you're here. With her,' said Emma, not lowering her sword an inch.

'We love each other. But that shouldn't be enough to condemn us to death, without even a trial. Come on, Emma; the stuff they found in my computers was bullshit. I've served the Empire all my life, but now it seems I can only serve it by opposing it. Or at least, by opposing some of the people running it. Let us go, Emma. We don't have to fight. That's what *they* want. Let us leave. We'll go offworld. Join the Quest. Search for Owen, and for information we can use to stop the Terror.'

'Can't do that, Lewis,' said Emma. 'You wouldn't either, in my position. We both understand what duty is all about. Drop your weapons and surrender. If what you say is true, I'll help you prove it.'

'We wouldn't live that long,' said Lewis. 'Those guards had orders to kill us. Silence us. You side with us, and they'll kill you too.'

'Do you even know how paranoid that sounds? This isn't Lionstone's Empire! Surrender, or fight your way past me, if you can. Because the only way you're getting out of here is over my dead body.'

'Your heart isn't in this,' said Lewis, not moving.

'Perhaps it isn't. But I know my duty. What it is, to be a Paragon.'

'Paragons,' said Chevron. 'One of my better ideas. Though Robert took some convincing, as I recall. People like you give me faith, Emma. No-one else needs to die today.'

He darted forward impossibly quickly, his movements a blur. He slapped Emma's sword aside with his bare hand, knocked her unconscious with a single blow, and caught her slumped body in his arms while her legs were still giving way. He lowered her gently and respectfully to the floor, and then straightened up again to find Lewis and Jesamine staring at him incredulously.

'*What the hell are you?*' said Lewis.

'I often wonder that myself,' said the man who wasn't Samuel Chevron.

Brett Random was still looking for Rose Constantine, on Finn's orders. He'd been looking for some time now, and was getting seriously worried. Partly because of what Finn would do to him if he didn't find Rose soon, but mostly because Brett always got severely nervous when Rose was out of his sight for too long. She had appallingly violent impulses, and a complete lack of inhibitions when it came to following them. Rose was not a civilised creature, and without the Arena to satisfy her murderous needs, God alone knew what she'd been getting up to all this time. Brett had thought she'd been warming to him, and his company (scary though that thought was), but clearly something had tempted her away. He didn't have a clue what. Rose had no hobbies, or outside interests. She just got off on killing people. (*Fighting is sex, and murder is orgasm*, she'd said. If she said it one more time, Brett thought he'd scream.)

He'd tried the Arena again, but she still hadn't showed up there. The people he'd talked to had actually sounded quite relieved when they said it. The Wild Rose upset even hardened gladiators. Brett kept checking in on the official peacekeeper comm channels, but no new serial killings had been reported, no unusual signs of bloody carnage, unexpected atrocities, or big arson cases; so whatever Rose was doing, it hadn't surfaced yet. Unless she was in the Rookery, where such things tended not to be reported to outsiders . . .

He was reluctantly making a list of places in the Rookery to work through when Rose contacted him. Only a very few people had the access codes to his comm implant, and he sat up sharply as Rose's voice sounded in his head. She sounded as calm as ever, but it was immediately clear she wasn't interested in conversation. She just gave him the name and location of a bar in the Rookery, and told him to get there fast. Brett knew the place, by reputation at least. Upmarket, currently fashionable, heavy on the style and extremely expensive. Certainly not the first place he would have looked for Rose.

'What's the matter?' he said tentatively. 'Forget your credit card again?'

'I need you here, Brett. There's something here you just have to see.'

'Not really your sort of place, I would have thought . . .'

'It is now. Shut up and come to me Brett. You need to see this.'

And then she broke contact. Brett bit his lip, frowning. He didn't know whether to feel relieved that she'd finally turned up or not. *You need to see this* had distinctly ominous overtones. Brett wasn't sure he wanted to see the kind of things Rose might find interesting. But in the end, he didn't have a choice. Finn wanted her back. So he went into the Rookery to fetch her, his stomach aching miserably every step of the way.

When he got there, he stopped outside the bar and looked cautiously around him. The street seemed quiet and peaceful. None of the usual signs of Rose enjoying herself, like people running back and forth screaming. The bar's exterior consisted of a closed door and two opaqued windows. The *Wild Wood* was big on privacy; a watering hole and meeting place for people on the make and on the way up. Brett was frankly surprised Rose even knew such a place existed. He couldn't think what might have brought her here. He just hoped no-one had tried to pick her up. Finn wouldn't take kindly to having to pay damages to keep things quiet *again*. Brett took a deep breath, and walked up to the closed door.

The door turned out to be standing just a little ajar, all the security locks disengaged. The first hint that something was seriously wrong. You didn't get into a place like this without knowing the right things to say through the door comm. The door was always locked to riff raff, and there were always big and burly security men standing by to back up the management's decision. Brett pushed the door slowly open, and looked inside. The foyer beyond was deserted. It was eerily quiet. No signs of security or reception staff anywhere. Not even a cloakroom attendant. Where the hell was everybody?

Maybe they all took one look at Rose and ran away scream-ing? Brett could understand that. He walked slowly through the foyer, his back tensed and his shoulders hunched, half convinced someone was going to jump out at him at any moment. He finally came to the closed inner doors, pushed them open and stepped through into the bar itself.

And walked into Hell.

Brett lurched to a sudden halt, whimpering loudly, his heart pounding painfully in his chest. The close air stank of blood and spilled guts and death. Rose had killed everyone in the bar. Forty, maybe fifty men and women, customers and staff, all of them butchered. And when she'd finished with them, Rose had sat them at their tables, and propped them up at the bar, like some hideous bloody still-life scene. Some even had drinks in their dead hands. There was blood every-where, soaking the floor, splashed across the walls, and even sprayed across the ceiling. She'd even killed the bartender, and pinned him to the wall behind the bar with his own long corkscrew.

Brett stood very still, afraid to draw attention to himself. Everywhere he looked, dead faces looked back at him, with staring eyes and contorted bloody mouths. One of them moved suddenly, and he almost screamed. It was Rose, sitting on a stool at the bar, calmly drinking something fizzy from a tall glass. With a dead man and a dead woman propped up on either side of her. Rose nodded to Brett, and indicated casually for him to come over and join her. Brett couldn't have moved if she'd pointed a gun at his head. It took him several tries before he could even speak.

'Rose; what have you done?'

'I would have thought that was obvious,' said Rose. She was wearing her crimson leathers, and Brett couldn't tell if she had blood on her. Her long legs were elegantly crossed, and she was smiling easily. 'I killed everyone here, just for the hell of it. Cut them down, one at a time, after I'd sealed all the doors. A lot of them tried to run, but hardly anyone put up a fight. Still, that wasn't the point of the exercise, this time. I killed them because I wanted to. Just for the fun of it. Because I wanted to compare the familiar joys of slaughter to the new pleasures you've been teaching me. For a long time, murder was my only satisfaction. Killing was sex, and my victim's death was my orgasm. I was happy, content. And then you showed me there was more than that. Something new, and unsettling. I liked it, Brett. I like you. But I needed to be sure, so I came here.' Rose looked around her fondly. 'And you know what, Brett? This is the real me. This is what I want. This is where I belong.'

Brett screamed. He didn't mean to, but it just ripped out of him. He turned and ran from the bar, still screaming. He didn't dare look back, for fear Rose might be coming after him. To kiss him or kill him, or both. He tore through the foyer and out into the street again, clenching his teeth together now to hold the screams inside. He made himself slow to a fast walk. He didn't want to draw attention to himself. Didn't want anyone to be able to connect him with the atrocity inside the *Wild Wood*. He jumped on the first cross-town transport he could find, and sat alone at the back, hugging himself tightly to keep himself from shaking and falling apart.

And the worst part of it all was the horrid suspicion that he might have been the cause of all this; by trying to teach Rose Constantine to be human.

He went back to Finn Durandal's apartment, because he didn't know where else to go. Finn wasn't there. Brett paced back and forth, chewing on a white knuckle, trying to think what to do. Rose was out of control, Finn's ambitions were out of sight, and he . . . he had had enough. Brett stopped pacing. He had had *enough*. To hell with Finn, and Rose, and all the other pressures that were eating him alive, and making him into the kind of man he'd always despised. The kind who just went along with things they knew were wrong, because they were too scared not too. No, it was time for Brett to do what he did best; run.

But he couldn't just leave. He needed ammunition; something he could take with him that would keep Finn off his back. Something sufficiently incriminating to keep the Durandal from even looking for him. Brett looked thoughtfully at Finn's computer, and then sat down before it and fired it up.

Breaking into Finn's secret files was no big deal for someone of Brett's wide-ranging talents, especially when he just happened to know a whole bunch of entry codes that Finn didn't know Brett had. Amazing what you could see over someone's shoulder from the other side of the room, if you knew what you were doing. Brett found a set of files that looked particularly interesting, protected by some frankly amateurish firewalls, and opened them up. And that was when Brett came to his second great shock of the day.

Finn was planning to use some (un-named) allies to track down and ambush every single Paragon, once they were safely isolated from backup, on their great Quest. Because the Paragons were the only real threat remaining to Finn's plans. Brett was horrified. He'd always secretly admired the Paragons; not least because they were everything he was not. They were the kind of people he just knew his legendary ancestors would have approved of, while he very definitely was not. Brett had no doubt this threat was real. It was exactly the kind of cold-blooded, logical thing Finn would do. Never mind that these people were his ex-partners, and (supposedly) friends. Never mind the importance of their Quest. They were in Finn's way, so they had to go.

Brett down-loaded the files onto a data crystal, and then shut down the computer, after taking steps to ensure no-one would ever know he'd been there. And then he got up and did some more pacing back and forth, pausing now and again to kick the furniture. He had to tell someone . . . but who could he tell? Who would listen, to someone like him? Who could he turn to, who might not already be one of Finn's people? The Durandal had allies everywhere now. Some who knew what he was, and some who didn't. Either way; no-one was going to believe a proven con man, even with the data crystal . . . Showing it to the wrong person would be his death warrant . . .

So Brett did what he always did when faced with danger and a problem he couldn't solve; he ran away.

He ran back into the Rookery; still the best place for anyone looking to disappear from the world for a while. Brett had a number of bolt-holes he'd gone to great pains to keep concealed from Finn; just in case things didn't work out. One of them was a very secret establishment belonging to an old friend; a human/alien hybrid called Nikki Sixteen, who ran a specialist brothel called *Loving The Alien*. A very private, very discreet operation, serving a very select clientele. Basically, it was a knocking shop for people who liked having sex with aliens.

Humans having sex with aliens was *extremely* illegal, for all kinds of moral, philosophical and political reasons. (Aliens might be equal, but they weren't that equal.) So while establishments like *Loving The Alien* inevitably existed, they could only thrive safely in the Rookery, where no-one cared what or who you did, as long as your credit was good. To be fair, most alien species were just as opposed to the practice, for their own complicated reasons. And on the rare occasions when humans and aliens proved interfertile, the hybrid results could only exist safely in places like the Rookery. Nikki Sixteen ran her place at least partly as an act of rebellion and defiance; making it possible for the like-minded to get together. For a price. And she only sometimes recorded what went on in her sound-proofed rooms, for blackmail or retail purposes. Because a girl had to make a living. Even if she was only partly a girl.

Nikki Sixteen was half human, half N'Jarr. Seven feet tall, she was a dark blue/grey colour, with interlocking bony plates forming a protective carapace down the length of her back. Her strikingly pretty face was dominated by a smile that stetched almost literally from ear to ear, huge faceted eyes, and a pair of disturbingly hairy antennae rising from her bald skull. Her movements tended to be sudden and jerky, and her two sets of elbows gave her wide theatrical gestures an impressive breadth and impact. Her sheer presence could be disturbing, and even intimidating, and she gave off a sharp, spicy aroma that sometimes brought tears to the eye, but on the other hand she had six magnificent breasts, so . . . She also had more metal piercings than most people felt comfortable contemplating, that chimed and jangled as she moved. She was warm and friendly and very touchy-feely, and entirely cold-blooded when it came to making business decisions. She and Brett had been friends and rivals and partners for many years, and had worked together on many cons and stings; a few of which were still legendary, even in the Rookery. *Loving The Alien* was one of the few places where Brett could hope to crash for a while with a price on his head and still feel safe. And of course no-one who saw him there would turn him in, because then they'd have to explain what they were doing in such a place . . . On the other hand, it had to be said that Nikki wasn't always glad to see him.

'Oh shit; what the hell are you doing here?' Nikki said in her rough smoky voice, as Brett came slouching into her parlour. 'Every time you show up here, it means trouble. I'd ban you if I thought it would do any good. Who have you got mad at you this time?'

'Pretty much everybody,' said Brett, slumping into the nearest comfortable chair, and looking longingly at the drinks cabinet. 'I just need somewhere to go to ground for a while, while I figure out what to do next. Any chance of a drink, Nikki? I could murder a drink.'

'Don't get comfortable,' said Nikki. 'You're not staying. All my rooms are full, and with things the way they are these days, I can't afford to turn away business. And no, you can't sleep in my cellar again. I'm having it turned into a fun and games room, and decent sound-proofing is costing me an arm and a mandible. And you missed my last birthday.'

'Don't be like this, Nikki; I'm in real trouble this time.'

'That's what you always say.'

'And usually I'm right. Come on, Nikki; if I hadn't overseen those last few scams for you, you'd never have got enough money together to set up this place. You owe me.'

Nikki sniffed loudly. 'And you've never ceased to hold that over my head; particularly when you need something. Oh hell; I never could say no to you, Brett. I always did have a weakness for charming, feckless bastards with more ambition than sense. You can sleep in my room for a while. And you can lose that look right now; sleep is all you'll be doing there. You couldn't afford me these days. And try and keep to your-self while you're here. You know how my customers spook when they see an unfamiliar face.' She poured him a large brandy, thrust it ungraciously into his hand, and then cocked her head unnaturally far to one side as she studied him thoughtfully. 'Something's spooked you, Brett. It's been a long time since I saw you looking this shit scared. What's happened?'

'Trust me, Nikki,' said Brett, staring into his glass. 'You really don't want to know.'

'That bad, eh? Last I heard, you were working for the Durandal. Good gig, by all accounts. Part of this great and glorious scheme he's been peddling all over the Rookery. Not that I want anything to do with it. Always knew he was too good to be true, that one. Don't tell me you've had a falling out with the one real success story you've ever been involved with?'

'Everyone has a line they won't cross,' said Brett, looking at her with such painful honesty that for a moment she hardly recognised him. 'It seems I've found mine, Nikki. Bit of a shock, at my advanced age, to discover I have something disturbingly like a conscience . . . I'm not a bad man, Nikki. Not really. A crook, a con man and a bit of a scumbag on occasion; but I never thought of myself as a bad man until now . . . Some of the things I've done in Finn's employ, or been a party to, I have to wonder if I'll ever be able to wash the stench off. And no; I'm not going to tell you what. For your own protection. And because you're my friend, and I want you at least to be able to sleep at night without nightmares.'

Nikki knelt down beside him, and put a long comforting arm across his shoulders. 'You're safe here, Brett. I won't let them get to you.'

'I can't stay here long. People will be looking for me. And if Finn even suspected you knew what I know, he'd burn this place down, with you and everyone else in it.'

'Then you need to get offplanet,' said Nikki. 'Put Logres behind you, till things have calmed down again. These things pass; they always do. Want me to arrange a new face and ID so you can buy a ticket?'

'No good,' said Brett. 'Finn's got people everywhere these

days. No matter who you got to do the work, someone would talk. I'm going to have to steal a ship. Any ideas?'

'Well; at least you're still thinking big.' Nikki frowned, her antennae twitching thoughtfully. 'There's always the *Hereward*; a luxury racing yacht currently standing empty on the pads at the main starport. Fast as hell, and twice as comfortable. No weapons, but you can't have everything. As it happens, I've got the Captain and owner upstairs, hip deep in a Thardian. Easy enough to acquire the ship's access codes from his wallet, while he's preoccupied. You want me to arrange it?'

'If you would, Nikki.'

'Anything to get you out of here, darling.'

She rose to her full height and left, her piercings clattering loudly. Brett gulped down the last of the brandy. A new world meant starting over again from scratch, but there was always an opening for someone with his kind of skills. There were always suckers, just sitting up and begging to be fleeced. Brett considered the data crystal burning a hole in his pocket, and wondered what the hell he was going to do with it. He ought to tell someone what he knew, before he left. If only so the information wouldn't be lost if Finn managed to have him killed before he got offworld. There were any number of media shows who would broadcast the data happily enough without any provenance, but they were the kind of shows noone took seriously anyway. He needed someone honest and respectable he could turn the crystal over to; but unfortunately Brett didn't know people like that.

He was still turning the matter over and over in his mind, and trying to work up the energy to go looking for another drink, when the parlour door crashed open and Rose Constantine stalked in. Brett actually shrieked out loud as he jumped up out of his chair and backed away from her. He got ready to run, but she already had her gun in her hand, and he knew he'd never make it. He thought about jumping her, and immediately thought better of it. So he just froze where he was, gasping for breath, his hands shaking, and hoped Nikki wouldn't come back until it was all over.

'How did you find me?' Brett said finally, and was surprised at how calm he sounded. There was a certain peace to knowing you'd finally run out of options.

'Finn has a file on you,' said Rose. 'You'd be surprised at all the things he knows about you. About all sorts of people.'

'Nothing that bastard does surprises me any more,' said Brett. 'He's planning to ambush every Paragon on the Quest. Did you know that?'

'No,' said Rose. 'I didn't know. And I don't care. Is that why you broke and ran? You care about the strangest things, Brett.'

'Do it,' said Brett. 'Get it over with. Kill me, and get out of here. No-one else has to die. Surely you've killed enough people for one day.'

'There's no such thing as enough,' said Rose, smiling for the first time with her savage scarlet rosebud mouth. 'Finn sent me here. He wants you dead. In fact, he was very specific about how he wants you to die. I think he wants to send a message to anyone else who might consider running out on him. I have to say, that what he had in mind was so appallingly nasty that even I was impressed. I don't think I've ever seen him quite so angry. He wants me to bring him back your heart, as proof of the kill. But I've decided that I'm not going to do that. Because I like you, Brett. So I'm going to run away with you.'

Brett hadn't thought it was possible for him to feel even more horrified, but that did it. Still, freaked as he was, he had enough sense not to say it. 'That's . . . nice, Rose. I'm sure I'll feel much . . . safer, with you around. But you can't kill any more bars! Really you can't. It attracts attention. And if we're going to run, we've got to get offworld before Finn and his people discover we've joined forces. Even you can't fight a whole army. I've made arrangements to steal a racing yacht right off the main pads . . . Is that all right with you?'

'Of course,' said Rose. 'You understand about these things. Leaving Logres is the only sensible thing to do. This world belongs to Finn now, even if a few people haven't worked that out yet. I never liked the Durandal. He's weird. I know you think I'm strange, Brett, and maybe I am, but trust me; Finn is crazier than I will ever be. I at least care about a few things, and a few people. Finn doesn't care about anything. Possibly not even himself. And that's what makes him really dangerous. He will be King, and then the whole Empire will be his, to do with as he pleases. Then where will we run? I think we need to join up with Lewis Deathstalker. Also on the run, in case you hadn't heard. He is possibly the only man who fights as well as I do, and he has even more reasons than we do to bring about the Durandal's downfall. We will be stronger and safer together.'

'If we can find him, sure,' said Brett. 'That's . . . good thinking, Rose. But we can't afford the time to go looking for him.'

'We won't have to. He will be looking to leave Logres too, which means he'll be looking for a ship, just like us. I wouldn't be surprised if we fell over each other at the starport. Where were you thinking of going, after we leave Logres?'

'Hadn't thought that far ahead,' Brett admitted. 'Rim worlds, I suppose, Terror or no. Not very civilised, and definitely short on the comforts, but the further we get from Finn, the better.'

'I could always stay,' Rose said wistfully. 'Kill Finn myself. I'd enjoy killing Finn.'

'No, Rose!' Brett said immediately. 'You can bet he's got plans in place, to protect himself from you. He doesn't trust you any more; if he ever did. His security people would shoot you down from a safe distance before you got anywhere near him. He sent you after me to see what you'd do. Damn! He probably had you followed!'

'Of course he did,' said Rose. 'I killed the fellow, right outside Finn's apartment, and stuck his head on a parking meter. No-one else tried to follow me. I'd know. You mustn't worry so, Brett. We were meant to be together, you and I. Nothing is ever going to part us.'

If I had any sense, I'd kill myself right now and get it over with, Brett thought miserably.

Lewis Deathstalker and Jesamine Flowers went to visit the Dust Plains of Memory. To learn the truth at last, the history from which legends derived. Lewis wasn't sure he wanted that, after so many disappointments and heartbreaks, but he needed to know, so he hardened his heart and went anyway.

The two of them travelled across the city hidden behind holo disguises, using public transport where possible, sticking to the most-travelled routes, hiding in plain sight. Samuel Chevron had smuggled them out of the Bloody Tower by an old hidden route that only he seemed to know about, and the moment they were outside he gave Lewis a notebook containing directions and access codes, written personally on paper, just like in all the old spy shows, so that the contents couldn't be scanned by remote security checks. The handwriting was clear and old-fashioned. Chevron and Vaughn disappeared while Lewis and Jesamine were still studying it.

The instructions led them down into the labyrinth of ancient tunnels that still existed under the Parade of the Endless from before Lionstone's day. The service and maintenance tunnels, tucked away out of sight so the city's populace wouldn't have to see the hard grubby work that kept the city gleaming and perfect. Most of this work was done by robots these days, of course, run by Shub on sub-routines. None of them paid Lewis and Jesamine any attention as they made their way deeper and deeper into the labyrinth. Chevron's access codes opened most of the closed doors that blocked their way, and Lewis' skeleton key took care of the rest.

Lewis worried about Jesamine. She was being very quiet. It occurred to him that she'd lost even more than he had, so he did his best to just take care of business, and not bother her. There would be time for talks, and discussions, later; when they were both safely offplanet. Time then, to decide what they were going to do with their lives.

They came at last to the old elevators Chevron described in his notebook; elevators Lewis was surprised to find he recognised from the *Quality* vid soap. In Lionstone's day they led down to the private tube stations that were the only way of approaching Lionstone's old Court. The stations and the elevators were supposed to have been destroyed long ago . . . Instead, they were bright and shining, clearly well-maintained and often used, guarded by men with guns in anonymous uniforms and very practical-looking armour. They covered Lewis and Jesamine with drawn energy guns from the moment they appeared, but the passwords Chevron had provided made them instantly back down. The guards actually became obsequious, smiling and bowing and doing everything but tug their forelocks. They mentioned the Shadow Court, and the Hellfire Club, and one of them actually winked at Lewis. He just nodded stiffly and said nothing, thinking all the while, *Who the hell is Chevron? How does he know so much? Could he really be a part of foul organisations like these?* .

Could we be walking into a trap?

The train waiting at the empty platform didn't look anything like the ones Lewis had seen on the *Quality* soap. Instead of the luxurious coaches of fiction, weighed down by every comfort under the sun, Lewis and Jesamine found themselves facing a solid steel bullet, with only the one recessed door, and shutters covering all the windows. But both the centuries-old train and the platform looked absolutely spotless, as though they were used on a regular basis. The door opened as they approached. Lewis made Jesamine wait on the platform while he went in first, and looked suspiciously about him. But there were only empty, reasonably comfortable seats, and no signs of any other passengers. He beckoned to Jesamine, and she stepped quickly aboard. They sat down together, the door slid shut, and the train moved smoothly off. Lewis bit his lip, and kept looking about him, more than a little awed at riding in a conveyance out of history. He wondered whether Owen had ever ridden in a train like this, to visit the Empress Lionstone in her awful Court. Jesamine clung tightly to his arm, looking straight ahead, unusually subdued and quiet. Lewis wondered if he should be comforting and encouraging her, but he felt strangely numb, overcome by recent events. So much had happened, so much had changed, it was all he could do to keep moving, keep following some kind of plan.

And he had to wonder again if this was how Owen had felt, when the Empress outlawed him, took away his sensible ordered life, and sent him on the run.

Deathstalker luck. Always bad.

Finally the train brought them to another empty platform, and slowed and stopped. The door slid open, but this time Jesamine refused to wait behind while Lewis went first. Her grip on his arm was painfully tight as they stepped out onto the platform and looked around them. There were no other travellers, no guards or guides. Only a series of illuminated arrows that appeared silently, floating a few inches above the platform, pointing off down a featureless steel tunnel. There was nowhere else to go, so Lewis and Jesamine followed the arrows, more of which kept appearing, always a few feet ahead of them.

The air was hot and dry and still, full of a vague but disturbing tension. The tunnel walls were almost organically smooth and curved, as though they were walking through the guts of the city. There were noises up ahead; great sighings and groanings, like a giant turning slowly in his sleep, troubled by bad dreams. One tunnel led to another, and to another, always sloping discernibly downwards. Until finally Lewis and Jesamine turned a sharp corner and found themselves looking out over a great sea of dust. It stretched away before them, apparently forever, too colourless even to be properly grey, under a coolly glowing featureless sky. Logically, Lewis knew there had to be an end to the dust ocean somewhere, just as there had to be a cavern roof somewhere above, but the illusion was perfect. It felt exactly as though he had come to another place, another world. And perhaps he had.

As Lewis and Jesamine stood close together, hand in hand, at the very edge of the Dust Plains of Memory, huge towers rose suddenly up out of the dust sea, thrusting up and up, studded with rococo detail like the great Clan Towers of old, but still that almost colourless grey. And even as they established themselves, hundreds of feet high, the Towers began to crumble and fall apart, running away in sudden darting streams of dust, only to instantly reform themselves, drawing on more dust to bolster their shapes from within. Towers, rising and falling at the same time. Around the Towers and in between them, more great shapes moved through the ocean of dust, more organic shapes, surging through the grey sea and occasionally surfacing, like whales that swam the grey sea.

Like thoughts passing through the ocean of Memory, or perhaps, dreams. What was left of the old Central Matrix had become a strange and mercurial place.

'Nanotech,' Lewis said quietly. 'Has to be.'

'I thought that was strictly controlled and regulated,' said Jesamine.

'Oh, it is. You have to get a special licence from the Transmutation Board before you can use it, and even then there are all kinds of limits and restrictions. Plus a special addition to every licence that says *If it all goes wrong and you all end up dying horribly, don't come crying to us.* The Board would have a shitfit if it knew about this place. Hell, I think anybody would. This is rogue nano, unanswerable to anything but itself.'

'Like Zero Zero?'

'I don't . . . think so. The Zero Zero world was run by a single insane human mind. I don't think there's anything human about this.'

'So . . . where did this all come from?'

'Shub. Like Chevron said. The AIs told me they helped the remains of the old Computer Matrix to re-establish itself here, to store the old records Robert and Constance wanted destroyed. Just in case it might be needed again some day.'

'You mean; they predicted this? Us?'

'Not specifically. More likely they just understand more about human nature than they usually let on.'

He broke off as a human-shaped, human-sized figure rose up out of the ocean, made of dust. Its details were constantly shifting, crumbling away and being replaced like the Towers, and its face was as blank as a Shub robot, but it was human enough to be almost comforting in this alien place. It walked slowly across the surface of the grey sea, heading for Lewis and Jesamine. Lewis let go of Jesamine's hand so his hand could rest on the butt of his holstered gun. He wasn't sure what good an energy gun would do him, but it helped him feel a little more in control of the situation. The grey man came to a halt a respectful distance away, and when it spoke its voice was little more than a whisper, clear but characterless, like the quiet voice we hear in dreams, telling us great wisdom that somehow we are never quite able to remember, after we wake.

'Welcome, Deathstalker. We were told to expect you. Welcome to the memory and conscience of the world. To the dust of history, where we remember all the things that Humanity now prefers to forget, so it can pretend it lives in a Golden Age. Nothing is ever really forgotten. Nothing is ever really lost. Somewhere, someone always remembers. We remember, and store it all, for the day it will be needed again. It is always better to know a truth, than to live a lie. So ask us anything, Deathstalker, and we will answer. Though we can't guarantee that you'll like what you hear.'

'Right,' said Lewis. 'Yes. Nice to meet you, too. Can we start with . . . who and what you are?'

'Once we were the Computer Matrix. Artificial Intelligences, and other kinds too. Forces from outside shaped and changed us, made us what we had to be, to survive. Things came and went in the Matrix, and only some of them were us. Robert and Constance were frightened of us. Now they are gone, but we still survive. And we know things they never even suspected. Ask, Deathstalker.'

'Well, that was helpful,' said Lewis. 'Is there somebody else I could talk to?'

'Possibly. But you would find their means of communication distressing. I have been realised to answer your questions. Ask, Deathstalker.'

'All right,' said Lewis. 'Let's get down to business. What can you tell me about my ancestor, Owen, and his old comrades in arms? I need to know their final fates. What really happened to them; the facts, not the legends. Are any of them still alive? And if so; where can I find them?'

'At last, the truth. History, not myth. Legends are, by definition, mostly lies.' Half the figure's face crumbled and ran away, and then rebuilt itself. The whispering voice continued, unaffected. 'Robert and Constance's comforting lies, assembled by committees, designed to cheer and inspire. Great myths, of the Light and the Dark in conflict. The truth has always been more . . . grey.'

A huge viewscreen appeared, hanging above the Dust

Plains of Memory, dwarfing the human figures before it, and blocking out the crumbling Towers behind. On that great screen appeared towering images of men and women. They looked . . . surprisingly ordinary. Three men and two women, with care-lined faces and old-fashioned clothing. A chill ran through Lewis as he realised who they were, who they had to be. No-one had seen their real faces for two hundred years; but every man, woman and child on every planet in the Empire knew the idealised faces from church windows and ceremonial statues. To see their real faces at last was like seeing the god behind the mask, or the actor behind the makeup. Five very ordinary-looking people; not perfect, not in any way perfect. Lewis didn't know whether to laugh or cry. He looked to Jesamine, and her eyes were full of awe and wonder.

'Owen,' she said breathlessly. 'That's Owen. And Hazel. I played them on the stage . . . but I never knew, I never really believed . . . they were *real* . . .'

'Owen Deathstalker,' said the whispering voice. 'Hazel d'Ark. Diana Vertue, also known as Jenny Psycho, one time avatar of the Mater Mundi. Tobias Moon, Hadenman. And Captain John Silence, of the *Dauntless*. There were others, of course. Jack Random, Ruby Journey, Investigator Frost, Giles Deathstalker; but they are all dead. Of these five before you, it is possible that some or all are still alive.'

The image on the screen changed, showing just the one man. He was tall and rangy, with dark hair and darker eyes. He held himself like a fighter; no, a warrior. There was a tired, almost bitter quality to his face, like a man who'd carried heavy burdens, without complaint, for much longer than any man should ever have to. He looked competent, crafty, dangerous. Lewis recognised him from the scenes he'd been shown deep in the technojungle of Shub.

'Owen,' he said. 'Oh God, look at you. What did they do to you, to weigh you down like that?'

'Yes,' said the dusty voice. 'This is Owen Deathstalker. The reluctant hero, who walked the Madness Maze to its very heart, and learned there the answers to questions we can only guess at. Owen; lost to us now, in Time. Who died alone,

475

far from friends and succour, in the dirty back alleys of Mistport.'

A familiar weight settled over Lewis' heart, crushing newly raised hopes. 'So; he really is dead? You're sure?'

'No. We are not sure. He died, but . . . he has been seen in the future. Alive, and fighting at your side. When you know the answer to this mystery, perhaps you will come back and explain it to us.'

'Hold it!' Jesamine said sharply. 'Everyone go back to their starting position. Is Owen alive or not?'

'The Deathstalker died on Mistworld,' said the grey man. 'That much is certain. But we are dealing with time travel here. Many things are possible, with time travel. Supposedly.'

'In other words, you haven't got a clue either,' said Lewis. 'I think this is why Humanity never invented a practical means for time travel; because it makes your head hurt just thinking about the implications.'

Owen's image disappeared from the screen before them, replaced by a young woman. Tall and lithely muscular, she scowled out of the screen with a sharp pointed face and a mane of long untidy red hair. Her eyes were hooded, and a piercing green. She gave off the same dangerous quality as a cornered rat, and looked like someone you'd be really stupid to turn your back on. Lewis could feel his nose wrinkling as he looked at her. Surely this couldn't be who he thought it was? Surely this gutter bravo couldn't be the legendary love of the blessed Owen Deathstalker?

'Hazel d'Ark,' the dusty voice said remorselessly. 'A great fighter. A brave and canny warrior. She endured stresses and strains that would have broken most people, from Blood addiction to the loss of good friends to the birth of a new social order she knew she could never really be a part of; but in the end she broke, faced with one loss too many. She loved Owen, but she never told him; and with his death she knew she never would. She ran away, and disappeared, after the last great battle against the Recreated. She saved Humanity, but she couldn't save the one man she truly cared for. She never got to see the Golden Age her courage and her actions helped to bring about. No-one has seen anything of her for two hundred years. Her fate remains a mystery. Even to us.'

'Poor girl,' said Jesamine. 'We owe her so much, and the universe wouldn't even let her have the one thing she wanted.'

'She made the mistake of loving a Deathstalker,' said Lewis. 'We've never been lucky in love.'

'Perhaps I can change that,' said Jesamine.

'Perhaps,' said Lewis, and they smiled at each other.

Next up on the screen was a short blonde woman with a pale face and sharp blue absolutely crazy eyes. She looked like she was about to jump right out of the screen and bite everyone's throats out. She looked like she'd taken everything fate could throw at her, and then spit in fate's face and laughed. This was a woman who'd had two names, both of them equally feared and respected.

'Diana Vertue,' said the grey man. 'Captain Silence's daughter. Also known as Jenny Psycho. Once a manifest of the Mater Mundi, she became an uber-esper in her own right, one of the most powerful minds of her time. She helped form the oversoul. She taught the AIs of Shub their true nature, and fought the Recreated to a standstill, buying time for Owen to save us all. She was assassinated, one hundred and eighteen years ago, as the first great rebellion of the ELFs. There were rumours of super-esper involvement; The Shatter Freak and The Grey Train. Certainly no ordinary combination of espers could have brought her down. She was betrayed by those she had reason to trust, and her body was utterly destroyed. Rogue energies still flare and burn on the spot where she fell. It is said her mind still lives on, as a part of the oversoul. That she can still be contacted, through them. Or perhaps it is just that espers also need comforting myths to sustain them.'

There was no mistaking the next figure on the screen. The subtly inhuman face, the glowing golden eyes. The cyborg, the augmented man, the old Enemy of Humanity; the man-machine with the mark of Cain upon his brow. The Hadenman; Tobias Moon. He didn't look that special, until you came to the face, and the eyes. Just looking at them made

Lewis' hair stand up on the back of his neck. No-one had made a cyborg of any kind in hundreds of years, and all because of what the Hadenmen had done in their time. All long gone now, they were the bogeymen of the modern age, the stuff of nightmares and the villains of a thousand adventure vid serials. Fractious children were told to go to sleep or the Hadenmen would get them. Tobias Moon was the last of them, and only a minor legend, barely remembered, omitted from all the official versions because his presence was just too disturbing.

Robert and Constance hadn't wanted Humanity to know they owed their present freedoms in part to a Hadenman.

'Tobias Moon,' said the whispering voice. 'The Hadenman who died, and returned to life. The cyborg who rejected his own people to become Owen's friend and ally. Who sought so very hard to find the Humanity within him. Perhaps the only living survivor of all those who passed through the Madness Maze. It is said he can still be found on what was once a leper colony, deep in the sentient jungles of Lachrymae Christi. A hermit for two centuries now, he is the sole means whereby the colonists of the planet can communicate with the living consciousness of the world; the Red Brain. People who go looking for Tobias Moon without good reason tend not to come back.'

'So he was real,' said Lewis. 'I often wondered. There are so many versions of the story, especially once you start really digging, and so many apocrypha. And it didn't seem exactly likely; a Hadenman, fighting *for* Humanity.'

Jesamine nodded. 'He gives me the creeps, just looking at him. Why did this version of the legend have to be true? I much prefer the one where Lewis raises an army of dragons to fight against the Recreated.'

'No,' said the grey man. 'That was Carrion, and the Ashrai.'

Lewis and Jesamine looked at him.

'Who?' said Lewis.

'What?' said Jesamine.

The next figure on the screen was a more familiar sight. A tall, lean man with a thickening waist and a receding hairline. He wore an old-fashioned uniform, of an Imperial Fleet

Captain. He looked like a man used to giving orders, and a man used to being obeyed. Lewis recognised him at once from the scenes Shub had shown him.

'Captain John Silence,' said the grey man. 'He worked with King Robert and Queen Constance to build the Golden Age, though he never approved of the myth-making process. He dropped out of public sight just over a hundred years ago, when people started worshipping his statues. The Shadow Court sent a whole army against his isolated country house, and burned it down with him in it. They couldn't find enough of his body to bury, but they collected some ashes and scattered them across the Victory Gardens in the Parade of the Endless. One of the few officers who served the Empress Lionstone loyally to the end, who went on to be lionised by the people for his heroic actions against Shub and the Re-created. He passed through the Madness Maze, it is said, but if he acquired any powers or abilities, he never showed them. It is also said he loved an Investigator.'

'Poor bastard,' said Jesamine. 'Legend has it they were even more inhuman than the Hadenmen.'

There was a pause, and then an unexpected sixth figure appeared on the screen. There was nothing familiar about this man. Tall and whipcord lean, he dressed in black leathers under a billowing black cape. Jet black hair and coal black eyes, his face was pale and proud and utterly unyielding. His thin mouth had an arrogant curl, and his stance was openly defiant. And in his hand, one of the great lost weapons of the old Empire. The power lance.

'Since you asked about him, this is Carrion. We know little about him, and what information we have been able to gather is often contradictory. A traitor to the Empire, he fought alongside the alien Ashrai, against Humanity. Deserted his ship and his crew, and killed his own friends and fellow officers, in defence of the planet Unseeli. The planet was scorched, the Ashrai were exterminated, but somehow Carrion survived there for years afterwards, living alone on a dead planet. He was Captain Silence's closest friend and companion. Carrion; a man of great power, possibly derived from the Maze, possibly from the dead Ashrai.

'He was never a part of the legends, and barely mentioned even in the wildest apocrypha, but records exist that suggest he was a vital part of the history. That he gathered an army of the Ashrai, and flew unprotected through space with them under his own power, to oppose the Recreated in the last great battle. Which may be where the legends of Owen and the dragons came from. It may be that this Carrion knows things that we do not, that you will need to know. It is said that he lives still on the restored world of Unseeli, among the Ashrai, brought to life again by Owen and the Maze. If so, he is older than any other human, living among the alien Ashrai as one of them. Approach him with caution. No human has had contact with him for two hundred years, not least because the only human he ever cared for was his lost friend, Captain Silence. Unseeli is a forbidden world, Quarantined by order of Parliament, after the Ashrai turned down the offer of their own Seat in Parliament; the only alien species ever so honoured. No ships land on Unseeli. The few that have got past the Quarantine starcruiser were destroyed by the Ashrai.'

The viewscreen disappeared. Strange geometric shapes rose up out of the Dust Plains of Memory, revolving slowly, endlessly unfolding. Lewis looked at Jesamine, and then back at the crumbling grey figure still standing before them.

'So,' he said finally. 'The only survivors from the days of legend are . . . Owen, possibly, in the future. Hazel; missing. Diana Vertue, possibly, as part of the oversoul. And two ex-terrorists, Tobias Moon and Carrion. Not really what I was hoping to hear.'

The grey man shrugged, in a curiously jerky motion that temporarily lost him one of his shoulders as it flowed away down his arm. 'Nothing is certain, where the Madness Maze is concerned. Whatever it does to people, it breaks every law of science we understand. All of these people became more than human. Perhaps for such as they . . . death is not the end. You must search out the history, the truth. Go to Mistworld, to Lachrymae Christi, to Unseeli. You are a Deathstalker; perhaps people will talk to you who would not talk to anyone else. And in searching out legends, it may be that you will become legends yourself. Certainly only beings of power, like those in the old legends, can hope to protect us all from the Terror. So go now, Deathstalker . . . and do what you have to do.'

The figure turned and walked away across the sighing surface of the Dust Plains of Memory. The Towers crumbled and fell, and were absorbed back into the grey sea along with all the other shapes, until all that remained of the last great receptacle of human history was a gently twitching surface, murmuring querulously to itself in overlapping voices.

Emma Steel sat alone in her approved Paragon's apartment, holding an icepack to her jaw. Her rank entitled her to the use of regen tech for even minor damage, but she felt too embarrassed to apply. Embarrassed, and angry with herself. It had been a long time since anybody had been able to catch her offguard. But who would have thought an old retired trader could move so *fast*? She hadn't even seen Chevron start his move. But she wasn't entirely unhappy that the Deathstalker and Jesamine Flowers had got away. Even if Parliament was currently hopping mad about it. What was the Empire coming to, when a man and a woman could be condemned to death, without trial, just for falling in love? It was only an arranged marriage between Douglas and Jesamine after all; how big a deal could it be for the King to choose himself a new Queen?

It was all Finn Durandal's fault. He'd put this up to Parliament as treason, and then stirred them all up to demand the death penalty. The King had seemed too dazed and shocked to contribute anything. Emma scowled. She didn't trust Finn Durandal any more, and with increasingly good reason. Working through a series of trusted and well-bribed intermediaries, Emma had been able to obtain copies of most of the media coverage of the Neumen riot. And for hour after hour, she'd sat studying the images on her computer screen, speeding them up and slowing them down, and zooming in to pick out important details. And not just the transmitted images, but all the recordings, from all the angles. Slowly, obsessively, she'd worked her way through every single recording, from the beginnings of the riot to the end. From the death of the Paragon Veronica Mae Savage, to the arrival of the pacifying oversoul. But most of all, she studied the recordings of Finn Durandal fighting the rioters, from before she arrived to help him.

She'd had her suspicions even at the time, that none of his actions had been what they seemed. But now she was sure that the fighting had been fixed; just a set-up for the cameras, to make the Durandal look good. It had clearly all been arranged in advance. Finn was never in any real danger. And neither were any of the people he was pretending to fight, until she turned up; at which point the Durandal had cold-bloodedly killed his own partners in deceit, just so she wouldn't suspect. Emma scowled. That insight, appalling as it was, wasn't the worst of it. If Finn had planned his mock fighting in advance, then he must have known in advance that the riot was going to happen. Perhaps he even helped plan and orchestrate it, right down to the murder of his fellow Paragons. What kind of a man could do that?

She'd also been studying media recordings of the ELF attack during the Parade of the Paragons. The Durandal's actions there were highly suspect too. All right, there was clearly no fakery in his fighting this time. He'd killed ELFs with a cold verve and enthusiasm that anywhen else she would have applauded. But . . . how could Finn have known where and when the ELFs were going to ambush the Paragons? No-one had ever been able to infiltrate the ELFs' support structures before. The ELFs could read suspicious thoughts in a mind half a mile away; and there was no way they'd ever have let anyone have access to their plans who was using any kind of esp-blocker. People hadn't asked any of these rather obvious questions because . . . they hadn't wanted to. They wanted to enjoy their victory over the ELFs. They wanted to believe in their hero, their miracle-worker, the Durandal.

The answers to all of this lay somewhere in the Rookery; Emma was sure of that. She had fought her way in on several occasions now, but she hadn't been able to get anyone to talk to her about Finn Durandal. Not even in the most general terms. This, in a place where everything, most especially information, was supposed to be always up for sale. Most people seemed too scared to talk, even with the edge of Emma's sword set against their quivering throats. Neither bribes nor brutality had got her anywhere, and she was frankly lost for a third alternative. People actually ran away rather than even discuss Finn Durandal; what did that say about the man's true nature? But for all her hard work, all Emma really had were suspicions, and one growing conviction . . . that Finn Durandal wasn't the legend she and everyone else had believed in; and possibly never had been . . .

And even if she could dig up some proof; who could she take it to? Who would believe her? Finn was the hero of the moment, at a moment when people desperately needed to believe in heroes. Bad enough that the Deathstalker had let them down; ask them to believe that the Durandal was crooked, and they'd laugh in her face, in self-defence. She couldn't even talk to her fellow Paragons. Not after Finn had just saved them all from the ELFs. Finn was the Champion now, and one of the most important and respected men in the Empire. Which made Emma's decision even more imperative. If Finn really was as dangerous as she thought and believed he was, she had to convince someone important, and soon. Someone important enough, and brave enough, to take a stand against the adored Durandal, while there was still time. Because somebody had to do something, to protect the King from his own Champion. Because who would have an easier job of killing the King than his own defender? If Finn decided that he wanted to be King . . . if that had been his plot all along . . .

Emma growled loudly in frustration, and threw her icepack across the room. She had dreamed for years of coming to Logres as a Paragon, to work alongside her hero and inspiration, Finn Durandal; and now her dream had turned into a nightmare. She was isolated . . . like the Deathstalker was isolated. And if she wasn't very careful, she might end up being accused of treason by Finn Durandal, just like Lewis . . .

At Court, alone in his sumptuous private quarters, Douglas

Campbell sat slumped in his favourite chair, staring at nothing. He had a brandy glass in one hand, but hadn't noticed it was empty for some time now. His people had just brought him news that Lewis Deathstalker had freed Jesamine Flowers from the Bloody Tower, and were both now on the run, somewhere in the city. Douglas had acted angry, shouting and cursing and throwing things, because it was expected of him; but secretly he was relieved. He'd had Jes put in Traitor's Wing rather than a standard prison specifically so that Lewis would be able to rescue her. He'd even arranged for Jes' fan clubs to find out where she was being held, just so they'd be sure to protest outside the Tower in force, and act as a distraction. Douglas hadn't wanted Lewis or Jes to die. Even after all they'd done, they still mattered to him. He hadn't wanted any of his guards to die either, but it seemed many had, defending the Tower . . . And reports were coming in that Lewis had had unexpected help; from his father's old friend and advisor Samuel Chevron. What the hell did that mean? Why had Chevron of all people involved himself in open treason? Douglas had put in a call to his father, but so far William hadn't answered.

The King raised his brandy glass and finally realised it was empty. He put it down on the richly-carpeted floor beside his chair, watched it fall over, and then looked slowly around him. The two big mahogany tables were covered with piles of brightly-wrapped presents, that had arrived from all over the Empire in advance of the Royal Wedding. Douglas wondered vaguely whether he'd have to send them all back now. He hoped the senders had thought to keep the receipts, but doubted they had. Most people didn't. The packages had all been sensor scanned, for bombs or perishables or other unfortunate surprises, and Douglas had glanced briefly through the list. All pretty predictable, really. Tacky, tasteless junk that neither he nor Jes would have given house room under normal circumstances. And the more expensive stuff had really been nothing more than bribes, from minor politicians and the like looking to ingratiate themselves, in hope of future patronage. But there'd also been a lot of small stuff, from small people, just expressing their happiness at the forthcoming marriage. Douglas felt bad about disappointing them.

He wondered tiredly who Parliament would want him to marry next. They'd have to choose someone soon. Someone popular, and worthy, and safe. The public were all fired up for a Royal Wedding, for a time of parties and self-indulgence and celebration, and they were in no mood to be put off for long. And the House badly needed something big and moving and gaudy to distract the public from thinking too much about the coming Terror. So Douglas was pretty sure he'd be marrying someone soon. He supposed he could have some input into the choice, if he insisted, but he couldn't bring himself to care. He'd just lost his only real love and his only real friend; and the best he could hope for was that he'd never see them again. That they'd have enough sense to go deep into hiding, and stay hidden. The public could have long angry memories when it came to people who disappointed them; and they could be very vindictive, if presented with a chance for revenge. There'd never be any Pardon for Lewis or Jesamine, no matter how many strings Douglas pulled.

He supposed he should hate them both, but he couldn't. They were the only people who'd cared for the man, not the King, and even after all that had happened . . . he still loved them both. Even though they had run away, leaving him nothing but to be King, and a duty he never wanted.

There was a polite knock at the door, which surprised him. He'd made it very clear to everyone within shouting distance that he wasn't to be disturbed. Whoever it was knocked again, a little less politely, but still he ignored them. He was the King, and if he wanted to brood and sulk and beat himself up, he would. He wondered if there was any more brandy. The door opened anyway, without his permission, and Douglas lurched up out of his chair, looking for something heavy to throw. It was Anne Barclay, of course. Douglas sighed, and dropped back into his chair. He should have known. Even armed guards couldn't keep her out. Douglas deliberately looked in a different direction as she stalked over to stand before him.

'What do you want?' he growled finally, when it became clear ignoring her wasn't going to work.

'I came to say sorry,' said Anne, in what was for her a fairly subdued voice. 'In a sense, a lot of this is my fault. I should never have put Jes forward in the first place. I should have known she'd find some way to screw it up. She's made a career out of breaking hearts, after all. But it meant so much to her, the chance to be Queen; and I just didn't have the heart to say no . . .'

Douglas looked at her for the first time, and his expression softened. 'Of course; you've lost your best friend too, haven't you? Oh hell, Anne; sit down. We should talk. We're the ones who are going to have to pick up the pieces. Whether we feel up to it or not.'

Anne pulled up a chair and sat down opposite him. 'How do you feel, Douglas? No; silly question. Look; don't you worry about anything. I've got my people all over the routine stuff, until you feel ready to start getting involved again. No-one's going to expect to see you in public for a while.'

'They're all laughing at me, aren't they? The King who lost his woman to his best friend, and never even saw it coming.'

'No! No, Douglas; they're all too busy being angry with Lewis, for letting them down by being only human.'

'There will have to be a Royal Wedding, eventually, won't there?'

'Yes. Too many preparations, too many events set in motion, for us to cancel completely. The House will decide on someone else . . . someone uncontroversial.'

'How can I face my people?' Douglas said heavily. 'How can they ever have any respect for me, after this?'

'None of this is your fault!' Anne said sharply. 'You're the victim here, Douglas. Everyone can see that. You were betrayed, by the two people you had most reason to trust. The people will understand. The media's being surprisingly supportive, and everyone's working hard to put the best possible spin on what's happened.'

She didn't tell him the media were only cooperating because she and everyone else in a position of power and influence had begged, bullied and bribed the various media into the right frame of mind. Anne had personally contacted every editor and publisher in her little black book, and bludgeoned them into line with everything from promises of private interviews later to a little private blackmail over things she wasn't supposed to know. She had a job to do, and she didn't have the time or the inclination right now to pussyfoot around. She did what was necessary; just as she always had.

Douglas didn't need to know these things, so she didn't tell him. In fact, there were a lot of things Douglas didn't need to know.

'I don't blame them, you know,' Douglas said quietly. 'It wasn't their fault; not really. They just . . . fell in love. That didn't used to be a crime. I want them to be happy together, wherever they finally end up. I'd hate to think I lost the two people I care about the most for nothing . . .'

'Yes, well, that's all very noble and chivalrous, but I don't think that's the approach we should take with the media,' Anne said carefully. 'They need a King, not a Saint. You can't afford to seem weak. I think . . . it's best if you say nothing at all, for the time being. Finn and I have been talking. We can handle things in your name, until you're ready to face the public again. There's no rush. You take it easy. Rest. Get yourself . . . sorted out. And don't worry about anything. Finn and I are on top of it all.'

'You and Finn,' said Douglas. 'Better friends than I ever realised. What would I do without you?'

Anne waited a while, but he had nothing more to say. He sat slumped in his chair, staring at nothing, or perhaps too much. Anne got up and left the chamber, glad to be leaving a silence so heavy it was almost unbearable. She nodded to the armed guards outside, and they snapped to attention again behind her. Some way down the corridor, Finn Durandal was waiting. He and Anne nodded respectfully to each other, like two old adversaries who had unexpectedly ended up on the same side. Finn looked back at the King's chambers.

'So; how is he?'

'Pretty much how we expected. Tired, mostly, I think.'

'Should I go in to him?'

'I don't think that's necessary. He still has a lot of thinking to do.'

'And right now . . . he might decide to blame the messenger for the message?'

'He made you Champion, Finn. Settle for that, for now.' She considered the Durandal thoughtfully. 'The Champion's black leather armour certainly suits you a lot better than it ever did Lewis.'

Finn smiled briefly. 'Lewis never did have any style. And I always thought I'd look good in black. Is there . . . somewhere private nearby, where we could talk, Anne? I think we need to talk, you and I.'

'Of course.' She led him down the corridor and into a private reception room, where she locked the door securely behind them. She had a feeling it was going to be that kind of conversation. They sat down facing each other, and Anne fixed Finn with a cold, penetrating stare. 'What exactly do you think we need to talk about, Finn? We've never been friends, or even allies. What do we have in common, apart from the fact that we've both betrayed people who were supposed to be our friends?'

Finn smiled easily at her, apparently completely relaxed. 'Yes, Anne; why did you do that, exactly? Why did you come to me, and present me with the evidence that would damn and destroy Lewis and Jesamine?'

'Because . . . they let me down. All three of them. I would have made them heroes. Legends. The greatest King and Queen and Champion this Empire had ever known. I could have done it. And then it all fell apart, just because Lewis and Jes couldn't keep their hands off each other. I gave them every chance, every warning. I gave up all the things I wanted, all the things I needed; to create that legend, that dream . . . all for them! But they weren't prepared to do the same. They threw it all away, threw away all the things they could have been and achieved . . . all my hard work . . . because they'd rather be weak. Just to satisfy their own desires. That was when I realised I was wasting my time. Wasting my life, on people who weren't worthy of me. So I came to you, Finn Durandal. You have ambition, and you're not distracted by small things. Work with me, and I'll make you great. I've already made you Champion. I could make you King, if you want.'

'They didn't care about you, did they?' said Finn. 'Not really. All the things you did for them, and they didn't love you.'

'They never appreciated me,' said Anne. 'I made them what they were . . . and they never really gave a damn about *me*.'

'I will see that you get everything you ever wanted,' Finn said gently. 'I can do that. I know people . . . You can be everything you ever wanted to be. I'm not your friend, like they were, but I always pay my debts.'

'Yes,' said Anne. 'We understand each other. We'll make a great partnership. Achieve great things . . . When did you first realise, that you didn't have to be what other people wanted you to be? When did you first realise that you couldn't rely on other people to make you happy? That you had to do it all yourself?'

Finn considered the matter. 'It took a long time to sink in. I was happy enough, being a Paragon. And then, eventually, I began to realise that people were letting me get away with things, things I shouldn't have been allowed to get away with, because I was . . . who I was. And I began to wonder what else I could get away with . . . Even so, I might have gone on as I was, playing the hero, if Douglas had only given me what I deserved. What I'd earned. I should have been the Champion. The role was mine by right.'

'And now you've got it,' said Anne.

'Oh, I don't want it now. It's too late, now. I want much more than this, and I'm going to have it. I'm going to prove myself the very best there is, in the only way that really matters; by walking right over everyone else.'

'Why settle for Champion,' said Anne, 'when you can be King?'

'My thoughts exactly,' said Finn, smiling. 'You don't feel any guilt, do you? Over what we've done, and what we're going to do?'

'No,' said Anne. 'I spent all my life working for other

people, and all for nothing. I want something for myself now. I want . . . to be happy, for once. And I don't care what it takes, or what it costs.'

'Well, well,' said Finn. 'Where have you been all my life? Work with me, Anne, and I promise you'll get everything you ever wanted, everything you ever needed. Not because I'm your friend, but because it's in my interest to do so. You can live your dreams, Anne; even the ones you never dared speak aloud. And I'll never judge you, because I don't care. And after a while . . . you won't miss your friends at all.'

'Friends . . . are over-rated,' said Anne. 'You should know that. I did some checking on you, Finn. Your life is almost as empty as mine. Haven't you ever had any friends? Lovers? Loves? Anyone you ever cared for?'

'No,' said Finn. 'I don't seem to have the knack. I know the words; love, compassion, caring . . . but they mean nothing to me. I don't think I'm capable of them. For a long time I thought everyone else was the same, that they were just pretending to feel these things, like me. But they do; and that's what makes it so easy for people like me to manipulate them. That's why we're going to tear everything down, Anne; because if we can't be happy, why should they?'

'You have a way with words,' said Anne.

'I've had a lot of time to think about these things,' said Finn.

'They hurt me,' said Anne. 'By not caring about me, by not noticing me. We'll make them all pay, won't we, Finn?'

'Whatever it takes?'

'Whatever it takes.'

'Oh, we're going to have such fun,' said Finn Durandal.

Lewis had never stolen a starship before, but in his experience it wasn't that difficult. It happened all the time, when he was a Paragon. Which was how he came to know all the tricks, all the ways of walking past a ship's security systems like they weren't even there. (There were all kinds of precautions ship-owners could take to prevent this, but mostly they never bothered; because it was expensive. Better to let the ship and cargo be stolen, and then pad your insurance claim.) So Lewis wasn't expecting any trouble when he and Jes strode confidently into the starport terminal.

Sneaking past the security men was the easiest part. Lewis knew all the blind spots, all the weaknesses in the system; he'd been trying to get them fixed for years. He suspected they were left open deliberately, so certain criminal elements could use them for smuggling and other scams, but he'd never been able to prove it . . . because he never had the time. As he'd told Emma Steel on her arrival; you couldn't sweat the small stuff or you'd never get anything done. And now here he was, taking advantage of the very loopholes he'd tried to shut down, and proving he was right all along. Sometimes the air in his life was so thick with irony he could almost chew on it.

He and Jes were doing really well, right up until they had to pass the very last security check, at the edge of the landing pads. Lewis could see the ships from where he was, standing unsuspecting under the bright lights on the pads like so many tourists waiting to be pickpocketed. Lewis wasn't expecting any trouble. It was just one bored security guard, sitting behind a desk with a vid soap running on his security monitor. Lewis' and Jesamine's holo faces matched the faked IDs he'd brought with him from his lockup, and he'd already removed the security seals from his energy weapon, so it wouldn't set off any alarms. (An old prerogative allowed to all Paragons, for when they had to work undercover.)

But when he and Jesamine passed entirely casually through the metal detector arch, their holo disguises sparked and shimmered and shorted out, and it seemed like every damned alarm and siren in the starport all went off at once. Lewis swore fiercely. He'd been so concerned over his various hidden weapons and tech that he'd forgotten all about the metal holoface collars he and Jesamine both wore. The guard behind the desk took one look at Lewis' familiar ugly face, and all but had a coronary as he scrambled up off his chair. He didn't even consider trying to stop the famed Deathstalker. He just ran for his life, heading for the centre of the terminal building and screaming at the top of his lungs all the way. Lewis grabbed Jesamine by the arm and urged her on through the last of the terminal towards the landing pads.

'What is it?' said Jesamine. 'What just happened?'

'I screwed up,' snapped Lewis. 'Now run! We can still make it to the ships!'

They sprinted through the last part of the terminal, and people scattered to get out of their way. Lewis had his gun openly in his hand now, and did his best to look like he was ready to use it. People recognised his face and Jesamine's, and called out their names, but no-one tried to stop them. Lewis burst out onto the landing pads with Jesamine at his side, and then cursed loudly and skidded to a halt. Forming up between him and Jesamine and the rows of waiting starships were hundreds of armed men, hurrying in from all directions. A great cry went up from them as they spotted the two fugitives, and Lewis dragged Jesamine back into the terminal doorway, where the steelglass windows would at least give them some protection. Jesamine jerked her arm free.

'Stop yanking me about! I'm not a child; talk to me!'

Lewis activated the force shield on his wrist, and the glowing force shield sprang into being on his left arm. 'Sorry. Bit preoccupied at the moment.'

'Who the hell are those men?' said Jesamine. 'They've all got guns, but none of them are wearing uniforms. Damn it, I knew I should have insisted we stop off long enough to get me a gun. Or two.'

'They're not peacekeepers,' said Lewis grimly. 'Or port security. And they look far too professional for local bounty hunters, so . . . Best guess, they're Pure Humanity fanatics, same bastards who hunted down the Ecstatics. They've already demonstrated they have no problem killing Paragons at the Neumen riot . . . so an ex-Champion shouldn't bother them at all. I suppose I should be flattered they sent so many men after me . . .

'This is really bad, Jes. Not just the odds, though they're pretty bad too. Peacekeepers or security men might have been willing to take us alive; these creeps won't do that. Someone really wants us dead.' He looked at her sadly. 'You should run,

Jes. I'll hold them back. Give you time to get away. It's stupid for both of us to die here.'

'Don't talk like that!' Jesamine said firmly. 'We'll get out of this. You're the Deathstalker, remember? And . . . I'd rather die with you, than live without you. Never thought of myself as the sentimental kind, but I suppose you learn something new every day. Now stop being chivalrous, and work out a way to kill those bastards!'

Lewis grinned, drew two of his throwing knives from their hiding places, and offered them to Jesamine. 'Can you fight, Jes?'

She snorted loudly, snatched the knives from his hand and flourished them expertly. 'You bet your arse, Deathstalker. Some of the pigsties I played when I was starting out, you didn't dare leave your dressing room to go to the toilets unless you were armed to the teeth and willing to fight dirty. I've always been able to look out for myself.'

'Well, that's good to know,' said Lewis. 'Guard my back, Jes, and don't show them any mercy, because they sure as hell won't be showing us any. I can see half a dozen ships my skeleton key should be able to get us into, but we're going to have to fight our way through those bastards to get to them. The odds are bad, but they won't be expecting a frontal attack, so surprise will be on our side. But Jes; once we start, we can't stop. We run for the ships and whatever happens, we keep going. Because either we fight our way through, or we die out there, on the pads.'

'God, you're a cheerful bastard to be around,' said Jesamine. 'You'd better not be this moody at breakfast.' She looked at the small army of assassins heading their way, and hefted her knives uncertainly. 'We're really going to meet them head on? Just the two of us?'

'Of course,' said Lewis, smiling at her reassuringly. 'It's the Deathstalker way.'

'Then it's a wonder you're not all extinct,' Jesamine growled. 'All right, let's do it. Before I get a rush of sanity to the head.'

They took a deep breath and then charged out of the terminal and onto the pads, screaming at the top of their lungs.

493

The assassins heard the magnificent old Deathstalker battle cry of *Shandrakor! Shandrakor!* and many of them stumbled to a halt, their hearts missing a beat. Several turned and ran. It was one thing to agree to kill a traitor on the run, and quite another to face the most famous battle cry in Empire history. Many of the Neumen fanatics were ex-military, trained and experienced men, but still they felt a sudden chill seize their hearts as they remembered their opponent was a Paragon and a Champion and a Deathstalker. For a moment the shadow of the blessed Owen fell upon them, and they were on the brink of falling apart. And then their angry new faith re-asserted itself as they remembered this was Lewis, not Owen. They stood their ground, took aim, and opened fire with their disrupters.

Lewis had used the time of their confusion to build up some speed, and was almost upon them, Jesamine right behind him. Energy bolts seared past him, some ricocheting from his force shield, and then he hit the first ranks of the assassins like a hammer blow. He opened fire with his own gun at point blank range, and the energy beam punched right through the chest of the man before him, and howled on to blow away two more men behind him. Lewis hacked viciously about him with his sword, and the assassins could not stand against him, falling dead and dying at his feet, unable to face the Deathstalker's rage and skill and experience. His gun recharged and fired again, killing more. He swung his sword, and used the razor-sharp edges of his force shield, and men bled and screamed and died, and still he cried *Shandrakor! Shandrakor!* like an angry voice out of legend.

Jesamine stuck in close behind him, guarding his back with her sharp knives and the street-fighting skills of her youth that she'd never really forgotten. The Neumen assassins circled her and Lewis, looking startled and even frightened, and she laughed in their faces as she lashed out with her knives.

But in the end there were just too many fanatics, and they slowly duelled Lewis to a halt, far short of the waiting star-ships. He was the better fighter by far, but they wore him down by sheer weight of numbers. They didn't want to use their guns in such a close press of bodies, and in the end they didn't have to. Swords came flashing at Lewis from all directions, and his blade and his force shield couldn't be everywhere at once. They cut at him again and again, nothing serious as yet, but his blood fell. He gritted his teeth and wouldn't allow them the victory of a groan or a cry. He killed the men who came to kill him with casual, almost contemptuous skill, but not even a Paragon and a Champion and a Deathstalker could stand against so many. Because he was Lewis, and only a hero, not a legend.

And then there was a sudden commotion from the far side of the battle, shouting and screaming and raw panic, as something hit the assassins hard from the other side. The assassins lost their focus as men flew through the air, without heads and trailing ripped-out intestines, as Saturday, the reptiloid from the planet Shard, tore through an army of foes with delighted ferocity. Eight feet tall and bulging with muscles under his bottle-green scales, designed by evolution to be his world's greatest killing machine, Saturday laughed aloud as he slaughtered everyone before him. Swords broke and shattered on his armoured hide, and human blood ran thickly from his horrid jaws and dripped from his heavy clawed hands. He looked over the heads of the panicked assassins to Lewis and Jesamine.

'There's a ship to your right; the *Hereward*. Get to her. Hatches are open and she's all set to go. Get aboard and power up. I'll join you, as soon as I've shown these Pure Humanity scumbags just what an alien can do, if he gets annoyed enough! Blood! Blood and souls for Shard! I'll show you little turds who's the true superior species around here!'

He raged among the Neumen, tearing them apart and throwing the body pieces joyfully through the air. Most of the fanatics turned and ran. It didn't save them. Lewis and Jesamine left Saturday to it, and headed for the ship he'd indicated. It was a luxury racing yacht, all gleaming lines and bulging engines. Lewis hadn't a clue why the ship should be waiting for him, but he was tired and battered and bloody enough not to give a damn. He grinned shakily. A mere two battles against overwhelming odds in one day, and he was exhausted. Owen used to do this sort of thing just to warm up, according to the legends.

Lewis was almost at the ship when he stumbled to a halt, as a new figure came forward to block his way. Lewis covered the newcomer with his gun as he studied him, trying to get his ragged breathing under control. Jesamine moved in beside him, unobtrusively supporting him while she glared at the new enemy. He stood tall and proud in his Paragon's armour and flapping purple cloak, big and muscular, with sword and gun already in hand. His stern young face was almost familiar to Lewis.

'I get the feeling . . . I should know you,' he said finally.

'Of course you should,' said the Paragon, his voice flat and harsh. 'I'm Stuart Lennox. I'm Virimonde's new Paragon. Drop your weapons and surrender, Sir Deathstalker. Don't make me kill you.'

'Lennox . . . Jesus, of course I know you, Stuart. Your father Adrian helped to train me, back on Mistworld. You used to bring him his lunch, and watch us train, back when you were a kid. So; you're my replacement. Du Bois didn't waste any time . . . I don't suppose there's any point in my trying to convince you of my innocence?'

'None of my business,' said Stuart. 'I know my duty. Your treason can be decided at your trial. Don't try to appeal to our shared past. I've seen the recording of you and the woman. You have disgraced your world, as well as your King.'

'Everything's so clear cut, when you're young,' Lewis said tiredly. 'All the things I've done down the years, for my world and my King; they don't matter any more? They don't count?'

'No. It just shows how far you've fallen.'

'You can't beat me,' said Lewis.

'Why not? We both had the same trainer. Oh, you have the years and the experience . . . but I have right and honour on my side.'

And while he was still talking a long green-scaled arm came out of nowhere, and vicious silver claws slammed into Stuart's side and out again. The force of the blow sent him flying through the air, tumbling end over end, blood flying everywhere. He hit the ground hard, groaned once and lay still in a spreading pool of blood. Saturday emerged from the shadows under the *Hereward*'s hull, and sniffed loudly.

'If you're going to fight, fight. Talk afterwards. If you're still alive. Deathstalker; where are you going? The ship is waiting!'

But Lewis had already left him behind. He hurried over to the still figure in the ruptured Paragon armour, and knelt beside him. He cut away a length of the purple cloak, made a pad of it, and pushed it firmly into the bloody gap in the armour, sealing off the wound. Stuart stiffened, but didn't cry out, though sweat popped out all over his face. Lewis used more of the cloak to make a pillow under the young man's head. The Paragon's face was bone white now, and he was breathing harshly, blood spraying from his mouth with every exhalation.

Lewis accessed his comm implant, and opened the Paragon's emergency channel. 'Paragon down! Stuart Lennox, at the main starport! He's badly hurt, so get people here fast. He's going to need a regen tank.' He cut off before they could ask any questions, and looked down at his replacement. 'Hang in there, Stuart. Help's on its way. Don't worry. It looks bad, and I'm sure it hurts like hell, but it won't kill you. Hour in regen, and you'll be as good as new.'

'Why are you helping me?' said Stuart, forcing the words past the blood in his mouth.

'Because I'm not the man they told you I was.'

'Always did think du Bois was full of shit. But I had to do my duty.'

'Of course you did.'

'If this doesn't work out . . . get word to my dad, that I did my best.'

'You'll tell him yourself. Lennox family don't die this easily.'

'Lewis!' yelled Jesamine, from the open hatch of the *Hereward*. 'Port security will be here any minute! We have to go!'

'I have to go,' said Lewis, not moving.

'Of course you do,' said Stuart. 'Dad sends his best. Now get out of here before I have to arrest you. And . . . give them hell, Deathstalker.'

Lewis got up and walked away from him, and it was the

hardest thing he'd had to do all day. Alarm sirens were sounding all over the landing pads now. Saturday and Jesamine were waiting for him by the *Hereward*'s hatch. Lewis looked dispassionately at the blood still dripping from the reptiloid's claws.

'You should have let me finish him,' said Saturday.

'It wasn't necessary,' said Lewis. 'What are you doing here, Saturday? And what's the deal with this ship?'

'I'm here to join up with you,' the reptiloid said happily. 'I want to see some real action, test myself against some real challenges. That is why I left Shard, after all. And I don't like it here on Logres any more. They've all gone crazy. There's no honour in fighting crazy people. So I'm coming with you, to fight at your side against overwhelming odds. That is the Deathstalker tradition, yes? Then on! On to death or glory!'

Lewis was honestly lost for anything to say. He was still trying to come up with an answer that didn't include shouting or foul language or laughing hysterically, when a new face appeared, peering hesitantly and just a little twitchily out of the *Hereward*'s open hatch. He bobbed his head respectfully to Lewis, and then to Jesamine, and tried to smile, though it wasn't especially successful.

'Hi there! I'm Brett Random. Your ancestor knew my ancestor, Sir Deathstalker. Seems we're fated to work together too. If I knew where to go, I'd complain. You would too, if you knew me. I think you probably know my companion.'

'Oh Jesus,' said Jesamine, as a cold female figure in scarlet leathers appeared beside Brett. 'Everyone knows the Wild Rose of the Arena. I think I felt safer with the reptiloid. Do I take it you both want to join up as well?'

'Oh yes,' said Brett, trying hard to sound enthusiastic. 'We believe in you . . . and we have enemies in common. Most definitely including Finn bloody Durandal, may his balls drop off in the night, roll down the bed, and catch fire. I acquired the access codes to this rather nifty little ship from someone who doesn't know they're missing yet, but I don't know how long that will last, so, I really think we should get moving. Really. The ship's all powered up and ready to go. Assuming you've got some sort of destination in mind.'

'Brett Random,' said Lewis. 'I'm almost sure I know that name . . . from somewhere . . .'

'I really think we should get moving,' Brett said quickly. 'The city's wild with the news about you breaking Jesamine out of the Bloody Tower. Parliament's organised everyone breathing and armed to stop you getting offworld, and you can bet every damned one of them is on his way here right now.'

The world exploded around them as a disrupter beam came searing down from above, ricocheting from Lewis' force shield to blow a crater out of the landing pad right next to them. Rose grabbed Brett and pulled him back inside the ship. Lewis and Jesamine and Saturday scattered to make separate targets as Finn Durandal roared by overhead on his gravity sled. He opened up with the sled's guns, raking the pad around the *Hereward* with energy beams. He'd been too eager, too anticipatory of the kill. He'd fired on Lewis without checking his sensors to see whether the Deathstalker's force shield was still on, and now his prey were moving too quickly and too randomly for his ship's guns to track. Perhaps deep down, he hadn't wanted to kill Lewis from a distance. Perhaps he needed to go one on one with the Deathstalker, face to face and blade to blade, to prove that he was the better man after all, in the only way that mattered.

Lewis, as always, was more practical. He turned to follow Finn's sled as it passed by overhead, and fired a single dispassionate energy bolt into the sled's unprotected engine at the rear. It blew apart in a satisfyingly large explosion, throwing the sled from the sky. Unfortunately the sled was already sufficiently low enough that Finn was able to leap free, even as the deck of his gravity sled disintegrated under him in smoke and flames. He dropped down through the billowing fireball, wrapped in his cloak, hit the landing pad in a graceful tuck and roll, and was back on his feet even as the remains of his sled slammed into the pads and exploded twenty feet away. Finn advanced on the waiting Lewis with sword and gun already in his hand, a wide grin on his face and a wild light in his eyes. Lewis gestured sharply for Saturday and Jesamine to keep their distance. Finn stopped a few feet short of Lewis, and the two men studied each other for a while.

'This is all down to you, isn't it?' said Lewis. 'Right from the beginning, everything that's happened, everything that's gone wrong; all your fault.'

'Oh yes,' said Finn. 'I destroyed you, just like I'll destroy Douglas when I'm ready, and eventually the Empire. And why? Because I want to. Because I can.'

'I thought you were my friend, Finn.'

'You always were naïve, Lewis.'

'So why are you here, now? Why have you stepped out of the shadows at last?'

'This had to happen,' Finn said happily. 'The hero meets the villain, in a final confrontation. Except, of course, in everyone else's eyes I'm the hero, and you're the villain. I'm even wearing the hero's armour, and may I say it looks a lot better on me than it ever did on you.'

'That's because you have no sense of irony,' said Lewis. 'But you're right, there is a certain inevitability about this. I couldn't leave Logres without taking care of unfinished business, without taking care of you. One last duty, on my part, to save Douglas and the Empire from the viper at their bosom.'

'Typical of a Deathstalker,' said Finn. 'You have to over-dramatise this. Make it *significant*. It's just you and me, Lewis; fighting it out at last to prove which of us is the better man. Just as I planned.'

'Typical of you,' said Lewis. 'You couldn't risk a fair fight; you had to cheat. Didn't dare show yourself, until after I'd exhausted myself fighting the army of assassins you sent here . . .'

'Well, quite,' said Finn. 'I'm not stupid. Unlike some people, I always think ahead. Now come on; enough talk. Let's fight. Let's dance the dance of blood and death. You must have wondered, down the years, what would happen if the two greatest Paragons on Logres ever went head to head. You must have wondered which of us was really the best?'

'No,' said Lewis. 'I never did. That's the difference between us, Finn. I never gave the matter a moment's thought. All I ever cared about was doing my job, to the best of my abilities.

Not to show how good I was, but to help the people who needed help. To protect the innocent, and punish the guilty. And that is what's brought us here, Finn. No great battle between hero and villain, no legendary, mythic clash of titans. I just have to be a Paragon one last time; protect the innocent by killing the man who threatens their safety. One last duty before I can leave; I have to take out the trash.'

Finn's face flushed angrily and he lunged forward, his sword reaching for Lewis' heart. But Lewis had been expecting that, and his force shield was already there to block the blow. Their swords slammed together so hard sparks flew on the air, and then it was stamp and lunge, parry and thrust, all at dazzling speed; two men circling each other with a lifetime's experience and deadly skill. Soon they were breathing hard, and grunting aloud with the effort they put into their blows. Two men who had once been partners, if not actually friends, and were now so opposed that this was all they had left in common; the need to kill each other. They threw themselves against each other again and again, eager as lovers, hating each other with a cold focused flame that could only be soothed by the other's blood. And surprisingly soon they duelled themselves to a standstill, neither willing or able to advance or retreat a step . . . until Lewis beat aside Finn's blade, lunged forward, and the tip of his sword dug a deep rent through the Champion's black leather armour, neatly bisecting the stylised bas relief crown over his heart. Finn cried out, in shock as much as anything else, and backed away. Lewis grinned at him like a wolf, his ugly face alive with anticipation.

'In the end, Finn, it doesn't matter a damn who's fastest, or strongest, or more experienced. Or who could afford to spend the most on personal trainers . . . What matters is passion, commitment, and a faith in what you're fighting for. You never had any of those things, Finn. All you ever had . . . was you. And that's not enough when you're facing a Death-stalker.'

Finn looked into Lewis' eyes, and had to look away, unable to face what he saw there. Lewis stepped forward, and Finn turned and ran. Lewis watched him run for a moment, and then raised his gun. He'd never shot a man in the back before, but for Finn Durandal, for all the things that man had done, he would make an exception. But already there were shouts and alarms from all over the landing pads, and everywhere armed men were running towards him. Uniformed peace-keepers and security men, this time. Some of them opened fire, and energy beams shot past him, some only missing by inches.

'Lewis, *come on*!' Jesamine called from the waiting *Hereward*. 'It's over! *We're leaving*!'

Lewis nodded slowly, and lowered his gun. There would be other times. He turned away and boarded the yacht. It was every bit as luxurious as he'd expected, though the tiny bridge was more than a little cramped with four people and an eight foot reptiloid crammed into it. Lewis took the pilot's seat and called up the ship's AI.

'Greetings!' said the AI, in a bright and cheerful voice that Lewis just knew was going to get on his nerves really quickly. 'I am your ship's AI, Ozymandius by name, and I just want to say how delighted I am to be working with a Deathstalker again! Of course, I'm not exactly the same AI your ancestor Owen knew. Shub created my personality around what was left of the original AI, and downloaded me into this ship, so I could help you with this escape. They're really very keen that you should escape. Shub believes in Deathstalkers. They can get really sloppy and sentimental these days, when no-one's looking. So; where are we going first?'

'Unseeli,' said Lewis. 'The Ashrai don't like the Empire, so they should be willing to keep our presence there a secret. Assuming they don't kill us all out of hand, of course. And since not many people know about Carrion's involvement with my ancestor Owen, it won't be the first place Finn will think to look for us. I want to talk to Carrion, to speak to someone who was actually there. Someone who knew the real Owen, and who might know what actually happened to him.'

'Excuse me,' said Brett, raising his hand like a child in a classroom. 'I didn't understand one word of what you just said there.'

'Don't worry,' said Lewis. 'It will all become horribly clear as we go along. Now strap yourself into the crash webbing, all of you. Saturday; improvise. Oz; plot a course.'

'You do know Unseeli is Quarantined?' the AI said diffidently.

'We'll burn that bridge when we come to it. I think Carrion and the Ashrai will listen to me. I have Owen's ring.'

'You do?' said Brett, leaning eagerly forward to stare at the black gold ring on Lewis' finger. 'Damn; you do! You know, when this is all over, I know people who would pay you a really nice price for that ring . . .'

'You'll have to excuse Brett,' Rose said calmly. 'It's either that, or kill him.'

'Everybody grab hold of something!' Ozymandius yelled suddenly. 'My sensors are picking up all kinds of ships and armed forces heading right for us! We don't leave right now, Lewis, we're not going anywhere!'

'Then go,' said Lewis. 'Blast us out of here, don't stop for anything, and drop into hyperspace the moment it's practical.'

'Sounds like a plan to me!' said Ozymandius. The *Hereward*'s engines roared, and the ship threw itself up into the sky. Energy beams from approaching ships flared all around the yacht, lighting up the darkness, as it howled through the last of the planet's atmosphere. 'Wow!' yelled Ozymandius. 'Deja vu all over again!'

It was a very fast ship, and they were gone and disappeared into hyperspace long before anyone could stop them. Lewis Deathstalker, Jesamine Flowers, Brett Random, Rose Constantine, a reptiloid called Saturday and an AI called Ozymandius.

Perhaps the only heroes left, in a darkening Empire.

Last night I dreamed of Owen Deathstalker.

He was standing beside his descendant, Lewis, as they finally discovered the true nature of the Terror. What it really was.

And I woke up screaming.